The Spy and the Seamstress

by SCOTT M. SMITH

Dedicated to Heidi, Alex, Sabrina and Garrett

AUTHOR'S NOTE

"Who Lives? Who dies? Who tells your story?"
Finale – *Hamilton, the Musical*

Hamilton, the Musical first hooked me on the Revolution – and inadvertently led me to Nathan Hale. Hale and Hamilton were both captains in the Continental Army serving in New York City in 1776. They were both the same age, both Ivy League graduates, both handsome, popular men. Yet, at the most dire moment in the war, when the Continental Army was surrounded by the full might of the British Empire, and commander-in-chief George Washington put out the call for an officer to go behind enemy lines, Nathan Hale was the only one to raise his hand. The rest is history – Hamilton went on to greatness and Broadway; Hale went to an unmarked grave and a book by me, an unknown author.

What passions prompted Hale – son of a prosperous landowner and a schoolteacher – to volunteer for an espionage mission well below his privileged station? What forces of the times propelled him from a carefree, bon vivant to a leader of men? What did his mission accomplish – then and now? As a history buff, patriot, and parent, I embarked upon this project five years ago in search of answers.

Originally, I expected to find eighteenth century New Englanders united in their pursuit of independence and morally conservative, if not Puritanical. Needless to say, I was surprised on both counts. The Revolution was a social and sexual awakening as well as a constitutional upheaval. To flesh out this turbulence, I intertwined the fictional Wheaton family, staunch Tories, not realizing until well into the writing that Anne Wheaton would become such a strong character in her own right.

With great respect, I have tried to stay true to the documented mileposts and surviving personal correspondence of Hale's life. Several of his college classmates have written, some with a tinge of jealousy, of his penchant for female companionship. Since Hale himself maintained gentlemanly discretion, the reader should know that his romantic entanglements in *The Spy and the Seamstress* are entirely my own invention.

For realism, I have written historical figures, both major and minor, into the story whenever possible, striving to portray them as they were perceived at that point in time. Of note, Lieutenant Colonel Robert Rogers of the Queen's Rangers was Hale's actual nemesis, Stephen Hempstead and William Hull were his true confidants till the end, and Sam Hale, Nathan's cousin, served the Crown with a vengeance. Eyewitnesses recounted that Nathan wrote a letter from captivity to his brother, Enoch, on September 22, 1776 which has never surfaced. Accordingly, I start *The Spy and the Seamstress* by re-creating it.

Although I have conducted extensive research into letters, diaries, and documents of the era, I apologize in advance for any factual errors. For readers inclined to separate truth from fiction, I have included maps, a bibliography, a timeline of actual events, and a listing of historical figures at the end of the book. Huzzah!

Table of Contents

PROLOGUE

Beekman Estate
New York

Brother Enoch,

I doubt I will again see a sunrise as beautiful as this one. The mist has just lifted off the East River. Its waters are still as glass. The last of the summer roses bloom a vivid pink. A stout oak arches its limbs not far from my tent, creating an oasis of shade. I believe the redcoats will hang me there.

The past twenty-four hours have been trying but I am at peace now. Major Rogers, my captor, treated me with respect during my transport here from Long Island, although, I must admit, I am disappointed that I fell victim to a man of such low character, whatever glory in his writings I once admired. I freely confessed my espionage to General Howe and have been judged fairly by him according to the doctrines of war. William Cunningham, Howe's provost marshal, however, is a vile fellow who denied me bible, quill and paper last night. Fortunately, those deficiencies have been remedied this morning.

I love my country and have done nothing but what duty demands. Every service necessary to the success of our Glorious Cause is an honorable one. Although my books and classroom are now but a distant memory, I cannot resist a last word borrowed from *Cato*:

> "I regret that I have but one life to lose for my country!"

My fellow Rangers are just a few miles away, so my eyes still search northward in faint hope of rescue. If so, I look forward to embracing you once again. If not, I will meet my fate resolute in my love of God, family and country.

Yours affectionately,

Nathaniel Hale
Captain, Continental Army

PART ONE
Boston
1775

"Our streets are again filled with armed men. Our harbor is crowded with ships of war. But these cannot intimidate us. Our liberty must be preserved. It is far dearer than life."

Dr. Joseph Warren
President – Massachusetts Provisional Congress
Address commemorating the fifth anniversary of the Boston Massacre
Old South Meeting House - Boston
March 6, 1775

CHAPTER 1 - APRIL 1775

"One if by land, and two if by sea..."
The Midnight Ride of Paul Revere
Henry Wadsworth Longfellow

The tom-tom beat of galloping hooves shattered the fragile calm in the red clapboard schoolhouse. I brandished my pointer, but would have had better luck teaching pigs to fly. My Union School class, boys aged twelve to sixteen, scions of the wealthiest families in New London, rustled on their benches, straining to hear if war had finally arrived at our doorstep.

"Back to ancient Greece, men," I announced, rapping my lectern. Nineteen, but already enlightened by four years of study at Yale College, I was only too ready to trade books and quill for musket and ball. Cocking an ear towards the window, I strained to hear the rolling drums of British troops on the move or the mustering of my fellow citizens, but all I heard was the lonely clop of four hooves receding down the street.

"Master Hale! The bloody-backs are coming!" Justice Mather, a mop-haired nine-year-old, shouted the dreaded alarm as he staggered down the steps from the attic where the younger boys were memorizing their multiplication tables.

"Mind your mouth, young man," I replied in a level tone that belied my own disappointment. "The British Army will not arrive on a single mount."

Laughter tittered as Justice whirled to face his classmates. "Give me liberty or give me death," he spit the words through gritted teeth, clenching his elfin fists as if he would lead the fight himself.

"You'll eat those words," Richard Wheaton, a mule-faced twelve-year-old, growled as he shoved Justice against the wall. From a Loyalist household, his father owned a shop on Bank Street that sold linens and fashionable clothes, Richard had been spoiling for a fight all week.

Taller than most men, and fitter as well (my long jump mark still stands unsurpassed on the New Haven commons), I easily separated the young combatants. After Justice grudgingly retreated up the stairs, I strode to the front door, peering towards the village green, watching a crowd gather around the rider.

While the redcoats might not arrive today, they would surely come soon. Last September, Thomas Gage, the commanding general of the Crown's army in North America, had occupied Boston, little more than a day's sail away, and imposed martial law. Parliament and King peppered him regularly to sally forth and subdue the rebellious colonists.

Although Philadelphia was our largest city and New York our busiest port, Boston, the site of the Massacre in '70 and the Tea Party in '73, was our beacon of liberty. My fellow citizens, descendants of the pilgrims who had fled across the Atlantic in search of the freedom to govern themselves, massed outside its gates, determined to drive the hated redcoats into the sea.

Returning to the head of my class, I poked the embers in the smoke-scarred fireplace as my students shifted behind my back. When satisfied they had settled, I turned, tapping my pointer on the plank floor as I quoted Socrates, "The greatest way to live with honor in this world is to be what we pretend to be."

The words of the great philosopher stung. How could I be an honorable man if I pretended to be a schoolmaster much longer? Thoroughly riled, I glared at my bellicose pupil. "Young Wheaton, what does Socrates mean here?"

Richard dragged himself up from his bench, fury still evident on his face, a spitting image of his older brother, Caleb, who had sat in that same seat last year. "Why don't you ask my sister, Anne? She was in your girls' class before breakfast, wasn't she?" he replied, fists clenched at his side.

"Yes, she was. But I'm asking now for your thoughts." As a tribute to my mother, Elizabeth, bless her departed soul, whose great-great-grandfather John Strong arrived in the New World in 1630, I had started a class for young women at five each morning. The fees added a modest supplement to my purse, while the opportunity to view the sunrise in the company of twenty members of the fairer sex, several of the first rank, was an unintended, but most agreeable, benefit as well.

"My thoughts are that no honorable man sits in his sister's seat. My father says that a proper school would never allow a female…"

A commotion outside drowned out the rest of Richard's answer. I tried to ignore the ruckus, but shouts from the parade of passers-by floated into the classroom.

"The redcoats broke out," a bald farmer, wobbling like an egg in the saddle of a lumbering draft horse, broadcast the news. "Attacked Lexington! Eight dead!"

"We rallied at Concord," added the butcher's apprentice, his slaughterhouse stench preceding him up the street. "Paul Revere got the Minutemen out in time."

With the boys' heads again craning towards the window, and my own attention blown to smithereens, I dismissed the class. Alone with my thoughts, I slapped my rod, the feeble instrument of a bum-brushing teacher, against the hearthstones, snapping it in half. Although I trained weekly with New London's Independent Company of Artillery, and pinned their black cockade to my hat with pride, the only way to prove that I was much more than a mother-coddled bookworm would be to join the fight in Boston. But, life wasn't that simple.

"Master Hale! Master Hale! Come quick," Richard, his truculence evaporated, burst into the deserted classroom. "Please! My father's in trouble."

Grabbing my frock coat and hat, three sides of the brim cocked to the crown, I followed him out into the street. At first, I thought I might be the victim of a prank, as the crowd had dispersed; but then a raucous cheer rose from the green.

"Down there. By the Liberty Pole," Richard pointed towards a ship's mast almost seventy feet high mounted in the middle of the grassy square, a mob of New Londoners bobbing like sea swells around it. With panic evident in his twisted expression, the boy searched for his father.

"There he is," Richard called out, tugging my sleeve, dragging me to the outskirts of the fray. Holding tight to his powdered wig, William Wheaton, impeccably dressed in a scarlet cloak and black breeches, was trying to forge his way into the Grosvenor Arms, a tavern where a toast to the King could have been uttered in safety not too long ago.

A gang of beefy seamen, the Sons of Neptune, their blue and gold trident banner held aloft, blocked Wheaton's path. Located at the mouth of the Thames River, New London was the largest deep-water port on the Long Island Sound, drawing flocks of working-class men and women to its waterfront.

"Still importing those fancy frocks from England, eh?" the leader, James Caulk, gray beanie pulled tightly over his ears, stepped forward, jabbing his finger in Wheaton's face. "Don't you believe in the embargo Congress put in place *last year*?"

"I saw the man taking notes down by the harbor an hour ago." Another dockhand, Pieter Sugarman, a caramel-skinned African whose lilting Caribbean accent belied the anger in his words, shoved Richard's father backwards. Wheaton tried to stand his ground but found himself encircled by a tightening noose of rebel musclemen.

"He's a British spy." The accusation launched like an arrow from deep in the crowd.

"He wants to see us hang," a third Neptune thug turned towards the mob, preying on its deepest fears. With New England now in rebellion, the Crown would have every right to punish its leaders. "Let's string him up first. There's an oak over there that will do just fine."

"Swing the Tory. Swing the Tory," a chant bubbled up. Richard wrapped his arms around his father's waist, tears leaking down his cheek.

I pushed through the perimeter, positioning myself between the Wheatons and the Sons of Neptune. It seemed like only yesterday the Wheatons were pillars of the community, but no one was willing to step up and defend them today. "What's going on here?" I asked Caulk.

"Wheaton's a spy," Caulk replied, his face inches from mine. "Now, get out of our way, boy."

"What proof of espionage do you have?" Although I had no doubt Wheaton was a Loyalist, I refused to budge. What was the point of tossing off the yoke of King George if tyranny of the mob took its place?

"Who're you in your fancy silk stockings?" An ink-smudged printer, Reuben Booge, challenged, stabbing a quill in my direction. "Wheaton's a Tory through and through. As sure as my apron's black."

"To hell with proof," another sailor growled as he lowered his beanied head and bull-rushed past Caulk, driving his shoulder at my midsection. I sidestepped, headlocking my now off-balance assailant and flinging him to the ground, a move I had perfected on the college wrestling ground.

"That's Schoolmaster Hale. He's a man of the book, but I would not mistake him for an easy mark." Stephen Hempstead, a sergeant in Coitt's militia, another local unit, as well as my neighbor and friend, broke through the crowd, positioning himself beside me to shield the Wheatons.

"Let Mr. Wheaton show us what he wrote down," Caulk demanded.

Wheaton untangled from his son and fumbled in the pocket of his waistcoat. "Here, here," he said, withdrawing a sheet of paper.

Caulk cleeked it, corkscrewing his eyes in a vain effort to read. "It's in code," he said, waving the page at the crowd like it was the British flag.

"Let me look," I asked, holding out my hand.

"Here you go, schoolmaster," Caulk sneered, complying nevertheless with my request.

"Mr. Wheaton writes in a flowing cursive, but his words are harmless," I announced, a practitioner myself of fine penmanship. "Five bolts of apricot damask; two bolts of lilac; one of rose."

"It's an order for my shop," Wheaton blurted.

"For cloth manufactured in England, I wager," Caulk countered. "A hot bath in tar and feathers will do you good."

At these words, two bearded hulks dressed in oily buckskin lugged a steaming cauldron to the inner circle. "Who brung the feathers?"

"What does liberty mean if all men are not free to act according to their conscience?" I shouted to no avail. The crowd jostled forward ignoring my lofty words. I gagged at the tar fumes but refused to separate from the cowering Wheatons.

"Break it up here. We won't tolerate bullies in New London," Judge Richard Law boomed. "There'll be a town meeting at seven tonight at Miner's Tavern to decide our course of action."

I pushed my charges away. William Wheaton caught a sharp elbow in his stomach as we slipped through the crowd but still managed to drag his son to safety.

"The Sons of Neptune don't give up!" Caulk called after us.

***

Anne Wheaton, eighteen years old, sat patiently at the table watching her younger brothers, Caleb, Phineas and Richard, drool in anticipation of the feast set before them. It was unusual to have such lavish fare mid-week, but, her mother, Abigail, had hastily organized the meal as soon as she learned of Father's ordeal that afternoon.

Located just off Water Street, their weathered gray clapboard house featured a keeping room, open to the kitchen, and parlor on ground level and two bedrooms upstairs. As the family's fortunes rose, Father had framed the hearth with pine panels and decorated the parlor with floral wallpaper imported from England. His prized possession, a Simon Willard tall-case clock personalized with the Wheaton name scripted on the face, stood against the far wall. To rectify the shortage of females in the household, he also purchased Becky, a matronly Black.

Anne was at least as hungry as her siblings. She had risen before sunrise to feed the chickens before heading to school. After class, she scrubbed yesterday's clothes in a tub of boiling water and mended Richard's coat. Then, she helped Father at the store, fitting Mrs. Goldsmith, one of their most finicky customers, into her new dress just arrived from London with a waistline two inches too tight.

"Anne, I believe tonight is your turn to say grace," Mother said, bowing her head. Her once crimson hair had grayed after the pox claimed her last two children, Grace and Phebe, before their fifth birthday, but she maintained a pleasant face and ready smile that always attracted greetings when she strolled along the harbor.

Anne waited for her family to link hands before offering thanks for their bounteous meal, good health, and the safe return of her father from the hands of the rebel mob. She paused, then added a word of gratitude for Schoolmaster Hale.

"You fancy him," Richard teased.

"I fancy learning," she replied, looking up and down the table, challenging any of the males in her family to dispute her right to exercise her mind.

"And what have you learned from that Yale dandy?" Caleb asked, tossing his unruly mane of flaming red locks. Sixteen and apprenticed to a New London tailor in preparation to take over the family business one day, he was fast becoming a man of the world. "I saw the way he gaped at you at the winter frolic at Miner's."

"He did look sweet on you when he supped here last month." Mother added with a coy smile. Father just huffed as he reached for the meat.

Anne dipped her head, staring at her empty plate to hide her blush. With a lashing tongue, petulant face and bosom as flat as a washboard, she was hardly a magnet to the young men in town. Did Nathan really fancy *her*? There were so many prettier girls in her class.

"No one kicks a ball as far as Schoolmaster Hale," Richard added, oblivious to the tenor of the conversation. "He cleared the trees…"

"Are you two going to bundle?" Phineas interrupted. A teenager himself now, he was just beginning to show an interest in the opposite sex.

Anne's face flushed as an image of Nathan, striding towards her, his queue of tawny hair swinging between his broad shoulders, ignited an urge that was completely inappropriate for a God-fearing, Christian woman. Since the first day of class last summer, she had harbored the fantasy of spending the night with her schoolmaster - even if they were both bundled in separate down quiltings with a board between them. Did her countenance reveal her thoughts? She glanced at Father, relieved to see him gnawing his fowl.

"Where would I sleep then?" Richard asked before gulping his cider. He had shared a bed with his older sister since he was a toddler.

"Anne cannot bundle with her schoolmaster," Mother interjected. "How would that look to the other girls in her class?"

"Those doxies are all from rebel families," Caleb spit out the words as if they were cherry pits. He was clearly learning to ferret secrets while he measured and stitched. "They wouldn't need any prodding to jump into bed with Hale."

"That would be a sight," Phineas contributed, his freckled face crackling with mirth. "Pass the turkey please."

"Enough of this nonsense. No rebel-leaning schoolmaster is going to bundle with my daughter." Father slapped the table, rattling the silver candleholders.

Anne flashed a furtive glance at Mother. They both knew Father's bark was far worse than his bite.

"I get assaulted by ruffians and you're all talking about courting," Father continued. He lifted his cap, which replaced his wig for evenings at home, and scratched his bald scalp. "The nerve of that rabble. How dare they manhandle a proper Englishman?"

This time, Anne couldn't help rolling her eyes. Father was born here in New London, inheriting the house, the silver and the store from his parents whose portraits hung in the parlor.

"Your Father's right," Mother said. "You must have been terrified, dear. If Schoolmaster Hale had not stepped in, who knows what would have happened," she added with a barely perceptible nod to Anne. "Did you do anything to incite the mob?" she asked while passing the tray to Phineas.

"Father was taking notes down by the harbor," Richard blurted proudly.

"Notes? In public? Again?" The tray in Mother's hand dipped, spilling juice across the tablecloth. "You're just asking for trouble."

"I was writing down some ideas for fall fashions. I think more clearly outdoors," Father replied.

"Really?" Mother steadied the tray, passing it to Phineas as Becky hustled over to clean up the mess.

"Yes, really." Father gripped a drumstick dripping with gravy from his plate and slanted it at his wife. "I will not be interrogated here at home. The Sons of Neptune are traitors to our King. And so is anyone else who supports them."

"The traitors are meeting at Miner's tonight," Caleb said, the cadence of his voice accelerating like a runaway stallion. "We can hide outside and…."

"Stifle yourself, boy," Father interrupted, his glare alone sufficient to lasso his eldest son's momentum. Mother coughed, then busied herself ladling vegetables to Richard.

"Anne, what do you think? Don't we all have a duty to obey our King?" Father asked, gnawing at his turkey. He washed it down with a spot of tea, ostentatiously displaying the imported brew that he purchased from smugglers in defiance of colonial edict. His cup, part of a creamware set glazed by Wedgewood in London, bore the monogram of the King, GR, Georgius Rex. "You must have read enough now to understand the law."

"How can we blindly obey King George when his parliament governs us without our consent? Our own Connecticut assembly is considering a resolution to declare the United American Colonies free and independent, absolved from all allegiance to Great Britain." she replied, secretly pleased that Father recognized her ability to comprehend a complex, "masculine" subject.

"Hogwash. King George has our best interests at heart," Father said, sliding his teacup away.

"Then why will he not allow representatives from the colonies to vote in Parliament?" she asked, pushing too far, but unable, or unwilling, to stop.

"That school has filled your mind with gibberish. It was a mistake to ever let you attend Master Hale's class." Father's face flushed as his temper boiled.

"But..." Father and his eldest son were so much alike, she thought as she yielded.

"But nothing, Anne. A woman's place is here at home. I've got a good mind to take you out to the shed for a thrashing."

"You'll do no such thing." Mother stood, her exasperation evident. "Where would you be without Anne's help at the store?" After motioning Becky to stoke the fire, she walked into the parlor, returning with a shawl wrapped around her shoulders. "Now, dear, do you believe the Sons of Neptune will harass you again?"

Father nodded, shrinking back into his seat. "I fear so. They're terrorizing Loyalists throughout the colony."

"Then we'll close up the shop and move in with my sister, Charlotte, and her family in Marshfield until the rebellion is over," Mother announced, her face displaying only a flicker of regret. "She writes that there is an Association of Loyalists there and a British garrison to protect them."

Now, Anne understood the feast. They would have to travel light.

***

Mrs. Hempstead's cornbread lay heavily in our stomachs as Stephen and I slipped into the rear of Miner's Tavern later that evening. Judge Law, dressed formally in black breeches, gray silk stockings, waistcoat and silver-braided frock, sat at a table facing the room, gavel in hand, with a roaring fire to his right and the bar, closed only for the duration of proceedings, on his left. Townspeople milled about until Law called the meeting to order with a brief prayer.

As heads lifted, Law scanned the room. "You've undoubtedly heard the rumors of British spies in New London," he said, pausing long enough to establish brief eye contact with men in the front rows. "While we still recognize our duty to King George, most here tonight believe that laws passed by his Parliament are illegal."

A Solomonic way to parse a delicate issue - and for Law to protect himself from charges of treason; but a bit timid, I thought, with a modicum of disapproval. Nodding heads throughout the tavern, however, confirmed the judge's words. I searched for the leaders of the Sons of Neptune, but they were not in attendance, no surprise since the sailors were neither property owners nor members of the Congregational Church, which generally were coincidental in Connecticut. William Wheaton and his fellow Anglicans were absent as well.

"We're here tonight to decide a course of action," Law continued. "If any man feels his loyalty to Parliament in London outweighs his loyalty to his neighbors, I'd ask him to leave right now."

No one moved. Josiah Barton, a cooper, his prosperity evident by the polished silver buckles on his shoes, was first to step up. "Let's stop dancing around like scared rabbits. Old Put's already on his way to Boston. Dropped his plow, saddled up his horse and rode off the minute he heard the news. New London needs to mobilize as well. Tonight."

Old Put was Colonel Israel Putnam, Connecticut's most famous military son. He had earned his reputation in Rogers' Rangers, fighting the French and Indians.

"John Stark's in Boston too. Another New Englander who tossed his Ranger uniform in the latrine," a grizzle-faced veteran added, tooting twice on a long-stemmed pipe before passing it on.

"Where's Robert Rogers now? He's the man we need to run the army," a baritone voice bellowed from the rear. The conversation bounced about the tavern, as did the communal pipe, each man snipping off an inch from the stem before taking his turn.

"Back in England, I heard. In prison."

"In prison?"

"General Gage hates his guts. Got Rogers tossed in jail on some trumped-up charges."

"Well, let's break him out. No one knows how to lead men in battle better than Robert Rogers."

"I read Rogers' *Journals* when I was thirteen," Stephen turned to me and whispered. Major Robert Rogers' account of the French and Indian War had been one of the most popular books in both the colonies and London in the late 1760's.

"I *dreamed* of wearing that green Ranger jacket," I answered, silently reciting my favorite passage: *It is the soldier not the scholar that writes...not with silence and leisure but in forests, on rocks and mountains, amidst the hurries, noise and disorders of war.* Rogers' victories in the wilderness – St. Francis, Montreal, Detroit – had stoked my boyhood dreams of glory and helped me overcome my grief at Mother's passing.

"Order! Order!" Judge Law banged his gavel. "Let's hear from Captain Coitt."

Dressed in his trademark scarlet and black cloak, William Coitt, a lawyer, detailed the readiness of his regiment, paid for out of his own pocket, the customary contribution of successful men to their town's defense. Should they march to Boston? When should they leave? How long would they be away?

Law's gavel slammed again. The meeting resolved that the patriot cause demanded immediate action. Coitt's men would leave for Boston at daybreak.

I jumped to my feet, leading the tavern in applause. What more honorable service could a man undertake than to fight for freedom alongside his fellow citizens?

***

The next morning, I watched my girls copy their vocabulary words in the attic classroom they shared with the younger boys. The thump of boots in the dirt drew our attention to the window. With the rising sun at their backs, Coitt's militia, dressed smartly in blue jackets and white breeches, marched past the schoolhouse. Stephen Hempstead, standing tall in the fifth row, waved farewell.

"When are *you* going to Boston, Schoolmaster Hale?" Prudence Richards popped the volcanic question from her seat on the back bench. Her blond curls peeked out from a pink cap tied neatly under her chin.

"As soon as the term is complete." I had wanted to leave sooner, particularly after last night's rousing meeting, but decided to fulfill my obligations here first.

"A great loss for the Union School, I'm sure," Prudence replied, swiveling her head, as if challenging her classmates to disagree. "But we all have to do our part now that the fighting's begun." Not surprisingly, the other girls all nodded in various degrees of enthusiasm.

"I thought you already enlisted. In the Artillery Company," Anne Wheaton piped in from her usual position in the front row.

"Yes, but..." I stammered.

"But that is a social club, pretenders parading around the green once a week and then getting drunk at Miner's."

"Your assessment is quite harsh." But largely correct, I thought.

"These are harsh times," Anne replied, standing. "Now, I must excuse myself. Mother needs my assistance this morning."

As Anne strode head down past her fellow pupils, I smiled at her ferocity. While she might look somewhat like a stork, her mind was as sharp as an eagle's talons, her wit honed to an even finer edge.

Anne's pursuit of learning reminded me of my mother. After I'd survived a particularly difficult infancy, Mother sheltered me, insisting that brother Enoch, two years my senior, and I pursue our studies while our three eldest brothers worked the family farm. When Mother passed on eight years ago, shortly after giving birth to her twelfth child, my father, Richard, a deacon of the Congregational Church in Coventry, honored her wishes.

I left for Yale shortly after my fourteenth birthday, accompanied by Enoch. Of course, I was much too young, and thoroughly spoiled, to appreciate this opportunity, so I pissed away my first two years drinking, gambling, sporting and chasing the local lasses (with some success at all four endeavors). Although a proud and prosperous landowner, Father threatened to pull me from school if I didn't straighten out.

As Anne disappeared down the stairs, I turned my attention to the other girls, albeit with slightly less enthusiasm. "Before I join the army, I must ensure that all you young ladies can spell," I said, strolling to peer over Prudence's shoulder.

With unblemished skin, pouting lips and a starkly white set of teeth, Prudence was, in my practiced opinion, the prettiest girl in the class. Even Enoch, studying for the ministry, would have skipped a beat in his sermon if she beamed at him from the first row of the meetinghouse. "And from the looks of your chicken scratches, Miss Richards, I have much work left to do."

Prudence had arrived in New London only a month ago, having been sent "abroad" by her father, a miller in the countryside, to further her education and housekeeping skills. She lived with her uncle, John Richards, a shipowner and Union School proprietor, and his wife. Coincidentally, or perhaps not, I also boarded at the Richards.

"We all can't be as smart as Anne Wheaton," Prudence barbed, picking up her quill. "The Tory bitch," she hissed with her head down so only I could hear.

"Mind your manners, Miss Richards," I replied, tapping my pointer on her desk. "Or you'll force me to bloody those delicate knuckles of yours." Unlike my fellow schoolmasters, I deferred from administering corporal punishment, though sorely tempted at times.

The boys filed in shortly after the girls departed for their morning chores. Prudence lingered on the schoolhouse steps, chatting with two of the older students. I had to shoo her away to start class on time. When Richard Wheaton didn't arrive, I wondered if he was ill, the flux had rampaged through town this spring, and Anne had left early to tend him. Only last week, I had spent an entire night sitting in the outhouse, freezing my bare arse off. Fortunately, I recovered the next day.

At four, I dismissed the boys and dipped my quill in the inkwell to draft my letter of resignation. Standing at the podium, I surveyed the room: neat rows of tables and benches already nicked by creative carvings, bookcases stuffed with favorite tomes, homespun curtains, a ratty blue muffler forgotten on the stairs, a fire simmering in the hearth. Yesterday, this schoolhouse was my castle. Within its walls, I reigned supreme, preparing my disciples to conquer the world. Today, I felt suffocated, choked by these same walls, barricades to my destiny.

But what was my destiny? Slipping two fingers under my cravat, I stroked the cluster of hair nestled on the right side of my neck as if it was the fuse on a keg of gunpowder. Any mark on that side was considered bad luck. A hairy one foretold an even worse fate. Death by hanging.

It was just an old wives' superstition, Father consoled when the mole first sprouted a week after my thirteenth birthday. But, wasn't great-grandmother Sarah accused of witchcraft in Salem? Did she make a covenant with the devil to escape with her life? Might I be the one to pay her debt? Death in battle seemed like a glorious alternative to the gallows.

A gentle rap on the open door saved me from further flagellation. Anne, wrapped in a black cloak and cap, stood on the threshold. "I wanted to say a proper farewell."

"Farewell?" I pushed the parchment aside and waved her inside.

"We're moving to Marshfield. Tomorrow." Anne closed the door and strode towards me. "We'll be safer there."

"That's true, unfortunately." I sidestepped, tossing a log on the fire, stirring the embers for several seconds to camouflage my disappointment. "The Sons of Neptune won't stop until they drive every Loyalist out of New London."

"Thank you for helping Father yesterday." Anne removed her cloak and laid it across the closest table. She approached the hearth, warming her hands, only an arm's reach away now.

"No thanks needed. It was the Christian thing to do." But was that the only reason I rushed to William Wheaton's aid?

"We'll return when the rebellion is over." She untied her white cap and swished her auburn hair.

"I doubt the rebellion will be so easily quelled." I stepped closer, noticing that Anne had donned a freshly laundered frock – and it wasn't for Sunday meeting. She had perfumed her hair as well, the lilac scent luring me like a stallion to stud.

She hesitated as if to gather courage. I loved the way her lips pursed while she worked through a knotty problem. Although I had enjoyed relations with other women, Anne was different.

"Great liberty, inspire our souls and make our lives in thy possession happy or our deaths glorious in thy just defense," she recited with a puckish smile.

"Addison's *Cato*." The tragic tale of a Roman senator, who chose to die rather than submit to the tyranny of Julius Caesar, was my favorite reading. I reached for Anne's hand, intertwining our fingers. Since she was no longer my student, I saw no reason not to advance our connection. Her smile beckoned me to proceed.

"I copied the quotation from your text." A lock of curls tumbled across her forehead. She brushed it away with her free hand. "I'll miss you."

"Stay then," I replied, the words leaping from my mouth.

"Stay in New London? And become a rebel?"

"Are you really a Tory?" I took her other hand, looking into her emerald eyes, losing my heart in their bottomless deeps. "Do you truly believe that our great continent should be governed by a despot on a tiny island across the ocean?"

"What I believe is not important. I'm a Wheaton, loyal supporters of the King for generations. If Father even knew I was here now, he…" She grappled with the words, anguish clearly visible in the scowl lines creasing her forehead.

"You know our cause is just."

"You're already a man of education, a man of property. What do *you* have to gain from this just cause?"

She must have rehearsed more than a few lines of Addison for this visit. I was flattered, but unwavering. "Liberty. Honor. Glory," I replied.

"Fine words, but are you willing to risk all to attain them?"

"Without hesitation. And you would as well, if your family…"

Anne shook her head, pulling her hands free. "I would never turn against my father or my brothers," she said, swiping at a tear. "Do you think the rabble that rousted Father could stand up to the might of the Empire? And, when the fight is over, the King will remember who stood against him. You'll be an outlaw in your own land. Or you'll be dead."

"The cost of freedom is never cheap." I reached for her again.

"It's a fairytale." She pushed my hands away, but her eyes never wavered, captivating me in their intensity. "And you're a dreamer."

"But we can make it come true." I gripped her wiry shoulders, our lips colliding in a kiss ripe with passion. Sliding a hand down her back, I cupped as much of her bony buttocks as I could through the flounce of her skirt and petticoat. She made no move to untangle.

The sun had dipped out of sight, leaving the classroom in the hush of approaching twilight. I thought to lock the schoolhouse door, but…

"Schoolmaster Hale? Are you in there?" Richard Wheaton pounded the knocker. "I came to say good-bye."

I grudgingly released Anne and retreated towards my desk. "Yes, yes, come in."

Richard's eyes shot open when he saw his sister, flushed and disheveled, but he held his tongue.

"I ask permission to write," Anne said, approaching me again, smoothing her hair, ignoring her younger brother. "To keep abreast of events here in New London, of course."

"I welcome your correspondence."

"Sister, you have to go. Mother needs you," Richard broke in, tugging on Anne's sleeve.

"In a moment, brother," she replied, refusing to drop her gaze from me.

I handed her the dog-eared *Cato* text. "Take it. A reminder of our time in New London."

"I'll treasure it." She tucked the gift into the pocket of her skirt. "Until we meet again."

Clasping her wrist, and reaching for Richard's as well, I bowed my head. "Let us pray."

CHAPTER 2 - MAY 1775

To George William Fairfax,
"…Unhappy it is to reflect that a brother's sword has been sheathed in
a brother's breast and that a once happy and peaceful plains of America are either
to be drenched with blood or inhabited by slaves. Sad alternative! But can a
virtuous Man hesitate in his choice?"
G. Washington
Philadelphia
May 31, 1775

After a lingering look back towards her schoolhouse, bathed in morning sunlight, Anne was the first of the Wheatons to climb into the covered wagon. She had survived a tense evening meal, as well as breakfast this morning, waiting for a storm that never broke. Richard had kept his silence, God bless him.

"Good riddance to Master Hale," Caleb whispered, following her gaze as he helped her up into the buckboard. "He's a rake – and a fornicator. You're too good for him."

"Hush, brother," Anne replied forcefully, looking around to make sure her parents were still inside. "It's a sin to spread lies and malicious gossip." Nathan was a rebel, and popular, but Caleb had gone way too far.

How far would she have gone with Nathan yesterday afternoon? She didn't know – and didn't want to.

"You'll see. I'll find proof." Caleb was remaining behind in New London, ostensibly to finish his apprenticeship and mind their house.

The wagon was stuffed with the Wheaton's household possessions, as well as two gowns and several bolts of fabric that Father thought would be necessary to establish his business credentials. Father and the boys loaded the Willard clock in last, but poor Stitch, their horse, wouldn't budge. They had little choice but to return it to the parlor.

"I'll defend our home with my life," Caleb vowed as the family boarded the wagon again.

Anne sat in the middle, where she could share the driving with Mother, while Father sat on her right, armed with his fowling piece. Phineas and Richard piled into the back, chatting and tussling.

"I know you will, son," Father replied.

"Don't be rash, Caleb. The Sons of Neptune are on the warpath," Mother added.

"Godspeed, brother," Anne called as Mother cracked the whip and Stitch plod forward, leaving Caleb a solitary figure in their yard. Her gut chilled as she realized this might well be the last time she saw her oldest brother alive.

Why were young men so eager for war? Although on opposite sides, Nathan and Caleb had much in common, she realized. Both would run towards the fight, not away from it. Brave or foolish? Only time would tell.

"Caleb will be fine, ladies. The Rangers will look out for him," Father said as the wagon rumbled past the outskirts of New London and onto the Post Road.

"Rangers?" Mother asked, scowling.

"The Queen's finest," Father replied, puffing his chest. "They'll teach that mob not to mess with the Wheatons," he muttered so only Anne could hear.

With the road a muddy bog in places from the spring rains, the journey dragged into a second week. As they drew closer to Boston, the thoroughfare clogged with refugees heading in and out of the city.

During an overnight stay in a tavern outside Wrentham, Father slipped away from the family table to engage in a conversation with a gaggle of fellow travelers that lasted well into the evening. Anne was awake when he turned in. Even with the candles out, she could see a spirit in Father that had gone missing since his encounter with the Sons of Neptune.

He sat on the edge of her bed to tell her the news. Mother's plan to move to Marshfield was out. General Gage had evacuated the garrison, as well as the Loyalist citizens of the town, to Boston immediately after the battles at Lexington and Concord. However, the growing concentration of Loyalists in Boston created business opportunities, particularly for someone who could move quickly.

Mother was distraught the next morning, although she agreed they had little choice but to ride into Boston. Her expression remained grim until they crossed the neck and entered the city, quickly locating an enclave of displaced Marshfield residents. They informed Mother that Charlotte and family had indeed sailed from Marshfield, but did not tarry long in Boston. Determined to escape the rebels for good, they had booked passage on a ship north to Halifax, Canada, site of a major British naval outpost.

Mother was tempted to follow, but Father persuaded her to stay, at least long enough for him to launch their business. Within a week, he set up shop in a compact, but well-stocked, storefront, vacated in haste by a tailor of rebel sympathies, on Wing's Lane, a narrow, tumbling cut-through near Dock Square and Beacon Hill. Displayed in the window under the freshly painted sign proclaiming "Wheatons - London Fashions" in elegant whirls, the two gowns, cascading with ruffles and intricate lacework, served as beacons themselves. Although trapped in a besieged city, the upper echelons of Boston society still craved luxuries, particularly those that might appear to have come right off the ship from the motherland.

"I'm sorry, Lady Pigot, but we don't have the daffodil one in your size just now," Anne apologized. She wore a cap and a simple, high-necked frock accented by a porcelain brooch handed down from her grandmother.

"Let me measure your waist," she added, tape in hand, not giving the portly matron time to object. "We'll create a new one that will look stunning on you."

"I'll need it by the thirtieth. For the final ball of the season," Lady Pigot said, sucking in her breath. Her face, coated with powder made from corroded lead, vinegar and flour, was a ghostly shade of white. Several silk patches, shaped like crowns and crescents, dotted her cheeks, strategically placed to camouflage smallpox scars. "It would be totally inappropriate for a Baroness to appear in her old rags."

"Of course, ma'am." While she knelt behind Lady Pigot, the bell tinkled.

"Coming, coming." Father, dressed in his finest crimson waistcoat, black breeches and silver knee bands, bustled to greet the new customers. He had even daubed a splash of powder on his cheeks, an artifice he had avoided in New London. "Sheriff and Mrs. Loring, I'm so pleased you could visit," he said at the door.

Peeking out from behind Lady Pigot's hooped skirt, Anne was gobsmacked by Betsey Loring, demurely wrapped in a full length, black velvet cape. With blond tresses framing sapphire blue eyes, Mrs. Loring's natural beauty was betrayed only by her rouged cheeks and fleshy lips, glossed to apple red with a mixture of beeswax and molten lead. A simple black dot pasted above her lip symbolized coquetry. Anne stared for a second too long before Loring sized her up - and dismissed her.

"You've settled in quickly, I see," Joshua Loring, the eldest son of a prominent Loyalist family, said, sniffing around the shop with an accountant's nose for detail.

"It's coming along," Father replied. "Your help was instrumental, of course."

"I expect a good return from…."

"The daffodil. I'd like to try it on." Mrs. Loring interrupted her husband. While not much older than Anne, she projected an aura of entitlement.

"Yes, of course," Father bowed.

"The triple flounced sleeves are new?" Mrs. Loring asked as she unfastened the silver clasp on her cape and laid it on a chair.

"All the rage in London," Father replied, struggling to keep his eyes off his prospective customer's powdered bosom, fully displayed by the low-cut bodice of her taffeta dress that matched the color of her lips. Anne felt like a bumpkin in her own modest attire and unpainted face.

The sheriff lingered behind his wife, content to watch her dominate the room. "Lady Pigot, you're looking well," he said. "It's good to see you out and about again."

"I was a bit bullied by the weather this winter," the Lady replied. "But, I am so looking forward to the Gages' fete. Welcoming the newly arrived generals."

"Gage's replacement will likely be among them," the Sheriff said, casually fingering a bolt of rose-colored silk. Father pushed a log into the stove, keeping Mrs. Loring and her husband in view.

"That is military life, isn't it? I'm sure General Gage longs for a return to his family's estate in England," Lady Pigot replied.

"I'm not sure his wife feels the same." Betsey twirled to face the Lady.

"Margaret's from New Jersey, isn't she?" Lady Pigot asked as if New Jersey was a leper colony. "Her loyalties must be twisted into a knot by this conflict. I don't know how she has kept up such a brave face."

"Whose side is Duchess Gage really on? The Crown's or the Jonathans?" the Sheriff asked, using the upper class British slang for the rebels. The reference to Brother Jonathan, a friend of the biblical King David, was a jibe at the Puritans' holier-than-thou forbears.

"All set now," Anne said, rising, startled by the opinions tossed about in the open. Boston fashions might be cosmopolitan, but its gossip sounded as provincial as New London.

"Aren't you going to write down my measurements?" Lady Pigot asked.

"I usually keep them in my head."

"Of course, she'll record them," Father said, sweeping the matron towards the overburdened table at the back of the store, fumbling among a gallimaufry of swatches, ribbons, patches and lace before holding up a quill and parchment.

"I'll be off then." Lady Pigot gathered her cloak. Anne curtsied farewell.

"I will need assistance in the fitting room," Betsey Loring, daffodil gown in hand, said as she strutted past Anne, beckoning her to follow.

Anne scribbled a few notes, primarily to please Father, before scrambling after Mrs. Loring. The fitting room, far removed from the stove, was cold, but the temperature did not appear to deter Betsey Loring. Whirling to face Anne, she unpinned her stomacher and extended her arms for assistance in the complicated process of undressing.

Mrs. Loring was a bit too eager, however. The toe of her shoe, high heeled with a swirling brocade, caught in a floorboard, sending her stumbling forward. Anne choked off a giggle as her customer's right breast popped out of her corset, more a serving platter than a garment of restraint. God is just, she laughed silently, although she was sure her riant eyes revealed her true thoughts. She quickly reached for the daffodil gown, holding it up as a screen to allow Mrs. Loring the privacy to corral her errant appendage.

"Now, who would you bet on to replace General Gage? Howe, Clinton or Burgoyne?" Father's voice filtered into the fitting room.

"My money's on William Howe," Joshua Loring replied. "He's the most senior of the bunch. And he distinguished himself leading his men up the cliffs outside Quebec in '59."

"I believe General Howe's revered older brother, George, fell at Ticonderoga in '58," Father said. "The Massachusetts' assembly funded a memorial in his honor in Westminster Abbey."

"Are you implying that William Howe might go soft on the colonists?"

"Not in the least, not in the least," Father said.

Betsey Loring cocked her head, clearly interested in the conversation, while Anne helped her into the daffodil gown. As Anne dropped to her knees to pin the hemline, the bell at the front door sounded again.

"Ah, Samuel Hale, glad you could join us," Joshua Loring boomed. Anne snapped at the Hale name, narrowly avoiding stabbing her customer in the ankle. Could Nathan Hale have a relation here in Boston? A Tory?

"Sam serves the Provost Marshal, the head of the military police," Joshua continued. "And where is your lovely wife today?"

"Mercy is home in bed, sadly. She was quite looking forward to perusing Wheatons' wares, but her digestion was not quite right this morning."

"Hale?" Father asked. "We had a schoolmaster in New London with that surname. Leaned towards the rebel cause, I believe."

"My cousin. A misguided youth."

Anne remembered Nathan's earnest voice, the strength in his fingers, the taste of his lips. His schoolhouse, its fireplace roaring, had welcomed her each morning into a world where her imagination could soar beyond the rigid intellectual boundaries confronting women of all ages and political inclinations.

She also recalled several classmates eagerly vying for their schoolmaster's attention. The new arrival, Prudence Richards, barely disguised her flirtations with her sly, pearly white smiles. She had actually seen the girl polishing her teeth with gunpowder and sea corals to achieve the dazzling look.

Would Prudence bait Nathan with an evening stroll on the beach? The friskier girls already whispered about their "adventures" to the strum of the waves. And the women of desperate means who sold their bodies in the dunes? Would Nathan use them to satisfy his desires while he waited for her? A practical solution, preferable even, she thought.

"Mr. Wheaton, I enjoyed reading your reports from New London. The Crown will miss them." Sam Hale's voice carried well.

"I am just a humble servant of King George," Father replied.

Anne scooted to the far side of Mrs. Loring and resumed her pinning. She was more startled by the appearance of Nathan's cousin than by the knowledge that Father had supplied news to Boston.

"New London is a strategic port. We need the flow of information to continue," Sam said, pacing about the store. "Can you recommend another loyal servant to continue your work?"

"Yes, most certainly."

"Please write down the man's particulars."

While Father wrote, Anne heard footsteps approach the fitting room. An eerily familiar face, albeit slightly older and powdered, peered out from underneath a gray wig fashioned into a queue, braided and bow-tied, trailing down the back. Underneath the cosmetics, however, Anne recognized the telltale Hale chiseled cheekbones and staunch chin. Sam Hale soaked in the scene for a beat longer than appropriate before he nodded farewell to the half-dressed Mrs. Loring and closed the door.

***

I sat at a back table at Miner's Tavern, quaffing drafts with Benjamin Tallmadge, a schoolmaster himself in Wethersfield, and Ebenezer Williams, both classmates at Yale and fellow members of its secretive Linonia debating society. After one spirited discourse back in '71, we all had drunkenly rampaged across campus, breaking windows and causing havoc. Enoch and I had to use our "emergency" fund without Father's knowledge to pay for repairs and avoid expulsion.

This close call, the imminent threat of returning in disgrace to life on the farm, put the fear of God in me. While I can't say that I abstained from my four favorite leisure pursuits, I certainly approached them with moderation for the remainder of my tenure at Yale. And beyond.

"A day, an hour, of virtuous liberty is worth a whole eternity in bondage," Ben proclaimed, lifting his flagon.

"Not Addison again," Eb said as he raised his glass to his lips. "You'll wear the good playwright's words out if you recite them one more time."

"He who loves not wine, women and song remains a fool his whole life long," Ben proposed, quoting Martin Luther this time.

"Here, here," Eb seconded.

"The ladies of New Haven were always most solicitous of our Nathaniel. Tell me, friend, are the ladies of New London as welcoming?" Ben asked, spreading his legs as he drained his ale in a single, long swallow.

"I do not lack for companionship," I said, smothering a grin. The Richards had left Prudence and me alone at home on several occasions, brazenly advancing their matchmaking efforts. While my doubts concerning her intellectual prowess hadn't changed, I was at least starting to enjoy her company. Not wanting to foul the nest where I slept, however, I kept a respectful distance. Fortunately, two other young ladies in town, both named Betsy, also vied for my attention, and had no conditions attached.

"I do remember a heartbroken lass you left behind in Haddam Landing. Didn't you write a sonnet in her honor?" Eb pressed.

"You were all in love back then," Ben teased.

In lust would be more accurate. I had been relieved to escape my teaching job in that backwater before incurring an obligation to marry the girl.

"Is there a *particular* lass here that has captured your fancy?" Eb would not let go.

"No," I answered most emphatically, and honestly. Despite my recent dalliances, I was still smitten by Anne; however, I saw no point in volunteering her name. Besides, Anne was in Boston now and a Loyalist, at least her family was. Too many complications to explain after too many beers.

"Of course, I do not object to polite *intercourse* with the fair sex, but I would caution against particular connections. Such *connections* at this tumultuous time in our lives, friend Nathan, are dangerous," Eb continued.

"None of us have yet proved able to withstand the *evil* that comes in the form of a beautiful female," Ben laughed, wiping the foam from his lips with the back of his hand.

"Enough of your foppery, gentlemen." I knew from experience that we could banter all night long about sexual relations using our familiar code words.

I stood, prepared to move on to more serious matters. "Our liberty, our very existence, is threatened. We must be prepared to sacrifice our pleasures, if not our lives, in its defense."

"Here, here," my classmates pounded their mugs on the table, spilling brew across the wood and onto the floor. A youthful barkeep, red hair flopping on his shoulders, hastened over with rag and mop in hand.

"Caleb Wheaton?" I asked. "I thought you moved to Boston."

"My family moved, Master Hale, but I stayed behind to complete my apprenticeship with tailor Appletree."

"Any news from…" I hesitated. "…your father?"

"None yet. No word from my sister either," Caleb replied before scurrying back to the bar.

I did not appreciate Caleb's tartness, but I would box his ears another time. I returned my attention to my classmates, raising my glass to recite Addison once again. "What pity is it that we can die but once to serve our country!"

A craggy-cheeked man with a crown of thinning gray hair appeared uninvited at my side. He was dressed in an elegant black velvet jacket sprouting officer's epaulets. "It will take more than platitudes to drive the British into the sea," he announced, hand resting on the hilt of the sword scabbarded at his waist. "My name is Charles Webb, Colonel Charles Webb. Fought the French and the Indians in the wilderness a few years back. Preparing to fight the Regulars now. Can I buy you men another beer?"

"A beer with a fellow patriot would be most welcome," I said, sliding over on the bench. "Please sit down and join us, Colonel."

"What brings you to New London?" Ben asked.

"College men like you," Webb replied as he motioned for refills all round. "I'm out recruiting officers for the Seventh Connecticut regiment of the Continental Army."

"The Continental Army? I didn't know we had one yet," Eb joked.

"We will soon enough. There's a few addle-plots left in Congress that abhor the concept of a national army, but they'll see the light any day now, I reckon," Webb replied.

"There's a gentleman from Virginia that I understand may be in line for command," I said.

"Charles Lee? An excellent choice. He has ample experience on the battlefields of North America and Poland," Webb answered.

"Lee was a captain in the British Army, only recently moved over to our side. Can we trust him now?" Tallmadge asked.

"I've heard men speak well of George Washington. And he's never worn a red coat." I sipped my beer.

"He certainly yearned for one, but the British command never granted his commission," Webb replied.

"Shouldn't a New Englander run the army? The fighting's all in the north anyway," It was Eb's turn to pepper the Colonel with questions.

"Enough noise, men. We're starting to sound like a Dutch concert." Webb stood, placing his draft on the table. "Now, who's ready to fight the British?"

Ben, Eb and I exchanged glances, the serious turn stifling our voices in a blacksmith's grip. The moment of truth had caught us unprepared. Eb coughed. Ben mumbled something about his teaching contract lasting one more year.

I pictured the surprise erupting on the faces of my older brothers when they first saw me in uniform. A velvet officer's coat. With epaulettes. I had fulfilled my obligation to Mother. Now it was time to break from my books - and the girls of New London.

Caleb wandered near the table, distracting me momentarily. Although the youth kept his head down, earnestly sweeping the floor, I had the distinct impression he was eavesdropping. Spying really. Like his father? Had I made a mistake defending William Wheaton?

A more mature man might have questioned the Colonel on the terms of service, but I was too eager to begin the grand adventure. Like a bull charging blindly at a red cape, I could not stand still and let the rebellion pass me by any longer.

"I'm ready Colonel," I announced, standing, separating from my friends. "Nathan Hale, currently a sergeant in the Independent Artillery Corps of New London." *Let Caleb report that to his masters. And his sister.*

"Excellent, excellent. I can see the makings of a fine officer," Webb said, reaching into his saddlebag for parchment, quill and ink.

"Sign right here. You'll wear the bar of a lieutenant. Enlist fifty able-bodied recruits and I'll promote you to captain."

"How do you define able-bodied?" I probed.

"Sixteen years and older. No cripples. And no slaves. Blacks and Indians are acceptable - as long as they hold proof of their freedom."

"But, the colony of Connecticut prohibits all Blacks and Indians from serving in the militia," Ben chipped in.

"Like I said, my regiment will be part of the *Continental Army* soon enough," Webb replied, standing to emphasize his point. "We'll need all the men we can get."

"And when will *our* regiment march to Boston?" I asked.

"In due time," Webb replied. "The men will be raw. We'll train here in Connecticut first."

I signed my name with a flourish, an officer at last.

CHAPTER 3 - JUNE 1775

"I wish we could sell them another hill at that price."
Brigadier General Nathanael Greene
Rhode Island

"Hold still, please, major," Anne Wheaton said as politely as she could with a needle and thread wedged between her teeth. Her first visit to a Beacon Hill mansion, she marveled at the opulence of its spacious public rooms, accented by shelves of thick, leather-bound books, plush carpets, ornately carved moldings and oil paintings of whalers and waves. Senior British officers billeted in homes previously occupied by wealthy rebels on this pastoral hillside away from the commercial bustle of the city proper.

"Almost done?" Major Geoffrey Stanwich, the twenty-five-year-old Lord of Runcorn, asked. A black patch lassoed his left eye, forcing him to turn his head to track Anne. His barrel chest, more appropriate perhaps for a ploughman than a nobleman, had proved a challenge for many an experienced London tailor, let alone a young seamstress in the colonies.

"Not quite. I want it to be as good as new, sir." The major, somehow known to Father, must have torn his uniform in revelry last night. His valet, Henry, had appeared at Wheatons early this morning blustering as if his master were mortally wounded. Father, apparently overwhelmed by bookkeeping chores, had sent Anne to the rescue.

"Do hurry, miss." Stanwich squinted with his good eye to assess the troop of redcoats marching along Treamount Street towards the Common. The calm waters of Mill Pond rippled in the distance.

Boston, a cloverleaf peninsula at the confluence of the Charles and Mystic Rivers, connected to the Massachusetts mainland only by a slender neck of land, was bursting with military activity. After the battles at Lexington and Concord, British soldiers and Loyalist sympathizers flooded into the city, driving the last remaining rebel families to the countryside.

"A vivid jacket, sir," Anne said, darting her needle into the scarlet cloth. She stitched with a steady hand despite her nervousness at being alone with a Lord. A quite handsome one too, she thought, looking up at his jutting chin. The dark stubble there hinted at a man of experience, a far cry from the peach-fuzzed boys of New London.

"My father first wore the scarlet fighting with General Howe in Canada," the major said. "This gorget was father's as well." He gripped the crescent-shaped silver ornament fastened by a black ribbon at the base of his throat. It was polished to a lustrous shine. "It displays our family seal – Neptune and Triton, the gods of the sea, flanking two liver birds native to our estate."

"The carving's impeccable, sir. It will certainly stand out on the field."

"Yes, well, today will be a good day to stand out."

"How is that, sir?" A droplet of sweat formed on her upper lip as Anne tied the final stitch. The high-necked bodice of her frock, as well as the shift underneath it, did not allow for much ventilation.

"The Regulars were supposed to march across the Neck towards Cambridge this morning, but someone must have warned the Jonathans. They dug in on the two Charleston hills overnight. Now we're going to have to cross the Charles and drive them out."

"All done." Anne stepped back, checking her handiwork. A speck of lint clung to the Major's epaulet. She pulled a red floral handkerchief from her sleeve and dusted it off.

He shot his cuffs and tugged on the hem of his mended uniform. "Well, then..."

Anne squared her shoulders as his eyes roamed her body. While her attire provided no boost to her meager bosom, the pannier belt she wore under her day-dress did fashionably broaden her hips. She dipped her right knee to curtsy. "God be with you, sir."

"You may be able to watch the fight from the rooftops," he said. "It will be a grand show."

"I'll be sure to tell Father."

"Your father's a good man. I'm sure he'll prosper here." The Major toyed with the hilt of his sword, now showing no rush to leave.

"He'll be pleased to hear that." Anne pocketed needle and thread through the slits cut into her skirt.

"You can tell him I'll be leading the grenadiers of the 63rd Regiment." Stanwich clicked his boot heels together and reached for his bearskin hat, a cone of black fur that added a good foot to his height. "My men are forming now."

"I'll pray for your safe return."

Anne skirted the Common on her way home, careful to avoid Mt. Whoredom, aptly named for the illicit activities that took place there day and night. She wondered how the Puritans who founded the Massachusetts Bay Colony would react to the sprawling den of iniquity.

The Common, a grazing ground for cattle and sheep, was overrun by soldiers today. Anne could see the crispness in the rows upon rows of uniformed men, hear the resolve in their officers' commands, feel the ground shake when they marched.

She walked past the granary and the graveyard, then along Hanover Street, the spine of the city, towards the North End. Warships in the bay spit fire at the rebel positions. Artillery boomed from Copp's Hill, the highest point in the city. Down at Freeman's Wharf, longboats bobbed, waiting to ferry the troops to the attack.

Looking across the Charles, a slender ribbon of blue from this vantage point, Anne could see the earthworks the rebels had constructed seemingly overnight on Breed's Hill, the red flag of New England flying overhead. What if the rebels had cannons up there? Could they destroy her new home? Her family?

She turned down **Charter Street**, towards the water. The steeple of the Old North Church, the tallest building in Boston as well as the launching point for the rebel Revere's ride of warning, loomed over her shoulder. Chief Narragansett, the wizened, pipe-puffing sachem, leaned against a tree on the corner, straining to get a better view of the action. Whistling the melody to "Rule Britannia", gray-haired Dr. Bradford almost knocked her into a pile of horse droppings.

The Wheatons' house, a mustard-yellow Georgian purchased for a song Father boasted to anyone who would stop long enough to listen, had a keeping room twice as large as their former home in New London, a sleeping space for slaves under the eaves in the attic, and a garden and root cellar in the back. The symmetry of the façade, five windows on the second floor lined up directly over the first-floor windows and front door, appealed to Anne's orderly mind.

While not as grandly furnished as the Major's Beacon Hill quarters, Anne guessed her house was older by the width of the knotted pine floorboards. Trees that wide were the first to be chopped down long ago.

"I told you, didn't I? This rebellion will be over by sundown." Father was back early from the store, his glee easily visible as he reached into the cupboard for a flagon of wine.

"Will Sam Adams hang?" Richard asked.

"Quite possibly," Father replied.

"Can we watch?"

"You'll do no such thing," Mother said, pushing her sons' lesson books across the table. "You'll return to your studies. Immediately."

"We can all go upstairs later. We'll be able to see the battle from there." Father savored his first sip. "If your schoolwork is done."

The boys' eyes gleamed with anticipation. "I wish Caleb were here," Phineas said.

"He'll join us when the Rangers are finished in New London," Father replied before tucking the *Gazette* under his arm and walking out back towards the necessary.

Finished? What were the Rangers planning in New London, Anne wondered, knowing full well it would be dangerous. And how did Father know of it?

Regardless, Anne had her own mission this afternoon. She tugged Mother into a corner. "I have an errand to run," she whispered. "It's my only chance. I must go now."

Mother nodded. "Be careful. The streets are not safe for a young woman."

Anne slipped out the front door. With Mother's blessing, she had written to Master Hale. He was a gentleman, a man of honor, not part of the mob of commoners who had rousted Father and forced Aunt Charlotte from Marshfield. In fact, Nathan had defended Father from the rabble. If Major Stanwich and his troops were successful today, Nathan could return to school and the Wheatons to New London. The healing process could begin.

Now she needed a courier to deliver her letter. As Postmaster General, Benjamin Franklin of Philadelphia had established a postal network throughout New England and the mid-Atlantic, but Boston was completely cut off for military reasons. Fortunately, Dr. Simeon Bacon, a pot-bellied widower who had visited the store with his young daughter, had a pass from General Gage to cross the Neck in route to tend to his dying mother in New Jersey. He was leaving this afternoon and had agreed to take her correspondence, provided he could read it first to insure there was nothing that either side would find informative or incriminating.

After a ten-minute walk, she reached the doctor's home on Lynn Street, also in the North End, fidgeting in the foyer while he read her seemingly docile words, written with the knowledge that they must survive the attention of prying eyes. She hoped Nathan would understand that the act of writing communicated much more than the message.

Dr. Bacon finished the single page, turned it around, flipped it upside down, held it to the light of a candle. No codes or invisible ink.

"You say your father approves?"

"He does not disapprove. Schoolmaster Hale did him a great favor in New London."

Scratching his bulbous nose, the doctor peered at Anne, perhaps searching her face for a scarlet letter, T for treason. He read the letter one more time, at last grunting his assent.

"Thank you, sir," she said. "I will be indebted to you."

"Yes, you will."

"A muffler? Red? I can knit you a warm one before winter."

"If I return…"

"Yes, of course."

"If I return, I might require more than a muffler for comfort."

Anne swallowed, his demand a foul tonic, wishing only to spit it into the fireplace. She sniffed the nosegay looped around her neck, as if it could ward off the evil airs. "Stockings as well then. I'll darn you a pair of stockings."

The doctor sealed the note without reply, dismissing her with a curt nod. Anne set off for home, walking along the shoreline. The rebels were in plain sight now across the river, no place to hide, no quarter would be given.

***

I dismissed my class just after mid-day, the news filtering down from Boston too distracting for both the boys and me. A major confrontation with the redcoats appeared imminent; I longed to be there on the front line with musket in hand, not trapped in a schoolhouse in New London. Donning my Artillery Company uniform, gold-buttoned white jacket and black leggings, I wandered over to Miner's to troll for prospects for my troop.

Lingering at the end of the bar, I picked at my dinner while re-reading the last letter from Enoch. My three older brothers had left to join the Army in May; I was jealous. Did they know I'd be commissioned as an officer as soon as the term ended? Between my time in college and my teaching assignments, we had seen little of each other for the past six years. Hopefully, we could catch up when my regiment reached Boston. Enoch also detailed his ministry preparations and provided mundane news on Father, our stepmother Abigail, and our younger siblings on the farm. I tucked the missive back in my pocket, restless to be off to war.

A lanky man with a queue of sandy hair tied with red, white and blue ribbons tapped his long, fine fingers on the far side of the bar as he conversed with Jabez Miner, the tavern's beefy, bearded publican. Several weeks of recruiting had taught me to listen without turning my head.

"Damn blockade," the man cursed. "Ships tied up at anchor don't need new sails."

"Suppose you'll be needing me to extend your credit again?" Jabez asked as he refilled the man's cup with ale. Sunlight, flooding through the open windows, glinted off the tin.

I saw an opening. My first thirty recruits had been eager volunteers, men determined to play their part in the creation of not only a new nation, but a new society promising opportunity for all. The last ones, however, had required some coaxing.

"Why don't you join the fight, friend?" I pushed my plate across the bar, slicing a sausage in half and gesturing to share it. "We'll drive those bloody-backs into the sea."

"I'm not a soldier, man. I'm a sailmaker."

"A sailmaker would make a fine addition to our regiment," I replied.

"Your regiment?" the sailmaker asked, stuffing the sausage in his mouth as he looked me over.

"Colonel Charles Webb's in command, actually. I'm just a lieutenant." I speared another piece of meat and offered it. "My name's Nathan Hale."

"I'm Elvin Parrish. But I ain't got military experience," he replied, again greedily chomping away. Jabez, a staunch supporter of the Cause, refilled Parrish's cup and turned his back to busy himself cleaning his flagons.

"No worries. I'm sure you'll make a fine soldier." While Parrish looked quite the dandy, I wasn't too particular right now.

"This ain't a good time for me to be leaving New London."

"If you're not making sails, why stay?" I asked.

"The Widow Appletree," he said, sporting a sloppy leer. "She's a right fetching woman in need of a man."

"Her husband just passed on a few weeks ago, didn't he?"

"Almost three weeks now. The bloody flux got him. And Darcy ain't got no children. None still alive at any rate."

"So the Widow will inherit the store?"

"And the house." Parrish sipped contentedly, white foam lingering on his thin lips.

"I understand that Paul Appletree put himself in quite some debt to build his business."

"Mmm." Parrish coughed into his ale.

"Might be why the Widow's so anxious to find a man," I said, now studying my own brew.

"Mmm."

"She might prefer a man with an income however," I added.

"And I might be willing to extend your credit a bit longer – if you were serving the Cause," Jabez chipped in as he swiveled to face us.

"I pay a bounty to each of my recruits. And your enlistment would expire on December 10th."

In fact, the enlistment of the entire regiment would expire then. Would my troop just pack up and leave? In the middle of a revolution?

"You'll be home for Christmas," the proprietor said, topping up Parrish's cup one more time.

"I'll set on it for a bit," Parrish replied, rising, but making no effort to pay his tab. "I promised Pa I'd mend the roof this month."

"Don't wait too long – I've just about reached my recruitment quota," I called as the
sailmaker walked out the door.

My enlistment efforts freed me from the cocoon of academia, forcing me to relate to men from all walks of life. Although two years out of Yale, I had only turned twenty this month. While teaching had taught me to command the room, I had no real soldiering experience. And my recruits knew it too. The fancy Artillery Company uniform didn't fool anyone - not even Anne, I thought ruefully. I would have to prove myself every day on the parade ground – until we got into a real fight.

Nevertheless, I was only three men shy of my goal. Two if Parrish signed up. Feeling full of myself, I decided to chase down Caleb Wheaton. His ears needed a boxing. I decided to see if he was still working at the tailor shop.

Elvin Parrish had an eye for women, I noted as Widow Appletree, pushing thirty but still in full bloom, answered my knock. Although leaning Tory, she invited me in – to my surprise- and offered a cup of tea. Bustling about the hearth in the parlor that also served as her storefront, she loosened her cap, letting her blond locks fall to her shoulders.

"Caleb's gone off to join the war," she said as she took the kettle off the crane. "In support of his King, I might add."

"I'm well aware of young Wheaton's political persuasion."

"But you're an officer on the rebel side, I gather. A dangerous proposition these days." She filled both our cups and sat opposite me, clearing a place at the table strewn with colorful rolls of silk, cotton and lace.

"I'm not afraid to fight for my rights, Widow." The steam warmed my cheeks as I sipped.

"Please call me Darcy." She uncrossed her legs, her bare ankles visible beneath her skirt. "I respect a man who stands up for what he believes in."

"And you? What side are you on?"

"That's complicated," she replied, standing, reaching high on a shelf for a jug marked with a crudely etched XXX. Her hem rode up to expose the lower third of a pair of sinewy calves. After pouring a generous helping into her teacup, she moved to fill mine as well.

I had flirted casually with mothers of my pupils, or they had flirted with me, but I had never been alone with an older woman. I was sorely tempted to test the adage from Ben Franklin's *Advice to a Young Man on the Choice of a Mistress*: "…below the girdle, it is impossible of two women to know an old one from a young one." Particularly, its emphatic conclusion: "They are so grateful!"

The battle between my brain and pindle raged for a full second before reason remarkably won the day. Elvin Parrish had already staked his claim to the widow, while I was inclined to disentangle myself from relationships here in New London, not embark upon a new one. I shook my head and stood to take my leave.

"Godspeed to you then, sir." Widow Appletree spit out the words before chugging her tea. "May our King grant you mercy."

***

Father had recited the British point of view so many times, Anne knew it by heart. Gage had been overconfident at Lexington and Concord, unaware of the sheer number of militia gathered in the countryside, hesitant to launch an all-out assault against men that he considered fellow Englishmen. The Regulars had been ambushed, rebel riflemen crouching in the woods and behind stone walls. General Howe would not make the same mistakes. Gage would soon be shipped back across the Atlantic in disgrace.

The sun was just past its zenith. The redcoats, at ease by the docks, waited restlessly for their final orders. She counted the longboats, factored in their capacity, and calculated the size of the assault force.

"A kiss for a soldier?" a cherry-cheeked private called out, breaking her concentration.

"A quick poke instead?" another jeered, bucking his hips.

Anne did not slow, accustomed to the taunts, grown saucier of late. One day she might prove they had underestimated her contribution. She quickened her pace, leaving the hecklers behind, when a familiar voice hailed. "Miss Wheaton. A moment of your time?"

"Major Stanwich. A pleasure to see you again, sir."

"Most fortuitous, yes." An awkward silence.

Anne shuffled her feet. "I must be going."

"Me as well. We board at two sharp." The major gaze flicked down towards the harbor. "A favor, perhaps?"

"Yes?" *Not another proposition.*

"Your kerchief? For luck. The gods of war can be fickle."

"Of course." Anne slipped the silk square from her cuff, observing Major Stanwich in a new light. Here was a man of experience, blooded in battle, aware of its capriciousness.

He tucked the talisman into the pocket of his waistcoat and bowed in thanks. "Until my return then."

Father and the boys were already upstairs by the time Anne stepped in the front door. Mother was chopping vegetables for supper, while Becky was out back making soap, the putrid odor of lye and animal fat drifting into the keeping room.

"Is it off?" Mother asked.

"Yes," Anne smiled. She would tell Mother the details later. "I'll help," she offered, reaching for the kettle hanging on the crane in the hearth.

"Father wants to talk to you first." Mother pointed up the stairs.

The afternoon sun blazed, baking the shingles on the roof. Richard and Phineas leaned out the attic window, craning to see across the river, while Father stood behind them, goblet of wine in hand.

"Has the action started yet?" Anne asked.

"Soon. General Howe had to wait for the tide. The last of his men are crossing now."

"I estimate two thousand at least," she said. Father's dark brows arched upward in surprise.

"Look at all the warships," Phineas called, recapturing his father's attention.

"There's the Lively, and the Somerset, and the Cerberus," Richard pointed out his favorites. "The Lively's the first to fire."

"Well done, son."

Father stepped back from the window, motioning for Anne to follow. "I didn't realize you were so quick with figures. Or so attentive to military matters."

"Pleasant surprises, I trust," she replied.

Father nodded, scrutinizing his daughter as if she was a mermaid fresh out of the sea. "Did all go well with Major Stanwich this morning?" he asked, returning to more familiar territory.

"Yes, Father."

"And?"

"And what Father?"

"Did he talk to you? Show any interest? In conversation, of course."

Anne blushed, her cheeks matching the scarlet of the Major's jacket. "We exchanged a few words."

"Good, good. He's a widower. Wife died of the pox last year, you know."

"We did not become that well-acquainted." Anne decided to keep mum about Dr. Bacon's advance.

"Well, I'm pleased to hear you're a modest girl."

"I hope you'll inform Caleb of that fact. He appeared to have some doubts."

"Your brother looks out for your welfare."

"And I look out for his." Anne checked to make sure Phineas and Richard were still occupied at the window. "What are the Rangers planning in New London?" she asked quietly.

"I know only it concerns a raid on the harbor." Father's smile was a cruel one. No wonder, since the harbor was the lifeblood of New London – and the Sons of Neptune.

"Father! Father! Come quick. I can hear the drums." Phineas shouted.

The family crowded into the window. A mass of British soldiers had assembled on **Moulton's Point** at the foot of Breed's Hill. The officers out front, followed by ruler-straight lines of redcoats. The formation marched to its right towards the beach, out of the Wheatons' view.

"Where'd they go?" Richard cried.

"To flank the rebel positions. General Howe will lead them," Father replied, tipping his goblet in a toast to success. "Brilliant move."

Musket fire popped. Clouds of smoke wafted from the hillside. The Wheatons waited.

"We should see our men atop the hill any second now," Father said at last, calmly sipping his wine.

"There they are," Anne pointed. The redcoats were streaming back towards their assembly point in disarray.

"They're retreating?" Phineas asked incredulously.

"Don't fret. A minor setback, I'm sure," Father said, stepping away from the window to refill his glass. "Howe will rally the men."

"Look, reinforcements," Richard said as another phalanx of red streamed from the boats up towards the hills. The Wheatons watched the men again form neat rows and columns and march straight up the pastures towards the rebel redoubt.

Another round of musket volleys. The tall grass weaved in the breeze. Gunsmoke drifted over the river. Anne thought she could hear the cries of the wounded on the wind.

Once again, a stew of red and scarlet leaked back into view. Father coughed up a mouthful of burgundy. The boys were silent.

"Is it over yet?" Mother called as she climbed the stairs.

"Not quite," Father replied, blotting the stain with his napkin. "We're forming up again. Third time's the charm."

The British charged straight up Breed's Hill again, climbing over their dead comrades, the carnage in plain sight. Mother blanched, pulling Richard away from the window by his ear, returning for Phineas, but he squirmed free, clasping Father's hand.

"We're gaining ground," Father shouted as the red mass inched closer to the rebel fortifications, leaving a trail of dead and wounded in its wake. A spasm of gunfire ripped through the British lines, halting the advance. The mass quivered like cherry jam, seemingly unsure which way to go.

"Are we going to retreat again?" Richard wailed.

The rebel guns fell strangely silent. A fife bleat from the hilltop.

"They're out of ammunition," Father shouted. "I knew it. I told Sam…" His voice faded away. So, Father was still in contact with the leering Mr. Hale, Anne thought.

"Fix bayonets! Charge!" The orders resounded across the river.

A blood-curdling roar emanated from the British ranks. The redcoats sprinted the remaining yards to the earthen berms. Up and over. Sunlight glinted off steel. Men screamed in anger, in exaltation, in agony.

The red mass blanketed the crest of Breed's Hill, while an array of blue, gold and brown coats slipped down its back side towards the neighboring Bunker Hill. The British were too battered to give chase, but the rebels did not tarry long. Their position was vulnerable to attack by land or sea.

By five o'clock, the battle was over. The Red Ensign, a scarlet flag with the Union Jack in the canton, flew on the hills, while the rebels retreated across the Charlestown Neck towards Cambridge.

"We've won," Father declared.

But at what cost, Anne wondered, watching a flotilla of empty longboats return to the city.

CHAPTER 4 - JULY 1775

Dear Friend Hale,
...I am informed that you are honoured by the Assembly with a Lieutenant's
Commission...When I consider you as a Brother Pedagogue engaged in a calling
useful, honourable & doubtless to you very entertaining, it seems difficult to advise
you to leave ... But when I consider our country, a land flowing as it were with
milk and honey, holding open her arms, & demanding Assistance in her sore
distress, a Christian's counsel must favour the latter...Our holy Religion, the
honour of our God, a glorious country & a happy constitution is what we have to
defend...

Ben. Tallmadge
Wethersfield, CT
July 4, 1775

"Forward march!" I ordered, leading my troop, four rows of ten men, around the New London green one more time. As a lieutenant, I expected to be in the front line at all times. It was a matter of honor.

While I wore my Artillery Company uniform, my recruits were still dressed in a motley assortment of deerskin britches, linen hunting shirts and other homespun garb. One private in the fifth rank even sported a beaver cap, tail flopping as he marched, too valuable to remove even on a summer afternoon.

A low ceiling of oyster-gray clouds signaled an approaching storm, but provided at least a temporary reprieve from the broiling sun. Whitecaps rippled the Thames River, rocking the craft at rest in the harbor. A lightning bolt pierced the distant sky above the Long Island coast.

My attention wandered for a second as I watched a rider canter up State Street and dismount in front of Miner's Tavern which also served as the local post office. While I had just about given up on a letter from Anne, I regularly exchanged correspondence with Tallmadge, still teaching school, and Williams, training three times per day with the Yale College militia.

I scanned the sky again. We might have an hour at most to drill before the weather hit. I signaled for the fife and drum to resume the Harriot, the Army's marching tune.

After thirty minutes, I halted the troop and aligned the men as if we faced the enemy. With gunpowder scarce, I rarely ordered my troop to shoot their muskets. Instead, we practiced formations, one line loading while another pretended to fire.

"Don't shoot until you see the whites of their eyes." I pounded the dictum into my recruits. Since muskets had little accuracy beyond sixty yards, it made little sense to fire any sooner.

On the battlefield, my most difficult task would be to maintain discipline in my men in the face of a British advance. Almost all the rebel casualties on Breed's Hill had been inflicted by British bayonets, not muskets.

How would I hold up against the redcoats? Only a real fight would test my courage.

Unfortunately, there was no word yet on the date of our deployment. General Washington had only arrived in Cambridge on July 2, the culmination of a two-week journey from Philadelphia, marked by frequent stops to greet local dignitaries as well as a celebrity-worshipping populace. While I suspected Washington would have preferred to hasten to the battlefield, the Virginia plantation owner had to win the hearts of New Englanders before he could win the war against the British. Fortunately, the broadsheets noted that the redcoats were busy fortifying Bunker Hill after their "victory" there last month and showed no signs of venturing out into the hostile countryside.

The clouds opened sooner than I anticipated, sheets of water deluging the green. My men started to fall out, one sprinting towards the cover of Miner's Tavern.

"Stop right there, Private Parish," I ordered, barely audible in the downpour. "Halt!" I yelled again, this time sprinting after the deserter. My men laughed as the comical chase unfolded. After thirty yards, my fingers snared the fop's ribboned queue as I tackled him into the muck.

"What in damnation, Lieutenant?" Parish grunted, spitting strands of grass from his teeth.

"Back in line. Third Company is not dismissed," I replied, shoving Parish towards the formation, the men clearly enjoying the diversion despite the downpour. They welcomed us back into the ranks with a volley of ribald comments.

"You two looked quite *tight* there."

"Tussling over Widow Appletree?"

"A threesome perhaps?"

I pretended to ignore the badinage as I reclaimed my position at the head of the company. An officer must command respect at all times, I realized, albeit too late. Had anyone seen me visit Widow Appletree's shop? Were the men laughing at me as well?

"Forward march," I ordered, leaning into the slanting rain, hoping to restore some semblance of my authority. We paraded around the green until the sun sliced through the clouds once again.

***

Major Stanwich stirred; the laudanum wearing off. Sitting in the rocker by his bedside, Anne tried to read his inscrutable face, pale from the ordeal, but patrician even in repose. Giving up, she gazed out the open window at the Back Bay, a spongy marshland at low tide, while her fingers absentmindedly twirled a ball of red yarn in her lap. The sun dipped to the tree line, time to change Geoffrey's bandages.

Although the British claimed victory, casualties on Breed's Hill were so high that Commander Gage prohibited the ringing of church bells at funerals. Anne shuddered at the memory of the morning after the battle when Father told her the "good" news - Geoffrey was one of the few front-line officers to survive. Perhaps, her kerchief had proved lucky after all. Then Father asked if she'd like to visit the major in the hospital tent the next day. She hesitated at first, but, upon Mother's urging, she went.

Her perception of good fortune changed when she entered that tent. Geoffrey was barely conscious, a jug of rum empty by his cot. A rebel musket ball had shattered his right leg, but his comrades had staunched the bleeding and the surgeons had amputated at dawn. His stump was now swathed in white linen and topped by a gray wool cap. Father said he was still in shock from the operation, which he noted was mercifully short. A British Army surgeon could saw through a thigh bone in less than a minute, he boasted.

Anne had sat by Geoffrey's bedside through that first night. Mother had warned her that the hospital would be ripe with noxious airs, but she had said nothing about the sights, moans and malodors of the wounded. These were professional soldiers, well-trained in the arts of war, yet they were now bloody, broken men. How could they ever become whole again?

Unfortunately, the narrow streets of Boston were not much better. The combination of summer heat, mosquitos, and cramped quarters created the perfect breeding ground for disease. Smallpox, in particular, was ubiquitous, contagious, and often deadly. Anne had seen its victims in the streets, faces ravaged by rash and pustules, ostracized by all but their closest kin. She had survived a mysterious illness when she was five, which Mother thought might provide immunity from the dreaded pox, but no one knew for sure.

Geoffrey emerged from the hospital minus one limb, but otherwise intact. Dr. Bradford visited regularly, bleeding the major and administering calomel, a mercury-laced laxative, to purge any poisons from his system. The doctor insisted that the windows remain shut to keep out the fresh air that might bring the poisons back. He also prohibited his patient from bathing since the practice might wash away the oils that protected the skin from disease.

With the heat and stench unbearable, Anne unlatched the shutters as soon as the good doctor left. A smile flit across Geoffrey's lips when she touched his hand. Mother had been right. It was her Christian, as well as patriotic, responsibility to help where she could. Now, a month into her bedside vigils, she had grown affectionate for her charge; yet, he was so often in pain, or opium-addled, that she could not gauge her true feelings. Or his.

Geoffrey shook the cobwebs from his head and struggled to sit up, clenching his teeth to fight the pain.

"You must rest," Anne said as she unwound the dressings. She dipped a cloth in a jar of herbal tincture, lavender and cinnamon, that Mother had prepared from her kitchen garden, and applied it to the stump.

"I've rested enough. I need to regain my wits." He reached for a feather pillow and flailed to put it behind his back. Anne took the pillow, as well as a second one, and propped them underneath Geoffrey's head.

"We should walk around the room today," Anne said, reaching for a crutch by the bedpost.

"Not yet," Geoffrey replied, waving it away.

A coach clattered to a halt in the street beneath the window. The Major's valet, Henry, a strapping, apple-cheeked private, appeared at the bedroom door. "General Howe here to see you, sir."

Geoffrey's eyes shot open in surprise. "The general? Here?" By sheer will, he forced his torso upright, his biceps straining with the effort. Anne moved to rearrange his bedding, but he shooed her off.

"Major Stanwich, you're looking fit. I was right next to you when you went down. Didn't think you'd make it," William Howe said as he stepped across the threshold. In full dress uniform, scarlet tunic tinseled with gold buttons, braids and epaulettes, bisected by a white sash, the general cut an imposing figure. He doffed his hat to Anne, revealing a softer countenance than she would have imagined for a man who had spent a lifetime at war.

"Yes, well, I'll be back up and about soon," Geoffrey replied.

"I'll go downstairs," Anne offered.

"No, no, stay. The Major may need your assistance," Howe commanded, keeping his distance from the bed. "I won't tarry long."

"My men tell me that you've fortified Bunker Hill," Geoffrey said.

"Yes. Quite impregnable now, I trust. We sacrificed too much blood to win that ground. We will not lose it."

Geoffrey looked down at his lost leg. "The army's staying in Boston then?" he asked, casting a sideways glance at Anne. She detected a hopeful tone in his inflection. Perhaps he savored their time together as much as she did.

"For now, at least," the General replied. "In my opinion, we should abandon this God-forsaken city. We're trapped here. Food is scarce. Wounded and sick overflowing in every barracks. If the rebels are smart, they'll just sit in their camps and starve us out."

"And Commander Gage?"

"He's of the same opinion, but we both await orders from the King."

"Where would we go?"

"New York would be my recommendation. It has a deep harbor and many more loyal friends in the countryside."

Anne kept her head down, shrinking back against the wall. *Father must hear this news. Our business would be lost, and our lives in jeopardy, if the Army leaves Boston.*

"I must be going," General Howe interrupted her thoughts. "Lady Pigot is hosting a farewell banquet for Mrs. Gage. She's sailing to England next week."

"Her sons attend school there, I believe," Geoffrey said.

"Yes, that is the reason. A mother needs to be with her family."

"I'm sure her departure will be a great relief to Commander Gage."

"The rumors of her inclinations to the rebel cause dog his steps every day," General Howe said.

"I, for one, can't believe she was a spy. Women simply don't have a head for military matters," Geoffrey said.

"I certainly hope not," the General smiled towards Anne. "I have a most attractive member of the fair sex waiting in my coach to accompany me this evening."

"Your secrets are safe, I'm sure," Geoffrey joked as the General departed.

Anne couldn't resist a glance outside. She recognized a familiar silhouette in the window of the coach. General Howe kissed her flush on the lips as he climbed in. Like a besotted schoolboy.

"That's Betsey Loring," she said, turning to Geoffrey.

"They make a handsome couple, don't they?"

"She's married."

"So is he, supposedly. The General's wife remains in England. And they don't have any children."

"But Betsey's husband is right here in Boston. He must know." Anne flinched as the coachman's whip cracked outside. The clip-clop of hoofbeats faded down the street.

"Of course, Joshua Loring knows Howe is rogering his wife. And he approves," Geoffrey said. "The next dispatch from the King will undoubtedly order Commander Gage to return to London. Howe will then become the Commander-in-Chief of the Crown's forces in North America. He will need respite from the heavy responsibilities of that office."

"So, Mrs. Loring's a respite, a trifle to amuse the General? While her husband…"

"You are a naïve young lady. Sheriff and Mrs. Loring are both providing a service to the Crown. I'm sure that General Howe will see that Sheriff Loring is well-compensated for his wife's efforts."

Anne looked at the soiled sheets and bandages piled next to Geoffrey's bed. Am I providing a service to the Crown as well? Will Father be compensated accordingly?

"England is your country too," Geoffrey added, fumbling for his crutch. "Now, my dear, I believe it's time for my walk."

"Yes, of course," she mumbled in reply.

***

After my troop dispersed, I strolled towards Miner's, surprised to find Prudence Richards waiting outside with a tin cup in hand. "Having a cider?" I asked, stripping off my jacket and smoothing it over the rail to dry. My wet shirt clung to my chest.

"Ginger beer," she replied with a wink. "I grew thirsty just watching you."

"I was a little rough on the men in the rain."

"When will you march to Boston?"

"Shortly."

"We'll miss you." She coyly sipped her beverage.

"I'm in need of refreshment as well." I pushed past, figuring that Prudence would soon voice whatever was really on her mind.

"Can I join you?" Prudence placed her cup next to my jacket, but it toppled over into the muddy street.

Her request took me by surprise. While women were welcome at Miner's during the day, the evenings were generally reserved for men unless there was a frolic or other social event.

"It's going to be a glorious sunset," I said, squinting into the glare from the golden orb hanging precariously above the tree line. "Why don't you join me for a walk on the beach later?" The proposition slipped from my lips without conscious thought, a cry for solace perhaps after my miscues on the parade ground. Regardless, Prudence would have little doubt of my intentions.

Before she could answer, a familiar voice boomed, "An ale or your mail, lieutenant?" Jabez beamed as he stepped into the doorway. "The first one's on me. Always pleased to serve the men who are serving our fair town."

"I'll meet you in front of the customs' house in thirty minutes." Prudence tugged my sleeve, reclaiming my attention. She nodded a farewell to Jabez then walked off towards home.

"Thank you kindly," I replied, cuffing the tavernkeeper's shoulder as I stepped inside. Taking my ale in one hand and a sealed but unmarked envelope in the other, I tried to quench my thirst and my curiosity at the same time, succeeding at neither.

I looked for a seat to read undisturbed. Elvin Parish was long gone to Widow Appletree's embrace, but four of my men surrounded the hook-nosed barmaid.

I swilled my ale before examining the anonymous message, turning it over twice in vain search of a clue. Breaking the seal, I removed the neatly folded page. The letter was from Ezra Selden, the first of my Yale friends to see combat. Three soldiers in camp at Roxbury, just outside the Boston Neck, were killed by small arms fire, another run through by bayonet. The account was sobering.

I skipped ahead, searching for any word of Boston itself. There…Ezra noted that the "inhabitance have done coming out of Boston almost." That's it? I read on. Nothing more.

A prick of guilt poked me as I thought of my upcoming shoreline stroll, but I brushed it away. It was foolish to even think of carrying a torch for Anne much longer. She had left New London three months ago. Besides, I was going off to war. Who knows when I might next enjoy female companionship?

Plumes of pink and orange streaked the sky as I slapped a silver coin on the bar to purchase a bottle of rum. I slipped out the rear door, avoiding my jabbering men. I did not want to keep Prudence waiting.

Before I advanced ten paces, a horse whinnied, providing just enough warning for me to sidestep a steaming dollop of dung. Pivoting, I thumped into a dark silhouette tensed by the hitching post, reins in hand. I recoiled, fearing a bear, but relaxed when I recognized a familiar face, his white irises standing out like lanterns on a black night.

"What the…" Asa Cobb paled in obvious fright. He stared wild-eyed for a full second before recognition set in. "Nathaniel Hale, you damn near scared the dilberries out of me."

Asa's mother, Florence, was a free Black, a paid laborer in our household in Coventry. His father was rumored to be a slave on a neighboring property, but no one knew for sure and Florence took her secret to the grave five years ago. Asa, two years older than me, had grown up on the Hale farm, joining my brothers and me on regular jaunts to take cattle and timber to the harbor in Norwich. Shortly after his mother passed, Asa declared that he was finished with farming life, choosing to seek his fortune hauling sails on a merchant brig instead.

"Enoch wrote that you were at sea again," I replied, pounding Asa's back. "It's good to see you."

"And you. And you." Asa's color returned.

"You're a free man. No need to be slinking around Miner's back door."

"Old fears die hard, I guess." Asa tethered his horse. "What brings you to New London, friend?"

"I teach school here. At least, I did until a few weeks ago. Now, I'm gathering a company of men to join the fight in Massachusetts."

"A noble cause."

"I want to hear all about your travels, but a young lady waits." I held up both hands as if helpless to resist.

"Some things never change," Asa laughed.

"Why don't we meet ..."

A ruckus inside the tavern interrupted their conversation.

"Nathan! You still out there?" Jabez called. "Come quick."

I sprinted back inside while Asa tagged behind. A dough-bellied man, water dripping from his ratty shirt and britches, doubled over and puked, the slop getting tangled in his stringy, gray beard.

"The Queen's Rangers attacked the harbor. Spiked our cannons. Set fire to the Customs House," the man, a jagged scar now visible on his plump cheek, spit out.

The Customs' House? Was Prudence safe? "Anyone else hurt?" I asked. A shoulder shrug of uncertainty was his only reply. "Where are the red devils now?"

"Down at the dock, loading up the Tulip. Plan to run supplies up to Boston." He swiped the phlegm from his lips. "I was on guard duty - the only one on board. Jumped off the stern." He retched again. "Not much of a swimmer."

"How many Rangers?"

"Seven."

"Men, get your weapons and follow me," I shouted, brandishing my pistol.

My men, mugs in hand, stared at me uncomprehending, their mouths gaped open. "We're outnumbered," one croaked.

"The whole town will be out soon enough!"

Still no movement. The barmaid shooed them away. "Off with you boys. You got work to do!"

Jabez Miner reached for a musket underneath the bar. "I'm coming too."

Tabitha handed me a lantern from the wall. "You'll need this."

"This is what we've been training for," I said as my four troopers finally assembled. I offered my own musket to Asa. "Another hand would be useful."

Asa nodded, raising his shirt to display a pistol tucked into his waistband. I slung my musket over my shoulder.

We raced downhill, several armed citizens joining our ranks. The harbor would usually be overflowing with ships, but the hostilities had ground commerce to a halt, leaving the dock almost deserted. Flames leapt from the Customs House; fire bells rang; Prudence was third in line on the bucket brigade, drawing water from the harbor to combat the conflagration.

Relieved to see her safe, I stopped under the tortured branches of an ancient beech, motioning my men into line. "Over there," I pointed out the Pink Tulip, forty yards away across open ground.

The glow of the fire illuminated the gauzy twilight. Most of the town was now harborside, either gawking or helping, but not paying much mind to the enemy.

I counted four masked Rangers, loading crates from a horse-drawn wagon onto the ship, plus one sitting in the buckboard and another tending a steer, pawing nervously.

"Ready?" I whispered. A burst of flatulence was the only reply. Time to learn if we could shoot straight.

"Fire!" I ordered, aiming at the driver. My arm jerked at the blast, the first time I had ever fired at another human. Instinctively, the Ranger ducked, dropping the reins, then popped up again. The volley from my men also sailed harmlessly into the night. Bucking wildly, the horse almost toppled the wagon, sending the remaining cargo tumbling into the dirt.

"Reload!" I swung my musket around, tore open a paper cartridge with my teeth, and primed the flash pan with a tinge of gunpowder. I poured the remainder of the powder into the barrel followed by a lead ball, tamping both down with my ramrod. An expert infantryman could load in less than fifteen seconds; I doubted my men and I could do it in thirty.

After cocking the firelock, I clamped the musket's stock tight against my cheek and aimed. "Fire!"

The cacophony of noise, light, and smoke stunned me for a full second after I pulled the trigger. Fortunately, my troop's second volley found its mark as a Ranger puddled on the dock. A cheer arose from the surrounding homes.

My musket must have gouged my cheek on recoil. I spit blood as I gave the command to charge. "Huzzah! Huzzah!" my men echoed, rushing the Tulip.

"Stinking skunks!" The Ranger captain cursed as he grabbed the bridle, struggling to calm the skittery horse. Leaping up onto the buckboard, he found the fallen reins and whipped the horse forward. The wagon rumbled away from the pier, steadily gathering speed as the untethered steer followed in its wake.

We chased but could only watch as the Queen's Rangers disappeared. Returning to the dock, I leaned over the fallen enemy, my own age, skull crushed by the musket ball, clearly dead. War was not so glorious up close. I replayed the skirmish in my mind, counting six Rangers, not seven, as the watchman had claimed back at the tavern.

I bent over, prying open a crate to reveal bushels of turnips and corn. If the Rangers were smuggling beef and vegetables, Boston must be in dire need of fresh food.

Footfalls pounded down the gangplank; a coarse voice shrieked an unintelligible war cry. I spiraled, but slipped on a corn stalk and fell. A mountainous Indian, face striped in red and black paint, lunged toward me brandishing a tomahawk in his right hand.

I rolled to my side, reaching for my pistol. The Indian stomped on my wrist, pinning it, sending the pistol scuttling across the dock. Eyes frenzied with desperation, the Indian raised his weapon to deliver the death blow. I lashed out with my right foot, knocking him off balance.

A shot rang out. The Indian's chest exploded, a crimson stain festooning his green Ranger jacket. Staggering backwards, the body splashed into the Sound. Asa dropped his smoking pistol and rushed to my side.

A crescent moon illuminated our way back to Miner's, its torches flickering a hero's welcome. We crowded inside along with a dozen men from the bucket brigade, who had successfully doused the fire. I looked for Prudence but couldn't find her.

"Nice shot," I said to Asa.

"Nice scar," he pointed to the jagged slash on my face. "You tucked your musket a little too close."

"It's just a scratch. The tomahawk would have done much worse."

"Deacon Hale would be mighty disappointed if I didn't look after his college boy."

"I'm quite grateful, myself."

I put my arm around Asa's shoulder. My wrist was swollen, but not broken. "Can I buy you that drink?"

"In Miner's? I'm still not sure my presence would be appreciated there."

"Don't be foolish, young man," Jabez Minor stepped up. "This round's on me."

Asa and I retreated to a back table, dimly lit by a drooping candle. Tabitha brought us two mugs of ale and a wedge of cheese. Asa surveyed the room one more time. "To your continued good health," he toasted, satisfied he was safe.

"And yours," I replied.

We sipped our brews in silence, decompressing from the evening's events. Two of my men went home, while the other two loudly regaled the barmaid with tales of their bravery.

"Do you always carry a weapon?" I asked Asa at last.

"Have you ever been to the West Indies?"

"When do you sail again?"

"Not for a while, I'm afraid. The Royal Navy doesn't look too kindly on rebel shipping right now." Asa sliced off a triangle of cheese with his knife. "I'm looking for interim employment."

"Join up with me then."

"The army? Connecticut doesn't allow Blacks to serve."

"I'm recruiting for the Continental Army, established by order of Congress in Philadelphia on June 14th," I said, signaling for another round. "I need good men like you. The Cause needs good men like you. To fight for Boston. And for freedom."

"Whose freedom would I be fighting for?"

"Freedom for all. The men in my company are from every trade – craftsmen, laborers, mariners. You're no different." I massaged my sore wrist.

"You keep forgetting I'm Black," Asa paused to let his words sink in. "Will your side enlist slaves?"

"No. We can't do that. It would be against the law."

"Oh, the law." He didn't have to say more.

While Father did not keep slaves, about one in five households in Coventry did. Just before leaving for Yale, I had gone fishing with Asa and his friend, Joseph, a Black whom I thought was also free. We got caught out in a storm and didn't straggle home until after dark. Joseph's master, Methuselah Bridgewater, was furious, thinking Joseph had tried to run away. All our explaining went to naught as Bridgewater made Asa and I watch as he whipped Joseph until his back was laced with crimson stripes.

When Father confronted Methuselah at the meetinghouse the next Sunday, the slaveowner noted that Joseph was his property and he could do with him as he pleased. The boy had needed a lesson in the law and he administered it. For good measure, he even recited the Bible, Luke 12:47, "the slave that knoweth his master's will, and doeth it not, shall be beaten with many stripes." A week later, Methuselah tore Joseph away from his family and sold him to a slaver sailing for Charleston.

"If the British win the war, we'll all be indentured servants," I broke the silence.
"Your people will trade one yoke for another."

"I wager you've ridden that slogan hard." Asa drained the last of his ale. "But, I'll think on it."

"Think fast. We'll be marching to Boston shortly."

Several more men, loud and thirsty, appeared at Miner's front door.

"I best be going," Asa said.

"Our rebellion is the first step to liberty for your people. We must walk before we can run," I said, the best I could do to reconcile my fight for freedom with the plight of the enslaved.

"Lieutenant," Tabitha Miner, a jovial woman whose girth exceeded her husband's, waddled over to his seat, holding up a letter. "Jabez forgot to give you this one. It was buried under the crockery at the bar."

I held the envelope up to the candlelight, my heartbeat soaring when I saw the initials, AW, scrawled in the top left corner. I forced myself to lay it on the table and gather myself.

"A traveling doctor delivered it. A kindly man. Tended to my bunions," Tabitha rumbled on, pointing in the general direction of her toes.

"A good excuse for me to take my leave, Lieutenant Hale," Asa said, shaking my hand before slipping out the back door.

I signaled for another ale, slit open the envelope and smoothed the newly arrived letter out on the table. The candlelight was dim, as were Anne's words. She was fine; their new home was grand; father's business was thriving. Her banality suggested that she too realized that distance and politics had snuffed out the flame of romance. Probably best - for both of us.

Anne had been the first girl in my class to seize upon the true meaning of *Cato*. It was a dark February morning, the snow falling so thickly that many stayed home. The fire blazed; the girls, bundled in their woolens, curled around the hearth to keep warm. I had selected Anne, not entirely by chance, to read the part of the beautiful Marcia. Our eyes locked as she recited, "I should be grieved, young prince, to think my presence unbent your thoughts and slackened them to arms."

"Why are you hiding back here, Lieutenant? Come celebrate your victory with the boys," a boozy voice called out from the bar.

I recognized James Caulk, William Wheaton's tormentor at the liberty pole back in April. *Mr. Caulk, where were your Neptune boys when the shooting started tonight? Why aren't they in the army?*

"In a minute. I have personal business to complete," I said, waving Anne's letter.

"Too high and mighty to mingle with us leather apron men, is he?" a murmur from an unseen face at the bar.

Still no sign of Prudence. Surprising - and disappointing as well, I had to admit. But I also wanted to finish Anne's letter which concluded with another paragraph of the mundane before her parting salutation leapt off the page. *Go on, and prosper in the paths of honor.*

I read the words again. And a third time. Innocuous at first glance, but they were from *Cato*, our secret bond.

"Hale, put down your books and come to the bar," Josiah Barton, the cooper, called stridently. Miner's was overflowing with ebullient townsmen.

I knew the second line of the couplet by heart: *Thy virtue will excuse my passion for thee,*
and make the gods propitious to our love.

Anne's message couldn't have been clearer, or more confusing. I had just about written off our romance when she was back in my heart – and stronger than ever. Even Ben and Eb would approve of Anne now. If only I could see her again…

"On my way, sir," my voice boomed as I rose, a huge smile creasing my face.

To my dismay, the mood in Miner's crossed to the dark side with the next round of ale. Someone held aloft a copy of General Washington's first orders upon arriving in Cambridge, reading them aloud between slurps, his mates stomping and guffawing in derision:
"All Officers are required to keep their Men neat and clean. They are also to take care that Necessarys be provided in the Camps and frequently filled up to prevent their being offensive and unhealthy…"

"His Excellency is a proper Virginia gentleman, is he?" James Caulk sang out. "Doesn't want to smell our shit?"

"We don't take too well to lairds of the manor here in New England," a cobbler's apprentice added in a clipped Scottish brogue.

"Or college boys who defend Tories like William Wheaton." Another leather apron man who hadn't forgotten.

"Lieutenant Hale is a hero, sent the Queen's Rangers slinking off into the night," the town constable came to my defense.

"Some hero you are," Reuben Booge, the printer, once again pushing forward into my face. "I heard a Black boy had to save your college arse or your brains would be leaking all over our fine dock." He whirled around, dropped his breeches and grabbed his knees. "You can wipe my arse, Lieutenant."

A black boot flashed from somewhere behind me, spanking the bare bum, sending Booge sprawling. A wire-thin man, pig tail swaying as he stepped forward, delivered another kick, this time into the fallen printer's midsection. "Anyone else want to insult the Lieutenant?"

The crowd shrunk back, forming a crescent around us. "Didn't think so," my mysterious defender said as he turned to face the bar. "My name's Zebulon Cheesebrough. Work a small plot of land about half a day's ride west. But I got dreams. Of a better world, for my two toddling sons if not for me. And I'm willing to fight for it. Die for it if the good Lord wills."

"Here, here," a murmur of agreement rippled through the tavern.

"I came to New London today to enlist," Zeb continued. "You got room for me in your regiment, Lieutenant?"

Zeb looked about the same age as me, but he sounded a decade older and wiser. "I'd be proud to serve with you, Mr. Cheesebrough," I replied, offering my hand.

"That's the spirit," Josiah Barton shouted, leading the way to the bar. "The next round's on me." Caulk and Booge drifted out into the night.

I rode a wave of good cheer for the next hour, my glass never empty, the fracas drowned in ale and rum. Three more men approached, volunteering to join my company. The crowd thinned. I gathered my hat and musket, checked to make sure Anne's treasured letter was secure in my pocket, and walked to the door.

The beat of a drum greeted me. James Caulk led a score of men and women, several with flaming torches in hand. They marched towards Miner's singing a bawdy take on a popular colonial tune:

> *Lift up your Heads my Heroes!*
> *and swear with proud Disdain,*
> *The Queen who would seduce you,*
> *shall spread her thighs in vain.*

Nested in the belly of the procession, Booge and the African, Pieter Sugarman, supported a fencepost on their shoulders. Seated atop the rail, legs splayed on either side, hands tied in his lap, was a young man cowled in the bloody hide and grotesque head of a steer. Innards, and who knows what else, smeared his shoulders, hair and face, but his expression was one of proud defiance. The formation halted in front of the tavern.

"We got ourselves a Tory conspirator here," Caulk announced, planting the Sons of Neptune standard in the dirt.

"Gave his chickens to the Queen's Rangers to ship up to Boston," another dockhand, bald pate glistening in the torchlight, added. Angry voices bellowed from other marchers.

"He was the look-out on the dock."

"Worships at the Anglican church."

"Drinks British tea, wears British clothes."

"Just like his father, a rich old bugger."

"We've given him a chance to denounce the King, but he keeps his bone-box shut," Caulk said.

Booge and Sugarman yanked on the captive's dangling legs, scouring the roughhewn wood into his private parts. I recognized Caleb Wheaton. No surprise at all, unfortunately. The mess slithered off Caleb's face, but he refused to cry out.

"Let's ship out, boys," Caulk ordered. "March him down to the Liberty Pole. Give him one more chance to see the light."

Then what? Has Connecticut descended into mob rule? Is this the liberty I'm fighting for? I clenched my fists and stepped forward.

Iron fingers gripped my shoulder. "It's not your fight," Zeb said. "I grew up with these boys. They've taken shit from the upper class, Brit and rebel, since they suckled their mama's tit. Now it's their turn to dish it out."

A woman, displaying the pink, puckered hands of a washerwoman, stepped from the mob to dump a bucket of offal on Caleb's head. He spit it from his mouth, wriggling against his bonds to no avail.

The formation marched around the New London green, torches burning, voices raised in song. Zeb and I trailed a respectful distance behind. The sailors stopped at the base of the pole. Ropey biceps, tattooed with anchors, the ocean voyager's universal symbol for luck, lifted Caleb off his mount, depositing him in a heap in the grass.

"Go on, boy. Tell us King George is a bunghole. Lower than whale shit on the bottom of the Atlantic," Caulk demanded.

Silence. The gathering appeared to swell in number. "String him up," a familiar female voice shrilled from the pack.

Prudence? What's she doing here? I didn't have time to get answers. I couldn't let anyone hang Anne's younger brother, even if he was a flaming Tory. Breaking from Zeb, I stormed forward, shouting, "Let him go. He's just a boy."

Caulk surveyed the crowd. I could almost see his mind churning, calculating whether murder was in his best interests. At last, he nodded towards me, his fervor subsiding. "We've done enough. He'll carry the message to his kind for us."

Someone cut Caleb's hands free. He stumbled like a drunkard. Another bucket of refuse was dumped on his head. He scrambled to his feet, looking frantically for an escape route.

"Is this your army, Schoolmaster Hale?" he screeched, a maniacal gleam in his eye. "They'll all hang soon enough. You as well, you fornicator. I'll be a Ranger myself one day and make sure of it." With that, he bolted into the darkness.

As the crowd dispersed, four seamen, passing around a jug, surrounded Prudence. She appeared to soak up the attention, keeping me waiting alone. I was just about to leave when she grabbed the jug and lurched away.

"I may not be as smart as Anne Wheaton but I'm a true patriot," she called out, swilling and spilling as she approached.

"Anne's not responsible for her brother's actions."

"Is that what her letter said?" Her bayonet-gray eyes, albeit bloodshot with drink, launched daggers at my heart. "I saw the letter on the bar at Miner's. Should have tossed it in the flames."

"Is that why you went off with the Neptune men?"

She bent over and dry heaved. "Seemed like a good idea at the time."

I put my arm around her shoulders. "Let me take you home before you sully your name beyond repair."

Prudence heaved again, this time spewing a chunky mix between my boots. After one more retch, she stood and wiped her mouth. "We should have lynched Caleb Wheaton when we had the chance. Mark my words."

"Duly noted," I replied, taking her elbow.

One of her former admirers, a brute with a ragged beard still housing supper scraps, walked towards us. He reached for his crotch, jerking his hand up and down. "Watch yourself, soldier boy. She's a bloody cock-teaser," he hissed. Prudence flinched, touching her cheek as if the insult had left a wound.

I started after him, but Prudence grabbed the sleeve of my jacket. "Leave him be. I've earned his disdain."

She held on as we shuffled towards the Richards' house. "What words of love did Miss Wheaton write?"

"We remain friends. That is all."

Prudence scrutinized my face, then shook her head. "You're a bad liar, Nathaniel."
She walked the rest of the way home without my assistance.

Whenever I thought I knew women, events almost always proved me wrong. Prudence avoided me for the next week, treating me to an assortment of scowls and grunts whenever we crossed paths at the Richards'. Didn't I see her home safely? Defend her dignity, whatever was left of it, from the rabble? She undoubtedly had a bee in her bonnet over Anne, but she had agreed to go to the beach with me *after* she had seen her rival's letter at Miner's. Regardless of Prudence's reasoning, I recognized the opportunity to watch the sunset together had passed.

I composed several replies to Anne, but struggled to commit one to paper. Getting correspondence into Boston would be difficult at best and might be read in the black chambers of either, or both, sides so I had to choose my words carefully. The New London Committee of Safety, which already had a reputation for intercepting suspect mail, could have no doubt of my loyalty to the patriot cause.

What did Anne actually know of Caleb's activities? How to describe his torture at the hands of the Sons of Neptune? Her parents were Tories, most likely supportive of their son's enlistment and opposed to their daughter's involvement with a rebel officer. Would they even allow her to read my words?

Finally, I decided I had an obligation to recount the facts, without any mention of Prudence, of course. Fiercely loyal to her family and King, Anne, at least, would understand my predicament. Another *Cato* couplet might help as well: *The hand of fate is over us, and Heaven exacts severity from all our thoughts. It is now not time to talk of aught but chains or conquest, liberty or death.*

I sealed the letter, stopping on my way to the parade ground to leave it with Jabez Miner, trusting him to see that it reached its destination. My men were waiting, anxious to begin the day's drilling. We all knew the time to depart for Boston was fast approaching. I readily pushed thoughts of the fairer sex to the back of my mind and ordered my troop to attention.

CHAPTER 5 - AUGUST 1775

"[On Oct 16] Major Rogers, who commanded his Majesty's Rangers in North-America during the last War, had the Honour to kiss his Majesty's Hand…"
New Hampshire Gazette
December 20, 1765

On the forecastle of the merchant brig, the *Baltimore*, shading his eyes from the unrelenting sun reflecting off Chesapeake Bay, Robert Rogers, still a major in the British Army, searched the coastline of his homeland for familiar landmarks. After spending the past five years in London, he realized with trepidation that he was much more familiar with the rivers, forests and mountains of North America than with its current political climate. Nevertheless, after two months aboard ship, bored to buggery and battered by summer storms, he longed to step on familiar soil. Already in his cups, he toasted the colonies with another swig of rum as the steeples of Annapolis came into view.

Born and raised in a frontier outpost in the New Hampshire wilderness, Rogers had been a fighting man since he was sixteen when a band of Iroquois had torched his family's farm. Fortunately, the Rogers escaped unscathed. Others were not so lucky.

He raised his first company of Rangers for the Crown in New Hampshire in 1755. Four years later, Rogers captained his men deep into the French territory of Canada, surprising the Ottawas at St. Francis. His heartbeat still raced whenever he recalled his troops hidden in the woods surrounding the sleeping village. "Kill quickly, no torture," he ordered.

The massacre turned the tide of the Seven Years War. Rogers shared command for the British victory at Montreal, then forged westward, paddling the St. Lawrence River and the Great Lakes in a daring feat of wilderness endurance to capture Fort Detroit. He was a hero then, feted in every port.

That was a simpler time, Rogers thought as the *Baltimore* glided to the dock. The colonies had united against an enemy clearly defined by the color of its skin. From reports circulating in London, they appeared divided now, Massachusetts alone in open rebellion while others still angled for reconciliation with the King.

Empty-handed, save for a tattered green jacket slung over his shoulder, he wobbled baker-kneed from the Baltimore's dinghy. The wharf bustled with sailors, soldiers, stevedores, and peddlers, but no one haled, or even seemed to notice, the once-famous warrior and author. How many had read his *Journals*? Memorized his twenty-eight rules of rangering?

It must be the beard, grown thick and matted. Or my appearance, soft and slovenly after the years away from the wilderness. Rogers vowed to return to form now that he was back home. At forty-four years old, he was not a young man anymore.

Remembering a tavern on the outskirts of town, the King's Arms, noted for its savory stew and welcoming women, indulgences sorely lacking on the *Baltimore*, Rogers trudged off.
He was proud of his hard-earned major's commission, an accomplishment matched by few provincials; but he feared the mood in the colonies had turned. Would his former comrades-in-arms now view him as a traitor, or even worse, a spy?

Rogers' memory had not failed him, although the tavern seemed a bit further away than he recalled and its name had changed to the Pigtail. The late afternoon heat blasted like the Devil's fart. His breath came in labored huffs, sweat leaked from his beard, his stained smock resembled a map of the Great Lakes. While pissing in the shade of a willow, he surveyed the entrance before putting on his jacket and squaring his shoulders. *Time to discover what America holds for me.*

Ranger green never failed to elicit a hearty greeting: rebel and Tory alike feared the Indians and appreciated the Rangers' role in subduing them. Fingering the meager coins in his purse, the major hoped that welcome would include a free meal as well.

The public house was almost empty. No uniforms of any color in sight. Two portly men, one carrot-pated, the other cribbage-faced, stood by the open door, while a second pair of cock-robins were locked in animated debate in the corner. Rogers ordered a bucket of flip and sat alone, but in earshot of both conversations. The rotting, gap-toothed smile of the wench behind the bar did little to stir him, but the view of her more desirable assets, showcased by a low-cut bodice, had a more salubrious effect. It had been too many months since he had wet his pintle.

Rogers was still legally married, although it had been five years since he had last seen Elizabeth, or his then newborn son Arthur. After retiring from wilderness command, he fell under the spell of the attractive twenty-year-old daughter of a respected New Hampshire clergyman and wealthy landowner. Elizabeth was as motivated to snare the famous war hero as he was to secure his financial future. Unfortunately, the union worked better on paper than in practice.

For Rogers, the scoldings and tirades of a shrill female were more threatening than an Indian war cry. His drinking, whoring and gambling, vices no longer shielded by the isolation of military camps or the company of fellow Rangers, added to his domestic plight. When Chief Pontiac stirred a confederation of western tribes to attack the British in 1763, Rogers had the perfect reason to muster out once more.

"A Ranger eh?" a raspy voice called out from the bar.

"Yes, sir." Rogers snapped to attention.

The gray-bearded stranger, tankard in one hand, cane in the other, hobbled towards him. Rogers recognized the telltale gait of a man who had lost several toes to frostbite.

"Where did you -" the stranger braked mid-sentence, brow furrowing, eyes squinting, mind churning to place the new acquaintance. "Major Rogers?"

"At your service."

"Well, I'll be danged. I never thought..."

"Please join me." Rogers swept his arm across his chest in a grand gesture for the stranger to sit. "And your name and rank, sir?"

"Private Tom Brown. Retired now."

"Tom Brown?" It was Rogers turn to gape.

"Alive and well. Mostly well, I reckon."

"I thought you were..."

"Dead. Wished I was. Several times actually. But the good lord had other plans, I guess."

Rogers had last seen Private Brown kneeling in the snow in the wilderness outside the French Fort Carillon almost twenty years ago. Leading a scouting party deep in enemy territory, exhausted and almost out of food, Rogers ordered his Rangers to take a shortcut home. Arrayed in a wide semicircle, the enemy, 250 strong, waited in ambush at the crest of a deep ravine. A French officer, resplendent in white jacket with blue waistcoat and red cuffs, gave the order to fire, but it was the Indians, bald heads and faces painted in garish red, yellow and black, that caused knees to wobble and bowels to weaken. At point blank range, the enemy's initial volley dropped several Rangers in their tracks.

Fortunately, Rogers had equipped his men with snowshoes, which the enemy lacked. The Rangers retreated, supported by covering fire from its rearguard, commanded by John Stark, and established a position on a nearby hill. They repulsed several enemy assaults before darkness fell.

His own wrist blasted to smithereens by an Indian musket ball, Rogers knew that his Rangers faced a long night. And a worse morning, if French reinforcements arrived. He ordered his men to kindle a fire, then another forty yards away, and a third, praying the illusion of encampment would fool the French for a few hours at least.

When the fires were blazing, Rogers detailed the healthy to help the wounded. "We're moving out," he said, heaving forward to lead the retreat. The haggard troop flinched at every hoot of an owl or snap of a branch, fearful that the enemy was catching up. All knew of the gruesome tortures that awaited Indian captives.

The spindly pines, petrified by frost, stood as silent spectators to the grim procession. The Rangers arrived at Lake George shortly after sunrise, collapsing onto the ice. All were accounted for except Private Brown.

Rogers knew most of his men could not move another yard. He could barely walk himself. "We can't go back," he said, praying silently that the private had died from his wounds in the night.

Private Brown had somehow survived, and now sat right in front of him. Was he friend or foe?

Brown laid his cane against the table and eased himself down. "Not your fault, Major Rogers. You had a whole company to look after. Did a damn good job getting those boys home safe."

Rogers breathed a sigh of relief. The loyalty of his men stood the test of time. "Spoken like a true Ranger."

"I got disoriented in the darkness. And the cold. Fell asleep maybe."

"Then?" Rogers hated to ask.

"The Ottawas took me. Kept me for two years before I escaped. Would never have survived without my Ranger training. I thank you for that."

Brown's eyes clouded. Rogers sipped his flip. The Battle on Snowshoes, the *Boston Gazette* had christened it in 1757: "The brave Rogers is acquiring Glory to himself in the field and in some Degree recovering the sunken Reputation of his Country..."

The broadsheet, the most influential in the colonies, claimed the intrepid Rogers' Rangers had killed more than a hundred French and Indians in the skirmish. After years of defeats and delays by the armies sent from London to protect them, British settlers on the frontier needed a victory to celebrate.

Several seconds passed as Rogers and Brown mulled the different roads their lives had taken. "Rumor was you was in London for a spell?" Brown offered at last, head down, his eyes boring a hole in the table.

"Your intelligence is correct. I am fresh off the seas."

"Never been to London."

"A majestic city."

"You gonna join the fight?"

"That is my intention."

"You been in correspondence with his Excellency?"

"I had a personal audience with King George."

Brown pinched his lips in puzzlement. "I was talking about George Washington, commander-in-chief of the Continental Army."

"George Washington? Commander-in-chief? He never..." Rogers stopped mid-sentence. He drained his glass and gathered his thoughts. The *Gazette* had once tried to compliment the militia officer from Virginia but the best the paper could write was "...a gentleman who has a deservedly high reputation of military skill, integrity, and valor, though success has not always attended his undertakings."

"The Continental Congress made the appointment in June. Right before the big battle," Brown said.

"Battle?"

"Breed's Hill. We showed those redcoats we could stand and fight."

"Was Washington in command?"

"No. He got to Boston too late. Colonel Stark did his share though. Manned the rail fence by the beach so Howe couldn't sneak around Putnam's flank. When his men ran out of balls for their muskets, they yanked the nails from the fence and fired them."

"Stark was a fine Ranger. Putnam too." *Why didn't I reach out to them sooner?* Too busy chirping-merry in London was the honest answer.

"A thousand British casualties, including a hundred officers in their freshly laundered scarlet coats and silver gorgets. They was sitting ducks."

"Foolish British pride," Rogers said. He knew it too well.

"General Howe won't underestimate us again."

Rogers head lifted. General Howe? Howe had commanded a ranger-type, light infantry unit in the French and Indian war. What happened to General Gage? Rogers' fortunes in the British Army could take a marked turn for the better if Gage was removed from the scene.

In fact, Rogers' fortunes could hardly turn worse. He had personally financed many of his Ranger expeditions in the wilderness, running up monumental debts. While he earned glory, the press pilloried his immediate superiors, Sir William Johnson, and his favorite son, Thomas Gage, then a colonel, for their inaction and outright defeats.

The British officers exacted their revenge by refusing to honor Rogers' drafts. In 1768, they concocted a story that Rogers, then commander of the wilderness fort at Mackinac, was going to sell out to the French, had him arrested for treason, and shipped back to Montreal in chains for trial. While Rogers was acquitted, he had to sail back to London to lobby for a new assignment that would allow him to clear his name and his balance sheet.

"Great to see the Rangers making their mark again," Rogers said, opting not to recount his tale of woe.

"Darn straight." Brown drained his ale and pounded the tankard on the table.

"No more militia then?" Rogers asked.

"There's still plenty of them. But Washington's in charge now. Told Congress he'd build them a real army and wouldn't take a shilling in salary for himself."

"A grand gesture."

"Congress ain't got no money anyway," Brown said.

"I've been out of touch for too long." While Rogers' patrons in King George's court enabled him to retain his major's commission, he was not assigned a new command. In 1773, he landed in debtor's prison, a victim of his own dissolute ways as well as the vengeance of Gage and Johnson. Robert's older brother, James, a Loyalist supporter and landowner in Connecticut, finally bailed him out and provided the funds for the return voyage to North America.

"But you came home to fight, right?" Brown asked.

"Yes, yes. I'm going straight to Philadelphia to offer my services to Congress." Rogers paused, crossing his boots under the table. "And I'll draft a letter to General Washington too."

Brown nodded slowly, taking the measure of his former commander. "Sounds like you've got a long walk ahead, Major. Can I buy you a bowl of stew?"

***

I was fiddling with my porridge when Prudence appeared in the kitchen. She dipped her cup into the kettle of coffee hanging over the hearth and sat down next to Mehitable Richards, a skeleton of a woman, approaching fifty. "Good morning, Aunt. Good morning Lieutenant," she said.

"Good morning, Miss Richards," I returned the greeting, barely looking up from my bowl. Prudence had not spoken a kind word to me in more than a week.

"You're not eating this morning, Nathaniel. Are you feeling ill?" Mrs. Richards asked. "I have a fine chamomile and saffron tonic in the cupboard."

"I'm fine."

"We could always try some snakeroot," Prudence chipped in, her teeth frozen in an angelic smile.

"Perhaps your friends from the Sons of Neptune can gather it with you," I replied, lifting my eyes from my breakfast.

"Sons of Neptune? I hope you're not associating with those ruffians," Mrs. Richards said.

"Just a casual acquaintance, Aunt. Nathan was a true gentleman and rescued me from their clutches."

"I would expect no less," Mrs. Richards noted as she passed a plate of bacon. I helped myself to three slices, but toyed with them on my plate.

"When my stomach ailed last month, Lucy Ballard suggested urine. Mixed with honey, of course," Mrs. Richards rambled on.

"I'll pass on the urine, thank you," I replied, slicing my bacon into ever smaller pieces, finally jabbing one into my mouth to prove my good health.

"Mehitable, you didn't listen to that old midwife, did you?" Mr. Richards snapped as he entered the room with a newspaper in hand. When no response was forthcoming, he sat next to me and spread the tabloid on the table. "News from Boston. The army is massing. General Washington seems spoiling for a fight."

I pushed aside my uneaten breakfast and scanned the article. The ink had smudged somewhat, but the gist of the message was clear. And held no surprises.

"When will your regiment leave New London?" Mr. Richards asked.

"We march in a fortnight. Colonel Webb relayed the orders last night."

"Excellent, excellent. You wouldn't want to miss the fight."

"No, sir." With enlistments expiring on December 10th, I was more concerned that my men would return home before the fight even started.

"Are you prepared?" Mrs. Richards returned to the conversation with an evangelical fervor. "Prepared to kill, to starve, to sleep in the mud, to face death?"

"Woman!" John Richards pounded the table.

"The boy needs to know war is no picnic. When my George came home from Canada in '62, he was a broken man. Died the next year. Left me penniless, too."

"Mrs. Richards, you are correct. War is a monumental undertaking," I replied. "My men and I could use more drilling, but the times do not afford us that luxury. I pray every night that I am up to the challenges that await."

Prudence studied my face, as if seeing it for the first time. Mr. Richards, however, was barely listening. "Wise words, Lieutenant. You respond to the call of duty like a true soldier."

Mrs. Richards picked up my breakfast dishes, still full of food. "Godspeed, young man," she mumbled under her breath.

"Girl, why are you not helping with the chores?" Mr. Richards shifted his attention to Prudence. "My brother will be most disappointed if his daughter returns slothful."

"I'm sorry, uncle. I was ...." Prudence stammered as she jumped up and reached for an apron hanging from a peg near the hearth.

"And, where were you last evening?"

"At a frolic."

"A frolic where?"

"At Miner's. To start the harvest season."

"You returned quite late. After midnight, I believe."

"Yes, sir."

"Quite inappropriate for a young lady. My niece, no less."

"It won't happen again, uncle."

I savored Prudence's scolding before excusing myself to return to my room. Mrs. Richards was right; with no military experience to draw upon, I was unsettled about the coming months. But then again, the entire rebellion was a step into the unknown. I opened my Bible for inspiration. The fight for liberty was just; God would be on our side.

I knew I had much to learn, and not just about battle. How could Prudence so easily read my face? Did I need to become more dissembling? Certainly not to lead men. Above all else, a commander needed to be trustworthy, inspiring men to follow his orders without the slightest question of his motives.

Prevarication, perhaps, came more easily to others. Prudence's beauty beguiled men, myself included, leaving me unsure whether her support of the Glorious Cause was a commitment or a convenience. Anne, however, was a simpler soul, never camouflaging her beliefs even under duress. Little surprise she still tugged on my heartstrings.

***

"A letter from New London at last." Father beamed as he burst into the Wheaton's keeping room waving an envelope in his right hand. Anne sat at the table helping Phineas with his studies. Her heart jumped – a reply from Nathan? Word from Caleb?

"It's from Tailor Appletree," Father said, crushing her hopes. Forging past Becky who was stirring a vile brew in the hearth-kettle, he reached for a knife to break open the seal. "Dr. Bacon delivered it to the store just ten minutes ago." Anne froze at the mention of the doctor, and the debt that she might owe him.

"He's dead," Father said, plopping down next to his son, his elation fizzling like a doused campfire as he read.

"Who's dead?" Phineas asked.

"Tailor Appletree. The flux got him."

"Then who wrote the letter?" Phineas again.

"He did. Before he died."

"Then how do you know he's dead?"

"His widow added a note." Father stuffed it in the pocket of his waistcoat. "Now mind your studies."

"Any word of Caleb?" Anne asked.

"Tailor Appletree wrote that he shows promise."

"Will Caleb be moving to Boston now?" Phineas knocked his ginger beer to the floor in his excitement.

"Pick up your mug and take it into the parlor. Now," Father exploded. "I need to talk to your sister."

Phineas trudged off while Anne remained, unsettled by the change in Father's tone. Did he want to discuss Dr. Bacon? Would the "good" doctor have requested permission to court her? Her confusion increased when Father walked to the fireplace, lit a candle and sat down next to her.

"Watch closely," he said, heating the tailor's letter over the flame. Another message appeared between the lines of Appletree's handwriting: *the rebels are out of gunpowder*

"Father, are you a spymaster?" Anne asked, her thoughts balanced like a scale between relief and concern.

"Of course not. I'm just an intermediary in the flow of information."

She read over Father's shoulder as the deceased man's words emerged as if by magic, detailing his reconnaissance from New Haven to Worcester, accompanied by Caleb most of the way. But the information was three months old. Where was Caleb now?

"Your brother can take care of himself," Father said, reading her mind. He folded the letter and handed it to her. "We need to get this information to General Howe. I wager the rebels couldn't fight off an assault by a flock of geese right now, let alone the British Army."

"The General and I are hardly on speaking terms."

"Your suitor, Major Stanwich, can deliver it to him."

Anne hesitated. Father's request represented a whole new level of their relationship. As well as her relationship with Geoffrey.

She had started visiting him every Sunday after church. Geoffrey's nobility had become apparent as he returned to health. His cheekbones and nose, both high and haughty, suggested a Roman lineage. A senator, like Cato, or a general, like Caesar, she daydreamed.

They had grown closer as Geoffrey had grown more confident, more alive. Venturing out together, first into the garden, then down to the Common, their words had become less formal. But words alone would not satisfy her. She longed for passion, willing Geoffrey to take her in his arms, to ravish her - or at least kiss her - but he hesitated. Hopefully, he would not wait much longer.

"Be off, then," Father said, handing her the decoded letter. "Where's Mother?"

"Upstairs, tending Richard. He has a fever." Fevers were a black omen, the deaths of Grace and Phebe rarely mentioned but never far from mind.

"Has she vomited him?"

"I haven't heard a retch yet," Anne replied.

"That explains the bitter brew warming on the fire," Father said, casting a sour glance at Becky. "I'll bring a cup to Richard while you're out."

CHAPTER 6 - SEPTEMBER 1775

To: John Hancock
President - Second Continental Congress
Philadelphia, Pennsylvania

Sir,
...It gives me great Pain, to be obliged to solicit the Attention of the
Honorable Congress, to the State of this Army, in Terms which imply the
slightest Apprehension of being neglected: But my Situation is inexpressibly
distressing, to see the Winter, fast approaching upon a naked Army: The Time of
their Service within a few Weeks of expiring, & no Provision, yet made for such
important Events. Added to these, the Military Chest is totally exhausted. The
Paymaster has not a single Dollar in Hand. The Commissary General assures
me, he has strained his Credit for the Subsistance of the Army to the utmost. The
Quarter Master General is precisely in the same Situation: And the greater Part
of the Troops are in a State not far from Mutiny...I know not to whom I am to
impute this Failure, but I am of Opinion, if the Evil is not immediately remedied
& more punctuality observed in future, the Army must absolutely break up...

Go: Washington
Camp at Cambridge Septmr 21st 1775

Colonel Webb's Connecticut troops were now part of the 39th
Regiment of the newly formed Continental Army. We proudly wore
our new uniforms, brown jackets with buff trim and pewter buttons.
Recently promoted to Captain, my cocked hat sprouting the yellow
badge of rank, I led the Third Company. The fetid odor of human
waste festering in the late summer heat greeted us as we climbed along
Charlestown Road towards camp on Winter Hill, one knuckle in a fist
of heights surrounding Boston.

The hundred-mile march from Connecticut had gone
smoothly: the Post Road firm underfoot, the surrounding countryside
green, and the populace rabid in their support of the rebellion. Many

farmsteads broadcast their sympathies by hanging crude effigies of lobster-jacketed British soldiers by the roadside.

Wealthy family, Yale education, well-paid schoolmaster, I had led a privileged life to date. This command had been my first real opportunity to lead men from diverse backgrounds. Looking back at my troop marching in neat formation, I beamed with pride.

Maybe Zebulon, Sergeant Cheesebrough now, had been right; men at the bottom of society's pecking order had to spit out the bile of their daily lives before they could move forward. But what would happen after the war was won? Could these men be trusted to vote, to hold office, to rule? While I was preparing to fight for liberty, my fellow patriots denied the most basic rights to men of different political opinions. And skin color. Passing an open latrine, I gagged, jolting from my daydreams of the future to the reality of the task at hand.

Fortunately, the bleat of fifes and beat of drums recaptured my imagination as we entered camp. Visible in the distance, the steeple of Boston's Old North Church rose above a checkerboard of homes and greenswards. I was here at last. To fight for freedom.

Boston itself was unimpressive, little bigger than New London, but its impregnability was obvious. With the exception of a narrow bridge of land, the town was surrounded by water and marsh. Mighty British warships like the Somerset, boasting more cannon on its decks than in the possession of the entire Continental Army, patrolled the harbor; redcoats manned berms studding Bunker Hill and the Neck; black-barreled artillery bristled on Copp's Hill in the North End.

The Continental Army headquarters on Winter Hill, a star-shaped log palisades, was engulfed by a hodgepodge of sailcloth tents, wobbling wigwams, tottering shacks, and stately officer marquees. Men, dressed only in breeches or loin cloths, lounged in the grass or gathered around the cooking fires dotting the hilltop. Hardly a uniform in sight. Where were the men who fought so bravely at Bunker Hill? Have their enlistments expired already? Our own December deadline was never far from my mind.

A shot rang out, startling me. Instinctively, I reached for my musket and spun around. Several of my men dropped to a knee, searching the tree line for the enemy.

"Damn beetleheads! Save your ammunition," an unseen officer barked.

"Establish our base on the far side of the fort while I check in," Colonel Webb ordered, pointing me to the north.

"Fall in!" I ordered, waiting for the ranks to form. As usual, Elvin Parish was the last to attention, but at least he had extracted himself from Widow Appletree's clutches.

When I had enlisted back in July, the regiment had been the 7th Connecticut, but George Washington had moved quickly after his appointment as Commander-in-Chief to organize the troops of the New England colonies into a unified force, at least on paper. Since each regiment still wore its own colors, Washington had also instituted a code of sashes and cockades to highlight officers and their ranks, distinctions critical to the commander's sense of military decorum.

"Move out!" I led Third Company forward, skirting the parade ground, a grass-starved meadow outside the fort's gate, where an officer, sporting an outlandish lime-green jacket, but absent the accents that would have signified a position in the Continental Army, struggled to mold fifty or so ragged recruits into a fighting unit.

I heard laughter ripple behind my back as my men watched a row of the trainees, armed only with farm implements and rundlets, most likely filled with rum, turn the wrong way and lurch into their comrades. Fists and epithets flew as the men piled up in the dirt.

One of the combatants broke from the scrum, sprinting towards my amused Connecticut troops. "Shut your bone-box!" he yelled, pointing his shovel in the direction of Asa Cobb.

I halted, whirling to face the threat. "We'll have none of that here."

"I didn't come up from Bristol to march with niggers." The militia man, a jagged scar splitting his right cheek, spat at Asa's feet. "His kind ain't even allowed in this army."

Several of Asa's peers surged in his defense, but he pushed past them, declaring, "I'm a free man, just like you. And I'm here to fight, just like you."

"No way a Black boy's going to fight with us. If you was back in Rhode Island, you'd be shining our boots," the militia man jeered, turning towards his mates crowding behind him. "Right boys?"

Asa grabbed his rifle with both hands and shoved his off-balance accuser in the back, sending him sprawling, the shovel sailing into the weeds. Embarrassed, the Bristol soldier leapt to his feet. "That's a hanging offense where I come from," he growled as he charged. Asa swung the rifle but missed; his opponent dropped low to tackle him. Soldiers from both companies circled the combatants as they wrestled on the ground.

The clatter of hoofbeats disrupted the melee. Emerging from a cloud of dust, a statuesque officer, dressed in a royal blue coat displaying polished gold buttons and gaudy epaulettes, cantered a chestnut horse, its tail swinging high, between the sparring parties. A stout, cherubic-cheeked Black, wearing the red and white livery of a personal servant, rode closely behind the officer, followed by a posse of uniformed soldiers.

My men quickly formed ranks. Asa stumbled back to his position but drew his chest up with pride. The Bristol troop demonstrated no such discipline.

"Who is in charge here?" General Washington demanded, adjusting the pale blue sash across his chest. His silver spurs and sword hilt sparkled in the sunlight. A cocked hat, adorned with a black cockade, rested atop meticulously coiffed reddish brown hair, touched with powder and queued down his back with a black ribbon. Given the general's patrician background, I was pleasantly surprised to see he did not wear a wig.

Over the summer, I had talked with Colonel Webb and assiduously read the broadsheets to learn the details of Washington's resume. The son of a second-tier plantation owner, Washington had entered the military at age twenty-one, seeking adventure, honor, wealth and the potential to ascend the social ladder. His first command, consisting of Virginia militia and Iroquois warriors, ambushed the French outside of Pittsburgh in 1754, essentially starting the Seven Years' War. When the Iroquois slaughtered several captives, albeit without Washington's approval, the French counter-attacked, capturing him at Fort Necessity. They allowed him and his men to return home unharmed where he resigned from the militia.

After failing to receive an officer's commission in the British Army, Washington next returned to the Ohio country as a volunteer aide to General Edward Braddock. Unwilling to listen to those more skilled in wilderness tactics, Braddock marched his redcoats into disaster at the Monongahela River in '55. When Braddock was mortally wounded, Washington galloped through the woods under heavy fire, rallying the panic-stricken troops into an organized retreat, saving hundreds of lives and restoring at least some luster to his reputation.

Nevertheless, the British chose to blame the embarrassing massacre on the "provincials" and again excluded George Washington from its officer corps. Virginia's colonial government, however, looked more favorably on its native son, rewarding him with the post of Commander-in-Chief of its militia.

Over the next three years, Washington applied the discipline learned with the British army, enforced by regular hangings and lashings, to mold the Virginia Blues into one of the most effective fighting forces in the colonies. He retired from military service in December '58, focusing his attention on private life until his country called in '75.

I approached the general, who towered over me like the impetuous Ares descending from Mount Olympus. "These are my men, sir. The proud Thirty-ninth from Connecticut, defending one of our own."

"You're newly arrived in camp?" Washington's gaze spotlighted up and down our ranks, stopping for an instant on Asa Cobb, a flicker of consternation kindling at the downturned corners of the general's lips.

"Yes, sir."

"Not exactly a sterling debut, but your men at least look like soldiers. Take them to their quarters for the night. I will personally watch you put them through their paces tomorrow morning at sunrise. Understood?"

"Yes, sir."

"Don't disappoint me. We'll need men who can fight in the next few days."

"Yes sir." Relief was soon replaced by anticipation. Fight? Soon? My pulse quickened. Two months had passed since the skirmish on the New London dock whet my appetite for action.

"And you, private?" Washington pointed to the Bristol man who had instigated the confrontation. "Speak up," he ordered as the soldier mumbled something unintelligible into his sleeve.

"Enos Cartwright, your Excellency, 4th Bristol militia."

Astride a sorrel mare, an officer about my own age, sporting a green sash symbolic of the General's inner circle, separated from the posse and trotted past Washington's valet. In addition to re-organizing the troops and distinguishing the officers, Washington had implemented a meritocracy, rare for its time, rewarding the best and the brightest with key positions. The aide pointed to an entry in a leather notebook and spoke in hushed tones that I could not hear.

Washington nodded and urged his horse forward, forcing the Bristol gang to separate. "Private Cartwright, it appears you've been accused of stealing a cow from the Bayberry farm last week."

"We was hungry. We haven't seen a penny of our pay in weeks. How do you expect us…?"

Cartwright's commander, the officer with the garish green jacket, finally surfaced. "Sir, I'm Captain Jeremiah King. In Rhode Island, I work for Mark DeWolf, as do these men. He is one of the largest traders in the colonies and will vouch…"

"I have purchased property from Mr. DeWolf on several occasions," Washington said.

I understood full well that Washington referred to slaves. Although the Hales didn't own any Blacks, my family, like most in New England, profited indirectly when we traded our livestock and produce for sugar and molasses grown on the giant plantations in the Caribbean. I cringed whenever I thought of my Yale tuition paid with funds earned from the labor of enslaved Africans, but now was not the time to proselytize on abolition to my commander-in-chief.

"Very good, very good. You will allow him to discipline his men as he sees fit then?" Captain King continued his plea.

"Mr. DeWolf is quite a wealthy man. Why are his men not paid promptly?"

"A clerical error, I'm sure. I'll see to it right away."

"Take Private Cartwright to the stocks," Washington ordered the captain of his guard.

"Mr. DeWolf will be quite upset at…" King protested.

"We can't expect the citizenry to support our cause if our own soldiers steal from them." The General scowled as if the militiamen were little better than the turds soiling the camp. "The rest of your men will dig latrines for the next week. Maybe that will impart the discipline necessary to contribute to the success of this army."

Washington tugged on the reins, wheeling his stallion towards the fort. The Bristol troops roiled, waiting for the General and his retinue to ride out of range.

"We'll get you, boy," Cartwright shouted at Asa before he was led away by two blue-clad soldiers.

***

Anne would miss Richard, even if he was often stubborn as a donkey. As far as she knew, he had taken their secret with him to his grave, never mentioning a word of her liaison with Master Hale at the schoolhouse. She fought back tears as she watched the men shovel dirt on top of the coffin.

The leafy cemetery, formerly a pasture, stood at the base of Copp's Hill. Richard would lie for eternity under the watchful eye of the Old North Church with the sea in full view. She imagined his beloved British warships firing off a salute as they sailed by.

The minister closed his Bible; the mourners lifted their heads and shuffled away from the yawning grave. The Wheatons lingered, saying a final goodbye. Mother, wilted like yesterday's rose, dabbed an eye with her handkerchief. Father whispered something to her then stole away. Setting her jaw like a proper Englishwoman, Anne squeezed Phineas' hand, tugging him towards their carriage. Mother remained at the graveside.

Father joined Sam Hale, Sheriff Loring and their wives, who retired after perfunctory words of consolation. Anne left Phineas with a friend from school and trailed after Father, hoping to catch snippets of the men's conversation.

"Life is short. We may all die of the pox tomorrow," Father said. Richard's death had sparked an anger that Anne had not seen in him before, as if it represented another bill for a debt he had thought long since paid.

"Boston is cursed. Food is scarce. Disease is everywhere," Sam replied.

"We must plan for our future. In New York," the sheriff said.

"Are you sure?" Father asked.

"Positively. My source is close to General Howe," Loring said.

"It's only a matter of time," Sam added, burying his smirk by gazing at the waves lapping the craggy coast. "William, we need your help."

Anne heard the scrape of a crutch behind her. Leaning into his good leg, Major Stanwich touched her elbow. "We should walk," he said. He wore his dress uniform, medals glittering on his chest. In deference to their service together, General Howe had taken Geoffrey on as an aide. Although not quite the same as a battlefield command, the position provided purpose to his every day.

"Yes, a good idea," she replied. "Let me have a word with Mother first."

She was doubtful that Mother would recover from this tragedy. Even worse, she blamed Father for keeping them in Boston. Her black dress hung limply on her now haggard frame; her eyes, once vibrant, sunk deep in despair.

"Phineas and I are going to join my sister in Canada," she said.

Anne nodded in agreement.

"I think you should accompany me, but Father demands your assistance here in Boston."

"He cannot run the store by himself."

"There's no one left to shop in the store." Mother spit out the words.

"The situation may change."

"Only for the worse. I'm worried about your safety. A young girl alone among desperate men."

"Father will watch out for me."

"Yes, of course. Like he watched out for Caleb." Mother looked briefly to the heavens before wrapping her shawl around her stooped shoulders.

"Caleb is a man now. He can take care of himself," Anne replied with less conviction than her words implied.

"Go on. I see Major Stanwich is waiting."

Anne returned to Geoffrey, taking his hand for comfort. His face had regained its full luster, the eye patch adding a dash of the devil, yet she still longed for their first kiss. *What was he waiting for?* It was time to hurry him along, like she had done with Richard when he was late for school. The memory of her little brother lollygagging down Bank Street brought a wry smile to her lips.

Geoffrey disengaged, gripped his crutch and swung his peg leg forward. Anne walked at his side, carrying her Sunday fan, silk with a floral design on both sides stretched over ivory sticks. The sea breeze refreshed her spirits momentarily.

"The general appreciated your father's report on the gunpowder situation in Connecticut. He would welcome more such intelligence," he said.

"Father will be pleased." She fluttered her fan slowly in front of her face.

"However, William would do well to steer clear of questionable company." Geoffrey glanced towards the trio of conspirators, heads still bent together in conversation.

"They have helped us settle in a strange city," Anne replied.

"Yes, I know. Sheriff Loring arranged the loan that enabled your father to purchase the tailor shop."

Her somber mood returned when she noticed Simeon Bacon waddling towards them. She tried to steer Geoffrey away, but it was too late.

"My condolences, Miss Wheaton. We have all lost loved ones to the pox."

"Thank you, good doctor." Anne sidled closer to Geoffrey, again taking his hand.

Bacon sneezed twice. "I detect a chill in the air," he said, wiping his nose with the sleeve of his richly embroidered French frock coat. "A portent of times to come, I'm afraid."

"The frost is still a long way off," she replied, closing her fan and striking it against her palm to signal the end of the conversation — at least on her part.

"Yes, well, we'll see. I would treasure these last days of summer. Mother Nature may shortly present her bill."

***

I winced as the cat-o-nine tails again flayed Enos Cartwright's bare back, the blood pooling in a puddle at his feet. Cartwright's arms were spread, crucifixion-style; his hands bound to two posts in the center of the parade ground. After snapping in agony at the first twenty strokes, his head now lolled lifeless on sagging shoulders.

Arrayed in formation, officers out front, the regiments quartered on Winter Hill watched the flogging in silence, its message clear. After thirty-nine strokes, the maximum allowed by Congress, General Washington, sitting tall in the saddle of Old Nelson, nodded for Cartwright to be cut down.

After the General and his retinue left the field, my men broke ranks, eager to return to camp and prepare for combat. Rumors of Washington's proposal to attack Boston had circulated on the grapevine for the past two days. If the British had any spies in camp, which they most certainly did, they would know the rebels were coming by now as well. The Continental Army's war council would meet this afternoon to review the battle plans.

"His Excellency will now retire to his mansion in Cambridge for lunch," Stephen Hempstead said, walking at my side.

"Mansion?"

"You didn't expect a Virginia gentleman to reside in a log cabin in the woods, did you? In fact, I heard the house the Massachusetts Committee of Safety reserved for him wasn't grand enough, so he moved into a bigger one on Tory Row."

Without comment, I kept moving towards my tent, but my friend continued with his harangue. "Estate overlooking the Potomac, the finest luxuries imported from England, ten thousand acres of tobacco plants, hundreds of slaves toiling in the fields... General George lives the life of an English lord. No wonder he looks down on us hardscrabble New Englanders."

"Washington will grow accustomed to northern ways soon enough," I said. "He didn't let his slave-trading get in the way of punishing that Bristol boy, did he?"

"He's been in Cambridge for three months and he hasn't freed his valet, Billy Lee, yet."

"Well, he's within his rights, for now at least." I struggled with my answer. "Hopefully, Congress will abolish slavery next year."

"Bullocks. Congress needs Virginia and the south if the colonies are going to present a united front against the British. That's why they named George Washington as commander-in-chief in the first place." Hempstead replied. "Just hope he doesn't get us all killed."

We separated when we reached the Connecticut encampment, ten rows of canvas tents in neat alignment at the foot of Winter Hill. I went to the supply depot to check on the regiment's allotment of gunpowder but could only find two barrels.

"Where's the rest? We were promised twenty barrels," I asked the quartermaster, who appeared pre-occupied whittling on the figure of a grizzly bear. Impressed by the 39th's performance on the parade ground the morning after the Bristol brawl, General Washington had proclaimed us battle-ready, loudly promising an ample supply of ammunition to lead the charge against the British.

"Ain't no more gunpowder. We got fifty spears instead."

"Spears? What in damnation are we supposed to do with spears?"

The quartermaster shrugged.

"Did you check with headquarters?" I pressed.

"Yep. Ain't got any gunpowder there neither."

"What about the armory in Cambridge? Or Roxbury?" Each town surrounding Boston maintained a stockpile of gunpowder for its own defense.

"Empty."

"But we were promised more." I calculated that each of my men would only have enough powder for ten shots at most. Hardly enough for a skirmish, let alone a full-scale assault.

What about our cannons? How could the artillery support our assault without gunpowder? On second thought, where were the Continental Army's cannons? I realized I had seen few batteries on Winter Hill.

"I figure Washington warranted every regiment more powder than he could deliver to fool the British. Hoped their spies would pass on the word that we were well-stocked, so they would sit tight in Boston," the quartermaster said, returning to his woodwork.

Fool our troops to fool the British? I was impressed with Washington's bluff. It might be the best way for the Continental Army to buy time. But then, why would the commander-in-chief want to double down on his weak hand by attacking Boston? That was a reckless gamble, pure and simple. With the fate of the entire rebellion on the line if he lost.

As the sun rose the next morning, I found myself again standing at attention at the forefront of my regiment, surrounded on the parade ground by the entire Winter Hill garrison. My men and I had spent a restless night, cleaning muskets, checking powder cartridges, however limited, and sharpening bayonets.

William Hull, a year ahead of me at Yale, had just arrived in camp to serve as a lieutenant in Colonel Webb's second company. A head shorter than me, Hull displayed the gelatinous stomach and pasty complexion of a young man who had spent too much time indoors studying for the bar, an exam he had passed shortly before his enlistment.

We shared a meal of bubble and squeak, fried beef and cabbage, washed down by rum and cider. Hull brought the good news that Enoch had passed his preacher's exam, as well as regards from several young ladies in New Haven. My mind wandered briefly, but the anticipation of my first venture against the Regulars forced all frivolities into retreat.

If we harbored any doubts concerning the seriousness of the moment, they were quelled by the sight of a hastily constructed gallows. The yardarm stabbed a shiv into my breast; the mole on my neck itched under my uniform collar, but I dared not scratch it. Who would be the unlucky soldier to climb those steps? After several minutes, General Washington and his retinue rode onto the grounds, pivoting to face the assembled troops.

Two blue-coats escorted a prisoner, hands bound behind his back, to Washington's side. The unfortunate soul, unknown to me, had fled when British pickets fired at his regiment last week.

One of the General's green-sashed aides kicked his horse forward. He reached into his breast pocket, withdrew the orders for the day, and cleared his throat, encouraging the suspense to build. The hangman's noose swung ominously in the background as he read aloud:

It is with inexpressible Concern that the General should find an Officer sentenced by Court Martial for Cowardice—A Crime of all others, the most infamous in a Soldier, the most injurious to an Army, and the last to be forgiven; inasmuch as it may, and often does happen, that the Cowardice of a single Officer may prove the Destruction of the whole Army and the cause of America.

Every Officer, be his rank what it may, who shall betray his Country, dishonour the Army and his General, by basely keeping back and shrinking from his duty in any engagement; shall be held up as an infamous Coward and punish'd as such, with the utmost martial severity; and no Connections, Interest or Intercessions in his behalf will avail to prevent the strict execution of justice.

Accordingly Lieutenant John Wainscott, now standing before you, will be cashiered and dismissed from all further service in the Continental Army.

General George Washington, Commander-in-Chief

The aide smartly about-faced and returned to his position. A drum beat prompted the General's retinue to trot off the parade ground. The blue-coats spun their prisoner around and marched him weak-kneed down the center aisle between the ranks of troops. A brown smear soiled the seat of Wainscott's white breeches.

The gallows had just been for show. This time at least. While Washington appeared determined to transform the rabble he'd inherited into an army, I was pleased to see him demonstrate some leniency; otherwise, I feared my men might leave even before their enlistments expired.

***

Although he had tramped into Philadelphia with an open mind, Major Rogers needed only a single day to recognize that he had no future in the Continental Army. Alerted by a post from Private Brown, the rebels' Committee of Safety had sent a representative to interrogate him the morning after his arrival.

Rogers had answered honestly: although a soldier by trade, he had no command and only received half-pay from the British Army, an amount insufficient for him to pay his bills. He had returned to the colonies to visit his generous brother in Connecticut, his own long neglected land holdings in New Hampshire, and his wife and son in Portsmouth.

When he left North America in 1769, those in opposition to the Crown, the Whigs, had been merely a fringe political faction, as were staunch Tories. The vast majority of his countrymen were more interested in economics than politics, confident that Parliament in London would legislate solutions to further the continued prosperity of the colonies.

While he was away, however, the Whigs, led by the men from Boston, had radicalized into a potent revolutionary force, virulently opposed to anyone with even the slightest connection to the Crown. "Tory hunters" prowled towns up and down the coast. The newspapers called Loyalists out by name, labeling them "enemies of their country", demanding their businesses closed and their property seized. If words failed, the Whigs delivered their own forms of rough justice: Anglican homes and churches invaded, their inhabitants chased in the street and beaten, or worse.

Accordingly, Rogers' officer's commission in the British Army, once his badge of honor, now weighed heavily against him. His desire to travel even on personal matters was met with skepticism. Would he spy for the enemy? Why hadn't he already volunteered for the Continental Army like his fellow Rangers?

The Committee of Safety demanded that Rogers gain approval of the Continental Congress to travel. Congress, however, was like a vast uncharted wilderness, a collection of representatives from thirteen colonies that shared few interests, other than a general disillusionment with British rule. How this body could agree on anything, let alone prosecute a war against the greatest empire on earth, was beyond him. Yet, he would have to navigate its corridors if he hoped to get his life in order.

He started by writing letters of introduction to representatives from his home state of New Hampshire, John Langdon and John Sullivan. He was skeptical about Langdon, a shipping magnate whose business was greatly impacted by the strife with Britain, but more optimistic about his chances with Sullivan with whom he shared a common background. They were both descendants of poor Irish immigrants and had served as majors in the state militia.

While waiting for a reply, Rogers scrounged for food, shelter and drink. Occasionally, an old Ranger comrade helped out, but more often he had to settle his bill with smooth talk and promises. His debts were again mounting. The Committee of Safety followed him day and night. If he couldn't leave Philadelphia within days, he would most certainly end up in jail once again.

***

Bible in hand, I went from campfire to campfire, helping my men check and recheck their weapons, sharing stories of home, leading prayers. The activity enabled me to quell my own fears as well.

Headquarters delivered extra rations of beef and rum, but they were poor substitutes for the gunpowder my men would need for tomorrow's assault. I retired early to write letters to Father, Enoch, and Ben Tallmadge, assuring them of my health, faith and commitment to the Glorious Cause. I could only hope that Jabez Miner had found a way to deliver my letter to Anne. If all went well, I might see her tomorrow in Boston.

"Captain Hale, a moment please," Colonel Webb called, approaching my tent.

"Yes, sir." I opened the flap and stepped outside into the cool night air, a harbinger of the winter months ahead. *Will I live to see the leaves fall?* I pushed the morbid thought away.

Webb led me a few steps from the soldiers huddled around the fire. "There will be no military operation tomorrow," he said, adjusting the sword at his waist. "Congress requires our commander-in-chief to obtain agreement from his senior staff on all key strategic decisions. And the generals voted against Washington's plan."

"Ward, Putnam, Lee, Gates and Sullivan?" I asked.

Almost all of the Continental Army's generals had fought in the French and Indian War. In fact, Charles Lee, as well as Horatio Gates, both Englishmen by birth, had served as officers in the British Army, and were George Washington's superiors on Braddock's ill-fated campaign in '55. Not surprisingly, both of these men were disappointed that Congress had passed them over for the top job and were not shy about undermining their leader.

"The War Council's vote was unanimous," Webb replied. "Washington's eager for a victory, but he must bide his time."

"What will the 39th do then?"

"Watch and wait. And dig. If we're not going into Boston, Washington wants to make sure the British don't get out. We'll be building fortifications around the city."

"A siege of Boston?"

"Exactly. We will all learn patience."

I returned to my tent both relieved and disappointed. If we weren't going into battle tomorrow, we might as well enjoy the extra rations of spirits.

As several junior officers gathered around a fire, William Hull raised his cup in salute. "To the jury that has rendered a just verdict on General Washington's reckless plan," he toasted, rum dripping from the corners of his lips.

"Spoken like a true lawyer," I replied before gulping a generous swig myself.

"Spoken like a practical man who has no wish to toss his life away in vain."

"But what honor is to be won in an interminable siege?"

"Honor?" Hull asked, laughing. "My friend, your head must still reside in the rarefied air of academia. Honor in the real world lies in living to fight another day. The British cannot afford to maintain a large army in North America forever. If the Continental Army can simply survive long enough, they will go home."

"If our Army does not go home first." I refilled my cup from the communal jug.

"True, but we still have cause to celebrate tonight." Hull stood and looked around the gathering. "However, it will be a dull celebration if we don't find some young women to enliven the evening." He bowed in mock deference towards me. "Captain Hale, you have much experience in this sport. Will you lead us?"

"You don't find many young women around the courthouse, do you?" I allowed myself a smile as I slugged another round of rum.

"Not nearly as many as flock to your schoolhouse."

***

The reply from General Sullivan arrived the night before Rogers' landlady was planning to kick him out into the street. It contained an introduction to the vaunted Benjamin Franklin, recently returned from a twenty-year stay in London, and the senior statesman in Congress. With Sullivan's letter in hand, Rogers wheedled two more nights of lodging and a bowl of lukewarm water to wash.

Early the next morning, after stitching a torn sleeve in his tattered green jacket and polishing its buttons, he presented himself at Franklin's house on Market Street. He showed his credentials to the butler who instructed him to wait outside. An hour later, the door re-opened and the butler escorted him through the parlor to the lintel of Franklin's walnut-paneled study.

Franklin, approaching seventy, motioned Rogers inside, but did not offer a seat. The great man himself, sporting a natty silver waistcoat and jacket, sat behind his desk in a high-backed "Speaker's" Windsor, a new creation of the Carpenter's Company for the leadership of the Continental Congress. Politicians in America, like politicians in London, knew how to look after their own creature comforts, Rogers thought.

"Do you miss London?" he asked, trying to establish a common bond. Although Philadelphia was home to 40,000 colonists, it was little more than a provincial outpost compared to England's capital, roughly twenty times its size.

"I don't have time for pleasantries," Franklin responded, head down, studying Rogers' petition. "Adams and Hancock are waiting at the State House."

"Fine men, but where would they be now if the French had won the Seven Years' War?"

Franklin looked up, unfocused, as if he had lost his train of thought. "Ah yes, your service in the wilderness," he said, returning to the present. "That's why I agreed to see you."

"I'm still in debt, sir, from that service. I need to travel to regain my financial footing."

Franklin grunted as he searched his desk, rumpling papers, his eyes finally alighting on his tortoise shell snuff box.

"You too are a man of humble roots," Rogers continued his plea. Franklin was the living symbol of opportunity in the new world, rising to wealth and influence on the strength of his brains and diligence. Such success would not have been possible in England, where birthright trumped all. Why then were the people here so unhappy? So anxious to rebel against the Crown that had nurtured and protected them?

"I have not forgotten my roots. Or my country." Franklin stopped his discourse to pinch a wad of tobacco under his lip. "You were once our brightest star, but you have fallen to depths I did not think possible."

Franklin picked up a report and read out loud. "Tried for treason, a fart-catcher at King George's court, debtor's prison, the demon rum, women of ill repute. The list of charges is a long one. How can the Continental Congress trust you now?"

"I'm determined to right myself, sir. I just need a bit of capital to get started." The uncharted lands on the far side of the Ohio River still beckoned. Rogers had once dreamed of leading an expedition to discover the Northwest Passage to the Orient. If he could raise funds, he could head west and bypass the rebellion completely.

"I will be leaving shortly to visit General Washington in Cambridge. To assess how Congress can better support our military endeavors. Would you serve if needed?" Franklin asked.

"Serve what? Supper? I doubt His Excellency wants me in his army." Rogers replied, struggling to keep the sarcasm from his voice. Washington was a second-rate militia man, while he was a proven battlefield hero; but the Virginian now occupied the general's mansion and he resided in a squalid boarding house.

Where did his life go wrong? Too much time in filthy, stinking jails, Rogers decided. First in Canada, then in London. No official from any colonial government had ever lifted a finger to help him, even though he had risked his life many times to defend the borders of his homeland. He'd had no choice but to turn to Lord Amherst and other wealthy patrons in London. King George himself had intervened on his behalf, while Franklin, Adams, Hancock and the others had remained silent.

"Unfortunately, you're right. Your services as an officer are not in demand," Franklin replied as he ambled to the windows and fumbled with the latch. An image of the elderly statesman's bare arse, flitted into Roger's mind, forcing him to suppress a chuckle. Franklin supposedly craved fresh air to the point of stalking naked around his private quarters, and was rumored to enjoy the company of young women in the same state of undress. At last, Franklin succeeded, flinging the shutters open to inhale the chill October breeze. "If I issue this pass, where will you go?"

"First to visit Governor Tryon in New York," Rogers said, straightening his posture and clasping hands behind his back. "I must collect my back pay and confirm the deeds to my lands in the north. Borders among the colonies may have changed while I was away."

"Times have changed. You'll find New York even more hostile than Philadelphia to men of Tory persuasion," Franklin said as he returned to his desk.

Franklin reached for a fresh page of parchment and dipped his quill into the inkwell. "Do you agree not to bear arms or scout for the enemy?" he asked.

"Yes, sir," Rogers replied. Talk was cheap, particularly when his survival was at stake.

"You will check in with the Committee of Safety within twenty-four hours of your arrival in New York. You will apprise General Washington in writing if your business affairs take you anywhere near his camps," Franklin continued.

"Agreed." Rogers maintained an earnest countenance. After years of gambling at cards and dice, he had little trouble concealing his true hand.

Franklin signed the document with a flourish, affixed his personal stamp, then handed it to Rogers. "Sign there," he pointed. "This will assure you safe passage throughout New England."

Rogers signed as directed. He carefully folded the treasured passport, placed it in the pocket of his jacket, and stood to leave. Franklin nodded a curt farewell.

"Understand clearly, Major Rogers." The statesman's reedy voice stopped him before he reached the door. "If you violate the terms of this agreement, you may well hang."

When the Crown puts down your traitorous rebellion, Mr. Franklin, you will hang. And General Washington will swing beside you.

To John Hancock,

…I find that a very great Proportion of the Officers of the Rank of Captains & under will retire—from present Appearances I may say half, but at least one third—It is with some Concern also that I observe that many of the Officers, who retire, discourage the Continuance of the Men & I fear will communicate the Infection to them.

Go: Washington
Camp at Cambridge
Oct. 30ᵗʰ, 1775

Ignoring the morning drizzle, I walked along the picket line at the crest of Cobble Hill. To my rear, row upon row of white tents stretched across the meadow to the foot of Winter Hill, our home base. I squinted in a vain effort to see through the fog that blanketed the river basin and harbor. It was just as difficult to maintain the discipline of my troop after weeks of construction work.

The monotony eroded my own spirits as well. Barracked deep in the countryside with thousands of other men, frivolities were few and far between. It had been too long since I had led William Hull and several other gentlemen on our celebratory jaunt, culminating in too many rounds of huzzahs and hard ciders at the Flag and Flagon in Mystic, a tavern I had heard was home to a covey of willing females. Sadly, the rumors proved as exaggerated as the estimates of our Army's supply of gunpowder. All we had found were a trio of haggard whores surrounded by a score of enlisted men, neither party particularly suitable company for officers of our rank. Nevertheless, we made the most of our evening, drinking and carousing until our purses were empty.

On the ridge, my company joined the other Connecticut regiments, humping over picks and shovels to shape an earthen berm for a new fort. Cobble Hill was a half mile closer to Boston; General Washington was tightening the noose.

"Lexington," I gave the day's code word.

"Concord," Asa, on sentry duty, replied with the countersign.

"Good man," I said, Would General Washington ever be able to forge a fighting force from this rabble?

"Nobody's coming," Asa said. "The redcoats are still licking their wounds from the thrashing we gave them in June. They're hunkering down for winter, just like us."

Boom! A flash of cannon fire from Beacon Hill appeared to belie Asa's assertion.

"They let loose a blast or two every morning. We'll soon oblige with a return salvo," Elvin Parrish, Asa's partner on duty, said. "After we're both done showing off, everyone'll settle down to the day's grunt work."

As the fog lifted, I pointed to the HMS Rose, its sails fluttering in the breeze as it headed south. "Somebody's leaving."

"Up to no good, I bet," Asa replied.

"Better for us if she leaves," Elvin said. "My cousin in second company heard that Washington wants to attack Boston."

"Again? Without any gunpowder?" Asa asked, shifting his musket from one shoulder to the other. "I'm down to my last nine cartridges."

"I heard Washington's stored a boatload of powder in the armory at Roxbury, but he's only got half the troops that Congress promised," Elvin added.

"What do you think's going to happen, Captain?" Asa again.

"I think you men should get back to patrol," I replied, having no information to add even if I was so inclined. "You ask more questions than my students back in New London."

Asa marched off, but Elvin but couldn't resist one more query. "Is it true we're gonna be wrestling the boys from Bristol up on Prospect Hill tomorrow?"

I nodded. "Captain King and I thought it would be the best way for our men to work off their animosity."

"They're gonna wrestle against Asa?"

"Asa will sit this one out. For his own safety."

"Who's going to take his place?"

"Looking forward to giving them a thrashing," I replied, a mischievous grin spreading from cheek to cheek. Although I knew I shouldn't fraternize with enlisted men, let alone repeat the infraction, I couldn't resist a competition in my favorite sport.

"I hear Mr. DeWolf's willing to put up twenty-five pounds on his boys. I do believe I'll take a piece of that action now."

I whistled in reply.

"Twenty-five pounds might not be much for a college man like you but it's a year's wages for me. More, when ship's don't sail." Elvin pawed the dirt with his boot. "How much you goin' in for, Captain?"

"You know General Washington frowns on gambling, particularly by his officers." I played checkers now, primarily for sport not sterling. The enlisted men played cards, but only in their tents; the officers were obliged to break up the games if they were out in the open.

"Won't stop the boys. This is their big chance to make some money. We'll be counting on you."

"I won't let you down," I replied, wheeling away to continue my inspection tour.

***

The once lush hillsides surrounding Boston were now almost bare, reduced to fields of knobby stumps. As we marched towards one of the remaining coveys of tall trees, I wondered what these lands might have looked like a hundred and fifty years ago when the Pilgrims first arrived. Where were the Indians, the original inhabitants? I thought of the Greeks and Romans – Socrates, Caesar and Cato. *Was this how a civilization progressed? Driving its predecessor deep into the wilderness?*

With winter fast approaching, the Continental Army faced the prospect of a cold, dark, protracted stalemate. My men grumbled: they had signed up to fight the British, not to battle pine, beech and oak. The adrenaline rush of axe slashing into bark was only a mild consolation for this ennui. How could I entice them to re-enlist when their terms expired in December?

General Washington's siege works insured that the redcoats had little chance of escaping Boston by land. Unfortunately, the odds of our army breaching Boston' defenses were just as slim. Colonel Webb had whispered last night that the council of war would reject another of Washington's ill-conceived plans of attack.

At least the food in camp was still plentiful, although no one knew how much longer the Massachusetts farmers would support the visiting army that occupied their countryside. I enjoyed a bowl of stew and the company of William Hull after the day's work. I looked up as two of my men strolled by, closer than usual to the officers' campfire.

"Kick their arse back to Newport, Captain," a red-haired private, a caulker by trade, called out.

"I've got my bride's dowry riding on you," his mate, a surveyor's assistant, added.

"What's that about?" Hull asked when the men had passed.

"A wrestling match tomorrow," I replied.

"And you're a combatant?" Hull asked, spooning brown gravy into his mouth.

I nodded sheepishly.

"You'll understand if I don't come out to cheer you on?" Hull delicately wiped his lips with his sleeve.

After retiring to my tent, I lit a candle on the empty keg that served as my desk and dipped my quill in ink. First, I recorded the troop's activities in my journal, bound in red leather. When I purchased this handsome diary, I had envisioned writing florid prose recounting glorious exploits on the battlefield, but instead I jotted terse phrases of yet another pedestrian day and sketched out a diagram of the camp. Nevertheless, the exercise sharpened my skills of observation which might someday, I hoped, be put to better use.

Next, I turned to correspondence. Enoch and my Linonia classmates regularly exchanged news. The "Betsies" from New London wrote as well, pleasant reminders of more enjoyable pursuits.

Still no word from Anne, unfortunately. While I could see Boston every day, the harbor might as well have been an ocean since I could not cross it. Where were her thoughts now? Had she found another beau? I pulled out her letter from my trunk and reread it. Perhaps I had been too reserved in my first reply.

A fellow officer had hinted that he knew a man who knew a man who could get a letter into the city on a fishing boat. I blackened my quill again, wrote of my aching heart and desire to see her again, closing with romantic sentiments from our beloved *Cato*: *Thy words shoot through my heart, melt my resolves and turn me all to love.*

What did I have to lose?

***

As the longboat pushed away from the docks of New York, Robert Rogers flipped a sarcastic wave at the two toughs from the Committee of Safety who had tailed him for the past week. The sun was at its zenith but could only peek out intermittently between the gaps in an armada of puffy clouds that appeared in no hurry. With little breeze, the steep bluffs of the coastline reflected in the pellucid waters of the North River.

The two British sailors grunted with each stroke of their oars as they ferried him out to the HMS Halifax, the new residence, temporarily at least, of William Tryon, the Royal Governor of the colony. While they had never met, Rogers was hopeful the forty-six-year-old, well-heeled Brit would welcome him as a fellow landholder, adventurer, and soldier.

During his previous stint as Royal Governor of North Carolina, Tryon had raised taxes to pay for the construction of an elaborate coastal mansion, dubbed Tryon's Palace. When two thousand farmers in the western wilderness, nicknamed the Regulators, rebelled, Tryon raised the militia, defeated them in battle at Alamance, and executed seven of its leaders under the power of a conveniently passed amendment to the colony's constitution. Based on this success, the King promoted Tryon to the governorship of New York, the most strategic port in the colonies and currently a cauldron of insurrection.

A fife and drum performed a lively rendition of the "British Grenadier" as the longboat glided next to the hull of the Halifax riding at anchor with sails furled. Its twin masts loomed majestically overhead as Rogers climbed aboard. An ensign led him to the governor's quarters, furnished with polished woods, gold and silver.

"Sit, sit," Tryon, ensconced behind a desk that consumed half the cabin, said. "I've read your communications. We have much to talk about."

A liveried servant offered Rogers a dram of whiskey, which he gladly accepted. "I'll need your seal on my land deeds in the north, and…"

"You'll have my approval, but that's not the reason I granted your audience today." Tryon adjusted his cravat and tweaked the ruffles adorning his shirt.

"No?"

"I'm more interested in the proffer of your military services to the Crown."

"You are?" Rogers coughed up his whiskey. "I mean, yes of course, your Excellency."

"The rebels grow more rambunctious every day," Tryon said, pointing out the window of his cabin towards the New York shore. "Washington is their hero. The Whigs practically threw flowers in his path when he traveled through the city in June. I was returning from London that same day. The town council asked me to wait out in the harbor until the parade was over."

"Quite appalling, sir."

"Washington is the symbol of the rebel cause, the unity of the northern and southern colonies against their king." Tryon continued his harangue.

"General Washington…"

"*Mister* Washington is a traitor and must be treated accordingly."

"What are you suggesting?"

"I'm suggesting that we need to apprehend the criminal and bring him to the King's justice."

"Kidnap Washington?"

"I want the rebels to see him swing from the gallows." Tryon pounded his fist on the desk.

"I have no love of Mr. Washington, but…"

"William Cunningham would be the man for the job, but the Sons of Liberty rode him out of New York on a rail."

Cunningham, Rogers knew from his days in London, was little better than a slave trader, luring men from the lower classes to sail to America with the promise of a better life. He crammed them below decks with meager rations, then sold them as indentured servants to pay off the fees for their passage.

"And where is good Mr. Cunningham now?" Rogers asked.

"In Boston as Provost Marshal. With a deep thirst for vengeance."

"I will leave the kidnapping of Mr. Washington to him then. I'm a Ranger, not a blackguard," Rogers said. He straightened in his chair and smoothed his green jacket. "I would like to petition you for the funds to capitalize a grand expedition to explore the lands west of the Ohio River. I believe we can discover a passage to the Orient. In the name of the King."

"You jest of course," Tryon laughed so heartily his wig almost slipped off. "The King is still in debt from that bloody Seven Years War with the French. Now, he's scouring Europe to hire mercenaries to put down this vile rebellion in North America. He has no spare funds for your fantasy."

"Rangering then. Surely, General Howe has need for men with experience fighting in the wilderness. I can rally the Indian tribes to our side."

"Yes, I'm sure you can be useful in that regard. I will forward your letters to Boston." Tryon straightened his hairpiece.

"Thank you."

"But, remember, you would be well compensated if you could deliver Mr. Washington to his date with the noose."

***

In route to the store, Anne glanced across the water, monitoring the activity of the Continental Army in the distant hills as best she could. Rumors of rebel plans to attack Boston circulated regularly, but she could not see any massing of men or ships to support such an endeavor. Her life, which had settled into an acceptable, if not pleasant, routine in the four months since Bunker Hill, would go on.

Since she had received no correspondence from Nathan, he had slowly slipped from her thoughts. She was almost nineteen. Living in a city at war, a city that might be overrun by low-life rabble at any time. Her brother's recent death was yet another reminder of the brevity of life. Geoffrey Stanwich was her man now.

Fortunately, he required little prodding to step up his romantic energies. Last Sunday after church, he had arranged for a picnic dinner at Windmill Point. Reclining on his regimental blanket, she closed her eyes and turned her face to the sun, soaking up the last warm rays of the season. When she looked again, he had propped himself on an elbow, his face only inches away.

He caressed her cheek and recited: *In this harmless grove no lurking viper hides, but in my breast the serpent Love abides/ Here bees from blossoms sip the rosy dew, but your Geoffrey knows no sweets but you.*

"Alexander Pope?" she asked, her fingers stroking the thick black hair curled over his ear. "How beautiful."

"Well done," he said, surprise evident in his expression.

"For a provincial," she added with a coy smile.

"Yes, for a provincial." He closed his one good eye and kissed her. After a tentative first brush, he withdrew, searching her face for approval. She licked her lips, savoring his taste, then kissed him again, and again.

That was as far as she would go, for now at least. She would not let her impulses drive her too far too fast, as had almost happened in the schoolhouse with Nathan. In hindsight, her brother's knock had proved most fortuitous, she assured herself.

Arriving at the store a few minutes early, she lingered outside, her mind still racked with improper thoughts. When would she finally lose her virginity? Would she, could she, wait until marriage? Would the first time be pleasurable? Or painful? Would she be skillful at the task?

Last summer, Martha Barrister's older sister had shocked the girls at a quilting bee by recounting the story of her wedding night, as if she had waited that long. How could something that big fit...? She looked down at her slim hips. Mother had tried to be helpful, but had faltered at the finish, telling Anne she was smart enough to figure out the last bits on her own.

Sex was like a difficult mathematics equation, she decided. Or stitching a gown from scratch. If she proceeded slowly but steadily, she would reach a satisfactory conclusion. Her mind drifted to this coming Sunday. Geoffrey had promised another picnic.

The sounds of men at work snapped shut her daydreams. On this side of the Charles River basin, the soldiers were demolishing vacant homes and public buildings to stockpile firewood for the coming winter. The silhouette of the town was beginning to resemble the gums of an old man, yawning gaps separating the few functioning teeth.

Father, however, seemed unusually bright this morning, sweeping the floor in the front room when she walked in. "Sam Hale said the army will be staying the winter," he said, broom in hand. "General Howe doesn't have enough ships to evacuate everyone."

"As well as Betsey Loring and her trousseau," Anne added.

"You jest, but Mrs. Loring will soon have occasion to wear her gowns. The officers are planning to turn Faneuil Hall into a grand theater, a fitting end to the rebel meeting house."

"And, of course, the other ladies in town will need evening attire as well."

"Yes, yes." Father put aside his broom and tossed a log into the stove. "We will do our best to satisfy their needs."

"I'd best get to sewing then," Anne said gathering a basket of scarlet yarn. Perhaps she could accompany Geoffrey to a ball.

"Not yet," Father said, warming his hands. "I need you to run an important errand. Across the Neck."

"Across the Neck? Into rebel territory?"

"The Crown has friends in the countryside too."

"But why me? I'm a …"

"Woman, yes, I know. But that is your security. No one will suspect you."

"Are you sure?"

"I'm in debt to Mr. Hale and Sheriff Loring. Business has been so slow I cannot meet my obligations. If we do not perform their bidding, …"

"I'm not a spy, Father."

"No, definitely not. You'd just be a courier, picking up a letter from a loyal Tory and bringing it back here. No different from your deliveries to Major Stanwich."

"I'll need time to consider." Anne pursed her lips. On one hand, Father was right. She had brought three of his communications to Geoffrey. Drifting along in the cozy fog of romance, she had successfully rationalized away the military and political significance of these actions.

Father took her hand. "Now's the time, daughter. Howe has sent his gunboats up and down the coast. There'll be havoc in Washington's camps."

"I said I'll consider it."

***

The men from Bristol, all fifty of them resplendent in their green jackets, massed on the far side of the wrestling ground, marked by four stakes at the rear of the Continental Army camp at Prospect

Hill. A wan October sun perched precariously on the edge of a cloudless, blue sky. In the background, the tent city rustled with the sounds of soldiers returning from a day's work. Smoke from cooking fires curled upward, the aroma of roasting pork wafting towards the combatants.

To the beat of fife and drum, I marched my men, wearing their browns, in two columns to the near side. Almost my entire command had come over for the show. Asa, despite my admonition to stay away, was in the last row. By mutual agreement, both sides had left their weapons home; however, I could see that my friend's right hand never strayed far from his hip. I would have bet a month's wages that Asa's pistol lurked underneath his shirt.

Captain King emerged from the sea of green with a black velvet pouch in hand. He held it high, jingling the coins inside loudly enough for all to hear. Zeb Cheesebrough handed me a leather saddlebag, stuffed with silver and currency. I met King in the center of the ring.

We were joined by Pastor Randall, a puckish septuagenarian who had agreed to safeguard the pot. He made a show of counting the Bristol silver first. All there. The New London collection, however, came up five pounds and two shillings short. I looked back at my troop but could see they were tapped out. I reached into my pocket and withdrew a silver watch, a graduation gift from Father, and tossed it to the Pastor. A roar went up from the Connecticut crowd. The match was on.

"Nigger lovers. Nigger lovers." The taunt rose from the Bristol side. Enos Cartwright took a long sip from his rundlet and tossed it to the ground. He peeled off his jacket and shirt, stepping forward to display the oozing scabs crisscrossing his back. "Now, it's our turn to administer a whipping."

"I'll go first, brother," John Cartwright, a squat, snot-nosed youth, said as he bared his chest and strutted past Enos. Planting himself in the center of the ring, he pawed the ground with his boots. Enos joined the cheering Bristol crew.

Attracted by the commotion, a score of soldiers wandered over from their tents. Two women, camp followers, their uncapped hair tumbling brazenly over bare shoulders, flirted with the spectators. A pig lolled along the perimeter of the crowd.

"I'll teach this lard-belly a lesson," Elvin Parrish said as he stripped off his shirt. He towered over his opponent as they slapped hands in a weak show of sportsmanship. A sergeant from a Worcester regiment announced two to one odds in favor of Elvin, taking side bets from all comers.

John Cartwright bulled Elvin out of bounds in less than a minute, returning to the center of the ground, rubbing his hands together in anticipation of his next victim. The match would continue until all challengers had their turn in the ring. The last man standing would claim victory for his side.

The next three privates from New London met the same fate as Elvin, but each lasted progressively longer. The cheers from the Bristol boys grew louder, bolstering their champion who was now sucking in gulps of air as he awaited his fifth match.

"A free one if you can run the table," one of the harlots called in encouragement, a wad of winnings in her hand.

The two women had now been joined by a third, a long-legged Native wearing a white feather behind her right ear and a fringed buckskin shirt, the top fastenings left undone to reveal an intricately woven necklace of red and white beads. Her hair, a shimmering blackstrap molasses, was braided into two strands which spilled over her shoulders before coming to rest atop the swell of her breasts. Feral green eyes, a regal nose and fleshy lips, asking to be kissed, stood out against her caramel skin. I was captivated.

Asa stepped past him to take a turn in the ring, but I recovered my wits in time to pull him back. "You're not wrestling today."

"I won't shrink like a coward in front of these white boys," Asa replied.

"These white boys will put your neck in a noose if you beat one of them in the ring."

"But..."

"I'm ordering you to stand down," I said, setting my yellow-plumed hat to the side and handing my shirt to Zeb. After weeks of construction duty, I spoiled for a fight. Even if it was with a fellow soldier in the Continental Army.

"Come on, you bungholes," John Cartwright called out. "Stop your cackling. I've got a lady waiting for me."

As I stepped into the fray, I couldn't resist a glance at the Indian to see if she was watching. Pleased to see that I indeed had her attention, I darted and danced, taunting Cartwright with every feint. The Bristoler pursued at a steady pace, undaunted by my antics, steadily closing the ground between us like a bear stalking its prey. Cartwright hemmed me against the boundary line, closing within range of his short arms, slapping me on the side of my head. When I ducked, he moved in for the kill, wrapping his arms around my waist, lifting me off the ground.

Inches from becoming Cartwright's fifth victim, I hammered my fists into his kidneys and twisted, creating just enough space to drop down to one knee and attack his legs. The air exploded from his lungs as he landed.

I sensed victory, but Cartwright kicked his way out of my grasp and sprung to his feet. With a guttural cry, he dove right back into the fray, catching me off balance and flattening me against the ground. Driving his shoulder into my spine, he wrenched my right arm, twisting it like a chicken wing. Eating dirt, I had little choice but to yield.

A roar surged from the Bristol crowd; their drummer beat a victory march. Pastor Randall shouted that the match was over and handed the prize money to Captain King. The Bristolers lifted John Cartwright on their shoulders and paraded around the wrestling ground.

"Damnation, Hale," Zeb stood over me, not offering any assistance. "You got yourself all lathered up over an Indian squaw. And got yourself beat."

"Captain Hale to you," I replied, rising to one knee, taken aback by Zeb's antagonism. It was the first time one of my men, let alone a sergeant, had sworn at me – to my face at least.

"You ain't my captain today." Zeb spit, narrowly missing my boots.

"I lost my watch," I offered weakly.

"Your daddy's gift. We'll pass the plate around to buy it back."

As the green jackets whooped their way back to camp, the object of my desire stepped from the shadows. She picked up my hat and strode over to where I still knelt in the dirt.

"Nice try, Captain," she said, tossing the hat at my feet. "But, if you give quarter to the redcoats, you'll be a dead man."

"I don't need any advice from…"

"My father, and grandfather, and great-grandfather were Mohegan warriors," she interrupted before turning to leave.

"Hey, where are you going?" I called.

"I'm at the Flag and Flagon most nights. Ask for Princess."

***

Anne stooped to pull the onions from the thin soil behind their home in the feeble light of a frosty dawn. Father had sent Becky with Mother and Phineas to Halifax rather than feed another mouth in Boston.

Although the snows were still several weeks away, food was already growing scarce. With the city surrounded by hostile forces, supplies could only come in by water. A swarm of lightly-armed rebel whaleboats, several hundred in number, pecked away at any British merchant ships that attempted to enter the harbor. The docks on Boston's Long Wharf were often deserted, its seamen out of work. The inhabitants of the besieged city wondered aloud if Parliament had forgotten them.

Anne carried a bushel of the onions down into the root cellar and tucked it away on a shelf. In addition to storing vegetables and salting fish, she would need to dip candles and boil a vat of soap. Father had already chopped whatever winter wood he could find and stacked it beside the house.

The loneliness of living in a city under siege could be overwhelming. Anne missed her mother, her brothers, her friends from New London, and her schoolmaster, whom she hadn't heard from in months. She didn't have a single female companion her own age. Instead, she was surrounded by frustrated, angry, leering men.

The blossoming romance with Major Stanwich was her one escape. She was young enough to feel no immediate pressure to find a husband, but she was not a beautiful woman, and her dowry would be modest. Although missing a leg and an eye, Geoffrey, the Lord of Runcorn, was an excellent match, perhaps the best she would ever find. And she had come to enjoy his company as well as his advances, which had grown more ardent each Sunday.

But Geoffrey had made clear, he would not stay in America longer than his military service required. Anne pictured herself as the Lady of the turreted castle overlooking the Mersey River, which Geoffrey had so vividly described.

Could she really leave America? Yes, she decided. British society had a sense of order, of place, that appealed to her mathematical mind.

Her family had strong emotional ties to England and might even join her. Caleb could partner with Father in the shop. There would be plenty of business opportunities on both sides of the Atlantic if the Crown won the war. If not, there would be little place for any of the Wheatons in America.

As for Father's proposed mission in the countryside, she would let Geoffrey decide if she should go. He might advise her to stay safely at home. He might also be sensitive to a woman, his woman, playing a more active role in the military campaign than he could. She would not want to overshadow her future husband.

The garden warmed as the sun rose. Anne removed her cloak, revealing only a simple shift underneath, and walked to the well for a sip of ice cold water. She filled a copper pot to heat over the fireplace, so she could wash before dressing to join Father in the store. A rustle at the rear door of their house startled her.

"Miss Wheaton, your father said I might find you here," Sam Hale said, his gimlet eyes roaming over her sweaty body.

She reached for her cloak, cinching it tightly. "And how may I be of service?"

"It is I who might be of service to you," he replied, reaching into the pocket of his intricately brocaded jacket to hand her an envelope. Anne's heart leapt when she recognized Nathan's neat penmanship. "Go ahead, read it. Take all the time you need."

She fumbled to open the envelope, noting that the seal had already been broken. She skimmed the words, then read them more slowly. Nathan's description of Caleb's treatment at the hands of the mob sickened her. Little wonder her brother felt such animosity towards the rebels. Were these ruffians running the country now? Where was the freedom that Nathan held so dear?

Most important, where was Caleb? At least he was alive, but surely, he hadn't returned to the tailor shop in New London. Anne was a Wheaton, loyal to family - and King.

She searched for a paragraph, a phrase even, that might convey Nathan's feelings, but could find none. His pathetic *Cato* quote conveyed more concern for his cause than for her sibling.

"How did you get this?" she asked Sam, trying to hide her disappointment.

"It is my job to monitor communications coming and going here in Boston."

Had Sam also intercepted her note? She had little doubt that Dr. Bacon would betray her in an instant to advance his position with the Crown.

"Do you still hesitate about venturing into the countryside on a simple errand for your father?" Sam continued.

"I planned to discuss it with Major Stanwich on the Sabbath," Anne replied, relieved that Sam Hale appeared ignorant of her earlier correspondence.

"I do not think that is a wise idea. In fact, I would strongly counsel against it."

"And why is that?"

"You're a woman. It is not your position to question my judgment."

"Yes, sir."

"Your father owes a debt. It is your familial duty to help him repay it."

Anne bowed her head, defeated by her own sword.

"You will leave tonight. A Native in my employ will row you up the Mystic River. There's a disorderly house just outside Winter Hill. The Flag and Flagon. A woman there will have a letter for you."

"How will I recognize the whore?"

"Smart girl," Sam said with a crude smirk. "She'll wear a white feather behind her ear. You'll ask if there is a Mohegan village nearby."

"And the countersign?"

"She'll inform you that the Mohegans have all but disappeared from the coast."

When Sam left, Anne stripped to the waist and tried to sponge herself clean, but she could not remove the filth that he had dragged into her home. After breakfast, a cup of tea and hard biscuit, she walked to the store. Father was alone. He busied himself with a page of figures and did not look up.

"I leave on the tide," she said. *For Caleb.*

***

I returned to camp for evening prayers after an eight-hour tour of marching, digging, chopping and waiting for nothing to happen. Although the temperature was dropping and there was no sign of a British attack, General Washington kept the army on a rigid daily schedule, pushing the troops to strengthen their bastions of defense for the assault not likely to come until the snows melted in the spring.

While the British Army remained bottled in Boston, the Royal Navy wreaked considerable damage along the coast. Evidently, roving bands of Queen's Rangers had spiked cannons, rendering towns defenseless. A fleet of warships had sailed north, burning Falmouth to the ground with incendiaries that left a thousand colonials homeless in the cold.

Since many soldiers on Winter Hill had left families behind, fear that the *Rose* and her sister ships might do similar damage in other coastal towns dominated conversation around our evening campfire. Several of my men wondered out loud why they were building breastworks outside Boston when they should be building them back in New London. I felt obligated to recite the patriot mantra, but stopped midstream, realizing my message fell on deaf ears at the late hour.

I retired to my tent, staring at the confining canvas of its sloping roof. I started to write another letter to Enoch but dropped my quill in frustration. Would I spend the entire winter cooped up here? Was this the military service I had enlisted for?

My mind wandered into black places. I wasn't afraid of my own death, the mole on my neck had forced me to confront that fate years ago, but I was terrified at the thought of failing my men. The wrestling match on Prospect Hill had weakened my position of leadership. Not only did I lose the bout, I had lost face. I sensed it in the field and around the campfire, the hesitation, the dropped head when I gave an order, the mutterings behind my back. Would my men re-enlist, or go home? Would I become a captain without a command?

As Princess had said, if I made a mental mistake against the British, the consequences would be severe. Was she a prostitute? Did it matter? She had to earn a living; the life of a single, unattached woman of meager means was a hard one, even more so for a Native.

While I had banked the fires of my libido back in New London, they now raged into a full-blown inferno. I was a college graduate, a captain, a virile twenty-year old entitled to female companionship.

How unlucky to have missed Princess on my first visit to the Flag and Flagon?

Tomorrow was a day of leave for Third Company. My clothes were filthy. There was a widow in Mystic who provided laundry services for officers. I could drop off my clothes and return to the tavern while they were washed.

Princess had claimed to be of noble lineage. Since my ancestors first arrived a hundred and fifty years ago, we had mistreated her people, driving them from their homes and hunting grounds. I had an obligation to hear her story. And perhaps sample her pleasures afterwards.

***

"Almost there," the bald Indian, Uncas, grunted as he guided the birch bark canoe towards the shore line in the dark. Anne perched in the front, wrapped in her mourning black cape and cap for concealment, per Sam Hale's instructions. She had studied Father's map and packed a supper of bread and cheese before leaving home.

The journey had taken her from Boston's North End around Moulton's Point, behind Breed and Bunker Hill, and past several floating batteries of British cannon. Even in darkness the twin hills looked formidable. She tried to imagine Major Stanwich standing on the beach at the front of his regiment, looking up at the fortified rebel positions, leading the charge into their guns. Would she have the courage to do the same?

Uncas had been careful to steer clear of contact with the British navy, laying up in the reeds for almost an hour to allow a patrol boat to pass. When they passed the vacant docks for the "Penny Ferry" connecting the road from Cambridge to Marblehead, she knew they were in rebel territory.

"We'll wait here until dawn," he whispered, his English fluent, as he steered around a half-submerged boulder guarding a crescent-shaped cove. He hopped into the rippling, knee-deep water, shoved the canoe up onto the bank, made sure it was firmly grounded, and climbed back in.

Anne guessed there was two to three hours of darkness left, but was too tense to sleep. Uncas had no such trouble, stretching out, his feet almost in her belly. Curled up, she counted stars and silently recited her favorite Bible passages until the first rays of light painted the sky, outlining the palisades of the rebel fort on Cobble Hill looming on the hillside.

According to Sam's briefing, she would have a half-day's walk at most, along the river path through Temple's Farm to Winter Hill. The Flag and Flagon was located in the village that had sprung up on the outskirts of camp.

Uncas had business of his own to attend. He clutched a saddlebag rattling with coins to his chest as he camouflaged the canoe, marking the spot with a cairn of five stones. He would meet her back here at sunset for the return trip to Boston.

***

I tossed all night anxious for dawn to arrive before at last drifting off into a sweet dream. *The Princess and Anne were naked, facing off in the center of the wrestling ground on Prospect Hill. Their breasts heaved as they grunted and grappled for position. I sat cross-legged on the sideline, reading Cato.* Princess was just about to shove Anne over the line, when the bugle sounded for reveille.

With a day of leisure ahead, the men of third company were in a much more jovial mood at breakfast than they had been the night before. Dressed in my nightshirt, I devoured a biscuit dipped in molasses as I warmed a kettle of water in the crane over the campfire. I took the kettle back to my tent, shaved and washed. While I admired my grooming in my handheld looking-glass, another gift from Father, Asa poked his head inside.

"Something important on your schedule today, captain?" he asked.

"No, no. Just chores and letters. Maybe laundry this afternoon," I replied. "You?"

"I think I'll enjoy the sunshine. Take a walk. Look up a friend."

"Be careful."

"As always." Asa tapped his hip.

I had an array of tasks to complete this morning before I would allow myself to leave. I laid my musket across my lap, cleaning the soot from the flash pan with pick and brush. I screwed a musket worm onto the head of the ramrod, wrapped it in flax, and worked it up and down the inside of the barrel. Finally, I polished the outside of the barrel with a paste of tallow and brick dust until it gleamed.

Satisfied with my weapon, I opened my cartridge box, the motto "Liberty or Death" proudly monogrammed on one side, and checked my flints and ammunition. Short one cartridge, I poured a thimbleful of gunpowder from my half-empty horn into a paper cylinder, tamped it down with a lead ball, and tied the end closed with a string. Now, I was ready for the battle that would most likely not occur until next spring.

I forced myself to walk at a leisurely pace, strolling out of camp with my laundry bundled over my shoulder. I arrived in town shortly after the sun began its descent. After a brief negotiation with the widow, I left my soiled clothes in her care.

Wearing a faded blue frock, open at the bodice, Princess was sitting on the porch of the tavern when he strolled by. "Captain, I thought you forgot about me," she called out.

"Duty before pleasure," I replied.

"Now, it is your duty to buy me a whiskey."

***

Penned up in Boston for six months, Anne had almost forgotten how the countryside looked and smelled. The path was dappled in the October sunlight; a scattering of auburn and gold leaves still clung to the trees; the fragrance of the last wildflowers of the season perfumed the air. A rabbit raced ahead of her before burrowing into the shrubbery. She slowed her pace, relishing the company of the river bubbling by her side. The stinking, starving, overcrowded city seemed a lifetime away.

A farmer, whistling a tune as he headed home from town empty-handed, a likely sign of success at market, nodded a greeting. She shivered when three blue-jacketed soldiers caught up from behind, but they passed without a word, deferential to her widow's black.

The Flag and Flagon, a tobacco-brown, two-story clapboard fronted by a narrow porch, loomed ahead. The red emblem of the New England colonies flew from a pole in the yard. She removed her cap and let her hair tumble over her shoulders. Rehearsing her lines, she gathered her resolve. Not nearly as challenging as the assault on Breed's Hill, she assured herself.

***

I curled next to Princess in the sagging center of a four posted, rope bed upstairs at the tavern. Our clothes were strewn on the floor; a fire blazed in the hearth. Her finger traced the faded musket scar on my cheek.

"A combat wound, captain?" she asked. I nodded, still breathing raggedly as her hand slid down my chest.

"Hopefully, you aimed before you pulled the trigger," she teased as her hand dipped lower, caressing me. "This musket went off a little too quickly today."

"Out of practice, I guess."

She rose from the bed, smiling at her own humor. I admired the muscled curves of her hips as she leaned over to retrieve her frock.

"Your first Indian pelt?" she asked, catching me ogling her. I nodded sheepishly.

"Our culture has no taboos on pleasure," she added, standing, defiantly comfortable in her nakedness.

"I noticed." The scratches across my back stood testament to her savagery.

Princess pulled the frock over her head, wiggling and tugging until it settled, then tucked a white feather behind her ear

"Where are you going?" I asked.

"A personal matter." She reached into a drawer for an envelope.

I scanned the room for my purse. "I haven't paid you yet."

Princess' head snapped around, her anger apparent as she returned to the bed. "I'm not a whore, Nathaniel."

"Why do you have a room at the Flag and Flagon then?"

"No reputable landlord would let a room to a Native." She tousled my hair and started for the door. "I'll be back in a minute. You stay up here and reload."

***

Anne had never been inside a tavern alone before. Although it was only mid-day, several uniformed soldiers stood at the bar. Heads turned her way as she approached. No sign of the British spy with the white feather. How long should she wait? What should she order?

Before she could decide, the Indian girl descended the staircase. About her own age. A striking face but foggy-eyed like she had just gotten out of bed. Wearing only a faded gown with no undergarments. The girl noticed Anne immediately – she must have stuck out like a lobsterback.

"Sister," the Indian called. "Here to try again to convert me to your Christ?"

At the mention of religion, the men turned away, burying their heads in their whiskey glasses. The Indian steered her towards the front door. Out on the porch, they exchanged sign and countersign. She never felt the Indian deposit the letter for Sam Hale in her pocket.

Anne was down the steps before realizing that the girl had about-faced and returned inside to the warmth of the tavern. She quickly headed back to the river path and her rendezvous with Uncas. The mission had gone smoothly, easier than she had feared and more exhilarating, her racing heartbeat confirmed. Although she had once thought she would rather sweep mouse droppings than deal with Sam Hale, she now hoped he had another assignment for her.

CHAPTER 8 - NOVEMBER 1775

"...And I do hereby declare all indented servants, Negros and others (appertaining to rebels) free that are able and willing to bear arms..."
Proclamation of Lord Dunmore
Royal Governor of Virginia – aboard the man-of war Fowey (Yorktown)
November 7, 1775

"Neither Negroes, Boys unable to bear Arms, nor old men unfit to endure the fatigues of the campaign, are to be enlisted..."
General Orders
General George Washington
November 12, 1775

"[Provincial forces] to be put on the most Respectable Footing [and] all Negroes, Molattoes and other Improper Persons who have been admitted into these Corps be immediately discharged."
General Orders
General William Howe
Commander – British forces in North America

Winter Hill earned its name as an Arctic wind scoured the camp; however, the frigid conditions didn't stop me from bolting down the road to Mystic after I dismissed my troop. For the past two weeks, thoughts of Princess had seared my brain. She had been both confident and uninhibited, different from any other woman I had lain with. But, how did she earn her money? I couldn't exactly ask around, even if I was discreet. I had to surprise her at the Flag and Flagon.

It would be easier if she was a whore. I could wait my turn, toss a few coins on the bed and be on my way. No need to deal with emotions. But, if she wasn't, what happens next?

For months, I thought I was in love with Anne, a Tory. Now, an Indian princess, well-versed in the ways of love and war, dominated my dreams. Reason would have to govern my romantic pursuits someday - but not tonight.

Frozen to the core, I slipped through a knot of soldiers surrounding the tavern's hearth. Two wore the uniforms of another Connecticut regiment, but, fortunately, none from my own command. I warmed my hands, gathered my courage, and approached the bar.

"I'm looking for Princess," I said, projecting a bravado that belied my churning stomach.

With outsized ears and a tomato-red nose, the rotund barkeep could have easily been mistaken for an oaf, however the squint in his dark eyes indicated he was not a man to be trifled with. He pushed an ale towards me and tilted his head towards the stairway. "She's in her room."

I tried to remain nonchalant, sliding a silver coin across the bar, but my expression must have conveyed my disappointment because the barkeep quickly added, "Alone." Yanking the sleeve of a pox-scarred boy who was swabbing tankards with a sudsy cloth, he ordered, "Go tell Princess she has a visitor. A captain by the cockade in his hat."

I nodded my appreciation and sipped my ale while waiting for a reply. Idly scraping through the grime, tallow and who knew what else that coated the bar, I uncovered a border of finely etched nautical flags and silver flagons, hinting at a more grandiose design for the tavern before ten thousand soldiers descended upon the surrounding countryside.

The stairway drew my glance every few seconds. Finally, my diligence was rewarded as Princess, bundled in a woolen night robe, descended.

"Captain Hale, I was hoping you'd visit again," she said, her voice as smooth as fine Madeira. She took my hand, sandwiching it between her own. Her scent, tinged with jasmine, percolated through the odors of whiskey, tobacco and sweat circulating at the bar. "You're ice cold. Let's go upstairs and warm up."

"I'm not disturbing you, am I?" I asked, relishing the hang-jaw stares of my fellow soldiers.

"No, I was just reading," she replied, turning to lead the way.

"Reading?"

"You sound surprised," she chuckled, pausing mid-stairway to look at him. "What did you think I was doing?"

"I wasn't sure." The words stuck in my mouth.

"A missionary preacher taught me to read when I was fourteen. In exchange for my eternal soul." She resumed her climb.

"You're Christian?"

"Sometimes," she answered over her shoulder as she opened the door.

The room, familiar from my previous visit, was furnished with only a desk, chest and bed, but brightly lit by a dozen candles. A war club, topped with a smooth-sanded wooden head about the circumference of a four-pound cannonball, rested against a bedpost, while a red and white checked quilt lay rumpled on the floor. A faded heather shirt and leggings hung from pegs on the wall.

I picked up the club, holding it with both hands, sensing its heft and balance. "This could hurt someone."

She took the club away and traced a string of eleven heads carved into its handle. "My grandfather killed eleven men with it." Pointing to four notches slashed into the wood, she added, "And was wounded four times."

"And where are your marks?" I asked with a light smile.

"Only one. So far," Princess replied. She flipped the club over to display a single skull. I swallowed hard. Whom had she killed? Why? I was quite sure Princess wasn't joking and could think of no suitable retort.

Moving on, I peered at the leather bound book open on the desk. "What were you reading?"

"*The Journals of Robert Rogers.*" Evidently, Princess had been writing as well because she hurriedly swept papers and quill, as well as the book, into a drawer. "Have you read it?"

"Many times. Would you like me to recite my favorite passages?"

"Later, perhaps," she laughed, stepping purposely away from her desk to add another log to the fire and stir the ashes. The wood ignited with a pop and cackle, quickly flowering into a full-throated blaze. Turning to face me, she swiped her right hand against her cheek, inadvertently war-painting it with a smudge of soot. "I thought I might help you thaw out first."

"Yes, that would be…" I swallowed hard as Princess dropped the robe from her shoulders, letting it slither to the floor.

She tossed back her braids and tugged her flannel nightshirt over her head. Her cocoa-tipped breasts swayed insouciantly as she dropped to her knees and reached for my belt.

Afterward, we spooned underneath the feather-stuffed quilt. The fire had calmed but still radiated a warm glow. Loud voices from the tavern were easily discernable, as were the aromas of fried oysters and roasting potatoes. Heavy footfalls sounded in the hallway, followed by a girlish giggle.

Princess propped herself up on one elbow, resting her free hand on my thigh. A braid of her hair fell across my shoulder.

"So, how was your day Captain Hale?"

"Most dreary. Until I saw you."

"You are growing weary of war?"

"No. I am growing weary of waiting for war. I want to fight already." I shifted my butt away, but she snuggled even tighter. The shutters slapped against the window pane.

"You'll have to wait until springtime, I'm afraid."

"How can you be so sure?"

"General Howe will not leave the gambling tables or the comfort of his mistress until the weather turns."

"How do you know General Howe has a mistress?"

"I have contacts in Boston."

"Within the British Army?" I sat upright.

"It's just girl talk," she backtracked, guiding me down under the coverlet. "Why shouldn't General Howe enjoy the pleasure of a beautiful woman's company on a cold night?" I was in no position to argue.

"Every officer, even the commander-in-chief, needs a diversion at times. To rest his burden," Princess whispered in my ear.

"General Washington is a faithful husband," I said.

"Are you sure? How well do you know your general?"

"Not well at all, really."

"He's a handsome man. And powerful."

"So?" The brush of her taut nipples against my back aroused me again.

"Some women find those qualities irresistible. There's a rumor that he picks his officers based on the beauty of their wives."

"I doubt that," I replied, burrowing back against her hard body.

"Do you think Washington will attack Boston before spring?" She ground her bush against my buttocks.

"Probably not."

"Are your men ready?"

"I've done my best," I answered, wishing she hadn't asked.

She marched her fingers over my hip. "Do you have enough powder for your muskets?"

"You ask too many questions," I grunted, rolling on top. Princess spread her thighs to welcome me.

Although the north wind still rattled, I didn't linger after the second coupling. Princess's interrogation had raised a bile in my mouth.

I looked back only once at the Flag and Flagon. All her candles were out.

The next morning, pellets of hail whipped against the sides of my tent, drowning out even the remotest possibility that anyone could hear the conversation inside. "Do you want the good news or the bad, Captain?" Zeb Cheesebrough asked. Camp food must have agreed with Zeb; his shirt, even when wet, no longer clung to his ribs.

"Looking at the weather, sergeant, I could use a little good news this morning," I replied.

"You won't have to worry about those green-jacketed bastards from Rhode Island any more. The Rose bombarded Bristol, so they marched off Prospect Hill yesterday to defend their hometown."

"Good riddance. And the bad news?"

"Our boys are ready to go home, too. All we do is grunt work. Haven't gotten paid in months. Ain't got much ammunition. Winter's here. You want me to go on?"

"No need."

"Truth is, we're losing faith in our commander-in-chief. General Washington's got as much sense as a cannonball," Zeb's shoulders sagged as he talked. "How can he kick Blacks – free Blacks - out of the army? He'll need every able-bodied soldier he can find if he wants to attack Boston in the spring."

"Washington's wrong, but it's not a simple task to forge men from thirteen colonies into a single army," I replied, sitting on my powder keg desk. "There's too many here that don't consider the Black an equal and won't stand next to one."

"Including the General himself. He'll always be a Virginia plantation owner at heart."

"Washington's only been north for a few months. Give him a chance."

"But we know Blacks can fight." Zeb stamped his boot. "Peter Salem at Lexington, Salem Poor on Breed's Hill. They're heroes."

"I heard several senior officers from Massachusetts are going to talk to His Excellency. They saw Poor in combat first-hand. Think he deserves a commendation." I checked the blanket wrapped around my musket to make sure the barrel stayed dry.

"What if the Blacks just turn around and enlist with the British?" Zeb asked.

"Dunmore's only offering freedom to southern slaves owned by rebels. It's a sign of desperation." I pounded the stock of my musket into the floor. "And General Howe doesn't want Blacks in his army in the north."

Zeb shifted his feet but remained silent.

"I already re-upped for 1776," I added, reaching under my bedding, pulling out a stack of papers, thumbing through them until I found the right one. "What about you?"

"Re-up? For a full year?" Zeb turned to peer out the flap of the tent. The hail had turned to rain, but showed no sign of relenting.

"Washington's got to know he can count on us." I stood and offered my quill.

"General Washington's going to get us all killed, mark my words."

"We're soldiers. We have to be prepared to sacrifice for the freedom of our country. You said so yourself only a few months ago, if I remember correctly."

"I did, I did. But most days now I feel like a common laborer, not a soldier," Zeb said. "If I'm going to build shelters and dig latrines, I might as well just go back to my farm. The wife can't manage by herself much longer anyway."

"You can't give up now."

"I can't let my children go hungry."

"I'll request a furlough so you can go home this winter." I put the re-enlistment papers back under my bedding. "I can advance you funds from my own pocket too, if that helps."

"My mind's set, Captain."

"Don't you want to fight the redcoats?"

"What fight? I ain't seen no fighting except on the wrestling ground. And I didn't get to fight there neither." Zeb turned up the collar on his great coat. "I'm going home on December 10th when my contract expires. And I'm afraid most of Third Company will do the same."

"I won't let that happen on my watch," I replied, strapping gaiters over my breeches for protection against the slop outside. "I'll talk to the men myself. Today."

"With all due respect *captain*, men were watching you over at the Flag and Flagon last night."

"That's a low blow."

"Can you deny it?" Zeb chuckled derisively. "How many times have you visited that disorderly house?"

"Don't I have a right to a private life – just like you?"

"Maybe. But it don't look good to see our captain out roistering like that."

I swallowed hard. I might have defended Princess, she was Christian and read Robert Rogers after all, but I now had my own doubts about her loyalties.

***

Anne bowed her head as she poured steaming tea, first for Lady Pigot, then for the four other women, all made up and bundled in furs, gathered at Wheatons this afternoon. Hardly a lover of the arts, Father had conceived a dramatic reading to attract customers to the store prior to the holiday season. He even instructed Anne to dress up for the day.

She wore her own creation: a white day gown embroidered with a pattern of sprawling red vines, looped into two puffs in the back. Her apron, kerchief, and cap were the Wheaton's finest linen. A heart-shaped pincushion hung at her waist, while a nosegay of winterberries and pine looped her neck. She had considered rouge and powder for her face as well, but Father advised against it; she was still a shop girl after all.

Scrutinizing her fashionable image in the looking-glass, Anne could hardly believe she had traveled rough on the Mystic River just last week, the adventure she had always dreamed about. She had not discussed the details of the trip with Father, who did not ask, or Major Stanwich, who would hopefully remain forever in the dark. Her body still shivered when she replayed the final stage of the journey in her mind.

"Did you meet a young woman at the tavern?" Uncas had asked as the canoe crossed back into British waters.

"Yes," she replied, shaken by his knowledge of her assignment.

"She's my daughter."

Anne lurched forward, almost falling into the river. Do you know your daughter's a whore, she came close to asking, but held her tongue.

"We are Mohegans, the wolves, a tribe of great warriors. We fought on the side of the British against the Narragansett and others for a hundred years." Uncas spoke steadily as he paddled. "And the British rewarded us by stealing our lands, infecting us with their diseases, and converting us to Christianity to pray for our lost souls. There's hardly any Mohegans left now."

"And you?"

"I survive as best I can. Occa too, my princess. She should be the wife of a great sachem, ruling this land. Instead…"

Anne could think of little to say as his voice trailed off. She searched the shoreline for the lights of Boston.

"Why are you here?" Uncas asked, then answered his own question. "Because you are desperate. I can smell it. You are in some debt to Mr. Sam."

"Yes, but…"

"Don't trust him. A woman alone is in a perilous situation. You do not know what service he will demand in repayment."

"Anne, dear, who baked these biscuits?" Lady Pigot's voice pulled her thoughts out of the canoe. "They're delicious."

"I did, ma'am."

"You're quite a talented young lady."

"Thank you, ma'am."

"I say Major Stanwich is fortunate to be the object of your attentions," Lady Evelyn, the youthful wife of another major in the army, said.

"A British lord would be quite a catch for a provincial shop girl," Elizabeth Pitcairn, a matronly Scot widowed when her husband fell on Breed's Hill, removed a biscuit from her mouth long enough to toss in the barb.

"His infirmity is your opportunity," Mercy Hale chipped in. She was a short, stout woman with a pinched face that did not reveal whether she was Anne's friend or foe.

"Lord Stanwich's father would roll over in his grave if he knew his only son was courting a commoner," added Lady Bingley as she coughed politely into her handkerchief. She had pasted a velvet dot on her forehead to signify the grandeur of her lineage. The Lady's husband, Anne heard while sewing in the shop, had purchased his officer's commission with her inheritance and had been the last man off the longboat in June.

"General Howe is enjoying a dalliance with a local as well, I understand," Widow Pitcairn tittered. "It is a shame that Mrs. Loring couldn't join us this afternoon. You provincials might have had a nice chat together." The jingle of the doorbell mercifully ended Anne's torture.

"Thank you for sharing your opinions, ladies. I believe our honored guest has arrived," Father said, bowing towards the dashing figure of General John Burgoyne. "I'm sure you know of the General's military prowess, but he also has a literary side. He's going to honor us this afternoon with a reading from his new play, *Maid of the Oaks*."

General Burgoyne, nicknamed Gentleman Johnny, wore full military dress, scarlet jacket with gold buttons and trim over a gold waistcoat and breeches. A scabbard hung at his hip and a black cravat circled his neck. His lips, almost feminine in their fullness, puckered as he opened the manuscript.

"I wrote this play, my first, in honor of the wedding of my nephew, Edwin Smith-Stanley, heir to the earl of Derby, to Lady Elizabeth Hamilton, daughter of the 6th Duke of Hamilton, at Lord Stanley's hunting lodge, The Oaks, last year. Since General Howe appears to have no intention of moving the Army out of this infernal city until the snows melt, I thought a tale of the countryside might be appreciated."

"Jolly good," Lady Bingley applauded.

Anne refilled the teapot with boiling water and tossed another log into the stove. As she brushed the ashes off her skirt, she realized her colonial roots might brand her forever as an outcast in British society. Maybe that was why Geoffrey had hesitated so long to kiss her. Fortunately, he now seemed intent on making up for lost time. But would he have the courage to marry her?

***

"Come in, Major Rogers. I'm honored to have such a famous warrior in my home," said Reverend Eleazer Wheelock, founder and president of Dartmouth College in New Hampshire. His formally-coiffed wig and black robe accentuated a stern appearance. "I'm so pleased you reached out to me."

"I grew well-acquainted with the Earl of Dartmouth during my time in London," Rogers replied as he brushed the season's first snow from the shoulders of his green jacket. "I wanted to volunteer my services to help his fine institution of learning."

"You've had a long journey, I gather," the Reverend said, sucking in his paunchy jowls as he eyed the Major's shabby appearance.

"Annapolis, Philadelphia, New York, Albany – got deathly sick there, then on to Kent to visit my brother. I have a pass to travel freely signed by Ben Franklin himself."

"An arduous walk for a man your age. You must be ravenous."

"I am a bit hungry."

Wheelock led the way into the keeping room, warmed by a roaring fireplace. An elderly trot with sagging jowls and vacant eyes tended a kettle on the crane over the flames.

"You've done a wonderful job educating the natives at your charity school in Connecticut," Rogers prattled on, but his eyes never left the stew pot. "Now, you're poised to implement your teachings on a grander scale, I gather."

"Dartmouth College will also be training men from good Christian families for the Congregational ministry." Wheelock reached into a cupboard. "An ale or something stronger?"

"A whiskey would be appreciated." Rogers sat, knocking back his first drink in a single swallow. "Rich men's sons, you mean. To preach in the Congregational church? You're a Whig then?"

"I support King George of course, but I do feel his Parliament has been too heavy-handed in its dealings with the colonies. General Washington and his army could go home if Parliament would relent." Wheelock refilled Roger's cup.

"To General Washington, our commander-in-chief. A fine military man," Rogers toasted, downing his second whiskey as quickly as the first.

"Have you met His Excellency?"

"No, I have yet to have the honor." Rogers pushed his cup forward hoping for another round. "But I do plan to call on him when I reach Cambridge."

"I'll write a letter of introduction for you then." Wheelock did not offer more whiskey, but instead motioned for his servant to ladle out the stew. "Where will you be headed next?"

"Portsmouth – to see my wife and son. It's been too long. I have land holdings there as well." Rogers reached for the knife in his belt, but Wheelock handed him proper dining utensils. He shoveled a spoonful of beef and vegetables into his mouth, mopping the gravy from his beard with the back of his sleeve.

"Will you join the Continental Army?" Letting his own stew cool, the Reverend watched the Major closely.

"I'm thinking about it. Been offered several commissions, but I'm still an officer in the British Army," Rogers said between mouthfuls. "Complicates things. Might just sit this war out."

"I see."

Rogers offered his bowl for a refill. "I could head back to London and raise money for your school. I have friends at court who might be able to arrange a grant of land," he said while waiting. "For a small agent's fee, of course."

"That won't be necessary," Reverend Wheelock replied.

***

The physical labor in winter camp suited me perfectly, providing an outlet for my frustrations and nagging doubts. Every time I drove an axe into a stump I thought of Princess. Every time I marched the troop around the parade ground I thought of Zeb's warning. Fortunately, my men were too tired and too cold to notice my distraction.

I wanted to visit Princess again. My body and mind ached to see her. But I had stayed away from the Flag and Flagon for the past ten days.

Not that I had eschewed all social life. I visited with my brothers in nearby camps and supped with senior Connecticut officers at General Putnam's residence, including the renowned Major Thomas Knowlton, an accomplished warrior who had made his mark rangering against the Indians in the north wilderness as a teenager and leading his company against the redcoats on Breed's Hill.

"To Captain Knowlton and battlefield glory," I toasted, wine bottle in hand, as I wandered through Cambridge with William Hull after the festivities.

My friend toasted back, a wry smile creasing his lips. "You will achieve glory in due time, Nathaniel. Knowlton spent twice as much time conversing with you as with me. He can see the fire in your eyes as well."

"It's only the wine," I replied, although flattered by the recognition.

Strolling by General Washington's residence, its windows still glowing with candlelight, William noted our commander's penchant for entertaining his senior officers and their wives. Even though Martha Washington remained in Virginia, he had added without expression. We tucked our bottles into our jackets when Zeb and another sergeant passed us on the walk back to Winter Hill.

"Captain Hale. Colonel Webb wants to see you in his tent." The Colonel's orderly greeted me immediately upon dismissal of my troop the next day.

"I'll wash up and..."

"I believe the Colonel wants to see you now."

The wan afternoon sun casted a flat light on the snow-swept humps and hollows of our camp. The flap to Webb's marquee, three times the size of my tent, was open when I arrived. The Colonel, stood at his writing desk, bundled in his great coat. Freshly shaved, he puffed on a clay pipe carved with intricate swirls, while perusing a letter, seemingly in no rush to greet me.

As I stood at attention, hands clasped behind my back, I fretted that I had not had time to put razor to cheek this afternoon. Disciples of the coarse General Lee might sport a shaggy beard, but any officer wishing to court the commander-in-chief's favor needed to be well-groomed.

"Captain Hale," Webb started without looking up, "I've got a petition in front of me signed by three sergeants questioning your captainship of Third Company because of conduct unbecoming the position."

I struggled to contain the panic lancing my stomach. "I know there's some discontent in the ranks, sir, but I didn't expect it to go this far."

"When men are restless, they look for a scapegoat. You've practically raised your hand to volunteer for the role."

I stared at my boots, noticing a crust of mud on one of the buckles. I knew where the Colonel was going. "I've made some mistakes sir, but…"

"Wrestling with the enlisted men. Gambling with them. Whoring too. You're an officer, a man of property, a man of honor. What were you thinking?" Webb took a drag on his pipe and exhaled a cloud of smoke.

I started to speak, but squelched the words before they left my mouth. I had been reveling in public places too often. Although Princess had never asked for, or taken, my money, she was a dirty puzzle by all appearances. And possibly worse. I searched in vain for a hole to crawl into.

"No, don't tell me what you were thinking. I've got a daughter at home your age," Webb continued.

"It won't happen again, sir."

"It better not. You've got the makings of a fine soldier. But a captain needs to set an example for his men. The right kind of example."

"I've erred, sir, but it's been on my own time. I believe Third Company has excelled on the parade ground and out in the field."

"So far at least." The Colonel paused, tapping a pinch of tobacco into his pipe. "Don't you see that you're on the precipice of a slippery slope to perdition? We're marooned here in winter camp, so it's easy to forget we're at war. But, every action that you take, or don't take, may have life or death consequences when we head into battle in the spring."

"Yes, sir."

"Loose women are dangerous, like opium. And just as addictive," Webb expounded. He exhaled a puff of smoke while studying my face. "You know there are British spies everywhere."

"I can only surmise, sir."

"In fact, I understand that our enemy prefers the weaker sex for this foul task. Particularly women of low morals. They have no honor left to sacrifice."

I wanted to puke, but struggled to remain at attention. "I can assure you I will not go within shouting distance of the Flag and Flagon again."

"We should just close that establishment down, but it would likely pop up again in another location. Men will be men," Webb rambled as much to himself as to me.

"Yes, sir."

Webb fixed his gaze on me as he returned to the situation at hand. "You were the first of your circle to volunteer for duty, Captain Hale. I haven't forgotten that." Webb paced behind his desk, puffing away while he mulled his next move. "I will interview the authors of this petition before I render judgment."

"Understood, sir."

"You're dismissed, Captain."

Reprimand? Demotion? Dishonor? A punishment of Biblical proportions for my lust and vanity. Angry and betrayed, I kicked a root on the walk back to my tent, almost breaking a toe. How could they? How could my sergeants, men whom I trusted, go behind my back?

Glumly, I realized that the sergeants had gone to Colonel Webb not so much to attack me, but to protect the welfare of the privates under their command. Here I was, believing I was the perfect captain, while I had lost the respect of my men. What would I say to Father, or my brothers, or my friends? Better to die an honorable death in battle.

I skulked inside my tent for a good hour before turning to my Bible for comfort and guidance: "Do those things that will show that you have turned from your sins (Matthew 3:8)."

I stopped by Zeb's tent before supper. "A game of checkers?"

The sergeant hesitated for a second before nodding for me to sit on his cartridge case. We set the board up on the dirt between us, playing several moves in silence.

"You signed the petition to Colonel Webb, didn't you?" I couldn't restrain myself any longer.

"Yup."

"Thought I needed a slap upside my head?"

"Yup."

"Why didn't you talk to me first?"

"I did, but you weren't listening too good. You're a twenty-year old captain, a natural leader, but you act like a spoiled schoolboy sometimes." Zeb double-jumped, crowning a king at the end of the board. "I'm twenty-two, but I ain't got your opportunity. Hate to watch you throw it away."

I visited three more tents, listening to the same message in varying forms. These were hard times, especially for men with families to support. And my men feared the worst was yet to come. I needed to smarten up.

I started by confining myself to quarters, transcribing the mundane instructions from my officers' manual into my journal by candlelight. "Every Officer & Soldier that mounts Guard must dress himself in his Regimentals as neat and clean as possible." I resolved to copy the entire document while I awaited Colonel Webb's decision.

The temptation awaiting me at the Flag and Flagon, however, was not so neatly tamed. Visions of Princess tortured my dreams. When carnal urges woke me, I walked the picket line, checking on our sentries.

After several sleepless nights, my brain turned to porridge. I swore I saw her slipping between the trees on the outskirts of camp. I heard muffled voices, her husky whisper floating on the breeze. Who was she meeting? When I stormed into the forest, she had vanished.

***

Anne huddled next to Geoffrey on the deserted beach at Windmill Point, the sky a whale gray, the wind whipping up swells in the harbor. She wore her maroon Sunday hat, trimmed with beaver fur, as well as cloak, scarf, gloves, and three layers of petticoats, the outer one quilted and stuffed with wool.

"I swear there's fewer Jonathans manning those barricades than last week," he said, putting down his spyglass.

"Can I see?" She notched the glass to her eye. "Maybe General Washington gave his men the day of rest for the Sabbath," she noted, squinting into the glass.

"Not likely," he said, drawing her closer. "Morale is low; troops are deserting Washington in droves; they're low on powder; they have few cannons at best."

"You can see all that in the glass?"

"Hardly, woman," he laughed. "General Howe has eyes and ears in the countryside."

"Why doesn't he attack then?"

"Howe watched too many good men fall on Breed's Hill," Geoffrey hesitated as he shifted his weight from his peg leg. "He won't assault a fortified position until he has overwhelming numbers, at least a three to one advantage."

"And when will that be?"

"The King has promised twenty thousand new troops by spring. Redcoats and Hessian mercenaries, too."

"So you think the rebels still have ten thousand men up there?" she asked, gazing off at the hills.

"No, not any more. But they might see reinforcements come April," Geoffrey replied as he struggled to catch up with the math. "You do have a head for figures, though."

"It will be a long winter." She looped her arm around Geoffrey's waist, allowing him to lean on her.

"Particularly if we remain caged in this town like dogs," he said. "The men are growing desperate already."

"They're hungry."

"That too." The major twisted away, signaling for Henry who was minding the coach, feeding an apple to Mersey, the twilight gray draft horse. "I have a present for you. It's been in my family for a century."

Her eyes widened in surprise. "For me?"

Geoffrey reached into the pocket of his greatcoat and removed a gold-plated pistol. "Do you know how to fire a flintlock?"

"Father taught me years ago," she replied, swallowing her disappointment. "Do you think the rebels will attack Boston?"

"No. Unfortunately, General Washington won't make such a grave error. The pistol's for protection from our own soldiers."

"The Regulars?"

"Last week, a maid in Lady Pigot's house – a provincial - charged a private in the 52nd with assaulting her - for the third time."

"And?"

"And nothing, sadly. His commanding officer conducted an inquiry and dismissed the charges."

Anne pursed her lips. "Does General Howe believe his army can ravish the colonies into submission?"

"Perhaps," Geoffrey replied, staring at his peg leg. "The General will never forget our losses on Breed's Hill."

"But that was war."

"As is rape. That is why you must learn to defend yourself – in case I am not here to protect you."

Henry propped a pumpkin on a stump ten steps away. Geoffrey loaded the pistol, cocked the trigger and handed it to her. Anne removed her gloves, gripped it with both hands, steadied her feet and aimed. The recoil sent her back into Geoffrey's arms. The ball sailed high. He tamped another ball down the barrel. She remembered Father's advice to slow her breathing. Her second shot exploded the base of the stump. The pumpkin appeared to laugh at her as it tumbled to the ground.

Henry set the pumpkin back on its perch. Geoffrey walked her closer, three steps away at most, and reloaded the pistol. "One more try."

Anne rolled her eyes. She imagined Dr. Bacon's leering face. Her third shot exploded the pumpkin into an orange mess.

"That's your range then." Geoffrey patted her shoulder and loaded a fourth ball. "Keep it with you whenever you venture in the streets." He pointed to the coach. "Time to go home."

As soon as Henry closed the coach door, he was on her, his lips peppering her throat with kisses. The thrill of shooting had stirred them both. After much fumbling, he finally loosened the laces of her corset. His eyes shone with a pilgrim's wonder as he scooped out her breast and rolled her nipple, already hard as an acorn, between his thumb and forefinger. She leaned back, savoring the sensations jolting her body, running her fingers through his powdered hair, knocking his hat to the floor as the coach bounced through the streets. Geoffrey now needed to be paced not prodded.

They parted only when Henry slowed Mersey to a stop in front of the Beacon Hill mansion. The valet first helped Anne down, then the Major. They could barely wait for him to stoke the flames in the hearth and leave the parlor before rolling onto the divan in another embrace.

Over the past three Sundays, Geoffrey had learned to maneuver his body and wooden limb to support his romantic forays. The barbs of the ladies at General Burgoyne's reading, however, still rang in her ear.

She gripped Geoffrey's hand after it had slipped under her skirts. He ignored her signal, forcing his fingers higher, hiking her petticoats above her knees. She would need a marriage vow, not a family heirloom, to surrender.

"Stop." She scissored her legs to no avail. His knuckles grazed her beard.

When Geoffrey reached to unfasten his breeches, she seized the sliver of an opening to scoot her hips to the side and wriggle away.

"It's time for supper," she said, smoothing her clothing back into place.

"Now?" he panted, falling face down on the divan.

Henry served them roasted lamb, gravy and sweet potatoes. She wanted to refuse, but hunger triumphed over pride. She hadn't eaten that well since last Sunday. The major, and his fellow senior officers, clearly had access to a more bounteous cupboard than anyone else in Boston.

"Henry, please pack that last piece for Anne to bring home to her father," Geoffrey directed when they had finished. He walked her to the door, brushing her cheek with a demure kiss. "Will I see you next Sunday?"

Anne sensed desperation in his voice. *Good!* She was willing, eager even, but she was no libertine. "Perhaps," she replied. "I will ask Father's permission. He has questioned me about your intentions of late."

"My intentions?" Geoffrey asked as if the question had flashed across the sky like a comet. "Yes, yes, I see," he added, although the bewildered look in his eyes indicated that he had not yet reached the appropriate conclusion.

"Well, I must be going then," she said, squeezing his hand in good-bye.

Henry helped her back into the coach for the ride home. "Did you eat?" she asked before he closed the door.

"No, Miss Anne."

"Take this then," she said, handing him the leftovers. If she was going to be Lady Runcorn one day, she'd do well to have Henry on her side.

***

With the lines already ten deep at the latrine trenches, I relieved myself in the weeds just after the drums beat reveille. I had spent another restless night awaiting Colonel Webb's verdict.

"General Lee requests the honor of our presence on the parade ground," William Hull said, as he approached, intent on the same task. Serving in the French and Indian War, as well as roles as a mercenary in Portugal and Poland, Lee had significantly more combat experience than Washington, but had nevertheless been relegated by Congress to a supporting role in the command of the Continental Army.

"To rally the men to stay, no doubt," I replied, fastening my breeches. According to leaks from headquarters, only ten percent of the ten thousand soldiers in the Continental Army had agreed to serve past Christmas.

With the scent of another storm in the air, I marched my grumbling troops into position. General Lee, dressed in tattered jacket and foully-used hunting shirt, followed closely by his two ever-present, slobbering hounds, stormed into the center of the hollow square formation. Although married to a Mohawk and adopted by the tribe, he was well known for his pursuit of liquor and ladies.

"Men, I do not know what to call you; you are the worst of all creatures," Lee steamed before frothing into a string of expletives. A short man with a giant nose, spittle lingering on the stubble of his unshaven face, he cut a comic, if not pathetic, figure. It was not hard to see why the Mohawks had nicknamed Lee, "Boiling Water."

Standing at attention, my heart sank. I thought of Princess, my visits to the Flag and Flagon, my inebriated stroll through Cambridge, and my wrestling wagers. *Will I end up like General Lee? A hollow man, snickered at behind my back?* Once a man lost his honor, there was no telling how fast or far he might fall; even worse, he might not even recognize he was falling until it was too late. The realization struck me like a sack of potatoes, knocking the breath from my lungs.

I believed in my heart I had done little, if anything, to justify a stiff penalty, but my legs still quaked when I thought of the options the Colonel might take. I vowed to redeem myself, regardless of Webb's decision.

When General Lee's energy finally dwindled, he dismissed the troops. Only his dogs voiced their approval, yapping loudly at his heels. There were no huzzahs or rallying cries from the troops, only disillusioned faces. I doubted the harangue had convinced even one soldier on Winter Hill to reenlist.

Colonel Webb stood on the fringe of the parade ground, shaking his head as Lee and his dogs scampered past. "Let's walk," he said as I approached.

Heavy, wet flurries tickled my face as I trailed a step behind my commander. My heart pounded as if Third Company's drummer was beating on it.

"It's hard to believe that some men in Congress still entertain the thought that that man can lead our army," he said.

"Congress would replace General Washington as commander-in-chief?" I asked.

"Lee takes credit for designing the web of redoubts surrounding Boston," Webb replied. "Washington will need a victory to silence his critics."

"But there is little opportunity for victory until the snows melt."

"Unfortunately, you are correct."

"Then I pray that Congress sees the value of our work fortifying our camps and preparing for the spring campaign."

"A wise comment, Captain Hale," Webb said, continuing to tread through the snow. "I have talked to your men and believe their respect for you is still intact. Accordingly, I am going to recommend that you retain your rank."

"Thank you, sir."

"Don't disappoint me."

"I will not, sir."

"You're dismissed, Captain." Webb continued his lonely march around camp.

I saluted and about-faced. I wanted to yell for joy, but confined my celebration to a grin that spread from one ear to the other.

The hard work, however, now lay ahead, I realized. I must justify my Colonel's trust and win back the unqualified respect of my men. I would also have to deal with Princess. Or not. The easiest solution would just be to stay away from her.

CHAPTER 9 - DECEMBER 1775

Sir [General Washington],

...I do sincerely entreat your Excellency for a continuance of that permission for me to go unmolested where my private Business may call me as it will take some Months from this time to settle with all my Creditors—I have leave to retire on my Half-pay, & never expect to be call'd into the service again. I love North America, it is my native Country & that of my Family's, and I intend to spend the Evening of my days in it—I should be glad to pay you my respects personally, but have tho't it prudent to first write you this Letter, & shall wait at this place for your Excellency's commands. I am Sir your Excellency's most Obedient & most Humble Servant

Robert Rogers
Medford, Massachusetts
December 14, 1775

Despite an ankle-deep blanket of snow, Winter Hill was a beehive of activity. Entire companies of troops marched home, while a handful of new arrivals trickled in. I only expected to lose half my men, better than many other units, justifying Colonel Webb's faith. My spirits lifted another notch when I received approval for a furlough to return to Connecticut, both to visit my family and to recruit replacements.

Third Company was foraging for tree limbs to bundle into abatis when shouts of exultation echoed from camp, the first whoops of victory I had heard since my arrival in September. I ground my axe in a fallen trunk and marched my men home, double-time.

Two sailors, wearing the green and white jackets of the newly christened navy, danced a jig around their banner planted in the snow. They were surrounded by clapping soldiers. In October, General Washington had personally financed the armament of a six-ship fleet of schooners and gained the permission of Congress to allow them to prey on British merchant shipping. Their flag, a towering pine on a white background with the inscription, "An Appeal to Heaven," had been a symbol of resistance in New England for a century, reflecting the Crown's attempts to regulate the harvesting of the trees which were ideal for the construction of ships' masts.

"Captain Manley captured The Nancy – with two thousand guns on board!" a rheumy-eyed sergeant stopped his celebrating long enough to inform the newcomers of the good news. "Powder and balls too."

"The crew will make a pretty penny on that haul," Asa, standing two rows behind me, muttered out loud. As incentive, Washington had commissioned his navy as privateers, allowing the captains and crew to keep one-third of the value of captured cargo for themselves as long as they did not mistreat any captives. Washington also named the first vessel, The Lee, in honor of his second-in-command, yet another attempt to keep his fellow general from Virginia in line.

"Sounds like you're tempted to return to the sea," I said to my old friend. The defection of Asa and Zeb hurt the most. Asa had saved my life in combat. Zeb had saved my honor. I had talked with them both about reenlistment until my face turned red, white and blue, but in the end, money talked louder. And the Continental Army didn't have any.

"I'm not sure I have a choice." Asa squirted tobacco juice into the snow. "Washington don't want Blacks in his army anyway."

Sensing a sliver of opportunity, I pressed. "Stay in camp until year end. I wager the general will come around by then."

"What makes you so sure?"

"Washington's no fool. When he sees the muster rolls, he'll realize this army needs all the good men it can get. And Congress will have to pay them."

"Even if they're Black," Elvin laughed, poking Asa in the ribs with his shovel.

"Maybe I'll give it another week or two then," Asa said.

That was a surprise, I thought, but I was certainly not in a position to question Asa's motives. At least right now.

"What about you, Elvin? What can I do to convince you to re-up?" I pushed my luck.

"Not me. I've got a sweet widow waiting back home," Elvin replied.

"Zeb? Change your mind yet? Going to stay and fight for your country?"

The sergeant shook his head. "I'm leaving on the tenth. We're going to have a little farewell gathering at the Flag and Flagon. Care to join us?"

"No thank you," I replied with a rueful grin. Although thoughts of Princess still haunted me, I had to stay away. Forever.

"That's what I wanted to hear."

William Hull caught up to me before I could reach my tent. "Come for a quick walk."

"Where to?"

"The mail tent."

"Why?"

"Just follow me."

We strode back across camp, still a ramshackle array of dwellings in varying shapes, colors and sizes. Ribbons of smoke spooled from cooking fires. Men, bundled against the cold, queued for their evening meal. Dogs barked hungrily, waiting their turn for scraps.

A solitary figure in a scuffed green jacket shuffled in front of the marquee that served as commissary and mail room. His paunch and graying beard confirmed that his glory days were a distant memory.

"That's Robert Rogers," Hull whispered. "I hear Washington won't meet with him, so he's trying to get an appointment with any general on the war council."

Word had thrashed around the cooking fires as of late that the legendary hero was on his way to Boston. Some wondered if Rogers sought a command in the Continental Army, others presumed he was a British spy.

"That old man?" I replied, my jaw agape. If only Princess could see him now, I chortled silently.

***

The brisk knock startled Anne. Who would come calling on a Tuesday evening? She placed the kettle of beans and salted fish back over the fire and trailed Father to the door. Peering over his shoulder, she saw an open sleigh, painted bright red, guided by a familiar horse and coachman.

"Good evening, Mr. Wheaton," Geoffrey said. "My apologies for the late hour."

"Come in," Father replied. "We're just sitting down to supper but I'm sure Anne can set another plate."

"Is she well then?"

"Much better, thank you," Anne answered for herself, concealing a smile. She had feigned illness and stayed away from both church and Beacon Hill this past Sunday. Perhaps, Geoffrey had gotten her not-so-veiled message.

"Good, good. I was worried about you." The Major shook the snow off his shoulders and shuffled through the doorway. Father took his coat while Anne clasped Geoffrey's hand, ushering him into the keeping room.

"Can I offer you a dram or a flagon of claret?" Father asked, as he caught up.

"I would like a word alone." Geoffrey broke from Anne to address Father. "With you."

Father's brow knitted in consternation. "In the parlor, then."

She stirred the pot until the stew turned to mush. The men stayed in the parlor for ten minutes, then twenty, their voices hushed. She tossed another log on the fire, refusing to let her thoughts jump ahead.

A great shuffling of feet preceded them back into the keeping room. Father could barely contain his smile.

"Your father and I have reached an agreement," Geoffrey announced. "Now, all we need is your concurrence."

"Whatever do you mean?" she asked.

Geoffrey leaned into his crutch and took her hand. "I would ask you to be my wife."

She hesitated for only a second, wanting to be certain she had heard the words correctly. "Yes." She wrapped her arms around Geoffrey's neck. "I will cherish you forever."

"A toast. We must toast," Father said, reaching for the spirits.

Geoffrey reached into his pocket, removing a silver sixpence already broken into two parts. He handed her one half. "To seal our engagement."

"When...?" Her voice trailed off before she could complete the question.

"We'll talk to Minister Dowell on Sunday during the break for dinner. My hope is he will read the first banns later that afternoon."

"And we can marry in January then?" The Anglican Church required marriage banns to be read aloud on three successive Sundays before a wedding ceremony could take place.

"Provided there are no objections, of course."

***

Flanked by two grim-faced guards, Robert Rogers tramped along the snow-packed path towards General Sullivan's tent on Winter Hill. His fellow New Hampshire man had again come through, setting up an appointment the day after Rogers had posted his request. Of course, he would have preferred to meet the commander-in-chief personally, but he was not in a position to complain.

Since he needed money badly, he would have to convince Sullivan to allow him to travel freely in the region to conduct his business affairs, as meager as they might be. A post in the Continental Army was too much to even hope for.

Rogers' shoulders slumped as he thought once again of his financial straits. The deeds signed by Governor Tryon confirmed that he owned land, a vast tract in the north, but he had signed over much of it to his wife years ago in the hope of evading his creditors and old gambling cronies. At least the paperwork gave him an excuse to travel. His brother, James, had been a prosperous man, but his assets were in danger of confiscation due to his Tory politics. Rogers would receive no further funds from this quarter either.

Not surprisingly, his recent reunion with Elizabeth had proved tempestuous. What was the point of marriage when his lawful wife wouldn't even lay with him, claiming fear of disease? Of course, he had fornicated with other women. Did she expect him to remain celibate during all these years apart? His son, Arthur, appeared to be a fine boy, but useless. Almost a teenager now, he couldn't find a pine tree in the wilderness if his life depended on it. Rogers prayed it never would.

The morning sun hid behind a veil of low clouds; the temperature was bitter cold; icicles crusted in the mangy, gray beard that protected his face. He hungrily eyed the cooking fires glowing in the distance as the faint aroma of frying bacon stirred pangs in his stomach.

Although the fortifications throughout the countryside appeared formidable, the camp itself still reflected a hodge-podge of men from thirteen colonies rather than a unified army. But he could see signs that Washington was gradually imposing order: sentries were well-posted, passwords exchanged, drum rolls and bugles called men to order, regiments drilled on the parade ground.

Rogers recalled his meeting with Governor Tryon. Perhaps, "Mister" Washington could still be kidnapped, but it would take a team of experienced Rangers to handle the assignment.

"We'll wait here until the general is free," one of his escorts, sporting sergeant's stripes and the grizzled visage of a wilderness veteran, announced after a quick disappearance inside the tent. Rogers watched with envy as a troop of blue-coated soldiers, led by a smart-stepping officer with a yellow cockade perched in his hat, marched across the white parade ground towards him. To be young again...

Burying his freezing fingers in the pockets of his green jacket, Rogers dropped his head and let his mind drift back to Ranger camps of long ago winters. The best times of his life, he realized now, even if they did not seem so at then. He first met Pontiac, the famed Ottawa sachem, on the shores of Lake Erie in November '60. Well aware of the Ottawas penchant for cannibalism, his men, all hardened Rangers, quaked when the war party approached. Fortunately, the regal chief, his ears and nose adorned with brightly colored trinkets, also respected Rogers' reputation as a warrior. The two leaders exchanged gifts and smoked a peace pipe, ornately decorated with black feathers and a wolf skull. Rogers left with the Ottawa's permission to travel on to Fort Detroit where he negotiated the surrender of the French force garrisoned there.

But where was George Washington in 1760? Exiled from the British Army and back home on the veranda of his plantation house supervising his slaves. How many Indian chieftains had summited with the Virginia militia man? None. If the natives knew Washington at all, it was as a land speculator. The General, among others, had accumulated ownership of vast tracts of wilderness in direct violation of the treaty line agreed to by King George with the French and the Indian chiefs in '63. Had Washington ever had an audience with the King or even walked the halls of Parliament? Hardly.

With the hillsides barren of trees, the wind whipped through the camp, frosting Rogers' ears a bright pink. A spot by a fire, or a cup of steaming tea, would have been courteous, he thought, but no offers were forthcoming. Rogers turned his gaze towards the sea and the spires of Boston in the distance. Had his message gotten through to General Howe? Had his friends in London reached out on his behalf?

"General Sullivan will see you now," the sergeant said, opening the flap of the tent. Rogers stiffened his spine and stepped inside. The tent's furnishings were spartan: a cot, neatly made, a plank desktop, empty of maps and papers, supported by two hogsheads, a field chair on either side of the desk and a roughhewn chest.

"Pleased to finally meet you in person," Sullivan, a decade younger than Rogers, said, as he unlocked the top drawer of his chest and removed several letters. He wore a knee-length, wool coat sporting polished gold buttons, the only sign of wealth that Rogers could see. The general's ruddy cheeks, a trademark of the Irish, stood out against his vast expanse of pale forehead. "Read your books. Several times, in fact."

"Those were good times," Rogers replied, playing to his own resume. Since Sullivan lacked any true military experience, he could only surmise that his mercantile success had paved the way to his generalship. "Nothing forges a man's character like combat."

"I was a bit too young to serve." Sullivan dropped his paperwork on the desk and sat down, motioning Rogers to sit as well.

Actually, you were studying law, Rogers thought as he accepted the general's invitation. "I killed my first Indian when I was sixteen," he said, pleased to get off his feet. "Fought them for ten years straight. From Montreal to Detroit."

"Reverend Wheelock writes of your recent visit to Dartmouth," Sullivan continued, scanning a letter while he talked.

"Yes, we had a nice chat over lunch last month," Rogers replied, leaning forward, making a half-hearted effort to see what other documents were in Sullivan's stack. "I offered to raise funds for his new college, but he was not so inclined."

"The Reverend was concerned about your financial situation. It seems the innkeeper in Hanover informed him that you failed to pay your reckoning the next morning."

"I told that rascal I'd pay him on my return. After I'd visited my lands." Rogers reached into his pocket and produced his passport from Congress. "That's why I'm here. Mr. Franklin requested that I receive His Excellency's permission to travel in this region."

"Mr. Franklin was concerned about your loyalties. With cause, perhaps," Sullivan steepled his hands. "Reverend Wheelock also noted that he received a report from friends in New Hampshire that you had journeyed into Canada, donned Indian garb, and assumed a command in the service of the King. Quite a serious charge."

"Indian garb? A command?" Rogers laughed. "Look at me."

"Perhaps your reputation with the natives exceeds your current state of affairs."

"Perhaps," Rogers beamed at the perceived compliment.

"Do you have any inclination to serve the Crown?" Sullivan asked.

"I am in no position to serve any cause but my own. I am here solely to assure both you and General Washington of my neutrality and desire to attend to personal matters."

Sullivan carefully read Franklin's passport before handing it back to Rogers. "All right. You may proceed with your travels. I will inform my commander-in-chief accordingly."

***

Flashing a pirate's smile, Anne pushed her chair back from the dining room table, a varnished rectangle of walnut shimmering with the light from a dozen candles nested in the chandelier overhead. She sipped the Spanish brandy that Henry had found cached in the cellar, an unintended gift from the rebels that were the home's previous occupants. Serving dishes strewn with lamb, carrots and peas, as well as scraps of fresh bread floating in brown gravy, sat as testament to their gluttony. The cloying sweetness of apples baking in the Dutch oven hinted at further culinary delights. Geoffrey belched before returning her mischievous glance.

With their first banns announced at church this afternoon, the couple had seen no need to delay the consummation of their relationship. They were barely able to sit still for the final hour of Minister Dowell's afternoon sermon. Skipping their customary walk on Windmill Point, they retired immediately to Geoffrey's bedroom, satiating one appetite while stimulating another.

The first time was less painful and bloody than she had feared, well worth the pleasure of Geoffrey's subsequent thrusts. Was intercourse, like stitching, an activity that might be improved with practice?

She patted her supper-swollen stomach. Might she be with child already? With half her siblings already dead, she yearned for a family of her own – seven, eight, nine children. Slender hips were not going to stop her.

"Please bring a plate to your father this time," Geoffrey said as scooped up the last crumbs of pie. "I will insure that Henry has his fill."

"Yes, dear." Anne wanted her whole family to share in the celebration. Communications outside Boston were difficult, but Geoffrey thought his contacts in the Navy might be able to deliver a letter to Mother and Phineas. She felt a stab of guilt for not involving Mother in her betrothal, but life moved too quickly in wartime. She had learned to make her own choices.

Could Mother be in touch with Caleb? She hoped so. Caleb would undoubtedly be thrilled to learn she was marrying a British officer. Maybe Geoffrey could even get her brother a position in the Army. He was old enough to serve now, and, knowing him well, frothing to do so.

Geoffrey offered to accompany her home in the sled, but she could see the day's fatigue etched in his forehead and insisted he stay to complete his paperwork for General Howe. They lingered over a farewell kiss.

"Where does the Major acquire such bountiful stores?" she asked Henry as he helped her down the ice-crusted stairs to the street.

"Excuse me, Miss Anne?"

"I will soon be lady of this house. I need to know how to feed my husband."

"Mr. Hale arranges the food deliveries."

"Samuel Hale?" The name steamed from her lips. "Go on."

"He has connections in the countryside."

"With rebels?"

"With men putting profit ahead of politics."

"A pretty profit, I would guess."

"Quite substantial, in fact. Less than a quarter of the supply ships that departed London have reached Boston this winter. The rest turned back due to weather or were captured by rebel privateers."

Henry placed a heated brick underneath her boots and tucked a grey blanket displaying the Runcorn family crest around her waist before climbing into the buckboard. He flicked the reins and Mersey clopped down Beacon Hill.

She digested Henry's news while the sled glided along the moonlit streets. Boston looked fairytale pretty under its white blanket, camouflaging the deprivation that all but a select few of its inhabitants endured. She was one of the fortunate ones, tonight at least. Of course, men like Sam Hale would find a way to profit from others' suffering, but she wasn't going to let thoughts of him spoil her evening.

Her cheeks were cherry red by the time they reached her home on Charter Street. She hopped down from the sled without assistance, anxious to deliver the plate of lamb to Father. But he was not in the front hall or the keeping room.

Sam Hale tended the fire in the parlor. "I asked your father to wait upstairs," he said, casually steering an errant log back into place. "I have a private matter to discuss with you."

"We have nothing to discuss," she replied, removing her bonnet but keeping her cloak secure.

"Ah yes, you are set to become a married woman. To an English nobleman, no less. If there are no objections..."

"Objections?" Her mind raced to Lady Pigot and Widow Pitcairn.

Sam reached into his waistcoat and removed another envelope. He slowly opened the seal. "From your lover, my cousin Nathaniel. A captain in the rebel army. Encamped on Winter Hill no less."

Winter Hill? But I was right there. Her knees weakened. "He is not my lover."

"His words say different." Sam slowly read Nathan's second letter aloud, starting with his return address. By the time he reached the *Cato* salutation, Anne's fists were clenched in despair.

How long had Sam withheld this letter from her? Did Nathan still yearn for her? Did she yearn for him? What did it matter now? The questions galloped through her mind. She grabbed at the paper, but Sam danced away. "I can't let you destroy the evidence of your treason."

"Treason? I have committed no treasonous acts."

"Treasonous or scandalous. Take your pick. Either will end your engagement to Lord Runcorn."

"Nathan was a schoolgirl crush. Geoffrey will understand."

"Of course. I will take my leave then." Sam reached for his coat. "The letter might cause quite a stir around town though. My superior, Mr. Cunningham, has contacts with Lord Runcorn's relations back in England. I'm not sure they'll approve of his marriage to the wanton daughter of a provincial dressmaker."

"Wanton? How dare you..."

"Taking advantage of a crippled man. You should be ashamed of your lustfulness."

Unless Henry had loose lips, which she thought unlikely, Hale was merely repeating well-worn bromides of female wickedness. Nevertheless, her defenses crumbled. She and Geoffrey were far from the first couple in their church to get a head start on their marriage, but they still had sinned in the eyes of the Lord. As a woman, she would shoulder the blame, and be cast out from the congregation.

"Ha! I can see in the blush in your cheeks that I'm correct," Sam pressed his advantage. "If Lord Runcorn denounces you now, you will be a fallen woman. You'd be fortunate to get Simeon Bacon to marry you."

"What do you want?" she asked, certain now that Sam knew of her letter to Nathan.

"That's better." Sam stepped close to her. She could smell the rum on his breath, see the smallpox scars underneath the powder on his cheeks. While the cousins shared a physical resemblance, Nathaniel was a man of honor, while Sam was a ...

He reached for the clasp on her cloak, toyed with it. She stood stock still, trembling, powerless. Except for the pistol in her pocket. Sam was well within her range.

"Don't worry. I'm a married man," he said, releasing the clasp without opening it. "You are a useful woman, and I will require your services again."

***

I sat on a stool outside my tent, polishing the stock of my musket with boot black and linseed oil. A log crackled on the campfire, sending a wisp of smoke curling into the dun sky. Soldiers, back from their day's toils, swirled around me, but I was oblivious. With the weather alternating between miserable and just plain ugly, the past weeks had proved difficult, the soldiering beyond dull. And, I had purposely withdrawn from after-hours socializing, even with my fellow officers.

Female companionship would have broken the tedium, but I would have to tread carefully before diving into those waters again. I missed bantering with Princess as much as I did strumming her. Maybe more. She had spent her whole life around warriors of one skin color or another, and understood the psychological elements of soldiering. She even read Robert Rogers at night. What other woman would do that?

Unfortunately, her contacts in Boston and her attempt to pry information from me still gnawed at my conscience. Was she a British spy? Was she in the woods that night outside camp? Or did I imagine it?

Despite my own sorry state, I had to keep Third Company's morale up. The loss of men, like Zeb and Elvin, weighed heavily on the ranks. My bible, checkerboard and quill proved useful.

I waited anxiously for the post to arrive each afternoon and wrote at least one letter each evening. Correspondence with my fellow Linonians reminded me of my carefree days at Yale, a time now as stale in my memory as week-old biscuits.

A letter from Prudence Richards was a most welcome surprise. She was still at her uncle's and would likely be there through spring. The new schoolmaster, lodging in my old room, was a stodgy goat who had discontinued the morning classes for girls. Not a great loss in her book. The big news - and she, of course, hated to be the one to tell me - was that Caleb Wheaton, wearing the green jacket of the Queen's Rangers, had been sighted on the outskirts of town. She signed off with an affectionate flourish, hoping to see me again whenever I returned.

I was re-reading the letter when a snowball splashed at my feet. "You're back?" I asked the tall, familiar figure, still sporting a flopping queue.

"Can't say I'm pleased to be here," Elvin Parrish replied as he dropped his pack in the snow. "But there's nothing for me back home anymore."

"The arms of the Widow Appletree have closed?" I asked, suppressing a smile.

"Her legs as well," Elvin laughed. "She's not a widow anymore. She's Mrs. Lamplighter now."

"Hard to believe she could find a better man than you."

"That's what I said. But her new husband owns the gristmill above Willow Creek. He's…"

"Save the details for supper. Three of the men are rattling with fever. I've got to check on them."

"Camp looks busier than when I left."

"The capture of The Nancy turned the tide. Reenlistments are over three thousand and new companies of militia keep marching in."

"Asa still here?"

"Yep," I replied, standing. I was pleased but knew that Asa always had an angle. Despite several long talks, I just hadn't discovered it yet. In the meantime, Third Company needed every man I could recruit. In my six months of command, I had learned that every soldier was a riddle. And I would never be able to solve them all.

"Other Negroes in camp, too," Elvin said, his frosted breath following the path of a pair of Black soldiers deep in conversation, their feet wrapped in rags.

"General Washington hasn't kicked them out." I belted my scabbard around my waist.

"He's desperate," Elvin said.

"I prefer to think he's recognized that the light of liberty shines on all men."

"That's a load of horseshit."

I couldn't choke my chuckle this time. "You're right, but it has a nice ring to it."

"You should write a book." Elvin hoisted his pack. "Speaking of books, an old student of yours in New London sends his regards."

"Really, who?"

"Caleb Wheaton. We met when he worked at the Widow's shop."

"Caleb sends his regards?"

"Well, actually, he still longs to see you hang."

"That sounds more like the Caleb I know." I stroked the mole on my neck.

"And his sister's engaged to a major in the British Army." Elvin turned to leave, not realizing his news had gut-punched me. Twice.

"Anne's engaged? To a redcoat?" Hanging might be preferable to seeing Anne in the arms of the enemy.

"You know her, I gather?"

"We're acquainted," my voice trailed off.

"Sounds like she found a better man." It was Elvin's turn to chuckle as he lugged his gear to his old campsite.

I retreated into my tent, retrieving Anne's note from June. I read the couplet from *Cato* again and again. How could Anne have fallen in love with an Englishman so quickly? And agreed to marry him?

Anne had sat in my classroom six mornings a week for almost a year. Although I had not seen her since she left New London seven months ago, I thought I still knew her well; but, once again, a woman had surprised me. Maybe that in itself should not be a surprise any longer.

I was a different man as well. Back in April, I would never have even fantasized about a romantic entanglement with an Indian princess. Or thought I might look forward to a reunion with Prudence Richards. War compressed time, changing everything and everyone in its wake.

***

My furlough couldn't start soon enough. Since I had advanced funds to my men, I arranged a loan collateralized by my January pay to carry me until I returned to Winter Hill. I would save money by walking the eighty miles to Coventry, rather than taking a coach or hiring a horse.

On the way out of camp on December 23rd, I visited Asa's tent, but it was empty. I hitched my pack and started off. Before I cleared the makeshift village where the camp followers lived, I swore I saw my friend up ahead bundled in a gray cape.

I stooped and quickened my pace, trying to follow, but not wanting to reveal myself. The lane was deserted; no one ventured outside in December unless necessary. The snow underfoot swallowed the sounds of my footfalls. Asa ducked in the face of the bone-chilling wind, seemingly unsure of which way to turn, before gaining his bearings and turning left. A harelipped harlot stole a few feet from her tent, found her footing and squatted to piss; we pretended not to notice each other as I slipped by. Asa stopped in front of a shanty, sailcloth supported on a tottering wooden frame, looked in both directions and barged inside.

I felt guilty for tracking my friend, particularly on the seamy side of camp. Maybe it wasn't even Asa but another soldier seeking the comfort of a woman's arms.

I stopped outside the dwelling, cautiously peering in the half-open flap. The gray cloak was strewn across a stool.

"I delivered my end. Now, I want my coin," Asa's voice pealed like a church bell.

"Talk to Mister Sam. He always pays late." This voice, silky and sweet, was familiar too. It was Princess. I nearly toppled into the snow.

"How am I going to reach Mr. Sam?"

"Then you'll have to wait," she said.

"There are men out in the countryside who trusted me."

"You wail like a hump-backed squaw. Nothing happens on schedule in wartime."

The pieces of the puzzle snapped into place as I watched a black hand lift the cape off the stool. Asa's decision to stay, Princess' post-coital questioning at the Flag and Flagon, and the voices in the woods outside camp all made sense now. I tossed my greatcoat into the snow, drew my pistol, and burst inside.

"Traitor!" I shouted, pointing my weapon at Asa. The whites of my friend's eyes blazed in surprise.

I never saw Princess's war club until she whipped it into my stomach, spanking the air from my lungs. My pistol flew from my fingers as I doubled over and fell to my knees on the ice-hard turf. My vision clouded. I rolled onto my back, gagging and sputtering. Asa and Princess stepped past me.

I feared I might die alone in the tent, but breath and reason slowly returned. I forced myself to rise. The point of impact was sore to the touch, but I could see no blood on my fingers. I was fortunate. Princess could have surely killed me with a head shot if she had wanted to, Asa with his pistol or knife. I stumbled outside, but the two conspirators were long gone.

Although grateful for clemency, I had no question about my course of action. I'd put the noose around Princess and Asa's necks myself if they were British spies. I shuffled as best I could to Colonel

Webb's marquee, questions rattling my mind. Where did they go? Would they return? Who was Mister Sam? What was delivered to him? Who else was involved?

Colonel Webb had already left for Connecticut. I requested a quill and paper from his aide and wrote down events and conversations as best I could remember. I signed the document, rolled it and dripped a hot candle wax seal.

The exercise forced me to recognize that the rebellion wasn't just *my* journey. While I had gone off to war as a grand adventure, hoping to bask in the glow of camaraderie and romance along the way, my friend and my lover had plotted behind my back. Everyone in the colonies had their own reasons to join the fight on one side or the other.

What did I hope to gain? Would I risk all to achieve it? Anne's questions at our parting in the schoolhouse floated into my thoughts.

I was no longer a carefree student or an imperious schoolmaster, but a commander of men. Nevertheless, my idealism was still intact, albeit tarnished. Leadership had only confirmed my belief that liberty for all was a Glorious Cause worth fighting for. *And, yes Miss Wheaton, I would risk my life to pursue it.*

CHAPTER 10 - JANUARY 1776

"Small islands, not capable of protecting themselves, are the proper objects for kingdoms to take under their care; but there is something absurd, in supposing a continent to be perpetually governed by an island."
Common Sense
By Thomas Paine
Published January 1776

The outward vestiges of war faded with every mile I hiked away from Winter Hill. The forests thickened, the roads unclogged of marching troops, and the air smelled of pine and heather rather than the grime of encamped men. The crunch of my boots in the soft snow beat a steady tune.

Whose side were Asa and Princess on? They were no longer my friends, that much was painfully clear. But were they my enemies? If so, they could have dispatched me easily back in the whores' encampment. Nevertheless, alone on the open road, I had turned several times and even drawn my pistol once at what turned out to be a scampering squirrel.

I tried to see a bigger picture. Asa had exhibited signs of disillusionment with the patriot cause from the first night we had met outside Miner's. And why not? How could any man fight for a liberty that did not free his own people? Princess too had justifiable grievances. Her people had been badly mistreated by my ancestors from the day they landed at Plymouth Rock. But, these evil practices had, in fact, flourished under *British* rule. The Glorious Cause at least offered a path towards a better world. I was so distracted I made a wrong turn outside Watertown, adding an extra four miles to my trek.

On my last night, I shared a room and pallet with three other travelers in a roadside tavern outside Pomfret, a half day's walk from Coventry. The food had been a miserable gruel, but the ale was sweet and the entertainment, a fast-fingered fiddler, had us all tapping our feet.

A cannonade of loud farts from one of my bedmates woke me well before dawn. The fire in the hearth languished and my breath frosted. I tugged my cap over my ears and ducked under the moth-eaten blanket as a witch's brew of emotions bubbled. After a year's absence, I was excited to see my sisters and brothers, but also dreaded facing Father. Although I was now twenty and living on my own for the past six years, the approval of my family still mattered.

I closed my eyes and recited a favorite passage from the Book of John, "In my Father's house are many mansions; if it were not so, I would have told you. I go to prepare a place for you." I drifted back to sleep, confident I would find a way to explain my foibles and maintain Father's faith in me.

I quickened my step as the familiar hillocks of our two hundred acre homestead came into view. The wind whipped across the unbroken landscape. Over the years, we had cleared most of the property of trees for our own farming and construction needs, transporting the excess timber to Norwich and New London for sale.

My eyes widened at my first sight of the new barn and the rambling, red clapboard house, wisps of smoke ribboning from its three chimneys. Undaunted by the gathering war clouds, Father and Abigail, married for six years now, had completed the buildings this past summer. Growing up, I had crammed into a far smaller abode with my eleven siblings. I scanned the horizon for my old home before realizing it was gone.

I tromped past the cider mill, between the symmetrical rows of the winter-bare apple orchard, and around the dormant vegetable gardens. As I approached the neat square of the herb garden adjacent to the back door, I waved to a familiar figure standing lookout in the window. My youngest brother, Billy, raced down the steps. Abigail and my sister Rose, a year older than me, waited at the doorway. They swept me into the long, rectangular wing encompassing both the keeping room and kitchen, the hearty aroma of freshly baked bread enveloping me like a tufted, feathery quilt.

I shook the snow off my great-coat and hung it on a peg by the yawning hearth, tall enough for me to stand inside. A servant girl, Sheila, her red hair and freckled face hinting at Irish ancestry, dipped her hand into the adjacent beehive oven to test its temperature. Joanna, ten years old and the youngest surviving child in the family, sat close to the fire, churning butter. She raced into my arms, followed by the twins, David and Jonathan, who leaped up from their checker game on the floor. Alice, a step-sister two years my junior, lingered by the loom with her new husband, a surprisingly older man, in tow. I recalled Rose, the family's most skilled seamstress, walking five miles a day while spinning cloth at that loom.

As I warmed my hands by the flames, Abigail informed me that Father and Enoch waited in the parlor. Given the many returning Connecticut troops, I had expected some news of my reprimand to have beaten me home. But what exactly did Father know? And how much should I tell him? Hopefully, Enoch, who had shared in several misadventures at Yale himself, would rally to my side.

The main body of the new house, three stories high, featured two social rooms, paneled with burnished pine, on the ground level. A musket rested in a place of honor above the compact, stone-framed fireplace in the front parlor which I surmised Father utilized as an office as well. I couldn't help peeking up the stairway to the sleeping floors. How many bedrooms were up there?

With five sons off at war, Father and Abigail must have felt an emptiness in their big, new house. They obviously built it with post-war plans in mind, I realized, when at least one of my older brothers would move back in, marry, have children, and take over the farm. As college graduates, Enoch and I were expected to travel other paths.

Father, a broad-boned man grown paunchier with age, and Enoch, looking older and wiser than his twenty-two years, sat in front of the crackling flames, a pitcher of cider between them. Father motioned me towards an empty chair, a most welcome respite for my blistered feet, and poured me a drink. Enoch topped up my cup with rum from his flask. The moment of truth had arrived.

I started by recounting the conflict between Asa and the Bristol boys on the parade ground. Father listened intently, his brow furrowing underneath his powdered hair. Since Asa was as close to family as a Black could be, I knew Father would second my efforts.

As I progressed to the wrestling match, Father shifted in his seat. "You wagered my gift?" he asked, barely containing his disbelief.

"I couldn't let my men down, sir," I replied.

"But you lost," Father said, shaking his head.

"Yes, sir. And the Bristol boys went home before I could buy it back."

"The British?" Father asked. "Did you engage the enemy on the field of battle?"

"General Washington attended one of my company's drills and commended us. I'm sure we would have seen action – had there been any." I didn't believe I was at liberty to discuss the Council of War's rejections of Washington's plans to attack Boston.

"I see." Father withdrew a palm-sized pipe from his pocket and slowly tamped a wad of tobacco.

"We've completely surrounded Boston with barricades. There's no place for the British to go – by land at least. I'm confident we'll assault the city this spring," I continued, hoping to detour Father into a military discussion. "Cannons would be helpful, however. We lack artillery."

"And your other transgressions, Nathaniel? Your brother, John, wrote home to tell us that Colonel Webb had reprimanded you."

"Minor misdeeds, sir. I'm new to command, but have learned my lessons. Colonel Webb interviewed my sergeants and confirmed my captaincy."

"Was there a woman involved?"

"Excuse me, sir?"

"I know you too well, son. When you stray, there's usually a member of the weaker sex at the root."

I nodded. I was committed to telling the truth, although not necessarily the whole truth. Father was an enlightened man, but was he enlightened enough to countenance a tryst between his son and a Native?

"Of course there was a *lady*." Enoch sailed to my rescue. "Nathan's always attracted the attention of the fairer sex," he added with a trace of jealousy in his voice.

"Was she a whore?" Father asked, clearly not fooled.

"No, sir." I replied softly.

"Unfortunate. The transaction with a whore is far more straightforward than a romantic liaison," Father continued. "Unless of course you intend to marry the young lady involved."

"Yes, sir," I said. "I mean, no sir. Marriage is not my intention."

"A lusty wife might be just what you need," Enoch interjected, a timber edging into his tone. "*Conjugal* relations, both for procreation and pleasure, are a critical ingredient for a pious life."

"Yes, Preacher Enoch," I said, shaking my head, still coming to grips with the fact that my brother, and fellow reveler, was now a minister in his own right.

"Your brother's right, however," Father said. "Young men with strong urges are best satisfied by a bride - or a discrete brothel. It's the middle ground that proves most treacherous."

"I'll remember that advice, sir," I replied.

"Are you still involved with this *lady*?" Father returned to the matter at hand.

"No, sir."

He reached over to rest a hand on my knee. "I'm disappointed in you, Nathaniel. And your mother would be as well. She wanted you to graduate college and pursue a higher calling. Yet, you seem perilously close to pissing that opportunity away."

I jumped to my feet at the mention of Mother. "Father, I'm a Yale man and Yale men carouse on occasion. It does not distract from my commitment to our Glorious Cause. I would sacrifice my life, if necessary."

Father's eyes widened as if he was seeing me in a new light. "I was not implying…"

"I'm a captain in the Continental Army, sir, and will make you and Mother proud."

"You said that Colonel Webb has reaffirmed your captaincy?" Father asked, retreating to the safety of his chair.

"Yes, sir."

"So the matter is settled?"

"Not quite." I recounted my discovery of Asa and Princess, describing her as a Mohegan warrior-princess with contacts in both the British and Continental armies.

"She sounds quite exotic," Enoch said, sipping from his flask.

"Quite." Princess was so many women rolled into one, I didn't know where to start, or where to end. But I did know my relationship with her was over.

Enoch sipped again, a longer draught this time, his gaze drifting away.

"Why did you not arrest them on the spot?" Father asked. Enoch shuddered and joined us once again.

"I thought it appropriate to gather more evidence before pressing such a grievous accusation," I replied, shame-skipping the wallop Princess delivered to my midsection. "I did leave a letter for Colonel Webb describing the incident and trust he will pursue the matter while I am home."

"I have great difficulty believing that our Asa's a spy for the British," Father said, slapping his palm on the table.

"I don't know for sure," I replied. "I do know that Asa, and others, are bitter over General Washington's hesitancy to accept Blacks into the army."

"Is that good enough reason to aid the enemy?" Father asked.

"I'm not sure Asa feels that the British are *his* enemy," I said.

"The Negroes must be patient," Father said. "We'll lose the support of the Southern colonies if we lecture too loudly on the immorality of slavery."

"We need to do more than lecture, Father." I was pleased to move the conversation away from my own misdeeds.

"I second brother Nathan's thoughts," Enoch added. He stood, refilling our cups from his flask.

"Yes, well, you would be wise to keep your opinion to yourself for a time at least," Father replied, looking towards the keeping room. Sounds of laughter and scurrying about escaped the portal. "I think the women are waiting for us."

The days stretched into a fortnight as I settled into the pedestrian tasks of farm life in winter, hunting rabbits, mucking stables and chopping wood with enthusiasm. I savored the comforts of home: a roof over my head, a warm fire by my bed, clean clothes, and the affection of my sisters and step-mother.

Since I had spent little time in Coventry since Abigail had joined the family, she shied from probing questions. John and Joseph, who arrived home together on the Sabbath after Christmas, also were not particularly intrusive. They knew most of the details already and seemed more interested in reuniting with their hometown friends than in grilling their long-absent, younger brother, perhaps in deference to my rank and college degree.

Rose, however, was not so reticent. While we tended the horses in the barn, she demanded the full story, including the identity of my mystery woman. "Were you in love with Princess?" she asked when I'd finished.

"I think so."

"Her betrayal must have stung twice as hard then."

"It did." My sister's barb reminded me of Anne, betrothed if not already married to a redcoat. I thought I was over "the Tory bitch," as Prudence Richards had once presciently called her, but she still gnawed at my heart.

"I want to fall in love someday," Rose continued, gazing out the window. "Of course, we'll court properly and have our banns read on Sunday." The twinkle in her eye indicated that she enjoyed a romantic life of her own. Had my beloved sister already indulged in an unholy connection with a man? I cringed at the thought.

With the end of my furlough fast approaching, the war and Winter Hill clawed back into my consciousness. After ice skating on the back pond with my youngest siblings, I sipped a brandy alone in the parlor, basking in the warmth of the hearth. A steady patter of voices from the kitchen had almost lulled me to nap when I was startled by a loud cough. Father filled his tumbler and sat down.

"It's been wonderful having you home, son."

"Thank you, sir." I shook the cobwebs from my brain and sat upright.

"Our Glorious Cause can change the course of history."

"Yes, sir."

"Promise me you'll make your mark, Nathaniel. There'll be plenty of time for romantic adventures after the war is won."

"I promise, sir."

***

Kneeling at Widow Pitcairn's feet in Wheatons' fitting room, pincushion in hand, Anne peeked upward at the rolls of delicate brocade cloth resting on the shelf above her head. Father had offered the fabric, his finest, and accompanying lace accoutrements, as part of her modest dowry. Rose or lavender? Anne wanted to decide this afternoon, leaving her ample time to stitch and trim her wedding dress in time for the big event.

Her wedding to Major Geoffrey Stanwich, Lord of Runcorn, was set for the last Sunday of the month, less than three weeks away, in the Old North Church. Minister Dowell himself would preside, adding the official Anglican seal of approval to the union. *That should quiet the gossips once and for all.*

The feast would be at Geoffrey's home on Beacon Hill. Although he had consulted her on the victuals, a positive sign for their marital relationship, Geoffrey insisted on settling the catering arrangements himself. He even had the gall to pontificate that women should not trouble their gentle minds with financial matters. *Hah! I'm much better with figures than Geoffrey – and he knows it.*

Nevertheless, she would rather clean night jars than spend time with Sam Hale, so Anne was not overly disappointed about being left out of the negotiations. Fortunately, Sam had kept his part of their bargain. Geoffrey appeared to have no knowledge of her correspondence with Nathan. But, when would Sam present the "bill" for his silence?

Determined to test Sam's black market network, Anne had selected a menu of chowder, oysters, roasted pig, duck, vegetables, corn bread and a pumpkin casserole. A fruitcake, spiked with rum, would be served for dessert. She wished she had a girlfriend in town to steer towards the lucky slice with nutmeg seeds hidden inside, an augury of impending marriage.

"Ouch!" Widow Pitcairn hopped away, a pin dangling from her ankle. "Where is your head this morning, young lady?"

"I am so sorry." Anne scurried to blot the droplet of blood. "There'll be no charge for the tailoring."

"I should walk out right now, but I need this gown fitted to perfection in time for the theatre at Faneuil Hall on Saturday."

"You're going see a play? How exciting." Anne threw her arms up in amazement, her best country bumpkin impression.

"*The Blockade.* Written by General Burgoyne himself," the Widow replied, her nose pointing skyward. "It's about Washington and the rebel army penning the might of the British Empire into a backwater town. A farce of course."

"Of course, ma'am. Sounds like great fun." Anne completed the hem and stepped back to exam her handiwork. She guided Widow Pitcairn to the looking-glass, so she could inspect it herself.

"Yes, that looks acceptable."

Anne helped the Widow out of the gown and into her day dress, then ushered her past Father, who had shrewdly kept himself busy arranging the window display. They both laughed after the door closed and their customer's capacious backside disappeared down Wing's Lane.

"I trust you didn't tell her that you will be at the theatre as well?" Father asked.

"A simple shop girl?" Anne replied with a mischievous grin creasing her face.

"Soon to be a grand dame of the realm," Father practically beamed with pride. "If only Mother could see you now…"

Anne returned to the fitting room to tidy up, her thoughts drifting to her absent family. It was Mother, not Father, who had steered her towards Geoffrey's sick bed. Mother had initially supported her correspondence with Schoolmaster Hale - until she saw the carnage at Breed's Hill. The war struck home that day; they never discussed Nathan again.

Mother would be disappointed to learn that her daughter still recited *Cato* when she was lonely, safeguarding the treasured text deep in her trunk. But Anne knew the past was an illusion; she could never return to that time and place. Nathan, barely out of his teens himself, had been nothing more than a schoolgirl's infatuation, their relationship a youthful fantasy. The war had aged her. She was a woman now and had made her choice.

Lavender. Her wedding gown would be lavender. A harbinger of spring. Would she be in England by then? Anne giggled out loud as she realized how quickly her mind had leapt forward. *Let Nathan have his busty, rebel girls. I have an English lord and a castle.*

She quickly chastised herself for her spitefulness and clasped her bible, always lying in view on the fitting room table. She prayed that Mother and Phineas were safe and healthy in Canada. She prayed for Caleb too. Had the news of her betrothal reached him? Would it temper his hatred of Nathan? She prayed that both men, directly in harm's way, could evade the ravages she had witnessed since arriving in Boston.

***

A package from Colonel Webb signaled the end of my holiday. I poured a slug of rum before breaking the seal, but breathed easier as I read the official notification that Congress had approved my commission as a Captain in the 19th Regiment of Foot in the newly reorganized Continental Army.

Colonel Webb also included a personal letter, noting that he had issued a warrant for Asa's arrest and sent a posse out to no avail. Since Asa had not reenlisted, I realized, he was no longer in the army but might still face the death penalty for treason. The final documents in the package were copies of General Washington's long overdue order to allow free Blacks to enlist, too late to save Asa, as well as an exhortation to spread the recruiting net far and wide. The Continental Army would now accept virtually any man willing to serve.

New recruits? Where would I find them? I had scoured the countryside last summer. Any able-bodied man with patriotic spirit was likely in the army already. To fill my quota now, I would have to lower my standards. But, would I even want to lead such men?

My pessimism was alleviated somewhat by the appearance of Asher Wright on my doorstep. Wright had attended school with me, but his family had fallen on hard times, forcing him into the labor force. Attracted by the Army's promise of an enlistment bounty, he sought to join my command.

Although I hadn't seen him in years, I offered Wright the opportunity to serve as my personal orderly rather than a private in the ranks. I hoped his hardscrabble background might help recruit other financially desperate men. After the near mutiny last fall, I also wanted someone close who could keep an ear to the rumblings of the troop. I did not want to be surprised again.

I spent my final night in Coventry supping with my family. My stepmother cooked an old favorite, baked ham with a sauce of mustard and raisins. After the meal, she presented me with a new shirt, dyed a pale blue, purchased from the weaver in town. Rose promised to knit a new suit of clothes for my return to civilian life whenever that might be.

While the women cleared the table, the men retired to the parlor to discuss Thomas Paine's *Common Sense*. The recently published pamphlet, providing an intellectual foundation for the Glorious Cause, was sweeping the colonies. It was impossible to participate in a tavern debate without a thorough knowledge of its passages. We did not go upstairs to bed until the clock struck midnight.

Sheila delivered a ewer of warm water to my room before dawn, refilling the basin that had crusted with ice overnight. Abigail insisted on a modicum of cleanliness in her new home, even during the winter months. I stripped off my sleeping woolens and quickly washed my face, chest and armpits before putting on my new shirt. My last real hot water bath had been in New London last summer.

Freshly scrubbed, I set off for New London, the first stop on my recruitment drive, in the saddle of Rambler, a chestnut roan. Asher followed close behind on a gray mare also from the Hale stable. By late afternoon, we were enveloped in a raging blizzard, snowflakes pinging our faces like grapeshot. With the road obscured, I steered the final miles by memory, pleased to arrive on the outskirts of town before dark.

Not bothering to shout into the roar of the storm, I held up five gloved fingers to indicate we were within minutes of their destination, Miner's Tavern. I silently rehearsed my recruiting pitch as Rambler plodded forward, the snow-swept rooflines of the town in view at last.

I gasped as I passed the spot where the Wheaton's house had once stood. It was gone now, reduced to a heap of stone and pilings, topped by a white frosting. Only the chimney remained erect, standing sentinel over the ruins. Where were the furniture and fixtures? The fine tall-case clock that Mr. Wheaton had prattled over when I dined there last spring?

I kicked Rambler hard, wanting to be away from this place as fast as possible. A vision of Anne, embracing me at the schoolhouse, mingled with the words of my favorite uncle, Sam, who had visited Coventry last week.

Uncle Sam, a former major in the Rangers and the current headmaster of the prestigious Latin School in New Hampshire, had worn his old green jacket when he rode up to our farmhouse.

"Don't you fall for a Tory wench," he counseled, while sipping his third after-dinner whiskey. "My Sam ran off to Boston last spring and I haven't heard a word from him since." The major spit into the hearth. "Probably never will, either."

"Tory wench?" I asked.

"Sam's wife convinced him he had a better future fighting for the Crown than against it."

"Sam's a redcoat?"

"I doubt he's in the front lines. My son's a lawyer, not a fighting man like you. He probably found himself a safe job behind a desk." Uncle Sam appeared to doze for an instant, then snapped awake. "That woman has expensive tastes. Only wants the finest, imported from England. She leads him around like a puppy."

I had only met my uxorious cousin Sam once, two years ago when I visited New Hampshire after my graduation from Yale. While our conversation had been agreeable then, I hoped we would not meet again.

I swiveled in the saddle for a last look at the Wheaton homestead before it slipped from view. I thought Anne would recognize the justness of the patriot fight and break from her family, but she had turned in the opposite direction. Had she too succumbed to the pomposity of British nobility, and the material comforts associated with it?

With my scarf-swaddled chin tucked against my chest, I rode past my old schoolhouse, so much smaller than I remembered. Miner's chimney puffed a welcome greeting as light and laughter spilled from the windows. I noticed the new Grand Union flag, the crosses of England in the canton on a field of thirteen red and white stripes, flying from its flagpole. The display of this symbol of colonial unity was a hopeful sign for the new year.

Jabez Miner's offer of free ale assured me an ample audience of boisterous men. I handed my snow-crusted great coat to Wright and went straight to the bar where a generous whiskey waited. I took a greedy swallow before turning to look for familiar faces.

Judge Law, Josiah Barton, John Richards and two other directors of the Union School encircled me. Had I met General Washington? What was he like? When would we attack Boston? The questions popped from several mouths simultaneously.

"Our commander-in-chief cuts the most impressive figure. He's out in the front lines with the men every day," I answered, my voice steadily rising as more men joined the conversation. "General Washington handles his white stallion like a born horseman. His uniform is regal; he commands the army with authority. No British general could be more gallant."

"Then why'd so many men desert?" An aproned smithy, wispy gray ringlets framing his ears, pushed forward, spilling ale on his boots.

"Only cowards deserted," I countered. "Good men went home when their enlistments expired. I can understand that. They have families to support."

"Here, here," a murmur circulated.

"But, I'm here to convince them to come back," I resumed. "To serve their country."

The room silenced. I chided himself. The mention of service might not have been the best initial approach. I would have to hone my message for future meetings.

"How's the chow?" a broomstick-thin sailor, swamped by a jacket two sizes too large, asked.

"The army's defending the people of Massachusetts and they feed us well in return," I replied, pleased to hear a ripple of approval circle the room.

"What about guns? Will the Army have muskets and balls for us?"

"You'd best bring your own," I answered truthfully, although I didn't see any reason to mention the shortage of gunpowder.

"I'm in," a voice squealed from the back of the tavern. The crowd parted. Several men laughed as a tow-headed boy, no more than fifteen, wriggled through.

"John Bell," the boy announced. "I'm ready to fight for my country."

"How old are you John?" I asked. The Bell boy had not been one of my students.

"Seventeen."

"Where's your father?" I looked around the room.

"Pa ain't been around in years. Ma can't feed us five boys much longer."

"You look a little young to fight."

"Tell that to Johnny Bristol," the youth replied, smacking his fist into his palm.

"I don't expect you'll get much opportunity to use your fists against the British," I said.

"Well, I can play the fife. And the drum."

"We don't have a drummer boy on our muster roll anymore," Wright interjected.

"Go stand next to my orderly." I pointed towards the bar. "Who's next?"

"Hercules Field." An African, thick beard laced with silver, shuffled forward. He was shoeless, feet wrapped in rags, a hitch apparent in his gait. "I'm here to enlist. Can't find no other job."

"Do you have proof of manumission?" I asked.

"Yes, sir." Hercules rummaged in his pockets. "Worked for Tailor Appletree my whole life. Gave me my freedom in his will when he passed. God bless his soul."

Tailor Appletree? While Hercules searched, I noticed a shock of red hair bobbing on the periphery. Caleb Wheaton? Would he dare to return to Miner's?

"Got it," Hercules produced his precious paper, running his finger over the lawyer's seal, then handed it to me upside down. I kept one eye on the unidentified redhead as I spun the document. Hercules' gaze never left the floor while I read.

"Please, look at me Mr. Field." The African raised his eyes slowly. I saw resilience, a man battered by life but still proud. With a mouth full of teeth. The only attribute that would automatically disqualify a candidate for the Continental Army would be a paucity of molars. Soldiers needed two working teeth on their upper and lower jaws to tear open gunpowder cartridges. Assuming the army obtained more powder.

I nodded my approval. "Welcome to the Continental Army."

As Wright explained the enlistment document to Hercules, the redhead barged forward, his cheeks freckled and pudgy, but his torso all hard muscle.

"Tom Peacock, how'd you get out of the stockade?" an authoritative, vaguely familiar voice chased after him.

"Sheriff said he'd let me go if I enlisted."

"He should cut off your hand for stealing from a brother seaman," James Caulk, flanked by a pair of well-fed stevedores, bulled his way through.

"I didn't steal nuthin'. Just took back what was mine," Tom replied, slinking past me towards the bar. As the Sons of Neptune closed within spitting distance, he tore the enlistment paper from Wright's hand, spilling ink all over it as he made his mark.

"The way you're goin' about things, Captain Hale, you'll get nothing but niggers, boys, and criminals for your regiment," Caulk said.

"And how should I go about it?" I asked.

"Money talks." Caulk rubbed his thumb and forefinger together.

"Congress will pay a bounty to each man who signs up."

"Congress ain't got no money." Caulk pointed his finger at my chest. "Your family's rich. You pay with hard coin up front – if you want good men."

"Good men like you?" I asked generating a titter of tentative laughter from the crowd.

"You can't afford me, Hale," Caulk replied, retreating a step. "But I can get you good strong boys for the right price."

"Boys like Asa Cobb?" Knowing that Asa was a seaman, I gambled that he was also a Son of Neptune.

"Asa's one of mine," Caulk replied, a wariness creeping into his tone.

"Well, he was one of mine too, but he's run off and joined the lobsterbacks now." The crowd whistled and hooted in derision.

Caulk turned his palms up as if washing his hands of Asa. "No telling what a boy's gonna do when he's got no money. I'll put some feelers out and see if we can reel him back."

"You do that, but make sure you tell him to stay far away from me. We're through." I stamped my boot on the floor. "I need men who are loyal to the cause of liberty." A huzzah emanated from the spectators.

"Those kind of men don't come cheap," Caulk returned to familiar ground. "Now, are you going to pay? Or keep on scavenging the dung heap for your recruits?"

"Are you looking for a bribe, Mr. Caulk?" I regained my footing, speaking loud enough for all to hear.

"I'm looking for my fair share." Caulk still talked big, but his stridency had shriveled. "The war's robbed me - and my men - of our proper wages."

"I'm recruiting patriots, not profiteers." I saw heads nod in agreement.

"You think I'm the only one trying to earn some coin?" Spittle spewed from Caulk's lips. "Mr. Barton over there sells his barrels to the army at twice their fair price. And sells them to the redcoats too."

Josiah Barton, his cock-hat bearing the blue bow signifying membership in the Sons of Liberty, coughed whiskey up all over his fine silk waistcoat. "That's a lie," he sputtered, searching the room for support, finding none.

"Mr. Barton, the best way to demonstrate your loyalty would be to enlist yourself," I said. "You're a few years younger than Mr. Field, I wager."

"Unfortunately, my responsibilities here in New London preclude my enlistment, Captain Hale," Barton replied stiffly. "But I'll pay a man in my employ to serve in my place."

"Three men, Mr. Barton. Good men," I said, steel in my tone.

"Three, then. They'll be ready to march in a week's time." Barton replied before scampering away.

"Well done, Captain Hale," Caulk bent at the waist in a mock bow. "I should add the commission for Barton's three to my bill."

"You can shove your bill up your arse," I replied.

"Fine words for a college man." Caulk's expression corkscrewed in contempt. "I can see you need more time to grasp the facts of your situation. Come look for me at the harbor when you're ready to talk." He pivoted and marched away, his two henchmen forging a path through the crowd which appeared to be losing interest in the proceedings.

I still seethed, but couldn't let the tavern empty without one more recruiting pitch. "Who knows where the King of America resides?" I proclaimed the words of *Common Sense* in my best Yale debating voice, pausing to let the question linger in the air.

"I say that He reigns from above and does not make havoc of mankind like the Royal Brute of Britain," a baritone voice boomed, completing the barb at King George.

"Stephen Hempstead, you are a most welcome sight." I smiled broadly as I hugged my old friend. "I heard you returned home when your term expired."

"I want to re-enlist," Hempstead announced, raising his glass. "Mr. Paine's words moved me to action, as they will everyone who hears them."

"Huzzah!" I toasted. I grabbed the contract from Wright and waved it in the air. "Now who else will join Mr. Hempstead?"

I had no more takers. As the crowd dissipated, John Richards tugged on my elbow, guiding me towards the end of the bar. "Will you be able to sup with us tomorrow evening?" he asked.

"Unfortunately, not. I leave for New Haven at dawn."

"Prudence will be disappointed. She was hoping to display her newly acquired culinary skills for you."

"Prudence has found a home in the kitchen?"

"It appears she has a talent for slaughtering and dismembering fowl. Mrs. Richards has put it to good use." Mr. Richards beamed with pride.

"I'm pleased the young lady's found an outlet for her considerable energies."

"Prudence has matured under our tutelage." Richards straightened his hat. "Did you receive her recent letter? I posted it myself."

"Yes, sir. It was a pleasant surprise."

"And did you reply?"

"Not yet."

"Well, young man, you are most tardy." Richards shot me a stern glance. "Young women from good *patriot* families deserve better."

"Yes, sir." I straightened. "I will be coming back to New London in a week's time. Perhaps I would be welcome at your table then."

"I will see to it. Good evening, Captain Hale."

After Mr. Richards left, I settled at a table fronting the bar with Hempstead and Wright. Jabez Miner brought another round. Six recruits, not a bad start, particularly for a snowy night, but I would need at least twenty more before I could return to Winter Hill.

"I lost track of you in camp," I said to Hempstead. "Why'd you leave?"

"I never got along well with my captain," Hempstead replied, shaking his head. "But I won't have that problem if I serve in your command, will I?"

"Not at all. In fact, I'm in need of a sergeant." I still ached over Zeb Cheesebrough's departure.

"Are you going to pay Caulk?" Wright asked.

I sipped my ale, wishing the decision were that simple. If I bought recruits from the likes of Caulk and Barton, I could meet my quota. But, was that any way to advance the cause of liberty? Any way to build an army that could defeat the British Empire? Who would own the loyalty of these hired hands? Would they follow me into battle? Or would they switch sides like Asa?

"Not if I can help it," I replied.

***

Summiting a rock-strewn ridge outside Medford, just across the Mystic River from Winter Hill, Robert Rogers bent over and puked a chunky broth of ale and stew into the snow. Chest heaving, breath ragged, beardless cheeks frozen raw, he hadn't felt this good in ten years. He looked back down the steep, forested slope, proud to see his snowshoe tracks still visible despite the blizzard. They brought back pleasant memories of past battles.

What motivated him now? Was it money? Or, his inability to gain a command from either the rebels or the redcoats? Or the furtive, pitying glances of recognition from the snot-nosed soldiers in the Continental Army camp? He didn't know for sure, and he didn't care. He just didn't want the war to end before he could get a chance to participate.

Rogers turned and trudged back downhill, grasping at branches to stay afloat in the swirling sea of snow. Only three more loops to go before dark. He was going to be a Ranger again – or die trying.

After completing his afternoon exercises, Rogers lurched into The Horny Goat, his home for the past month. Josiah Gold, the proprietor, dipped a flagon into a bucket of flip and slapped it on the counter. "You made it." His guffaw mixed with a thick Scottish brogue as he nodded towards the two rough dressed men standing at the bar. "Your mates would nigh wager a shilling on your return today."

Rogers downed the drink in a single swallow, nodded his appreciation and lurched towards his room. Separated from the rear of the tavern by a flimsy door and heated only by a squat, soot-blackened brazier, the accommodations offered little privacy and fewer comforts, but the price was right. Gold, a retired Ranger and closet Loyalist, provided room and board in exchange for Rogers' presence in his establishment each evening, regaling patrons with tales of Indian pow-wows, hard-loving squaws, royal audiences, and London jails.

Rogers stripped off his snow-drenched green jacket, hung it on a hook over the smoking coals, and examined his face in the cracked looking-glass for the telltale burn of frostbite. In violation of his own rules for winter survival, he had shaved off his beard; but he wanted to feel the cold this time. Satisfied that he had survived the day's activities no worse for wear, he flopped down onto the pile of straw that served as his bed and surrendered to exhaustion.

Crouched behind a pine tree on the edge of a dark forest, he scouted the clearing ahead. Two Continentals in blue jackets, gold buttons shining in the sunlight, stood guard over an officer's marquee.

"For the King!" he shouted. A war party of ten Iroquois, their faces daubed a lurid red, leapt out of the forest to join his attack. Arrows whistled past his ear, puncturing the hearts of the sentinels who crumpled at his feet. Pistol in hand, he ripped open the door to the tent. General George Washington, attired in his impeccably tailored uniform, sat at a table, sipping a glass of claret, his African manservant behind him. He felled the servant with a single shot, then reached for his tomahawk. Washington cowered in fear...

"Rogers, get your sorry arse out of bed," Gold rapped on the door, rattling its hinges. "There's someone here to see you."

Rogers rubbed the sleep from his eyes as he rose, every muscle aching. The image of Washington lingered for a last, delicious second. He pulled on his breeches, cinching the belt tight, pleased to note he had progressed another notch in the past week. Might even need to take in the waistline soon. After washing in the icy water remaining in his basin, he shouldered his jacket and stepped into the tavern.

A lissome Indian girl stood next to Gold, a frown of impatience marring her otherwise flawless face. Her faded hunting shirt was open at the neck to reveal a red and white beaded necklace; her leggings had the telltale wear of saddle time; a war club rested in a sling over one shoulder. Rogers shook the cobwebs from his brain, fearing he might still be dreaming.

The girl looked him up and down, her expression unchanged. "It is an honor to meet the great Robert Rogers, *once* the formidable warrior of the wilderness."

"At your service." He deliberately ignored the barb.

"The years have not treated you well."

"Who are you?"

"My name is Princess. Mr. Gold will vouch for me."

Gold nodded. "Princess is a useful woman. She brokers information between General Howe's command in Boston, the Queen's Rangers in the countryside, and the tribes in the northwest."

"I need a military man to scout rebel positions in Canada and New York. A man who can travel in rough country."

"I'd be taking orders from a tavern wench?" Rogers asked, scratching his crotch somewhat absentmindedly. Although he knew from experience that the wives of Indian chieftains often sat at war councils, he did not envision his return to the Crown's service beginning this way.

"I didn't ride here in the storm to be insulted by a sleep-addled old man."

"This old man still has enough gumption to plow your furrow."

"If your scrawny prick so much as sticks out its head, I'll cut it off," Princess replied, her right hand tapping the hilt of the hunting knife scabbarded at her waist.

Rogers reached for his own blade, but Gold intercepted him. "If you want to prove your mettle to General Howe, you'd best work *with* Princess," he said.

Rogers muttered an Iroquois curse under his breath.

"You remember our language," Princess noted as she pulled a familiar book from her pack. "My agents write their reports in code. I'll show you how it works."

***

Anne held Geoffrey's hand in the back of their coach, waiting in a long line of coaches outside the entrance to Faneuil Hall, a squat brick building topped by a majestic domed steeple. She was bubbling with anticipation of her first time at the theatre, an almost unfathomable experience for a Puritan New Englander. Massachusetts had actually banned plays in 1750 and Congress had followed suit at the start of the war. Unfortunately, her betrothed was gruff, his thoughts distant, leaving her to stare out the window in silence at the frostbitten streets.

Although the temperature had not approached the melting point in weeks, the late afternoon sun hovered over the hills, providing a cruel tease of a distant spring. It cast a waxen glow over the fashionably dressed Boston couples as they stepped delicately from their carriages and paraded into the hall.

A smattering of commonfolk, ill-dressed for the cold, gawked from the sidewalk. Instinctively, she searched their gaunt faces, as she did every face, for signs of the pox, still rampant in Boston.

Anne was mindful to stay a beat behind Geoffrey as they climbed the steps to the entranceway. She nodded to Widow Pitcairn, who trailed them into the hall.

"Major Stanwich, Miss Wheaton," the Widow said, forcing the greeting with only the slightest movement of her lips. She had bolstered her brows with mouse skins to brighten the appearance of her eyes.

"Widow Pitcairn, so pleasant to see you," Anne replied, doing her best to contain her gloat. "I'm so looking forward to the performance."

"Yes, well, I was as well. Until I learned I would be seated in the last row of the theater. The best I could hope for as a widow, I suppose."

On the opposite end of the marital contract, Anne felt there was little she could say in commiseration. She turned to Geoffrey, but he was clearly not minding the conversation.

The "First Couple" greeted guests just inside the front doors. Betsey Loring, attached at the hip to General Howe, sported Wheaton's daffodil creation with the bodice modified to exhibit her ample bosom, cleaved by a dazzling diamond pendant. Sable mittens and matching muff completed her wardrobe. Joshua Loring was nowhere to be seen.

Having taken her pick of the leftovers at the Wheaton shop, Anne wore an understated mauve gown, lightly etched with floral lace, and a gray petticoat. Although the high neckline revealed little, she had tightened her silk stays to at least suggest the presence of a bosom underneath. Father had beamed as he rouged her cheeks and pasted a heart-shaped patch on her cheek before she left the house.

Geoffrey cut a positively dashing figure in his dress scarlet, adorned with medals from past campaigns as well as his service in North America. She would have let him ravish her right there, but they had agreed to abstain until after they said their vows next week.

"Lady Wheaton, I am so excited about your wedding," Betsey Loring's gushing voice lured Anne and Geoffrey forward. "It will be wonderful to have another woman of continental birth as a friend."

"I look forward to our association as well," Anne replied hesitantly.

Geoffrey and the general separated a step, but Anne tilted her head to hear their words.

"A clear sky," Howe said, gazing upward. "And a calm sea." "Good omens," Geoffrey replied.

Anne pursed her lips in a tight smile, pretending to listen to Betsey's prattle about dresses and jewelry.

"Yes, tomorrow will be a fine day to sail," Howe said.

Panic lanced Anne's stomach, but she refused to acknowledge it.

"I won't let you down, sir." Geoffrey nodded farewell to Mrs. Loring and nudged Anne forward. Walking down the center aisle, she forced herself to stay silent, searching for familiar faces to calm her growing anxiety. Mercy Hale wore Wheaton's most elaborate gown, adorned with an abundance of lace and ruffles, topped by an equally overdone hat festooned with sprigs of winterberries.

Anne followed Mercy's gaze to William Cunningham, Hale's superior, sitting alone two rows forward. As Provost Marshal, he ran the prisons of Boston with an iron, and often bloody, hand. Rumors ran rampant that he regularly hijacked the rations and clothing allocated for his prisoners and sold them on the black market. The wail of his captives begging for bread through barred windows was testament to the veracity of these charges.

"Where are you going?" Anne asked Geoffrey, the words waterfalling out of her mouth as soon as they settled in their seats.

"To Halifax. I will be commanding my old regiment." Geoffrey whispered, bursting with pride.

"Command? But your…disability?"

Geoffrey gave her only a stern look in reply. They sat in silence as Anne contemplated her future. Geoffrey was still a soldier. If she was going to be his wife, she would have to accept the vagaries of army life. After only a few seconds, she nodded her acquiescence, slipping her hand into the crook of his elbow to reassure him of her support.

A drum roll signified the start of the play. The audience at Faneuil Hall, senior officers and their wives or mistresses, perhaps one hundred people in total, clapped as General Burgoyne bowed from stage right. The musical conductor, also a major in the dragoons, returned the salute and snapped his baton at the orchestra. The flutes and horns launched into the opening number.

Joseph Addison did not have to fear competition from John Burgoyne, but the play was entertaining. Anne laughed heartily as the junior officers effected high pitched squeals in the women's roles and

General Washington's over-powdered wig slipped askew. When a soldier, costumed in scarecrow's garb with straw bristles for a beard, rushed onto the stage shouting about the rebels attacking Charlestown "tooth and nail," the audience clapped heartily in delight. A barrage of artillery fire shortly followed, sounding scarily authentic, as if it came from the batteries on Bunker Hill.

A uniformed messenger rushed to General Howe who disengaged his hand from Mrs. Loring's to listen to his words. Anne, Geoffrey, and everyone else looked around in confusion. The General quickly jumped to his feet, waving frenetically to silence the orchestra. "The rebels have landed. Turn out! Turn out!" he ordered as soon as he could be heard.

Officers jumped over chairs, bowling over several ladies and their fancy hats, as they scrambled for the exits. Mercy Hale's berries squirted a purple juice on the tails of her gown when a captain stomped on them in haste. Geoffrey grabbed Anne's hand and tugged her towards the General. The two men conferred for a minute before Howe bolted for the door. Betsey Loring looked lost until an aide guided her towards her coach, which had jumped to the front of the line.

Geoffrey allowed the crush to subside before he signaled for Henry to bring their transport around. He had mastered climbing into the coach without assistance. When the door closed, he turned to Anne, an expression of excitement on his face that she had not seen since the morning of the battle on Breed's Hill.

"What's happening?" she asked.

"The rebels have launched a raid. Only a small force, but commanded by Major Knowlton, a formidable opponent. We'll repel the incursion, but it is an ominous sign nevertheless," he replied.

"And you?"

"I sail tomorrow to Halifax on General Howe's flagship, the *Chatham*," he said, his eyes gleaming with pride. "I will be leading men again."

"But, why lead men to Canada?"

"The General wants a man he can trust to evaluate our options."

"We're going to evacuate Boston?" The coach jolted through a pothole, bouncing Anne a foot in the air.

"You know I can't discuss military plans, dear."

"When will you return? What about our wedding?"

"We'll have to postpone it. But only a few weeks. Three most likely. Four at the most."

"If you're sailing to Halifax, could you bring Mother and Phineas back to Boston?"

"I could. If they wanted to come to this hellhole. But I don't expect we'll be here much longer." Geoffrey clasped her hand, but his mind was elsewhere. After several minutes of silence, he seemed to remember that she still breathed. "You'll keep your pistol with you at all times?" he asked.

"Yes, dear. It will remind me of you."

"Good, good." Geoffrey missed her sarcasm. "And you've been practicing your marksmanship?"

"Regularly."

"Well done." Geoffrey paused as if gathering his courage. "Perhaps we might practice *our* marksmanship this evening?"

"You are truly a wicked man."

"Wickedly in love with you." His face bore the sloppy grin of a hungry hound. She had spawned a devil but would see that he sailed away content.

**

I arrived back in New London early enough in the day to visit my favorite barber for a proper shave and hairdressing before supper at the Richards. After a week of hard travel and hard recruiting pitches, largely to hard men of modest intellect, I found myself looking forward to a civilized evening of good food and stimulating conversation.

As with Father, I would need to make sure that Mr. Richards recognized my new status as a Continental Army captain, not a militia man or schoolteacher. Accordingly, I donned my well-worn Connecticut uniform, albeit with my stepmother's new shirt, freshly laundered, and strapped on my saber.

I paused before lifting the doorknocker on the two story, slate gray Georgian, a comfortable home but not nearly as large as our family's new farmhouse in Coventry. How should I handle Prudence? The Richards' intention to match us had been clear since the day she moved in, but I still had no interest in matrimony. Yet, the young lady possessed spunk - in addition to first rank beauty.

John Richards greeted me with a welcoming shoulder clap. Upon entering the front hall, my nostrils perked at the pungent aromas of coriander and cayenne. Mrs. Richards had always taken a Puritanical approach to cooking, eschewing any ingredients that might add spice to her meals. There was obviously a new chef in residence.

The parlor also boasted a new look. A blue pillow, embroidered with the outline of a schooner, rested on Mr. Richard's favorite chair; a curlicued Oriental rug warmed the floor; whale oil lamps replaced candles on either side of the entrance; and a freshly burnished copper plate hung over the fireplace. The room seemed more colorful, more alive, than I remembered, as if it was trying to entice me to stay.

Mr. Richards proudly ushered me into the kitchen to witness Prudence, clad in a gravy-stained apron, at work. She flashed her teeth in a mischievous smile before returning her attention to a turkey roasting on the spit.

The dining room table was set for only four. Their boarder, the new schoolmaster, was visiting relations and wouldn't return home this evening, Mrs. Richards explained. Claret was a casualty of the British blockade, but ale and hard cider flowed freely, slowly loosening tongues.

I made sure to praise the meal; Prudence, seated immediately to my right, reveled in my words. Her cheeks had lost their schoolgirl blush, but her eyes retained their dare-me sparkle.

"I'm pleased to see your appetite has returned, Master Hale," Mehitable Richards said as I gobbled my second portion of turkey.

"The military experience is not all bad, dear. It can bring out a certain wisdom in a man," John Richards added.

"Are you wiser now, Nathaniel?" Prudence teased, her pearly smile glimmering.

"In the ways of men, perhaps," I replied.

"Touché," Mr. Richards said, waving his index finger like an imaginary sword. "The fairer sex will always remain a mystery to me."

"We do have a certain utility, though. Don't we dear?" Mehitable asked, as she passed a pumpkin dish to her husband.

"Of course, of course. A man needs a partner in life's work."

"As Nathaniel will realize one day," Mehitable said, casting a sharp glance in my direction.

Fortunately, the servant girl saved me, wheeling out an apple pie fresh from the oven, its crust sprinkled with cinnamon. While I was stuffed, Prudence devoured the sweets, running her tongue over her teeth to capture the last clots of whipped cream.

"You'll stay with us tonight," Mr. Richards asserted as the dessert plates were cleared.

"With great respect, sir, I cannot," I replied, standing. "I'm boarding at the Hempstead's and must take my leave shortly."

"Why go out into the cold at such a late hour?" Mrs. Richards asked, tapping her husband's thigh. He took the cue and rose to add more wood to the hearth, poking the logs until they blazed.

"I have obligations, military obligations, to complete this evening with Sergeant Hempstead and my orderly. We march to Boston with our new recruits tomorrow."

"A toast then. To victory," John Richards withdrew a bottle from the cupboard and set four tumblers on the table. "I've saved this madeira for a special occasion."

After the toast, Mehitable rose. "Why don't we let the young people have some privacy? They haven't seen each other in months."

"I do believe there's some wine left," Mr. Richards added.

"Captain Hale, you are welcome to stay as long as you like. I'll fix your bed in case you decide to change your mind," Mrs. Richards tossed out the offer like breadcrumbs to a goose as she climbed the stairs, her husband in tow.

"Aunt Mehitable…" Prudence huffed, her eyes alight with embarrassment. Nevertheless, she refilled my glass and her own.

Welcoming the opportunity to talk with Prudence, I sat back down. "Your letter was a most pleasant surprise. It brought sunshine to a dreary day."

"I thought you might appreciate some cheer."

"My apologies for not replying, but my duties…"

"I'm sure you were busy day and night with your troops," she replied with an innocent smile.

"Yes, and now I'll have to train new men. Almost half my troop failed to reenlist."

"They lack the backbone to defeat the British." Prudence sipped her wine.

"No. They have families to support. And we haven't seen many redcoats. Up close at least. They've stayed snug inside Boston." I toyed with my cup but didn't drink.

"As has Anne Wheaton, I gather. I've heard she's betrothed," Prudence said. "Quite disappointing, I'm sure." Her eyes, peeking above her cup, however, did not reflect any dismay.

"It was a shock, but I've moved on."

"Have you?" She leaned closer, her lips tantalizingly close to mine.

I reached for her hand. "Please don't take offense, but I really must go."

Prudence let her fingers linger in my grip. "Go then."

I stood, taking small pleasure in the surprise registering on Prudence's face. She was not accustomed to rejection. "I would like to call on you again. When my duties permit."

"Duly noted, captain."

The next morning, the sky was a pure Continental Army blue, lacking even the trace of a cloud. Stepping from the Hempstead's porch with Stephen and Asher Wright in tow, I whistled "The Girl I Left Behind Me." I had struggled to fall asleep last night, but, to my pleasant surprise, had no regrets today. And I did plan to visit Prudence again.

We marched to the docks, our boots crashing through the crust of frost on the street. While ice clogged the Thames upriver, the New London harbor still looked passable, its gray, forbidding waters rippling into the Sound and the Atlantic Ocean beyond. A dual-masted schooner, the Laughing Lady, was lashed to the pier. Three steam-breathing stevedores loaded cargo on board from a wagon that had skated its way mid-ships. Caulk himself appeared to be supervising the operation from a perch at the aft.

"Where are these headed, Mr. Caulk?" I rapped my knuckles on a crate.

"No matter to you," Caulk replied as he jumped on to the pier. "Seamus and Ian will be ready to leave as soon as they finish up here. They don't talk much, but they'll follow orders."

"Isn't that from the Wheaton house?" I asked as a familiar tall-case clock appeared on the shoulder of one of the stevedores.

"We confiscated it under Connecticut's High Treason Act," Caulk replied, hurrying his man along. "You're not going to defend that Tory family again, are you?"

"No."

"Good. Then we can do business." Caulk picked an icicle from his nostril and flipped it at my feet. "Do you have my coin?"

"Half now. Half later. Jabez Miner will hold the balance until I send word."

The idealism that I had harbored just a few weeks ago had died somewhere along the road to New Haven. As news trickled through the colony of the defeat of Colonel Benedict Arnold, Connecticut's own son, outside Quebec, men backed away from my pitches. I had little hope of commanding a unit capable of fighting the redcoats without Caulk's two Irishmen, as well as Barton's men. Once we left New London, I would do whatever necessary to mold them into honorable soldiers and win their loyalty. In the words of Cato, *"Valor soars above what the world calls misfortune..."*

"If you cheat me, college boy, you'll regret it."

"You're a true patriot, Mr. Caulk."

Wearing several layers of woolens under my uniform, I led my men, eleven in all, dressed in a variety of homespun, on to the Post Road just after the mid-day meal. The recruits from other towns would meet us in camp on Winter Hill in five days' time. Young John Bell drummed the Harriot for the first mile, attracting waves and cheers from bystanders.

At a rest break, I sought out Hercules Field who was unwrapping the layers of rags covering his feet. "We'll get you some sturdy boots in camp," I said, grimacing at Hercules' calloused, misshapen appendages.

"That would be most appreciated," Hercules replied, as he massaged some color back into his toes and applied a homemade balm.

"When you worked for Tailor Appletree did you ever meet his apprentice, Caleb Wheaton?" I asked.

"An evil boy." Hercules didn't bother to stop his ministrations.

"Have you seen him around New London lately?"

"No sir. Don't care if I never see him again neither."

"Did you have a run-in?"

"No, sir. I stayed as far away as I could." Hercules bound his right foot back up again and looked at me. "Out in the yard one morning, I watched Mr. Caleb pick up a baby owl. Couldn't have been more than a week or two old. Must have fallen from its nest." Hercules paused to tend his left foot. "Mr. Caleb snapped its neck like a twig. Then tossed it into the bushes." Hercules stood. "Don't need to know any more about a boy than that."

We marched north through Connecticut and Massachusetts, stopping only to eat and sleep. I stayed again in the tavern in Pomfret and in the home of a family friend in Uxbridge, while my men bivouacked in the woods. I could sense their anxiety grow as we approached Winter Hill on the third day.

I too was nervous about my arrival in camp. When I had left in December, morale was low, as was faith in General Washington. Arnold's defeat, as well as a month burrowing in the snow, could hardly have improved spirits. Were there enough soldiers and ammunition to mount an attack on Boston? Or defend the ramparts if General Howe advanced?

Where were Asa and Princess? What had come of their conspiracy? I wanted to confront them and learn the truth, but doubted they would appear anywhere near camp again. I tabbed the yellow cockade onto my hat and marched my men past the sentries.

I noticed the cannons before we reached the parade ground. Soldiers were unloading them from sleds. How did waddling Henry Knox, who might have weighed more than three hundred pounds, engineer those sleds up snow-covered hills and down icy slopes all the way from Fort Ticonderoga to Boston? Yet, the colonel and his men had obviously accomplished the impossible. With sixty artillery pieces now under his command, General Washington had the firepower to bring the British to their knees.

CHAPTER 11 - FEBRUARY 1776

"Bows and Arrows are more easily provided everywhere than Muskets and Ammunition."
Benjamin Franklin
letter to General Charles Lee
February 11, 1776

The rap on the front door startled Anne as she sat down to supper with Father. They were down to their last bushel of onions in the root cellar, but fortunately, Henry had delivered a barrel of salted fish and several bottles of claret upon Geoffrey's departure for Halifax. Not quite a feast, but better than what most Bostonians would be eating tonight. The knocker rapped again, this time with a greater sense of urgency.

"Who could be out in this cold?" Father asked, nearly spilling his wine as he rose. He fumbled with the latch for several seconds before finally opening the door.

Sam Hale's valet, Livingston, outfitted in scarlet and buff livery, stepped inside without waiting for an invitation. He removed his hat and stamped his boots on the rug.

"Yes?" Father asked.

Livingston sneered in response, stepping past Father to address Anne. "The Deputy Provost Marshal requires your presence at his office this evening," he announced.

"This evening? For what reason?" Anne replied, still sitting at the table.

"My master did not provide an explanation. His coach is waiting outside."

"It would be inappropriate for my daughter to visit Mr. Hale alone at this hour," Father said, reaching for his coat. "I will accompany her."

"I'll be fine, Father." Anne stood. "Please give me a moment to freshen up."

She climbed the stairs to her room, lifted her undergarments and squatted over the chamber pot, picturing Sam Hale's face at its bottom.   After washing, she primed her pistol and buried it in the pocket of the belt she wore over her shift.   Remembering the intimacy of their last encounter, the rum on Hale's breath and the smallpox scars on his cheeks, she smoothed down her skirt, slipping a hand through the slit to make sure her weapon was within easy reach. Just in case.

Livingston sat across from her in the coach but did not say a word as the blades glided along the ice-hard streets. Anne shivered as they approached the prison on Queen Street, site of the offices of the Provost Marshal and his staff, but they kept going down towards the docks and the sea.

Geoffrey was out there somewhere, Anne thought, praying briefly for his safe return. All she wanted to do was pay her debt to Sam, get married, and move to England. If they had to stop in Halifax for a few months, so be it. Mother and Phineas would be a welcome sight.

The coach swayed as the driver braked hard at the base of the Long Wharf and skidded into a right turn. They came to a stop fifty yards later in front of a dark, weather-battered warehouse.

"Shall we?" Livingston hopped down and offered his hand.

"Where are we?" Anne asked. The cold bore through her woolens, wrapping her rib cage in its chilling grip.

"Mr. Hale's private office." Livingston appeared impervious to the elements.

Anne's heart raced as he latched the warehouse door behind her. The wind whistled through the walls, circulating the unpleasantly familiar odor of salted fish and pork. They walked between a row of pickle barrels, stacked to the ceiling, towards candlelight flickering in the far corner.

"Miss Wheaton, good of you to come," Sam Hale called out as he rose from his cluttered desk, a pine plank supported by two barrels next to a potbelly stove. A map of Boston and the vicinity was tacked to the wall. Sam shoved a log into the stove and warmed his gloved fingers over the flames before motioning for Anne to sit in a rickety chair across from him.

He sat, poured himself a drink, but made no move to offer her a glass. After sipping, he opened his lock box, the ubiquitous GR monogrammed into the leather, and withdrew several papers. He read the top page, shuffled the stack, and scanned the next page. He shook his head and sighed, appearing to surrender. Reading upside down, Anne could make out a shipping laden and receiving documentation.

"Your father said you're good with figures," Sam said.

"I've been schooled in them, yes."

"By my cousin, the rebel, no doubt."

"By my mother, actually."

"No matter." He lifted the pile of paperwork and dropped it on the tabletop. "I need someone I can trust to take inventory and do the bookkeeping."

"Me?" Steam plumed from her lips.

"Yes. These papers relate to private affairs. I believe I can trust your discretion. As you can trust mine."

Anne heard a rustle in the warehouse.

"Do you approve, Mr. Cunningham?" Sam asked, looking over her shoulder into the darkness.

She turned her head, staring into the vulpine eyes of the Provost Marshal, clamping her thighs shut to keep from pissing herself.

"She'll do," Cunningham replied.

***

News of the arrival of Colonel Knox and his cannons spread like wildfire down the frost bound New England coast. Army recruits and militia units piled into the Boston area, swelling the ranks of the Continentals to more than ten thousand soldiers, although many still lacked munitions and uniforms. One militia company actually wore red coats. The camp flew the Grand Union flag, its message of colonial unity more wishful thinking than reality, I thought, as I marched my men around the parade ground.

With artillery now in hand, General Washington was eager to launch the killing blow.

If Howe sailed his army out of Boston, where would he likely land? Washington had already sent General Lee to New York City to plan its defense.

The Connecticut regiments moved camp from Winter Hill to Roxbury, the gateway to the Boston Neck. As a privilege of my rank, an army wagon transported my trunk of personal belongings to my new home. I was both excited to be in the front line, the British sentries were within view of my spyglass, and relieved to be away from the temptations of the Flag and Flagon.

With Asa gone, Elvin saw no reason to cover for him any longer. He stepped forward, telling me that Asa often snuck out of camp after hours. Assumed he had a lady friend but couldn't be sure.

"Did Asa have coins in his purse?" I had asked.

"Yes," Elvin answered, finally coming clean.

Unusual for any soldier, let alone a Black, I noted. Also unusual for any man with a mistress. So, who was paying Asa? And Princess? Was it Mister Sam?

"Company halt!" Despite the frigid temperature, I drilled my troop every day. Fortunately, the 19th Infantry now had "Young John" Bell for amusement. Someone would invariably slap John's back and shout "ring the bell" to start every march. John alternated playing fife and drum to entertain the men during the hours of drudgery.

A covey of horses kicked up a cloud of snow as they approached. My heartbeat quickened as I recognized the tallest rider, sitting imperially erect in the saddle.

"Ground arms!" I barked as General Washington approached. Each soldier stood at attention, the butt of his musket touching the ground by his right boot. The commander-in-chief inspected the ranks, his head swiveling from right to left and back again. I willed my men to remain motionless.

"As you were, Captain," Washington said, peeling away to rejoin his coterie.

"Huzzah," I shouted, as soon as the General was out of earshot. I felt like a schoolmaster whose students had just graduated with flying colors. Only my "students" might be marching into battle any day. I was sure Washington was out surveying the troops to assess their readiness for the long awaited invasion of Boston.

"Company dismissed." My men had earned an early break for supper.

"Where's my musket?" Elvin Parrish shouted. A ripple of laughter surged through the ranks as Young John appeared, marching with a gun on his shoulder.

"I can shoot better than you with my eyes closed," John replied, kneeling to take aim at a distant tree.

"I'll teach you a lesson you won't soon forget!" Elvin booted John in the butt, sending him and the musket sprawling. I would have been upset if the musket was loaded. But, with gunpowder scarce, no unit drilled with weapons primed. Stephen Hempstead and several other men came to John's defense, but it was unnecessary. Morale was high, the men spoiling to fight the British, not each other.

I was exhausted but pleased as I watched my men drift back to their quarters. While most slept in the barracks constructed last fall, Elvin and his new bunkmate, Tom Peacock, dug a shelter into the hillside, burrowing out a chimney as well as scavenging a timber door and straw bedding. They invited "Young John" and "Old Hercules", still bootless unfortunately, to join them.

Bowl of beans in hand, I wedged myself next to William Hull at the feeble campfire of the captains' mess. With the army swollen in size, firewood and food had grown scarcer every day. Many meals were now eaten cold, frostbite an ever-present enemy.

"I saw General Washington checking the ice in the Back Bay yesterday. He actually jumped up and down to see if it's thick enough to march across," Hull said, shaking his head.

"And?" I asked.

"He's ready to attack. As usual."

"Washington inspected my company this afternoon. I think he was pleased."

"Our commander-in-chief needs to be patient. The army's not ready yet. Did you hear about the skirmish in Dorchester the other night?"

"Six of our men taken prisoner," I said.

"The redcoats sent our troops running and burned several houses."

"Washington won't let that stop him. Nor should it."

"You're always spoiling for a fight."

"That's why I enlisted." I blew on my fingers in a futile effort to warm them.

"Maybe Martha will talk some sense into her husband." Hull leaned over and whispered. "Did you hear about the Spanish fly?"

"Spanish fly?"

"I have a friend on the General's staff who said our leader ordered four tinctures of aphrodisiac."

"Enough folderol," I replied. "We prepare for battle."

***

185

Anne watched the sea-smoke spiral skyward off the ice-strewn harbor as she turned into Dock Square. The failing sun outlined the edges of a low-hanging cloudbank in a bright orange hue. Walking briskly, she inhaled the comforting fumes of firewood burning in the chimneys of homes still fortunate enough to have a log pile in the yard.

Geoffrey had been gone for over two weeks. No news was good news, she thought. It seemed like only yesterday she was at the theatre hobnobbing with the British elite. Until he returned, and they wed, she had to return to her life as a shop girl. No sense fretting about it. Father needed the help.

While her own wedding gown remained unfinished, she worked at the store measuring and cutting fabrics for the gowns of Wheaton clients to wear at the final gala of the season. Everyone understood they would be leaving Boston and none too soon. Good riddance to this cold, dark, depressing skeleton of a town. What would become of it after the Army left, no one seemed to know, or care. Although Anne still had stitching to do, Father, looking gaunter every day, insisted that she leave before dark. If he knew about the contents of Sam's warehouse, he never let on.

A scratching noise in an alleyway along the wharves startled her. Anne reached for the pistol, primed and loaded, in her pocket. She tested the cock, notched in safety mode, with her gloved fingers. A rat, as big as a rabbit, scurried out into the light, then scampered back to its den. Anne released the weapon and hurried away.

Head down, she passed three redcoats, drunk from the sound of their banter, stirring a foul-smelling kettle over an open flame. Beary, she guessed, a brew of shoe leather and animal remains; dogs and cats, she heard whispered in the store. She quickened her gait as footsteps and a pungent male tang followed her. Uncas, standing guard at the entrance to the warehouse, waved as she approached. The trailing footsteps faded.

The warehouse door swung open, and William Cunningham barreled out. His bald head and beady eyes peeked above his black cloak like a dragon rising from its lair. Anne gasped as he bumped into a shoddily jacketed Black pushing a wheelbarrow, full of dung, by the foul odor emanating from it, along the side of the street. Fortunately, the Black steered his load clear of Cunningham and kept on his way.

The soldiers, who must have lingered in the shadows, cackled at the near miss. Cunningham snapped, spittle frothing from his lips. He whipped his cane into the slave's back – once, twice, three, four, five times – while ranting about some obscure law requiring the enslaved to walk their loads in the middle of the road. The poor man buckled to his knees, head drooping as he mumbled an apology. The soldiers kicked up a racket as they stumbled back into the darkness.

Cunningham slashed the fallen Black twice more before striding towards Anne. She wanted to disappear as well, but there was no place to hide. Instead, she forced herself to silently recite a couplet from a poem by Phyllis Wheatley, a freed slave whose work was popular among Boston's more far-sighted citizens: *"Remember, Christians, Negroes black as Cain/May be refin'd, and join th' angelic train."*

"Good evening, Miss Wheaton," Cunningham said as he passed. As if nothing had happened.

Anne helped the Black to his feet, wrapping her scarf over his bloody shoulders. He nodded his thanks. Enraged, she bulled past Uncas, who had watched the incident without a word, and entered the warehouse.

She turned to shout at Uncas but caught herself. What could he have done? Cunningham was the law; Indians were just barely above slaves in Boston's social hierarchy. Wheatley's poetry was the exception, not the portent of a changing tide. Anne realized that she was powerless as well. Women, even the wives of officers, had few rights of their own in British or colonial society.

Anne's frustrations faded as she counted barrels of pickled pork and fish, corn meal and turnips, recorded their value and mapped their location in the warehouse. She barely noticed the briny smell. Where did the food come from? Why was it here? Neither Sam nor William Cunningham, would look favorably upon her questions. Growing hungry, she pried a lid open and helped herself.

Loud voices from the front of the building interrupted her snack.

"What's in there worth guarding, red man?" Someone asked in a sloppy Irish brogue.

"We're the King's soldiers. Let us take a wee, little peek." Another Irishman.

"No," Uncas replied.

"Not hiding any food, are you?" The first voice again.

"We ain't had full rations in a month," the second soldier said. Anne choked on her pork.

"I'm hungry too," Uncas said. "Shall we take our complaints to Provost Marshal Cunningham? He's due back here any minute."

The Irishmen grumbled, but their voices faded. Cunningham wouldn't return until morning, but Uncas' bluff appeared to have worked. Anne returned to her bookkeeping. She had another hour before Uncas would walk her home.

***

I surveyed the checkers on the board, but didn't need more than a second to see the triple-jump. Stephen Hempstead groaned in defeat, handing over a silver coin.

"I'm tapped out," the sergeant said, blowing on his hands for warmth as he stood to leave.

I flipped the coin back. "Buy your ensigns a round on me."

"In Boston," Stephen said, smiling. He whistled Yankee Doodle as he left the cabin.

Yes, in Boston, I thought. I was too excited about the prospect to sleep.

I shared the quarters with William Hull and two other captains, but they were on duty tonight. Perhaps they would have news of Washington's plans when they returned.

I settled another log in the stove, sat at my desk, and re-read the letter from Prudence Richards which had arrived yesterday. Sprinkled with rose water, it contained only light news without mention of my sudden departure last month. And, she looked forward to my return to New London. Her resiliency whet my appetite to see her again. I dipped my quill and began to draft a reply.

A blast of icy air snapped me back to the present. I stashed the letter and scrambled to sit up.

"Friend Nathan, I hope I'm not interrupting," Asa said, stepping into the cabin and closing the door.

"How did you get into camp?"

"It wasn't hard. The picket line is manned by raw recruits. Old men and boys."

I reached for my pistol, but Asa beat me to the draw.

"Is this what we've come to?" Asa asked, his pistol hand unwavering.

"You're a spy."

"No. I'm not."

"Do you deny that you're employed by the Crown?"

"I profited from the Crown, as did many others here in Massachusetts. The people in Boston need to eat. I played a small role in filling that need."

"And Princess?"

"The young lady wears many hats." Asa lowered his weapon. "She wants to talk to you."

"I have no interest in talking to her."

"She has information that might prove invaluable to General Washington."

"Let her call on the General then."

"She's waiting outside." Asa pointed to the door. "Probably half frozen to death. Can she come in?"

"In here? My bunkmates may return any minute."

"Would you prefer to talk somewhere else?"

"Why me?" I stood.

"Because she trusts you. She knows you're an honest man and a true patriot."

Asa was right on both counts. "Let her in," I said.

Asa opened the door and waved Princess into the cabin. She wore man's leggings and baggy winter woolens, war club slung across her shoulder. She removed her fur cap, letting her braids tumble free. "It's good to see you alive and well, Captain Hale."

"I wish I could say the same," I replied. Princess' haughty visage still took my breath away, but her spell over me was broken. "What do you want?"

"There is no need to attack Boston. General Howe plans to evacuate within weeks, if not sooner."

"How do you know?" I asked.

"I have my sources in Boston. Howe has sent a trusted major north on his flagship to scout out a new base."

"North? To Canada? I thought Howe would head south to New York."

"He'll get there eventually. But New York's another viper's nest of rebels. He wants his men to recuperate and train before sailing there. And he's waiting for reinforcements - Hessians and redcoats. The King has raised a new regiment to fight in North America."

I said nothing in reply.

"Even if Washington can get your army across the ice, an attack would be suicidal," Princess continued, reaching inside her jacket for a parchment. "The town is too well-defended. Here is a map of Howe's fortifications."

I scanned the map, more richly detailed than the ones I had sketched in my diary.

"Why are you giving me this? What do you have to gain?"

"My only concern is my people." She tapped her club in the dirt as she spoke. "The Mohegans will only survive if we side with the victor in this war."

Princess was playing both sides. She would sell me out in a minute if it helped her cause. Nevertheless, I would relay the information to Colonel Webb and let him take it up the chain of command, if he thought it worthwhile.

"And you, Asa? Have you joined the tribe?" I asked. Princess' lips curled into a wry smile at my question. I searched her face for a sign of affection – for me or Asa – but saw only indifference.

"No. As usual, my skin is the wrong color," Asa chuckled. "I'm a pirate at heart, so I'll be going back to sea with Mr. Caulk. Captain Caulk now actually. He has obtained a letter of marque from our very own Congress."

"Stay away from camp. There's a warrant for your arrest. And I'll execute it myself."

"Godspeed, my old friend," Asa replied. "I fear we will all need His help before too long."

***

Geoffrey could return any day, Anne thought, as she departed Wheatons the next afternoon. The brisk breeze blowing off the harbor rattled her bones; nevertheless, she welcomed the fresh air. The streets of Boston stank worse than a week-old chamber pot. She scanned the sea for sails, but the roiling waters resembled an endless, uninhabited desert.

Would Geoffrey approve of her nocturnal activities? Not likely. But Anne realized she didn't want to quit. Not yet at least. The air of secrecy was exciting; the side benefits kept her and Father from starvation; and, Sam, for all his skeevy ways, treated her with respect.

Yes, she was undoubtedly involved with the black market, but so was almost everyone in Boston. Maybe she could tell Geoffrey she was engaged in a project for the Provost Marshal. No one, not even a major, wanted to cross William Cunningham.

As she hurried past the Irish soldiers huddled with heads down around the fire, she could feel their eyes, like needles, jab her back. She prepared for their ribald taunts, but they were silent. No crude banter or sexual suggestions trailed her wake. They were beaten men, hardly capable of challenging a woman let alone the fiery rebels.

Was that a ship rising on the horizon? Without a spyglass, she couldn't be sure. Sails were difficult to distinguish against the backdrop of snow and ice shrouding the harbor islands. She wanted to race down to the customs house but gathered herself. It might just be an illusion, the twilight playing tricks. Even if it was the *Chatham*, and Geoffrey, please God, was on board and unharmed, he would have to report to General Howe. She would have time to finish her evening count and be home before he arrived. *Don't act like a foolish girl. Let him come to you.*

Uncas opened the warehouse door and waved Anne to hurry inside. He peered into the gloaming behind her for several seconds.

"Something is wrong," he said, tuning all his senses to the street. "A shadow follows you."

"It's probably just one of those hideous rats." Nevertheless, Anne was relieved when she was safely inside, and Uncas latched the door. Sam had left a fresh woodpile by the stove and two lanterns burning. She warmed her hands before reaching for quill and paper.

The columns of figures would not cooperate tonight. She made an error in tabulation and had to start over. *Damnation!* She was starting to curse like a soldier. Anne pursed her lips in concentration, but her attention wandered to Geoffrey. Finally, she gave up and walked to the front of the warehouse.

"All quiet?" she asked Uncas, pacing to keep warm.

"Seems so," he replied.

"Good. Please go down to the customs house and inquire if the *Chatham* has signaled." Anne unlatched the door.

"I should stay here."

"I can't get a thing done tonight. I need to know if my beloved is home."

"He will dock soon enough." Uncas moved to re-lock the door, but Anne blocked his path.

"I order you to go." When she straightened to full height, she was a head taller than Uncas, though only half as wide. "You'll be back in thirty minutes, less if you hurry."

Uncas shook his head, but Anne reached for the gold-plated pistol in her skirt pocket and aimed at a pickle barrel. "I can defend myself, you know."

Uncas only smiled in response.

"Go. You can lock me inside until you return."

After the lock clacked, Anne marched back towards the lights flickering in Sam's lair. If Geoffrey was indeed home, would he demand to lie with her tonight? Her carnal desires stirred from hibernation. They could marry within a fortnight. She would be the Duchess of Runcorn forevermore. The castle in England beckoned.

She carefully placed the pistol on the desk and stared into the dark reaches of the warehouse. She had not been truthful with Geoffrey. Gowns and chores and the inventory count had taken priority over her marksmanship practice.

Her fingers clenched at a distant rattle. It's just the wind, she soothed herself, but her heart still pounded double-time. She reached for the flask that Sam kept on the shelf. The liquid burned all the way down her gullet, but it had the desired effect. Her breathing slowed. The warehouse quieted. The figures fell into place once again.

A crash of steel on timber shattered the temporary calm. Anne jumped in her seat, splashing ink all over the page of neatly aligned columns. She grabbed lantern and pistol and raced towards the noise.

An axe protruded from the front door. It was soon joined by a second blade, splintering the planks. One kick, then another, opened a gaping hole. A black boot stepped inside.

"Alone now, are ye lassie?" A lanky redhead sporting an unkept beard thick enough to house a sparrow's nest, flashed a cheeky smile as he flicked the wood chips off his road-weary red coat. Anne could smell the liquor on his breath at twenty paces.

"We'll feast tonight, Sean," a second infantryman barged through, a lopsided black-toothed grin leaked towards his left ear as he inhaled the aroma of the stored food.

"Aye, Harry. Tell John to join us." A third redcoat crammed inside. Blond ponytail, peach fuzz tufted on creamy skin, and blue eyes.

Anne pointed her pistol at Sean, struggling to keep her hand steady. "You'll leave right now. That's what you'll do. If you don't want to face the wrath of William Cunningham."

"That ruse worked once, but it won't fool us again," Sean said. He walked towards her, axe at his side. "Put that pistol down, and you won't get hurt."

"One more step and I'll shoot."

"You'll need to release the safety first." Sean lunged before she could react, slapping her hand down, sending the pistol clattering across the floor. He backhanded Anne across the cheek. "The next one won't be a love tap."

"Now get out our way, woman," Harry shoved her aside, his grotesque grin frozen in
place. Anne stumbled and slipped to her knees.

"John, you watch her while we reconnoiter the premises," Sean ordered.

"With pleasure," John replied, his eyes turning icy hard.

"I'm a Loyalist," Anne said, fear creeping into her gut. "On your side."

"We're privates. No one's on our side."

"I'm engaged to a Major." She needed to stall for time.

"Are you now?" John stepped closer, putting a finger under her chin, lifting her head. "Not much meat on your bones, is there, dearie?"

"He's a grenadier with the 63rd Foot."

"And I'm a knight of the Round Table. Call me Sir Lancelot." John mockingly bucked his hips at her face.

Anne couldn't see Sean and Harry, but she heard axe crash into wood again, followed by a roar of wonder. "John, come quick. There's pork here. And rum," Harry called.

"I'll be along shortly."

"Geoffrey is due to meet me here any minute," Anne said as she started to stand, searching for help.

John grabbed her hair and twisted her back to her knees. The rank scent of horse flesh emanated from his uniform. A cavalryman.

"Not so fast, dearie. You don't sound like a proper Englishman's lady to me."

He unbuttoned the top of his breeches with his free hand and ground her face into his groin. "I bet you're just his tart. No harm in sucking another English cock is there?"

Anne grabbed the cavalryman's hips for balance. Her eyes darted forward. Sean and Harry pried open another barrel. After weeks of privation, they were crazed with gluttony. She screamed for help.

"I'm next, John," Harry said, waving a tin cup, rum splashing to the floor. "Always wanted to mount a rebel mare."

"We'll hang for this," Sean said, reaching for Harry's arm.

"Don't be such a macarony." Harry pulled free, spittle spraying from his lips. "She's just an American. No one will mind if we climb in her saddle."

John's hand cupped the back of Anne's head, forcing her mouth towards him. His breeches dropped to his ankles. She twisted her head and spit at his feet.

Footsteps sounded at the front door. The scrape of a peg leg? A dull thwack resonated above her. A warm ooze gushed over her neck and shoulders. John sank to his knees, a tomahawk implanted in his heart, then toppled into her arms. She tossed his limp body aside, his blood painting her face.

Uncas raced towards her. A shot rang out. A red crater burst across the Indian's stomach, his intestines spiraling out as he crashed to the ground. Geoffrey, following close behind, swung himself into the fray.

Sean's pistol smoked as he reached for his powder horn to reload. "She really has a major," he said to Harry. "We're dead men now."

Harry puked all over his boots, but recovered quickly, drawing a dagger. "Nothing to lose then."

"Geoffrey, praise God, you're home," Anne said, tears streaking her crimson cheeks. Her fiancé looked like a bull about to charge, grinding his teeth so vigorously she thought he might try to bite Harry's head off.

"Slow down, Major. We're all Englishmen here," Sean said, ramming a ball down the barrel. "We don't want to hurt you."

"A red man and a doxy ain't worth dying for, is it?" Harry added. "You've got one leg. We got four." Harry kept up the patter, as he glided towards Geoffrey. "Think of the odds."

When Harry got within arm's reach, Geoffrey swung his wooden leg back, cast his crutch at the soldier's knife hand and launched his body. His wig sailed to the left; his crutch flying to the right. They distracted Harry just long enough for Geoffrey to dive past the flailing knife and tackle the soldier.

On the ground, Geoffrey had an even chance. His forearms, fingers and upper body were blacksmith-strong. He grabbed Harry's knife wrist with both hands and ripped his teeth into it, drawing blood and freeing the knife. Harry roared in agony. Geoffrey replied with a keeling war cry that seemed to rise from his loins. He headbutted Harry until the private's eyes rolled up into his sunken forehead.

Anne watched in amazement at Geoffrey's ferocity. Now she understood the difference between an elite grenadier and an ordinary soldier.

Sean snapped out of his own stupor, aiming his pistol at Geoffrey's back. Anne screamed. Sean pulled the trigger. A flash in the pan but no ignition. A misfire.

He tossed his weapon aside and dove at Geoffrey. They rolled on the floor, Sean coming out on top. He tried choking Geoffrey, but her fiancé fought him off. They wrestled again. Geoffrey was tiring.

Anne regained her wits. She searched the floor for her own pistol, crawling to it, releasing the safety. She stood, still woozy, and wiped the blood dripping into her eyes.

Sean had a knife in his boot. He gained the advantage, his knees straddling Geoffrey's midsection. He plunged the blade downward, but it clanged off the silver gorget guarding Geoffrey's throat. Sean was unfazed, forcing the gorget to the side, resuming his attack.

Anne approached the two men, heard their heavy breathing, smelled their sweat and fear. Ten feet away. She quickened her pace. Five feet. Geoffrey grasped Sean's knife hand but could only slow its advance. Three feet.

One more step. Sean's back provided a broad target. His blade hovered over Geoffrey's jugular. She would not - could not - miss from here. Geoffrey let loose his war cry as he jackknifed his torso, aiming the tip of his skull for another headbutt.

Anne's trigger finger jumped. Sean's back exploded, his knife clattering harmlessly away. Geoffrey slumped to the floor, clutching his chest, his fingertips drenched in his own blood. At close range, her bullet had ripped through both men.

Anne screamed. She dragged Sean's carcass off her fiancé and dropped to her knees to cradle Geoffrey's head.

"My love, my love."

"Good shot," Geoffrey replied, forcing a smile, his once-ruddy cheeks draining to a parchment pallor

"I'll go for a doctor."

"No. Stay with me." He squeezed her hand, but his grip slowly faded.

***

Robert Rogers shivered in the woods on the perimeter of the Continental Army camp at Roxbury. The moon cast a spectral glow over the icy landscape. He touched the boulder, vaguely resembling a crouching grizzly, the one Princess had designated for their meeting.

Where was she? He chafed at the thought of taking orders from a female, let alone a girl half his age, but General Howe had not replied to his missives. The Indian bitch was his best, if not only, chance to prove his resurrection to the British command.

He moved closer to the rock. A bit warmer there. The rebel pickets were less than thirty yards away, stomping in the snow, trying desperately not to freeze to death. One of them could enter the woods to take a leak at any moment.

He heard the crunch of a frozen branch before he saw the silhouette, relieved that his wilderness awareness remained intact. A man. White irises on a black face. He withdrew his pistol and tracked him as he led the way for Princess, telltale war club across her shoulder.

"You're late," he said, lowering his weapon.

"Is the great Rogers now afraid to be in the forest alone at night?" Princess stepped forward, while her sentinel faded into the shrubbery.

"The pox on you." His epithet prompted a pistol to cock behind him.

"What do you have for me?" Princess asked.

"I watched fast riders circulate all day. Something must be up," Rogers replied.

"That's not news. Washington's camps leak like sieves. What does he expect when so few of his men are in proper uniforms?"

Rogers reached into his jacket, his fingertips numb as he fumbled for a page lined with columns of figures. Each number corresponded to a page, line and word in the book Princess had given him, his own *Journals*. "I've learned the code. Here's my report on the defenses surrounding Boston."

Princess held the page up to the moonlight. "Well done," she replied, tucking the document into her jacket.

That's all? Princess gave away nothing in conversation, the mark of a good spy. "You'll get that to General Howe?" he asked, desperately trying not to sound like a beggar.

"With my next dispatch." Princess turned to look at the rebel cooking fires flaring in the distance. Her companion rustled in the trees.

Rogers understood that he was about to be dismissed. "I'll head north at dawn."

"You've memorized the inns and campsites that are safe?"

He nodded, hating the fact that his situation left little choice but to trust the Indian. Other men did as well, he consoled himself.

"Leave your reports with the proprietors. Asa or my father will retrieve them."

"You've built quite a network."

"I have much at stake."

***

Anne awoke to the sounds of Sheriff Loring and his constable sloshing through puddles of blood, swinging their lanterns over the dead bodies. She didn't know how long she'd been unconscious, but it was still black as tar outside.

"This one's from the fifty-second," Loring said. He gagged as he kicked over John's body, the tomahawk buried in his chest.

"An Indian over here," the constable, a short, fat man, added. "Probably got drunk and started a fight."

"No," Anne shouted, bolting upright, Geoffrey's head still in her lap. "That's Uncas, Sam Hale's man. He tried to save me."

The two men jumped, as if startled to find a survivor. Anne realized she must be a ghastly sight, caked in blood. "The soldiers would have … if …" she broke down, sobbing as the images flooded back. "Geoffrey's dead too," she mumbled numbly, lifting her fiancé's head, his skin now a translucent white. "I shot him."

"You shot Major Stanwich?" Loring asked.

"I didn't mean to."

"Dead privates is one thing. Those lard asses quarrel every day. But a murdered major's a barrel of trouble," the constable said.

"Shut up, Horatio." Loring dropped to Anne's side, examining Geoffrey's body. "He's dead. From a bullet wound in his chest."

"I'll go for the magistrate." Horatio turned to leave.

"You'll do no such thing," Loring roared, freezing his constable in his tracks.

"We can't have an investigation…here." Loring swiveled his head around the warehouse stocked with containers of black market goods. "Go fetch Sam Hale. Tell him to come quickly. Don't say a word to anyone else or I'll have you flogged till your skin peels off. Understand?"

As the constable hustled away, Anne's senses returned. Loring cared more about the location of the murders, than the victims. And she was the only witness. She needed help. Geoffrey was dead. Uncas was dead. There was only one person left whom she could trust.

"I need to go home. Father will be worried sick."

"You're to go nowhere until Sam Hale arrives."

Sam had at least as much to lose as Loring if the warehouse is discovered. William Cunningham too.

"Look at me," Anne screeched, throwing her arms wide open, doing her best play-acting. "Blood everywhere. I must wash." She pulled at her hair and rubbed her hands up her flanks. "Wash, wash, wash."

"There must be a cloth here to clean your face." Loring stepped to the rear of the warehouse, searching Sam's desk and the shelves behind it.

Anne calculated that she had enough of a head start to reach the street. She sprinted for the front door. Loring ran after her, but she didn't slow, leaping over the splintered timbers. His footsteps faded as the cold battered her face and lungs. Loring would not want to explain why he was chasing a barefoot, raving lunatic female in the dead of night. And he knew where she was going anyway.

Fortunately, the streets were deserted. Anne didn't stop running until she arrived at Charter Street. Father was asleep in his chair, a goblet of wine on the table, logs smoldering in the hearth. He jumped up when she burst through the door, his eyes flaring when he took in his daughter's condition. "Praise God. You're alive."

"For now." She hugged him until her shivers subsided. He heated water for tea as she told her story.

Father interrupted only once, asking if she was sure Geoffrey was dead. When she nodded, tears streaming down her cheeks, he embraced her again.

He poured another spot of tea, adding a slug of rum this time. They sipped in silence for several minutes. After her cup was empty, Father guided her up the stairs, stirring the fire in her room while she peeled off a layer of woolens. He helped her into her sleeping robe and tucked her under the quilts with a kiss on the forehead.

Anne awoke at noon to the pounding of the knocker on the front door. She ran her fingers through her hair, untwisting it from the cavalryman's assault. The image of his cock poking up from a nest of golden pubic hair cudgeled her brain. She forced herself to think of Geoffrey. He had thrown himself into the fray to save her. And she had killed him.

Every fiber of her body ached. She stood shakily, slid the chamber pot from under her bed and vomited into it. She rinsed her mouth with the cold tea Father had thoughtfully left by her bedside. Wobbling to her door, she listened to the conversation downstairs.

"I was expecting you, Sam," Father said. "Anne's asleep. In a state of shock, I fear."

"That's understandable. She had a difficult evening," Sam Hale replied, barging straight into the keeping room. "But I must talk to her immediately."

"I'm awake, Father." She knotted her robe and stepped gingerly down the stairs. Father took her elbow and guided her towards the bench near the hearth. Sam crossed his arms over his chest. She had worked with him long enough to know that his mind was set.

"We moved the bodies across the street to the pier," Sam announced, staring straight through her. "You wandered down there to watch your fiancé's ship sail into the harbor. A foolish move, but you're a young woman in love."

Anne nodded. *I was a young woman in love. Now I am…what? A widow? A mistress? A murderess? A smuggler?*

"You were attacked by three of our own regulars, regrettably. Since they're already dead, there's no need for a messy investigation." Sam continued as if he were reading a story from the Gazette. "Major Stanwich died trying to defend your honor. A true British gentleman."

"And Uncas?" Anne asked.

"He ran off." Sam shrugged. "No one will miss an old Indian."

"What do you want Anne to do?" Father asked.

"Disappear," Sam said, resuming his pacing. "She's distraught. Preferred to grieve with her relations in the countryside. I'll handle the details in Boston."

"Anne did no wrong," Father said.

"But, she's a woman." Sam pushed right into Father's face.

"Yes, I know."

"With a woman's wickedness. She might have provoked the entire incident."

"My daughter did no wrong." Father clenched his teeth so tightly Anne was afraid one might fall out.

"Tell that to William Cunningham. He has no love of women or provincials," Sam replied.

"And he has a tremendous sum at risk," Anne added, twisting a strand of hair around her fingers.

"As you alone well know," Sam chortled with a sinister glare.

"Mr. Cunningham does not strike me as a man who forgives, or forgets, Father."

"I will see to my daughter's journey."

"And you will stay here in Boston with us, William," Sam said. "After all, it is your name on the warehouse lease."

Father hung his head, avoiding Anne's eyes. "I have no plans to depart."

"Excellent," Sam said, drawing his cloak over his shoulders. "Then I will take my leave."

"Good day, sir." Father tended the fire rather than see Sam to the door.

"Ah, I almost forgot." Sam reached into his pocket. "I'm sure Major Stanwich would have wanted you to have these." A sneer curled his lips as he handed her Geoffrey's gorget and his half of the coin signifying their engagement.

She understood his meaning completely. *This is all I will get.*

"Thank you." She fondled the silver pieces in her lap. They would have to suffice.

Anne and Father stared at each other for several long seconds after Sam Hale had left.

"I'm in his debt, but you have a chance to start anew," Father said, patting her shoulder.

"You're his hostage, Father, so he owns both of us. That's why he's letting me leave."

"I'll be fine, dear. You have done more than I could ask of any daughter." Father sat next to her on the bench. The fire waned to a flickering glow but still warmed their backs.

"Where should I go?" she asked.

"New York, of course," Father replied. He found a quill and paper, and wrote a brief note, signing it with a flourish. "Here is an introduction to Nehemiah Longfellow. He owns a shop on Long Island and might be in need of a seamstress."

"I shall travel alone?"

"Caleb will guide you."

"Caleb?"

"His letter arrived last week. He plans to enter Boston this evening." Father smiled sadly. "He planned to surprise you on your wedding day."

***

We were scavenging at the base of Bush-Tree Hill on the far end of the Dorchester Peninsula, two miles from camp, when Hercules stumbled upon a man's body, half-buried under a pile of snow and pine needles. Elvin helped him drag it into the open, their eyes wide with disbelief. Little John Bell ran to see, but turned away in disgust, retching all over a tree stump. The torso had been stabbed repeatedly, blood coagulated across chest and throat, and the initials GR carved into his forehead.

"That's old Elias Goode," Elvin gagged. "A fisherman. Asa and I bought eels from him last year."

Did Asa do this?

"Queen's Rangers," Stephen Hempstead declared, pointing his musket at Goode's forehead. That's their mark."

"Bastards," I muttered, horrified, but secretly relieved that the murderers were not from our army.

"From the looks of the body, they killed him recently too," Stephen added.

"Maybe they wanted his dinghy," Elvin chipped in.

"He won't be needing his boots anymore, will he?" Hercules asked, his feet still wrapped only in rags and shreds of leather.

I had tried, in vain, to secure footwear from the commissary for Hercules, the only shoeless man in my troop. "No, he won't," I replied, turning my head as Hercules removed the dead man's boots.

With the ground too frozen to dig a proper grave, I instructed my troop to gather twigs and stones to bury the mutilated body. I marked the grave with a crudely constructed cross and said a brief prayer. For the march home, I deployed Tom Peacock's squadron as scouts flanking the main column, in case any Queen's Rangers were still lurking about. Was Caleb Wheaton among them? How would Anne react to the atrocity?

I reported to headquarters as soon as I got back to camp. Colonel Webb indicated he would notify the next of kin and send out a patrol to search for the Rangers.

William Hull sat at his field desk, writing furiously, when I returned to our cabin. Hull jumped up, a broad smile creasing his face. "The war council's overruled our commander-in-chief once again. There will be no attack on Boston."

"A damn shame. The British have just attacked us right here." I recounted the grisly discovery out in Dorchester.

"I wager old man Goode stumbled upon a ring of spies. The Crown has sympathizers all over our camps," Hull replied. "They were probably trying to get back to Boston with word of our attack."

"A possibility, I'm sure."

"I heard Washington was livid when his plan was rejected," Hull returned to his favorite subject. "After waiting all winter for the Back Bay to freeze solid, he couldn't believe that his generals still thought the enterprise too dangerous."

"We don't have enough powder for a full scale assault anyway," I said, stripping off my soggy gloves and warming my hands by the stove. I was pleasantly surprised at my inner calm, the stewardship of my men foremost in mind.

"Washington has bluffed the British, but he can't fool his own army," Hull said, joining me at the stove.

"We have Knox's cannons. Washington will find a way to put them to good use."

"I heard a rumor that we're going to haul them up to Dorchester Heights."

"We were reconnoitering in the vicinity this morning. It would be a grand location. The city and the entire British fleet would be within range." I sat down and began to clean the barrel of my pistol. It had misfired when I shot at a wild turkey earlier in the day. "Howe would have to evacuate immediately or come out and fight."

"I don't see how we could get those big guns up there," Hull replied. "The slopes of Dorchester are steep and in plain sight. The British would cut us to ribbons."

A rap on the door snapped us to attention. Colonel Webb entered without waiting for an invitation.

"As you were, captains. New orders. Just in," he said, withdrawing a scroll from his pocket. "We're going to gather brushwood and stones to build fascines here in camp. Starting this evening. We have no time to waste. Washington wants them ready to move to Dorchester in two days' time."

"The commander-in-chief has a new plan then?" I asked, hopeful that my days as drillmaster and earth mover would soon be coming to an end.

"Yes. Quite daring. And quite brilliant," Webb replied.

CHAPTER 12 - MARCH 1776

*"My God, these fellows have done more work in one night
than I could make my army do in three months."*
General William Howe
Boston
Morning of March 5, 1776

Anne didn't want Caleb to see her cry, but tears insisted on trickling down her cheeks. She brushed them away and leveled her head.

"Sit still, sister," he said, scissors in hand. "This is for your own good."

She closed her eyes, listening to the sound of Caleb's shearing while imagining her auburn locks floating to the floor. *I should be a married woman, preparing to sail with my beloved to our home in England.*

"Done," Caleb said, stepping back to examine his handiwork. He handed a looking-glass to Anne, but she shook her head, the knowledge of a shorn scalp punishment enough.

She looked instead at her brother, sixteen years old but a man now. Six months living off the land with the Queen's Rangers had hardened him. A winter beard burnished his cheeks with a coarse scarlet stubble; hair fell wild across his shoulders; biceps rippled; blue eyes cut like steel. And he stunk worse than a skunk. But, she loved him, and, more important, trusted him. She was as much a Loyalist now as he was. And they would likely live, or die, together.

Caleb rummaged about the keeping room until he found a linen tablecloth. He squinted, measuring her with his tailor's eye, then sliced the cloth in half. "You can bundle your chest with this."

"I haven't got much in the way of tits," she replied.

"True," he chuckled. "But we can't take any chances."

Anne retired to her room to dress. She removed her shift, swaddled her breasts, and reached for her petticoats. *Men don't wear petticoats.*

"I thought you might need these," Caleb appeared at her door with woolen pants, hunting shirt, boots and green jacket.

She fumbled to cover up, but he shook his head with a bemused smile. "Not what a Ranger would do."

She wrapped three silver coins, including her engagement pieces, in a kerchief, then tucked the kerchief into a pair of socks. Finally, she bundled the socks into a shirt and stashed it under the tea, hard cheese and biscuits in her satchel. Not much else to take. They would be traveling light and fast with little opportunity to change or even wash. She would probably end up smelling like Caleb soon enough. What a horrible thought, she laughed to herself.

Her fingers wrapped around Geoffrey's gorget, safe in her pocket. Tears welled again but she fought them back. She took one last look around her room. Father promised to deliver her trunk to New York whenever he arrived. And she could dress as a proper female once again.

She turned around at the top of the stairs, hurrying back to her bedroom. *Cato.* She couldn't trust it to Father.

Her first steps dressed as a man were tentative, but Caleb nodded in approval. Encouraged, she dared the looking-glass. The clothing fit as well as could be expected, Caleb had skill with a needle, but what remained of her hair was an abomination. He had left her with only a pubic patch of tight curls on top of her head.

"Here you go," he said, offering his beaver hat, complete with long tail. "You'll need this to stay warm." Caleb had done his best, Anne duly noted, as she fitted the hat over her ears and returned to the glass. "Much better, sister."

"You mean brother, don't you?" she asked.

"Yes, brother." Caleb smiled. He reached into his pack for a muffler, unwrapping it to display a dozen coins. "Father gave me silver before he left for the store this morning. To help pay for our journey."

"How thoughtful."

"What name should I call you?" Caleb asked.

"Silas."

"Grandfather's name. A good choice."

"One last item," Anne said, reaching into the cupboard for her pistol. She tucked it into her waistband. "I had hoped to retire it permanently."

"You look quite the wilderness warrior now," Caleb replied as he slung his musket over his shoulder. "Ready to move out?"

A full moon waited impatiently on the horizon for the sun to complete its day's work. Anne sensed an early thaw on the breeze, giving hope to the end of this dreadful winter, but the streets were still ice-hard. They marched out of the North End but barely reached the Commons before the ground shuddered from a thunderous artillery barrage.

Anne froze, her senses assaulted by the deafening roar, the flashes of fire, the acrid smell of gunpowder. Caleb ploughed on until a cannonball smacked into the pasture thirty yards ahead, burrowing a hole wide enough to swallow him. He wheeled around and scampered back to his sister.

Rooted in place, they watched the newly installed battery on Mt. Whoredom return fire, the ten-man crews scampering to reload the big guns. Windows shattered, a child wailed, a woman screamed. Another ball whined overhead. Two more pounded the Commons. The rebel gunners were finding their range, the intensity of their shelling unrelenting. The long-dreaded assault on Boston had likely begun.

A company of regulars double-timed towards the breastworks on the Neck - straight into the teeth of the cannonade. A lieutenant gave them a 'what in damnation' glare as he passed.

"Turn around," Caleb screamed into Anne's ear, pointing back the way they had come.

She shook her head, snapping out of her stupor. Her life would be in just as much danger at home if Sam, or even worse William Cunningham, discovered she was still in Boston. She pointed up Beacon Hill towards Geoffrey's mansion, seemingly out of range of the rebel guns. "Follow me."

They slogged up the road, heads down as if in silent prayer. Caleb had to slow down twice to wait for her. She sucked in large gulps of air before climbing the steps to the front door.

Henry answered the knocker. While his cheeks had sallowed over the long winter, his blue eyes still glowed with youthful exuberance. A dozen soldiers appeared to have set up camp in the parlor behind him. "What do you want?" he growled. "We have nothing for beggars here."

Anne stepped back, shocked at his disdain. "Henry, it's me."

"Who?"

She brushed the splatter off her jacket and doffed her hat. "Me."

"Miss Anne? What in heaven's name…" A smile softened Henry's countenance.

"This is Caleb, my brother. Can we come in?"

Eyes still wide in disbelief, Henry waved them into the foyer, by habit taking Anne's coat from her shoulders. "Spruce up, men," he shouted. "There's a lady in the house."

"A lady?" Francis, a portly private, wearing only breeches and boots, replied as she approached the hearth. "I don't see no lady."

***

I waited in line on the outskirts of Roxbury, along with twelve hundred soldiers and 350 oxen tethered to flat-bed wagons, for the last rays of sunlight to peter out. Our monumental mission was to ferry cannons, balls, gunpowder, and earthworks to the summit of Dorchester Heights before dawn. General Washington wanted the British to wake up to the sight of a newly constructed, impregnable fortress looming over Boston.

I kicked the frosted ground, barely denting it. Although the temperature had finally climbed, ice still carpeted the track. A good surface for moving heavy loads. Even better, fog swirled upward, bathing the lowlands in a spectral mist and obscuring all but the closest wagons from view. If I couldn't see the caravan, it might be invisible to the British sentries as well. Until it was too late.

The ear-splitting boom of artillery resounded from both sides of the harbor. In my six months in camp, I had never heard a barrage this intense, let alone be trapped in the middle of it. A battery of Knox's big guns positioned on Cobble Hill and Lechmere Point launched balls at Boston, while Howe's artillerymen responded as hoped for, lashing out in the direction of Cambridge. If the British aimed their cannons southward, they might destroy the caravan before it got rolling.

The Continental bombardment was supposed to last all night, providing further cover for the army's movements. British spies had undoubtedly reported that the rebels were short on gunpowder, so a lengthy barrage might also sow doubt in Howe's mind. General Washington was throwing all his chips on the table.

I nudged Sergeant Hempstead to inspect the wagon wheels, wrapped in straw to insure a quiet which hardly seemed necessary now. Hercules Field, proudly booted, whispered in the ear of a restless beast; Tom Peacock whelped a barking hound, sending it whimpering back towards camp; Little John Bell, his musical instruments replaced by a sack of biscuits, paraded up and down the line parceling out the evening's rations. I sent Asher Wright ahead to check in with Colonel Webb's staff.

I was excited to be part of a major military operation for the first time, even if I wasn't in the vanguard. General John Thomas, a Massachusetts doctor and commander of the Army's southern flank, had hand-picked the units who would lead the way. They were already on Dorchester Neck, setting up bundles of hay to screen the caravan from British eyes. They would be first up to the summit as well, keeping a look-out for enemy activity in Boston.

Of course, if my regiment had stayed on Winter Hill, our role might be different. Four thousand men under the command of Generals Putnam, Greene, and Sullivan were waiting there to board bateaux to launch an amphibious assault on the city. Washington hoped that Howe would be so incensed at the rebel's fortress atop Dorchester Heights that he would attack it, leaving Boston vulnerable. The Continental force would land on the far side of the city and fight its way across to the shoreline opposite Dorchester.

According to the map provided by Princess, I knew our men would have to overcome a maze of narrow streets, steep hills, and well-fortified barricades. Why would Washington take this risk? What if the weather turned and his army was stranded in the harbor or stymied in the city? How had he convinced his council of generals to agree?

The surprise assault would either wipe out the British army in a single stroke, or decimate our own forces, or possibly both. William Hull thought Washington was going mad with frustration, architecting complex plans that required more coordination than his green troops and the unpredictable winter weather would allow.

My troops stirred, sensing departure time at hand. At last, the order to move out whispered down the line. Hull's company, immediately ahead, inched forward then gathered momentum - as much momentum as oxen pulling wagons loaded with cannons could generate. The men, dressed in wilderness browns and greens, trudged behind the wagons, like a procession of monks heading to midnight mass.

We were out on Dorchester Neck now, fully exposed. Between the mist, the muffled wheels and the silent men, the caravan looked like the Continental Army was stealing the precious cargo, rather than delivering it.

Peering over the protective bales of hay, I saw dots of orange, the enemy's campfires, glowing across the water. An ox bellowed as the procession started uphill. John Bell stumbled and fell, sliding in a spray of scree. I cringed, expecting balls to fly any second. But the British remained blissfully oblivious.

Three quarters of the way up the slope, the fog lifted, revealing a full moon and our army's earthen walls under construction on the summit. The cannonade continued from both sides of the harbor. Fiery trails arced across the starry sky.

We lumbered over the crest, the ridgeline a beehive of activity. General Thomas himself directed the placement of the guns. Joining a construction crew, we raised ten foot chandeliers and stuffed our fascines between them to create a makeshift wall. We dug trenches, tossing the icy sod upward to fortify the breastworks, and filled barrels with rocks to roll downhill into climbing redcoats.

By ten o'clock, the fortress was complete. Flanked by Wright and Hempstead, I took my place on the ramparts. Dorchester Heights rose over one hundred feet, taller than Bunker Hill. Only Beacon Hill was higher. Houselights still burned near its summit, taunting our cannoneers who obviously could not reach them. The rest of Boston, cloaked in darkness, spread out before us. Now came the hard part - waiting for dawn and General Howe's revenge.

***

Henry's introduction ended Anne's charade before it actually began. She knew several of the men in Geoffrey's company by sight if not by name, and vice-versa, so it would have been difficult to fool them for long anyway, despite her massacred locks.

"Hello, Francis," she said, removing her cap.

"Miss Anne? Is that really you?"

"We heard you was gone to the countryside," Richard, a bristly-whiskered sergeant said, jumping up to greet her.

"We're on our way," she replied honestly. "With all the rebel activity, my brother Caleb thought I should travel in disguise." Caleb nodded as the attention shifted to him, a mere provincial Queen's Ranger among all the regulars.

The men gave Caleb a quick inspection, duly noting the family resemblance, before gathering in a tight circle around her, offering their condolences and laments.

"He was a good man. Tough but fair."

"Pleased as a peach to be back in command again. We won't see another officer like him for a long while."

"You was the apple of his eye."

"Died with his sword in his hand. Defending his lady's honor, I might add."

"From his own countrymen, sadly." Richard, the elder statesman of the platoon, chipped in, sensing Anne's discomfort. "Now, let's give the lady some space. She's had quite a shock."

"A seat would be most welcome," she said, hoping to provide as few details as possible about the true circumstances of her fiancé's death. The men did not need to know of Sam's warehouse or her role in cataloguing its contents.

Francis, now shirted, swept his coat, once a bright scarlet like Geoffrey's, off a chair to make room. From the looks of the detritus on the table, the men had clearly helped themselves to the mansion's cellar and food stock. Henry started to apologize, but she dismissed him with a wave.

The wail of an infant cut short any further conversation. She hadn't noticed the ragdoll-thin girl about her own age, suckling a baby on the floor in the corner of the room. The mother, her raven hair modestly capped, glared at Anne with the ferocity of a she-wolf protecting her cub.

"That's Jemma and Francis, Jr.," Richard provided the introduction. "She usually camps with the baggage, but we thought it'd be alright if she joined us tonight."

"Of course," Anne replied, pleased at the diversion. "She can stay as long as she likes."

"We won't be here long," Henry said. "General Howe's had his fill of Boston. We'll be moving out by land or sea any day now."

The boom of a cannon punctuated Henry's comments.

"Time to teach the rebels to respect their king," Richard said.

"Bunch of bloody farmers think they're better'n us. Don't want to pay any taxes. King George won't stand for that."

"Hang the lot of them, I say."

"Here, here."

Despite Anne's protestations, Henry insisted on clearing Francis and his family from the master bedroom. Jemma refused to look at her as she bundled up their meager belongings with one hand while holding their baby with the other.

That could be me one day. Not anytime soon, however. Her monthly had flowed last week right on schedule, a disappointment at the time but a blessing in disguise now.

Remaining fully dressed, Anne shared the big bed with Caleb, just like their toddler days. The steady throb of the bombardment rocked her to sleep.

The bleat of a bugle woke her just after dawn. She rolled over, noting immediately that the cannons had silenced and Caleb was gone. She peeked down the stairs. The parlor bustled with the nervous energy and outhouse odors of men preparing for battle.

Caleb was topping up ammunition boxes, nimbly pouring gunpowder and tying off the tip of the cartridge, while the regulars donned their uniforms. She wandered into the kitchen where Jemma stirred porridge in a kettle on the hearth. Her son slept on a blanket nearby. When he awoke with a mighty cry, she took the spoon and nodded for the girl to look after her baby. The men filed in, trenchers in hand.

"Damn rebels. They fortified Dorchester Heights last night," Richard muttered. "Our sentries must have been bloody sleeping. Every ship in the harbor's in artillery range now."

"We muster on Long Wharf in an hour," Henry said.

"Howe can't let that fort stand," Francis added. "He has to attack."

"Getting up that slope will be hell," Richard said, shaking his head as he dipped his finger in the porridge to test its temperature. "Then we'll have to breach those damn walls."

Anne cringed as she looked at Jemma and little Francis who had fallen back to sleep on her shoulder. Howe had tried the same tactic on Breed's Hill. And she had seen the results first-hand.

***

After a futile attempt at sleep, I returned to the breastworks just after dawn, two steaming cups of coffee in hand. "Your turn to grab some shut-eye. I'll wake you if anything happens," I said to William Hull, handing him a cup.

We stared silently at the panorama unfolding below. The morning sun broke through a light cloud cover burning off the last traces of fog. The temperature remained relatively mild, the breeze light. The red and white striped flag flying overhead hung limp.

"I can't believe we did it," Hull said, sipping his brew. "Right under Howe's nose."

"You have to give Washington credit."

"Partial credit. We've gained the advantage, but the battle has yet to begin."

"Look." I pointed at the scarlet tentacles streaming from the city towards the wharves. "The redcoats are starting to form."

"I'd give ten pounds to see their faces this morning."

The boom of cannon from Boston's south battery halted our conversation. I held my breath, waiting for the ball to land. It crashed into the hillside, thirty yards downhill. Two more followed with the same result.

"Their guns can't aim this high!" I pounded my now empty cup on the woodwork in excitement.

"General Howe will have to come get us," Hull replied.

"Let him come."

"He's here! He's here!" Little John Bell ran up and down the ramparts. "General Washington's in the fort."

Sure enough, the commander-in-chief rode into view on his stallion, flanked by two aides. He wore a royal blue jacket, black cockade in his hat and short sword on his hip. The sunlight glinted off his gold buttons. With no action imminent from the British, the men turned to try to hear the words of their leader.

"It is the fifth of March…avenge the death of your brethren."

I couldn't discern the entire speech, but these phrases echoed up and down the line. March 5, 1770 – The Boston Massacre. The first shots the British fired against the good citizens of Boston, leaving five dead. My men responded with a rousing huzzah as Washington trotted off.

The red mass coagulated at the waterfront. Transports bobbed in their moorings waiting for the troops to board. Spectators checkerboarded the surrounding hills, anticipating the battle. The breeze picked up, unfurling the colors of the thirteen rebellious colonies.

"When do you think they'll launch?" Hull asked, scanning the horizon, shivering as the temperature once again plummeted.

"With the afternoon tide," I replied. With any luck, Boston will then be vulnerable to surprise attack from Cambridge. Washington's plan could work to perfection.

***

Anne wanted to leave Boston immediately, but Caleb wouldn't miss the fireworks. Sam Hale, like everyone else would be preoccupied with the coming battle, he reasoned; no one would notice them. Nevertheless, she wrapped her chest and donned her beaver cap to be safe.

They found a good viewing spot on Beacon Hill, settling on a blanket to savor the sunshine until the action began. Several "ladies" whose dress, or lack thereof, suggested previous employment on Mt. Whoredom wandered over to sit nearby. Caleb sipped from a flask which he offered around to his newfound friends.

"My turn?" Anne asked, when it had completed the circle.

"It's whiskey," he said dismissively.

"I didn't think it was ginger beer," she whispered, yanking the flask from his hand and downing a hearty swallow. Caleb gaped as she wiped the fiery liquid from her lips with the back of her hand. "There's a lot you don't know about me," she added in a louder voice. Too late, she realized her voice gave away her identity.

"You tell him, sister." A buxom, freckle-faced whore clapped in delight. "Don't fret, we can keep a secret."

"They're off," Caleb jumped up, oblivious to the girl-talk, pointing to the harbor where the first transports eased away from the pier. "Sergeant Richard told me they're going to assemble on Castle Island and launch the assault from there."

The breeze, gathering force, sent Anne's beaver dancing up the hillside. She chased after the cap, a bit of a wobble in her gait, to the delight of her fellow spectators.

"They'll be too late," Miss Freckles said, studying an angry gray mass of clouds forming behind them as if she were a ship's captain. "There's a nor'easter coming."

"How do you know?" Caleb asked, surly from the alcohol.

"Me husband was a gunnery mate on the *Rose*. Until he drowned." She grabbed the flask from Caleb and swigged. "The bastard."

"What would a woman know…" Caleb muttered so only Anne could hear. The transports were halfway to Castle Island when they appeared to lose their way.

"The wind's tossing them like babes." Miss Freckles appeared intent on providing a running commentary. "It's only going to get worse."

Within minutes, the sky overhead had darkened as if God in his wisdom had drawn a curtain. The wind shrieked; the temperature dropped; rain, then sleet, pelted down, but no one left the hillside. The lead transport crashed into the shoreline near Windmill Point, the troops piling onto the beach where Anne and Geoffrey had picnicked a lifetime ago. And where he had given me that cursed pistol.

"The boys ain't getting to Dorchester today," Freckles concluded.

"They might need some cheering up then," one of her cohorts chortled before the women bundled up as best they could and stumbled off downhill.

Anne and Caleb trudged uphill, back to the mansion. Her jacket was sodden and her lips blue by the time they reached the portico. Jemma was tending the fire and Francis, Jr at the same time. Anne made Caleb turn around while she stripped to the waist and hung her jacket and shirt up to dry. Topless, she skipped up the stairs to the master bedroom.

Several of Geoffrey's shirts were still hanging in the closet. She hesitated for only a second. The shirt still smelled of him, but it was warm and dry. He would have wanted her to wear it.

The men piled in an hour later, peeling off wet clothes and gathering their belongings. Hailstones pinged the roof; the gale uprooted a tree in the front yard.

"We'll tarry here long enough to dry out," Sergeant Richard said. "Then we're off to the barracks. General Howe wants to launch again at first light."

"We'll not launch anywhere if this storm doesn't subside," Francis, Sr replied, taking the infant from his wife.

"No matter, we're due at our bunks for roll call. For God and King."

"I'll come too," Caleb volunteered. "You'll want dry cartridges."

"No need," the sergeant replied. "Howe learned a lesson on Breed's Hill. No stopping to reload our muskets this time. We're going up with bayonets fixed."

Francis clasped his wife's hand and tried to lead her to the stairs. "We have time," he said softly.

Jemma shook her head. "Not while the baby's awake."

Anne stepped forward, taking Francis Jr from his father, cuddling the tiny bundle against her shoulder. "Go ahead. Use the bedroom. I'll tend to him."

"You're sure?" Jemma asked, her eyes circling the parlor. No one paid them any mind.

Anne nodded. "A soldier should leave home content."

Francis winked. Privacy was a rare treat. "We'll name her Anne."

***

The dawn brought light to Dorchester Heights, albeit in muted gray tones, but it brought no warmth. The Continental Army had neither time nor materials to build shelters atop the ridge, completely exposed to the raging storm.

Standing guard, I swore at the wind, the sleet, the cold, and the British in that order. Icicles leaked from my nose; my cheeks were frosted red; I barely had feeling in my fingers, and my toes could well have been frostbitten. Otherwise I was ready for battle.

But there would be no battle in this weather. Boston was still. No mass of redcoats gathered at the wharves; no seamen unfurled sails or dipped oars in the whitecapped waters.

"This might help," William Hull said, pouring a dram of whiskey into my cup.

"Hot coffee would be better," I replied.

"And a nice plump partridge on the spit."

We laughed. We were young, alive and in command of the Heights.

"To our commander-in-chief," I toasted.

"Yes, to General Washington." Hull raised his cup. "May he always be this fortunate."

"Fortunate?"

"This storm is a blessing from the heavens. Howe can't attack Dorchester, so Washington can't attack Boston. Hundreds, possibly thousands, of lives will be spared."

"Howe will come tomorrow, or the next day," I said, stamping my frozen feet to stop my shivers.

"Let's pray General Howe is not as rash as our own fearless leader."

***

Anne woke to the hearty wails of little Francis, his fuzzy head peeking out from under the weighty quilts. Jemma, sleeping on the far side of the big bed, stirred and gathered the baby to her breast, quieting him. The sky was gray but brightening, although rain still plinked the window. Anne stood, bracing against the cold. She stirred the embers in the hearth, trying to remember the last time she had slept this late.

Where was Caleb? He had slept on the floor at the foot of their bed but must have gone out before they had woken. Downstairs was even colder. The storm had tossed a tree branch through a kitchen window.

Anne cleared the broken glass but there was no way to repair the damage. She closed the kitchen door, lugged two logs, each as big as her leg, into the parlor fireplace, and struck the flint until the tinder sparked. She poked the logs and blew gently on the flame coaxing the wood to cackle.

Returning to the kitchen, shivering, she found a teapot, filled it from a jug of water, and took it back to the parlor to boil over the slowly building fire. The tea service brought back memories of evenings with Geoffrey. She lingered in the past for several minutes, her final luxury of the morning.

Jemma, holding little Francis, hobbled down the steps, her belongings in tow. "Thank ye for your hospitality, but we best be going," she said.

"And where are you going in this weather?" Anne asked.

"To the camp. We best not be late."

"Late for what?"

"For evacuation. We'll all be leaving shortly."

"No, *we're* not. *We're* going to attack Dorchester Heights as soon as the storm passes."

Jemma shook her head.

"How do you know?" Anne pushed.

"Can't you smell it?" Jemma sniffed the air. "The bread. They wouldn't be baking so much if we weren't leaving. For good."

Anne tried to convince her to stay until her husband returned, but Jemma was adamant. She had to reclaim her place in the baggage train if she wanted to be sure of a berth on board ship.

"Godspeed, then," Anne said.

"To you as well." Jemma bumped into Caleb as she left.

Her brother was chock full of vim and vigor. "We sharpened bayonets all morning. The rebels will soon get a taste of British steel."

Anne could see the outline of the rebel fortress across the harbor. It appeared to have grown even more imposing overnight. She prayed for the safety of all the men she knew who might soon be engaged in mortal combat, and their women.

***

Rain pounded Dorchester Heights, softening the turf, creating swamps of slush that swallowed wagon wheels. I leaned into the caisson, loaded with eighteen pound cannon balls. Parrish, Peacock, and Field grunted beside me, while Hempstead led several men on the far side of the wagon. Little John Bell played a lively tune on his fife, encouraging the team to inch forward.

General Thomas pointed towards the battery in need of ammunition. General Washington rode up and down the line, inspecting the fortifications. The Continentals had used the weather delay to strengthen the redoubts, adding more firepower and barricades. The presence of our senior officers, out in front despite the storm, boosted morale.

After delivering our load, I gazed down on Boston once again. Where was Anne? If the Continentals had to fight their way through the city, no quarter would be given to soldiers or civilians. Only God could protect her. I saw a mass of redcoats on the Commons and in the streets leading down to the water, but there was no movement, no sign of an imminent assault. Was Howe losing his nerve?

***

Cannons on both sides were silent that morning, their fury spent. Anne cleaned the mansion, upstairs and down, as best she could, the activity providing a much-needed outlet for her energy - and grief. She and Caleb left just before noon. Again, she wanted to escape Boston, but Caleb would not hear of it.

Despite the rain, he dragged them down Beacon Hill and along Summer Street until Windmill Point and Griffin's Wharf were in view. Companies of regulars lined the streets, nervously awaiting orders. Dorchester Heights loomed across the water. "I want to see the rebel blood flow," Caleb said, as if testing her loyalty or her squeamishness.

Neither would be an issue, Anne thought. But the quiet on the docks was worrisome, as was the paucity of spectators. The hillsides were strangely vacant.

A flurry of activity at the head of the quay attracted her attention. A messenger arrived. Officers conferred. A major broke away, mounting his horse and galloping uphill towards the Commons.

Within minutes, pandemonium erupted. The neat lines of regulars disintegrated. Townspeople, all fellow Loyalists, poured from their homes, despair etched on their faces. A rebel battery atop the Heights fired a single ball which splashed harmlessly into the water. Above the ramparts, rebel hats flew into the air, while shouts of celebration rained down on the city.

Word spread like Greek fire. General Howe had called off the attack and ordered his army to evacuate. He would negotiate a peaceful surrender to General Washington or burn the city to the ground.

The siege was over. Boston had fallen. The rebels, the rabble, had won. Caleb cried.

***

I hugged Stephen Hempstead. My men downed their daily ration of rum in a single swallow and went looking for more. Little John banged out Yankee Doodle on his drum over and over. Cheers of huzzah echoed throughout the fortress.

The troops looked for their leader, but General Washington had returned to his headquarters in Cambridge shortly after the British dispersed. I knew our commander-in-chief frowned on excessive drinking but would not want to dampen the army's spirits today. Captains, like myself, would have to contain the men.

Later that afternoon, I found William Hull, alone at a corner of the redoubt, sipping from his canteen.

"To victory," Hull slurred, offering a toast.

"Yes, to victory," I replied. "And to General Washington."

"To General Washington," Hull acknowledged with another splash of rum.

"Howe went quietly, didn't he? As if he never wanted this fight."

"Some will surely say that," Hull replied, finishing off his drink. "But the war is not over. The redcoats will return, and you'll get your chance to fight them."

I looked out at the harbor. An armada of ships, flying British flags, were anchored just out of range. "Will Howe be able to evacuate troops and civilians?"

Hull shrugged. "I'd hate to be a Loyalist in Boston after the redcoats leave."

I remembered the Sons of Neptune's rampages in New London. Vengeance will be brutal. I offered a silent prayer for the safety of Anne and her new husband, and her family, even Caleb.

***

Despite a pounding headache, Anne roused Caleb at dawn the next morning. They had helped themselves to the last three bottles of Geoffrey's claret last night, passing out on the divan in the parlor. She pissed into the chamber pot in the front hall closet, already full from the reek of it. A welcoming gift for the rebels upon their return.

While her brother dressed, she went upstairs to the master bedroom for a final nostalgic tour. The four poster bed, the cozy hearth, the closet still filled with Geoffrey's clothes…this was supposed to be her life. She cradled the gorget in her pocket. It was all she would ever have of him, besides the memories. And his shirt.

Passing the looking-glass, Anne laughed at her herself, clumsily dressed as a man. She should have washed this morning but there was no time to heat a pot of water. *Do I smell like a man?* Perhaps Geoffrey's lingering scent might help her disguise.

"We have to go to Wheatons," Anne said, returning to the parlor. "Father will need help preparing for evacuation."

"I thought you would want to leave immediately," Caleb replied, buttoning his breeches.

"Our inventory is too valuable to leave for the rebels. We would face bankruptcy if we lost it all."

"Bankruptcy?"

"Father has debts to pay."

"Father has debts?" Caleb was not the brightest candle in the chandelier, but the implications finally registered. "What about me? I stand to inherit those debts."

"Then you'd better follow me."

Wheatons was not far from Beacon Hill, but the muddy streets churned with soldiers and civilians in great haste. They followed the flow which seemed to be heading towards Wing's Lane anyway. She noticed people carrying household possessions – linens, woolens, crockery, silver. A muscled African wearing a red muffler and cocked hat, too warmly dressed to be a slave, pushed a cart laden with smithy's tools. The caravan queued up in front of Wheatons storefront. Two regulars guarded the door.

She nudged Caleb, tilting her head towards the Black.

"What's going on?" her brother asked him.

"General Howe's orders. Any goods that might be of value to the rebels must be delivered here or destroyed."

"Why not take them aboard ship?"

"No room."

"No room?" Caleb was incredulous. "The greatest navy in the world is short of space?"

"I heard they's dumping barrels of pork into the harbor."

Sam's warehouse, Anne thought. He'll lose a pretty penny there. "Are you going to get paid for your goods?" she asked the Black, pointing to his cart.

"Excuse me, ma'am?"

"My brother's got a high voice. Sounds like a girl sometime," Caleb jumped in.

"Supposed to."

"Paid in silver?" Caleb asked.

The Black shrugged, pushing his wagon as the line inched forward.

They circled around to the front of the store. It was a frenzied scene that could have easily turned into a riot if the redcoats had not been present. She could see Father inside, inspecting goods and signing papers. Sam Hale and Sheriff Loring were at his side.

She ducked, pulling Caleb away. A man, a lawyer or magistrate from the looks of his wig and fine clothes, exited Wheatons, cursing as he walked their way.

"Excuse me, sir," Anne intercepted him. "What recompense did you receive for your goods?"

"Paper. A worthless piece of parchment signed by the Provost Marshal." He tossed it into the street and stomped, sending a spray of mud in Anne's direction. "About the only thing it's good for is to wipe my arse."

That's the scheme, Anne thought. Sam will use his black market contacts to move the goods after the evacuation. From the looks of the loot piling up in the store, he, and his syndicate, would easily recover their losses on the food.

"Are we going to look in on Father?" Caleb asked.

"No need," she replied. "He's in good hands. We should go before it's too late."

As they hiked out of Boston, she plotted the route to New York. "I want to pass through New London."

Caleb shook his head. "There's nothing there for us anymore."

***

I watched Boston disintegrate from the ramparts of Dorchester Heights. On March 9th, Howe launched a furious, but futile, artillery barrage before agreeing to terms of surrender. The Continentals would allow the British Army and all Loyalists to evacuate unharmed, while the British would preserve whatever structures remained standing in the city.

Supplies and weaponry were another matter, however. Redcoats spiked their cannons and wheeled them into the sea. Foodstuffs and furnishings floated on the swells; horses, cows and pigs wandered aimlessly on the shore. Townspeople crammed onto the first brigs to enter the harbor, choosing to wait for evacuation day on board rather than risk getting left behind.

Washington had hand-picked five hundred soldiers, all immune to smallpox, to enter Boston once the British had gone. He would not risk infection sweeping through his army. In a gesture of modesty, he selected Major General Artemas Ward, a Massachusetts man, to lead these men across the Neck in triumph.

As the birthplace of the revolution, Boston had tremendous psychological significance, but held little strategic military value. New York, sitting at the mouth of the mighty Hudson River, was much more crucial. If the British could control the Hudson from Canada to New York, they could isolate New England and split the colonies in half. Accordingly, Congress demanded that New York be defended at all costs.

The Connecticut troops were among the first to leave Massachusetts, departing before the British had even evacuated. We would fast-march to New London and board ship there for the rest of the journey. Colonel Webb's 19th regiment would now be part of a newly-formed command under General William Heath, a Massachusetts man boasting battlefield experience at Lexington and Concord. Washington wanted his best men in New York to complete its fortifications before Howe and his redcoats arrived.

Although we had not fired a musket or faced a bayonet charge, the Continental Army's conquest of Boston stirred my soul. Asa and Princess' conspiracy, whatever it was, had failed. I couldn't wait to teach the bloody-backs another lesson.

***

Robert Rogers watched in disbelief as a paunchy middle-aged man, cheeks a bright scarlet from exertion, huffed down to the beach near Windmill Point, tossed his cloak into the reeds and ran into the sea. After a few splashing strides, he dove into the swells in a laughable effort to swim out to a British transport anchored in the harbor. The man lasted a dozen strokes before he flailed, sputtered and submerged, resurfacing only once. He had heard that the Loyalists of Boston were fearful of reprisal, but had not expected insanity.

"Damn fool," Asa Cobb said, shaking his head. He pointed to a crude map of Boston that Princess had prepared for them. "Wheatons is on Wing's Lane."

He wasn't pleased to be traveling with the Black, but Princess had promised him a share in the profits. The journey into Boston had been child's play. The barricades on the Neck were formidable, but unmanned, as the regulars were already on board their evacuation vessels.

Rogers led the way up Summer Street, detouring around another deserted breastwork. Scavengers and looters prowled the streets. Other residents wandered about with the ghoulish stare of the walking dead.

"There it is," Rogers said. Wheatons was hard to miss. A squadron of redcoats guarded a treasure trove of household goods spilling out into the street.

William Wheaton quickly ushered them inside. "It's all yours," he said, spreading his arms wide. "If you have the silver."

Rogers nodded, and began counting coins, Spanish pieces of eight, from the purse Princess had given him. He stacked them in three columns on the table while Asa stood by his side, pistol holstered on one hip and a cutlass scabbarded on the other.

"You're short," Wheaton said, sweat beading on his forehead. He looked anxiously out the window towards the harbor. "The price was arranged."

"And you're running late," Rogers replied, fingering the four coins he had left in the purse. "You wouldn't want to miss the last boat out, would you?"

"No, I wouldn't."

"You should be off then," Asa added.

Wheaton pursed his lips and looked at the soldiers waiting outside. No way the tailor would involve them in this squabble, Rogers thought. They would only demand their share of the loot. Wheaton harrumphed and swept the coins off the table.

"Right then," Rogers said. The tailor gave a last look around his cluttered shop before marching out the door and down the street, followed by the regulars. Rogers handed a coin to Asa. "Your share."

The Black, a pirate to the core, shook his head. "It's not enough. And I'm not in a hurry."

Rogers handed over another piece of silver. In fact, he was the one in a hurry. "I'm to meet with General Howe," he said. "I trust you can manage here."

"I'm sure the great general is anxiously awaiting your arrival," Asa replied with a smug smile lighting up his face. When Rogers did not respond, Asa waved him away. "No worries. I won't be alone long. The *Laughing Lady* docks on the afternoon tide."

Rogers strode down King Street and the Long Wharf, following two dozen paces behind Wheaton and his bodyguards. *Ordered about by a woman. Brushed off by a Black. How low must I sink?*

Howe's flagship stood a lonely vigil at the end of the pier, the final British vessel to leave Boston. Wheaton trotted up the gangplank, relief apparent on his face. The grenadiers guarding the *Chatham* remained in place, the gangplank stayed down. The ship was not sailing yet.

Rogers wagered that General Howe had not boarded. Of course, he had no appointment with the General, but he was determined to have his say. While waiting, he scanned the harbor, counting at least a hundred ships – schooners, merchant brigs, towering men-of-war – in a line over a mile long stretching out to the Atlantic.

He whirled around at the clatter of hoofbeats. A coach rambled down the wharf. The grenadiers snapped to attention and formed a cordon leading to the gangplank. General Howe stepped down and saluted. He was accompanied by a richly-attired, voluptuous blonde, who had somehow managed to maintain her radiance through the long siege. She had to be the infamous Mrs. Loring. Everyone in Massachusetts knew of the Sultana, an obviously well-earned sobriquet for the general's consort.

"General! General Howe!" Rogers shouted. A guard shoved him back, but he sidestepped, calling out again. Howe stopped, looking around, while Betsey Loring continued on. "It's Robert Rogers. Major Robert Rogers."

The guard manhandled him away. "Leave the general alone, old man."

"Wait," Howe commanded. "Let him be."

The guard stepped back. Rogers straightened his green jacket and drew himself to full height.

"Major Rogers," Howe said. "I've seen your reports. Excellent work."

"At your service, sir."

"You look in fighting trim. Ready to return to command, eh?"

"Yes, sir." Rogers beamed.

"Good, good." Howe grasped the hilt of his sword as he turned to leave. His mistress waited at the *Chatham's* rail. "I must be going."

"But…"

"There's no berth available anywhere in this flotilla, I'm sorry to say."

"Yes sir."

"The fleet will be in New York by spring. Meet me there. I will likely be in need of your services." Howe pivoted and marched away. The grenadier nodded to Rogers, according him newfound respect.

Rogers shuffled back up the pier. With nowhere urgent to go, he wandered aimlessly around the deserted city. Howe had blocked every street with earthworks, gabions piled with stones, and cannons. Washington and his army would have been slaughtered had they tried to take Boston. Unfortunately, the Heavens intervened.

He jingled the coins in his purse, a rare and most welcome sound. Enough for a week's lodging and entertainment. A celebration was in order.

Fortunately, the Green Dragon was open for business, replacing the Red Ensign flag with the stars and stripes. The place was deserted except for the barkeep, an older man whose bald pate was ringed by a crown of scraggly, gray curls, and a tavern wench, the barkeep's daughter by the resemblance, which was not exactly a tribute to her beauty. But at least she had nice, plump tits.

He checked his pocket to make sure the travel pass signed by Benjamin Franklin was still legible. It would suffice if anyone questioned his presence in Boston. The barkeep gave him a withering glance, but the plunk of a silver coin on the counter earned a friendlier nod. Hungry enough to eat a horse, he ordered an ale and a bowl of stew, gambling that he was not, in fact, eating a horse.

A cannon blast from the *Chatham* signaled Howe's official farewell. Within an hour, he heard the rhythmic footfalls of soldiers marching in formation. The Continental Army had arrived. He ordered a whiskey, then another, and another.

Rogers awoke with a blistering headache as the first streaks of sunrise painted the sky. He rolled over, wiping slobber off his chin as the past evening's activities came into focus. He was alone in the Green Dragon's "patriot parlor". What a joke, but he had been in no condition to argue when the barkeep put him to bed. He sat up, tugging his jacket around his shoulders, listening to the clink of the two remaining coins in his purse. The food, drink, lodging and a furtive coupling with the tavern master's daughter had taken its toll on his silver. He hadn't splurged on the luxuries of life in years.

Basking in the memory of General Howe's recognition, he puffed out his chest as he walked down the stairs. Unfortunately, the tavern was dark, no one there to share his good cheer. He sipped stale ale from a jug on the bar before stumbling outside.

The city stirred with signs of renewal. A finely cloaked man appeared to be dictating notes to a clerk, trailing with quill in hand. A mother swept the steps of a red brick Georgian that had miraculously survived the siege intact, while her two young daughters chased a chicken around the yard. The patriots were returning.

He walked along the outskirts of the Commons, a ghost town of deserted barracks and storm ravaged tents. Untethered horses nibbled on whatever grass they could find. A herd of sheep waddled by.

Rogers stepped aside as an immaculately coiffed, blue-sashed senior officer trot past him sitting tall astride a chestnut charger. George Washington himself, he gasped. Trailed by two aides and surrounded by six ramrod-stiff, neatly groomed soldiers, a far cry from the typical Continental, the commander-in-chief appeared intent on inspecting the fortifications Howe had left behind.

The security detail had to be members of the newly formed Life Guards, the talk of the countryside over the past week. Washington had evidently sent out an order to all regiments requisitioning "clean, handsome, well-made, and well-drilled" men to serve as his personal bodyguards. The General must have realized that he was now *the* hero of the patriot cause, and, as such, the most obvious target of British vengeance.

Governor Tryon should have moved sooner, Rogers thought. He would now have to penetrate the formidable shield of Life Guards to get to Washington. Rogers again congratulated himself on his decision to cast his lot with General Howe. Howe had vastly superior numbers and would surely crush the Continental Army in New York. And he would be there to share in the spoils.

Slowly, word spread that George Washington was in Boston. Heads poked out of houses and hovels, men and women trailed the great man down the street. Everyone wanted to be seen on the winning side. Someone tossed a wreath at the hooves of the General's horse. He sidestepped it and continued with his study.

Let Washington savor his victory. It will be his last.

PART TWO

New York
1776

"...We hold these truths to be self-evident, that all men are created equal..."
Declaration of Independence
Read publicly in the city on July 9, 1776

CHAPTER 13 - LATE MARCH/APRIL 1776

To John Hancock
It is with the greatest pleasure I inform you that on Sunday last, the 17th..the Ministerial [British] Army evacuated the Town of Boston, and that the Forces of the United Colonies are now in actual possession thereof. I beg leave to congratulate you Sir, & the honorable Congress—on this happy Event…

To Brigadier General Stirling
…we shall have an Opportunity of securing & putting the Continent in a tolerable posture of defence, and that the operations of the Summers Campaign will be not so terrible, as we were taught to expect from the accounts and denunciations which the [British] Ministry have held forth to the publick.
Go: Washington
Head Quarters Cambridge
19 March 1776

Crouching behind a boulder, Anne heard the militia men stroll by, their voices raised in verse:

When to Boston he came, with his prick in a flame,
He shewed it to his Hostess on landing,
Who spread its renown thro' all parts of town,
As a pintle past all understanding.
So much there was said of its snout and its head,
That they called it …

She focused on the two ladybugs crawling across the rock, inches from her face, in an effort to keep still. Her boots and breeches were caked with green slime; her toes were wet and cold; her thighs cramped; and her stomach grumbled. She wanted to go home. But she had no home. And the countryside rollicked with inebriated soldiers and roving bandits – was there a difference? – looking to prey on Loyalists fleeing Boston.

As the last strains of the bawdy song faded down the path, Caleb emerged from the shrubbery, a toothy grin spread across his bearded face. He dangled a rabbit, guts spilling out, from his left hand. "We'll eat well tonight, sister."

They hiked to their bivouac from the previous night, nestled under a rocky outcrop, ten feet above the Mystic River, swirling and gurgling from the melting snows. Anne foraged the hillside, while Caleb skinned and spit the rabbit.

"Can we risk a fire tonight?" she asked, returning with an armful of twigs and branches. Her hands shivered as she nestled them into a pyramid in the dirt.

"Do we have a choice?" Caleb didn't wait for her answer. He picked up a stone and struck his flint against it. Sparks flickered. On the fourth strike, the kindling ignited with a pop. He cupped his hands around the wisps of smoke and blew gently to encourage the flame. "Warm yourself while I fetch more wood."

Anne tended the fire until her hands stopped shaking. Caleb had taken charge as soon as they left Father at the store. She had expected to leave Boston by foot across the Neck, but he steered her down to the shore searching for a cairn of five stones. The stones marked the spot where a fisherman's ketch lay hidden under a screen of brush. She climbed in as soon as he pushed off without asking how he had come about the craft or the origins of the blood stains on the bow.

The war, she realized, had numbed her sense of morality, blurring her once vivid distinction between right and wrong. All that mattered now was survival. And survival meant getting to New York.

Caleb had rowed them around the Charleston peninsula, following the same route, as far as she could tell, that Uncas had navigated on their mission to Mystic last fall. Unfortunately, the surging river forced them to put in several miles from the town. They had been holed up here now for two days, waiting for the rebels' euphoria to subside.

Caleb trimmed four branches of roughly equal length, knotted them into two X's with leather cords from his pack, and planted the crosses on either side of the fire. He placed one end of the spit in the crook of each X so that their supper dangled above the flames. "You mind the rabbit, while I stand guard," he said, priming his musket.

Anne slowly rotated the spit, her insides dancing in anticipation of the feast. She whistled when the meat was done; Caleb didn't need to be called twice. He sliced strips off the carcass, filling her trencher first. She stuffed a piece into her mouth, juice dripping down her chin.

"Aren't you going to say grace?" Caleb asked, flicking a louse off his beard and into the flames where it sizzled like a firefly.

Anne stopped chewing, trying to figure out if her brother was really waiting for a benediction. He torched another louse, smiling this time. "You're disgusting, brother," she said and resumed her meal.

"You will be too, sister, soon enough. By the way, it's worse when they get into your crotch."

Lice crawling in my beard? Anne spit up, catching the scrap with her biscuit and stuffing it back into her mouth. After devouring the meat, she licked the last drops of grease from her fingertips.

She only had two bannocks left, and no cheese. "We should go into Mystic for supplies."

"It's too risky," Caleb replied. "There's a safe house two day's walk away. We'll stop there."

"Are you sure it's still safe?" *Two day's walk for you – three for me.*

Caleb shrugged. "Get some sleep. You'll need your rest."

"It's not as cold tonight. Spring will be here soon." Anne fastened her jacket across her shoulders, tucked her beaver cap over her ears, and curled near the fire.

Caleb set the two Xs that had held the spit on either side of Anne and hung his tarp over them, creating a modest shelter for his sister. "I smell rain."

"How do you know?" she asked, drowsily.

"I know."

She was on her knees, the cavalryman leering above. Her petticoat tore. Uncas raced towards her. A shot rang out. He stumbled, flailing to the ground. Geoffrey burst into the warehouse. A second shot boomed. No, too loud for a pistol. Anne fought to emerge from her nightmare. A third stentorian blast wracked the ground. Thunder.

She wiped the sleep from her eyes. A lightning bolt flashed across the western sky, backlighting Caleb who paced in a lonely vigil on the far side of the dying embers. Seconds later, the heavens erupted in a deluge; an angry wind cartwheeled the tarp into the bushes.

Anne rolled to her stomach, crossing her hands futilely over her head as a driving rain pelted her backside. Her nightmare lingered. Uncas had died trying to save her; she had an obligation to tell his daughter of his heroism. Even if his daughter was a whore. Anne sprung to her feet, slung her pack over her shoulder and slip-slid down the hillside towards the river.

"Sister!" Caleb roared but his voice was swallowed by the storm. "Silas!"

Anne stumbled over the fallen branch of a rotted tree but lurched ahead like a wayward child. Caleb caught up just as she reached the path, rutted and muddy as any pigsty. He grabbed her arm, forcing her to halt.

"Anne. Wait," he commanded. Rain dripped down his forehead and matted his beard. She shook her head violently, trying in vain to break free from his grasp. He pulled her close, his lips inches from her ear. "If you break your leg, we'll never reach New York."

"Mystic. I must go there." She gulped for air. "And tell Princess."

"We'll go together." Caleb drew his knife from his belt. A jagged flash of lightning illuminated its blade, honed to a razor's edge. He sliced the tip of his index finger, drawing a trickle of scarlet. "Now, give me your hand."

Anne obeyed. Caleb pursed his lips, wiped his eyes dry with the back of his knife hand, and pricked her. Eyes gleaming, he pressed their bleeding fingertips together. "Blood brothers. Forever."

"Forever." Anne nodded her agreement. The storm abated to a steady drizzle. They climbed back up to their campsite, gathered their scattered belongings, and trudged side-by-side into Mystic.

***

With the snow melted, crowds lined the main street in Medford to welcome the victorious Continental Army. Men waved flags, both the stripes and crosses of the Grand Union and the pine tree of Massachusetts, women tossed garlands of holly, and children broke from their parents to step in line with the troops. The first floral scents of spring were in the air.

Regiment after regiment strutted through the town square, marking the waning hours of the first day of our 225-mile journey to New York. I set the pace at the head of my company, slowing only to doff my cocked hat to the prettiest girls. Little John Bell, a grin stretching from ear to ear, beat his drum and twirled his sticks, a trick he had learned from a veteran drummer in the last days in Roxbury.

Stephen Hempstead brought up the rear, urging the stragglers to keep up.

The Connecticut men were fortunate; we would be sailing from New London to New York, cutting our march in half. Nevertheless, the 19th would need to travel at least twenty miles per day over troop-trampled, spring-melt roads for the next four days to keep on schedule. If my men stayed healthy and the weather cooperated, I calculated we might even arrive a night early. In which case, I could visit Prudence.

I had thought about the British, and the tasks that lay ahead, but the miles seemed to pass much quicker when my mind lingered on Prudence's lascivious lips and pert bosom. From the raillery I could hear in the ranks, my men also eagerly anticipated entanglements with the fairer sex, although without the romantic attachments.

"Five hundred whores in one square mile. Can you imagine?" Elvin Parrish asked to no one in particular.

"*The Gazette* says New York has the finest bawdy houses in the colonies," Tom Peacock added. "And the bitchfoxy jades are just waiting for us."

"The only thing that's waiting for you at those establishments is a good dose of the French pox," Steven Hempstead chipped in.

"French? Do you want me to try a French tune?" Little John asked, fife in hand.

"We'll find a young lass in New York to tickle your instrument," Elvin guffawed. "That'll make a man of you."

Little John stared at his feet, electing to trudge along without providing musical accompaniment. Stephen cozied next to the sour-faced youth. "Why don't you play *Three Blind Mice*," he requested. It was Little John's turn to laugh as he limbered his fingers.

I forced my mind back to the redcoats. Word had spread that the British had evacuated Boston, but no one was quite sure where they were headed. The last I had heard their flotilla, stretching a mile long, was still anchored at the mouth of Boston harbor. Since the rebels had no navy of their own, the British could sail unopposed to any port in North America.

Would General Howe set a course straight to New York? Where would he land? When? The city was located at the southern tip of Manhattan Island, surrounded by two rivers and the Atlantic Ocean, providing the British with unlimited options. How could General

Washington plan the defense of New York if he was completely blind to the movements of an enemy at sea? The Continental Army desperately needed intelligence.

The gray gauze of twilight cloaked the road as it spilled out of town and snaked through rolling farmland. A breeze stirred the tree canopy, hinting at a change in the weather. An owl hooted, the call answered by its mate. My men marched silently now, eagerly approaching each turn, hoping it might reveal their resting place for the evening.

Washington had outsmarted Howe once, he would do it again, I told myself, although the task would be much more challenging the second time. In Boston, Washington could pick the time and place of attack; in New York, the British owned the advantage.

Why not just order the Continental Army to bypass New York and pick a more favorable battleground? That question was rife with political and financial implications. The wealthy merchants of New York, at least those who supported the Glorious Cause, would not look too kindly on their abandonment. Accordingly, the Continental Congress would ultimately have to make the evacuation decision. It was well above my pay grade, and probably Washington's too, I realized.

Torchlights beckoned up ahead, the silhouette of a roof line visible. Just in time, I thought, as raindrops splattered the road. The order came down the line for the troops to camp in the fields for the night. Colonel Webb and his captains, however, would billet in the tavern. I pumped my fist. Hot food and a warm, dry bed awaited.

***

Robert Rogers sipped an ale, a solitary figure at the bar at the Flag and Flagon on this godforsaken evening. A slice of lamb pie, quite tasty for a house of this reputation, snuggled in his stomach. Silver clanked in his pocket. A berth waited for him in a common room upstairs. With rain pelting the shingles, it would be a good night to sleep indoors. He was not certain when he would enjoy this luxury again.

He hated to admit that Princess, or any woman for that matter, was responsible for the positive turn in his fortunes. Somehow the squaw had built a network of contacts stretching from the backwoods of Canada to the New England coastline. She was a demanding superior, more so than any of the British generals whom he had reported to in the past, and knew every nuance of the intelligencing trade. Even General Howe recognized her contribution to the Crown.

Before she retired this evening, Princess had sketched a map of his route to Quebec. She wanted him to assess the strength of local militia and the depth of support for the rebel cause. Most important, she had doled out an advance to cover his expenses. He would leave at dawn.

The arrival of two youthful stragglers, drenched as if they had swum all the way from Boston, interrupted his reverie. The taller one, bearded and shawled in a fine black cloak, had the confident stride of a wilderness man. The other, although cosseted in faded Ranger green, pigeon-stepped behind. A watery trail followed them to the bar.

"What can I do for you gentlemen?" the red-nosed barkeep asked, his tone anything but welcoming.

"Two ciders to start," the tall one replied, shaking droplets from his beard.

"I don't serve Queen's Rangers here." The barkeep tilted his head towards the shorter man. "He'd best leave before trouble starts."

"That's our pa's coat. He fought with Rogers at St. Francis in '59. It's all my little brother's got."

"Did he now?" Rogers squared up, his eyes rounding in surprise. "And what's your pa's name?"

"William Wheaton. I'm Caleb, his oldest son."

"I don't recall a Wheaton in my regiment." Rogers hand slipped to the dirk scabbarded in his belt. "But I do recall a William Wheaton running a fancy-dress shop in Boston. A scarlet-to-the-bone Loyalist."

"Meet Major Robert Rogers himself," the barkeep said, reaching under the bar for a pistol which he cocked as he aimed squarely at Caleb's chest.

Caleb's jaw dropped open wide enough to swallow a sparrow, while his eyes darted between Rogers and the barkeep. "You're Robert Rogers? *The* Robert Rogers?"

Rogers bowed low as he had learned in the royal court of King George many years ago. "Now, what do you two boys really want?"

The pigeon-toed Ranger stepped forward, tugging off her fine beaver cap. "I'm Anne Wheaton and this is my younger brother," she said, running her fingers thru the damp stubble of hair that barely covered her scalp. "We're here to see Occa."

"Who?" he asked.

"What business do you have with her?" the barkeep interrupted, his gun barrel unwavering.

"I have news of her father," Anne replied.

"What's her father's name?" the barkeep asked.

"Uncas. He brought me here last fall."

The barkeep lowered his weapon. "Princess is upstairs. I'll go fetch her."

"Are you a Ranger, boy?" Rogers asked Caleb, while they waited.

"Yes, sir. Out of New London."

"A dangerous place to support the King." He sipped his ale, but kept his right hand near the hilt of his knife. "Done any killing?"

"Yes, sir."

Heads turned as Princess swooped down the stairs. She wore a modest, chocolate-brown sleeping robe, knotted securely at the waist, but her free-wheeling hair, unbraided and lush, suggested the mystique of the unexplored wilderness. Although Rogers still harbored fantasies, he accepted that he had a better chance of a knighthood than a night in Princess's bed.

"What news do you have?" the Indian asked before her bare feet touched the floor. Her shoulders steeled for the news.

"Your father's dead," Anne said.

"Did he die a warrior?"

"Yes. With tomahawk in hand, defending my life."

"A good death then. He rests in peace." Princess's face remained a stoic mask as Anne summarized the battle at the warehouse, as well as Sam Hale's decision to deposit Uncas's body in Boston harbor.

"Hale's the son of a poxed strumpet," Princess cursed. "But I want to hear more of his doings." She reached for Anne's hand. "Come upstairs to my room. You can hang your clothes by the fire while we talk."

Anne shook her head. "I'll stay with my brother."

"He can come too, if he wishes."

"To your room?" Caleb's tone sounded as if Princess had suggested a visit to the moon. "That would not be proper."

"As you wish," Princess replied. "Your sister will wrinkle like a pickled cod if she stays down here much longer." She turned to the barkeep, trailing obsequiously behind. "These men can drink on my bill tonight. I'm sure Major Rogers has many tales to tell of his wilderness adventures in days gone by."

"Go upstairs, sister," Caleb said, clearly intrigued by the prospect of an evening with the famous warrior. "The hearth down here will serve me fine."

"Are you sure?"

"Your lips are blue. We'll resume our journey in the morning."

Rogers' eyes tracked the two women to Princess's door. If Princess was half as promiscuous as the natives he had had the pleasure of knowing over the years, Anne's evening would be far from restful. He would gladly empty his pocket of silver for a view through the keyhole.

***

Anne would have followed the devil upstairs if she promised a warm bed and dry clothes. Princess tossed two logs on the fire and stoked it until flames leapt up the chimney. Anne hung her sodden green jacket and waistcoat on an empty peg, wrinkling her nose at the fug of mud, sweat and animal droppings emanating from them. She hadn't removed her outerwear for three days, and wasn't sure when she would have the luxury of doing so again.

Turning her back to the blaze, she basked in its heat. Her "under" clothes, Geoffrey's shirt and neck stock, were heavy with moisture. The shirt, fortunately, was long enough to reach below her knees, providing a layer of insulation from the chafing of her leather breeches, soaked through as well. She longed for a dry frock and satiny petticoats.

Sitting, she peeled off her boots and woolen socks, so stiff with grime they could practically stand by themselves. Cherry-red chilblains scarred the tips of her toes.

The door latched behind her with a clang. "You can take off your shirt and leggings. No one will disturb us," Princess said.

Anne swiveled her head to keep an eye on Princess, the Indian's breasts swaying freely underneath her robe. She could not imagine a Christian woman sleeping in the nude on a hot summer night, let alone on a night this cold.

"Why are you still wearing those wet clothes?" Princess tested the water in the copper pot hanging over the fire. "Now, off with your shirt."

A wash would be heavenly, Anne thought, unbuttoning. The linen strip binding her chest still provided a measure of decency, although dampness had rendered it translucent.

"You'll catch your death if you spend another night in that."

Anne couldn't argue with the logic. She turned her back to unwrap the swaddling.

"You Englishwomen are so prudish. What are you hiding?"

"I'm not the prettiest flower in the garden, but I've nothing to hide." She faced Princess with her swaddling in hand.

Princess looked Anne up and down. "You've been to the Flag and Flagon before, haven't you?"

"Yes, your father brought me."

"He told me about you. Said you were good with sums. And Sam Hale trusted you."

"I'm not sure that's a compliment." Anne shivered. "Do you have a shift I could borrow before my tits freeze?"

Princess dug into her chest, tossed a nightgown on the bed, and turned her back. "Why do you work for Sam?" she asked over her shoulder.

"I could ask you the same question," Anne replied as she wiggled out of her clammy breeches and tugged the threadbare, but dry, linen over her head.

"Hale's needs were simple. He smuggled food into Boston, which farmers here were eager to supply, and he paid in silver. Now that the British have sailed away, I doubt I'll ever see him again."

"Did Major Rogers work for Sam Hale too?" Anne winced as she said the Hale name. Nathan's second letter had originated on Winter Hill. Was he still camped nearby? She was tempted to ask, but held her tongue for fear she would sound like a lovesick schoolgirl.

Princess turned to face Anne. "No. The major works for me, collecting intelligence for General Howe."

"You're a spy?"

"I run an intelligence network."

Anne was flabbergasted that a woman could be the leader of one organization, let alone two. Strong women, like Mother, might rule in the privacy of their home, but they would never command outside of those four walls. "Men follow your orders?"

Princess removed her war club from its peg, balancing its heft in her hands. "I beat them if they cross me. And the ones I can't beat, I fuck."

Princess was serious on both counts, Anne realized. And General Howe was brilliant for employing her. No one would suspect a woman, an Indian no less, capable of gathering military intelligence.

"And you? Why do you work for Hale?" Princess asked.

"My father's in his debt."

"He will bleed you dry then. Where do you go next?"

"We're to meet Sam and Father in New York. He provided a letter of introduction to a tailor there."

"It will be a dangerous journey. Every town on the coast is a boiling pot," Princess replied, twirling her war club at her feet. "You should stay here and work for me instead."

Anne hesitated, pursing her lips. Should she try to profit from this war – as others clearly did? The merchants, who took no side for too long, would likely be the survivors, while the true patriots, like her brother and Nathaniel, would be the ones to sacrifice their lives. But, family came first. "We must go."

"You are too headstrong for your own good." Princess pounded her club on the floor to emphasize her point.

"Is everything all right?" Caleb's voice floated up the stairs.

"All is well, brother," Anne called. "I will be down shortly."

"You can sleep up here." Princess lifted the corner of her quilt. "I have good whiskey to warm us."

"I prefer to sleep next to my brother."

"As you wish." Princess smoothed the quilt back down. "It would be safer for you to travel by way of Long Island. You'll find many more friends there."

"But we'd need to secure a boat to get there," Anne said. Certainly not beyond Caleb's capabilities, she thought.

Princess paused, as if waiting for kindling to catch. "I have contacts in New London who might be of service."

And now I will be in your debt as well, Anne thought.

***

Rogers awoke before the sun, tossed back the thin coverlet, its yellowed stains reflecting years of hard use, and stepped smartly into his boots. He had no desire to linger next to the pustule-popping man sharing his mattress. At least, there were no other bedmates, last night's storm discouraging travelers. He would head north at dawn, the first step towards redeeming his military career.

The meat pie had worked its way through his digestive system, declaring its intention to exit with a rolling gurgle that would not be denied. Tavern etiquette decreed that shits be taken in the privy out the back door rather than in the night jar in the common room. He took the steps two at a time, but nearly tripped over the inert forms of the Wheatons curled by the banked fire in the Flag and Flagon's main room. Miss Anne had come downstairs much earlier than he had expected last night. And, not surprisingly, had offered no explanation of the thumping in Princess's quarters.

A fog, thick as potato soup, clouded the turf, but could not cloak the foul airs haunting the privy. Nevertheless, Rogers lingered on the thunder-mug until a rap on the door interrupted his repose.

"Be done in a minute," he growled.

"Get off your arse," Princess ordered. "I'm going to fatten your wallet."

Rogers didn't need any further motivation. He buttoned his flies and brushed his wiping hand on the seat of his breeches as he stepped outside. The eastern sky simmered with the first rays of dawn. "At your service."

Princess was already bundled for the road, her war club slung over her shoulder. "There's been a change in plans. The Wheatons will need your assistance."

"Humph," he grunted. No surprise there.

"They'll be traveling to New London, not New York. You'll accompany them." She opened her palm to reveal three Spanish coins, good pay for little more than a week's journey roundtrip. Rogers eyebrows arched with interest. Princess continued, "And you'll report on the Continentals in New London. I'll want a list of the regiments departing by sea. They'll be Washington's finest."

"New London will be crawling with rebels," Rogers slow-talked, even though he was pleased at the opportunity to prepare another report that would likely reach General Howe. He eyed the coins but made no move to take them. Princess clearly had a personal motivation to see the Wheatons safely delivered. She added another coin to the pot. He still didn't reach.

"I'll double it upon your return."

He smiled and palmed the money. "Done."

"You'll bring the Wheatons to the smuggler's cove outside of town. Asa Cobb will meet you there with a dory to take them across the Sound to Oysterponds."

Rogers frowned at the mention of Asa. He had no desire to see the Black again, but he had already pocketed the coins. "Will you contact Asa?"

"No. I have business in Boston now that the British are gone. Asa checks for messages at Tailor Appletree's shop. You can leave word for him there."

"Are you sure Miss Anne will be able to keep up?"

"She'll ride Ehnita." Princess pointed to a pale gray mule, long ears perked, tied to the hitching post outside the Flag and Flagon. "There's an extra blanket and dry stockings for her in the saddlebag."

"You're going to a lot of trouble for a woman."

"Women with balls are hard to find."

***

After four days bouncing atop Ehnita, which Rogers had informed her was an Indian name for the moon, Anne's backside was as battered as waulked wool. But she never could have kept up on foot. The major had set a blistering pace from sun-up to sundown, as if he carried a hot coal in his pocket. He led them on Indian trails through the woods, paralleling the Post Road, to avoid the legions of rebel troops marching south from Boston. Nevertheless, they scurried for cover whenever the crunch of boots, beating of drums, or crisp commands of sergeants floated through the trees.

The Wheatons had made the same journey, albeit in the opposite direction, less than a year ago. Anne could hardly believe how much the times, the countryside, and her life had changed in that short span. She now masqueraded as a man and carried a loaded pistol. They were in enemy territory, Rogers cautioned; friends were few and far between. They camped without fire each night, avoiding travelers, towns and taverns. She slept fully dressed, shivering until exhaustion finally overwhelmed the cold. And, like the men, she was prepared to fight to the death.

Putting up outside Stonington, a half day's walk from New London, Anne wiped down Ehnita and settled her for the night before looking after her own sleeping arrangements. She swept leaves, pine straw and loose branches into a rough rectangle next to a covey of black chokeberry bushes that would at least provide shelter from the wind. "What do the people in London think of this war?" she asked Rogers as they sat for supper.

"They're divided. Some believe King George should put down the rebellion as ruthlessly as his grandfather put down the Scots at Culloden in '46. Others recognize the value of trade with the colonies and the need to retain a somewhat warmer relationship," Rogers replied, nibbling on dried peas and corn meal, old favorites from his wilderness days.

"Washington should be hung, drawn and quartered. Like the traitor he is," Caleb replied, gnashing his teeth on a strip of salted pork.

"The Crown can't rule the colonies with an iron fist forever," Anne answered, ignoring her brother's comment. "London is too far away and North America is too large."

"You're right Miss Wheaton. But I fear the rebel victory in Boston will inflame both sides. The radicals in New England will use it as justification to push for independence, whatever that means, while the King will be so embarrassed when the news arrives in London that he will be forced to unleash the full might of the Empire," Rogers said.

"So, we will have a long war," Anne said, quartering an apple with her knife. Although the extra woolens that Princess had packed had made the journey almost tolerable, she longed to sleep with a roof over her head and shed these wretched breeches. The Native's offer of employment was looking better every day.

By the time Anne awoke the next morning, Rogers was already gone. "The Major went ahead to make arrangement for our passage to Long Island," Caleb said. "We're to leave here two hours before the sun sets. That should get us to Smuggler's Cove comfortably before midnight."

"Until then?"

"We chase rabbits." His tomahawk gleamed far brighter than his teeth.

***

After four days of hard marching, the 19th regiment approached New London on the Post Road. Sunshine and a scatter of pillowy clouds, zephyring across the pale blue sky, ushered us home. The early arrival of spring portended well for the Glorious Cause, I thought, and for the second half of our journey.

Although we would be sailing in the relatively sheltered waters of the Sound, I had never traveled any distance by ship, let alone spent four nights on the water. I prayed my stomach would prove up to the journey. The prospect of barracking in a big city for weeks, months or even years was another cause for anxiety. How did so many people live so closely together? Where did they grow their vegetables? What dress was fashionable? Was there a proper church? The upcoming campaign in New York, both daunting and exhilarating, had kept me tossing in my bedroll the past few nights despite my exhaustion.

While General Howe had elected to head north to regroup in Halifax, as I had learned yesterday, there was little doubt of his ultimate destination. When would the British Army arrive in New York? In what numbers? Would they be reinforced by the dreaded Hessian mercenaries? *Would I finally get a chance to fight?* Today, however, was not the day to dwell on difficult questions.

The New London citizenry turned out in force to welcome its returning heroes. A fife and drummer, hobbled, gray-haired men unfit for service on the front lines, played a well-practiced Yankee Doodle. Obviously inebriated seamen stomped their feet out of tune with the music, while their women banged on washboards. The Artillery Company fired a salvo out into the Sound.

I searched the crowd for familiar faces. Justice Mather was not so elfin anymore; Josiah Barton, waving a Grand Union flag, appeared to have recovered his patriotic fervor; John and Mehitable Richards stood on their front stoop, smiling like proud parents; Zeb Cheesebrough and his wife, wide as a plough, stood next to their wagon while their two young sons clambered in the back. I saluted my former sergeant but did not slow.

Widow Appletree, Mrs. Lamplighter now, smartly dressed for the season in a pink shawl, stood with her husband in front of their shop, neither one noticeably enthusiastic. I thought the Widow leaned

Loyalist, but she must have taken the oath to Congress to have stayed in town. Elvin Parrish spit a stream of tobacco juice in her direction as he marched past.

The Wheatons, of course, were gone. I wistfully recalled the sense of innocence and community that had fostered my romance with Anne. The anger aroused by the rebellion had destroyed those values, just like it had destroyed the Wheaton's house and the properties of other Tories. Once the war was won, the colonies would have to rebuild the bonds of neighborliness, or at least civility, to move forward.

A gaggle of former students, including two Betsies, congregated outside the Union School. Where was Prudence? There! She stepped from the pack to blow me a kiss. Huzzah, I cheered silently. Tonight would be a memorable reunion. The Richards might again grant free rein of their parlor, but, if not, the early arrival of spring assured we would have little trouble finding privacy outdoors.

The parade ended down by the harbor, schooners and brigs lashed to the docks awaiting the soldiers' arrival. I would billet at the Hempsteads, while my men would either spend the night in homes or camped on the green. All would board prior to the morning tide. As my troop dissolved, I set off on a quick inspection tour.

"Ahoy, Captain Hale," James Caulk hailed from the deck of the Laughing Lady.

I braked. "Mr. Caulk, a pleasant surprise to see you in the service of the Army."

"Captain Caulk, son," Caulk corrected with a mock salute. "Service, hell. Congress is paying a pretty penny to transport the army to New York."

"I thought there would need be a pecuniary angle for your participation."

"Did my boys hold up well in Boston?"

"They did, sir. And I will authorize Jabez Miner to release the remainder of your silver this evening." I nodded farewell and resumed my walk.

"Much obliged. Continentals are barely worth the paper they're printed on," Caulk called after him.

Satisfied with the seaworthiness of the fleet, not that I really knew what flaws to look for, I strolled towards Miner's Tavern. I kept an eye out for Asa but was relieved not to see him. William Hull and

Ben Tallmadge, much to my surprise, were already drinking at the bar. I pulled Jabez aside for a private word, instructing him to conclude the transaction with Captain Caulk, before joining the group.

"No school today, Ben?" I teased as I hugged my dear friend. Despite all his bold talk last summer, Tallmadge had elected to complete another year as schoolmaster in Wethersfield.

"I signed my enlistment papers this morning," Ben replied. "I'll be joining you in New York as soon as the term ends."

"If we haven't already sent the British packing by then." I thumped on the bar for emphasis, and motioned to Tabitha for an ale. We quaffed brews and exchanged small talk for the next thirty minutes.

"Captain Hale, there is a young lady outside who demands your attention," Stephen Hempstead declared as he burst into Miner's to join us. "I'll volunteer to take your place here while you address her needs."

"Only one lady waiting? I'm disappointed in you, Nathaniel." Hull toasted his own riposte.

"Beware of connections, Friend Nathan," Ben warned with a mischievous grin.

I skedaddled to the porch where Prudence was pacing, fetchingly dressed in a sea-blue frock and black cloak. I started to apologize, but she cut me off.

"I've waited three months for you."

"Just one more hour, then." I clasped her hands. "I must sup here first."

"The Richards are expecting you." Her lips formed a moue of disappointment.

"Can you convey my regrets?"

"I'll tell them you had last minute responsibilities with your men."

"Much obliged. I'll meet you out back as soon as we're done."

"Whatever do you have in mind?" Her teeth shone brighter than a full moon.

"I believe I still owe you a stroll on the beach."

***

Leaning against a moss-covered boulder nestled above the bank of a fast-running stream, Anne sat barefoot reading *Cato* until the sun rose high enough to burn off the morning frost. After watching a school of catfish dart by, she put the play aside and stepped ankle-deep into the water. Her toes were just about frozen when she spied a silvery streak heading her way. She bent low to guddle it, splashing and thrashing, but came up empty-handed. With her shirt now half-soaked, she had a better idea.

Stripping, she plunged to her waistline, the water gripping her thighs in its icy tentacles. She sponged her torso and face before high stepping to the safety of the rocks. After checking her pubic hairs for lice, praise God there were none yet, she toweled off with her shirt and hung it to dry. Cleansed, and as content as possible under the circumstances, she stretched out in the grass, the first rays of springtime caressing her winter-pale skin.

She drifted off, dreaming of a frigid morning by the hearth in the Union Schoolhouse, acting out *Cato* under Nathan's tutelage. He was just about to reach for her hand when a thrashing in the foliage snapped her awake. With tomahawk in hand, Caleb tramped towards their campsite. Fortunately, he seemed lost in his own thoughts.

"Caleb, turn around. I'm bathing," she called.

"Why bathe?" Caleb chuckled. Clearly, the idea had not entered his mind. She dressed quickly, tucking the play under her shirt.

The afternoon dragged, her only chore the care of Ehnita. She peeked skywards every few minutes to check the position of the sun. When it dips to three fingers above the tree line, it will be time to leave, she told herself.

"Ready, Silas?" Caleb asked at last, his load hoisted on his shoulders.

"Ready, brother," Anne grunted, affecting her most manly voice. Caleb shook his head sadly. They would be in trouble if Anne had to speak.

She mounted the mule, riding silently by Caleb's side for two hours, maybe longer. He knew the way from his days hiding out with the Queen's Rangers. The trail was deserted, other than the occasional appearance of a rabbit or squirrel. As the moon rose, they ventured out onto the Post Road, little wider than two wagons at this point.

"Couldn't we sneak into town?" Anne asked. "Just for a quick look."

"There's nothing to see," Caleb replied.

"Our house?"

"Burned to the ground by the mob. After they looted it, of course."

"The meetinghouse?"

"Chopped down for firewood."

"Our friends? Father received correspondence from Tailor Appletree and his wife."

"She remarried. Didn't have much choice," Caleb replied. He marched five more steps, then added in a conspiratorial whisper, "Darcy might help us in a pinch, but I wouldn't count on it."

So, Caleb's on a first name basis with Widow Appletree, Anne noted, looking at her younger brother in a new light. War changes everything, and everyone, she reminded herself.

"Damn them all then," Anne cursed, surprising herself at the outburst. The mule whinnied in agreement.

"Steady, Silas," Caleb replied, a grin curling his lips in appreciation of his sister's vitriol. "We'll be across the Sound in Oysterponds before dawn."

A thin veil of clouds sheathed the moon, reducing visibility to just a few feet ahead. Dropping down over a swale, they pulled up just short of a dray horse, foaming at the bit and pawing the dirt in frustration. The beast was harnessed to a wagon that had deposited its left front wheel in a sinkhole. Ehnita eyed the situation warily.

"I'm scairt, Pa," a child called out from the buckboard.

"Me too," a brother echoed.

"You boys sit tight. We'll be moving again soon enough," a motherly timbre commanded from somewhere down below.

Caleb tugged at the bridle to lead Anne around the wreck. They just might pass in the inky blackness without notice. She stared at the children, bundled in sleeping woolens; Caleb tugged again.

Before Ehnita cleared the wagon, a man's head, capped by a tricorn bearing the bright cockade of a militia officer, popped up from the rear. "Huzzah, strangers. Your assistance would be mighty appreciated."

They were trapped, but Caleb reacted smoothly. "Need another hand back there?" he asked.

"Need all the help I can get."

Caleb stepped forward, seeming to forget his sister. Who was masquerading as his brother, Anne remembered a beat too late. She dismounted, but couldn't help noticing the puzzled expression on the militia man's face. *If we help him get moving, he won't be inclined to ask questions.*

Anne couldn't see a means to harness Ehnita to the wagon, so she tied her reins around a sapling. Caleb gripped the near corner of the wagon, while the militia man took the far side. Anne positioned herself between them, her fingers too delicate and uncalloused for a man. The other woman helped her two boys down, then joined the trio at the rear. The older boy stroked his horse's nose, coaxing the beast into one more try.

"One, two, three." Anne did not join in the count. The foursome heaved, cursed, and heaved again, but could only budge the wagon a few inches before it rolled back into its hole. They stepped back, huffing from the exertion.

"Zeb Cheesebrough," the militia man introduced himself as they rested. "My wife, Hilda, and our sons, Davey and Tom."

"Caleb Smith," Caleb replied. "And my brother, Silas. We're heading to Lyme to assist our cousin in raising his barn. Started a bit late in the afternoon."

Anne nodded, relieved that her brother stuck to the script they had rehearsed. And wisely hinted that they couldn't tarry long.

"I told Zeb we should leave New London sooner, but he and the boys couldn't get enough of the soldiers," Hilda said, tactfully scolding her husband.

Zeb looked crossly at his wife, but didn't argue. "One more try then?" he suggested, ushering the foursome into position. Unfortunately, they achieved the same frustrating result.

"Would you be staying the night in town?" Zeb asked.

"That's too rich for our purse. We'll just find a spot to set our bedrolls," Caleb replied.

"We'd appreciate it mightily if you could just pass through then. My old unit, the 19th, is billeted there. Some of the men might be inclined to come out and help me get rolling again."

Caleb hesitated; Anne flared her nostrils impatiently; Ehnita chewed a cud of grass in no hurry to go anywhere. Zeb tossed a glance over his shoulder at his wife. "Would get me out of hot water with Hilda as well," he added.

"Certainly," Caleb replied, grinning. "Wouldn't want you to have to sleep in the barn."

"Ask for Captain Hale. Nathan Hale. He's probably dining at Miner's," Zeb replied, gratitude apparent on his face.

Anne lurched at the mention of Nathan, but strangled her thoughts in her throat.

"Are you all right, man?" Zeb asked.

"A touch of the ague," Caleb reassured, taking Anne's arm. "I wouldn't let your boys get too close."

"I've got a comfrey potion in my satchel," Hilda offered. "Might help…your brother."

Zeb's expression darkened as he mulled his wife's words. Anne could practically see his butter churning as he looked at her and then back again at Caleb; but he remained silent. *Zeb needs us.*

"We best be going if we're to bring help." Caleb took command.

"You best then," Zeb answered, giving them the evil eye once more.

Anne mounted the mule and they parted without another word. Distracted by thoughts of Nathan, she slipped off the saddle as Ehnita stumbled over a kettle-sized rock in the road; Caleb caught her before she fell.

"If you go near Hale, I'll kill him," he said, his beard so close it tickled her chin.

"No worries, brother." The knowledge that Nathan was nearby had overwhelmed her senses like a stampeding bull, goring her heart more deeply than she would have reckoned. Nevertheless…

"Good, then." Caleb kept her close, wanting to believe her. "We'll stick to our plan and bypass the town."

"Rebels be damned," she replied, as if she meant it.

"Mind your arse now," Caleb said, taking the lead. The siblings trudged silently on without a backwards glance.

***

Rogers crouched behind the trunk of a fallen oak watching the Wheatons approach. With the hullaballoo surrounding the arrival of the Continental troops, he had slipped unnoticed into the tailor shop in New London. Mrs. Lamplighter, a most comely woman, was just about to close for the parade, but had agreed to see his message delivered to Asa by nightfall. Accordingly, he had doubled back along the Post Road to shepherd his charges to their rendezvous.

He was just about to step out into the road when he sensed a fourth presence. One footfall too many, a careless crack of a branch, the scampering of a rabbit that should not have scared - the years in London had not dulled his wilderness skills. Rogers retreated to his hiding spot and let the Wheatons pass. Sure enough, a lone figure trailed them, keeping his distance, stopping when they stopped, pistol at the ready.

Keeping to the woods, Rogers tracked the threesome for two hundred yards to be certain the shadow was alone. Since the Wheatons moved at a woman's pace, it was child's play. Satisfied, he darted ahead until he found a boulder large enough to hide behind.

He breathed deeply, slowing his heart rate. There was silver at stake, but, more than that, his reputation. If calamity befell the Wheatons, Princess would blame him. General Howe would never reinstate him to command. He would be ruined.

He tapped the cheek of the tomahawk looped at his waist. A decade had passed since he had last killed a man, but he had not forgotten how. Closing his eyes, he willed the energy to flow through his body.

Rogers assessed his enemy as he passed: spry, confident of his step, comfortable outdoors. A soldier perhaps. *Let's see if he's easily distracted.* He scooped a handful of loose stones and tossed them across the road, clattering in the shrubbery on the far side. The man stopped in his tracks, whirling to face the threat, exposing his back to Rogers. *He's not a ranger.*

Yipping like a hawk, a traditional Native war cry, Rogers leapt across the open ground, tomahawk in hand. He slashed down viciously, driving the blade through the muscles of his victim's exposed neck. Blood spurted like a fountain, drenching his fingers and forearm. The man crumpled at his feet, dead before he hit the ground, pistol slipping from his grasp. It landed atop a jagged rock and fired loudly, but harmlessly, into the woods.

Rogers knelt, extracting his blade from the body. He looked around, expecting no one, seeing no one. A squirrel darted up a tree trunk; a wolf howled in the distance.

Grabbing the almost severed head by the hair, he sunk his tomahawk into the forehead, peeling back the scalp. If the mutilated body were found, it would look like a murderous Indian was on the loose. He dragged the carcass body deep into the woods, camouflaging it with soil and loose shrubbery. After a pause to catch his breath, he wiped his blade clean and set off after the Wheatons.

***

Ehnita had been skittish ever since they left the Cheesebrough family. She whinnied, pricked up her ears, and twisted her head in a vain effort to turn around. Could she sense someone following? Anne quickly dismissed the thought. There was nothing behind them but endless darkness. Ahead, however, lay Smuggler's Cove and a boat to take them across the Sound, if they arrived in time. She drove her knees into the beast's sides and jerked the reins to keep her moving in the right direction.

The pistol shot set the mule off again, but the wolf howl was the last straw. Ehnita reared her hind legs, then bolted forward, almost tossing Anne from the saddle. Her hat toppled to the ground. She wrapped her arms around the beast's neck and held on for dear life. Caleb chased after the runaway mule but couldn't catch up.

Too late, Anne saw that Ehnita had taken the wrong fork. They were heading into town, rather than down to the shore. Caleb screamed, but his words died on the breeze. Seconds later, the lanterns of New London came into view. Ehnita trotted towards them.

Milling on the green, soldiers first laughed at the runaway mule and its haggard jockey, but quickly recognized they were not gallivanting for sport. Beers in hand, they cornered the beast, who had finally tired, and helped Anne dismount. Caleb barged into the circle with his eyes flared and mouth agape.

"Brother Silas, are you all right," he shouted. Then, tugging her elbow, he whispered, "We must leave, sister."

Unfortunately, they were surrounded. Soldiers jostled closer, tossing out questions, growing hostile when the Wheatons mumbled their answers.

"What's the hurry boys?"

"Why are you out riding after dark?"

"What's in those saddlebags?"

More troops gathered, trapping the Wheatons. Anne searched frantically for a familiar face. Where was Major Rogers?

Miner's Tavern was in sight. Could she reach Nathan? Would he help? Did they have *any* friends left in New London?

There! A classmate! Prudence Richards. No! Anne keeled over to hide her face, but it was too late.

***

Miner's was crammed with officers, their families and friends, including a few intrepid women dressed in their Sunday finest. Their pinks, daffodils, and lavenders brightened the smoke-filled tavern, while the aroma of roasting chickens accented the usual odors of stale ale and tobacco. I wiped the smear of rhubarb pie from my lips and rose from my bench. "Friends, I must take your leave."

"Duty takes precedence over revelry, of course," Schoolmaster Tallmadge said.

"Duty to whom, my fellow captain?" William Hull asked, smirking as he remained planted in his seat. Stephen Hempstead buried his grin in his beer.

"Yes, well, a young lady wishes to bid me farewell," I replied, shrugging my shoulders. "How can I deny her request on my only night in New London?"

"To a most ardent farewell then," Hull toasted.

"Huzzah," my friends rejoined, pounding their mugs on the table.

I stepped outside into the spring evening, pleased to see the full panoply of stars overhead and only a gentle breeze whispering off the Sound. A grand night for a stroll on the beach. And a farewell tumble in the dune grass. Now, where was Prudence?

The ruckus down by the green doused my fire. There must be a brawl, I thought, eyeing the milling soldiers. My men had prickled all day in anticipation of the journey to New York. Duty did call, after all; I shook my head as I strode over to the melee.

"That's Anne Wheaton! And her brother the Queen's Ranger!" Prudence's strident cry rose above the fray. I rattled as if a cannon barrage had rumbled the ground under my feet.

"Look at her — she masquerades as a man," Prudence continued her harangue. "They're spies. Do they take us for fools?"

I shook off the shellshock.

"Let the captain through. Let him through," Elvin Parrish called, parting the crowd with a broad sweep of his arms. His eyes danced mischievously as he recognized my predicament. Little John acted as a one-boy wedge, brushing recalcitrants from my path. By the time I reached the Wheatons, they were each securely in the grip of two soldiers. Muskets pointed at their chests.

"Nathan, praise God you're here," Anne called out, a ray of hope lighting her countenance. Defiant as ever, Caleb twisted in vain to free himself, finally drooping his head in defeat.

"Little good *he* will do you," Prudence, well-lubricated with liquor, answered, searching my face for confirmation. I felt as if each arm was lashed to a horse, stampeding in opposite directions.

I searched for Colonel Webb or Justice Law, but neither was in sight. I was the ranking officer on the scene. The respect of my men, my captaincy, if not my entire military career, hinged on my actions in the next few minutes.

"Anne, I wish I could say I was pleased to see you," I said, having already decided that Caleb was not worth my attention. "What *are* you doing in New London tonight? In costume no less."

"Intelligencing for the Crown, what else?" Prudence would not be denied. She swept her arms over the array of soldiers present. "Why else would they travel under cover of darkness if not to gather information on our troops and their movements?"

"We're doing no such thing," Anne asserted. "Please ask these men to release me."

I nodded my assent. Prudence spit at Anne's feet.

Anne rubbed her bruised biceps and wiped a crust of snot from her nose. "Although New London's been our family home for generations, we recognize we're no longer wanted. We're here to gather our belongings and move on."

"Who are you meeting in New London?" I asked.

Anne pursed her lips. "No one. Caleb and I travel alone."

"Your brother has lurked about town for months. Surely, he has told you that you have no belongings left to gather," I replied. Anne's pursed lips were a tell that she was thinking. If she had to think, she was probably lying. "The truth now, please."

"Here, here," the crowd murmured. Little John punched his fists rapid-fire in the general direction of the Wheatons.

"Your husband's an officer in the British Army, is he not?" Prudence accused, pointing a finger at Anne.

"Major Geoffrey Stanwich is dead. I am his widow. With no inheritance, I might add," Anne replied, quieting the murmurs.

"All the more reason to spy," Prudence countered.

Anne lunged towards her antagonist, but soldiers blocked the path. Her pistol dropped from her pocket, eliciting several gasps.

"And why are you armed?" I asked.

"The roads are dangerous," Anne replied promptly.

"Miss Wheaton, you stand accused of a heinous crime. Do your sympathies still lie with King George?" My question aroused a chorus of hisses and catcalls from the audience. I prayed Anne would recognize the gravity of her plight, and answer accordingly. Even if her words were false.

Anne exchanged a glance with Caleb. The crowd hushed, sensing the crucible was at hand. Stephen Hempstead pushed his way through, leading the town's two constables, older men with grizzled faces. Hempstead reached my side, but then retreated, as if he understood this battle was personal. Anne raised her chin and looked directly in my eyes. "God save the King."

The green erupted in a tidal wave of noise, yet Prudence's cry again rose above the din, "You'll hang for that!"

Damn Anne's petulance! I balled my fists in frustration, but would not shrink from my duty. "You leave me no choice then. Connecticut has laws against high treason. I must ask the constables to detain you both until Judge Law can conduct a proper trial."

Anne's hands were bound behind her back; Caleb looked with pride at his sister as he too was cuffed. Prudence flashed a victory smile.

Stephen led the procession towards the town jail, shielding the prisoners as best he could from the chicken bones, turds and whatever else spectators tossed. Little John trailed, tooting Yankee Doodle on his fife. Ben watched from the porch at Miner's.

Hands clapped my back; words of praise fell on my ears. I turned away, breathing deeply to ease the pressure caving my chest. There was no glory tonight. I prayed that justice would be fair - and merciful, if need be.

William Hull caught up to me. "You had a *connection* with Miss Wheaton?"

"Briefly, yes, although not as you imagine," I replied.

"The evidence against her is circumstantial at best."

"Will it matter in these times? Governor Trumbull himself has urged all citizens to hunt down Tories." I admired, envied even, Anne's courage, her honor, her passion, but the mob demanded blood. I fingered the mole under my cravat.

"Surely Miss Wheaton was not the young lady who wished to bid you farewell?"

"No." I looked towards the liberty pole; Prudence, standing alone, waved.

"Ah, your damsel awaits," William noted. "Go, captain, and enjoy her company. We sail in the morning. You would be wise to keep your distance from Miss Wheaton."

Although my thoughts remained clouded, adrenaline still coursed through my veins. "Sage counsel, friend," I replied, clapping William on the shoulder. Anne had chosen her path; I had chosen mine. I would write a letter tonight praising her character and ask the Hempsteads to deliver it to Justice Law. I could do no more.

"You did well, Nathaniel," Pru said, displaying her brilliant smile as she took my hand. She had pasted a black silk heart at the corner of her right eye, a fashionable symbol of passion. We wandered in silence for several minutes until we reached the shadows, sheltered from the flickering illumination of the town's lanterns. "All the more difficult because your feelings for Anne have not subsided."

"How could you…"

"Your face is an open book…" Pru reached up, cupping the back of my head and drawing me close. "…but, it is most handsome."

The tension in my chest snapped like the spring of a bear trap. I pushed her against a hitching post. Our lips locked in a greedy embrace. She tasted of rum and sweets; the scent of roses wafted from her neck.

"I pray your cock is not blind," she whispered, grinding against me until I thought her petticoats might melt.

***

Anne ducked a mass of slop as the constables shoved her up the steps of town hall, the site of New London's courtroom and jail. She thought she caught sight of Major Rogers, lingering on the outskirts of the mob that taunted them. Not much good he could do now.

Prudence Richards – Anne spit out the name. At least the tart's teeth were starting to rot, the telltale yellow now creeping from the roots. Another sign the Continental Army was running out of gunpowder, she chuckled silently.

Little wonder how Prudence weaseled her way into Nathan's graces. Nevertheless, he was pleased to see me, Anne thought, the frisson lighting his noble face unmistakable. As I was him. How did we grow so far apart so quickly?

She had also noticed the trace of a v-shaped scar on Nathan's cheek. It had not been there last spring. The faces of many British soldiers in Boston were similarly marked. A residue of musket fire, Geoffrey had explained to her.

Nathan was an officer in the rebel army, by definition a traitor to his King; but, he had acted honorably, given her every chance to state her case. To meet him halfway, perhaps. But there was no middle ground any longer.

She was a loyal subject of King George. The monarchy and Parliament provided an order to society. Without them, the drooling rabble would rule. She could only hope the Crown would give Nathan the opportunity to redeem himself when the rebellion was put down. Dropping her head, she prayed that she, Caleb, and Nathaniel survived to see that glorious day.

Sheriff Gray, a barrel-bellied man with fleshy jowls melting into his neck, waited at the door, a gravy stain smearing his waistcoat. He had dined at their home only a year ago, helping himself to seconds on all courses. "You're kin, you say?" he asked as if he didn't remember.

Anne shook her head in disbelief. "Yes, sir."

"Then I'll lock you up together and save some space. You're going to be here awhile."

"What's the cause of the delay? My brother and I have done no wrong and would like to be on our way as soon as possible."

"That's all well and good, but Justice Law's traveling the circuit this week. Believe he's in Coventry today. Won't be back in New London until Saturday." Gray ushered them downstairs to the basement.

The stench of human waste was overwhelming; termites had feasted on the wooden beams supporting the ceiling; there were no windows, only air vents, less than a foot wide, up near the top of the walls. A rat scurried across the dirt floor.

"That's six nights down here?" Anne croaked, struggling to remain upright.

"You're the smart one, aren't you?" Gray turned a key to open a door, unfortunately the only stout block of lumber in sight. The cell was barely as big as the warming room off the kitchen in their home in Boston.

He signaled for the constables to free their hands. "In you go."

"Where's the privy?" she asked after noting only a lone night jar, half full by its stink, topped by a soiled rag for wiping. And they would have to share the straw pallet on the floor with a colony of roaches.

"Brothers and sisters don't have secrets," Gray chortled along with his two constables as they locked the door and left.

"At least you bathed this morning, sister," Caleb cracked before skulking into a corner.

They sat silently in the darkness for a good hour, maybe longer. Anne's eyesight adjusted, but her stomach would not. When she dry-retched, Caleb hopped to his feet, helping her stand as well. Arm in arm, they paced around the four walls, seemingly impregnable. When she heaved again, he got down on all fours underneath an air vent. "Up you go," he said. "Tell me if there's any way you could wriggle through."

Anne stood shakily on her brother's back. She wasn't tall enough to reach the sill, but could see that there was no way even her slender frame could fit. She angled her head to view a pauper's slice of stars, sucking in gulps of air until her nausea subsided, although she was sure it would return again. She clambered down, her steps weighted by the enormity of their plight.

She finally nodded off, sitting upright, counting spiderwebs, but got no rest, a hangman's noose torturing her dreams. A racket upstairs awakened her; the vent showed light, indicating mid-morning. Caleb paced back and forth.

Footsteps, several sets, shuffled outside her door. A woman's voice shrilled, near hysteria but familiar. Hilda Cheesebrough. Anne's brain started to function. What could she want? Is she here to complain that we didn't send rescuers last night?

"Recognize these two?" the sheriff asked as he stepped into the cell. Hilda and the two constables trailed behind.

"That's them." Hilda stabbed a finger first at Caleb then at her. "The Smith brothers."

"The *Smith brothers*, you say?" Gray asked.

"That's what they told us before they left us stranded in the middle of the road."

Anne started to respond, but realized it wouldn't be worth the effort. Unfortunately, she was right. Only worse.

"We know them as Caleb and Anne Wheaton," Gray said.

"Anne?" Hilda was clearly puzzled. "He's a woman? Where's my husband?" Hilda's voice rose in anger.

"Your husband?" Anne replied. "He was by your side the last we saw him."

"Zeb smelled a rat, so he went off tracking you two down the road. Haven't seen him since."

"Neither have we," Caleb chipped in.

"You killed him. I can smell it." Hilda crossed her index fingers, forming a crucifix and pointing it at Anne. "You're a witch. I hope they burn you at the stake."

Anne shuddered. While a witch hadn't been executed in Connecticut for over a century, tales of the trials in Salem and other New England towns still brought dread to women from all walks of life.

"That might be a bit harsh, Mrs. Cheesebrough," Gray said, steering her away from Anne. "Perhaps, your husband went on ahead to your farm. Or got lost in the night. He could have fallen and not been able to get up."

"Not my Zeb." Hilda aimed her evil sign at Anne again. "She killed him. And she'll burn for it."

"Maybe a band of Iroquois caught him and scalped him," Caleb offered. Anne wasn't sure if he was trying to be helpful or just sarcastic.

"We haven't had any Natives on the warpath around here in quite some time," Gray said. "We took a tomahawk from your belt," one of the constables pointed at Caleb.

The accusation took the steam out of her brother's kettle. "I didn't kill nothing but rabbits," he mumbled.

How did Caleb acquire the dory in Boston? Anne had never asked about the blood stains in the boat that got them to Mystic.

"Let's not get ahead of ourselves here. White men don't scalp," Gray said, looking sternly at his constable. "This boy's from a good Christian family. And he's in a heap of trouble as it is."

"Where's my Zeb then?" Hilda asked, a tear streaming down her chubby cheek.

"We'll find him. Don't you fret."

***

Hunched behind a corncrib, Robert Rogers kept vigil all night. If the Wheatons didn't escape, they'd likely hang as spies. While he himself held the incriminating papers from Princess, the fact that Anne and Caleb, confirmed Tories and offspring of a suspected spy, followed the Continental army troops into New London would be damning. He'd never seen a woman swing from a yardarm before, but bet that Anne would shit her breeches same as any man. She might get off with a bath in tar and feathers, but that could easily prove as deadly if the tar was hot enough. And quite possibly even more painful.

Since the Wheatons had been captured on his watch, Rogers knew his future was almost as much in jeopardy as theirs. If he didn't spring them, his aspirations for a command in the British Army would evaporate. Princess would see to it. Without an officer's commission, he'd run out of funds soon enough, and die a drunkard's death. He'd killed one man already to insure their safety. He'd kill more if he had to.

The air vents, barred with iron grates set into the foundation of town hall, were a good indication that at least one holding cell was located in the basement. How many guards were down there? Where was the key? When would the Wheatons be tried? Had they been beaten? Were they still fit to travel? He had many questions, but little chance of finding answers while the town crawled with soldiers. Fortunately, most if not all the troops appeared to be assembling in preparation for their imminent departure.

Just after dawn, Rogers left his hiding place with his hat pulled low. He bought breakfast, a stale breadcrust and an apple, from a pushcart peddler down by the docks. Needing a cover for his surveillance, he negotiated the purchase of the peddler's entire bushel of fruit. Lugging it back towards town hall, he noted the colors and cockades of the regiments marching in formation to the harbor, as Princess had requested. He grudgingly gave Washington credit for molding the New England farm boys into soldiers.

A stab of jealousy pricked his gut when Israel Putnam, a brigadier general now, paraded by, surrounded by youthful aides exhibiting the swagger of men who had yet to see combat. Rogers ducked his head, feigning interest in a steaming pile of horse droppings. If he were recognized, he would most certainly join the Wheatons on the gallows.

He set his bushel down in the dirt kitty-corner from the front entrance of town hall and sat himself, cross-legged and head down, next to it. Two goats and several raggedly dressed children besieged him, but he shooed them away. Before the sun had gained much height, he sold four apples, and gave one away to a toothless, hunchbacked woman in exchange for the information that the Wheatons' trial would be delayed a week until Judge Law returned from his duties in the countryside. While the provider of that tidbit appeared disappointed there would be no execution today, he was quite relieved.

He watched a mother, hard-featured and heavy-bottomed, and her two young sons enter town hall, but thought little of it. Thirty minutes or so later, they left, accompanied by one of the town's constables. An uneasy feeling settled in his stomach as they headed up the Post Road together.

"Two more apples if you can find out how many constables are still inside," he offered the hunchback.

"Why you want to ken?" she asked in a thick Scottish brogue.

"None of your business."

"Four apples, then."

"Three."

She moved spritely for a hag, mingling with passersby, briefly entering town hall, and returning with the information that Sheriff Gray and Constable Goodbody remained on guard. He allowed her to sort through his bushel in order to keep her talking.

"Constable Prescott left with the farmer's wife, Cheesebrough's her name, and her two bairns. It'll cost ye another apple..." When he nodded his assent, she continued. "Cheesebrough's husband, Zeb, disappeared last night. They went lookin' fer 'im." She examined each apple, tucking four with the least blemishes into her skirt, and had the good sense not to ask him why he wanted to know. "God save the King," she whispered with a wink before shuffling away.

He had underestimated the hag; she was no fool. And she would sell him out in a heartbeat – if she hadn't already done so. He glanced at the front door of town hall. Still closed, fortunately, but it was time for him to move on.

With the judge gone, there was no need to force the Wheatons' escape, especially since he was outnumbered, and soldiers still lingered around town. Would Widow Cheesebrough find her husband's body? The discovery of his scalped victim could actually work in his favor. If the sheriff was in fear of murderous natives, he might put his constables out on patrol and neglect the Wheatons. *Might even have to move Zeb's carcass out where someone could find it.* Rogers left the rest of his rotten apples for the urchins.

***

Anne thought Constable Prescott might have pissed in their supper again. It had yellow streaks like week-old snow, same as yesterday's evening meal which she had refused to eat. A third miserable night in jail, however, had worn her resistance down. She dipped her spoon into the rancid stew, swirled around until she found a scrawny string of meat, and tentatively chewed. Hunger must have been the missing ingredient.

About the only good news they'd had was no news. There'd been no sign of Zeb Cheesebrough, and Hilda had not returned to the jail.

"They have no case against us," Anne declared after mopping up the last of the gravy with a crust of bread. She paced about the cramped cell, stepping over her brother's outstretched legs at each turn.

"Are you a lawyer now, sister?" Caleb asked. He hadn't moved from his spot on the floor since yesterday afternoon except for a lengthy and loud seating on the chamber pot this morning. He clenched and unclenched his fists over and over, as if seeking to defend himself from an invisible attacker.

"We have every right to be here. New London's our home," she declared. Her oratory reminded her of morning classes at the Union School. She hoped Nathaniel wouldn't be at her trial - and its aftermath. When Caleb only snorted in reply, she continued, "Where's the evidence of spying? We had no maps, no codes, no contact list. Gray checked everywhere."

"Prescott thought you might have hidden notes up your cunny."

"He would have checked too, if the Sheriff didn't stop him." Anne instinctively checked the flies of her breeches.

"You don't understand this town any more. The leather apron gangs - the Sons of Liberty, the Sons of Neptune – play the fiddle now. Everyone must dance to their tune. Or else…"

"The bastards are just out to fatten their wallets." Anne spit in the dirt. "The rebellion's merely a convenient excuse to riot and plunder."

The rattle of a key in the lock ended their conversation. Sheriff Gray entered, flanked by his two constables. "Judge Law has cut short his tour of the countryside and returned early to New London. Your trial will begin tomorrow morning," he announced, his voice as flat as an undertaker's.

"Don't get all choked up about the good news, eh," Prescott guffawed at his pun.

"Do you need anything to prepare yourselves?" Gray asked.

"A bible perhaps?" Prescott interjected, earning a nasty glance from his superior.

"A quill and ink would be helpful," Anne said, struggling to fight the sensation that she was being sucked under by a swirling riptide. *Father? Mother? Phineas?* She wouldn't let herself wallow in self-pity tonight.

"An ale as well," Caleb added.

"I'll see to it," Gray replied as he led his men out of the cell. Prescott slammed the door shut. Caleb dropped his head, too late to hide the tears welling in his eyes. He's still just a boy, Anne thought, as she turned away to avoid embarrassing her younger brother.

Gray returned shortly with writing materials, a pitcher of frothy beer, and two flagons. His goons waited at the door, clearly entertained by the flirty chatter of a vaguely familiar female voice behind them. "You have a visitor," he announced.

"You are the sly one, Constable Prescott," Darcy Lamplighter giggled as she parted the constables and swept into their cell, a wicker basket in hand. She was fashionably dressed in a forest-green dress and white apron, accented by a lacy buffon draped across her low-cut bodice. Her grand entrance somehow knocked off her cap which floated to the floor. "So careless of me," she exclaimed, bending over to retrieve it, captivating the attention of all four men. Her appearance clearly breathed new life into Caleb.

Darcy corralled her blond tresses, unleashing notes of lavender perfume in the process, and retied her cap. "I baked an apple cobbler for the Wheatons, and for you men as well," she said, opening the lid of her basket to show off her creation. "Heaven knows, the air in here could use some sweetening."

"The Wheatons stand accused of treason," Gray said solemnly. "It's not a sweet offense."

"I pray they will see the error in their ways. As I have," Darcy replied.

"A little late for them," Prescott chimed.

"That cobbler sure does smell good, though," Constable Goodbody said, leaning over the basket.

"Let me cut you a slice," Darcy replied, removing a kitchen knife from her apron. She carefully cut slices for each of the officers and tucked the knife away.

"Can't be leaving that in here," the sheriff said, nodding at the knife between mouthfuls.

Darcy opened her eyes wide. "I'm insulted, Sheriff, that you would even imply such an ill motive."

The sheriff allowed a few minutes of simple conversation before signaling that the visit was over. Anne saw the eager look on her brother's face as he hung on Darcy's every word, but she barely acknowledged his existence.

"My man Rogers will come round later tonight to retrieve the crockery," Darcy casually tossed the words as she stepped towards the door.

"Rogers, eh?" Gray asked. "Don't believe I've met the man."

"I'm sure you'll have the opportunity soon enough."

As soon as their cell door shut, Anne clasped Caleb's shoulders, barely containing her excitement, and whispered in his ear, "We have friends after all, brother. They'll be coming for us shortly."

"We don't have much packing to do," Caleb cackled as he rubbed his hands together. She was pleased to see him laugh, even if it brought the return of a killer's gleam to his eyes.

They didn't have long to wait. Within an hour of Darcy's departure, pandemonium broke loose upstairs in the courtroom. Anne and Caleb pressed up against the door of their cell, but could only hear fragments of the shouting.

"Cheesebrough was scalped!"

"Indians on the warpath!"

"Defend our women and children!"

Boots spanked the floor above their cell. Then quiet. Absolute quiet. Anne could barely breathe as several agonizing minutes passed in silence.

A scuffle, scraping outside their cell door, broke her trance. Its grunts and curses were music to her ears. *Who was standing guard tonight?* A pistol fired; a body slammed against the door, followed by the moan of a wounded man. A key turned in the lock.

Major Rogers entered, his pistol still smoking, followed by a well-built Black, armed with knife in hand and pistol tucked into his belt. "Move," Rogers ordered.

The Wheatons didn't need to be told twice. Sandwiched between their two rescuers, they stepped around Constable Goodbody, slumped against the wall with blood stains flowering in his right shoulder, and up the stairs. Should have been Prescott, Anne thought, but she had no time for regrets.

The courthouse was dark and deserted. Rogers led the way down the center aisle between the empty benches. With the moon veiled by clouds, the front steps were pitch-black as well. Rogers must have plunged the torches outside the entranceway into the rain barrel on his way in, Anne realized.

The major whistled twice. A horse-drawn wagon rumbled up; Darcy Lamplighter sat on the buckboard, reins in hand. Ehnita, the runaway mule, lagged behind.

"Up you go," Rogers said, offering a hand to Anne.

"Where are we going?" she asked.

"West." Darcy replied. "I have relations in Greenwich who share our sympathies, albeit behind closed doors. You can easily slip over the border to New York, if you like."

"But your new husband and your shop are here," Anne said.

"My husband beats me." Darcy dropped her head. "I took the silver. He can have the shop."

"Let's go ladies. Or, do you plan to gossip all evening?" Rogers asked, patting the bed of the wagon. It was covered by a tarp, anchored by sacks of grain. "Crawl underneath and stay put until I tell you it's safe to come out."

Anne snatched one last look: her old house, the Union School, Miner's, the village green, the meeting house, town hall. Although New London had been her home for so many years, she doubted she would ever return.

"Asa, you take that donkey back to Princess. She'll want to know where the Wheatons are headed." Rogers commanded the Black as he climbed up to the buckboard. Resting one hand on Darcy's thigh, he snapped the reins and the wagon clattered away.

Anne ducked under the tarp, offering a silent prayer of thanks. Seething like a jilted lover, Caleb crawled next to her. They were off to New York.

***

So far, so good, Rogers thought as the wagon rolled westward, leaving New London in its wake. A little more moonlight would have been helpful, but the road was traveled enough here to be easily discernable. He listened for the sounds of pursuing horsemen, but heard only the chirp of crickets.

His ruse might have worked. He had paid the hag good silver to claim that she saw the Wheatons heading towards Smugglers' Cove. Asa had scuffed up the beach there to look like a skiff had grounded and then pushed off. Sheriff Gray would have little reason to search once he had evidence the Wheatons were at sea, headed to Long Island, essentially a foreign territory still full of Tories. And the wounded constable would likely live, so there would be no murder charge to motivate him to seek vengeance. Finally, His Excellency, General Washington, was due to stop in New London any day on his journey from Boston to New York. The sheriff, as well as the entire town, would want to ogle the great man rather than pursue a wild goose chase.

Rogers kept his eyes fixed on the road, one pothole could derail their journey, but his mind wandered to what might have been. In '65, a scant decade ago, he stood at the pinnacle of British society. He had published his journals, received a personal audience with King George, and secured a commission with full pay to serve as commandant of Fort Mackinac on the northern tip of Lake Huron, England's westernmost outpost in North America. He was in an ideal position both to repay his debts from the Indian wars and launch an expedition to discover the fabled Northwest Passage, a route through the continent to the Pacific Ocean and the riches of Asia. His name could have been emblazoned in history along with other great explorers, like Cortes, Hudson or LaSalle; and, he would have shared in the bounty of gold and furs. Instead, the debts of the Empire, squabbles at the King's court and the jealousy of Thomas Gage brought him to ruin.

Rogers' free hand roamed higher on Darcy's thigh. She didn't appear to object. At least he'd have a woman tonight, if Caleb Wheaton didn't get in the way. "It's plain the boy has puppy eyes for you," he said, tilting his head back towards the bed of the wagon.

"I know," she replied without looking at him. "He apprenticed in the shop for a year and helped around the house after my first husband passed."

"Is he going to be a problem?"

"No." She shook her head. He decided there was little to be gained by pressing further.

It was just as obvious that Caleb had Ranger potential, but Rogers needed to find out if the boy was tough enough for the life. Could he march for weeks at a blistering pace on frostbitten toes? Could he scavenge for worms and insects when his food supply ran out? Would he eat the flesh of his dead comrades to survive? How would he react to the screams of a man staked to the ground by Indians, his guts slit open and left as a feast for the buzzards? Rogers' two years in a London jail were a walk in the park compared to his time in the wilderness.

Around midnight, he steered the wagon towards a copse of birch trees beside the Connecticut River outside Old Lyme. They would camp there and find a ferryman to row them across in the morning. The Wheatons, exhausted from their ordeal in prison, were asleep under the tarp.

He kicked Caleb. "Get up boy. There's chores to do." Caleb shook the sleep from his eyes, rising slowly to his knees with a sullen glare. His sister remained motionless. "I just saved your neck boy. Don't give me the stink eye."

Caleb stepped down from the wagon, checking his surroundings and stretching his legs. "Where are we?"

"Safe. For a few hours at least." Rogers planned a little test of Caleb's toughness. "Unhitch the mare. Get her watered, fed and wiped down," he ordered. "And don't hurry back. I'll be attending to Miss Darcy for a bit."

While Caleb walked the horse down to the riverbank, Rogers set about starting a fire. Darcy sat cross-legged beside the flames, watching him raptly, a jug in hand. He kneeled next to her and took the jug. She removed her cap and flounced her hair over her shoulders. He wiped his chin with the back of his hand.

They both had emotional axes to grind and little interest in conversation. She lay back and parted her legs; he undid the flap on his breeches. The bushes by the river path rustled; Caleb had returned early, as expected.

Good, let him watch, Rogers thought, as he took a long slug of whiskey, the fiery liquid spilling over his lips. Safely out of Darcy's sight, a spectator wasn't going to spoil the fun. While the rutting was violent and loud, as fornication in the woods with another man's wife should be, Rogers didn't take his eyes off Caleb.

The boy stood stock still, silhouetted against the expanse of the river. He tied the mare to a tree limb, withdrew a duckling from the shelter of his pocket, and cradled it in both hands. When he was sure he had Rogers' attention, Caleb snapped the duckling's neck.

Rogers stopped mid-thrust. Damn, that boy has a set of balls. He'll make a fine Ranger. If he doesn't kill me first.

After completing matters with Darcy, he buttoned up his breeches and curled next to her for warmth. If all went well, they'd be in Greenwich in two more days. He'd leave the women there and head up north with Caleb on his original mission to scout the rebel positions.

CHAPTER 14 - APRIL/MAY 1776

"It would grieve every good man to consider what unnatural monsters [Tories] we have as it were in our bowels. Numbers in this colony, and likewise in the western part of CT, would be glad to imbue their hands in their country's blood...It is really a critical period. America beholds what she never did before."
Nathan Hale – letter to Enoch
May 31, 1776

Yet again, I found myself with spade, rather than musket, in hand. Long Island's Guana Heights, named for Gowaine, an Indian warrior, was little different than Dorchester Heights, featuring steep embankments, slopes thick with rocks and vegetation, and a bird's eye view of the city below. If the British ever occupied this ground, Washington would have to abandon New York, much like Howe evacuated Boston.

Flanked by Hempstead, Hercules and Elvin, I shoveled underneath the perimeter of a rounded boulder, roughly half the heft of General Washington's four-wheeled phaeton. The commander-in-chief had ordered the handles of all tools branded with the legend "C XIII" to mark them as property of the thirteen colonies, a sad sign of the rampant theft prevalent in our army.

Third Company was clearing ground on the ridgeline to build a redoubt to block the road up to the East River from the village of Flatbush. The ramparts would be fifteen-feet thick in parts, complete with musket holes, firing stands and sally ports. The task was so monumental, and so vital to the defense of the city, that soldiers and civilians, White and Black, freemen and slaves, worked side-by-side. Freemen, however, got days off, while slaves were not so fortunate.

When I sensed the stone wobble, I tossed aside my shovel and leaned my shoulder into it. We heaved twice before it inched from its resting place. Another push and it tottered forward. A final exertion sent it over the edge.

Too late, I saw Little John Bell pissing behind a bush on the slope directly in the boulder's path. Fortunately, the boy heard the crash of shrubbery and jumped clear, tumbling tail over tea kettle. He arose with a big smile, breeches at his knees, and waggled his flopping carrot to the hoots and hollers of his fellow troopers above.

I was down the slope in three strides, boxing his ears before the laughter stopped. "Chafe your yardarm in public again and I'll see you thrown in the brig," I said. "Am I clear, private?"

"Yes, sir," the boy mumbled, tugging at his breeches. "Just having some fun."

"We'll see how much fun you'll have when the Regulars charge up this slope with their bayonets pointed at your prick."

We needed to raise our game. While the construction work here was as drudgerous as it was outside Boston, the situation was totally different. Winter was over. The shipping lanes were open, bringing fresh supplies and reinforcements, including the Hessians, to the British Army. General Howe could hibernate no longer. He would have to attack, and New York was both the most strategic and most vulnerable port on the coast. The redcoats would be coming soon enough.

I kicked Little John in the arse, sending him sprawling again. The laughter atop the ridgeline stopped, my message sinking in.

I was relieved to be stationed on Long Island for the next few weeks at least. With our quarters in New York located on Bayard's Mount just west of the Bowery, only a short walk away from the famed Holy Ground, I had talked myself ragged warning my men of the dangers of its bawdy houses and gin mills. Ironically, this den of iniquity had taken root virtually underneath the steeple of Trinity Church, the tallest structure in the city, on a plot of land owned, in fact, by the church itself.

Manhatta, native for "hilly island," had looked so pristine when my transport first anchored in Turtle Bay the month prior. The waters of the East River sparkled, the beach was sandy and smooth, and the Beekman Mansion, a butternut clapboard retreat nestled in lush greenery and fruitful orchards, loomed above. How restorative it would be to spend a night there, I had thought. The three-mile march down the Post Road passed through rolling hills and verdant countryside, a farm house or country estate occasionally visible through the foliage.

However, New York City itself, located at the southern tip of the island, was already girded for war. Under the guidance of General

Lee, whom Washington had dispatched from Boston in January, the army had dug trenches and set timber barricades across every street accessing the waterfront. Half the population, over twenty thousand at its pre-war peak, had evacuated, leaving homes and belongings behind. While Continental Army troops appropriated these vacated properties for their barracks, General Washington had issued several orders warning the men against theft and vandalism. He had also convinced Congress to increase the maximum penalty for disobedience from thirty-nine lashes to one hundred.

Washington himself had arrived in mid-April, establishing his military headquarters in the two-story stone mansion built by British Navy commander Archibald Kennedy at 1 Broadway, fronting Bowling Green and, ironically, a gilded statue of King George on horseback. Befitting the commander-in-chief, the mansion represented the height of colonial architectural excellence, featuring a fifty-foot parlor, grand staircase, and cupola overlooking the Hudson River. Its gardens tumbled down to the shoreline.

Broadway was a stately boulevard, lined with shade trees, fine Dutch-gabled and Georgian-brick homes, and steepled churches; oil lamps hung on every seventh house, lit by a corps of city servants each evening. It ran parallel to Queen Street, the major commercial thoroughfare. Over the past century, business had grown so brisk that New Yorkers had steadily expanded the footprint of Manhattan with landfill to accommodate docks and warehouses.

Although the war had recently curtailed maritime commerce with England, New York's riverfront throbbed with the sounds of Dutch, Spanish, French, Italian and African voices. Tobacco, furs, indigo, rum, sugar, silks, spices and slaves were still traded here. Gunpowder was also in ready supply as merchant vessels evaded the British Navy on "powder cruises" to Europe and the Caribbean.

The iron fist of King George, however, was never far from view. The massive man-of-war, *Asia*, had sailed down from Boston to set anchor in New York harbor. It both protected the *Duchess of Gordon*, home of William Tryon, the titular Royal Governor of the colony, and threatened the city with its sixty-four guns.

Standing alone on the outskirts of camp, set on a plateau several hundred yards back from the Guana ridge, I watched traffic scurry through the waterways. A merchantman unfurled its sails, heading towards the Narrows, the passage between Long Island and

Staten Island that led out to the Atlantic Ocean. Ferries shuttled back and forth to New York. A slaver, traveling into the harbor, reeled in its riggings, its sad cargo of men, women and children in chains visible on the deck. Once again, I struggled to reconcile the fight for independence with the institution of slavery; and, once again, I realized it was a moot point unless the Continental Army proved victorious.

As the sun sunk towards New Jersey, I ruminated about my life after the war, assuming our side won. *I'll study law and enter politics. That's the only way to influence the debate over slavery and the myriad other issues the thirteen colonies must resolve if we hope to unite and form a new nation. As important, I'll marry and have children. A whole brood of them.*

Prudence might prove a suitable wife. She was a handsome woman brimming with energy and patriotic fervor. Father would approve, as would the Richards; but, I was far from ready to settle down.

Sadly, I could not see a renewed relationship with Anne Wheaton in my future, even though she was widowed. Her intellect, wit and passion were all characteristics I hoped to find in the woman I would someday marry, but she was now fully and publicly committed to the wrong side in this war. A year ago, our differences seemed ephemeral, a fissure that we might easily cross. But the distance had gaped into a chasm, and there was no middle ground.

Could I convince Anne to forgo her King and become an enthusiastic citizen of an independent America? I shook my head. Even if we both survived, I knew we would have difficulty casting aside our politics whenever the war ended, regardless of which side won.

I tapped the pocket of my waistcoat, the envelope there growing heavier by the second. It bore Prudence's seal, her first letter since we had parted. If the Continental Army could only protect New York as well as she had defended her maidenhead, the British would surely sail away in frustration. Yes, Pru had been generous with her hands and lips on the beach in New London, but never lifted her petticoats.

Assuming Pru's letter brought news of the Wheatons' trial, I had tucked it away until I could carve out a private moment after supper. While I didn't want to believe that Anne was a spy, I had no doubt she was capable of the task. I thought back to Anne's searing question in my school house only a year ago: would I be willing to sacrifice all? Now, she was the one possibly facing the ultimate sacrifice. I tore open the envelope and steeled myself for the worst.

Dearest Nathaniel,

I have much to tell you. Genral Washington stopped in New London last month. The entire town turned out to greet him. He cut quite the impresive figure astrid his handsum steed. He was surrounded by Life Gards, well bilt men who pledge their lives to protect our leader from his emenies. By chance, I had the pleasure to gain the acquantence of one such man. His name is Tom. He lived in Wethersfield before the war which he believes will be over by fall. He pledged to return to New London and marry me then which is good since I am carrying his child. You did not want to marry me anyway.

By the way, your beloved Anne and her cursed brother excaped from jail. They shot Constable Goodbody. He died. They had a boat waiting and sailed for Long Island. Looks like Asa Cobb helped them since he is gone too. There is a bounty now on their heads. We will hang them yet.

That is all.

Prudence Richards – soon to be Mrs. T. Hickey

I read the letter three times, slowly absorbing the news and calculating its implications. Although I could not blame Anne for escaping (I would do the same if captured by the enemy), she had participated in a violent act against my countryman, and must eventually pay the penalty. Was she the one who shot Constable Goodbody? I doubted she knew which end of the pistol to hold, but it didn't matter. Anne, like her brother, was a sworn enemy now. I would hunt them down himself, if I wasn't shackled to a spade.

How did Asa get involved? The only explanation was that they were all part of a spiderweb of spies. I turned to look at the fort under construction on Guana Heights. If the British found out the details of the Continental Army's defenses, they would know precisely where to attack. My men would die, as would my dream of a new nation.

Did the Continental Army employ spies? We certainly needed them, but I didn't know. Nor should I know, since spies by definition needed to operate in secrecy. It was a lonely, and most dangerous, assignment.

I should have felt disappointment or anger or jealousy at Prudence's betrayal, but, in truth, I only felt relief. She had not been shy about her quest to marry, and had obviously, and correctly, chosen not to wait for me. Although I was surprised that she had yielded to another man so quickly, I could see the attraction of her new beau.

Outfitted in blue coats, red vests and white shirts, Washington's Life Guards stood out among our largely ragamuffin army. I would have to inquire which lucky Guard was Tom Hickey. Or rather which honey-tongued man was Hickey, convincing Prudence the rebels could win the war by this fall. The Continental Army might be able to hold New York till then, but I doubted the British would just sail away defeated. The only way the war could be over quickly would be an overwhelming British victory this summer. I feared Pru had spread her legs for a beard-splitting rake and would bear the consequences alone.

After straightening my hat and fiddling with the sword at my hip, I stood tall, vowing to leave a more lasting impression on my next female connection. Stephen Hempstead trotted towards me. "Primping for a young lady, captain?" he asked.

"Not at all," I replied, embarrassed at my obvious self-indulgence.

"Just as well. We might have to get ourselves over to New York. Little John missed roll call."

"Have you asked around?"

"Elvin saw him heading towards the ferry landing. Thinks he might have returned to the Holy Ground for a second helping."

"The little whippersnapper. We'll have to flog some sense into him."

With the night warm and windless, Stephen and I rowed across the river to Murray's Wharf. After exchanging sign and countersign with the sentries guarding the bulwarks, we hied across the cobblestones of Wall Street. Although the Watch had already lit the evening lanterns, the stench of cattle guts still lingered over the meat market on the corner of Queen Street. We passed the Old Dutch Church, City Hall, Presbyterian meeting house, and Lutheran Church before reaching the steps of Trinity Church, an Anglican house of worship. The religious diversity in New York still amazed me. I had heard there was even a Jewish synagogue and cemetery uptown.

A chorus of drunken sailors welcomed us into the Holy Ground. Originally Church Farm, known for its neatly furrowed fields and rolling pastures, the property was subdivided in 1731 into small lots for working class housing in the name of urban development. Taverns, gambling houses, bear-baiting arenas and brothels sprung up as well. Close to the wharves, King's College and the stately homes on Broadway, these houses of sin gained popularity among all classes of New Yorkers and now dominated the neighborhood.

If the mythical Hades had a bazaar, I thought, it would undoubtedly look like this maze of narrow streets, eerily illuminated by lanterns sheathed in red cloth and cloaked in foul vapors from smithies' forges and tanners' vats. Prostitutes, hair uncapped and faces brightly rouged, beckoned from ramshackle log cabins and tottering tents, crammed tightly together in a motley mosaic. The human stink of sweat, shit, piss and puke stalked the alleyways.

Scattered clapboard tenements housed the more upscale establishments, smoke spilling from their chimneys. My hand slipped protectively over my genitals as we passed one such brothel where the bodies of two missing soldiers were found castrated in late April. I prayed Little John had not met the same fate.

"Elvin said they visited the whores in here," Stephen said as he pushed open the door of a crude tippling house, aptly named The Ramrod.

I choked on the tidal wave of tobacco fumes that greeted us. Standing on a sawed-off powder keg, a bearded fiddler played *Highland Laddie,* while a bald dwarf in a tartan kilt danced a jig in front of him. A harelipped trull jiggled her tits, pestering the crowd to stuff coins down her dress to pay for the entertainment.

I tossed a palmful of hacksilver on the bar, immediately garnering the attention of the barkeep, a Chinaman with a long queue trailing down his back, and signaled for two ales.

"Here you go," the barkeep said, sliding a single beer in our direction and swiping all my silver from the bar.

"I ordered two."

"You only paid for one."

"That's larcenous. Taverns on Broadway charge half that."

"You're on Holy Ground now, captain," the barkeep sneered.

I slung an even larger handful of change on the bar. The Chinaman dutifully brought a second beer and palmed half the coins.

"Looking for a good time officers?" a freckle-faced wench asked as she tossed her mane of red-gold hair in their direction. She had a black star patched on the right side of her forehead to signify her support for the rebel cause.

"Not tonight, dear," I replied, scanning the tavern for Little John.

"Queer, are you?" Her green eyes twinkled.

Stephen spit out a mouthful of ale. "No."

"I didn't think so," the whore said, pursing her lips, like Anne, I thought. "I'll do both of you at the same time for a good price. You can even bugger me if that suits your fancy."

"We're here on business," I said, now concerned that some old poofter might try to bugger Little John.

"D'ye think I'm here for laughs?" the whore cackled, revealing a mouthful of black teeth. "My name's Lara. I'll be around till dawn if you change your mind."

"There he is!" Stephen pointed at the stairway. Little John bounded down, a broad grin splitting his face.

"Take this." I swept my loose change off the bar and deposited it in Lara's hand.

"How much do you think she would have charged for buggery?" Stephen laughed as we hustled towards our young private.

"You're under arrest, Private Bell," I hissed, grabbing Little John by one elbow, while Stephen took the other. We frog-marched him out into the street. None of the other patrons paid much notice.

"It's not what you think," Little John stammered. "Well, it is what you think, but it's more than that."

"Are you drunk?" I asked, my grip still iron tight.

"No. I was intelligencing. And whoring."

"Intelligencing?"

"While I was waiting my turn, I talked to a man with a fine pistol. Silver-plated. I asked him where he got it."

"And?"

"Said he was a gunsmith. Just sold a crateful of pistols to Governor Tryon himself. For a pretty penny."

Weapons were scarce in New York for both soldiers and civilians. The Committee of Safety regularly ransacked homes of known Tory supporters and confiscated their guns. Supplying the *Duchess* with pistols was a hanging offense. "What was the man's name?" I asked.

"You don't exactly ask a man his name at The Ramrod," Little John replied. "But, he said if I wanted to earn some coin I could meet him back here the night after next."

"You may have just saved yourself a flogging," I said, releasing the young man.

***

Anne bowed her head to pray, a tear welling in her eye. *Glory to the Father, Son and Holy Spirit*...She hadn't attended a proper Anglican service since Geoffrey died. She remembered her giddiness when Reverend Dowell read their banns for the third time. Now she was hiding out in Greenwich and worshipping in a clandestine service with curtains drawn in the parlor of David Bush, a cattle farmer with Loyalist ties. God works in strange ways.

She added a brief prayer for the soul of Constable Goodbody. He had treated her fairly, unlike Prescott, yet he was the one to catch a slug. She flinched when the post rider brought the news from upstate but had little time for sentimentality. War was unfair, yet it was her destiny to be caught in the middle of it, her fate pre-determined.

Facing a certain death sentence if arrested, Anne knew her trust in God would be tested. Fortunately, Greenwich, located on Connecticut's western border with New York, the colony most loyal to the Crown, was as safe a place for her and Caleb as any town in New England. While ostensibly governed by a Committee of Safety supporting the rebellion, Loyalists were numerous in the Greenwich countryside, and well-armed. Darcy's aunt, Hephzibah Merritt, a widow, and her four grown children, lived on a farm five miles from town on Round Hill Road and offered shelter, at least temporarily, to the fugitives.

After shepherding them here, Major Rogers did not linger long. He recruited Caleb to join him on a journey north, but, while sorely tempted, her brother refused, much to Anne's relief. Although she didn't want to be an anchor around Caleb's neck, she needed him. Darcy didn't appear to shed any tears over the major's departure, but neither did she demonstrate the slightest fancy for Caleb who seemed more interested in winning the acceptance of her two cousins, young men his own age, than in regaining her affections anyway. Anne closed her devotion with a prayer that their current domestic arrangements would last a while longer.

A benefit of the secret church service was its brevity: the sermon, warning against the evils of profanity and lewdness, lasted only an hour. Straightening her skirt, she felt the weight of her pistol in the pannier beneath her petticoat. All the Merritt women, except for fifteen-year-old Remember, traveled armed; the Continental Army had not been kind to suspected Tories during its march from Boston to New York. She stepped out into the spring sunshine, allowing herself a moment to bask before taking Caleb's hand to walk towards the wagon for the ride back to the farm.

While still the Sabbath, no one in the Merritt household could afford the luxury of rest, not with the British army expected to arrive shortly in the New York area. Anne joined the women at the kitchen table to knit socks for the Regulars; she had learned firsthand in Boston how cold and hunger could drive a man to depravity. Caleb galloped away with Shubal and Bezaleel, muskets slung across their shoulders.

The rambling farmhouse was a picture of bliss. A fire burned in the hearth; a kettle of boiling water hung on the crane; a silver teapot, creamer and sugar dish, all engraved with an intricate pattern of leaves and vines, gleamed on the table. Anne stitched effortlessly, the heft of thick yarn and needle a welcome reminder of happier times.

"You ladies have fast fingers," Widow Hephzibah, a hogshead of a woman with fleshy, pitted cheeks and short stubby fingers herself, said, admiring first Anne's, then Darcy's, work. After about two hours of sewing, both women were more than halfway up the calf of a sock, while the Merritt women were still working the ankles.

"Our families were tailors and dressmakers. We didn't have much choice," Anne replied. She didn't want to compete, but she *was* further along than Darcy.

"Your socks are so smooth. Mine always bulge," Remember, blessed with blonde curls and an unblemished complexion, said, dropping her needles on the table in frustration.

"If you paid more attention, you wouldn't lose track of the count," scolded her twenty-year-old sister, Thankfull, who, like her mother, bore the scars of smallpox.

"If I could attend school, I'd know my sums and tables," Remember countered.

"Hush your nonsense. A young woman don't need schooling," Hephzibah answered. "Now, get back to your knitting."

Anne placed her own sock down and picked up Remember's. Her little sisters, Phoebe and Grace, would have been about Remember's age had they lived. "You only did seven stitches here, and here," she pointed out. "You need eight. And eight purls back. Just follow my lead." Anne handed the sock back to Remember and reclaimed her own, slowing her handiwork so the girl could follow.

"Humph," Thankfull retorted, burying her head in her own yarn.

"Pass the sugar, please," Hephzibah asked, apparently ignoring both her daughters for the time being. She held out her cup, flicking out her pinky to affect an air of formality. A comical gesture for a frumpy, farmer's widow in rural Connecticut, Anne noted smugly.

"We're almost out of tea, Mother," Thankfull replied. "Perhaps our new *friend* has relations that can help us refill our pantry."

"It's not Christian to ask friends for favors, dear," Hephzibah scowled. "But, Anne, we would all love to hear more about your time in Boston."

"Were you really betrothed to a lord?" Remember fumbled in her pocket, pulled out a horn-carved comb, and stroked her golden locks. Her pale blue eyes danced, oblivious to the tension building in the room.

"Anne's been through quite an ordeal. She'll tell all in due time," Darcy interjected, her fingers working furiously.

"I think the time is past due." Hephzibah said.

"What do you think she's hiding?" Darcy asked, stopping her knitting. "Do you think she's here to spy on us?"

"I make no such accusation, but our family and farm are at great risk should she have *friends* on both sides of the aisle."

"Didn't Major Rogers vouch for her?" Darcy continued her defense, her voice rising in anger.

"Who will vouch for Major Rogers?" Hephzibah replied. "Some reports have him in the Continental camp; others with the British."

"And the letter of reference he gave you?"

"From a Native. A woman no less. Hard to put much stock in that."

"Humph," Thankful seconded her mother's opinion.

"His name was Geoffrey, Major Geoffrey Stanwich of the 63rd Regiment of Foot. He lost a leg driving the Jonathans off Breed's Hill," Anne said quietly, surprising herself with her use of upper-crust idiom. She looked up briefly from her knitting to be certain Widow Hephzibah saw the grief shrouding her words. "He also held the title of Lord of Runcorn, a family estate in Northern England going back generations. Banns were read, we were set to marry. I was to assume the title of Lady Runcorn, and move to England," Anne continued, casting a quick glance at Darcy's progress. "But I was attacked by drunken regulars at night on the Long Wharf. My beloved died bravely defending my honor."

"That's so sad. But so gallant," Remember said, looking dreamily at Anne.

"Tell us more, dear," the Widow asked.

Returning to her stitches, Anne recounted her story from the first meeting with Geoffrey in the mansion on Beacon Hill. She finished her sock, a few purls behind Darcy disappointedly, about the same time as she described her escape from jail in New London.

"How convenient that the town hall emptied the night before your trial," Thankfull said while studying an errant stitch.

"Except for Constable Goodbody," Darcy said. "Poor man, he did like my apple cobbler."

"And no one's come looking for you down here," Thankfull continued to probe.

"Yet," her mother added.

Anne felt she had said enough. She picked up a ball of yarn and started another sock.

"Did you have a new gown to wear at your wedding?" Remember asked.

"A lavender one. I made it myself. And a velvet shawl to match."

"I'd love to see it. Someday."

"My father promised to bring my belongings to New York. And my mother and brother, Phineas." Anne wondered how Mother had fared in Halifax. Not well, she expected, but it couldn't have been worse than Boston. It would be grand to see her again. And Phineas always made her laugh.

"Are you with child, dear?" Hephzibah interrupted.

Although she knew the answer, Anne instinctively looked down at her belly. She was taken aback by the bluntness of the question, but it was not unwarranted. Hephzibah was both the head of household and mother of two bachelors. "No, although not for want of effort," she replied.

Thankfull arched her brows, while Remember's jaw dropped open. "I appreciate an honest woman." Hephzibah said, returning to her knitting.

"When will you leave here?" Thankfull asked. "To meet your family, that is."

"As soon as we get word the Navy has sailed from Halifax."

"That could be any day now," Hephzibah added.

"You don't have much time to lure Caleb into your bed then, sister," Remember teased, quickly ducking her head. Thankfull threw down her knitting and stalked from the table.

"Caleb always has a place here," Hephzibah said, looking after her eldest daughter who had disappeared into the parlor.

And me? Hephzibah's unspoken words hurt, reminding Anne of her tenuous position as a single woman without family, money or property.

The women resumed their knitting, needles twirling in silence until the sun dipped below the tree line. Remember lit candles, while Thankfull brought out a tray of cold meats and vegetables for supper. Hephzibah passed around a jug of homemade moonshine. Her daughters sipped, while Darcy swallowed lustily, much to her dismay. Anne took her turn last, but was still unprepared for the potency of the brew. Her eyebrows ignited and gullet blazed, but she forced a smile of approval.

At the thunder of approaching hoofbeats, Hephzibah removed her firelock from its rack above the hearth. Although a bit wobbly, Anne reached into her pannier and cocked the hammer of her pistol.

"Probably just the Cowboys, Ma," Remember said, taking another swallow from the jug. The Cowboys were a gang of rough men who supported the Crown and defended Loyalists in the Greenwich vicinity, at least that was what Caleb had told her when he rode off with them last week.

"Too many horses," Hephzibah replied as she slowly opened the door with her weapon now on her hip. The four other women crowded behind her. Fireflies buzzed the portico; the chickens clucked in their coop as if they smelled an approaching fox. The old goat looked up from a cud of grass as a throng of at least ten riders galloped up the path.

"That's young William Sharpe out in front," Remember pointed out. "He's constable now that so many of the other men went off to war."

"A Skinner too, ain't he?" her mother asked.

"I do believe so," Thankfull replied. The Skinners were supposedly a rival gang that favored the rebel cause. Anne drew her pistol from its hiding place.

"Put that away, dear," Hephzibah said, dropping the barrel of her musket. "Old man Sharpe's been our neighbor for twenty years now. The Skinners don't mean us no harm."

Cowboys and Skinners riding together? Anne was thoroughly confused, but she obeyed the widow. She breathed a bit easier when she saw Caleb and the two Merritt boys in the middle of the pack.

"Good evening to you, Widow Merritt," Will Sharpe said as he dismounted. A tall dashing youth with dusty, un-queued hair slapping his shoulders, he wore a bandolier across his chest that holstered a pistol at the ready under each armpit.

"And to you," Hephzibah replied. "What brings you calling at this late hour?"

"We came across your boys and their house guest on the road. Wanted to make sure they arrived home safely." He was close enough for Anne to count his missing teeth.

"Much obliged," Hephzibah replied warily, now cradling her musket in her arms.

Caleb, smiling broadly, hopped off his horse and unfastened his bulging saddlebags. A palm-sized, silver box, engraved with a detailed curlicue pattern, tumbled out, spilling black stars, half-moons and dots into the dirt.

"I've brought you a present sister," he called as he gathered up the patches. "And a scarf as well."

What is my brother doing with a sterling patch box? And a silk scarf? Before she could ask the questions, one of the Skinners kicked the flanks of his horse, a gray sorrel, and bore down on Caleb. Anne screamed, but it was too late. The Skinner swung the stock of his musket, clubbing her brother on the back of his head. Caleb went limp as a rag doll, sprawling in the dirt, loot spraying out of his saddlebags.

"Lookee here. Your guest's been raiding the good citizens of Greenwich," Will Sharpe said, pointing a pistol at the baubles now littering the yard. He nodded to his men, who drew their weapons and surrounded both the Merritts. "Your boys too. I heard they roused Elder Mead and his wife. Live all alone now since their sons marched off with General Washington."

"I'll make sure you get your share," Hephzibah said. Anne saw the widow's trigger finger twitch, but they were badly outnumbered.

"I'm sure you will, but that ain't enough."

"What do you want then, Mr. Sharpe?"

Remember and Thankfull sidled backwards into the house. Anne tightened her grip on her pocketed weapon. Darcy stood her ground next to Anne.

"*Constable* Sharpe," Will corrected, as he sighted his pistol over the widow's shoulder. "I've got the brother. I want the sister too. There's quite a bounty on the Wheatons up in New London."

Anne froze. There was no place to run. And she couldn't leave Caleb. Even if he had turned into a common highwayman in the name of the King.

Hephzibah aimed her musket at Will's chest. "Come on inside, Constable Sharpe. I've got a fresh batch of shine and some victuals on the table. I do believe we can work out an arrangement suitable to both our interests."

The women stepped back as Sharpe and four of his men, one of whom had Caleb's inert body slung over his shoulder, barged inside. Thankfull took her mother's cue, grabbing Remember by the elbow and tugging her into the kitchen. Darcy passed the jug to Sharpe, while Anne tended to her brother who had been dumped into a chair. She sensed the Skinners' pistols aimed at her back, but refused to face them.

"You take the whole load from the Mead house." Hephzibah started dealing even before she and Sharpe sat down.

"That might be a fair price for your boys," Sharpe countered, nodding towards the door, left open to allow some air flow in the crowded room. His men held Shubal and Bezaleel at gunpoint in the yard. "But not for them two murdering Wheatons."

"We didn't kill anyone," Anne said.

"You can tell that to the judge," Sharpe replied, standing as if to leave. One of his men, dead-eyed and greasy-palmed, took Anne's left arm. She struggled but couldn't shake free.

Hephzibah pushed the silver tea set forward. "Take this too."

"I can burn this whole damn house to the ground if I want," Sharpe said, pounding his fist.

"Yes you can," the widow replied in a voice that betrayed no fear. She took a swig from the jug, wiping the drips from the corner of her mouth with the sleeve of her dress. "But then the Cowboys'll be round your pappy's house right quick. Not to mention the King's Own when they march into town."

Sharpe sat down again. His wheels didn't turn too quickly, but, after several seconds, he swept up the tea set. "For which one?"

"Both of them."

"Nope."

"The boy then." Hephzibah pointed to Caleb.

"No," gasped Darcy. Anne's knees wobbled. She wanted to draw her pistol but was too slow. Another of the Skinners grabbed her right arm, yanking her away from Caleb. Remember slipped back into the room bearing a plate of food.

Sharpe whistled in admiration at Hephzibah. "You looking to marry the young buck?"

"Not me, you fool," the widow replied. "Thankfull's the one that needs a husband. Not too many eligible bachelors left in town."

"Mother…," Thankfull moaned.

"Hush daughter, and go look after your man. He's starting to come to."

Thankfull tossed her head, but tripped over her skirt as she hurried to Caleb's side. She wiped his forehead with her kerchief without ever taking her gloating eyes off Anne.

"We can't let them take Anne," Remember said. She rushed towards Anne, but was repelled by her captors.

"We can't hardly stop them. She's worth a pretty penny," Hephzibah said, standing to signal the end of the negotiation. "I'll see you and your men out then?"

Remember took a bounteous swig from the jug. "You'll need a wife yourself soon enough, Will," she declared, bursting past her mother.

"The Wheaton woman?" Sharpe guffawed, looking around the room to make sure his men laughed along. "She's a Tory, and not a particularly pretty one at that. I might use her, but I wouldn't want to wake up next to that horse-face every morning."

"Not her. Me." Remember pushed the curls off her forehead and angled her bosom forward. "I'd be right pleased if you chose to come courting."

"Stifle yourself, girl," Hephzibah commanded. "You're much too young for that talk."

"I'm old enough, Mother. Since I can't go to school, I might as well get hitched." Remember took Sharpe's hand. "And you'd be a good provider, wouldn't you Will?"

Sharpe looked Remember up and down, as if he was inspecting a side of beef. "I do believe I would," he said slowly, a leer crossing his lips.

"No!" Anne shouted. "You can't give yourself to that pig. Not on my account."

"It's settled then," Remember said, refusing to even look at Anne. "You'll come courting for the next year. Until we're ready to marry. And Anne will live here with us."

"What if she runs off before the wedding?" Sharpe asked, pulling his hand back from Remember's touch.

"She won't. I'll lock her in the cellar if I have to," Hephzibah said, reaching for her musket. "Do we have a deal?"

"I reckon we do." Sharpe cupped Remember's chin. "I believe I'll pay my first courting call tomorrow evening."

"We ain't going nowhere," Hephzibah said, moving towards the door. "But it's getting late now. The candles are guttering."

Caleb groaned and lolled his eyes. Thankfull cradled his woozy head. Anne's captors relaxed the grip on her arms. She sunk back against the wall.

"We're almost done," Sharpe said.

"Almost?" Hephzibah asked.

"I *am* the constable now. What will the people think if I don't enforce the law?" Sharpe signaled for two of his men to seize Caleb. They shoved Thankfull to the side and dragged Caleb to the table. "You don't want me to bring him in front of the judge now, do you?"

"What do you have in mind?" Hephzibah's shoulders sagged as the words rolled from her lips. Caleb's eyes began to focus. He struggled in vain to free himself.

"An ear or a hand," Sharpe said, unleashing the tomahawk from his belt loop. "I have to show the Meads some measure of justice, now don't I?"

"No!" Thankfull, Darcy and Anne shouted simultaneously, but Sharpe ignored them, tapping his blade on the table.

"A finger. The boy'll be your relation soon enough," Hephzibah countered. "You might be working this farm together after I pass on."

"All right then. A finger." He pointed for his men to bring Caleb's left hand forward and pin his wrist to the table. He separated four fingers, leaving Caleb's pinky exposed.

"Please God, make it a clean strike," Thankfull prayed in a hushed tone. She fainted, crumbling to the floor as the blade sliced off the digit, blood squirting into the tray of meats.

Caleb clamped his jaw shut, staring in shock at his mangled hand, refusing to acknowledge the pain. The Skinners marched victoriously out the door, loot and trophy finger in hand.

Hephzibah held the poker in the fire until it glowed. She forced a rag between Caleb's teeth before pouring a thimble of whiskey into his wound and cauterizing it. Caleb passed out again, his head rattling the table. Anne bandaged her brother's hand while he was unconscious. Remember and Darcy cleared the dishes.

***

I had never flogged a man before, but I had little choice this evening. There was no greater vice in a commander than ease, both Washington and Lee had pounded the dictum into me and my fellow captains back in Cambridge.

Stephen Hempstead had caught Seamus McElroy, one of Captain Caulk's Irishmen, in the mansion of Governor's Island with two silver salvers and a pocketful of spoons. After completing our work on Guana Heights, the 19th had been reassigned to the sparsely populated island, strategically located in the harbor within swimming distance of both Long Island and New York, to fortify its defenses.

I understood the temptation. My soldiers were worked hard, paid infrequently, fed poorly, and surrounded by the trappings of wealth, often owned by Tories; nevertheless, the charges against McElroy had gone up the chain of command, a brief court martial ensued, and the sentence handed down.

Little John beat a somber tune on his drum. My entire company stood in formation while the thief, a hirsute grizzly of a man, was stripped to the waist, tied to a post, and offered a bullet to grind between his teeth. I prayed silently before setting to the task.

The Army must maintain discipline if we hope to become a potent fighting force. I bit my lip as I delivered the first blow, the cat-o-nine tails slicing into the private's back. My arm tired at fifteen lashes; sweat dripped into my eyes. McElroy, to his credit, refused to cry out. I paused for only a few seconds rest before continuing the flogging.

We are the defender of our homeland, not a foreign invader, and need to treat our fellow citizens accordingly. Elvin, standing in the front rank, fainted at twenty-five strokes, but Hercules held him upright. The old Black man had undoubtedly seen worse in his years as a slave. McElroy's eyes wobbled in their sockets like sloops in a storm, but he remained silent. Little John continued his drum roll.

The citizenry, multiplying rapidly and spread over a giant land mass, can be the Army's greatest asset over time. After a blister burst on my right thumb at thirty-three lashes, I rested again. I motioned for Sergeant Hempstead to offer McElroy a sip of rum, but the private bared the gnawed bullet between his teeth in refusal. Hempstead swabbed the blood off McElroy's back before the punishment continued.

New York is the crucial test. If we can weather the British assault this summer, we can win the war. Soaked in sweat, I dropped the whip after thirty-nine lashes. I could see McElroy's suffering reflected in the eyes of my men. But I also saw the spark of grim determination, a recognition of the need to rise to the difficulties ahead. I prayed that I was up to the task of leading them.

Hempstead cut McElroy, unconscious now, down. Two of his bunkmates carried him away. I dismissed the troop, relieved that my obligation here was complete.

"General Washington would approve," Hempstead said as we walked back to our tents. Cooking fires glowed; drums beat to announce supper time.

"I hope to do more to gain the General's attention than flog a man," I replied.

"Tonight's the night then."

Little John had been recruited by his contact at the Ramrod to row a skiff from Red Hook on the Long Island shore out to the *Asia* after midnight. While stealing from civilians was taboo, intercepting supplies headed for the British definitely was not. If our mission succeeded, my troop could end the evening with a celebration.

Hatless, shirtless and barefoot, I led ten men, skillful with fists and knives, down into the reeds on the shoreline. All claimed to be strong swimmers as well. Hempstead followed me in line, just ahead of Ian Lawrie, Caulk's other recruit, whose diminutive height belied the power of his punch. I especially wanted Lawrie along to keep an eye on him after his mate's flogging.

Little John, sporting a yellow peacock feather in his cap, had gone on ahead. I had planned to shield the boy from danger for as long as possible, but the boy was a man now in more ways than one.

The stars twinkled and the moon was full, bathing the harbor in an eerie glow. A breeze rustled the treetops, but the waters were calm. My feet sunk into the mud, gentle wavelets nipping my ankles. The tide was out, leaving the Buttermilk Channel between Governor's Island and Long Island a squishy quagmire, stinking with the smell of dead fish. I signaled for my men to halt, while I surveyed the harbor with my spyglass.

The *Asia*, torchlights flickering from its thirty-two gun ports, sat defiantly in deep water no more than a good swim away. It towered over the *Duchess of Gordon* which had gone dark for the night. As the *Asia's* watchman called the hour of eleven from the poop deck, four marines climbed over the taffrail into a skiff tethered to the mother ship.

A beacon flashed from the tip of Red Hook. Oars splashed as the skiff steered towards it.

"Weren't expecting the lobsterbacks, were we?" Hempstead whispered.

"No," I replied. Little John had led me to believe we would be dealing with Loyalist civilians, not soldiers. None of my men, including me, had faced the British regulars in actual combat. The moment of truth approached.

"Can ye trust the lad?" Lawrie whispered. "He'll not lead us into an ambush?"

"I've no cause to doubt him," I replied confidently. Little John's judgment might be suspect, but his loyalty was not.

"His pintle's out of his breeches now. That's cause enough."

"Not for me." I stepped forward. There was no more time for discussion. We would have to move fast, an arduous task in the muck, to reach the rendezvous before the British loaded up and pushed off.

"Move out men," Hempstead seconded, touching his finger to his lips to signal silence.

An hour later, we approached the end of the channel. The water line reached my knees. Sounds of exertion, men cursing and splashing, filtered down from the point.

I clambered up onto the rocky shore, turning to count my men. All there. We would be seen at any second. I nodded to Hempstead as I drew my pistol. "Huzzah!" I cried, leading the charge.

The battle was over before it began. There was only one Loyalist, the gunsmith presumably, who fled into the night. Three of the redcoats dropped their loads, mouths drooping open in surprise as they raised their hands to surrender. "Damn ye cowards!" the fourth, an ensign, cursed before he dove off the skiff and began to swim back towards the *Asia*. I grabbed the hawser to reel in the prize.

The loot included two dozen pistols and two hundred balls, as well as a cask of Madeira, two kegs of buttermilk, a trunk of cheese, a fat ham and a pouch of sealed letters. The armaments, paperwork and prisoners would have to be turned over to General Putnam in the morning, but I planned to share the beverages and foodstuffs with my entire company.

By evening muster the next day, word of our foray had circulated throughout the Continental Army's encampments. I soaked in adulations for the next week, the schoolteacher with the musket scar who had tweaked the nose of the mighty British. While the loot itself was insignificant to the defense of New York, our daring escapade was a welcome omen to men who checked the horizon hourly for enemy sails.

CHAPTER 15 - JUNE 1776

"Upon information that Major Rogers was travelling thro' the Country under suspicious circumstances I thought it necessary to have him secured. He was taken at South Amboy and brought up to New York. He... pretended he was destined to Philadelphia, on business with Congress...the Major's reputation, and his being an half pay Officer has encreased my Jealousies about him..."
George Washington
Letter to John Hancock
June 27, 1776

An inner calm settled over Robert Rogers as he hiked alone through the northern wilderness, home for the best years of his life. The towering trees goaded him onward; the crisp scent of pine breathing new life into his aging limbs. For the past month, he had surveilled upper New York and Canada, returning twice to a farmhouse outside Crown Point to leave coded reports for delivery to Princess, and hopefully General Howe as well.

These reports contained positive news for the British. The Continental forces, which had remained camped outside Quebec after their defeat there in December, were in disarray, poorly supplied and rife with disease. Men were deserting in droves. Their commander, John Thomas, a respected veteran who had led the fortification of Dorchester Heights, lay dying of smallpox. It was a cruel twist of fate as Thomas had prohibited inoculation fearing the risky process would weaken his troops, if not kill them outright, before the summer fighting season.

Rogers had urged the British to press the advantage and swoop down from Fort Quebec, the guardian of the strategic St. Lawrence River, into the Hudson River valley. If Howe captured New York, as he most certainly would, the British would control both the coastal and inland waterways of North America, strangling the colonies' war efforts. Furthermore, redcoat reinforcements, already en route, could pour into both entry points, trapping Washington and his army between them. The rebellion could be put down before Christmas.

Recent information gleaned from conversations in taverns and campsites, however, had led Rogers to reconsider this recommendation. Brigadier General Benedict Arnold was supposedly building a fleet, dubbed the Mosquitos, in a shipyard at Skenesborough, south of Ticonderoga, that could ambush the British navy in the narrow straits of Lake Champlain.

The men, the true fighting men, of the Continental Army adored Arnold and would follow him to the Gates of Hell – again. Their journey through the wilderness last winter to reach the gates of Quebec had been as rigorous, if not as foolhardy, an expedition as any Rogers himself had led twenty years ago. Furthermore, before the war, Arnold had captained a merchant schooner, a smuggler most likely, providing firsthand experience with naval skirmishes and tactics. He was the general that Howe should fear, not George Washington, in Rogers' professional opinion.

Fortunately, the Continental Congress appeared to be doing its best to keep Arnold down. After Quebec, Congress had pushed him to Montreal, away from the front lines, and now to Skenesborough. Lesser generals, Wooster and Gates, appeared to be in ascendancy even though Rogers thought they couldn't defeat a herd of cattle on the battlefield. John Sullivan, Rogers' interrogator on Winter Hill, was rumored to be heading to Quebec to replace the dying Thomas, but he also had never led troops in combat. All the while, Philip Schuyler, the titular head of the northern army, never left his cozy mansion in Albany.

Regardless, Rogers needed to see Skenesborough for himself before filing his next report. He skirted Fort Ticonderoga, its ramparts largely devoid of cannon thanks to the herculean efforts of Henry Knox, and boarded a flatboat ferry to cross Lake Champlain, sparkling in the morning light, to the eastern shore. A long day's hike took him south to the Poultney River which fed into Skenesborough harbor. Camping by the bank, he caught a trout for dinner with his bare hands.

He completed his journey to Skenesborough in the pre-dawn darkness, settling into a prone position underneath a lush blackberry bush, set in a grove atop an overgrown hillside that tumbled down to the waterside. Wildflowers, pink and purple, tickled his nose. *I never noticed the colors of the blooms before*, Rogers noted as he shifted his gaze to the waterfront.

He didn't have long to ponder the meaning of his awakening as fife and drum resonated before sunrise. Arnold himself, easily recognizable by the pronounced limp resulting from British shot during the assault on Quebec, led a torchlight procession of fifty-odd men to the quays. The first rays of daylight revealed four fighting boats already at anchor.

Rogers watched as the Continentals went quickly to their tasks. Saws cleaved tree trunks into masts; scissors trimmed canvas; searing fires heated cauldrons of pitch. The skeletons of two more vessels rose on drydock, shipwrights scrambling over gracefully curved ribs like bees returning to the hive. Arnold was everywhere, urging his men onward, lending a helping hand, cursing the King.

Absorbed by the choreography down at the harbor, Rogers never heard the soldiers' approach until a pistol cocked behind his right ear. He slowly extended his arms, palms down in the grass, and cranked his head around to assess the situation as best he could.

"Enjoying the view, old man," a lanky lieutenant, marked by the cockade in his hat, drawled.

"Beautiful sunrise," Rogers replied. A boot thumped his rib cage, driving the breath from his lungs.

"That'll teach you to be saucy," another southern voice twanged.

Rogers curled to protect himself from the next blow as well as to gain a peek at his captors: three soldiers, all dressed in the oat-white, fringed hunting jackets of Morgan's Rangers from Virginia. The two privates carried long guns, rifles with grooved barrels that were far more accurate at distance than a typical smooth-bored musket. The Virginians' sharpshooting was legendary, particularly targeting any British officer foolish enough to stick his head above the ramparts in Boston and Quebec.

"We should've just shot him when we spotted him," the second private spit through a thatchy beard that draped down his chest.

"Weren't no challenge in that," the first private, cleanshaven and reeking of lavender cologne, countered. "The geezer stood out like a peacock."

"Spying's a hanging offense," the lieutenant said. "But I do believe General Arnold will want to interrogate the man before we string him up."

"You've made a mistake." Rogers' comment earned him another boot in the stomach. Before he could regain his wind, his hands were wrestled behind his back and hog-tied with a leather cord. The two privates jerked him to his feet.

"Let's go meet the General," the lieutenant commanded, shoving Rogers downhill.

Rogers stumbled, barely keeping his balance. His mind raced ahead, trying to concoct a story that might save his life. Of course, he was spying. What else could he claim to be doing hiding in the bush above the harbor? And he was still officially a major in the British Army. But he was no amateur. There were no notes or maps hidden in his boots; he kept all the details in his head. All he had in his pack was his own book, *Journals,* but they wouldn't know it was the basis of his coded communications to Princess.

The quartet entered a dense grove of pines, the trail swathed in shadow, the harbor obscured from sight. An Indian battle cry split the silence. He sensed the swish of the war club before he heard it crack the lieutenant's skull. As the body hit the ground, Princess pirouetted to face the two privates. Her braids slapped against her cheeks. She twirled her club once above her head, gathering momentum, then smashed it into the bearded private's midsection. He doubled over and dropped to his knees. The cleanshaven private reached for his weapon, but a long gun was not much use at close range. Princess backhanded her club into his face, splitting it open like a pumpkin.

Rogers shuffled uphill towards the fray, but Princess didn't need any assistance. He swore she grinned as she approached the gagging private, still on his knees. With her left hand, she grabbed his beard and jerked his head skyward. With her right, she unsheathed her knife and slit his throat. He died face down in a gurgling scarlet puddle.

"We need to move fast," Princess said, as she cut Rogers free.

"Why...? How...?" Thunderstruck by the ferocity of Princess's attack, he could barely croak out syllables.

"I'm here because I didn't believe your messages. My contacts in Albany read Schuyler's mail. He thinks his army in Canada is thriving and ready to assault Quebec again." Princess wiped the blood off the head of her club, the warlight fading from her eyes. "I followed you quite easily from the safe house. You're getting sloppy Major

Rogers," she continued. "But you were right to come here. Arnold is dangerous. We must get word to Howe."

Rogers nodded in agreement, finally regaining his bearings. He picked up the bearded Virginian's long gun, its stock engraved with an intricate pattern of gold vines, and sighted down the barrel at an imaginary target.

"Let's move," Princess said, stepping out of the grove of trees into the sunshine.

Another rifle puffed from a rock formation two hundred yards to their left. Princess's head snapped backwards as the bullet perforated her chest. She slumped into the dirt, but had enough sense, and strength, to crawl behind the trunk of a fallen tree.

Rogers stayed in the shadows, searching for the shooter. How many were out there? He couldn't help Princess until he knew the answer. He counted slowly to five, then ten; no more shots were fired. Only one rifleman left on patrol. He knew it took at least thirty seconds to reload a long gun; the bullet had to be threaded down the barrel. That was his window. He kneeled and aimed at the rocks. The Virginian stood to ram powder and ball. Rogers was an expert shot but had never fired at this distance. Fortunately, age had yet to diminish his eyesight. He cocked the firelock, aimed at the rifleman's chest, a bigger target than a head shot, and squeezed the trigger.

Rogers' rifle recoiled from the blast, slamming his shoulder. The Virginian keeled over. Rogers rushed to Princess's side. She was sitting up, her back against the tree, her complexion paled. He scraped together a bed of pine boughs and laid her flat.

"A lucky shot," Princess said, smiling wanly.

Rogers peeled open her shirt and examined her shattered breast. Princess winced as he probed for lead but refused to cry out. He lifted her shoulders, the bullet appeared to have exited cleanly, so there was hope, but only if he could staunch the bleeding. Slicing his spare shirt into strips, he stuffed the wound, lifted her arms, and bound her chest.

Princess's lips were cracked and brittle. Rogers cradled her head to help her sip from his canteen. The rum might dull the pain.

"Thank you," she said.

"You need to rest," he replied. They both knew there was nothing more he could do.

Princess dozed in his arms for a minute, then snapped awake. "The Continentals will be coming soon. You need to leave me."

She was right. Rogers thought of Tom Brown, the private he had left to the Indians twenty years ago. It was the law of the wilderness. He covered Princess with her sleeping roll, placing water, two strands of jerky, and her war club next to her. She reached out to stroke the handle of the club, like it was a loyal hound. "Three more skulls…" she whispered.

He took her hand and placed his pistol, primed and cocked, in it. "This may serve you better."

"Go!" she commanded, coughing up blood as she rested a finger on the trigger.

Rogers wiped the spittle from her lips and smoothed her braids, wanting to say more than goodbye but the words wouldn't come. He slung his pack and musket over his shoulder, deciding to leave the long gun behind. It would only raise questions he didn't want to answer.

"A warrior's death…," Princess murmured, smiling contentedly as she closed her eyes, her breathing ragged. Rogers headed south towards New York.

***

After three weeks strengthening defenses on Long Island and Governor's Island, my regiment returned to Manhattan, billeting a mile north of the city in an abandoned Anglican meetinghouse. This morning, I awoke before reveille, my night shirt drenched in sweat, my mind shuttling between the two unpredictable, but mortal, threats facing the Continental Army – the British invasion and the pox. Combined, they could easily end the rebellion right here in New York this summer.

Just yesterday, I learned that General John Thomas had succumbed outside Quebec. Thomas, a former physician himself, had appeared indestructible only three months ago; now, he was gone. Even worse, rumors circulated that the pox had decimated the entire Northern Army, filling barns in Canada with sick and dying soldiers.

No one was quite sure what caused the disease, how to prevent it, or how to cure it. Once the telltale pustules broke out, the victim was in God's hands, the odds of survival little better than 50/50.

Fortunately, history had demonstrated that an individual who lived through the ordeal would be immune for life. After surviving a sickly infancy and a bout with the measles in college, I believed I was one of the lucky ones.

Who would be next? Could the epidemic reach New York? Could a depleted army repel the British forces on land and sea?

Sunrise revealed the full scope of the challenge posed by the geography of Manhattan. It was a long, pencil-thin island, only two miles across at its widest point. The Hudson River stretched to the horizon on one coast, while the East River did the same on the other. There was simply too much waterfront to barricade against an amphibious assault. If the British landed en masse anywhere, they could cut off New York City completely. Unless Washington had a network of spies to provide critical intelligence, I concluded, the British would likely prove a more formidable enemy than the pox.

As my company formed up for roll call, I counted heads. A third of my men had failed to muster. I headed back inside where several soldiers wallowed in their own filth. I forced myself to walk from berth to berth, repeating a few kind words to each man as I scanned his face. McElroy was still recovering from his flogging, but his cheeks showed a healthy color. Lawrie was sallow-faced and sweating. He had likely drunk well or river water, both equally fetid, or too much rum. A yellow complexion, however, was better than pimples and pus.

I was more concerned with Elvin Parrish; the private had fought a fever for the past two days. The next twenty-four hours would be critical to see if the fever broke or developed into something more serious. An image of the dead wagon rolling up to collect Elvin's body shuddered my thoughts. Little John had simply overslept. I kicked his bedroll until he snapped awake.

After breakfast, we marched north to forage. On a scout yesterday   afternoon, I had discovered a cluster of empty homes, a little "Tory-town", just outside the village of Bloomingdale. While gunpowder was now plentiful, lead, necessary for bullets and cannonballs, was scarce. Accordingly, the army ripped apart vacated Tory property, while patriot families generally volunteered their pewter, ornaments, and tableware to be melted down for the cause.

"When do you suppose General Washington will return?" Asher Wright asked me on the march. Strong and loyal as a mule, and generally as taciturn, my orderly had largely lived up to expectations. "It's been almost two weeks now."

"Don't know," I replied brusquely, having asked myself the same question the last few mornings. The commander-in-chief was off meeting with Hancock and the Congress in Philadelphia right now.

"The men are getting restless." Asher switched his musket to his left shoulder. "There's one rumor that Washington's going to resign and return to Mount Vernon. Another man thinks he's been sacked by Congress and replaced by General Lee. A third thinks he's got the pox."

"Washington survived the pox at nineteen," I said, squinting into the rising sun to find the trail. "He'll be back soon enough."

I prayed Washington would return with permission to evacuate the city and burn it to ashes. The army would be in better position to fight both the British and the pox that way. We could easily find much stronger defensive posts in Harlem Heights or Westchester; we would be out in the countryside, away from the cramped, filthy streets as well as the temptations of the Holy Ground; and, the British would be denied both a strategic port and the comforts of winter quarters.

"What if the British attack while he's gone?"

"You sound like a scared schoolgirl."

"I thought you wanted me to keep you informed about the concerns of the troop."

"I did. I did," I said, wheeling the formation left at the oak with the forked dead branch that served as my marker in the dense woodlands. I wasn't at liberty to tell the men that Washington had established a network of signal flags and a relay of fast horses to whisk him back to the city if a British fleet appeared on the horizon.

A yellow farmhouse with gabled roof sat deserted in a clearing ahead. I set my men to work stripping metal from door frames, window sashes, and hearths under Hempstead's direction, while I went on ahead with Asher to check the next house.

Unfortunately, Isaac Sears and his Sons of Liberty, waving their flag of nine alternating red and white vertical stripes, had beaten us there. A successful privateer turned merchant and shipowner, Sears became the de facto "king" of the city when Governor Tryon moved out. While he had stayed clear of military matters since Washington's arrival, Sears still ruled the streets with an iron hand.

And George Raleigh, the owner of the second house, was about to feel his wrath. I saw buckets of tar and feathers hidden at the back of the crowd as Asher and I pushed through to join Sears on the front steps.

"You're a Tory," Sears, a gaunt, gray-haired man in his mid-forties, stabbed a bony finger in Raleigh's chest. "We saw a candle in your window on the King's birthday."

"We've not declared for either side," Raleigh declared with all the innocence of youth. He couldn't have been more than twenty-five with the soft features and paunch of a man well-fed. His hook-nosed wife and two toddlers stood proudly behind him.

"That's not good enough. The captain here needs your house," Sears said. "Don't you, captain?"

"We were coming for the lead," I explained. "You could make a donation to the cause."

"Yes, well, I think Charlotte could find some things that would suit you," Raleigh answered. He shooed his wife and children into the house on a scavenger mission.

"And you'll sign an oath swearing your allegiance to Congress and denouncing King George." Not surprisingly, Sears had the parchment and quill at the ready. His gang hooted and hollered behind him; the pungent odor of tar grew stronger. They must have moved the bucket up front.

Raleigh swallowed hard, his queue of sandy hair bobbing up and down as he read. He looked at the mob, shuffling and frothing in place, and returned his gaze to the oath. "I can't sign this. It's a death warrant," he croaked. "Perhaps a change here…"

"Take him boys," Sears commanded, his eyes as dead as stones. Five men rushed up the steps, grabbing Raleigh's arms and legs and lifting him skyward. A rail, a roughhewn fencepost, appeared in the middle of the crowd. "A little ride might clear your mind."

"No!" A loud soprano wail sounded from the vestibule of the house, but it was too late. Raleigh was already adrift on a sea of hands. They seated him on the rail and bound his legs in place with rawhide. With wicked grins smearing their faces, two bearded men tossed buckets of bubbling tar over his head. Raleigh loosed a blood-curdling scream as the viscous liquid coated his hair, face, clothes and bare skin.

A gap-toothed strumpet rushed forward to add a dollop of goose feathers to the mix. To the chorus of Yankee Doodle, the Sons of Liberty bounced their prize down the lane towards the city.

"Take what you need, Captain," Sears said, doffing his cap in farewell.

Although I could never approve of mob violence, I had hardened to it. Last summer, I had defended William Wheaton, but no more; my idealism succumbed to reality the moment Princess smashed her club into my gut. The war was here. The Raleighs refused to stand with us, so they were de facto against us.

Would the British show mercy if the rebellion was crushed? No. Washington and others would surely be executed in a public spectacle, just like the leaders of the failed Jacobite rebellion in Scotland only thirty years ago. Tories would gleefully dance a jig as they returned to their homes, kicked out their neighbors and confiscated their property. I prayed that I would not live to see that day in America.

"See that the woman and her children are safe," I ordered Asher. "I'll go get our men."

Afterwards, the troop rolled two wheelbarrows of treasure back to camp. As my soldiers dispersed, I hastened to the meetinghouse to check on Elvin. I jumped back in horror when I reached his pallet. The private now had a vile, checkerboard rash creeping up his nose and an ulcer on his lower lip.

"I've got the pox," Elvin murmured lifting his rheumy eyes.

"I'll summon the doctor," I said. I'd have to summon the ambulance wagon as well. Infected men were quarantined on Montresor's Island in the East River.

"I did it myself," Elvin added, lying back contentedly as if he had just gorged himself on the last piece of pie.

"What?" I exploded. I had heard rumors of men self-inoculating, but it was a risky procedure. And against orders.

"Paid a guy two shillings for a swab of his pus. Sliced my forearm and rubbed it into the wound."

"You could infect the whole company. Wipe us out completely." I had also heard that inoculation worked. If all went well, the victim got a mild dose, recovered in a few weeks, and was immune for life.

"Couldn't stand to wait for it to come and get me. This way at least I'll have a chance."

I dragged Elvin outside by his boots. The bastard could lay there all night until the ambulance arrived.

The next morning, we were foraging close to camp when a fast rider galloped up with an announcement: George Washington had returned from Philadelphia. There would be a parade feting his arrival this afternoon in the city. Tossed hats and loud huzzahs celebrated the news.

I shaved, nicking my chin in my haste; Hempstead polished his buttons; Hercules buffed his cherished boots; Lawrie popped out of bed to trim his newly-grown mustache; Little John beat the call to arms on his drum.

I herded my men into place for the march south. We connected with regiments from Massachusetts, New Hampshire and western Connecticut, the procession stretching a quarter mile over Bowery Lane. Several soldiers tipped their hats, recognizing me from my successful heist of the *Asia's* supply boat. In the city proper, we paraded down Broadway to the Bowling Green, circled the statue of King George, and marched back uptown to the Common. There, we waited in formation to see our leader.

Astride his chestnut mount, Washington did not disappoint, exuding dignity, confidence, and control. Six Life Guards, riding tall in their dress blues, flanked our commander-in-chief. Was Tom Hickey among the six bodyguards? Was I just a bit jealous of Prudence's lover? Regardless, I knew that Washington needed protection, having seen firsthand the angst his extended absence had caused. I didn't even want to imagine the consequences should the general fall victim to a foul plot.

In good health and full uniform, blue jacket, sash, and gold epaulettes, Washington sauntered up and down the ranks, inspecting the enlisted men and saluting the officers. Black men now comprised roughly ten percent of the corps. Although Washington had only reluctantly admitted them into the service, and still owned slaves back in Virginia, he made no public distinctions in New York, either on the parade ground or in his daily written orders. The army needed all the fighting men it could attract, plain and simple. Washington accepted that he would have to rise above his ingrained prejudices for the good of the country. I returned the commander-in-chief's salute crisply, proud to be part of this man's army. After Washington had been seen by all, he rode home to the Mortier mansion.

While there was no official announcement, it quickly became obvious that Congress had quashed any thought of abandoning the city. Instead of packing for retreat, we dug in further, constructing river defenses including floating artillery batteries and chevaux-de-frise, containers of stones topped by iron spikes to be sunk in the harbor to rip apart the hulls of British ships. In case these measures were not successful, we also fashioned fire arrows to launch from the shore at enemy sails. New York would be defended to the death.

***

Anne was on her knees, wrestling with a cabbage plant in the Merritt's kitchen garden, when Hephzibah charged out of the house like it was on fire. Evidently accustomed to their mother's outbursts, Thankfull and Remember, turning the soil next to Anne, barely moved. Darcy was in the kitchen, mending clothes.

"The British are coming! The British are coming!" Hephzibah shouted, already huffing from her trot.

"When? Where?" Anne sprung to her feet.

"General Howe has sailed for New York. With twenty thousand regulars and ten thousand Hessians." Hephzibah bent over at the waist to catch her breath. "They should arrive by the end of the month."

"Are you sure?"

"Shubal just returned from the harbor with the news. There's going to be a meeting tonight at Toad's Tavern."

"A meeting?" Anne asked.

"Just the Loyalist families. To plan our welcome."

"Caleb and I will attend, Mother," Thankfull said, standing slowly and brushing the soil off the knees of her skirt. "An evening out with likeminded fellows might be just the tonic he needs."

He needs to be rid of you, Anne thought. As a result of the Mead raid, Caleb had not only lost a finger but gained a bride-to-be, and a shrewish one at that. Not that he didn't deserve punishment for plundering the home of an elderly couple. Nevertheless, Anne had bought Caleb some time by insisting, as his older sister, that the couple follow proper marriage decorum. The third and final banns were set to be read this Sunday.

"I'd like to attend as well," Anne said. "I'm quite familiar with the British Army."

"You'll stay here with me," Hephzibah said, hands on hips. "Constable Sharpe would not approve of you wandering about on your own."

"Come with me then," Anne said. "As my guardian."

"Go ahead, Mother," Remember urged. "You like to dip your finger in every pot."

"Mother's place is at home," Thankfull screeched, her voice grating like a poorly tuned fiddle. "As is Anne's," she added in a more melodious key.

"My sister's place is at my side," Caleb boomed as he stepped from the house into the middle of the conversation. Thankfull looked disdainfully at her betrothed but remained silent, obviously deciding not to cross him, before the wedding at least.

"Constable Sharpe won't even notice Anne's gone," Remember offered, taunting her mother with a coquettish smile. "I'll make sure of it."

"You'll do no such thing, young lady."

"It will be for the King, Mother." Remember winked conspiratorially at Anne.

They left at the rise of the crescent moon. Although Will Sharpe had yet to arrive, Darcy volunteered to stay home to chaperone the young lovers. Caleb took the reins of the wagon team with Thankfull and Hephzibah seated snugly on either side. Anne climbed into the back, flanked by Shubal and Bezaleel, both armed with musket, pistol and dirk. The stars peeked through the tree canopy as they bumped along the dark road.

Endearing memories of Geoffrey – picnicking on the beach in Boston, resplendent in his dress scarlet at the theatre, naked in their four-poster bed - flooded in. She lolled in the past until more pressing questions forced her back to the present. Could she be welcomed as a war widow? How was Father? She never thought she'd miss him so much. And Mother and Phineas too, of course. Would Sam Hale and William Cunningham leave her be? She shuddered at a jarring memory of the redcoats who tried to rape her. Only time would tell.

If Howe had thirty thousand soldiers, plus the fleet, the Jonathans had no chance. According to dinner table gossip, Washington could only muster ten thousand healthy men at most.

Would Nathaniel survive the rout? Although he must surely suffer some consequence for rebellion against his king, Anne found herself thinking of him more fondly of late. Nathan was a man of vision and ideals, albeit misguided. Since Geoffrey's death, she had been surrounded only by men of much meaner pursuits, her brother included, unfortunately. Anne bowed her head and gave a brief prayer for her schoolmaster's safety.

Hephzibah gave the sign, "Tyburn", at the tavern door. Tyburn was the execution ground in London, featuring a three-sided gallows that could hang twenty-four felons at once. The guard lowered his musket and replied with the countersign, "noose". The Loyalists were feeling plucky these days, Anne thought. Not surprisingly, the tavern, occupying the ground floor of a weather-beaten clapboard just off the Post Road, was packed. The imminent arrival of the British fleet had obviously sprung many Loyalists from the shadows.

It also launched David Matthews, mayor of New York and Governor Tryon's right hand man, on a tour of the countryside. With the mottled cheeks of a middle-aged man familiar with the demon rum, Matthews stood on an overturned crate to preside over the meeting. "God save the King," he intoned to capture everyone's attention.

"God save the King," men and women murmured in unison, looking furtively at their neighbors to confirm their complicity.

"Good and loyal citizens of Greenwich," Matthews began. Topped by a powdered wig that drooped precariously, his round head bobbed with the fervor of a Sunday preacher as he began what appeared to be a well-rehearsed plea:

"The Crown requires your assistance if we are to put down this troublesome rebellion and restore law and order to the colonies. Rest assured, you are not alone. There are more than two hundred Loyalist militia companies operating in towns across New York, Long Island, the Jerseys and Connecticut. While they have been operating independently until now, Governor Tryon will forthwith be directing events through his trusted lieutenants. The Governor asks you all to agree to take up arms when the British invasion begins, to seize the rebels' supply depots, to sabotage roads and bridges that might aid the rebels' escape from New York, and, most important of all, to recruit rebel soldiers to join our cause before it is too late for their salvation. To each Continental who sees the light, the Governor promises a cash bounty, payable immediately upon signing an oath, and two hundred acres of land after the rebellion is crushed."

Men banged their musket stocks on the dusty, planked floor in agreement; women smiled grimly as they nodded their capped heads. Would Nathan switch sides, Anne asked herself? Never. But others surely would. The reward was too rich. General Washington might soon find his army hollow at the core.

Matthews leaned over and opened a chest at his feet so that all could see its contents. Stacks of currency. "Continental dollars. All counterfeit," he exclaimed, as if he had just unveiled the Holy Grail. "Made by the finest artisans in the printing craft. We're going to drown the Congress in its own paper. No one will be able to tell the queer from the originals. No respectable merchant will supply the Continental Army. No rebel soldier will be able to feed his family with his pay."

The mayor dug his hands into the chest as the crowd gasped. He passed around packets of bills to spectators in the front row, urging them to circulate them back while he reached for more.

"Here! Here!" men exclaimed, stuffing their pockets with the fakes.

"I'm going to need volunteers to shove the queer on Long Island. We have many friends there who remain true to their King," Matthews asked, raising a flagon to signify that his speech was near its end.

"To the King!" Caleb stood, saluting. Bezaleel and Shubal joined him. Hephzibah looked on proudly at her clan. Strepitous men and women pushed forward, engulfing the mayor with their babble. Ale flowed freely at the bar.

"We should be going, Mother," Thankfull said as the crowd began to ebb. She clung to Caleb's elbow.

"Not yet," Anne replied. "I'd like a word with the mayor."

"Well, get on with it," Hephzibah ordered, clearly bewildered by Anne's request. "We have to get home to Remember."

Anne pushed through the thin circle of men surrounding Matthews. "Your honor," she curtsied. "I'd like to volunteer my assistance. People say I have a good head for figures."

"And which figures would that be lassie?" a kilted Scotsman guffawed, his breath rancid enough to kill lice. "Your figure could use a little fattening, eh?"

"You'll need to track the currency, real and queer, going in and out of the till, won't you Mayor?" Anne brushed a stray hair back under her cap. "I've had some experience keeping inventory for the British Army in Boston."

Matthews head snapped back. Squinting his eyes, he examined Anne as if she were a rare coin. "You wouldn't be Anne Wheaton, would you?"

"At your service." Anne curtsied again.

"Sam Hale suggested I keep a lookout for you."

"Sam?" She winced at the name.

"Hale and I do business from time to time. He wrote me a letter from Halifax. Said you were quite a resourceful young woman," Matthews continued.

"Thank you, sir." Anne breathed a sigh of relief. The foul-breathed Scotsman stepped back, a look of respect now in his eyes. As long as he keeps his mouth closed...

"Wait till I'm through here," Matthews said, tilting his head to a corner of the room. "We'll talk then."

Hephzibah wasn't pleased with the delay, but she couldn't argue with Matthews. Thirty minutes later the Mayor signaled for Anne to join him.

"A libation?" he asked. They were alone at the end of the bar, shielded by the mayor's bodyguard and out of eavesdropping range from the other remaining patrons.

"A whiskey would be appreciated," she replied.

Matthews contained a smile as he commandeered the barkeep to bring over a bottle and two tumblers. He filled them both, handing one to Anne. "To the King."

"To the King," she replied, shooting the fiery liquid in one gulp, calming her frayed nerves. Matthews refilled both glasses, scanning the room to see if anyone was watching. Pray he's not going to proposition me, Anne thought as she pushed the refill away. "How can I help?" she asked.

"I'll need you to deliver a message in New York City."

"When?"

"You should leave at sunrise. Can you ride?"

"I've had some experience."

"Excellent. My valet will arrange a horse."

"Where do I go?"

"First to a safe house run by the Raleighs, outside Bloomingdale. They'll direct you onward."

When she nodded, Matthews continued. "The rebels have formed a secretive Committee on Conspiracies and may have wind of our plans. Their security will be tight."

"I'll take every precaution."

Matthews withdrew a cloth-covered button from the pocket of his waistcoat. Hiding it under the palm of his hand, he slid it across the table. "It's hollow. There's a coded message folded inside."

Anne slipped her hand under his to claim it. "I'll find an appropriate hiding place."

"The Crown is counting on you. If our plan is successful, the war will be over this summer."

"Your message will get through." Anne would go to any length to hasten the end of the war, and lift the death sentence awaiting her in New London. But she would need to escape her prison in Greenwich first. She briefed Matthews on her situation. And Caleb's. "Perhaps he can provide protection to me?" she asked.

"You'd best travel alone, my dear," Matthews said. "A nine-fingered companion may raise difficult questions at the rebel checkpoints."

"Caleb can't stay here."

"I'll have a conversation with Widow Merritt." Matthews poured himself another whiskey and smiled. "Your brother can join my guards. We return to Governor Tryon in the morning."

"Constable Sharpe may not approve."

"He will look the other way, or he will face the justice of the Crown when the redcoats arrive."

Unfortunately, the widow did not see eye-to-eye with the mayor. "The Crown be damned," she said, pointing her musket directly in Matthews chest. "I'll sprinkle your guts in the sawdust before I let Caleb leave without doing right by my daughter."

"Madame…" Matthews tried to reason.

"Don't sweet-talk me," Hephzibah said, waggling her weapon in the mayor's face. Anne heard the click of triggers cocking as Shubal and Bezaleel backed their mother.

"I'll marry Thankfull," Caleb said, stepping in front of Matthews.

"You will?" Thankfull's high-pitched squeal of joy nearly cracked a glass decanter on the bar. "Praise God."

"You don't have to," Anne interjected, tugging Caleb's sleeve and earning Hephzibah's scowl. "Blood brothers, remember."

"I'm a man of honor. And I've a debt to repay," Caleb said. Hephzibah lowered her weapon, as did her sons.

"When?" Thankfull practically panted.

"Tonight. The minister's still here," Caleb replied, nodding towards the corner of the tavern. "He can perform the ceremony. And I'll leave with the mayor tomorrow."

"We can spend our wedding night upstairs," Thankfull said. "I'll inquire if the bridal suite is available."

Anne shook her head in surprise. Her little brother might be more of a man than she thought. And he would have a night of conjugal relations with Thankfull, although she wasn't sure if that would be reward or penance.

"It's all settled then," Mayor Matthews concluded, splashing his whiskey glass down on the bar. He took Anne's forearm and scuttled her away from Caleb and the Merritts. His treacly breath tickled her ear. "I'll be at my country home in Flatbush tomorrow evening. Meet me there after your mission."

"As you wish, your honor." Anne curtsied again, hoping he didn't detect the sarcasm in her words.

***

Benjamin Tallmadge had finally left school and joined the Army. I was ecstatic to see my best friend in New York sporting a crisp blue jacket and pink cockade of a lieutenant in Colonel John Chester's Connecticut regiment. Although Asher regularly mended and washed my brown and buff coat, as well as my shirts and breeches, they still showed the strains and stains of twelve months of hard labor.

If we can gain one more victory like Boston, Congress might be able to raise the funds to purchase new uniforms for everyone, I thought wistfully. At least, the legislature had backed up its decision to defend New York by paying the troops in recent weeks and even offering a ten dollar bounty to new recruits. I noticed more paper currency around camp of late, although the value of Continental dollars was still variable from one transaction to the next. Silver remained king, however, and I was fortunate our family farm in Coventry remained successful enough to stake my military service.

Ben celebrated his arrival by treating William, Stephen and myself to a feast, a turkey purchased from a butcher's cart and a bottle of aged Scotch whiskey brought from home. We built a fire on a verdant hillock overlooking the Hudson and took turns swimming, and bathing, in the river while the bird roasted. Although the sun had dipped to the New Jersey tree line, the air remained hot and humid. We dressed languidly after our dip and sat staring at the flames.

Ben handed the bottle to me. "My apologies for missing your birthday, friend. June 6th, I believe."

"Twenty-one years old," I replied proudly, swigging the whiskey and passing it along.

"To many more," Ben toasted.

"Here, here," Hull and Hempstead joined in.

A silence, like a thundercloud, darkened the mood for a brief second, each of us pondering the obvious. We were men at the prime of our lives, the world our oyster bed; yet, with war approaching, none of us could be confident of seeing another birthday. I broke the spell by standing and turning the spit.

"You certainly took your time reporting to camp, Friend Benjamin," I teased as I poked the turkey with my knife. Satisfied the meat was done, I banked the fire. "What was her name?"

"If only it was a scrape with an ardent female," Ben laughed. "I had my inoculation for the pox. Took me three weeks to regain full strength."

"So the inoculation works?" Steven Hempstead asked, peeling off a drumstick dripping with juice.

Ben spread his arms wide. "I'm alive and well as far as I can tell. General Washington now requires all recruits to get inoculated when they're first supplied. He even insisted that Martha undergo the procedure in Philadelphia."

Under these circumstances, it would be difficult to punish Elvin Parrish too severely when he returned from quarantine, I thought.

"And your face is as pretty as ever," William Hull teased. "You'll be a welcome sight at the Holy Ground."

309

"We'll have to pay a visit to Lara at the Ramrod," Hempstead suggested between bites. "Perhaps she'll offer a group discount."

"To Lara," Hull offered, raising his cup.

"To Lara," Hempstead, Tallmadge and I laughingly replied.

"Speaking of Philadelphia, I understand Congress is drafting a document articulating our grievances with King George," I said, returning the conversation to a more serious bent.

"Thomas Jefferson from Virginia will be the author, I believe," Hull said. "Mr. Franklin will be lending his ideas as well."

"Huzzah," I cheered. "Both men are known for their independent thinking. I'm anxious to read their words."

"The troops need a clear definition of the Glorious Cause. A reason to stay here and fight, rather than return to their farms and families," Hull said, slicing a triangle of white meat from the spitted bird. "Delicious," he added, licking his fingertips.

"I fear Congress will not venture far enough," Hempstead said. "They're lawyers and politicians after all."

"And don't want a noose around *their* necks if *we* fail," Hull replied, returning for another go at the turkey.

"*We* can't fail then," I said, my gaze drifting out to the river, visualizing the redcoats splashing from their ships and climbing up the slope.

After supper, we separated to return to our respective camps. Bloated and slightly inebriated, Stephen and I tramped together through the underbrush in the wan moonlight. The ground was rocky and uneven, requiring our full attention to remain upright. Dipping under the sprawling limbs of an ancient oak, we stumbled into two men whispering in the shadows.

"I'll be off then," one said with a trace of Irish brogue before stalking away as quickly as the terrain would allow.

I couldn't discern a face, but from the man's silhouette and nimble feet I assumed he was a soldier. Struggling to recall who was on picket duty tonight, I rehearsed the day's sign and countersign; but no challenge was forthcoming. My hand reached for the pistol at my belt. Hempstead cocked his weapon as well.

"Captain Hale? Is that you?" another Irishman called out.

"Private Lawrie?"

"Yes, sir. Just out for an evening stroll, sir." Lawrie stepped out from concealment.

"And who were you meeting out here in the dark?" I asked, my finger still on the trigger. Stephen shuffled at my side, the moonlight reflecting off his pistol barrel.

"A friend from the Old Sod. County Clare to be precise," Lawrie replied. Eyeing the two raised weapons, he raised both hands, palms up and empty. "One of the commander-in-chief's Life Guards," he added proudly. "No harm done."

"What's the man's name?" I pressed.

Lawrie hesitated. "Thomas Hickey."

I holstered my pistol. "Hickey from New Haven?"

"I do believe that's where he resided before the war."

"He's betrothed to a former pupil of mine in New London. A staunch patriot."

"Thomas did mention a lass he was keen on."

"I trust he's a good man?"

"Loyal and true, sir." Lawrie scraped the grass with his boot.

"I'd be pleased to meet him one day."

"I'll see to it, sir."

***

Fortunately, Salt and Pepper, Anne's mount, aptly named for his black and white speckled coat, was docile, content to amble along the Post Road without much need for guidance. Regardless, she held the reins so tightly her knuckles whitened. At every bounce, she clamped her knees to the saddle, pleased that she had donned her well-traveled breeches for the journey.

What message could Mayor Matthews fit onto the head of a button? What code did he employ? How could he fold a paper so tightly? Anne's curiosity almost got the better of her last night, but she had bit her tongue. The message was likely a short one. *Go…or kill. Kill whom? George Washington? Washington was the head of the snake. If he were killed, the snake would die. No other message could carry such importance.* She nervously checked the neck of her shirt, where she had triple-stitched Mayor Matthews' button. It was still secure.

Anne hoped to reach the Raleighs before sundown without forcing the pace; however, the unsettled sky, a potpourri of grays, threatened her timetable. Boldly, she kicked her heels, and, to her pleasant surprise, Salt and Pepper responded by picking up his gait. So far so good, Anne thought, as they trotted through Mamaroneck, passing a milk wagon, a vegetable-seller's cart, and a farmer leading two hairy white goats. She searched the roadside houses for rebel flags, but found surprisingly few flapping in the summer breeze.

Traffic coming at her thickened midafternoon as Anne approached the northern reaches of Manhattan Island. She tugged over to the side of the road as one fast rider, than another, galloped by, grim expressions etched in the faces of the young messengers clinging to the saddle. Had the British fleet arrived?

Although the sky had darkened, Anne and her mount needed a rest. She stopped at Bronck's River, allowing Salt and Pepper a noisy slurp, then guided him to a stand of beech where she dismounted to snack on corn meal and dried peas.

Fear tip-toed into her thoughts. She was alone in the woods without Geoffrey or Caleb or Major Rogers or Uncas or even Father to look after her. She was in enemy territory carrying a message that could spell her doom if discovered. To reach its recipient, still unknown, she would have to talk her way through a gauntlet of rebel checkpoints. But what was the alternative? Sit in the Merritt's kitchen and darn socks? She had the opportunity to play a role in ending the rebellion and had to seize it.

Looking towards Connecticut, she accepted that she had no home there any longer. Even worse, she held little hope that her family would be welcomed back after the rebellion was squelched. On the other hand, if she could safely navigate New York and reach Flatbush, a covey of Loyalists from all she'd heard, she could start a new life.

Thunder growled in the distance. Her dead siblings, her angels – Richard, Grace and Phoebe – were playing at bowls up in heaven. Would she join them shortly? If she was to die, she prayed for a quick death, not a tortured dance dangling at the end of a rebel rope. A bolt of lightning flashed. Her destiny called.

Anne pulled a sailcloth poncho, coated with a thin layer of tar for waterproofing, out of her saddlebag and slipped it over her head. Salt and Pepper bucked in disapproval as she untied him, but an apple and a few kind words proved calming. Climbing into the saddle, she rode into the storm.

With sheets of rain lashing like a cat-o-nine-tails, she clung head down to the saddlehorn, relying on her mount to navigate. Thunder boomed. The earth quivered. Salt and Pepper reared and bolted forward, but Anne held fast, intertwining her fingers into his mane. And cursing the beast to hell. Fortunately, the Post Road quickly dissipated into a muddy bog, moderating the pace.

They stumbled onto the King's Bridge before she saw it coming. The bridge, a wooden structure reinforced with stone bulwarks, crossed Spuyten Duyvil Creek and represented the northern boundary of Manhattan Island. Smoke wisped from the chimney of the toll collector's house, but no one ventured out as she crossed. Salt and Pepper grew winded, slowing to a canter then a walk as the sky brightened. Anne checked the button. Still fastened tight.

The rain stopped completely by the time they passed the ramparts of Fort Washington, standing guard on a hill overlooking the Hudson; the sun streaked through the breaking clouds as Salt and Pepper picked his way through the puddles on the climb up Harlem Heights. Stopping for another rest, welcomed both by her arse and her horse, Anne stuffed the poncho back in the saddlebag and shook out her hair to revel in the warmth.

"Halt! Who goes there?" A dusty-haired, pimpled youth challenged, musket at the ready as he blocked her path. His jacket was adorned with a blue badge from a Rhode Island militia company.

"You're supposed to ask for the sign, pigeon-brain," a second militiaman, swarthier but still too young to grow a full beard, scolded as he stepped out of the bushes.

"Sign?" the first sentry corrected himself.

"I'm riding south to look for my husband. I've received a message that he fell ill," Anne replied, frowning. "I pray he's recovered but I fear for the worst."

"What's his unit?" the raven-haired sentry asked.

"The 19th Regiment of Foot. From Connecticut."

"Don't know them in particular, but there's a whole slew of Connecticut men down near Bloomingdale."

"I trust I'm going the right way?" Anne moved the conversation forward. She was surprised the sentries didn't ask for her surname, but saw no point in volunteering the information which she had rehearsed for the eventuality.

"I do believe so," pimple-face said, puffing out his chest. "But we've only been on the front lines for a week ourselves."

The front lines? Anne swallowed her laugh. Looking out at the mighty Hudson River, however, she realized the boy might be right. The British fleet could attack anywhere.

"What's in these bags?" Raven-hair rested a hand on her saddle.

"A wet sailcloth. And some healing herbs."

"That's all?" He unfastened the buckle on one saddlebag, lifted the flap and poked a hand inside.

"My supper as well. And a proper frock and bonnet."

"Any silver?" He rummaged around for a few seconds but came up empty.

"No. Just Continentals." Anne reached inside the saddlebag on the other side of Salt and Pepper and withdrew a hefty wad of Mayor Matthews' counterfeit currency "Is there a toll to travel on this road?

"Continentals are practically worthless."

Practically worthless, but not completely. "I'd be pleased to contribute - generously - to ensure safe passage to my husband's side."

The soldiers' eyes opened wide as she peeled bills off the roll and handed them over.

"What about the rest?" raven hair asked.

"She'll need to save some for her husband's care," pimple-face said.

"I'll make another payment upon my return."

"That's fair." Pimple-face stashed the cash, clearly pleased at his good fortune. "You ask for Luke and Zach now, you hear."

If these are the "men" defending New York, General Howe will be residing on Broadway soon enough, Anne thought as she rode away. She urged Salt and Pepper into a lope once they descended the heights and were out on the Harlem Plains.

The checkpoint at McGowan Pass, manned by regulars from the Connecticut Line, not militiamen, was more challenging. The pickets brusquely demanded that she dismount, then dumped her saddlebags in the mud, ruining her frock. They clucked like hens at the remaining Continentals, but didn't pocket any.

Anne thought she was clear until a pristinely uniformed officer with a pink cockade in his hat, stepped from the shrubbery where he had likely been watching the proceedings. "Lieutenant Willow, at your service, ma'am. A woman traveling alone raises my suspicions," he said, circling Anne slowly. "We're expecting the British to flood the island with spies. Are you a spy, ma'am?"

"No. I'm looking for my husband," she replied. "He's ill. Quite seriously, I'm afraid."

"Yes, you said that to my men. But yet you don't appear particularly distraught."

"That's my nature, I guess."

"The redcoats prefer women for espionage," he said loud enough for his pickets to hear. "Please remove your boots."

"And stand in my stockings in the mud?" Anne protested but complied.

"The perils of war." The lieutenant said as he examined the insides of each boot and tapped on the heels to see if they were hollow. "And your breeches, I'm afraid."

"I'll do no such thing." Anne clamped her hands on her hips defending her dignity. "I'm a married woman."

"I haven't forgotten." The lieutenant appeared to be considering his options. "Empty your pockets and turn up your cuffs." Anne did as ordered. What would be next? Her pulse fluttered like a butterfly's wings as she forced herself *not* to look at the button on her shirt.

"From New London, are you?" he asked as he knelt to feel around her ankles.

"Yes sir." Anne wiggled her toes in the mire.

"There are some New London men camped just outside the city." The lieutenant stood apparently finished with his search.

"That's where I need to go then," Anne said.

"Your husband's name?"

"Elvin Parrish." Darcy had suggested Anne use the name of her old beau if she was in a pinch. No one outside his unit would likely know him, and, if she accidentally ran into him, he might help her out. Elvin's allegiance to the rebellion was marginal at best, and he might have heard that Darcy left her husband.

"Don't know him myself," the lieutenant replied.

"May I go now?" Anne reached for her boots and belongings.

"You may, but be certain I will inquire as to your husband's health. If there are any discrepancies in your account, I will track you down myself."

Anne turned right at the fork, the only turn Matthews said she'd need to make, on to a cross road heading west for the last mile to Bloomingdale, named by the Dutch for its verdant hills and wildflowers. She halted several times to look for pursuers, but there were none that she could see.

Brilliant shades of pink and orange streaked the sky as Salt and Pepper lumbered to a halt in front of the Raleigh house, or rather what was left of it. The doors and windows had been ripped out, furniture lay strewn in the yard amidst shards of pottery and tableware, and the front yard trampled. Looking around, Anne realized the neighboring homes had been tossed as well, as if a hurricane had swept through the clearing. She dismounted and tied Salt and Pepper to the hitching post, which miraculously still appeared intact. Where were the Raleighs? Were they even alive?

"Hello," Anne called as she ventured across the transom. The elegantly decorated parlor had obviously been ransacked. She heard a rustling back in the keeping room and called out again. A young woman emerged, musket in hand albeit shakily. A boy and girl, neither likely older than five, peeked out from the doorway. Anne raised her empty hands. "I'm a friend. The Duchess sent me."

"Ah yes. You'll need to see my husband then," Charlotte Raleigh said, dropping the barrel of her gun. "Wait here."

"I can't wait long."

"Unfortunately, George is not well. He was assaulted…" Charlotte fought back tears. "I'll see if he's awake."

"Assaulted by whom?" Anne asked, although she could easily guess the answer.

"Let's talk back here," her hostess replied, eyes darting furtively, her fear apparent.

Anne followed her into the keeping room. The aroma of bread baking in an oven tucked into the hearth suffused a normalcy to the otherwise chaotic surroundings. Her husband lay on a straw pallet on the floor, covered only by a thin cotton sheet. His bald scalp, as well as the skin on his face, was a mass of puckered red blisters and open sores, intermingled with smudges of black tar. His lips had been burned to a crisp, his nose warped at a right angle, and one eye swelled shut.

"George. A woman is here to see you," Charlotte said, patting her husband's forehead with a wet cloth. "She used the password from Mayor Matthews."

"The Duchess sent me," Anne repeated.

"George was lucky," Charlotte continued, as if reassuring herself. "The rebels only gave him a 'genteel' bath. They left his clothes on. It could have been much worse."

"Which rebels?"

"A Captain Hale and his men. From Connecticut."

"Captain Nathan Hale?" Anne seethed.

"You know him?" Charlotte asked.

"Regretfully now, I'm afraid."

George forced his head up and reached for his wife with a scorched hand. He whispered in her ear and Charlotte nodded. "Is the Duchess well?" she asked.

"He's a bit seasick," Anne completed the authentication sequence. George nodded and drew his wife close again.

"You're to meet with Lara. She poses as a trull at The Ramrod in the Holy Ground," Charlotte said.

"And then what?"

"That's all we know," Charlotte shrugged. George fell back, his eyes closed.

Anne beckoned for Charlotte to follow her outside. Her children trailed along as well. "Lavender and cinnamon," she explained, pinching a handful of herbs from the pouch in her saddlebag. "Mix them into a salve for your husband."

Salt and Pepper was not pleased to be back on the road again, but Anne gave him little choice. She kicked his flanks viciously, wishing it was Nathan she was kicking instead. How could he? What had he become?

The moon was almost full, providing ample illumination for her ride. The Bloomingdale Road was double-track and deserted, nevertheless she kept to a trot to avoid arousing suspicion. How long until the lieutenant contacted Elvin Parrish, learned he had no wife, and came looking for her? She had to leave Manhattan by daybreak.

About a mile from the city limits, the road turned into Bowery Lane, even wider still. On either side of the road, fires glowed, and men shifted about in the shadows, but no sentries stepped forward to challenge her. The tang of roasting meat rose from the camps. The acrid scent of gunpowder as well. Was Nathan billeted here? She'd shoot him herself if she didn't have a mission to complete.

Bowery Lane led directly to the city gate. The watchman, impossibly tall and skeletal-thin, appeared to be asleep standing up but snapped to attention as she approached. "And where are ye headed at this hour, lass?" he asked, shining his lantern into her eyes. His free hand rested on the hilt of a pistol tucked into his waistband. "There's a curfew in place, ye ken."

"The Ramrod," Anne replied, too nervous to breathe. "I've heard it's in need of a woman with my skills."

"Your skills?" the giant belly-laughed. "And what skills might those be?"

Anne was about to say "healing skills" when he waved her through with a snicker. "Skills? Can't say I've ever heard that one before. Don't tarry in the street now, ye hear."

She was in the city! The lamps on Broadway revealed a grand boulevard transformed into a military camp. To avoid being mistaken for a whore again, she slowed Salt and Pepper and capped her hair.

Riding down the middle of the broad avenue, she could not help but marvel at the degradation of her surroundings. Ancient oaks had been chopped down to stumps and flowerbeds ripped out. Half-dressed soldiers crammed into the brick mansions that once housed the city's elite. Fortunately, all muskets were pointed east and west towards the rivers where the British might shortly land. A solitary traveler received scant attention. Anne reached Trinity Church without a challenge. Its dark spire pierced the night sky, a worthy symbol of the den of wickedness beyond.

Despite, or perhaps because of, the imminent threat of invasion, the streets of the Holy Ground pulsed with energy. Although Anne had seen Mount Whoredom in Boston, it had been from a distance. The debauchery here overwhelmed her senses. Whores walked the streets with one, or both, breasts exposed; a couple copulated in an alleyway; three soldiers shared an opium pipe; hawkers beckoned with a crooked finger from every doorway.

A stubby Black, wearing lime-green livery, crossed her path, obviously in a hurry.

"Sir, sir," she called, but he did not slow. "Sir," she leaned over in the saddle and tried one last time.

"Are you addressing me, madam?" he asked, his sweating, bald head bowed as he stopped. "I am unaccustomed to that sobriquet."

"I'm in dire need of directions."

"And where in these holy grounds might you be headed?" he replied, eyes still glued to the dirt.

"Speak up." Anne was surprised at the stridency in her voice.

The Black raised his head dramatically, revealing a patch over his right eye. "Forgive my reticence. I've already had one eye gouged out for speaking with a woman of Caucasian descent. I can ill afford to lose the other."

She gasped, speaking so fast that the words tumbled into one another. "I'm looking for The Ramrod."

"A coarse establishment for a young lady."

"I'm to meet someone there."

"Well, then, you are quite fortunate. That is my destination as well," the Black replied, dropping his head again. "My mistress has sent me to fetch her husband."

The Black resumed his brisk walk while Anne followed. "May I inquire as to whom you are to meet?" he asked stopping in front of a ramshackle structure, marked by two red-sheathed lanterns. The din of loud voices, the twang of a fiddle and a cloud of smoke spilled out from its swinging doors.

"Lara," she replied.

"Ah, my master's favorite strumpet."

"Would you be kind enough to ask her to join me out here?" Anne feared Salt and Pepper would not be waiting if she ventured inside.

"Whom shall I say is calling?"

"The Duchess."

Anne's eyes tracked the green jacket into the bawdyhouse. The Black carried himself with a dignity far above his station. How did he come to speak the King's English? What did he do to earn his master's wrath?

The crash of a table, and all its crockery, inside The Ramrod commanded Anne's attention. She heard the scrape of a chase, followed by the lusty laughter of female voices.

"You snot-nosed turd!" A Chinaman shouted as he tossed a youth out into the street. "I'll slice off your tiny balls if you step foot in here again."

The boy, wearing the brown jacket of a Connecticut soldier, landed at her feet. The shock of recognition flashed like a lightning bolt. He was at the forefront of the mob at her arrest in New London. One of Nathan's "men", if you could call him that. And he recognized her as well. The boy jumped up, started to speak, but stifled his words at the shrill of a constable's whistle. He darted off into the night, leaving Anne trembling against the flank of Salt and Pepper.

With tendrils of flaming red hair slithering in all directions like Medusa's snakes, a freckle-faced whore emerged a few minutes later and sidled next to Anne. "You're the Duchess, eh?" she asked, stroking the horse's forehead. "Looks like you've seen a ghost."

"I'll be all right." Anne replied.

"'Tis troubled times we live in. But that's good for business." The whore's face brightened as she jingled the silver in the pocket of her loose-bodiced green gown which left little of her décolletage to the viewer's imagination.

"The Duchess sent me," Anne wanted to complete her delivery as quickly as possible and find a ferry to Flatbush.

"Is she well?" Lara replied.

"He's a bit seasick."

"Chamomile will cure him." That was the final phrase in the recognition sequence. "You have something for me?"

"I thought I was to make delivery… to a man," Anne replied hesitantly.

"No one's getting close to my man. It's too dangerous. For him and you."

Anne fingered the button on her shirt. "Here."

"Follow me then. We must be quick." Lara led her to the alley behind the Ramrod. It stunk of vomit and horseshit.

Anne snipped the button off with her knife. Lara placed it in her mouth and rolled it around with her tongue. Arching her overgrown eyebrows, as if to say, 'watch me', she reached up underneath her skirt, pulled out a bloody rag, stuffed the button up her cunny, and wadded it back in place with the rag. "That'll keep for a while at least," she noted, smoothing down her skirt.

Unless you return to work, Anne thought.

"Where do you go from here?" Lara asked.

"Away."

"We're short a girl tonight. You could cover for her and make some easy silver."

"I don't think that line of work suits me." And I'm out of practice, Anne thought.

"It's not too difficult. Just lay on your back and close your eyes. The soldiers are randier than rabbits."

"My brother is waiting."

"Godspeed then," Lara said stiffening her shoulders. "You'd best leave now. I'll watch your back."

Anne mounted Salt and Pepper and walked him down Broadway. The life-sized statue of King George raised on a white marble pedestal stopped her cold at Bowling Green. It seemed so out of place in this rebel fortress. She noticed four soldiers, impeccably uniformed in red, white and blue, standing at attention in the doorway of an elegant mansion adjacent to the green. Candles sparkled in its front parlor. Whom were they guarding? It had to be General Washington. What was keeping him working late this evening?

As she tugged Salt and Pepper's reins to move on, she noticed Lara out of the corner of her eye. Her fellow spy was walking down Broadway towards the mansion, now sporting a flouncy mob cap and shawl, curled over her shoulders and knotted to cover her cleavage. She had also patched a black star to the right side of her forehead, completing her transformation from Holy Ground harlot to prim soldier's wife. Anne tarried a second longer, watching as Lara stopped at the front of the mansion to chat with guards on duty there. They appeared to be on familiar terms. Were the guards patrons from the Ramrod? Or fellow conspirators? Anne burst with pride at the thought of playing at least a small part in a mission that might bring down General Washington and end the war. *If only Father could see me now…*

She would put them all at risk if she didn't move on. Anne rode past the fort and the battery at the tip of Manhattan, the tension apparent in the men manning their battle stations around the clock. The wharves and warehouses on the East River side of the city, however, were dark and silent. A handful of travelers waited at Murray's Wharf for the last ferry of the evening to Long Island. She joined the queue, her nerves prickling like bacon in a skillet.

The ferry, a flat-bottomed, single masted scow, glided into the dock, propelled by crewmen on both sides wielding poles and oars.

Anne waited patiently as a squadron of soldiers, Maryland men, marched off. They were hard men with jutting chins and sunken eyes, a far cry from the boys she had encountered outside Fort Washington. They reminded her of Geoffrey, she realized. Salt and Pepper nickered in exhaustion as she prod him to board.

Fortunately, the crossing was brief, the evening breeze on the East River a welcome respite from the day's heat. Moonlight danced off the ripples in the calm waters. She turned for a farewell look at New York, surprised to see a torch burning in a belfry window at Trinity Church. She swore the steeple had been dark when she passed it earlier this evening. She blinked and the tower was dark once again.

Munching on the last of her peas, Anne steeled herself for the final part of her journey. Fortunately, she did not expect any difficulty navigating to the Mayor's farmstead. The main road led directly from the ferry landing up through the Flatbush Pass in the Guana Heights and down into the village proper. And safety.

Astride a coal black mare, Caleb waited at the dock. Anne bolted upright in her saddle at the sight of her brother. Relief coursed through her veins like a fine whiskey, providing a much-needed shot of adrenaline. She kicked her heels to urge Salt and Pepper down the ramp.

"You did well, sister," Caleb said as they walked their horses side-by-side.

"How do you know?"

"A flare at Trinity Church confirmed that your message was delivered safely to its intended recipient. We watched for it on the Heights."

"I thought the rebels controlled the Heights?"

"The Mayor has friends everywhere."

"What's next?" she asked as the horses began the steep climb to the pass.

"Our plan is in motion. We must wait for news of its success."

"Praise God," Anne replied, bowing her head.

"The mayor is at his farm, preparing for Governor Tryon's triumphant return to New York. I'm to bring you to him."

They arrived at the farmhouse precisely at ten according to the tall case clock in the front parlor. The mayor wore a scarlet sleeping robe trimmed in black silk and a matching cap for his wig-less head.

"Well done, Private Wheaton," he said to Caleb. "You are dismissed."

"But…" Anne started to protest before the Mayor cut her off. "Your report to me must be made confidentially. The safety of others is at stake."

"It's all right, sister." Caleb said. "I must see to the horses anyway."

"Good man, your brother," Matthews mumbled as he closed the door. And latched it. "I want to hear all the details," he said, ushering Anne into his pine-paneled study. He ordered his valet to bring a tray of meats and filled two crystal tumblers with a ruby Madeira.

"To the King," he offered.

"To the King," Anne replied as she sank down into a floral-brocaded wingback chair, its plush cushions a welcome relief for her saddle-weary glutes. The story of her day gushed from her lips. Matthews listened intently, prodding her with questions. Since he appeared thirty years or even older, she had thought he must be a married man, although she could see no indications of a woman's touch in his home and he made no mention of his family situation. Twice, he stood to stare out the window, but saw nothing save darkness and returned his attention to her.

Anne had no intention to rut with the mayor, nor did he coerce her. However, she was giddy with success; the traipse through the Holy Ground had stirred her juices, dormant since Geoffrey's death; the Madeira was silky smooth; and, wickedly perhaps, she wanted to prove to her brother that she was a woman now. None of these factors alone would have lured her upstairs into the massive feather bed, but the weight of all four tipped the scales.

Between the sheets, Matthews presented a most welcome contradiction – the voracity of a young man and the artistry of an older one, proving particularly adept at pleasuring her in ways that Geoffrey never had. With her lust satiated, she lay naked, loosely covered by an indigo and white checked quilt, when the platoon of rebel soldiers banged on the front door sometime after midnight.

The mayor scrambled for his robe as his valet tried to stall the intruders in the parlor - to no avail. Footfalls pounded up the stairs. Ten soldiers at least, maybe more. Anne had no night shift at the ready, so she sunk deeper under the covers.

"David Matthews?" a tall barrel-chested officer demanded as he brandished his saber. "I am General Nathanael Greene of the Continental Army. You are under arrest for treason."

***

I waited patiently until Third Company settled into formation for evening review, Hercules the last man to shuffle into place. We had just completed a backbreaking day under a scorching sun digging artillery entrenchments outside Greenwich Village, all the while checking the river for enemy ships. My shirt, once white, was sweat-drenched, while my men were mostly bare-chested. The aroma of roasting fowl reminded me to be brief.

A green-sashed aide from headquarters stomped across the parade ground, handing me the day's General Orders to read out loud. The man was sitting at a desk all day, why does he look so glum, I thought. Then I read the communication silently, its message settling like a funeral shroud. But I didn't have time to grieve as my mind raced back to the night of my chance encounter with Ian Lawrie outside camp.

Private Lawrie had not mustered for today's work detail, citing the flux, a common enough malady. I had thought little of it this morning, but now had the sickening feeling that the man was a traitor. I ordered Sergeant Hempstead to keep the men in formation, listening to their groans as I sprinted to the barracks. Sure enough, Lawrie's pallet was empty, and his belongings gone.

Private McElroy, however, was up and about, although he dropped his head at my entrance. *He's here, a testament to his loyalty, but he knows.*

"Where's Lawrie?" I asked, knowing the question was purely rhetorical. With a full day's head start, Lawrie could easily be in Long Island or the Jerseys by now. McElroy shrugged.

"Stay here. We'll talk as soon as the men are dismissed," I commanded before hastening back to the parade.

I nodded to Little John for a drum roll. If the news shocked me, it would undoubtedly rattle my men as well. When I was sure I had their attention, I read:

Thomas Hickey belonging to the Generals Guard having been convicted by a General Court Martial ... of the crimes of "Sedition and mutiny, and also of holding a treach'rous correspondence with the enemy, for the most horrid and detestable purposes," is sentenced to suffer death. The General approves the sentence, and orders that he be hanged tomorrow at Eleven O'clock ... All the officers and men off duty...to attend the execution...

Thomas Hickey.   The soldier that Ian Lawrie had met clandestinely. The man, according to Prudence's letter, who was the father of her unborn child and soon-to-be husband. The connections to the insidious traitor were too personal.

Unfortunately, McElroy had little hard information. Lawrie had hinted there was silver and land to be earned simply by signing a pledge of support to the Crown.   That pledge would also be an insurance policy if a Continental was captured by the British Army when it barreled through New York this summer. When McElroy didn't take the bait, Lawrie had stopped talking.

"Why didn't you come directly to me?" I asked.

"I didn't know if I could trust you," McElroy said, biting his lower lip.   "I saw you and Hempstead talking to Lawrie in the shadows."

After finishing with McElroy, I walked alone along the heights above the Hudson, my mind spinning like a wind-whipped weathervane. Had other men in my command accepted Lawrie's offer? Would Hickey be the only man to hang? Was he a spy? A saboteur? An assassin? How were the British able to corrupt someone so close to the general? Were other Life Guards involved?

Could Prudence have had any role in the plot? While I could not envision her involved with the Tories in any way, she might be implicated, simply by association.

What would have happened if Hickey had succeeded in his dastardly plan? Who could possibly replace George Washington? Could the Continental Army even survive without him? Could the Glorious Cause? I knew these answers, and they roiled my guts.

Although flawed, Washington stood alone at the crossroads of history, the only man able to bridge the northern and southern colonies, parley with politicians, and lead men into battle. For the rebellion to have any chance of success, every soldier would have to do whatever necessary to protect the life of their commander-in-chief. Revolution demands sacrifice; I steeled myself for the challenge.

William Hull was so agitated at the officer's campfire he nearly spilled his entire trencher of chicken. "I heard that Hickey was just the tip of the iceberg," he said, picking a drumstick off the grass. "Another Life Guard is already in jail, and three more are implicated. They were planning to assassinate General Washington, blow up the ammunition in the magazine and spike our cannons as soon as the British landed."

"Tom Hickey's a private. He could not have been the mastermind," I replied. "His orders had to come from higher up. Governor Tryon, I wager,"

"Mayor Matthews has been implicated. He was arrested in Flatbush last night," Ben Tallmadge chipped in. "My source said he was caught *in flagrante* with a young trollop when General Greene knocked down the door."

"Lieutenant Tallmadge, you have only just arrived, yet you already have cultivated sources in headquarters," I marveled. "You are surely marked for a career in intelligencing."

"Tell us more about the trollop," Hull asked with a leering chuckle. "Was she arrested as well?"

"I believe she was let go," Tallmadge waved his hand in dismissal. "A mere housemaid."

"A juicy one, I trust," Hull laughed. "It may be the mayor's last supper."

"Do you think Matthews will hang?" I asked.

"He has not been tried yet. Hickey is the only man condemned - so far," Ben said.

The next morning, I shaved, polished the silver buckles on my boots, donned my blue shirt, and buffed the buttons on my jacket before assembling my men on the parade ground. We marched in silence along Bowery Lane joining a procession of companies from all four brigades stationed in New York.

At an open field north of the city, the men drew up in front of their respective commanders, Generals Scott, Stirling, Spencer and Heath, and waited. Our eyes were fixed on the gallows, its platform high enough for all to see, a single noose swinging slowly from its yardarm in the morning breeze.

I was awed by the size of the crowd, ten thousand soldiers in formation and probably as many civilians lining the outskirts, undoubtedly the largest public spectacle in the brief history of the colonies. It appeared that everyone living on Manhattan Island was here, except George Washington, at least not as far as I could tell. I wondered whether Washington's absence was for security reasons, or a demonstration that the commander-in-chief was at his post, the war effort proceeding without interruption. I preferred to believe the latter.

Just before eleven, a plangent drumbeat called us to attention. A guard detail, composed of twenty soldiers hand-picked from each of the four brigades, materialized at the rear of the field and marched towards the gallows. Hands bound, head up, defiantly staring out at the spectators, Thomas Hickey strode at the center of this entourage. Provost Marshal William Maroney, appointed by Washington in January specifically to oversee the discipline of the troops, as well as the hangman and a chaplain, waited on the platform.

The prisoner, now flanked by only four guards, mounted the steps. He exchanged words with the chaplain – no prayers would save Hickey from damnation, I thought – and appeared to wipe a tear from his eye.

What occupied Hickey's mind at his final moments? Did he seek solace in his cause – whatever that might be? Did he recall the kindness of his parents? Or the pleasures of the flesh? Did he think wistfully of Prudence and the unborn child he would never see? Did he notice the colors – the blue of the sky, the green of the trees, the yellow of the dandelions? Did he feel the breeze upon his face? Did he hear the church bell toll eleven o'clock?

Hickey's time on earth was near an end. The hangman placed a black hood over his head, followed by the noose. After cinching the knot, the executioner stepped back. The Provost Marshal waited for two seconds, letting anticipation build, then signaled with a gesture of his hand. The platform flapped opened. Hickey swooshed down.

I had never before witnessed a man hang; death came excruciatingly slow. As I watched Hickey dangle, my right hand moved on its own accord, stealing up to rub the hairs imbedded in the mole on my neck. *I want to make a mark before my turn comes.*

Hickey's body swung for minutes before it stopped twitching. The burial party had to dodge the shit leaking from his breeches to load him into their wagon. Washington's message had been sent, and received; the drum roll to dismiss the troops couldn't come soon enough.

I asked Little John to toot Yankee Doodle on the march back to camp. Hickey had received his just reward; it was time for us to return to the tasks of preparing for the British attack. I listened to the jabber of my men as their spirits steadily lifted.

An aide bearing General Washington's daily orders was again waiting on the parade ground. I was anxious to hear my commander-in-chief's comments on the execution and its aftermath, but frankly found his message confusing:

...And in order to avoid those crimes the most certain method is to keep out of the temptation of them, and particularly to avoid lewd women, who, by the dying confession of this poor criminal, first led him into practices which ended in an untimely and ignominious death....

Was Washington referring to a specific lewd woman? Surely not Prudence. Or, was he again playing the patrician elder, taking yet another swipe at the low character of his troops? With battle nearing, the men would not welcome a morality lecture.

Unfortunately, Washington's order omitted any news from Philadelphia. For almost three weeks now, Thomas Jefferson and his committee had been drafting a document to present the justification for the rebellion to the country, if not the world. Surely, they must finish soon. What would be the next step? Must Congress debate and vote before it could be published? How long would this parliamentary process take? The manifesto could be a huge boost for morale, if it was worded strongly enough. That's what the troops needed to hear.

Nevertheless, I had little choice but to read Washington's daily missive aloud and do my best to enforce it. Little John tried to scurry away as soon as I finished, but I chased him down. The boy had tasted the forbidden fruit of the Holy Ground and would be tempted to return there, if he hadn't already done so.

"Did you hear the warning of our commander-in-chief?" I asked, scolding like a schoolmaster, or even worse a preacher.

"Yes, sir."

"I'll have you flogged like Private McElroy if I learn you've visited the Holy Ground again." I hated to threaten, but I needed to scare Little John.

"But..." Little John started to speak.

"No 'buts.' It will be the lash if you yield to the sin of fornication." *Minister Enoch would be proud.*

"Yes, sir." Little John hung his head.

A shout from Stephen Hempstead ended the conversation. He held a spyglass in his hand as he ran towards me. Three red and white striped flags flew from the Jersey shore, the signal that General Howe's flagship, the *Greyhound*, and more than a hundred additional ships of the line had been sighted. "All London's afloat," shouted a sentry on the shoreline.

Lanterns blazed late in the barracks that evening. Sleeping pallets were empty as soldiers milled silently in grim knots, grinding knives against whetstones, filling cartridges with powder, and corkscrewing rags down the barrels of muskets. Little John sat alone writing a letter; Hercules sliced a strip of rawhide to fashion new laces for his boots; Tom Peacock mended a tear in his breeches, pausing often to guzzle from his jug. Like a skunk's spray, the scent of fear fouled the room. The British were here.

CHAPTER 16 - JULY 1776

"...the famous Major Rogers is in custody on violent suspicion of being concerned in the conspiracy [at New York] ..."
Thomas Jefferson to William Fleming (Virginia Senator)
Philadelphia
July 1, 1776

"...The Congress have judged it necessary to dissolve the connection between Great Britain and the American Colonies, and to declare them free & independent states; as you will perceive by the enclosed Declaration..."
John Hancock to George Washington
Philadelphia
July 6, 1776 (received July 8)

"...The eyes of all America are upon us. As we play our part, posterity will bless us or curse us..."
General Henry Knox to wife, Lucy
New York
July 8, 1776

Robert Rogers blistered the soles of his boots pacing the boundaries of his prison, the now deserted barracks built to house the Associators – a fancy name for the militia of the Pennsylvania colony – who had marched off to join the rebel army in New York. His interrogation by General Washington, four days ago, had not gone well, resulting in his transport under armed guard to Philadelphia. Although voicing suspicions, Washington had not actually charged him with any crime, leaving that prickly task to Congress which had ordered his confinement but appeared in no rush to decide the matter.

In the worst case, Rogers allowed he might again face trial for treason. At least, he wasn't in shackles, as he had been in Canada in 1768, when General Gage, the arseworm, had him shipped back from Fort Mackinac in the hold of a trader's brig stinking from otter furs. Then, however, he had influential friends in London to arrange his acquittal; now, he had no one.

Yes, he had been spying for the British, but he carried no incriminating evidence – coded papers crammed into a button or maps hidden in his boot heel; his information was all in his head. General Howe needed to know about Benedict Arnold's flotilla and the lack of rebel fortifications on the Staten Island shore. He was shocked that Charles Lee, whom Washington had entrusted to plan the defense of New York back in January, had constructed only a signals fort there. The British could anchor their fleet in the Lower Bay and bivouac troops on the island with no fear of rebel bombardment. General Howe would surely pay handsomely for this intelligence, if only Rogers could reach him.

Could the rebels have learned of his surveillance of Skenesborough harbor? The riflemen who had apprehended him were dead. As most likely was Princess, he thought with a twinge of sorrow. Were there other witnesses? He had not seen anyone else, nor had he been followed south. He decided to stick to his story: he was visiting his land holdings in northern New York with the intention of returning to Philadelphia to volunteer for service in the rebel cause. Let Congress prove otherwise.

With little else to do, Rogers replayed his audience with Washington over and over again. It was the first time he had met the general. Although Washington did not offer a handshake, they saw eye-to-eye, both tall men for tall times. They stood in the commander-in-chief's oak-paneled office in the opulent Kennedy mansion, the perfect setting for the plantation squire from Virginia. Four Life Guards, burly men in crisp, clean uniforms, were in the room at all times, their eyes riveted on Rogers as if he were a threat to their leader. Aides scampered in and out, whispering hushed messages. Rogers caught references to the machinations of a secret committee.

A light breeze had drifted off the harbor, but did little to cool the room. Ironically, Rogers could see a statue of King George on horseback outside the open window. The statue was commissioned in recognition of the British victory in the Seven Years' War, a victory that he was proud to have played a major role in, a much greater role than Washington in fact.

Sweat leaked from Rogers' grimy hunting shirt; he had had no opportunity to wash after his apprehension. The commander-in-chief, however, looked the part of the regal leader, the burnished gold furnishings on his immaculate uniform worth more than Rogers' entire estate. Could Washington someday be crowned King of America?

Rogers had purposely avoided traveling through New York City, but Washington had somehow learned of his presence in the region and sent men to hunt him down. If Washington had not learned of his espionage, why did he go to such trouble to have him arrested?

Rogers would have welcomed the opportunity to chat about the old times in the wilderness, but Washington was in no mood for small talk. "What are your dealings with the Royal Governor, William Tryon?" the general asked.

"I visited him on the *Duchess* last October," Rogers replied truthfully, relieved that there were no questions about Skenesborough. "I needed him to certify that my land grants in his colony were still valid."

"That is all?" Washington appeared to study the monogram on his handkerchief as he wiped a bead of perspiration from his upper lip.

"That is all," Rogers had answered, less truthful than before. The twinkling of Washington's eye signaled trouble. Tryon is the issue here, he realized too late, already knee-deep in horseshit. *Washington must have learned of the Royal Governor's kidnapping plot and his efforts to recruit me. Therefore, I am guilty of conspiracy or guilty of failing to disclose a conspiracy. Either charge would undermine my claim to support the rebel cause.*

Rogers skulked around his prison in Philadelphia, angry that he had underestimated the rival he had once disdained. How did Washington flush Tryon's machinations out into the open? The general must have established a counter-intelligence organization. Washington had grown quite rapidly from a mere militia man into the commander-in-chief of a national army.

Looking out the window across the square, Rogers could see the Pennsylvania State House, a majestic red brick building sporting a soaring steeple. The bell, housed in the lower reaches of the steeple, chimed frequently summoning Congress to session. His warden had told him the legislature was debating a document, written by Thomas Jefferson from Virginia, that would declare the colonies' independence from Great Britain.

A declaration of independence was a bold gamble, bolder than he thought possible from a covey of pickthank politicians. While it might rally support for the rebel cause both in America and Europe, any man who signed the document would not be able to hide from its consequences. The penalty for treason against the Crown was death and forfeiture of all property. Congress had raised the stakes of the game considerably, while it held no aces.

Rogers forged a grim smile. The declaration might be just what he needed to reverse his fortunes. If he could help the British defeat the rebellion, he would be in line to reap his due reward. A plantation in Virginia perhaps?

***

Colonel Webb unscrolled the broadsheet, delivered fresh off the printing press from Washington's headquarters, as his captains gathered around. Peering over the colonel's shoulder, I could only read the headline set in bold black type: *A DECLARATION by the REPRESENTATIVES of the UNITED STATES OF AMERICA.* William Hull bounced with excitement on the far side of the colonel. The break from England was finally out in the open, no turning back now.

The concept of a "United States of America", declared to the entire world, sent my head spinning. I recited the four words out loud, listening to them roll off my tongue, savoring every syllable. With its abundance of natural resources, unexplored wilderness, coastline stretching from Massachusetts to Florida, and its booming population, White, Black and Red, the United States of America could become the greatest nation the world would ever know.

Of course, I had many questions, governance and slavery foremost, the devil was always in the details, but they could wait. I would fight for these United States, die for them if God willed.

"You'll have to wait until six o'clock, boys," Webb announced as he rolled up the document and tied it with a blue ribbon. "General Washington wants all the troops to hear the Declaration at the same time."

"Has New York ratified it yet?" I asked.

"Finally," the Colonel replied. "The provincial Congress convened up in White Plains early this morning. All thirteen colonies are now united."

"Took them long enough," Hull muttered under his breath. New York had been the only abstention when the Continental

Congress had ratified the document five days ago on July 4th in Philadelphia.

"White Plains?" I chuckled. "Wanted to be as far away from the city as possible."

"Not exactly a vote of confidence in the Continental Army," Hull added.

"Let's prove them wrong then," Webb countered as he trundled back to his quarters.

Anticipation crackled on the Common that evening, July 9th. Through the hush of twilight, my men and I strained to see our commander-in-chief regally walk his horse to the head of the formation. His blue-jacketed Life Guards and green-sashed aides melted into the background. A drum roll called us to attention. Washington fiddled with his hat, stretching out the moment before unrolling a parchment.

A shroud of silence settled over the Common. Although the assembly was less than a quarter of the size of the audience that had watched Hickey hang, we recognized that tonight's event was far more important. We were witness to history and didn't want to miss a word.

Washington bellowed, but it was still difficult to hear. He began with his general orders, which I had been fortunate enough to read earlier that afternoon:

The General hopes this important Event will serve as a fresh incentive to every officer, and soldier, to act with Fidelity and Courage, as knowing that now the peace and safety of his Country depends (under God) solely on the success of our arms: And that he is now in the service of a State, possessed of sufficient power to reward his merit, and advance him to the highest Honors of a free Country.

Washington stopped, rerolled his parchment, and cantered Old Nelson backwards several steps. On cue, Colonel Webb and the other regimental commanders stepped forward and began to read the Declaration itself:

...We hold these truths to be self-evident, that all men are created equal, that they are endowed by their Creator with certain unalienable Rights, that among these are Life, Liberty and the pursuit of Happiness.--That to secure these rights, Governments are instituted among Men, deriving their just powers from the consent of the governed, --That whenever any Form of Government becomes destructive of

these ends, it is the Right of the People to alter or to abolish it, and to institute new Government…

Colonel Webb intoned for a quarter of an hour, the troops' attention never lagging, lapping up the concepts even though I was sure that Jefferson's multi-syllable cramp-words had never before entered their lexicon. The document enumerated both the general rights of the newly formed states as well as a list of specific grievances against the King. I counted twenty-six such charges, leading my men to huzzah at the mention of taxation without consent, the dissolution of our legislatures, the restriction of immigration, and the blockade of international trade. How could Britain expect the colonies to acquiesce to such barbarities without a fight?

With each cheer my men, as well as the regiments surrounding us, grew more agitated, the Common rocking to the beat of stamping feet. Colonel Webb had to shout the Declaration's final words:

…for the support of this Declaration, with a firm reliance on the protection of Divine Providence, we mutually pledge to each other our Lives, our Fortunes, and our Sacred Honor.

"Our Sacred Honor!" I proclaimed, thrusting my saber in the air as Webb pocketed his parchment and turned towards General Washington. Exuding dignity and gravitas, our commander-in-chief sat stock-still upon Old Nelson until the last colonel had completed his oration. He held this spell for a final second before spurring his mount off the field, trotting north towards his residence with his Life Guards in tow.

"Company dismissed!" The order echoed from regiment to regiment, but no one moved, a pregnant pause sweeping across the Common as each man searched the countenance of his fellow patriots. Where do we go from here? We were on the precipice of independence, whatever that meant, but hesitant to leap into the unknown.

"Topple King George!" The cry first came from the back ranks, then gathered force among the civilians milling about the fringes of the formation, and finally broke over us like a clap of thunder.

Men drifted towards Broadway, then surged down the avenue. I was swept along, proud to be present at the birth of our nation. Hull,

Tallmadge, Hempstead – we all bobbed in the sea of celebration. Drums beat, fifes bleated, women cheered.

By the time I reached Bowling Green, two men, stevedores by the looks of their caps pulled low over their ears, had already climbed atop the marble pedestal supporting the statue of the King astride his stallion. The mob, predominantly white but peppered with a handful of Blacks, hurled insults. The red and white stripes of the Sons of Liberty flag unfurled from a townhouse window.

A knot of three roughhewn men, the wear of a long journey staining their hunting shirts and breeches, stalked the sidelines. One held a slate-gray pit bull, growling and tugging at the end of a leash. They scanned the crowd, seemingly uninterested in the proceedings atop the statue.

"Topple the King! Topple the King!" The shouting gained urgency, morphing from a rallying cry into a command. Someone tossed a rope, then another. The seamen grabbed them and started to scale the monument. As one reached the King's shoulders, his beanie fell off revealing a bald scalp tattooed with the trident of the Sons of Neptune.

Losing sight of familiar faces, I slipped to the perimeter, content to watch the action unfold. Ben Tallmadge, standing on the steps of the Kennedy mansion, caught my eye and waved me over. I hustled past two rouge-cheeked whores soliciting customers for their establishment in the Holy Ground. One was Lara, I realized, but she didn't appear to recognize me, and I didn't stop. Hull was already by Tallmadge's side when I arrived, but Hempstead was still missing.

The seamen looped the nooses around King George's head and shoulders and nimbly worked their way back down to the pedestal. Sons of Liberty and Sons of Neptune men jostled for position on the ground, wrapping the ropes around their beefy biceps, digging their heels into the dirt readying for the big pull. Isaac Sears stepped forward, the mob yielding in his path.

"Down with the King!" Upon Sears' order, the men leaned in, grunting and groaning. The crowd urged them on. The King's head snapped off, clanging to the ground. Huzzahs boomed; rum flowed freely. Before long, the entire statue lay shattered on the Common. Someone mounted the King's head on a pike, and the mob paraded it on a victory tour through the streets of New York. Church bells pealed in celebration.

"I bet there's thousands of pounds of lead lying there," Hull said as the Common emptied. "We should melt it into ammunition."

"A fitting end for our King," Tallmadge added.

"I for one will be most pleased to fire His Majesty's balls from my musket," I replied.

"I believe a libation is in order," Tallmadge said, pointing the way towards Fraunce's Tavern, a red brick townhouse close to Washington's command post that served as the favorite watering spot for Continental Army officers.

The three grizzled travelers I had noticed on the Green blocked our path down Pearl Street. They surrounded a stocky Black, festooned in green livery, a patch covering one eye, cowering at each lunge of the leashed pit bull.

"Winston smells a runaway," the leash holder said, giving it a bit more slack. His two henchmen, armed with both pistols and truncheons, bunched closer cutting off the Black's escape. "Are you a runaway, boy?"

"No sir. I belong to Mr. Vincent Van Cliff, a well-established landowner in Flatbush village."

"He's one-eyed. And short. And Black," one of henchmen laughed, tugging his beard which straggled down his chest. "That's sure fits the description in the warrant, Jackson."

"I am quite certain several men meet those criteria," the Black answered, his eyes flicking between the slobbering beast and Jackson.

"You talking back to me boy?" Jackson asked, unravelling more slack in the leash. Winston nipped at the slave's boots. "We traveled all the way up north from Virginia tracking you. We ain't going back empty-handed."

"You may well be," I said breaking towards the tight circle.

"Leave it alone, Nathaniel," Hull whispered, tugging on my sleeve. "It's not our fight. Not tonight at least."

"General Washington's a slaveholder. And a fellow Virginian," Tallmadge added. "He would not look kindly on your interference here."

"Let's walk around this mess." Hull stepped towards the far side of the street. Tallmadge followed. Their current tugged at me.

Winston barked, lunged at his prey, sunk his teeth into the Black's calf. Obey screamed in pain. The blight of slavery had festered in my conscious since my chance meeting with Asa at Miner's last summer. I could not look away any longer.

"Restrain that beast. Or I will shoot it," I commanded, breaking from my friends and drawing my pistol.

"Mind your own business, soldier," Jackson replied, a cold steel in his tone, yanking Winston back nevertheless. The Black, his pant leg bloody, hopped a step away, but did not have much room to maneuver.

"This man has rights. You can't just kidnap him off the street. Not here in New York," I said, holstering my weapon, hoping, foolishly perhaps, to reason my way through the situation.

"What rights does a slave have? Here or anywhere in the colonies? You don't think Mr. Jefferson was including slaves in his high-minded Declaration, now do you?" Jackson asked, arching his furry brows extended in a ridgeline as formidable as the Guana Heights. He snorted a wad of snot in my direction, then wiped the back of his hand across the damp swamp of gray hairs sprouting from his nostrils. "All men are created equal? Ha!" he added. His fellow slavecatchers guffawed in agreement.

"His master, Mr. Van Cliff, has rights then," I countered.

"If Van Cliff lives in Flatbush, then he's most likely a Tory. And Tories are traitors. They ain't got no property rights any more. Ain't that right?"

Lara and the other whore walked by on their way back to the Holy Ground, but steered clear of the confrontation. "Next thing you'll tell me is women have rights too," Jackson taunted, loosing another snotball. Lara flipped him the bird before hastening away.

"We may be out of line here," Tallmadge said, stepping to my side, followed by Hull.

"Let's whistle for the constable," William added.

Jackson chuckled wickedly. "How do you think we found the nigger? The constable's in for a share of the bounty."

"We'll take …" I looked at the Black.

"Obey's my given name."

"We'll take Obey to the city jail ourselves then and see if his master claims him," I said.

Jackson looked us over, shuffled his feet, surveyed the street, several more soldiers approaching. "Forty-eight hours. Otherwise he's ours," he hissed. The slavecatchers and their dog marched off.

I didn't feel like celebrating any more after we parked Obey in a cell underneath City Hall. Jackson was right. I had no legal grounds to defend a fugitive. The words of the Declaration of Independence were aspirational, a vision of what our new country might someday be. Right now, unfortunately, these freedoms only applied to white men of property who supported the Glorious Cause. Still, it was all we had. And we had to start somewhere.

Stephen Hempstead, his jacket disheveled, caught up to me on Bowery Lane as I headed back to camp. A smudge of gunpowder scarred his pistol hand. "Caleb Wheaton. I saw him on the perimeter of the Green tonight. He was up to no good, I'm sure," he said.

"What happened?"

"I chased him down to the East River, but he escaped to Long Island. Probably had a rowboat hidden in the weeds."

If Caleb was close by, so was Anne. Was she an outlaw in hiding? Or a revered widow of a British officer? Why did I still care?

***

Anne rather enjoyed her role, however temporary, as lady of Mayor Matthews' Flatbush estate, a far cry from her position on her first night here, a scant two weeks ago. Naked, scared and scandalized, she had buried herself beneath the quilts while the Mayor dressed under the watchful eye of General Greene and his men. Greene at first sought to question her, but Matthews dismissed her as a trifling servant girl, a description that steamed her ears at the time, but, in hindsight, might have saved her life.

After the rebels had carted the Mayor away, she dressed and made her way downstairs, stopping on the landing at the sound of voices.

"Is *she* still 'ere?" a shrill female asked in a cockney brogue.

"Upstairs," George, the valet, chortled. "Ridden hard and put away wet, if I know my master."

A rather accurate description, Anne thought, but a rather pleasant experience. She found herself stirring once again.

"'e does enjoy the ladies' company, don't 'e?"

"And why not? My master has no marital ties." Although disappointed to learn several others had shared Matthews' bed, hardly a surprise in the cruel light of the morning after, Anne breathed a bit easier knowing she was not an adulteress.

"Shall we give'er the boot, then?"

"Unfortunately, no. Upon his departure, the Mayor informed me that the woman has his permission to stay as long as she likes. And be treated with the utmost respect for her service to the Crown."

"And what service might that be, eh?" The servants shared a lusty laugh.

Their lewdness flipped Anne's arousal to indignation. She thought of Betsey Loring and General Howe. Would she now be viewed as David Matthews' concubine? What would Geoffrey have thought of her service to the Crown?

She thudded down the final steps, pleased to see the surprise register on the faces of her taunters. "I've worked up a hearty appetite," she said. "Please set a table for one. Meat and cheese will do. Whiskey as well."

George's jaw dropped, but he only hesitated a second before shooing Rose, gray-haired and horse-faced, dressed in the livery of household help, to the kitchen. "Of course, ma'am," he replied. "Would you prefer to dine in the parlor or the study?"

With the Mayor in jail, quite possibly due for a worse fate, Anne enjoyed free roam of the estate. George had somehow learned of her bookkeeping experience and sought her assistance with the household accounts. She steadily expanded the scope of her responsibilities, soon overseeing a swarm of servants, stable hands, and slaves, who, unlike in Connecticut, comprised the majority of the labor force here on Long Island.

After an inspection of the watermelon patch and vegetable gardens, and a hot bath, which she required Rose to draw, a trite yet satisfying retribution, Anne dressed in a fine cotton frock, dyed a deep blue and accented with lace imported from India, recently purchased from the weaver in Flatbush. She strolled barefoot into the parlor to supper on the "Japanned" table, lacquered in black to copy highly fashionable furniture made in the Orient, which rested on an intricately woven rug thick enough to nestle her toes. The room, an Anglophile's delight, featured damask wallpaper decorated with a menagerie of birds, monkeys and flowers, as well as a mechanical orrery displaying the orbit of Mercury, Venus, and the earth around the sun. If only Father could see it, she thought.

The table was set for two, but, as usual, Caleb was late. She sipped a '60 Bordeaux, the Mayor kept an excellent cellar, and watched the summer sun set languidly below the treetops. There was not another farmhouse in sight. Long Island, at least this end of it, was lightly populated, less than three thousand people in all, including slaves.

George had thoughtfully left the latest edition of the *New York Gazetteer*, Tory in its politics, for her perusal. The rebels were acting quite plucky, particularly with the British army now at its doorstep. Perhaps, the thwarting of the plot against Washington had spurred them on. While Mayor Matthews and several others were still imprisoned and under investigation, Thomas Hickey was the only one to hang, so far at least. The longer the rebels delayed in reaching a verdict and executing a sentence, she reasoned, the better the Mayor's chances. He might yet live to welcome General Howe to his city.

Today's headline blared news of a Declaration, signed five days ago by the Continental Congress in Philadelphia, now sweeping across the colonies. She would have liked to read the incendiary document in its entirety, but the broadsheet only contained snippets and hearsay. From what she could glean, the Declaration might inspire true believers, like Nathan, who needed little further inspiration, but offered few details as to how this new nation, if it ever came to be, might actually run.

Typical for politicians, she thought, to incite the populace with high-minded verbiage, but to omit the nuts and bolts of their proposals. Nevertheless, if the Declaration was half as bold as the tabloid claimed, its signatories had, in fact, signed their own death warrants. The King would show little mercy to any man who fomented open rebellion.

Could this Declaration prompt France to enter the war on the rebels' side? Geoffrey had often talked of the French, a country of hated papists in his view, as lying in wait to revenge their humiliating defeat in the Seven Years War. The French navy alone would certainly provide a much-needed boost to Nathan and his compatriots.

She wondered how rebel newspapers, like the *New York Journal* or *Pennsylvania Evening Post*, would cover the Declaration. Most likely aggrandize it into the Second Coming of our Savior. On occasion, George had come across opposition broadsheets and would show them to her, if she asked. It was like reading the news from another country.

Anne rang her bell summoning the valet. He appeared promptly, bearing a tray of turkey, sweet potatoes and turnips. "Dining alone, ma'am?"

"Hopefully not. My brother should be back soon enough. But there's no need for you – or Rose - to wait. We can clean up ourselves."

"Thank you, ma'am. We'll see you in the morning then."

Anne nibbled at her food while she read further. At the sound of approaching footfalls, pleased that Caleb had returned at a reasonable hour, she looked out the window. All she saw, however, was a Black, barely discernable in the dim light, hurrying up the path. She called for George, but her voice echoed in the empty house. Reaching into the cupboard, she withdrew her pistol, checked the barrel for ball and powder, and cocked the trigger. She glanced out the window again, her pistol at the ready, the Black now on her doorstep.

It was Obey, Mr. Van Cliff's man whom she had first met outside the Ramrod. She had run into Obey twice in the village, but, aside for a cordial greeting, had kept her distance, respecting his recalcitrance at talking to white women in public. Breathing a sigh of relief, she put her pistol in her skirt pocket. What was he doing here? At this hour? On second thought, Anne decided to keep a finger on the trigger as she opened the door.

"Miss Wheaton, my sincerest apologies for disturbing your supper," Obey said, his hand shaking, complexion pale, green jacket torn and dust-splattered.

"How can I be of assistance?"

Obey glanced furtively left and right, like a squirrel caught in the middle of the road. "May I come inside? Please. It is most urgent."

"Of course." Was Mr. Van Cliff in need of assistance? He had but one arm after all, his left crushed in a fall from horseback several years ago. A petite Oriental woman, Chinese most likely, tended the house, and was rumored to be his wife, although she did not appear at Sunday meeting.

Anne stepped aside; Obey followed.

"Is Caleb home this evening? It is his assistance that would be most valuable."

"No," she replied, then added, "But I expect him at any moment."

"May I wait then?"

"Only if you explain the reason for your visit."

"I went to New York this afternoon. To listen to General Washington recite the Declaration of Independence."

"Why would you do that?"

"I wanted to hear myself if the document promised freedom for all men, as I had heard rumored."

"And did it?"

"It offered a glimmer of hope, but…" Obey choked off the sentence, trembling.

"Go on."

Obey told the story of his torment at the hands of the slavecatchers and their pit bull.

"Why would slavecatchers come after you? Don't you belong to Mr. Van Cliff?"

"I fit a description on a bounty notice. They claimed to have tracked me all the way from Virginia."

Anne ruminated for a second. "And did you run away?"

"Look at my eye, Miss Wheaton," Obey ripped off his patch and pointed to his mutilated socket. "My mistress, Constance, English by birth, took a liking to me. She taught me to read and write. In violation of Virginia's laws. When her husband found out, he put out my eye. And would have put out the other one if Miss Constance had not intervened. And this is not the worst of my scars."

Anne shuddered at the sight of Obey's wound. She had grown up viewing slavery as a benign institution. Becky was part of the family; Father would no more harm her than he would harm one of his children.

Nevertheless, Anne knew she was on shaky ground now, harboring a fugitive slave was punishable by death in many colonies. New York might be more lenient, but her position on the Matthews' estate was far from unassailable. She checked the window, staring down the path for five full seconds, but saw no movements in the darkness. "Does Mr. Van Cliff know of your past?"

"Yes, ma'am. He offered me refuge in exchange for my labor. I believe he is an Abolitionist at heart."

There was obviously more to Mr. Van Cliff than his frequent visits to the Holy Ground would suggest, Anne thought. Obey must return to him as soon as possible. "How did you escape the slavecatchers?" she asked.

"Three Continental officers rescued me. And marched me to the city jail to await my master."

"Since you are here alone, I gather you didn't wait."

"No ma'am. Captain Hale paid a boy to run a message down to Flatbush, but how could I be sure it would reach Mr. Van Cliff in time?"

"Captain Hale? Nathaniel Hale?" She couldn't dowse the light in her eyes.

"Yes, Ma'am. A bold and intrepid man. Pledged to do everything he could to end slavery in the United States – once the war was won," Obey shuffled his feet, as if he had said too much. "Do you know him?"

"He was my schoolmaster in New London - a long time ago." Anne sat down, digesting the latest twist in Obey's story. "Please continue."

"Miss Lara, the strumpet you met at the Ramrod, and an associate must have watched my arrest. They followed me to City Hall and, shall we say, entertained the jailhouse guards while I slipped away."

"And the slavecatchers from Virginia?"

"They will undoubtedly have learned of my escape by now."

"And will track you…here," Anne concluded.

"Yes, ma'am. That is why I came looking for Caleb. I know him to be a man of action. And sympathetic to my cause."

Caleb, an Abolitionist? She was not aware her brother had ever thought about the subject, but tonight was already full of surprises. Caleb and Nathan on the same side? She prayed she would live to see that day.

A fierce pounding on the door knocker rattled the candlesticks. The slavecatchers had arrived. Obey slipped towards the kitchen.

Anne opened the door a crack, her pistol firmly gripped. Three road-hard men and a fierce dog waited politely outside.

"Evening, ma'am. My name's Jackson," the leader said, removing his hat and tilting his protruding brows in her direction.

"And this here's Winston," he added, yanking hard enough on the leash to produce a growl from the pit bull. "Is your husband home?"

Teeth flashed from Jackson's associates, forced smiles, too sly for Anne's taste. "Sorry to disturb you so late," one muttered obsequiously.

"My husband is out, but will return this evening," she replied, flicking her gaze up the road. Where was Caleb? Why had she dismissed the help so early? "You can return tomorrow if you have business with him."

"We're looking for an African, a one-eyed African, who absconded from his master in Richmond. Stabbed a man to death in the process." The men showed no signs of leaving.

"Sounds like a dangerous man." She relaxed her trigger finger. One bullet wouldn't stop three men. Not these three anyway.

"Most dangerous. Have you seen him, ma'am?"

"No sir."

"Are you certain. He's hard to miss." The dog prowled towards Anne.

"No sir. I trust you'll be on your way then." She started to close the door.

Jackson half-turned, then wheeled and kicked it open.

"What...?" A backhand slap to her cheek stifled the question stillborn.

"Lying bitch," Jackson said, his ice-blue eyes still as stones. "You have no husband. You're Mayor Matthews' whore." He motioned his henchmen inside, closed the door, and dropped the leash, allowing his mutt free rein to sniff around the parlor. "And you're man's not coming home tonight, now is he?"

"I do believe he's awaiting his date with the hangman," a henchman added, his scraggly beard insufficient to muffle his giggle.

Gripping Anne's shoulders, Jackson shook her until drool dripped down her chin. "We had to beat a man silly on the Flatbush Road before he'd tell us which way the nigger went. We'll do worse to you if you don't give him up." The bruises and blood stains on his knuckles, visible in the candlelight, confirmed his story.

Jackson tossed Anne to the carpet like a rag doll. He ordered his men to take the dog and search the house while he stood over her, sweat dripping from his hair-stuffed nostrils. Crockware crashed against a wall in the kitchen. The thump on the ceiling above her head signaled the destruction of the great featherbed in the master bedroom. Anne curled into a fetal ball.

Jackson stalked to the hearth, grasped an iron poker, and paced the parlor. He stopped in front of the orrery, admiring it, toying with its bronzed rings and levers. "This must be English," he said. "Your man's a Tory."

Anne didn't reply.

"You're living in sin with a supporter of the King. Fornicating with him too, I reckon." He tapped the orrery gently with the poker, then smashed it down, a wicked gleam firing his eyes. The porcelain ball, delicately painted with the blues and greens of the earth, shattered into pieces. "Now where is that runaway?" Jackson demanded without raising his voice.

Anne curled tighter, expecting the slavecatcher to attack her, but he strolled towards the hearth, twirling the poker in the flames. "My boys better find Obey. For your sake."

The men converged in the parlor, empty-handed. "Hold her still," Jackson commanded, the iron glowing red, then orange.

Anne tried to scuttle away but she had nowhere to go. The men each grabbed an arm and dragged her to her feet. The dog slobbered as if expecting a treat. Jackson appeared in no rush. "Where did Obey go?" he asked maintaining the even tone of an undertaker.

"He's Mr. Van Cliff's man. I sent him back to his rightful home. Make a left in the village. It's about a mile down the road." Anne forced herself to croak out an answer.

"Why did he stop here then?" Jackson held the poker inches from her face.

"I don't know." She would never give up Caleb.

"We'll soon see about that." With his free hand, Jackson reached for the bodice of her dress, ripped it open and grabbed her breast. The heat from the poker seared her aureole; her nipple swelled like a cherry waiting to be plucked. Anne bit right through her lower lip.

"We're going to teach you some respect for the law," the henchman with the long beard hissed.

"Last chance, whore," Jackson said.

"Wait!" Obey shouted as he floated like a black ghost from the kitchen.

"That's better," Jackson replied, turning towards the slave. "Take him, boys." His men dropped Anne's arms, tossing her back to the floor, and clambered towards Obey. Winston nipped at the slave's feet, waiting for its master's order to attack.

The front door splintered open. Caleb burst inside, a pistol in each hand. His first shot felled the pit bull in its tracks; the second caught Jackson in the right shoulder, knocking him to his knees, the poker falling from his grasp, steaming a hole through the Oriental carpet.

Obey must have concealed a vest-pocket pistol in his palm. His shot split the forehead of the bearded slavecatcher, dropping him cold. The third slavecatcher lunged, but stumbled. Obey whipped out a shiv from behind his back and drove it up into his pursuer's throat. The man toppled in a fountain of blood.

Anne scrambled for her pistol before Jackson could crawl too far. Firing from point-blank range, she didn't miss. Jackson collapsed face-forward but somehow found the strength to roll over, scarlet blooming from his chest. "Nigger lovers," he gurgled through a mix of spittle and blood flickering from his lips.

Anne screamed in primal rage, a war cry any Indian would have envied. Tossing away her smoking pistol, she grabbed the poker, plunging it into Jackson's groin, taking satisfaction in the sizzle and stink of his burning flesh. Again and again, she stabbed. Jackson cried out loud enough to wake the cows; his eyes bulged; his legs kicked in a macabre dance.

"He's dead, sister," Caleb gently removed the iron bar from her grasp and wrapped her in his embrace. Shaking, her ordeal over, Anne cried softly on his shoulder.

"I'll put the bodies in the wagon," Obey said. "There's swampland just below Guana Heights. No one'll ever find them."

"Or miss them," Anne added, wiping away her tears. Jackson leered at her even in death, but she had had the last laugh.

***

The news from John Richards hit me hard. I crumpled his letter and stuffed it into the pocket of my waistcoat. Although I was exhausted from another dog day of shoveling dirt in the July heat, my quarters offered little promise of comfort. Nor did I have any interest in the camaraderie of my fellow officers. I arranged for my sergeants to handle the evening muster and stalked out of camp.

Turning off Bowery Lane, I sought solitude in the woods. Perched atop a pumpkin-shaped boulder overlooking a meandering brook, I read the missive again:

Captain Hale,

Prudence is dead. In her last week on this earth, she had grown sullen and irritable, far unlike her normal temperament. Accordingly, Mehitable suggested a visit with midwife Lucy, who admitted afterwards that she had recommended a potion of tansy. On his beach patrol the next morning, Constable Prescott found Prudence's body in a pool of blood. An urn with a residue of the golden petals and an empty bottle of rum were nearby. I considered pressing charges of witchcraft against the midwife, but Mehitable implored me not to do so. She remains distraught with grief.

Sheriff Gray certified that Prudence's death was due to natural causes, no foul play involved. My brother requested a private funeral ceremony and had his daughter buried in his family cemetery.

You shared a close connection with Prudence. Mehitable and I prayed it would blossom into a marital union, but it was not God's will. I must confess I held you responsible at first for my dear niece's melancholy, but my wife assured me that was not the case, although she refused to provide any more particulars. Nevertheless, as one honorable gentleman to another, I ask you forever to restrain from utterances that might tarnish Prudence's memory. She was an impetuous young lady who most fervently supported our Glorious Cause. May she rest in peace.

Godspeed.

John Richards' parting paragraph stung like whiskey on an open wound. After practically tossing his niece into my bed, he blamed me for abandoning her? If anyone was at fault for Prudence's intercourse with Tom Hickey, it was the Richards.

Parsing Richards' words with those he left unwritten, I deduced that Prudence might have shared what she had once thought of as good news with Mehitable, but had wisely not announced it to all of New London. A savvy reader of men, as I could well attest, she likely began to doubt Tom Hickey's moral fiber well before his treachery became common knowledge.

Once news of his execution circulated, the brunt of carrying the traitor's unborn child likely became more than Prudence could bear. I harbored no doubt that her visit to the midwife was prompted by the desire to free herself of shame one way or another. I resolved to burn Pru's final letter as soon as I returned to camp, and prayed she had not confided her secrets to anyone else.

Silently, I eulogized Pru to an audience of squirrels, rabbits, and pigeons, choosing to remember my friend as a casualty of war, dying a noble death, although she had never fought on a battlefield. Tom Hickey had killed Pru, as surely as if he had stabbed her with his bayonet. Her cherubic face, gleaming smile and boundless energy were gone forever. She had made her choice freely, if naively, and bore the consequences alone.

A hawk landed on a tree limb above my head, his darting eyes vibrant with interest in my unspoken soliloquy. I closed with an ode to martyrdom I had read in the *New York Journal*: *"I was born to die and my reason and conscience tell me it is impossible to die in a better or more important cause."* These words were published anonymously, but I had recently met the author, Captain Alexander Hamilton, a King's College man my own age, at Fraunce's Tavern. We bonded over our common interests, notably the Revolution and beautiful women. He would have enjoyed Prudence's company, as she would have his.

When I finished my silent speech, the hawk soared into the dusk. I lingered on my boulder until the boom of cannons cut short my mourning. A barrage of balls whistled over the treetops. The British were coming!

I thrashed towards the ridgeline overlooking the Hudson. Like a pair of fire-breathing dragons, the warships, *Phoenix* and *Rose*, familiar from Boston harbor, sailed upriver, their canvas billowing defiantly in the breeze as their gunners expertly raked Manhattan with broadsides. I scanned the swells for longboats ferrying redcoats to shore, but was relieved to see none.

To my left, I did see a familiar face. Captain Hamilton and his recently formed New York Provincial Company of Artillery had set up a temporary battery on a rock-strewn outcrop. With horses few and far between, they must have dragged the half-dozen squat black cannons across Manhattan from their post atop Bayard's Mount. To my envy, his men boasted crisp, new uniforms - blue coats, brass buttons, white shoulder straps, and buckskin breeches, courtesy of John Jay, a wealthy New York merchant and King's College alumni.

I watched as Hamilton, resplendent in a red-feathered hussar's hat, gingerly stroked the barrel of the lead gun as if it were a favored hound. He set its elevation with quadrant and plummet, then stepped away as his men performed a seemingly well-rehearsed minuet to load the weapon. Soldiers alternated ramming and sponging the barrel, before the gunners primed the piece with powder and wadding. A well-run team could launch a hundred shots per day, although few, on our side at least, could actually hit a moving target, as the continued advance of the *Rose* and *Phoenix* attested.

After Hamilton bellowed the order to fire, an explosion detonated in his nest. Steel, hay, blood and body parts spewed well into the air, like lava from a volcano. A severed arm landed at my feet. I first thought to return it to its rightful owner; unfortunately, its rightful owner would have little use for it now.

Hamilton rose from the dirt, seemingly unhurt although his uniform was no longer unsoiled. "Damnation! A misfire!"

"I'll fetch an ambulance and corpsmen," I shouted. My troops were safe in their barracks, while the carnage below demanded attention. Sprinting downtown towards King's College, now serving as the primary hospital for our army, I passed gaggles of soldiers standing hang-jawed on the bluffs, looking out to the river as if spectators at a carnival show.

Although the sun was well past its zenith, the city baked. Smoke and fire rolled up Broadway, the might of the British Empire apparent for all to see. The sound of drum beats calling men to arms mixed with the high-pitched shrieks of women and children. Constables and fire marshals set up bucket lines to draw water and dowse the burning buildings. I looked skyward, hopeful of an evening thunderstorm, but no clouds were in sight.

Civilians, the few who had not yet evacuated, appeared intent on rectifying their mistake as quickly as possible. They tossed their belongings into pushcarts, or piled them on their backs, and trudged north towards safety. Sons of Liberty patrolled street corners, urging people along and offering to relieve them of any excess baggage.

After notifying the medical authorities of Captain Hamilton's dilemma, I commandeered three privates to stretcher a bloodied matron, wearing a lime-green taffeta gown that she obviously couldn't bear to leave behind, and a child, a native girl no more than five years old, to the hospital, stepping around cannon balls that had come to rest in the street.

The barrage lasted two hours before the *Rose* and *Phoenix* sailed past Fort Washington, thumbing their noses at our shore-mounted guns. The British had made their point most emphatically: New York was at their mercy.

At nightfall, I crossed Hamilton's path outside King's College, his old stomping grounds. Last year, he first earned notoriety for his sharp tongue by holding off the Sons of Liberty with a verbal barrage while Myles Cooper, Dean of the College and a flaming Tory, escaped out the back door. Hamilton assured me he had no sympathy for Cooper's politics, but detested mob rule even more, a position much to my liking.

My fellow captain was unusually, but understandably, morose. Two of his men had died at their post while another two lay mortally wounded. Although his shirt and breeches were soiled with blood, Hamilton's hat was still fastened securely under his chin and his shoulder strap in place diagonally across his chest, maintaining a look of professionalism. I tucked in my own shirt as we trudged uptown together towards our barracks. Although embers sizzled on rooftops, the fire brigades had largely contained the damage. The streets were deserted.

"To a good death," Hamilton offered as we passed a legless corpse. Boyish in feature and slight in build, at least a head shorter than me, he seemed even smaller tonight. Having assumed his command fresh from university, leapfrogging several more experienced candidates, he had to be concerned how the day's events might reflect upon his resume.

"Here, here," I seconded. We walked in somber silence for at least fifteen minutes. A half-moon hung like a beacon over the Hudson as we approached Hamilton's battery, deserted now. "What caused the debacle?" I asked.

"Two pudding-brains failed to clean their cannon properly." He spit out the words in disgust. "What do you expect from men recruited in the tavern, and bribed with liquor? I have to drag them from the Holy Ground almost every night."

"At least they died at their post. Better than bed-ridden with syphilis."

"The rabble will never learn. The passion which arouses them to oppose tyranny naturally leads them to contempt for all authority." Hamilton shook his head sadly, but then appeared to jump back to life. His eyes gleamed with a fire that could bore through steel; his words flowed as relentlessly as a snow-swollen stream. "The United States will need a strong federal government after the war. A central bank, a professional army, a single set of laws that apply to all citizens in all states. That's the only way our country can claim its rightful place in the world."

"You're getting a bit ahead of yourself aren't you?" I asked.

"Did I forget something?"

"We must win the war."

"Ah, yes. An important detail." Hamilton chuckled. "But, we do not necessarily have to win the war on the battlefield. We can gain our victory at the bank."

Although somewhat baffled by Hamilton's words, I nodded as if in complete agreement, encouraging him to continue, which he did, most ardently. "If the Continental Army can simply hold out long enough, the British treasury will be emptied and the Crown will have to withdraw its forces from our colonies. King George has an entire empire to consider."

"And slavery?" I just realized that I hadn't seen the three slavecatchers in the city. Hopefully, they were on their way back to Virginia empty-handed. "The Declaration of Independence states clearly that 'all men are created equal' but those words do not appear to apply to Blacks."

"Slavery is a delicate issue, but the United States must abolish it as soon as feasible. I saw its horrors first-hand on the plantations in the Bahamas in my youth. How can our country ever stand for freedom if a fifth our population is enslaved and abused?"

"But, your mentor, Mr. Jay, owns slaves, I believe."

"They are a vestige of his family. He is an Abolitionist at heart."

"I would welcome the opportunity to visit with him one day."

"Excellent idea, Nathaniel. I will see to it."

And I was beginning to see that ambitious men like Hamilton, as well as my friends Tallmadge and Hull, saw the war as much more than a noble adventure. It was the means to advance their careers. Not that they weren't staunch patriots, risking their lives for the Glorious Cause, but they also had a personal agenda. I would need to find a mission myself if I was going to keep pace. What better place than right here in New York with the British on our doorstep?

The evening after the bombardment General Washington gave vent to his frustrations in his daily orders:

"The General was sorry to observe… many of the officers and a number of men instead of attending to their duty…continued along the banks of the river, gazing at the ships. Such unsoldierly conduct must grieve every good officer and give the enemy a mean opinion of the army …"

Sorry to observe? Grieve every good officer? What was Washington trying to accomplish with this message? These were the men we had, and we had no time for self-pity. I thought of Stephen, Hercules, Elvin, Little John and the others in my troop. I was proud of them, and would be even more proud to lead them into battle. Of course, our army's spirits would improve markedly if we all had uniforms like Hamilton's artillerymen; the ragtag collection of homespun that most men in New York wore grew more wretched every day.

I would undoubtedly get my long-awaited opportunity to fight before the summer was out. After supper, Colonel Webb summoned his captains together and relayed our orders for the coming weeks. Admiral Richard Howe, commander of the British Navy and General William Howe's brother, had sailed his flagship, the *Eagle*, into New York Harbor that morning. The rest of the British fleet, carrying thousands more troops, could not be far behind.

My company, as well as several other Connecticut regiments, would return shortly to Long Island where we would camp outside the village of Brooklyn and dig in to await the British assault – if, in fact, the redcoats chose to attack through the Island. Alternatively, they could land anywhere on Manhattan. Or they could do both, and pincer our army between its claws.

How much did Washington know of the size of the British force and its intentions? Outnumbered and outgunned, the Continental Army would have little chance of defending New York without intelligence. I prayed that we had spies aplenty in Long Island, Staten Island and the Jerseys.

Sergeant Hempstead approached as the captains' meeting disbanded. "Seems like our comrades in Philadelphia were lax at their post as well," he said, handing me a handbill with a crude caricature of a uniformed army officer:

Wanted – Dead or Alive
Major Robert Rogers
$50 bounty
Payable by Philadelphia Committee of Safety

"What happened?"

"Rogers walked right out of town while his guards were celebrating the Declaration."

"How did you get this?"

"Little John found it."

"And where did he find it?"

Stephen shook his head, delaying his response. "It was posted in the Ramrod. And likely other disorderly houses, I wager."

As with Captain Hamilton, I could only do so much to keep my men from the temptations of the red lanterns. If the British didn't attack soon, our army might wither away from venereal diseases. Robert Rogers might well end up a victim of the demimonde too, I thought, remembering the decrepit officer I had seen searching desperately for a patron at camp on Winter Hill.

"Do you think Rogers will rejoin the British army?" Stephen asked.

"Little good he will do them," I replied, my mind already churning ahead to the more pressing challenges that lay across the river in Brooklyn.

***

Perched precariously on a limb of a stout oak above the Staten Island shore, Robert Rogers scanned the Lower Bay. Cluttered with the masts of British ships, it more resembled a pine forest than a harbor. The sixty-four gun *Asia* and *Eagle*, flying Admiral Howe's flag, a red cross on a white field, and the *Bristol* and *Preston*, boasting fifty guns each, dominated the scene, but smaller warships like the *Rose, Phoenix* and *Halifax* were also visible standing guard on the periphery.

Counting troop transports, supply vessels, and merchant brigs, Rogers estimated there were at least four hundred British craft lying in wait off New York, quite possibly the grandest armada in military history. While he was never particularly good at figures, he calculated that the fleet might have landed as many as twenty-five thousand troops, including crack Hessian and Scottish Highlander regiments. George Washington and his pitiful Continental Army, rumored to have less than ten thousand healthy men, didn't stand a chance.

Rogers' stomach growled as the aromas from the evening cooking fires drifted skyward. Since his escape from Philadelphia last week, he had traveled only at night, sticking to the woods and jumble-gut back lanes whenever possible. It was a slow journey, and a hungry one since he had no weapon to hunt game.

His mind drifted to a plantation in Virginia, Mount Vernon he believed it was called, the Potomac River lolling past the door, fields of tobacco stretching as far as the eye could see, slaves to fulfill his every want. Although he had railed too many Indian squaws to remember, he had never had a Negress. His breath quickened at the thought of dark, pendulous breasts swaying to a jungle beat. Yes, Mount Vernon would prove an idyllic spot for his retirement - after the rebellion was put down.

At last, he identified the *Greyhound,* a twenty-gun frigate flying both the Red Ensign and Red Lion insignias. He shimmied down the tree trunk, resolved to remain in hiding until morning when its tender would likely come ashore for supplies. The Staten Island coast was littered with the white tents of British troops; Washington had made a grave error not fortifying it. And the Staten Island militia, four hundred strong, had recently switched sides in a public ceremony of allegiance presided over by Governor Tryon himself. Although confident he could gain an audience with General Howe, Rogers saw little reason to chance an encounter with an overeager patrol of either redcoats or militia.

His prudence was rewarded at dawn. Before the dew lifted, the *Greyhound's* tender pushed off, an officer standing regally at the bow. It was General Howe himself, Rogers realized as the boat approached the shore. After tucking his grungy hunting shirt into his breeches, not exactly his Sunday roast meat clothes but the best he could do, he scrambled down the slope to greet him.

Rogers stopped ten yards up the beach, his hands empty and clearly visible, as two marines leaped off the longboat, splashing through the shoals to guide the vessel. They eyed him suspiciously but made no move in his direction. Once the craft was secured, General Howe was first ashore, followed by four more marines and another high-ranking officer from the look of his uniform, as well as two subordinates.

Howe and the other officer wore their battlefield reds, making the statement they were here for work not show, and were freshly-shaven and powdered. Rogers scratched his mangy beard, thick enough to store acorns.

Howe stared for a long second before recognition dawned. "Major Rogers?"

Rogers stood at attention. "Reporting for duty, as you requested, sir."

"Last I heard you were held captive in Philadelphia."

"I escaped, sir. And came straight here. I have information that I believe will prove valuable."

"Walk with us then," Howe said, ushering Rogers into his circle but keeping his distance. "Allow me to introduce my second-in-command, Major General Henry Clinton."

Clinton offered his hand but then thought better of it as he came within orbit of Rogers' ripe body odor. The generals maintained several feet of separation as they strode down the beach. Rogers filled them in on Benedict Arnold and his fleet under construction at Skenesborough, well-positioned to intercept the British forces in Canada if they sailed south to link with Howe's army.

"Arnold is an intrepid fellow, the best field commander the rebels have as far as I can tell," Howe said.

"But he has jealous rivals. And Washington appears slow to recognize his worth," Clinton added.

"We should reach out. If Arnold's resentment boils over, he might prove ambidextrous one day," Howe replied.

"But Arnold is not in New York, fortunately. And the capture of that city is our immediate concern," Clinton said, pointing across the bay. "I believe we should attack up through Long Island."

"Have you explored the Island, Major Rogers?" Howe asked, stopping to gaze out to sea.

"No sir."

"I took the opportunity to examine the terrain myself en route to the Carolinas earlier this year," Clinton said, smoothing a circle of sand with his boot. "It is conducive to landing and supplying a large force. The locals are highly supportive of their King."

"From the maps I have seen, the Guana Heights appear to be a formidable natural barrier," Rogers said.

"And our spies tell us that Washington has entrenched them heavily," Howe replied.

"He must split his army between New York and Long Island," Clinton interjected. "The Royal Navy can sail through the Narrows and cut them off. We will trap the rebels and destroy them."

"Just last week, I offered General Washington clemency for his men, if he surrendered," Howe said, shaking his head. "After the *Rose* and *Phoenix* torched New York, I thought he might see the futility of his position. But, sadly, he has not."

A high-pitched squeal erupted from the dunes to their left. A woman, skirtless, struggled to climb the sandy slope, her flowing blond tresses slapping the pink cheeks of her naked arse. Two British soldiers, bare-chested but still wearing their white leggings and black boots, trotted after her, apparently in no hurry.

"Just a little sport with the locals," Clinton explained with a chuckle. "The troops are in high spirits."

"I can see," Howe said, his glance pivoting away from the chase.

"Washington will need to send out his own intelligence agents soon enough," Rogers said, steering the conversation back on track. In his excitement, determined to receive more than fiddler's pay for his efforts, he narrowed the gap with Howe. "I would be well-suited to lead a force to apprehend them."

"Rangers?" Howe asked, coughing politely into his fist. "The Queen's American Rangers, I like the ring of it."

Rogers nodded enthusiastically, the prospects of full pay plus plunder, particularly if Howe turned a blind eye, dangling like sugar plums. "I'll recruit the men myself, sir, but we'll need a sound ship to patrol the Long Island coast."

"You shall have it. Make Washington pay for his impudence."

CHAPTER 17 - AUGUST 1776

"I only have time for a hasty letter...the event we leave to heaven."
Nathan Hale to Enoch Hale
Long Island
August 20, 1776
(last letter)

"The time is now near at hand which must probably determine whether
Americans are to be freemen or slaves.... The fate of unborn millions will now
depend, under God, on the courage and conduct of this army.... Our cruel and
unrelenting enemy leaves us only the choice of brave resistance, or the most abject
submission. We have, therefore, to resolve to conquer or die."
General George Washington
Address to his troops before the Battle of Long Island
August 27, 1776

Salt and Pepper shuffled up the Flatbush Road, pulling a load of watermelons harvested on the Matthews' farm. David was still imprisoned in New York, the Continentals seemingly in no rush to pass judgment. The execution of a royal mayor was much more complicated than that of a simple private. Anne thought to visit him, but decided it was not worth the risk to enter the rebel-held city: she was still wanted for murder in New London. In fact, the current situation, Matthews in jail and the farm in her hands, was quite satisfactory, although she knew a reckoning would someday come.

Since Caleb had left several days ago to hike through the Jamaica Pass, the easternmost crossing of the Guana Heights, and rendezvous with a sloop taking Tory volunteers to Staten Island, Anne had asked Mr. Van Cliff if Obey could escort her this morning for her protection. He had secluded Obey on his property since the run-in last month with the devil-men from Virginia, only releasing him today after Anne had explained the true purpose of her journey, to reconnoiter rebel positions on the Heights.

As the sun rose above the tree line, the August humidity settled like a damp shawl on Anne's shoulders, sweat beading her forehead. Sitting on the buckboard with reins in hand, she fanned her face with her bonnet, but could find little relief. The road itself, a former Indian trail widened to accommodate wagon traffic, was baked and firm underfoot. The slope steepened as they neared Battle Pass, the surrounding hillside an impassable jungle of vegetation. Sweat frothed from Salt and Pepper's mouth, mosquitos buzzed his ears. She snapped the whip tartly on the horse's flank, keeping him on task.

"There," Obey pointed to the earthworks of Fort Greene looming up ahead, standing sentinel over the road. A pair of Continental Army soldiers, neatly uniformed in buff and gold, lolled in the shade of a towering ash. As the wagon approached, they stepped into the sunlight, bayonet-tipped muskets at the ready.

"Will you need my assistance with the pickets?" Obey asked. Anne's eyes narrowed into a "did-you-not-see-me-kill-a-man" stare.

"Ah, then I will play the dutiful Black," Obey answered his own question.

"Morning," Anne said to the sentries as she reined the wagon to a halt. Salt and Pepper whinnied in appreciation.

"And to you, ma'am," the lead soldier, bushy sideburns devouring both cheeks, replied. "What's your business?"

"Taking fruit to market in Brooklyn." Anne recognized the uniforms, the same as the hard men she had seen on her first ferry to Long Island.

"Fruit, eh?"

"Watermelons. Can I offer you a slice?" she asked. Handing the reins to Obey, she climbed down from her seat, smoothed the frills of her skirt, and walked towards the back of the wagon. She lifted the tarp, revealing a formation of oval-shaped green husks.

"Much obliged."

"Where're you from? Anne asked. "You don't sound like Long Islanders." She cut three generous slices of luscious pink fruit, handing one to each of the soldiers and keeping one for herself.

"Baltimore, ma'am. Smallwood's battalion." Juice dripped from the corners of the soldier's mouth as he replied.

"Judging from your neat attire, Mr. Smallwood must be a wealthy man." Anne spit black seeds into the dirt, in no rush to leave.

The soldier puffed out his chest at the compliment. "New muskets too. And plenty of powder. More than I could say for many of the other regiments on the Heights."

"Bet they'll be thirsty, though," Anne laughed, patting an uncut melon.

"Sure enough," the Marylander replied, turning at the crunch of another wagon approaching. "Best get on your way."

"Good day to you then." Anne climbed back up to the buckboard, disappointed that she had not learned more. She flicked the reins, Salt and Pepper rumbling reluctantly forward. They crossed a hundred yards of open ground, stripped of boulders and brush, a killing field for rebel marksmen stationed inside the fort.

"On to Brooklyn," Obey said looking back ruefully at the watermelons.

***

I called for Little John to bang his drum for reveille well before dawn, enabling my troop to be first in line at the East River ferry landing. Although we were in fine physical condition, I saw no need to waste energy marching in the heat of day. We would have a battle to fight soon enough. And, taking a cue from Captain Hamilton, I wanted to demonstrate initiative to my superiors.

Once the boat docked, we had only a short walk to Brooklyn, the road meandering through fields and orchards, flat and easy on the legs. I sensed the men, myself included, were relieved to be out of New York. The city rotted in the summer heat, as sorely used, foul-smelling and disease-ridden as a Holy Ground hag. One poorly-tended campfire, or well-placed torch, could set it all ablaze.

Elvin's clear tenor led the men in song, starting out with "A Bashful Maiden of Fifteen," prompting ribald taunts at Little John, who, to his credit, played along on his fife. They segued into "A Captain's Tart", a particularly bawdy verse bringing back memories of Princess, although she was most certainly not a tart. The last time I had enjoyed the uncomplicated affections of a loose woman might as well have been during the reign of Queen Elizabeth.

When we reached the village, roughly two dozen houses scattered around a crossroads, the sun had risen above the treetops. Brooklyn was one of six hamlets on the Guana Heights connected by a well-trodden network of paths. Five forts, which we had helped to build this past spring, guarded the ridge line.

Our orders called for us to lug supplies and munitions up Cobble Hill to Fort Corkscrew, so nicknamed because of the sharp switchbacks on the road to its summit. With hay scarce, a cavalry company from Connecticut had actually returned home because Washington refused to feed their horses, we had no choice but to hitch our backs to the wagons and drag them up the steep slope.

After the first round-trip, I signaled for a respite under a grove of pink-flowered tulip trees. Taking a knee in the welcoming shade, we sucked on our canteens, each man judging for himself how much precious liquid to leave for the next break, whenever it might come.

Because an embarrassing experience with New York's foul well-water had required me to purchase a new pair of breeches, I drank only beer on the road. And didn't inquire what beverage my men chose to consume, as long as they could keep marching. After all, alcohol aided digestion, cured colic, and boosted stamina, according to our army physicians.

"Found a strawberry patch," Little John's voice sing-songed through   the   hedges. Off alone answering nature's call, I heard several of my men scramble to join him. After tidying up with a handful of moss, I tracked down the foragers stomping through what had been neat rows of plants. "That's enough boys," I ordered.

"Just one more," Little John pleaded, his fingers stained red, juice dribbling down his chin. "Can't play the fife if my whistle ain't wet."

"One more," I replied, in recognition of Little John's musical efforts, but realized my mistake before the words fully escaped my lips.

"What about me? My whistle's as dry as an old Goody's tit," Elvin said, puckering his lips. Three other men lined up behind him, proving my intuition correct, unfortunately.

"Got to respect property," Hercules, a step behind me, intervened. No one disputed his words. In fact, the former slave, and the oldest man in my troop by at least ten years, had emerged as a voice of wisdom, as much a leader among white men as he could possibly be.

I was proud of Hercules, as well as Asher, Elvin, Peacock, and the others, including McElroy, who had recovered from his flogging and the desertion of his friend to pull his weight in the ranks. Even Little John, despite his rambunctious ramblings, which I excused to youth, had become a soldier, willing to risk his life for the Glorious Cause with a smile on his face.

The concept of liberty united men from all walks of life, although it might hold a different meaning for each. Unlike Hamilton, and perhaps my own Yale classmates, I had learned to respect the "rabble," and relished the opportunity to lead them. Resting my hand on my saber hilt, I prayed I would prove worthy of that honor in the heat of battle.

Sadly though, for the first time, I was beginning to doubt the men in charge of our army, even General Washington, although I recognized his options were limited by Congress' mandate to defend New York. Unsure where the British would attack, Washington had divided our army between Long Island and Manhattan, leaving us perilously short-handed in both locations. He had placed Nathanael Greene, his best commander, in charge of Long Island, but Greene had just recently fallen gravely ill forcing Washington to promote John Sullivan to the post with precious little time to reconnoiter the ground he would have to defend.

If British warships, like the *Phoenix* and *Rose*, again sailed up river, our forces could be isolated and crushed. But, who was I to question my commander-in-chief? I had captained little more than a company of pack mules for the past year.

The sun was unrelenting all afternoon, frying us like potatoes on a skillet. Sweat oozed from every pore in my body. Battle would be a welcome relief to this mind-numbing labor. A cheer went up from my men as we delivered our last load. I ordered Little John to pick up the marching beat so we could be first in line for supper.

We reached Brooklyn just before the watchman cried five bells. The village, and its surrounds, were now crowded with troops from our regiment as well as others. Colonel Webb had established his headquarters in the Ferry Tavern. Messengers from Washington's central staff, split between the Kennedy Mansion in New York and the Cornell House on this side of the East River, raced in and out. A "telegraph" pole towered by the tavern porch, manned by an aide who raised and lowered flags to communicate with the forts.

"Good work, Captain Hale," the colonel said, barely looking up as he pushed a most welcome flagon of brew across the table, followed by my troop's orders for the morrow. "Direct from Major General Sullivan."

"And General Stirling?" I asked, trying to mask my disappointment. William Alexander, who preferred to be known as Lord Stirling, in reference to his claim on lands and title in Scotland, was a New Jersey man well-familiar with the terrain of this region. Wealthy in his own right, he spent a considerable sum outfitting his own regiments – with bayonets too, I noted jealously. Our regiment had been shuttled between his command and Sullivan's during our deployment in New York.

"Stirling is guarding our right flank, down on the Shore Road where I expect the first action will be."

I longed to be there serving under him, right in the teeth of the enemy assault. Sadly, our orders for tomorrow read the same as today. Dig in and wait for our call.

"You and the other captains will billet upstairs tonight. The men should pitch camp in the fields," Webb added.

The fields that I had defended from my men's plunder this morning would surely be trampled by them tonight. There was no way for the countryside to escape the ravages of our invading army, which is what in fact we were.

***

Anne steered the wagon off the road, stopping under a thicket of leafy beech trees intersected by a waist-high stone wall. Marshland, its tall grasses bleached by the sun, coddled the tree line. Beyond the marsh, a pasture, speckled by wild flowers, stretched over low-rolling hills. No soldiers were in sight.

"We're almost in Brooklyn," Obey said, remaining in the buckboard.

"Salt and Pepper needs a rest. And I need privacy," she replied, her lips pinched in discomfort. She dismounted, lifted her skirt above her ankles, and scrambled over the wall.

"Ah, nature calls," Obey said, stepping to the ground. "Slaves are whipped in Virginia if they cannot control their bodily functions."

"But, we are not in Virginia," she called from her squat, before reemerging, her relief apparent. She stroked the horse's forehead, cooed soft words into his ear as she fed him an apple, watching affectionately as he chomped away. Obey raised his eyes and assumed a lookout position with a view of the road.

"The rebels are too well-entrenched," Anne whispered to her mount. "Their forts may hold against even an overwhelming force." Salt and Pepper whinnied, either in agreement or in hope of another apple, which she obliged, savoring the peaceful moment.

She thought of Nathan and his readings of ancient Greece, the tale of the battle of Thermopylae in particular. Three hundred elite Spartan warriors had held off tens of thousands, if not hundreds of thousands, of invading Persians at a narrow mountain pass, buying their fellow Greeks precious time to rally. Sparta, however, was the military powerhouse of its age. Her young men emerged from the womb with sword in hand and trained their entire lives for battle, far unlike the Continental Army, formed of cobblers, butchers, millers, and schoolteachers taking leave from their day jobs.

Yet...she shivered despite the heat, recalling the open ground Her Majesty's troops would have to cross before they could breach the formidable palisades of Fort Greene. How many redcoats would fall there? General Howe would do well to find another way, another pass, a backdoor, as did the Persians, who eventually slaughtered the Spartans at Thermopylae to the last man.

Atop a hillock on the far side of the pasture, Anne now noticed the bare backs of men, sunlight glinting off their shovels as they dug. Shouted commands drifted across the still air. The men, antlike, appeared to be carting off the dirt to build a berm. She would have liked to map the defense works in the countryside, not nearly as visible as the forts up on the heights, but had purposely traveled without paper and ink for her own safety.

The marsh rippled, unnaturally so, as there was no breeze. The tip of a long gun sprouted atop the wall, followed by another, and another, and another, the four soldiers attached to them emerging shortly thereafter. Anne spun frantically. Obey still stood sentry by the road, looking in the wrong direction.

"Afternoon, ma'am," a cinnamon-haired officer, sporting a looping mustache, drawled in a too familiar Southern accent. He doffed his cap and bowed graciously. "Lieutenant Archibald Lee of Richmond at your service."

Richmond? Virginia? Panic battered Anne's gut like a hurricane. She wanted to run, to scream to Obey to run even faster, but they were trapped. "A pleasure to make your acquaintance," she replied, forcing a smile.

"Is that your wagonload of watermelons?"

"Yes, sir. Can I offer you one? At no charge of course."

"Why, I'm right offended by your offer, ma'am. Do we look like men in need of charity?" Lee swept his hat towards his squad, dressed in a ragtag assortment of homespun buckskin and linen, a far cry from the crisply outfitted Marylanders who had stopped her at the pass. Smirking, the men, militia most likely, lowered their weapons, obviously enjoying her discomfort.

"Certainly not, Lieutenant. I meant no offense…" Anne could hear herself tripping over the words, prayed the Virginians had never seen the bounty notice for Obey.

"No offense taken," Lee replied. "There's a company of powerfully thirsty men toiling upon yonder hill."

"I see."

"I'm not sure you do." Lee motioned to one of his men, who stepped forward with a purse of jangling coins. "We'll take the whole load."

Relief flooded Anne's cheeks and rolled out her mouth in a hearty laugh. "I wasn't planning to sell the whole load. Not just yet at least."

"Trying to hold out for a better price, are you dearie?" Lee asked, taking the purse from his man and balancing it in his palm.

"No. No. Your offer took me by surprise. That is all."

"We have a deal then." The gallantry drained from Lee as he handed the purse to Anne. His pupils narrowed to needles, raking her face. "For your melons, your wagon and your horse."

"What?"

"You can keep your nigger," Lee added, as two more of his men appeared, prodding Obey along with their rifles. "We got enough of those."

Anne sensed the tension coiled in Obey. "You drive a hard bargain Lieutenant," she said, stuffing the purse into her satchel before the Black could explode. And get them both killed. "We'll be off then."

She stalked imperiously past Obey, treating him as the Virginians would expect her to treat a slave, and headed down the road towards Brooklyn. A victory whoop echoed behind her but she refused to turn. Even for a last look at Salt and Pepper.

Obey caught up at the first bend in the road. "With all due respect, Miss Anne, I have seen just about enough Virginians to last the rest of my life."

"Quite understandable."

"I'll be returning to Flatbush. You'd do well to accompany me."

"I'm not finished here." She was determined to scout as much of the countryside as possible before nightfall.

"You may prove the death of me yet," Obey muttered, but followed Anne deeper into the countryside.

***

I stood by the door of the Ferry Tavern, watching a thunderhead advance from the west, quickly flipping dusk to darkness. Lightning zig-zagged across the sky; thunder boomed like an artillery barrage. Within seconds, a damp, cool breeze littered the Brooklyn green with bramble, followed almost immediately by sheets of rain. After only a fleeting glance back, catching the innkeeper striking a flint at the hearth, I turned up my collar and headed into the deluge to help my men set camp.

If I was going to lead, I needed to lead by example, weather be damned. Asher followed me out the tavern door, his sour expression conveying disdain for my decision. Fortunately, Hempstead and my other sergeants had picked a meadow only a hundred yards outside the village. Hercules, Elvin and others struggled to peg their tents; the wind, gale-force, tossed the canvas like square-rigged topsails on the open ocean. Peacock chased his hat through a patch of purple wildflowers, while McElroy stripped naked and enjoyed a shower. Hempstead and Little John stood in the midst of the chaos, sharing the sergeant's spyglass to squint up at the sky, perhaps tracking lightning bolts like Benjamin Franklin.

I pitched in with Hercules, wrestling his canvas to the ground but unable to do much more with it. Giving up, rain streaming down our cheeks, we sat on the tenting and shared a swig of rum from his canteen.

Fortunately, the storm subsided quickly; stars twinkled in the evening sky. The troop pitched their tents and built fires to prepare supper. I helped Hercules settle in, allowing my shirt and breeches time to dry. Men who happened to pass by nodded in recognition, or perhaps in appreciation of my efforts.

My head spun with thoughts of redcoats on my walk back to town. *When? Where? How many? What more could I do to prepare?* I must have been strolling exceedingly slow because a Black, head down, pumping his stubby legs, churned right by me. His profile, round and droll, was a welcome sight. "Obey?" I called out.

The Black jumped, as if shot, at the sound of his name. He turned, struggling to identify me in the darkness. I could smell his fear, well deserved after his brush with the slavecatchers. "Captain Hale?" he asked, a tremor in his voice.

"I am most pleased to see you safe," I replied, clapping his shoulder.

"Yes, yes. As safe as can be."

"Your master claimed you, I gather."

"I am back at my post in Mr. Van Cliff's household."

"And those bounty hunters returned home empty-handed?"

"They did not inform me of their plans."

The tremor in Obey's answers did not quite set right, but he was a slave responding to an Army officer. "You appear in quite the hurry. What brings you to Brooklyn this evening?" I asked.

"An errand, sir. For my master. Lodging just outside of town."

If Obey's master was in fact a Tory, then his appearance here, in the midst of our defenses, was suspect. "I would much like to meet this Van Cliff."

"Meet him?"

"Yes, take me to his lodgings."

"Now?" Obey replied. Bold of him to question me, I thought. Then a candle appeared to light in his eyes. "Of course. I believe my master would most enjoy the opportunity to discourse with you."

With my bluff called, I had little choice but to turn on my heels and follow Obey along the path, past our camp, towards Red Hook. We didn't go far before stopping at a thatched roof cottage, nestled in an apple orchard. The door was ajar, a rocker empty out front, a ribbon of smoke curling from the chimney. I kept a hand on the grip of my pistol but didn't see any signs of redcoats or anyone of suspicion lurking about.

Obey knocked. "A visitor," he announced, then stepped away to permit my entrance.

An elderly couple sat at a table sharing a jug and slab of cheese with a young woman, her back to me. "Excuse me for interrupting your supper," I said, removing my hat which, to my dismay, dripped on the floor. "I'm looking for Mr. Van Cliff."

"There is no Van Cliff here," the old man, still bearing a purpled patch on his cheek from a long-ago battle with the pox, replied.

Perplexed, I turned towards Obey, but, before I could speak, the young woman shot up, spilling her drink, a frothy cider, in her lap. Her hair, uncapped and flowing across her shoulders, was a familiar shade of auburn. "Nathaniel?" she stammered my name, one syllable at a time.

"Captain Nathaniel Hale at your ..." Recognition of Anne Wheaton cut short my response.

"I believe you two are well-acquainted," Obey said, sporting a fox's grin.

"Anne? What are you doing here? In Brooklyn?" I wished my words were more eloquent, but a torrent of conflicting emotions robbed my oratory skill. After dreaming of this reunion, lusting for it in fact, my duty as an officer of the Continental Army now overruled my heart.

"I was selling watermelons from the farm where I board. In Flatbush." Anne appeared to regain her composure. "A lieutenant from Virginia bought my entire load, as well as my horse and wagon. So I am forced to rent a bed in the home of this kind couple for the night."

"For the second time, I have found you *coincidentally* in the midst of my Army."

"Let's talk outside." She strode towards me, but I grabbed her wrist before she could pass.

"You should be in jail."

"I've done no wrong, Nathaniel," Anne replied, disappointment, if not pain, evident in her eyes. "My belongings are there, by the hearth." She shook loose of my grip, walked back into the room, and emptied her satchel on the floor. A purse, filled with coins, a petticoat, and a summer scarf tumbled out. Her hosts appeared frozen in place. Obey had slipped inside and stood guard at the door.

Anne reached into the pocket of her skirt, still wet from the rain, and withdrew her pistol, laying it on the table. "Search me if you want. You'll find nothing of value," she said, spreading her arms wide.

"There's no need," I said, turning, pushing past Obey. "Let's go for a walk, then."

Anne followed. The moon, almost full, lit the way through the orchard. I stopped under an arching limb groaning with fruit and turned to face her. "Prudence wrote that you murdered Constable Goodbody, a loyal servant of the people of New London."

"That is false. I murdered no one."

I could not deny my feelings for Anne, but, sadly, those feelings alone were no reason to trust her. "How then did Constable Goodbody perish?" I asked.

"He died in a skirmish at the jail. It is wartime. More men will die. Women too."

Anne's boldness did not surprise me, but her heart had grown colder. "And Caleb?" I asked.

"He serves his country." Anne reached for my hand. In a moment of weakness, I let her take it. "You and I still have much in common, Nathaniel, despite what Prudence says - or does."

"She is dead."

"What?"

"Prudence is dead. The pox. She went quickly last month." I invented the lie to keep my promise to John Richards and Prudence's memory.

"I did not like the woman, but I am truly sorry to learn of her passing." Anne squeezed my hand, a gesture of shared sorrow.

"Me as well."

"Were you betrothed?"

"No. I was not prepared to make such a commitment. Prudence pledged her affection to another man after I sailed for New York."

"You were wise, Nathaniel. Your cause demands your passion. Even if it is a lost cause."

"I do not believe that is so." I disentangled my fingers from hers.

"You and your army will feel the full wrath of King George soon enough."

"To die in the service of the Glorious Cause would be a most honorable death."

"I pray you will earn other honors then."

I retreated another step, gathered myself. "Anne, you must go. I would be remiss in my duty to allow a known Tory, even a woman, to linger behind our battle lines."

"I will not linger. I'll return to my lodgings in Flatbush immediately. Obey will walk me home safely."

"Goodbye then."

Anne did not leave. "Nathaniel, I serve my King but I share your passion for liberty," she said, stepping closer, turning her face up to mine. "Liberty for men and women of all skin color. Can you say the same? Have General Washington or Mr. Jefferson proclaimed plans to free their slaves?"

Her words stung. "No," I replied. "Not yet at least."

"Then your cry of liberty rings hollow."

"It is a start. We will forge a new government that one day will deliver on the promise of equality for all."

"I fear neither of us will live long enough to see that day."

"You may be right. But it is better to take the first step than take no step at all."

"Rest assured, Nathaniel, I have already taken steps to defend the rights of the Negro." Anne took my hand again. "As have you, from what Obey has told me. And I am proud of you for it."

"How can you talk of rights when your King sends his armies to subdue his subjects who seek only to have a voice in their own governance?" I asked.

"It is more than that now, Nathan."

"Yes, it is more," I replied, allowing my hand to remain in her grasp. "Our army fights for the workingman, for his opportunity to achieve a better life. Your army fights for the aristocracy, for their profits and plunder."

She sighed, reaching for my shoulders, pulling me closer. Her tongue darted across her lips, moistening them. "We have this moment, alone together. Let's not squander it."

I broke our embrace before it progressed further. "Go. Before I change my mind and have you arrested."

Anne stepped away, but raised her chin, her eyes saucy with defiance, looking, and sounding, more like her brother, Caleb, than ever before. "If you challenge a King, Nathaniel, you must succeed...or die."

"To die *for* a King is a death wasted." I met her gaze squarely, hoping, foolishly, she would relent.

"Farewell, Sir Galahad. I hope you find your Holy Grail."

"If e'er we meet again, it shall be in happier climes and on a safer shore." *Cato* seized my tongue before Anne turned her back and retreated into the night.

***

Church services were mercifully short, ending by noon, on Sunday, August 25th. Everyone knew the British Army had landed in force, tens of thousands of men, at Gravesend Bay on the 22nd, and would be marching up the Flatbush Road any day.

Standing at the window of the Matthews' manor, Anne bounced on her toes with excitement at the first sight of the advance guard, light infantry men carrying axes to clear the woods rather than bayonets. The heavy infantry, including grenadiers in their tall bearskin hats, arrived later in the day. Thousands of redcoat regulars and green-jacket Hessians marched in formation, flags waving, drums beating, officers calling out commands in both English and German. She searched for familiar faces, but saw none.

I'd love to see Nathaniel's face when he first confronts this onslaught. How could he have rejected my advance? Why doesn't he see the futility of his struggle? He's just a foolish young man, not a battle-hardened veteran like my Geoffrey. Yes, the Continentals have their forts, but they can't barricade themselves inside forever.

Anne stepped outside, waving a Red Ensign flag that Mayor Matthews had hidden away for just this occasion. George, Rose, and two kitchen slaves trailed behind her.

"Those cabbage-eaters are a mean lot," George said, spitting into the dirt as a Jaeger unit paraded by to the toot of a hunter's horn, an instrument much more suited to a speedy advance over uneven ground than drum or fife. "Mercenaries. The House of Hanover dragooned them right off their farms and sold their services to King George."

"Get paid a bounty for each rebel killed, I h'rd," Rose added. "Won't be taking prisoners, I'll bet you that."

The British Army stopped well before sunset, carpeting the fields with white tents for as far as Anne could see. From the front porch, she watched as foragers ransacked her vegetable gardens and carted away the last of the watermelon crop. Little she could, or wanted, to do to stop them. It was a small sacrifice, but she wondered how long the army would stay.

Expecting senior officers to billet at the Matthews', Anne instructed George and Rose to prepare an evening meal. She went down to the wine cellar herself to select the claret. While deciding between a Palmer or a Lafitte, she heard a familiar voice call her name.

"Father!" she cried, bounding up the stairs. Father's smile stretched from ear to ear as he wrapped her in his arms. Caleb stood in the doorway, grinning as well.

"Your brother told me about your…adventures," Father said after they disengaged. "I couldn't be more proud of you."

"I serve my King," she replied. "Mother and Phineas? Are they well? Are they here?"

"Yes, and yes. But I cautioned them to remain on Staten Island until we have taken New York."

"And snuffed out the rebellion," Caleb added.

Anne stepped back, taking stock of her men. Father had fattened like a Hogmanay goose during his five months in Halifax, a fullness in his cheeks not seen since New London. Guiltily, she realized the extent he must have gone hungry in Boston, while she dined at Geoffrey's table. Caleb sported a bright new jacket, Ranger green.

The arrival of a contingent of four senior officers, obvious by the gold braid draped across their starched scarlet jackets, and their retinue interrupted the Wheaton family reunion. "Major General James Grant," an aide announced. "Laird of Ballindalloch and Member of Parliament," a second aide amplified.

Anne curtsied, while Father and Caleb bowed. Grant was portly, to be kind, even his finely tailored uniform could not camouflage a bulging gut and double-stuffed chin. He had led men into battle against the Highlanders at Culloden and the French in the wilderness at Fort Duquesne, but was now well past his prime, in his fifties at least, maybe older. But he had not mellowed, Anne thought.

Grant's vitriolic comments in the House of Commons had earned him the disdain of all but the staunchest Tories in America.

The men retired to the parlor for brandy while she checked the bedrooms upstairs. Grant would have the master of course and would allocate the other rooms as he saw fit. The four aides would likely sleep in the parlor or the barn, as would the Wheaton men, if they could stay. Anne set her bedroll in the keeping room next to the kitchen, hanging a blanket from the lintel for privacy. She hoped it would only be for one night.

George set eight places at the dinner table with the Matthews' finest Wedgewood and Waterford. After lighting the candles, not a simple task with two twelve-pronged silver candelabras, he announced supper at six. Having changed from her day dress into her finely laced blue frock, she ushered the officers and aides to their seats.

"Surely, Miss Wheaton, you have miscounted," General Grant said, as his men stood at their places waiting for him to sit. "I insist that you join us this evening. Mayor Matthews has written of your great service to the Crown."

Anne thought she heard a snicker from one of the aides at the mention of service, but she ignored it. "I am most flattered, Lord. But I have not seen my father in months."

"Your father can join us as well then. If that's what it takes to bring your fair countenance to our table," Grant replied, his eyes twinkling in Anne's direction as he adjusted his wig. He motioned for the aide at his right hand to slide down, creating room for Anne to sit next to him.

"We would be honored to join you, sir," Father said, nodding in appreciation to his daughter as he took a seat at the far end. Caleb slipped away into the kitchen.

Henry served turkey, two huge birds bursting with stuffing and dripping with gravy, as well as all the fixings. He selected the '62 Palmer, a good choice, Anne thought, since the cellar had ample supply. The men were gluttonous after their day on the march, although she had trouble believing that the General spent much time on his feet these days.

Anne was hungry as well, but sat erect and ate daintily, exhibiting the manners she believed were expected of an upper crust Englishwoman. She hoped to have time alone with the general after the meal to fill him in on her reconnaissance of the rebel defenses, much weaker in the countryside than atop the Heights.

Evidently, Grant envisioned a private liaison as well, as his hand slipped under the table to rest upon her thigh. She froze, shocked at the advance from a man old enough to be her grandfather. Grant was fortunate to still have his teeth, let alone…She tried to catch Father's eye, but he was engaged in conversation with one of the lesser officers.

"These rebels are *farmers*, not soldiers. My army could march clear across this continent in a month's time…and geld all the males as well," Grant declared, clearly reveling in the attention his bold words provoked.

"I wager our Hessians have much experience gelding farm animals," Major Richard Whitcomb, a classically handsome man roughly Geoffrey's age, contributed with a smirk that snaked around the table.

"I understand you have informed the Hessians that the rebels stabbed their prisoners in Massachusetts with pitchforks? And boiled them alive?" Grant asked Whitcomb, squeezing Anne after each question before removing his hand to cut his meat. She exhaled when her thigh was finally free, but grew incensed at the tone of the conversation. The rebels were *not* cannibals!

"Yes, yes," Whitcomb answered. "Want to make sure the peasants are properly motivated."

"Well done. King George paid well for his mercenaries," Grant said, taking a large draught of wine, his cheeks taking on a ruddy glow. "Don't want them to waver at the sight of the rebel forts. The going might prove difficult."

"It most certainly will," Anne said, forgetting her place. "I've seen those forts. Just last week," she continued, ignoring the eyebrows raised in disapproval of her forthrightness. Only Father appeared interested in her opinion.

"Have you now, dear," Grant said, stabbing and slicing his meat.

"I counted five. Formidable redoubts well-situated with clear fields of fire."

"Do you doubt our ability to take them?" Whitcomb asked. "Based on your ample military experience, of course."

"We can take them, but at what cost?" Anne refused to surrender to these men. "Much better to circle around…"

"General Howe is most frugal with the lives of his troops," Grant cut her off. "Particularly after our casualties on Breed's Hill last summer."

"My betrothed, Major Geoffrey Stanwich of the 63rd, fought next to General Howe…"

"Your   betrothed?"

"We were betrothed, but Geoffrey died before we could marry."

"Most unfortunate."

"And you are now unattached?" Major Whitcomb asked.

"Yes."

"A difficult situation for a young woman," Grant said, patting Anne's hand for all to see.

"My daughter is a skilled seamstress and dressmaker. She will assist me in reopening Wheatons' emporium in New York," Father interjected. "I'm quite confident we will serve the fashion-minded women of that fair city as well as we did the matrons of Boston."

"Society women…" Grant mused, the subject apparently more interesting to him than Anne's thoughts on the rebel positions. "We must keep the fairer sex amused. A proper autumn ball and theater in New York would do nicely." He pointed his knife at his aide. "Make a note of it."

"At once, sir," the aide replied, rising from his seat to search for quill and ink.

"General Howe will be delighted," Grant continued, a jaunty glint to his eye. "He loves to display his beautiful bauble, Mrs. Loring, at every opportunity."

"Mrs. Loring was a regular patron of our shop on Wing's Lane," Anne said, earning a nod of approval from Father. "She was most intrigued by our evening gowns, the latest designs from London, of course."

"Latest designs…" Grant said, patting Anne's hand again. "You'll have to tell me all about them…after supper."

The candles guttered before the men finished the dessert puddings. After draining the decanter of claret, the General signaled the official end of the meal with a mighty belch. He pushed back his chair and stood, lips pursed in discomfort, followed immediately by the rest of the men. Anne was the last to rise, letting the lecherous old man stew in his juices while she meticulously wiped her lips with her napkin, before pointing him towards the water closet. She signaled for George, instructing him to serve port in the study. Pipes and snuff boxes materialized as the men shuffled off, Father as well, engaged in conversation with Major Whitcomb.

Anne knew well enough to stay out of the study. She busied herself helping Rose clear the table, the scuttling about providing an excuse to catch snippets of conversation, as well as the rather pleasant aroma of tobacco, reminding her of evenings with Geoffrey. She considered retiring early to avoid Grant, but then again, he might prove a powerful patron, if she could manage him. What would *that* entail? At his age?

Could Father rescue her? He wouldn't be here in Flatbush if he did not have some value to the army besides dressing the officers' women in fine fashion. With Rose busy in the kitchen, Anne lingered by the open door, trying to parse the cacophony of conversation. Sam Hale! She started at the mention of his name, although she could not discern the speaker. If Sam was in the vicinity, then William Cunningham was here as well. A powerful patron would be absolutely necessary if those two scoundrels were still set against her.

"Miss Wheaton, your hospitality was most welcome this evening," Major Whitcomb said, stepping from the study, surprising Anne, silently scolding herself for not anticipating the arrival of Hale and his master.

"I am most pleased to be of service."

"Yes," Whitcomb interrupted his reply with a cough. "General Grant has asked me to secure the pleasure of your company upstairs after our assembly in the study concludes."

"Upstairs? In his bedroom?" Her voice squeaked.

"I believe so, yes."

"My father is here."

"Your father is a merchant. His fortunes will improve significantly if he remains in the Major General's favor."

Could Father be bought off as easily as Joshua Loring?

"Miss Wheaton, I knew your betrothed quite well before this war. We attended Eton and served together in the Highlands, quite a dreary place by the way," Whitcomb continued. "… although I wouldn't repeat that last remark in front of the Major General."

"I miss Geoffrey greatly."

"Yes, Major Stanwich left his mark on all who knew him," Whitcomb said, his countenance softening. "I can inform the general that you are still in mourning, if you wish. Besides, you must be exhausted after hosting such a lavish meal."

"Your offer is most appreciated," Anne replied. "Although I was hoping to provide the General with my intelligence on the rebel defenses."

"Ah yes, your military intelligence." Whitcomb gently clasped Anne's forearm and drew her near the hearth. "Rest assured, Grant, as well as Generals Howe and Clinton, are well aware of the strength and weaknesses of the rebel fortifications."

"They are?" Anne stuffed her fist in her mouth in a vain effort to stifle her vacuous question.

"Yes," Whitcomb whispered. "And have devised a most daring plan of attack."

"Then I believe I will retire for the evening."

"And I will apprise General Grant accordingly."

***

Entrenched between the villages of Brooklyn and Bedford, I stewed in anticipation of the coming battle, although the redcoats were still out of sight. As the sun rose over my shoulder, the crack of musket fire floated up the Guana Heights. Puffs of gun smoke and the acrid smell of powder tempted me like the aroma of a Sunday roast. Were the lobsterbacks advancing? Or was this just another skirmish down in the flat lands? I had no way of knowing.

Colonel Webb had briefed his captains before dawn, the British were massed on both the Flatbush Road and the Shore Road, likely preparing for a two-pronged assault. He also informed us that Washington had appointed General Putnam to share command with General Sullivan, surely not a vote of confidence in the latter.

Even more disappointing, our regiment was again to be held back in reserve, ready to buttress any weak point that developed in our front lines which stretched for more than a mile. Furthermore, we were positioned towards the left, or eastern edge of the Continental Army's defenses, overlooking the Jamaica Road, where no attack was expected.

I assumed the point position while Sergeant Hempstead dug in to my right, followed down the line by the rest of third company, muskets at the ready, aimed over the earthworks across an open pasture. Would we stand fast in the face of a bayonet charge? Would anyone turn and run? If so, I was required to shoot him dead. I prayed that moment would never come.

Over the past weeks, I had talked with each man, checked their weapons and ammunition, read the Bible to them if they were so inclined. I was confident in our steadfastness, but accepted I could not be certain until the moment of truth. With little to do but wait, I looked over my troop one more time. Elvin Parrish was the most unpredictable, I decided, making a mental note to stand beside him when the enemy first marched into our sights.

Around mid-day, General Putnam, astride a coal-black stallion, trotted behind us, leading two companies from Pennsylvania. To my envy, the Pennsylvanians marched around our lines and down towards Battle Pass and the Flatbush Road. Putnam shouted an huzzah and galloped off towards Cobble Hill. An hour later, we saw more soldiers streaming off in direction of the fighting. Cannons boomed from three of our forts to support our attack. Again, I received no word whether the British were coming, or not. The uncertainty, the waiting, the monotony, tried my soul.

General Washington's appearance enlivened the afternoon. He rode, surrounded by aides and Life Guards, from fort to fort, stopping at our position as well as the other entrenchments along the way. Afterwards, Colonel Webb informed us that the commander-in-chief would be shifting more troops from New York to Long Island. Five hundred riflemen would strengthen our position, surprising since we were not supposed to be in the line of the enemy's advance.

At sunset, the Pennsylvanians returned, whooping in victory. The Hessians had retreated from Flatbush. It had just been a skirmish then, not the beginnings of the assault. Would the British Army retire from the field? Return to England without a real fight? Highly unlikely, I thought. Another sleepless night lay ahead.

I perched beside William Hull at supper, a stew of rabbits and other varmints. "How well do you think our commanding officers know the Long Island terrain?"

"A little late to be asking that question, isn't it?" he replied, quaffing his ale.

"I fear Washington may be having second thoughts about the Jamaica Pass." I pointed to the arriving riflemen. "It's the only crossing of the Guana Heights he did not fortify, but now he's reinforcing us."

"This waiting is addling your brain. Jamaica's too far east to be a viable point of attack." Hull picked about his trencher for a piece of meat, then stabbed it with his knife. "If Howe started to march his army in that direction, we would have ample time to shift our resources. I'm more concerned that the British landing on Long Island is just a feint. The real thrust of their attack will come behind us. In New York."

"It is rare that you are on the same page as our commander-in-chief."

"Yes, well, times change," Hull chuckled.

"I would feel better if we had more intelligence about our enemy's plans," I said, standing up, looking around the camp, busy with the activity of an army settling in for the night.

"I'm sure we have friends in the countryside to keep us informed."

***

Anne was not sorry to see Major General Grant and his retinue evacuate her home on Monday afternoon. Howe had recalled the advance guard to resettle with the main body of his army in the Flatlands rather than engage in meaningless skirmishes. She was in no danger, the rebels had already retreated back up the Guana Heights, and looked forward to supping with Father whom she had invited to lodge, at least temporarily, at the Matthews'. He had walked to Howe's camp that morning to attend to business but planned to return by sundown. Caleb, as usual, was off to his own devices.

Rose was in the kitchen, carving a fowl, while George set the table. After the visit from the Virginia slavecatchers, Anne vowed never again to dismiss the help early unless there was a man in the house. Still dressed in her calico day frock, she sat on the porch, sipping a claret while watching for Father. The sunset had just flared a vivid pink and orange, when an elegant carriage, pulled by a pair of white chargers, rolled up the road.

Betsey Loring, a scarlet summer shawl draped over her shoulders, her blond ringlets piled high in what Anne imagined was the latest London fashion, was the first to step out. "Miss Wheaton, so good to see you again," she said, her tone quite formal. "And dressed so simply for supper. How colonial."

"I was not expecting guests this evening."

"No matter." Betsey air-kissed besides both of Anne's cheeks. "We never had the opportunity to say a proper farewell in Boston."

"I was pressed to leave the city," Anne replied. By your husband's cabal, she wanted to add, but didn't. Mrs. Loring had never let on how much she knew of Joshua's dealings, the rewards he received for her affair with General Howe.

"I do want to express my condolences for your betroth's untimely passing. Such a gallant man." Betsey squeezed Anne's hand. Father emerged from the chaise carrying several bolts of fabric.

"I miss him greatly," Anne said. So this is a working visit, not a social one, she thought. No surprise really, and more straightforward.

"I'm sure you do." Betsey waltzed into the Matthews' parlor. Father chased after her. "But I see you've adapted well to your new circumstances," Betsey added.

"Can I offer you a claret, or a cider?" Anne asked.

"After my fitting perhaps." Betsey undraped her shoulders, revealing a forest green frock, elaborately embroidered with silver thread, and an unsurprisingly deep décolletage. "Your father said you'd be back to dressmaking shortly and I will need new gowns for the fall season in New York."

"How many gowns will you require?" Father asked.

"General Grant mentioned a ball and a play, so I will require three."

"Of course," Father replied, pushing aside the place settings on the dining room table to provide room to spread several rolls of taffeta. Anne smiled inwards, sensing Father calculate their profits as he displayed the wares. "The finest silks, from Italy of course. Emerald green – to match your sparkling eyes; a coral pink – to complement your delicate complexion; a brilliant vermilion – to highlight your exquisite jewelry." Father smoothed his hand over each roll as he talked. "Anne, of course, will add unique touches with lace from the Orient and gold trimmings. Perhaps an ermine collar to keep out the chill?" he added.

Where did Father acquire these luxurious items? Anne wagered that Sam Hale was somehow involved.

"Perhaps," Betsey muttered as she inspected the fabrics. "The latest designs from London?"

"Of course. Nothing less will do for a woman in your position," Father said. Anne muffled a chuckle.

"What do you think?" Betsey asked, holding the pink fabric up against her chest.

"It's you," Anne said. "I have a classic pattern in mind, only I will drop the neckline, bone the bodice, and design a bold farthingale to accent your hips. I would suggest interlacing ribbons of gold silk for your stomacher."

"How exciting!"

"And we'll do the underskirts in dove white."

"I can't wait!"

Father had a parchment and quill out before Anne had finished her description. "We'll just need your signature right here, Mrs. Loring, so my daughter can get started."

Betsey started to sign, but then hesitated. "Perhaps William should see the fabrics first."

"Of course," Father said. "I will bring them to him directly in the morning."

"I'd like to seek his approval tonight…before he marches off to battle," Betsey said, then lowered her voice. "One never knows…"

"Battle? Tonight?" Anne couldn't stop the questions from tumbling out.

"I shouldn't have rambled so, but, yes, the army marches when the clocks strike ten."

Anne wanted to press for more details, but held her tongue. Where was the army going? Was it going to attack the rebels while they were asleep? How ungentlemanly.

"Then I will accompany you back to General Howe at once," Father replied, gathering up his wares in such haste he knocked over the bottle of claret.

"No worries. I'll clean this up," Anne said, scrambling to pick up the bottle and contain the mess with a napkin.

"David Matthews has provided you with no help?" Betsey asked, looking towards the kitchen for the cavalry to arrive. "Difficult, considering his confinement I imagine, but you deserve better, my dear."

"Rose! I require your immediate assistance," Anne called, realizing with horror that she sounded exactly like Betsey Loring. *Was this where her life was headed?*

Rose appeared from the kitchen, although in no apparent hurry. "Yes, Miss Wheaton?"

"Here." Anne handed her the soiled linen. "Please finish cleaning up while I see Mrs. Loring out."

Three goats had wandered over to the front door, bleating farewell as Betsey and Father boarded the coach. Anne dined alone.

Afterwards, she took a decanter of port out to the porch. The moon, a crescent, was up, but she could see only an inky blackness beyond the silhouette of the barn. The tall-case clock in the parlor chimed nine times. Father must have chosen to spend the night in Flatlands, no need to worry, she told herself as she sipped her second port.

The clock rang ten. Was that a drum beat in the distance or a roll of thunder? She strained to hear the sounds of men, but only heard the hoot of an owl. An entire army could not march in silence. Betsey Loring must have erred. Surprising, since the woman was no fool.

Anne dragged up the stairs to the master bedroom and changed into her night shift, but was still uneasy about the Army's movements. Where was Caleb? And Father?

Shaking the drink from her brain, she left her room, taper in hand, and strode to the end of the hallway, capped by a bookcase, seemingly laden with leather-bound volumes. She withdrew *The Iliad,* translated by Alexander Pope, reached inside and released a latch, which allowed her to roll open the otherwise false façade, revealing a ladder that led up to the attic and down to the scullery at the back of the kitchen. George had only showed her the secret passage the morning after the attack by the slavecatchers, whom she had described as marauding highwaymen since she did not know, or trust, his views on runaway slaves and their accomplices.

The attic had no window, so it broiled like an oven, soaking Anne in sweat before she reached the top rung of the ladder. Stocked with a sleeping pallet, several woolen blankets, and a chamber pot, the snug room was always kept ready for occupancy. She tugged on the half-height door opening to a widow's walk, which would have appeared purely ornamental to anyone down below, and wiggled out.

A breeze tweaked the weather vane atop the shingled roof, but the sky was cloudless, the stars out in force. Standing tall, she could see across Flatlands. Campfires twinkled for miles. Perhaps Betsey Loring lacked the head for military matters, she thought with satisfaction. Caleb and Father were safe. The British Army was not going anywhere tonight.

***

On Tuesday August 27th, I walked the midnight watch on the front line, prodding and chatting to insure all stayed vigilant. The night was still, the moonlight revealing no movements save the buzzing of fireflies and the rustle of leaves. The martial fetor of gunpowder, tobacco, and men, entrenched and fretful, overwhelmed any floral scents in this once pastoral setting.

Did we really have friends in the countryside, as Hull had suggested? The citizens here were primarily Dutch, descendants of the region's first settlers who had arrived soon after Henry Hudson's expedition in 1609. Upon the arrival of British warships in 1664, the Dutch turned over the port without a fight, and had lived peacefully and prosperously under British rule ever since. Owning lush farmland and ample slaves, they stood to gain much more from a quick defeat of the Continental Army, I surmised, and the withdrawal of soldiers from both sides, who already outnumbered civilians here by more than ten to one, than they did by any extended struggle for the vague concept of freedom. If the locals were to provide us with any intelligence, it would have to be because Washington paid for it, which, by definition, impugned its reliability.

With a terse nod, Sergeant Hempstead relieved me at two o'clock. Coffee in hand, Hercules led Little John, wiping sleep from his eyes, to the front line. The strain of waiting for an attack, amidst the knowledge that we were most certainly outgunned, squelched any banter. I retired to my tent, set fifty yards back, lit a solitary candle, and scribbled a brief update in my red leather diary. Since my arrival in New York back in April, I realized, despite my good intentions, I had only inked a handful of entries at most. An indication of my frustrations. I closed my journal and sought peace in my bible instead before attempting sleep, fully dressed.

Wandering on the bluffs above New London, I heard cannons boom, drums roll, and boots, thousands of them, pound the road down below, but I could see nothing. I was blindfolded, my hands bound behind my back. I ground my teeth in frustration…

"Captain Hale, wake up," Little John said, pinching my shoulder. "The battle has begun."

"Are you sure?" I asked, sitting up, but hearing no gunfire. "Who sent you?"

"Hempstead. Colonel Webb ordered him to turn out our men," he replied, squatting back on his haunches. "A messenger arrived from General Putnam. There's fighting on the Shore Road."

"What time is it?"

Little John shrugged. "Still pitch black out though."

I jumped to my feet, squared my hat on my head, then thought a second, took it off and removed the yellow cockade, an act I had mulled for several days. "No sense standing out for the British sharpshooters," I explained, squaring the hat again.

Campfires blazed as our Army prepared for the fight. Orders were shouted; men checked cartridge boxes and sharpened knives; others lined up at the latrines. A prayer circle formed around a preacher on a stump. Little John tooted *Yankee Doodle* on his fife; Colonel Webb stalked behind the earthen ramparts, stopping every minute or so to peer out into the gloaming. Signal lanterns were lit up on Cobble Hill to communicate with headquarters in New York in the darkness. I yelled a quick roll call before taking my own position behind our berm, looking down the barrel of my musket towards the Jamaica Road.

Sunrise revealed a calm countryside, no redcoats in sight, although pandemonium was breaking out behind me. General Washington himself, as well as several hundred reinforcements from New York had arrived. Uncharacteristically, the commander-in-chief was on foot, although still flanked by four Life Guards.

A drum beat called us all to attention. Brandishing two pistols, Washington shouted words of encouragement, although I could only catch snippets: "…I will fight as long as I have a leg or an arm…I will not ask any man to go further than I do…" The General talked briefly with Colonel Webb, then mounted up and trotted off to the next regiment.

Although I still harbored doubts about our strategy here on Long Island, I was proud to serve in this man's army. A leader who stood in the front line, risking his own life side-by-side with his men, commanded respect, if not awe.

***

Anne awoke at dawn to the crunch of boots marching up the Flatbush Road, understanding before she even rolled over that the long-awaited assault was underway. Shouts of "Vormarsh!" and the beat of kettle drums filtered through her open window for thirty minutes, maybe longer. Sounded to her like the Hessians would form the vanguard - and take the heaviest losses. The mournful bleat of bagpipes signaled that the Highlanders were next in line. While washing her face, she tried to square General Howe's concern for the lives of his troops with an assault directly into the teeth of the rebel defenses. That's the role of mercenaries and outlanders, she reasoned.

By the time she buttoned her day frock and capped her hair, the marching had stopped. Only a regiment, perhaps two, could have gone by. Where were the Regulars? Where were Father and Caleb?

After picking at a bowl of porridge, Anne resolved to find out. As the sun peeked through the trees, the sky a broad expanse of indigo blue, she walked down the Flatbush Road towards the acres of white tents, aligned like a gigantic checkerboard on the green fields. She was the only traveler, no wagons or pushcarts rolling to market, unusual for this time of day, or any time of day for that matter. Off in the distance, the pop of musket fire and the blast of cannons was unmistakable, coming from both Battle Pass behind her as well as the Shore Road to her right, the battle already engaged on multiple fronts. She quickened her step.

The British camp, housing ten thousand men yesterday, was a ghost town this morning. Anne wandered up and down the neat "streets", finding no soldiers. Canvas flapped; cooking fires smoldered; chicken bones and bread crumbs lay scattered; a cartridge box sat open and empty. She hurried by a man-sized stake driven into the dirt, adorned by the brown-red stains of dried blood. The Regulars had clearly marched, but in what direction?

On the far side of the field, just before the King's Highway, she opened a gate in a low, rambling stone wall. It led to a lane winding through the woods to the Van Cliff manor, grander than the Matthews' farm house, and free from the scavenging of the Crown's forces: its vegetable garden remained untrammeled and chickens still pecked about.

Peter Van Cliff was outside inspecting the orchard, trailed by his female companion. Seeing Anne, he waved and vectored towards her.

"Good morning, Miss Wheaton," he said, doffing his tricorn with his right hand then tucking it under the stump of his left arm. His powdered hair, weaved into a tight braid that dangled between woodsman's shoulders, glistened in the sunlight. Anne guessed that Van Cliff was in his forties; his companion, however, looked significantly younger and more fragile.

"And to you, sir. And ma'am."

After a pregnant moment, the silence chafing, Van Cliff clasped his companion's gloved hand. "Let me introduce you to my wife, Elizabeth."

A most proper English name, Anne thought, for a most exotic woman. "Pleased to meet you."

Elizabeth only nodded in reply. Her oval-shaped eyes, flat nose, and ruler-straight, coal-black hair spoke of her heritage from an Asian shore.

"Ah, your father harkens," Van Cliff said quickly, dropping his wife's hand to point towards the yard, ending another awkward moment of silence.

"My father?"

"He spent the night."

"Daughter, you are a most welcome sight," Father called, standing beside the well, bucket in hand. "Come join us for a late breakfast."

The Van Cliffs started towards their orchard, but Peter pivoted for a parting word. "I almost forgot. Obey asked me to relay his farewell, Miss Wheaton. He has gone off to join your brother in the Rangers."

"Under Colonel Rogers' command?" Anne asked.

"Yes, Rogers has quite an unsavory reputation, but it will be far safer for Obey there should anyone from Virginia return."

Obey might also earn his freedom by serving the Crown, Anne thought, as the Van Cliffs retreated, hand in hand. She followed Father into the house, elaborately furnished in hues of heather, burgundy, and goldenrod. Sam Hale sat at the parlor table, which appeared to be carved from a single trunk of walnut, his fingers greasy with bacon. Startled, she turned for the door, but Father touched her shoulder and nodded comfortingly towards Sam.

"Ah, Miss Wheaton. So good to see you safe and sound," Hale said, although he did not rise.

"And you as well, Mr. Hale," she replied. Father pulled a high-backed chair away from the table and motioned her to sit. A teen-aged Black, dressed in a lime-green frock covered by a crisp white apron, hastened over to pour a steaming cup of tea. Another runaway, Anne wondered.

"I understand you have tended Mayor Matthews' estate quite capably during his incarceration," Hale said, reaching for a biscuit and smearing it with butter.

"I have tried, sir," she replied, sipping her tea. "Do you have any news of the Mayor?"

"I believe David has been carted off to a prison in Connecticut. The rebel leaders are fearful to hang him, lest they themselves be hung for treason someday, but are in no hurry to release him either."

"I will pray for his safe return." Anne smothered a smile. This scenario could prove quite satisfactory, at least until the rebellion was squelched. "…and continue my duties on the farm. Unless you have an objection?"

Sam shrugged. "You'll find no objection from me. Major General Grant – he billeted here last night - spoke glowingly of your charms. As a hostess, of course." He nodded towards Father as Anne blushed. Grant's patronage was already useful.

"Where is the good General this morning? The camp is deserted."

"Grant's marching up the Shore Road. His men will hold the rebels' attention until Howe, Clinton and Cornwallis storm across the Guana Heights with the majority of our army," Hale replied.

"*Across* the Heights?" Anne asked. "How will they gain the Heights in the first place?"

"We should be well through the Jamaica Pass by now," Hale answered, sporting a pirate's leer.

"The Jamaica Pass? We have caught the rebels by surprise?"

"General Howe kept the campfires burning all night and confined the locals to their homes to keep the march a secret," Father interjected. "That's why I couldn't return to Flatbush."

"I sincerely doubt that Mr. Washington is in good spirits this morning," Sam said. "He fortified all the passes over the Guana Heights except one."

"And your brother Caleb led our Army there," Father said, positively beaming with pride.

"Your boy will make a fine Ranger," Hale added, signaling the slave girl, Sally, to refill his plate with more eggs. "That old goat, Rogers, is fortunate to have him in his company."

"If there's any rangering to do after Washington surrenders," Father said, raising his coffee mug in a mock toast.

"The Continentals will not retire so easily, I'm afraid," Hale replied. "Men, like my young cousin, Nathaniel, are zealots. We may douse their fires on Long Island but they will rekindle throughout the countryside. We will be snuffing them out for years."

"A sad truth," Anne said. Captivity would not squelch Nathaniel's ardor, or that of her fellow rebels. She rose, walking over to the kettle hanging on the crane over the hearth to refill her own teacup.

"Not sad at all, my dear," Hale said between lusty bites of bacon. "War creates hardship – which, in turn, creates opportunity for profit."

"Mrs. Loring gained her paramour's signature for our gowns last night. Four of them, in fact," Father said. "Daughter, you must start dressmaking immediately."

"You are thinking small, William," Hale said. "Broaden your horizon. The Crown may soon host thousands of rebel soldiers in her prisons."

"What profit is there in prisoners?" Father asked.

"Prisoners of war need to be clothed, housed and fed," Hale said. "Like dogs," he added in a whisper of disdain.

Anne wanted nothing more than to dump her tea on Sam Hale's white hair. Nathan was a fine man, misguided perhaps, but not a dog. He deserved to be treated with respect, even in defeat. Geoffrey would have understood that.

She thought back to her conversation with Nathaniel outside Brooklyn. Could men of coarse motives like Sam Hale and Father, she hated to admit, truly triumph over men like Nathan, who would willingly sacrifice their lives for their Glorious Cause? No, the realization hit her like a brick. The British might win a battle, but they could never extinguish the flame of liberty.

Defeat defines a man far more than victory. For the first time since leaving New London, Anne found herself rooting for Nathaniel and his cause - and doubting her own role in this war.

The clatter of hoofbeats interrupted the conversation. Two white chargers snorted outside the parlor window, General Howe's coach in tow.

"Ah, Mrs. Loring has arrived," Sam said, standing. "We're off to observe our grand triumph. Will you join us?"

***

Before the hoofbeats of Washington's horse faded from our palisade, I heard the blast of British signal guns. In short order, drum rolls pulsed up the Jamaica Road from the east. I swept my gaze across the fields, the morning dew had lifted, but I saw nothing amiss. Then, a prick of red appeared on a distant hillock. It swelled into a trickle, then a ribbon.

"The British are on the road! Stand fast! Hold your fire!" My men grumbled as they readied themselves for the onslaught. I squinted through the eye of my spyglass, but I no longer needed magnification to see the enemy.

The ribbon had avalanched into a swath of redcoats, spilling into the fields. The Regulars advanced at double time, officers galloped on horseback, cannons rolled along the road. Drumbeats grew louder; commands pierced the air. The swath was now a sea, flooding the entire countryside in scarlet.

It appeared that the entire British army confronted us. I looked down our long, thin line, suitable to defend against skirmishers, but having no chance to repel an extended assault by grenadiers and heavy infantry.

While I could still hear musket fire behind me, coming from the Guana Heights and the Shore Road, I realized we had been fooled. Howe's forces in the Flatlands had been feints; his main thrust was right here. His army must have marched all night in silence up and over the undefended Jamaica Pass. Washington had been out-smarted.

The Continental Army was virtually surrounded now. Our ring of forts were formidable obstacles to an enemy climbing the hillside, funneling into narrow passes, but were much less imposing to British regiments that had already gained the heights and outflanked us.

Amazingly, the scarlet horde halted several hundred yards from our line, safely out of firing range, but, nevertheless, massed for battle. I aimed my musket, and waited. Voices rose in false bravado from our ranks.

"Come on, you damn bloody backs, we're ready for you!"

"Come and get it, dung eaters!"

"King George can kiss my arse."

I turned to see if there was a weak link in my company, a deserter, but my men, even Elvin Parrish, stood firm at their posts. Nor did I hear any drum roll to signify retreat. The telegraph flags were silent as well. We would defend this ground to the last man.

The sun passed its zenith. Musket fire continued to resonate to our rear, a battle raging below the Heights, but still the redcoats did not charge. Without the benefit of tree cover, we baked as we fidgeted. I removed my hat and ran my fingers through my sopping hair. My stomach growled with hunger. What were they waiting for? Did the British fear *us*? Perhaps, they overestimated our forces. Or hesitated to march into the mouths of our cannons, situated up in our forts. My heart raced, grasping a shred of hope.

Wiping the sweat from my eyes, I looked across the open field once more. The damnable redcoats now had spades in their hands and were digging trenches to parallel ours. They set mortars, then wheeled a cannon into place, its barrel seemingly aimed right at me. Then another. And another. Howe was going to lay siege to our fortifications, rather than attempt a frontal assault, unwilling to risk his army as arrogantly as he had on Breed's Hill.

While I breathed easier knowing I would live to see another sunrise, I realized the hopelessness of our position. We were vastly outnumbered and had nowhere to go. British warships would likely be sailing up the Narrows and into the East River right now, cutting off any possibility of our retreat to New York. Furthermore, the British, boasting artillery on land and sea, could bombard us into submission at their leisure.

I thought warmly of Father, my stepmother and young siblings still at home, my three brothers now scattered among the troops in New York, and Enoch at his pulpit. Our revelries together at Yale seemed a lifetime away. I prayed to see them all again – on this earth.

Why had General Washington no intelligence of the British maneuver? Would he surrender, dooming us all to languish in British prisons? Or hang as traitors.

***

Mid-way up the Flatbush Road, near the Matthews manor, the carriage slowed to a crawl, swarmed by green-coated Hessians trotting towards a fork in the road which veered towards the Shore Road. Horns tooted while the men, blooded from battle, barked their guttural marching songs. Sam Hale clambered down, accosted a German officer, and, after much pointing and pantomiming, returned with a broad smile.

"The Jaegers overwhelmed the rebel front line just below Battle Pass. They're off to the coast now to continue the attack," he explained. "We'll follow and watch the fighting there."

The carriage careened to the left along a cut-off, quite bumpier than the main road, rumbling uphill for perhaps a mile before stopping atop a hillock. Sam jumped to be first out, then extended a hand to Mrs. Loring, dressed rather demurely in an olive day gown topped by a simple white neck bow and matching bonnet. Anne and Father followed.

The foursome stood to the side of a clique of camp followers, flaunting uncapped hair and abundant bosoms, and local farmers, who gawked more at the bawdy women than at the soldiers massing below. A hunchback with a lazy eye peddled cider and pies from a donkey-drawn cart.

The battleground was a mix of orchard, pasture and marsh, centered around a two story, stone farmhouse, home of the Cortelyou family, and its picket-fenced vegetable garden. On the right of the house, the Shore Road wound up into the Guana Heights. To the left, it rolled down in the direction of Gravesend Bay, the site of the British landing. On the far side, the Gowanus Creek trickled into the rippling blue waters of the Narrows.

"General Cornwallis has beat us here," Hale announced, bouncing jauntily on his toes as he pointed to the standard waving atop the farmhouse and the regiment of redcoats burrowed into its gardens. Cornwallis was noted for both his bravery and his fidelity to his wife back in England, a rare combination. He must have marched clear across the Guana Heights and down the other side, Anne realized. The Hessians pouring in from Flatbush further supplemented Cornwallis' firepower. "The rebels are trapped," Hale added.

"Where *are* the Continentals?" Mrs. Loring asked.

"There." Father gloated as his index finger traced southward down the Shore Road, stopping on a phalanx of troops, their jackets all colors save scarlet. Anne picked out the buff and gold of the Marylanders she had encountered last week. Father's finger continued down the road. General Grant and his army of red-coated Regulars marched north with drums beating. She wondered where the handsome Major Whitcomb stood.

"I believe *Lord* Stirling commands the rebels. Those are his men in the crisp blue coats," Hale said. "His lordship's first time on a battlefield, I believe."

It was plain to see that the Continentals, no more than two thousand men, were caught in a vise between the two British forces, each easily equal that number. As the morning progressed, the armies exchanged fusillades, but at a distance. Cornwallis rolled cannons into place to increase the pressure. The Continental force slowly dwindled as men fell, while the redcoat armies swelled with a steady flow of reinforcements.

A handful of Continentals, slatternly outfitted, broke from their ranks, trying to reach the marsh. Hessians, goaded to the hunt by the blare of horns, sprinted from the farmhouse to chase them down. Anne silently urged on the rebels, but they were too slow. Green jackets quickly surrounded them. The Continentals tossed their muskets to the ground and raised their arms; one waved a bandanna in surrender.

The Hessians tipped their bayonets towards their encircled prisoners. "Vormarsh!" The command rang clearly, sending a shiver down Anne's spine. A trapped Continental squealed in terror as he realized what was about to happen. Advancing at a walk, the Hessians tightened the noose. With nowhere to run, the Continentals fell on their knees, begging for mercy, but the German juggernaut did not relent. The Jaegers stabbed over and over, laughing as they impaled one rebel after another like pigs at the slaughterhouse. The massacre ended in seconds.

"Damn brutes," Sam Hale spat. "No rebel will surrender now."

A farmer cheered in Dutch, drenching his wife's Sunday finest in cider; a whore puked on her bare feet. The Hessians trotted back to the farm house, the ground behind them grotesque with gore.

Anne was not squeamish at the sight of blood, and well understood the brutality of battle, but what she had just witnessed was cold-blooded murder, not warfare. *How could we ever expect to rule this land if we unleash animals like the Jaegers on its citizens?*

The Continentals had also witnessed the massacre. Their fire intensified in both directions. They dug fox holes and rolled dead bodies into place to serve as bulwarks. But they were still trapped, their efforts reeking of desperation.

Around mid-day, Stirling split his forces. His blue coats, along with a motley stew of others, faced south, keeping Grant and his Regulars in check, while the Marylanders, which Anne knew to be crack troops, formed up opposite Cornwallis and the Jaegers.

Sunlight glinted off steel as the men in buff fixed bayonets. They were going to fight their way out, in the hope that at least some would reach the safety of the forts up on the Heights and live to fight another day.

Suicide, Anne thought. Four hundred Continentals, by her rough count, charging several thousand of the Crown's finest infantry, entrenched behind stone, supported by artillery and marksmen, their rifles poking out of the farm house's upper story windows. But, what other options did the Continentals have?

The Continental drum roll began slowly, gradually reaching a crescendo. Time stopped as all eyes fixed on the men in buff and gold, crouched and coiled. A bugle wailed. The Marylanders rose as one, their huzzahs echoing across the field, and charged the stone house.

"I'll be damned!" Sam cursed. "Lord Stirling is out front."

"His bravery is no longer in question then?" Anne asked, earning a sharp elbow from Father.

The redcoats waited, unflinching. Officers stalked up and down the front line, bravely enforcing discipline. British cannons fired the first shots, riddling the attackers with grape as they crossed open ground. Muskets smoked, clouding the field in haze. Marylanders twisted and fell, but the tide did not recede. Several reached the stone wall, dove over, then disappeared under a swarm of scarlet.

The Continental bugles blared again; the Marylanders retreated. "It's over," Father shouted.

"Not yet," Anne said, pointing to the buff and gold mass forming again. Another bugle call, another charge. Lord Stirling again leading the way.

The redcoats wilted, perhaps surprised by the audacity of their enemy, perhaps caught reloading their guns. The Marylanders crashed through the fences, reached the farm house, and battered open the door. Now, it was the Crown's turn to beat a retreat, although only a few yards. Anne saw Cornwallis behind the line, shouting orders to his aides who scurried back to the fray. The Hessians led the counter-attack, overwhelming the undermanned Marylanders, reclaiming lost territory.

"Quite the surprise," Mrs. Loring said, wringing her hands as the Marylanders formed up yet again, and charged. "Those rebels are such brave men." Like Spartans, Anne thought.

She shifted her gaze to the far side of the battlefield. The Continentals facing General Grant were gradually drifting away – solo and in packs - slipping into the marshland while the Hessians were occupied at the farm house. She almost called out to stop the deserters, but a new voice in her head squelched the words.

Stirling and the Marylanders charged six times before the day waned, reaching the farm house once more. But, the Crown's force, supplemented regularly by new arrivals, was simply overwhelming. Broken bodies, swathed in scarlet, green, buff and gold, littered the gardens, draped over walls, and hung out windows. A handful of Marylanders hobbled back to the main body of Continental troops, but otherwise the ground was still.

"Now, it's over," Sam Hale said. No one on the hillock disputed his claim. He signaled for the peddler to serve refreshments to all.

While the Hessians tended their wounded, fresh Regulars swarmed forward to deliver the decisive blow to the remains of the rebel army. Fighting for almost ten hours now, the Continentals were depleted, exhausted and surrounded. Musket fire quickly faded as hands were raised in surrender.

Anne blenched, fearing the worst for the prisoners. The camp-ladies sharing the hillock were likely thinking the same as they turned to walk back to Flatbush; the farmers and their wives, however, appeared in no hurry to leave.

"Let those men be!" Mrs. Loring shouted in the direction of the Regulars holding the captives.

"Do not fear," Sam replied, gently lowering Betsey's arm. "We will have ample rebels to fill our ships before the day is out."

"Ships?" Anne asked.

"William Cunningham, with Mr. Loring's assistance, has secured two ships to house our 'guests' and insure they do not return to the battlefield."

"Will the ships sail to England?" Anne pressed.

Sam laughed heartily. "No. They will be anchored stoutly in the middle of New York harbor where we can keep a close eye on our prisoners."

Anne watched as the redcoats led the Continentals away. She supposed confinement on board ship was preferable to a Hessian bayonet, but, knowing Hale, Cunningham and the Loring's, she wasn't quite sure.

Eyes turned back towards the farm house, swarming with Regulars and Hessians, their exhaustion obvious. Jackets and muskets littered the ground, men lined up ten deep at the water buckets, others sprawled underneath the few shade trees. A score of bare-chested prisoners were tasked, like teams of oxen, with dragging cannons from one end of the property to the other in order to aim them up the Guana Heights.

On the front step, General Cornwallis conducted a formal surrender ceremony. Lord Stirling, who miraculously had survived, delivered his saber.

"Stirling is a true Spar – a true soldier," Anne corrected herself just in time. "I hope he is not treated to the King's hospitality on board ship."

"General Stirling will be housed in quarters appropriate to his position until the rebels can arrange for his exchange," Hale replied. "If the rebellion continues beyond this evening, that is."

"Do you think Washington will surrender tonight?" Father asked, visibly agog at the possibilities.

"He will find himself surrounded on land and sea by nightfall," Hale said. "He may have little choice in the matter."

"That would be quite convenient. A winter in New York would be wonderful," Mrs. Loring interjected, sounding quite like Father, their thoughts already far away from the battlefield. "Halifax. Flatbush. I'm so bored with backwater billets."

"As we all are," Hale said, his sarcasm apparent, at least to Anne.

"William, of course, will select the grandest mansion in New York for our residence. We'll host our first ball before the snow falls," Betsey continued.

"Why don't we press the attack immediately?" Anne asked no one in particular.

"An insightful question, Miss Wheaton," Hale replied.

"It appears we've won the battle, but have yet to achieve the victory that will end the rebellion," she continued.

"Perhaps General Howe believes our army needs to rest and regroup to ensure the next assault is the final one. He is most considerate, some might say overly so, for the well-being of his men. I would be most surprised if we did not launch again at dawn," Hale said.

"Why rush? The rebels have nowhere to go. We can take them at our leisure," Betsey said, a frown creasing her face. "Besides, if the war ends too soon, my William might get recalled to London before our season can even begin."

"I suppose you're right, my dear," Hale said, taking Betsey's elbow and steering her towards our waiting coach. "Mr. Washington is most certainly trapped."

Like a caged bear, Anne thought. Dangerous until dead.

***

All night, we burrowed deeper into the ground as well as into our hearts, fortifying both for the inevitable charge; but Wednesday dawned and the redcoats stayed put. As the morning progressed, they appeared content to dig their trenches and prime their cannons, sending occasional skirmishers to probe our lines. I fired my musket twice, wounding only myself, inflaming the scar on my cheek.

By mid-afternoon, the wind had changed course, coming now from the north, preventing the British Navy from sailing up the Narrows. I assumed General Washington would capitalize on this good fortune, which might prove fleeting, to evacuate our army, but no such order was forthcoming. Instead, our commander-in-chief raced over a steady stream of reinforcements from New York, who marched from the ferry with a resounding fanfare of drum and fife. We were going to double down on Brooklyn. I would have the opportunity to fight, and die, for my country right here on this ground.

Just before suppertime, my friend, Ben Tallmadge, landed with Colonel Chester's regiment, as usual bringing news. General Sullivan, as well as General Stirling, had been captured yesterday. Ten Marylanders, out of four hundred, had miraculously reached safety after their assaults on the Old Stone House. Smallwood's regiment was now dubbed the Immortals, a sobriquet of extreme honor, their ultimate sacrifice a point of pride for us all. The Declaration of Independence might have been signed in ink in Philadelphia, but it would be signed in blood in Brooklyn, the vow passed up and down the line, confirmed with determined nods and muttered curses.

By sunset, the wind strengthened to a gale, dropping the temperature and peppering us with rain and hail. Fully exposed to the elements, we shivered in our positions, drenched and miserable into the wee hours. I did not even try to sleep, pacing the line in fog thick as porridge, prodding my men to stay alert. The silver lining, I told them through chattering blue lips, was that the storm would force the British Navy to remain at anchor for yet another day.

At four bells, Hercules came to fetch me. Little John had broken, curling in the muck around his musket. "I've sinned, Captain. At the Ramrod. More than once," he cried softly, his eyes puffed and red.

"We've all sinned," I replied. "If the Army weeded out sinners from its ranks, there'd be no one left."

John allowed himself a brief smile, but his snivel quickly returned. "I want to see my Ma again."

"You will, John, you will," I assured him, although I could not in all honesty say whether it would be in this world or the next. "And she will be mighty proud of you."

"She will?"

"Most certainly. You have grown into a fine man – and taken your place with other brave men serving our Glorious Cause." I pointed down the line at the huddled shapes.

"I'm not ready to die, Captain," he said, wiping the running snot from his nose.

"None of us are, John. But we are all ready to fight." I helped him up and back into place. "We are going to serve the redcoats a warm welcome of lead and steel should they venture across that field."

"Yes, sir. A warm welcome." Little John pointed his musket out into the swirling mists. I moved on to check my other men.

The rain slackened by daybreak, and the fog lifted, but still the redcoats did not charge. They appeared content to complete their siege works and hurl epitaphs that no woman should ever hear. I allowed my men to break from the line in shifts to visit the breakfast fire. *What was Howe waiting for?*

A drum roll to my rear marked the loud arrival of yet another regiment of reinforcements, fishermen from Marblehead, Massachusetts, wearing tight blue coats and duck-white breeches. To my eye, they looked more like sailors in the Royal Navy than soldiers in the Continental Army. Perhaps, the loud arrival of our reinforcements has persuaded the British to delay, I thought, although we still held a far inferior hand.

At our mid-day captains' briefing, Colonel Webb delivered the news we had been waiting for. "There will be a Council of War at the Cornell House this afternoon. General Washington has commandeered any craft that floats to assemble at the ferry landing by dusk. I know not our destination, but keep your men at the ready to move out on a moment's notice."

I pulled William Hull aside after we were dismissed. "Washington is prone to bold gambles," I said, confident that my words would not travel further than my friend's ears. "I would not be surprised if we now try to outflank our enemy."

"Sail east to Jamaica Bay?"

"Or possibly west towards Gravesend. Either way our army could miraculously appear behind the redcoat lines when the sun rises on the morrow," I replied.

"A miracle on the scale of Moses parting the Red Sea," Hull said, his eyes gazing towards the heavens. "I know little of weather, wind or currents."

"Nor do I. We will have to ask the Lord's blessing."

Hull shook his head. "My money still rides on New York. I believe General Washington remains determined to fulfill the wishes of our Congress and defend the city at all costs."

"We will learn our mission soon enough, friend." I clapped William's shoulder, praying silently this would not be our final farewell. "Huzzah."

Still wet and cold, my men were as skittish as newborn foals that afternoon. While I did not volunteer any information, they sensed an end to the stalemate, one way or another. We supped in relative quiet, a light fog returning to shroud our camp as well as the entrenchments of the enemy. Sergeant Hempstead informed me that Elvin and Peacock had swiped extra biscuits and peas, earning a rebuke from our cook, but I told him to ignore the infractions. We would all need additional fortification this evening.

At eight bells, Colonel Webb gave the order to move out with all our belongings. As the hazy gray of twilight faded away, company after company left the line, marching in strict silence, not even a cough tolerated, along a muddy path that quickly deteriorated into a bog. I was quite certain we were headed towards the ferry landing, although I knew not our ultimate destination.

Not all regiments retreated, I noticed. Chester's troop scrambled to take our place, stealthy apparitions spreading thin to fill gaps, maintain fires, and provide the illusion that our army's entrenchments were still at full strength. Ben gave me a crisp salute as we passed.

I did not know the logic behind the order of deployment but recognized that my friend would be among the last to leave, facing grave danger should the British gain wind of our movements. My own thoughts were as raveled as one of my sister Rose's yarn balls, tangled between relief at leaving the line and disappointment at not being selected to stay until the end.

I did not have time to ponder as the mucky path that snaked through fields and orchards required my immediate attention. We stepped over, or around, discarded baggage, broken wagon wheels, and a horse's corpse. A cannon lay on its side, its touchhole spiked with nails, confirming that our army would not be coming back. I hustled up and down our line moving my men along and enforcing the silence demanded by my superiors.

The tasks were manageable until we neared the waterfront, the torches of New York beckoning across the river. Sensing they were headed to safety, not battle, men broke pell mell, as if a swarm of bees had attacked the head of the line.

In the wan moonlight, we watched privates ignore the shouts of their officers and sprint to the river, clogging the landing with their bodies and gear. Crafts of all shapes and sizes, from four-passenger dories to double-bowed bateaux to sail-rigged Dutch doggers, hovered near the bank. A longboat seesawed precariously as men piled in, packing themselves like strips of salted pork in a barrel.

"Out!" General Washington yelled, stomping and splashing his boots towards the nearest boat in the shallows. Panic was so intense that few even recognized their commander-in-chief, even though he was as finely hatted and impeccably uniformed as ever. He reached into the bank, yanked out a stone the size of a man's head, and held it aloft, ignoring the mud dripping on his jacket. "Out, or I will sink this skiff right here and now."

Spitting and muttering, four men clambered to shore to wait their turn for the next boat. The men from Marblehead, the same men I had seen earlier, heaved their cloth-muffled oars, propelling the bateaux, riding a bare six inches out of the water, away from Long Island. Washington climbed the riverbank to dry land, but did not go far, his presence confirming the importance of this evacuation, the last chance to save our army.

I kept my men together as we shuffled ever closer to the landing, the probability of reaching safety increasing with every step. Little John was not the only man to peer over his shoulder every five minutes to look for a redcoat charge. When we were one company away, Elvin and Peacock celebrated by sharing their purloined rations with their fellows. Chester's regiment, and others at the front, were still safe, I thought. Finally, just past eleven bells, we were first in line.

"Halt!" General Washington's low voice carried as he stepped down from his perch. "Captain Hale from Connecticut, correct?"

"Yes, sir," I answered in a similar subdued tone, proudly stiffening my posture.

"Your men will step back."

"Yes, sir." I herded my men away from the departure point, ignoring their grumblings. A company of New Jersey men rushed to take our place in the bateaux. What did Washington have in mind? A rumble resonated in the heavens, seeming to come from the Heights. Cannons or thunder, I could not tell. Little John shook, his gaze frantic. Hercules calmed him. Were we going back to the front?

Another rumble, this time much closer at hand, but far less threatening. An overloaded wagon, drawn by two plough horses, splashed through the muck. General Thomas Mifflin, Washington's chief aide and quartermaster, steered from the buckboard. A Pennsylvania Quaker by birth who had been expelled from his faith for joining the army, Mifflin was well-respected by the troops for his efforts to supply us despite the financial constraints imposed by Congress.

Mifflin drew the reins hard as the horses' hoofs splattered mud all over my breeches. When the wagon was stopped and steady, he stood and waved a signal lantern. The signal was returned from one of the larger vessels out on the water which then appeared to swerve towards our shore. "Muskets, munitions and medical supplies. You must see they reach safety," he said, while steadying the horses.

The ship, a merchantman, glided to the tip of the pier extending out into the river. Its frame looked familiar from the docks in New London. Asa Cobb was the first to jump down from the *Laughing Lady*, lashing its lines to the stanchions. I was taken aback, quite surprised to see my old friend serving the Cause once again, but this was no time for pleasantries. We loaded the crates of valuable supplies in the hold and crammed ourselves on the deck shoulder to shoulder as Captain Caulk gave the order to cast off. Little John broke out his fife as soon we were clear, but I slapped it away before he could toot a note. Silence would be enforced until we reached the far shore.

The breeze was light, the waters smooth, as the *Laughing Lady* glided towards New York, towering over the myriad of other vessels, traveling in both directions. The silhouettes of Generals Washington and Mifflin stood out in the moonlight as they directed the evacuation. While we had clearly lost the battle on Long Island, out-maneuvered before a shot was even fired in truth, the Continental Army looked like it might survive to fight another day. I prayed that history might one day view our escape as the first step towards our victory.

When we tied onto Murray's Wharf in New York, my men and I unloaded the cargo. We would have to hump it to the armory, a task we were quite familiar with. I directed Sergeant Hempstead to take charge, while I lingered to talk to Asa.

"Captain Hale, I'm pleased to see you safe," he said, stepping down the gangplank. He drew close, as if he was going to embrace me, but then thought better of it. In the torchlight, I noticed Asa's hair had thinned and his cheeks had hollowed. Had my countenance lost its youth as well?

"I've yet to truly engage the enemy," I replied, fumbling with my load, as well as my next words. "I'm surprised to see you here, serving our Cause. Is there a profit in it?" I asked at last.

"No profit, Hale." Caulk jumped into the conversation from his perch on his ship's rail. "We freely answered General Washington's summons. Couldn't let our boys be trapped by the damned bloody-backs."

"Most appreciated then."

Asa started to loosen the knots fastening the *Laughing Lady* to the pier. "We must return to Long Island for another load while the tides are favorable."

"Godspeed, friend," I replied, offering my hand.

"Until we meet again," Asa said, clasping it firmly.

CHAPTER 18 - SEPTEMBER 1776

To Major General William Heath
"…As everything, in a manner, depends upon obtaining Intelligence of the Enemys motions, I do most earnestly entreat you … to accomplish this most desireable end…leave no stone unturn'd, nor do not stick at expence to bring this to pass, as I never was more uneasy than on Acct of my want of knowledge on this Score…"
General George Washington
New York
Sept 5th, 1776

"…Some scrubby fellows ought to have gone…"
Testimony of Asher Wright
1836

On a sun-drenched afternoon, Anne stood high atop the ramparts of Fort Stirling, looking across the harbor at the rebel flags fluttering over New York City. How had the Continental Army escaped from Long Island? Why did General Howe not press the attack and finish them off? The questions had hissed from the mouth of every Crown-loving citizen in Flatbush for the past week, accompanied by a great deal of head-shaking.

"Anne, dear, are you going to join us?" Betsey Loring's voice floated up from the parade ground inside the fort. A score of scarlet-clad officers and their aides gathered around a long table, fashioned from hogsheads and planking, set with linens, sterling and crystal. A pig roasted on a spit, a silent observer to the decadence. "Dinner is almost ready. And General Grant has just arrived," Betsey called.

Anne waved, but made little progress towards the ladder leading down from the palisades. Her heart trilled as she glanced again at the stars and stripes. The rebellion still lived, a dying gasp, perhaps, but a breath nevertheless. She took care to mask her exhilaration before descending.

"Come, come, don't look so glum, dear," Betsey said, tugging Anne off to a quiet corner, handing her a flute of champagne. They stepped over an empty cartridge case and around a spiked cannon. "We have not yet taken New York but we still have much to celebrate."

"We do?"

"Well, I do," Betsey whispered, tipping her crystal to her lips, finishing off the last drops of bubbly. "A rather lengthy list, I'm pleased to say."

"Do tell," Anne said, swirling her champagne but not imbibing, surprised that Betsey appeared ready to let down her guard. To her.

"We've taken over a thousand prisoners. And stand to make quite a tidy profit on their upkeep."

"We..." Anne said hesitantly.

"General Howe has appointed my Joshua to be the Deputy Commissar. Reporting directly to William Cunningham."

"A well-earned position...for your husband." Anne tried to keep the bite from her words.

"Don't be such a prig, dear. Joshua and I have an understanding. I will entertain General Howe during his stay in America while he amasses our fortune. Then our marriage will resume a more traditional course."

"Quite a partnership."

"Perhaps you will be so fortunate one day."

Never, Anne prayed. "And how will you manage your living arrangements, if I may be so bold to ask?"

"General Howe has selected the Beekman estate, overlooking the East River, as his residence. I will visit him there at his convenience."

"Don't we have to evict the rebels from New York first?"

"You've seen the rebel position," Betsey tilted her flute towards the ramparts. "It's indefensible. We can evict them at our leisure."

"And when will that be, do you surmise?"

Betsey shrugged. "William doesn't tell me everything."

"I am honored you have chosen to confide in me." Anne dipped her bonnet, pleased that the sarcasm in her gesture went unnoticed.

"I believe we may see much more of each other this winter season."

"We will?"

"William is outfitting the *Britannia* to properly host his soirees.*"*

"The *Britannia's* a merchant vessel, isn't she?" Anne vaguely recalled the ship from her walks along the docks in Boston.

"Was a merchant vessel," Betsey corrected. "He will be knocking through two decks to create a ballroom, lacquering the walls and trimming them in gold."

"A perfect setting to wear your new gowns," Anne replied, taking her first sip, hoping it would encourage Betsey to continue. "You'll look stunning."

"There's more." Betsey signaled for a liveried waiter to refill her glass, staying mum until he was out of earshot. "The master stateroom will have a broad expanse of glass so William - and I - will have a magnificent view of the harbor."

"Truly palatial." Little wonder General Howe appeared in no rush to end the war, Anne thought.

"And there will be two more grand staterooms. For our guests."

"How thoughtful."

"Perhaps you and General Grant will join us."

Anne coughed to camouflage her surprise. Although they were close in age, she never thought of Betsey Loring as her friend.

"Ah, the good general's approaching now," Betsey continued.

Waddling was more appropriate, Anne thought. Put an apple in Grant's mouth and he could pass for a suckling pig. Would she have to lie with him after all? Smothered by his sagging skin and florid face? General James Grant symbolized the arrogance, pomposity and decay of the Empire. *Where was Nathan?*

"Ladies, what wickedness are you contriving?" Grant asked, chuckling at his own cleverness. Sprigs of gray hair sprouted at the edges of his wig.

"I was just admiring the view…of the harbor," Anne replied.

"Ah yes, you have a head for military matters," Grant said, clasping Anne's elbow and leading her towards the feast. "Quite unbecoming for a young lady, you know."

"It will pass, I'm sure."

"I do hope so." Grant's eyes twinkled at the thought. "Besides, I doubt there will be any more military matters to trouble your brain."

"Truly? The rebel flags still fly quite defiantly over the city."

"Not for long, my dear. Not for long. The rebels have been thoroughly thrashed. I wager they will never stand up to the King's troops on the field of battle again."

A seductive smile crept across Anne's face. "Can I be so bold as to assume the other side of that wager?"

***

Leaving our camp on Bowling Green, I picked my way up Broadway, past the crumbling facades of once stately mansions, around an overturned copper brewery vat, over a mangled settee, its lavender upholstery well-gashed, and far clear of a still steaming mound of feces. Smoke spiraled from campfires scattered randomly along the street. Soldiers, at least those that could still stand, lingered in grim knots, their broken spirits obvious from tattered uniforms and mangled weaponry strewn uselessly in the dirt. Others lay about, either drunk or diseased. Yes, our flags still flew overhead, but the Continental Army was barely alive.

Nevertheless, my spirits were hopeful as I walked north. My troop had escaped Long Island unscathed, and, unlike so many of our comrades, appeared willing and ready to fight. To my surprise, Tom Knowlton, recently promoted to Lieutenant Colonel, had sent a messenger this morning, summoning me to his quarters on Harlem Heights. I had not come into direct contact with Knowlton during my months in New York, although I had seen him at a distance. To the best of my knowledge, Knowlton and his company had remained in defense of Manhattan and thus missed the fighting on Long Island. While I did not know the reason for my summons, I assumed it was not simply to discuss the weather.

Arriving on the Heights in late afternoon, I repaired straight to Knowlton's headquarters, a spritely, two-room farmhouse overlooking the Hudson. Unlike the chaos downtown, this camp maintained its martial aura. Pickets patrolled the perimeter, tents were set in neat rows, companies drilled at a brisk pace. Of course, these men had yet to taste defeat or the tremors of a midnight retreat with the British hot on their heels.

Knowlton, a squat, barrel-chested man sporting mutton-chop sideburns, kept me waiting only a scant minute or so. The front room, serving as kitchen, parlor and office, reeked of smoke. An aide offered me coffee, or whiskey. I took neither.

"Captain Hale, our situation on this island is quite perilous," Knowlton began, standing up, a faded, red clay pipe in hand, to point at the map spread across the table. "Mr. Franklin and Mr. Adams have returned with empty hands from a parley with Lord Admiral Howe who threatened to sail his ships of war upriver if we do not surrender unconditionally."

"Never, sir," I replied, resting my right hand on my saber.

"Exactly the sentiments of General Washington. And myself, I might add." Knowlton approached, puffing heartily, clearly savoring his tobacco. "Accordingly, the General has tasked me to form an elite company to serve as the vanguard of the Continental Army. We will gather intelligence of our enemy's positions and intentions, and skirmish when necessary."

"Rangers?" I asked, my youthful readings of the exploits of Robert Rogers flashing in my thoughts. I restrained from volunteering immediately, forcing myself to wait for an offer which I prayed would be soon forthcoming.

"Yes, rangers. Men who are extraordinarily brave, cunning and fit. Men who have no fear of dangerous missions, or their consequences. Men who can serve as a shining example to the rest of our army, which, sadly, is in dire need of such motivation." Knowlton paused, as if waiting to unveil the grand prize at the county fair. "Your brothers, John and Joseph, have already signed on," he added.

I was relieved to learn my two brothers were alive and well, and esteemed as soldiers, but also a bit jealous that they were now Rangers. I wanted to wave my hand, like an overeager student in the front row of the schoolhouse, to commit as well, but, fortunately, there was no need. "I've watched you from afar the past few months, Captain Hale, and been most impressed with your leadership," Knowlton continued.

"Thank you, sir. I only wish to have engaged the enemy more directly."

"You will fulfill your wish soon enough." Knowlton paused and puffed his pipe. A cloying, cherrywood aroma filled the space between us. "I have asked Colonel Webb to permit you to join my new command with all haste. At your current rank, of course."

I shook the colonel's hand, my head spinning with excitement as I exited the farmhouse. I was a ranger at last. And a captain at that. One of four, the colonel had explained. Two from his current command. As would be most of the other men in the unit. No other officers or soldiers from Colonel Webb's regiment had been invited. I could bring only a second, Sergeant Hempstead, and my orderly, Asher Wright.

I dismayed at the prospect of leaving my troop, but this was the opportunity I had yearned for since my enlistment over a year ago. Made even more sweet by the opportunity to serve alongside my brothers, whom, Knowlton had noted, would not be under my direct supervision.

I couldn't wait to write Father and Enoch, but I would have to. My new commanding officer had informed me that all personal communications, both letters and diaries, were prohibited while I was in his unit for fear the enemy might learn our whereabouts. A small sacrifice, in my opinion. Knowlton's Rangers, the words skipped off my tongue as I walked back downtown.

***

As the sunset cast a honeyed glow over Fort Stirling, the catering staff discreetly retired to the shadows while the coterie of senior British officers and their mistresses lounged around the parade ground in various states of sobriety and undress. Scraps of pork lay scattered, attracting a flock of geese who flapped noisily as they pecked. An empty champagne bottle floated in a tub of ale; a half-full demijohn of claret balanced on its side in the grass. The makeshift table now sported a new centerpiece, a pig's head impaled upon a dagger, a linen napkin, inscribed with the initials GW in red lipstick, tied neatly around its neck. Sipping a ruby Madeira, Betsey Loring sat on General Howe's lap while he fondled her bare breast.

The depths of the bacchanal, which had unfurled gradually over the course of the evening, had taken Anne by surprise. Still fully clothed and clear-headed, she skipped away from General Grant, who pranced in pursuit, clearly enjoying the chase. Major Whitcomb unfortunately was not present this evening to rescue her.

Accepting her need for a powerful sponsor, Anne had plied Grant with alcohol of all colors betting that he would totter off before her reckoning was due; however, his capacity appeared bottomless. She spied a ladder leading up to the ramparts. "I want to see the view at night," she called over her shoulder, calculating that the ascent might prove too formidable for her suitor.

Unfortunately, she had underestimated Grant's speed of foot, or overestimated her own in her high heeled shoes. His hands circled her waist before she reached the third rung. "I am enjoying the view right here," he replied, burying his nose in her petticoats.

Anne reached down to tousle his wig, buying herself time. If she protested, would anyone hear her scream? Or care? Grant loosened his grip. She kicked off her shoes and scooted up the ladder. The General labored to follow.

"The rebels built this fort quite well," she said, running a hand over a gun port carved out of the palisade.

"Yes, they did. I'll grant them that," Grant huffed. He too couldn't resist a glance across the panorama of forts and harbor. "Quite formidable defenses. Almost as formidable as yours."

Anne had to chuckle at Grant's first sign of wit. She crossed her hands over her chest. "But I will not abandon my breastworks as easily as did the rebels."

"No, no. I see you are determined to put up a lusty fight. More so than Mr. Washington I might add."

"Were you surprised at the rebels' retreat?" she asked, dropping her hands.

The mirth disappeared from Grant's eyes as he scanned the ramparts to make sure that no one was within earshot. "Quite so. If I had been allowed to press my advantage, the rebellion would be history."

"Why did you halt then?"

"Howe's orders," Grant replied, shaking his head. "But, you are again taxing your brain with military matters, my dear. Is it merely a ruse to distract me?"

"I am not a woman of schemes and subterfuge." Anne curtsied towards the general.

"No. I thought not." Grant looked skyward, appearing to count the stars. A woman's shriek pierced the air, resonating more of fright than frolic. "Your message is quite clear, so I will scabbard my sword and see you home with your honor intact."

"And yours as well."

***

I fretted over my farewell to my men, but, as with correspondence, the decision was cast by my superiors. Given that I could not disclose where I was headed, Colonel Webb thought it best if I left camp immediately. While Asher packed my belongings, I made a brief round of our tents.

"I volunteer to join you – wherever you're going," Little John gamely offered, tapping out a rat-tat-tat on his drum.

"Always knew you were fit for grander things," Hercules added, saluting.

"Who's taking your place?" Elvin, ever the sly one, asked as he sloshed down a healthy dose of rum.

"You'll report to William Hull, captain of second company, until Colonel Webb sorts things out," I replied. "He's a good man."

"He's a lawyer," Elvin spat.

"That too." I had no time to list my friend's more admirable qualities.

I left Bowling Green for the second time that day just before darkness settled, along with Asher and Stephen. We took only what the three of us could carry. Asher had packed the remainder of my belongings to be shipped up to our new camp later that week.

We barely exited the city limits before I felt faint. I walked another quarter-mile before my stomach cramped. I dropped my haversack, racing into the hedges to void my bowels. Afterwards, I tried to remount my pack, but it felt as if an ox had climbed inside it. My limbs turned to jelly; my forehead burned. I could do little more than kneel on the road. And retch.

While my body revolted, my mind raced. Would this illness pass? Or claim my life? I fingered the mole on my neck. I am not fated to die in bed, I thought as Stephen rolled me on to my back. He propped up my head and offered a sip of ale from my canteen. I prayed that I would recover in time to join my new unit before the battle for New York was over.

"There's no blood in your shit," Asher said as he knelt beside me. "Probably just the flux."

"We'll make camp here until you recover," Stephen added hopefully.

I nodded then surrendered to a fitful sleep. In the morning, Asher summoned an Army physician who bled me to drain the evil humors from my system. But still the fever raged. I tossed and sweat for the next forty-eight hours. Asher and Steven alternated vigil, bathing my forehead with cold compresses and feeding me a thin soup, although I could scarcely recognize one from the other. I do vaguely recall listening to a bible passage read out loud, fearing it was my last rights.

The fever broke just after dawn on the third morning. My sleeping roll was so drenched, I swore I had pissed myself. Asher burned my blanket and dressed me in a fresh white linen shirt. He thought another bleeding might be helpful, but I persuaded him to wait a few hours at least. By mid-day, I was able to sit up and read scripture. My appetite returned by nightfall. Despite Asher's protests that I needed more rest, I instructed Stephen to go ahead to Harlem Heights and inform Colonel Knowlton that I would arrive in the morning.

Asher and I did not make great time, but we still walked into the Ranger camp before breakfast was finished. An aide pointed to the farm house, informing me that Knowlton was meeting with his officers. I hastened over, lingering on the periphery of roughly a score of men, several of whom I recognized but none I knew by name.

"Gentlemen, I will ask again," the Colonel said, his voice rising. Men skulked, casting their eyes downward as if searching the floor for lost silver, as Knowlton continued. "Our commander-in-chief has requested a volunteer to venture behind our enemy's lines on Long Island and gather intelligence. We must learn when and where the redcoats will attack if we have any hope of defending New York. The mission should last a week, no longer."

"Washington's begging for a *spy*, ain't he?" a bald-pated lieutenant asked.

"Our commander does not beg," Knowlton replied, struggling to keep his tone even.

"But he can't *order* any soldier to spy, can he? That job ain't befitting a dog," the lieutenant countered.

"No. Washington can not command any of you to spy, but he implores you to consider it for the good of the Cause."

"Washington lost Long Island, not us," a voice charged from the back ranks. "Now, he just wants to save his own neck from the noose."

"I'll willingly die on the battlefield, but I'll be damned before I swing on the gallows," another officer barked, but did not step forward.

"I do not want to return empty-handed to our commander-in-chief so I will ask for a volunteer one more time," Knowlton said. He paced across the front of the room, looking each man in the eye. The silence stretched like a putty that refused to snap. Men shuffled their feet, folded their arms, scratched their balls, but no one raised a hand. Knowlton turned his back, staring out the window. A fly buzzed his ears.

I knew I should keep silent and bide my time. Learn my way around my new unit. Meet my men. We would see combat in a few days at most. Like my friends Hull, Tallmadge and Hamilton, I was a college graduate, destined to play an increasingly significant role in the birth of our nation. The reasons to duck this assignment were manifold, but I couldn't resist, once again playing the bull chasing the matador's cape.

"I'll do it," I said, pushing my way forward, heads turning, mouths agape. "For the past year I have been attached to the army and not rendered any material service. I am prepared to undertake whatever assignment General Washington deems necessary to secure our victory."

"Well done, Hale. You are a true Connecticut man," Knowlton said, a broad smile stretching from ear to ear. He strode towards me, clapping me on both shoulders. "General Washington will be most pleased, and proud, to learn of your eagerness to serve."

My fellow officers couldn't exit the farm house fast enough. A few tossed a huzzah in my direction, or offered a tepid welcome to the Rangers, but most avoided me as if I were a leper. No true soldier associates with a spy. I was relieved my brothers were not present.

"You should report to Mortier House for your briefing at once," Knowlton said, ushering me to the door. "And go alone. Leave your man here to fix your billet."

I scarfed down a double helping of biscuits, jam and bacon and returned to the Bloomingdale Road, fighting a tide of pedestrian and wagon traffic heading north. As I passed the village, I thought of the rough justice the Sons of Liberty had delivered to George Raleigh and offered a brief prayer for his recovery.

Pulling over a lieutenant wearing the blue jacket of my home state's militia, I learned that General Washington had at last received Congress' permission to abandon the city. Only General Putnam and his regiments would remain on guard until the evacuation was complete. If we had torched New York months ago, we would not be in this predicament today. Nor would I be volunteering for espionage.

With the army in retreat, there was little wonder Washington now conducted all business uptown, Life Guards stood duty on the front porch, flanked by two soaring Greek columns; aides scurried in and out, jumping on and off horseback to deliver their messages; our commander-in-chief's phaeton was tethered by the stables, a vestige of better days.

I climbed the steps with great trepidation, the gravity of my mission weighting each footfall. The thump, scuffle and grunts of men packing in haste resonated from the parlor to my left. "Captain Hale reporting for duty, sir," I said to the aide sitting at the desk in the foyer at the foot of a spiral staircase. "Lieutenant Colonel Knowlton sent me."

The aide's head jerked at the mention of Knowlton. "Yes, we were expecting a volunteer from his command. Welcome to Mortier House, captain." He stood and ushered me into the cloakroom. "Colonel Reed will be with you shortly," he added before closing the door.

With no place to sit, I paced about the tight space for what I estimated to be an hour until Reed, Washington's adjutant, burst in, his jacket unbuttoned and hair askew.

"All hell has broken loose, as you can well see," he said, pointing out the open door to the foyer. "The British sailed up the East River this morning. Six troop transports and four men-of-war. One hundred and fifty cannons. They bivouacked opposite Kip's Bay. We fear an attack any moment."

"I understand we're quitting New York," I replied.

"Yes, Hancock has yielded all discretion to His Excellency. We're moving Continental Army headquarters north to Mount Morris tonight."

"And the troops?"

"We'll evacuate the sick and wounded first. As well as our supplies."

"My mission…?" I left the question hanging.

"More critical than ever. Washington needs to know if the route north to the King's Bridge will be blocked. Will Fort Washington be assaulted? What are the British plans to fortify New York should we choose to counter-attack? What's the situation on eastern Long Island? Friend or foe? The questions are vital to the survival, and ultimate success, of our army."

"I see."

"Do you?" Reed stepped towards me, pointing a finger at my chest. "Are you up to the challenge, Captain? Do you have experience in rangering and intelligencing?"

"I have no history in those arts, but I am confident that I will rise to the task. My mind is keen and my oratory skills are of the first rank."

"A silver tongue will be useful in this endeavor."

"What codes should I use? I have heard spies employ invisible ink for their messages."

"Latin? Are you well-versed in Latin?" Reed swiveled to glance out the door, his impatience obvious.

"Quite fluent, sir."

"Then you should record your observations in Latin and tuck them into your boot."

"Yes, sir." Not exactly the answer I expected. "Are there supporters of our cause behind the enemy lines who can provide aid should I be in need?"

"Most certainly. If you listen closely to tavern discourse, you will uncover them." He reached into his jacket for a parchment which he handed to me. "An order signed by His Excellency enabling you to command any armed vessel in our service to ferry you across the Sound. I suggest you begin your mission in Huntington and work your way back to the front lines."

"Understood. I will embark north immediately." I had so many more questions, but realized Reed lacked any good answers.

"Good luck, Captain Hale. I must return to my duties," he said. "I look forward to receiving your report in seven days' time."

I stood alone in the cloak room, an island of calm in the turbulent sea of Mortier House. How desperate our army must be to send me off this way.

I shuffled into the foyer, trying to stay out of the way of the aides lugging trunks out the front door. My mind was so clogged I didn't notice George Washington himself emerge from the parlor. He met my gaze straightaway, held it for a brief second, started to speak, then squelched his words.

I'm a spy now, I realized. I must learn to live in the shadows. I turned to leave, but Washington's voice stopped me. "Godspeed, Hale."

It was dark when I stepped outside, torchlights providing only a meager illumination, but the grounds of Mortier House still hummed with activity. I couldn't linger with so many people about. And I needed to start my journey.

Before I reached the Bloomingdale Road, I made three decisions: I would rest overnight at Harlem Heights; I would ask Stephen Hempstead to accompany me until I secured a vessel for my transport to Long Island; and, I would assume the role of schoolmaster canvassing the countryside for a position for the fall term.

"Captain?" a female voice sallied from the hedges.

My hat still bore its yellow cockade, I realized. I would need to alter my wardrobe before I reached enemy lines.

"It's Lara. Remember me?" she called again, a brogue apparent in her lilt. She stepped out into the road blocking my way. "You appear in a quite the hurry. Are you off to meet a lassie?"

I brushed by, having no interest in a harlot this evening, or any evening for that matter.

"Quite rude tonight, aren't you Hale? I took you for a man of honor."

I kept walking, unnerved slightly by the unwanted recognition.

"Flog your own pintle then," she called before I strode out of range.

I was exhausted by the time I reached the Ranger camp. A sentry, expecting my arrival, pointed me towards my new billet. I stopped first at Stephen's tent, nudging him awake. He readily agreed to my plan.

Asher had pegged my canvas and stood outside, stoking a gentle campfire. "Captain, your brother, John, asked me to give this to you." He handed me a silver pocket watch, similar to the one I had lost wrestling against the boys from Bristol. "He said your father would have wanted you to have it."

I turned it over gently, reading the inscription etched in a swirling cursive: *Godspeed your safe return.* One of the Ranger officers present when I volunteered must have told my brothers of my mission.

Asher shook his head wryly and retired to his own tent, leaving me to thoughts of my family. But, I was not alone. Much to my astonishment, William Hull sat by the flames.

"Dear friend, your orderly informed me that you might have volunteered for a hare-brained assignment," he said, his distress clearly evident.

"How could Asher have reached you so quickly?"

"He is not weakened by fever. Nor am I." Hull stood, squaring his fists on his hips.

"He knows no details."

"Asher knows your mission is hastily conceived, hardly necessary and of doubtful propriety for a man of your character."

"I cannot stand idly by while our Army is surprised again. We will not survive another defeat as we experienced last month."

Hull clapped my shoulder. "Nathaniel, we have been friends for many years. How can you become a spy? Your countenance is too frank and honest for deceit."

"I was a thespian on the stage at Yale."

"This role will prove much more challenging," Hull chuckled ruefully. "You are incapable of acting a part foreign to your habits."

"I will surprise you then with my pretensions and prevarications."

"Even if you prove successful, you will stain your honor and sacrifice your integrity."

"Every service, necessary to the public good, becomes honourable by being necessary." I kicked a pile of loose pebbles into the fire, hopefully signaling the end to this argument.

"You're as stubborn as a mule," Hull replied gathering his musket. He turned, striking on a new tack. "Tallmadge will likely be here in camp tomorrow when the evacuation of the city is complete. Talk to him before taking action."

Didn't Hull realize I had thought this through? My country needed me now more than ever. I would not allow my conviction to waver.

"Your brothers. They're patriots too – engage with them." Hull's shoulders slumped.

He was a true friend, but sensed his words fell on deaf ears. "I pray you rest your body and mind before undertaking a mission that will likely end badly," he continued. "Most badly, I fear."

"I will reflect and do nothing but what duty demands."

"Sleep well, Nathaniel. I pray to see you here on Harlem Heights at breakfast."

In fact, I slept little. Since my trunk had miraculously arrived in camp, I had some choice as to my wardrobe. I selected a brown woolen suit and buff waistcoat with simple pewter buttons, knit by my sister Rose, and round-brimmed hat, which I planned to don prior to reaching Long Island. I tucked my Yale diploma, critical for credibility as a schoolmaster, into the waistcoat pocket. After leaving a note for Asher to transfer my remaining belongings should the Ranger camp move north, Stephen and I departed before the roosters crowed on Sunday Sept. 15th.

***

Cannon blasts assaulted Robert Rogers' eardrums as the Royal Navy bombarded the rebel fortifications on the embankment above Kip's Bay later that same morning. He stood shoulder-to-shoulder with fifty of his finest Queen's Rangers, waiting anxiously in their flatboat, one of eighty in the amphibious armada which formed a scarlet and green cloak spanning the East River. He thought back to his exertions on the snow-covered hills of Massachusetts; his lust for blood and plunder now whetted to a fine edge.

Rogers had spent the past six weeks recruiting in New Jersey, Westchester, Connecticut and Long Island, striving to reach his quota of four hundred Rangers. At first, progress had been slow, but, after the British victory on Long Island, men had poured in, wanting to join the winning side in time to share in the spoils. His requirements were low: a mean streak and proficiency with either musket or blade. The recruits needed little training. They would be raiding and pillaging, not marching in formation.

At ten o'clock, the barrage halted, and the invasion of New York began. Four thousand Regulars and Hessians, all under the command of General Clinton, spearheaded the landings, encountering little resistance, apparent to Rogers from the surprising lack of return fire.

By the time he and his men splashed ashore and charged up the ridge, the rebels had been routed. Many threw down their weapons and ran vigorously away from the battlefield towards the presumed safety of the interior. Rogers had never seen such cowardice. He fired his pistol at a fleeing arse for sport.

***

The unmistakable boom of artillery rolled unobstructed across the waterways of New York harbor. It resonated in the compact, white clapboard meeting house in Flatbush just as Anne took her seat between Father and Sam Hale. Knowing glances flitted up and down the ten rows of parishioners, the invasion had begun.

Minister Wyndham, who had celebrated his sixtieth birthday only last week, bellowed a welcome on this joyous day and led the opening hymn. He maintained a steady cadence for the next hour, but the energy required to out-shout the cannonade took its toll on his vocal chords. He soldiered on for another thirty minutes before cutting short his sermon and dismissing the congregation into the morning sunshine.

"Our lucky day," Major Whitcomb said as he sidled up to Anne, close enough to be heard without shouting. He wore his dress scarlet, although she noted his silver gorget was unadorned with any coat of arms.

"On multiple accounts," she replied, her gaze drifting towards the Guana Heights and the battlefield beyond. She separated from Father, who was too engrossed in conversation with Sam to notice, and walked towards the village green. The major followed.

"What brought you to Flatbush?" he asked. "A young widow on her own in a strange land, let alone one who appears to be supervising a significant estate, is quite rare."

"You flatter me," Anne replied, stopping under the shade of a sprawling oak. "After Geoffrey's death, there was little to keep me in

418

Boston. And Father had contact with a tailor here on Long Island who, it turned out, had long since moved on."

"A most perilous journey, particularly in wartime." Another distant boom punctuated his comment.

"That it was," Anne said, suppressing a rueful chuckle. "I did not travel alone, fortunately. My brother, Caleb, and Major Robert Rogers, whom he know serves, accompanied me most of the way."

"And Mayor Matthews?" Whitcomb asked, dipping his head slightly to avoid eye contact. "He has turned out to be a most fortuitous patron despite his incarceration."

"I delivered a message for the mayor – for Governor Tryon actually – to an agent in New York. He offered me shelter on his farm afterwards. For my safety."

"I understand the rebels apprehended Matthews right here in Flatbush. Dragged him out of bed in the middle of the night. Quite rude."

"And what about you, Major? What winding road have you traveled to Flatbush?" Anne asked, flashing her sweetest smile.

"Not nearly as adventurous as yours, I'm embarrassed to say. My father is a barrister in London. Done well, well enough to ship me off to a proper school and purchase my first commission in the Army, but he's no peer of the realm."

"No skeletons in your closet?" Anne swept down a low hanging branch, masking her face behind its leaves.

"Skeletons? No. But I am the proud father of two sons, Willie is 9 and Harry is 7. I miss them sorely."

"And their mother?" Anne let the branch snap back up.

"She passed, going on two years now. I miss her as well."

"My sympathies, Major." Anne's countenance softened.

"Please call me Richard."

"Major Whitcomb," General Grant barked as he waddled in their direction. "Your presence is required at headquarters. Immediately."

"Yes, sir." Whitcomb saluted. "Good day, Miss Wheaton."

"Perhaps, we could stroll," Grant asked, offering his elbow to Anne. "I expect our guns will silence shortly and the landing will begin."

"Where, if I may ask?" She hesitated briefly before accepting the general's offer.

"Kip's Bay. General Clinton's men will be first ashore. My command will remain on Long Island for the foreseeable future. In case the rebels counter-attack."

"I'm relieved to learn we are so well-defended here."

As Grant had predicted, the artillery barrage stopped as they walked back towards the meetinghouse. The General's coach had pulled up outside, its two horses pawing the dirt. Father and Sam stepped aside, gawking. Anne feared Father, who positively beamed at his daughter's good fortune, might kneel to Grant as if he were king.

"I am going to Fort Putnam on Wallabout Bay to watch the action. It should be a grand spectacle," Grant said. "Most suitable for your military mind. Will you accompany me?"

"I do appreciate the invitation, General, but I am going to demure." The words tumbled out spontaneously; she could no more stop them than she could halt a brook from gurgling or a mother hen from clucking.

Grant flushed cherry red at Anne's rejection. In public.

Realizing the gravity of her faux pas, Anne patted her forehead. "I have a touch of ague this morning. It is best if I return to the farm and lie down."

Father was aghast as Anne walked past him and headed up the Flatbush Road. She thought she might regret her decision, but felt no such twinge. At least not yet. She kept her head down as the General's coach thundered by.

***

Rogers watched bayonets flash and stab as the Crown's forces cleaned up whatever rebels remained behind above Kip's Bay. Caleb Wheaton, whom he had promoted to sergeant, bared his tomahawk, but there were no unfortunates left to slaughter. After spending months fortifying Manhattan, the Continental Army had yielded without a fight.

Or so Rogers thought. He almost dropped his pistol when he spied a chestnut charger burst from the distant tree line, its rider sitting tall in the saddle. George Washington himself was scrambling to rally his fleeing troops. How brave – but foolhardy! The depths of the general's pent-up frustration had turned him into a madman. He must have outrun his Life Guards, a rashness unpardonable in a senior officer, let alone the leading man on the American side. Rogers recognized the opportunity immediately.

"Charge!" he commanded, leading a sprint across the open ground, the prize less than a hundred yards away. If only the British had landed cavalry as well as infantry, the rebel general would be trapped.

Washington horsewhipped one soldier then another, seemingly oblivious to the approaching threat as he tried to halt their flight. It was a futile effort. Desperate rebels swarmed past their commander-in-chief, paying no heed to his safety. The Rangers closed to fifty yards.

Four Life Guards galloped from the forest. One grabbed Old Nelson's bridle and yanked the horse around. The anger seeped from Washington's scowl as his trusted men formed a shield, leading him from the battlefield.

Rogers turned, frustrated, his once-in-a-lifetime opportunity slipping away. He looked back for help, but his Rangers stood alone. The bulk of the Crown's forces had halted, awaiting orders. Washington had escaped yet again.

His Rangers marched south, along with the Regulars and Hessians, now numbering nine thousand troops. Apparently, Howe had ordered Clinton to secure the city immediately rather than march across Manhattan Island and cut off the Continentals' evacuation.

***

Anne spent the afternoon tending the vegetable garden behind the house, out of sight from the main road. Whether planned or not, she accepted that she had crossed the Rubicon at least in her own mind. She pruned and clipped, but, more important, considered her options.

The rebellion would likely be over shortly, possibly even this afternoon. She would not be Grant's concubine, or anyone else's for that matter. Yet, what other role could she play? A wife? Major Whitcomb's probes this morning perhaps indicated his romantic interest, a much preferred alternative to General Grant, although that was an admittedly low bar. Anne hoped she had encouraged Whitcomb with proper coyness, but the Major could not compete with his superior for her favor. Why did she have to attach herself to any man to gain a place in society?

Did the rebel cause offer an alternative? Did their Declaration's promise of liberty for all extend to women? To Blacks? She thought not. Was it a first step in that direction? Quite possibly. Men like Nathaniel had the vision of equality, and were willing to sacrifice their lives in pursuit of it, but other so-called patriots, like the slavecatchers from Virginia, she shivered at the memory, certainly did not. The argument was moot, of course, if the rebels lost. Her mind spun circles like a dog chasing its tail.

Anne washed up in the scullery. Without thinking, she cleared the dross that artfully hid a door. She pushed. It creaked, opening to the ladder that descended from the secret room up in the attic.

At the clop-clop of an approaching wagon, she closed the door and replaced its camouflage. After capping her hair, she walked around to the front of the house, just in time to see Father storming up the steps. Sam Hale waited in the buckboard.

"How could you?" Smoke practically steamed from Father's ears. "Your future, our future, would be assured if…"

"If what Father?"

"I am going to Staten Island on the evening ferry to fetch your mother. Perhaps she can talk some sense into you. We'll return tomorrow."

***

Not surprisingly, New York was empty of rebels when Rogers arrived in late afternoon. General Putnam and his four thousand man garrison, fully half of Washington's forces, must have escaped north up the Bloomingdale Road, likely passing within a mile of the British troops marching in the opposite direction. While Howe had achieved his strategic objective with little British bloodshed, the Continental Army had survived to fight another day.

The city was a shithole, far from the booming seaport he had visited only a year ago. There was no point in seeking plunder, whatever riches had once gilded its mansions were long since gone. Tories, however, had somehow survived, emerging like rats from the underworld to greet the conquering redcoats. The British flag soon fluttered above the Battery, shouts of "God Save the King!" resounded in the streets, the whores in the Holy Ground decked themselves in scarlet while the disorderly houses offered free grog to anyone in uniform.

Rogers led Caleb and three other sergeants to a table at the front of the Ramrod, the loudest and most raucous establishment. Its ramshackle frame rocked to dancing feet and a fiddler's tune. The night was hot and dry, the swinging door and open shutters providing little relief. Candles flickered everywhere, casting a macabre glow across the room.

Rogers sipped his ale, but kept an eye on an oil lamp tottering behind the bar. If it fell, he wanted to be the first one out. He didn't see the strumpet with the red-gold hair until she spit at his feet.

"You Major Rogers?" Lara asked. "Of the Queens Rangers?"

"Lieutenant Colonel Rogers," he replied, tipping back his chair. "Who's asking?"

"I understand you're the chief rebel spycatcher here."

"I am." In the mood to celebrate, he was somewhat disappointed that the woman had sought him out for business, not pleasure.

"I'm in possession of information you might find useful."

"What kind of information?" This encounter might prove worthwhile after all, he thought, as he nodded for Caleb and the others to leave them alone.

"It'll cost you ten shillings."

"Three."

"Seven, and I'll throw in a bagpipe," she said, licking her lips, burnishing them to a succulent shine.

"Deal. I'll take the bagpiping first though." He didn't have much confidence in the tip anyway.

Lara led him up the back stairs. Fifteen minutes later, Rogers returned to his men, seven shillings poorer but with a sloppy grin spreading across his face. Unbecoming for a man his age, but it had been so long...

"Anyone know a Captain Hale?" he asked.

"Nathan Hale?" Caleb snapped, spilling his ale in his excitement. "He fawned over my sister back in New London. Poisoned her mind with rebel talk."

"He was seen coming and going from Washington's headquarters late yesterday. First time he's ever been there. Then he left Knowlton's Ranger camp before dawn, accompanied only by a valet. Heading north. Away from the front lines."

"You think he's going to circle around behind our lines?" Caleb asked.

"Washington is desperate. You saw him on the battlefield today. He's going to have to send spies out into the countryside or his neck may soon be fitted for a noose. A Ranger would make sense."

"I doubt Hale's the man. He's too smart and God-fearing to spy. And he's got a powder flash on his cheek that marks him as a soldier." Caleb downed his brew and waved the barkeep to refill his tankard.

"Do you want to track him or shall I assign someone else?" Rogers asked, his frustration apparent. Foiling Washington…his own plantation…the prospects kept him awake nights.

"I'll leave at once." Caleb stood, slashing his tomahawk into the table. The blade splintered the pine and shimmered in place.

"Take five good men of your choosing."

Caleb nodded. "I've a debt to settle."

***

After stopping twice to rest, my endurance still not up to snuff, Sergeant Hempstead and I reached the bustling harbor in Greenwich, Connecticut just before suppertime. Tories were out in force, openly celebrating the capture of New York. The news, combined with the joy on the faces of my enemies, pummeled my guts. Proudly wearing our brown jackets from Colonel Webb's regiment, we stalked up and down the docks, sending the Tories scattering like geese.

I was burning to sail for Long Island. Unfortunately, no schooners flying the stars and stripes were in sight, likely scampering up the Sound to evade the Royal Navy.

"We should return to camp," Stephen said. "Your journey is superfluous now."

"I'm not turning back," I replied. "Washington still needs intelligence to get our army off Manhattan intact."

"If there's much of an army left. The British may have trapped Putnam's division in the city." Stephen looked around the waterfront, frowning at five men of military age who had clustered outside the Cardinal and the Crow, sensing their swelling belligerence.

"We'll walk to Stamford or Norwalk. I'm sure we'll find a friendly vessel there." I started to trek uphill back towards the Post Road, my head down, learning to melt into my surroundings.

"Stubbornness does not become you, Nathan," he called, following my lead nevertheless. I thought to reprimand Stephen for forgetting my rank, but we were alone, and true friends – to the bitter end, if God willed.

"Captain Hale? What a pleasant surprise to see you," a female voice warbled, an undertone of sarcasm apparent.

"Good evening to you, Widow Appletree," I replied as evenly as I could manage. So much for incognito. "Is there a frolic in Greenwich this evening? On the Sabbath?" I couldn't help returning the sarcasm. The widow looked fetching in a lavender frock and matching cap, attire completely inappropriate for the Lord's Day.

"We're out for a stroll. To learn the news of the day. Most disappointing for the rebels, I understand," she answered.

"For *all* good citizens who pledged their loyalty to Congress." How quickly Darcy had forgotten the oath she must have sworn to remain in New London.

Ignoring my barb, Darcy tugged forward her companion, a pox-marked woman whose homely appearance was barely enhanced by a floral patterned mauve day-gown and scarlet apron. "Allow me to introduce my dear friend, Thankfull Wheaton."

"Wheaton?"

"If I remember correctly, you are acquainted with her husband, Caleb Wheaton," Darcy added.

I started at the name, but my first impulse was as a man not a patriot. What circumstances had driven a strapping youth like Caleb to take up with a hag like Thankfull?

"Captain, we should go," Stephen said, taking my arm. "We have an appointment to keep."

"My husband serves with Colonel Rogers of the *Queen's Rangers*," Thankfull said as she curtsied.

Caleb Wheaton…a Ranger now, like me. I had come to terms with Anne, at least in my own mind, accepted she would likely marry another officer of the Crown and raise a family either here or in England, but the news of Caleb unsettled me. He would remain a formidable foe until his dying breath. Rogers might add weight to his challenge - if the old gizzard could raise an entire company of hotheads, scoundrels and picaroons. The Colonel had shown his true colors, the opportunity to pillage and plunder overwhelming any loyalty he might have ever had to the Glorious Cause. The significance of my mission grew larger: the Continental Army must successfully move north to protect our faithful from men like him.

The throng from the tavern appeared to be snaking closer. Although eager for a fight, I swallowed my pride and bid farewell to the ladies.

***

Rose was in the kitchen, gutting a fish, when Anne informed her she would be supping alone. Would she risk her own life for liberty? The question had started as a spark, which she first thought to stamp out, but it had flickered and flared, refusing to die. She went upstairs, rummaged in her trunk, retrieved her gift from Nathaniel, and returned to the parlor to read. Engrossed in the verse of *Cato*, she did not hear the rap of the doorknocker.

"General Grant to see you," George announced.

"Me?" Anne stuttered in surprise, or fear, as she rose, gathering her wits in time to tuck the treasured book underneath the quilt covering the settee.

"Miss Wheaton, you are looking well," the General said as he crossed the threshold, not waiting for an invitation. Gold braid and a row of medals adorned his scarlet jacket. "It appears you have recovered from your ague."

"A trace still lingers." She struggled to find some reassuring feature of Grant's countenance, or his nocturnal visit.

"A claret might do you well then." Grant signaled to George who scampered off to the kitchen.

"Please sit down." Anne steered the general to a wing chair by the hearth, not the settee.

George returned with a bottle and two glasses, then retired. Grant poured the wine and raised his glass. "To King and country."

"To victory," she replied.

"I am pleased to report that New York is ours. With hardly a fight, as I expected."

"The rebels evacuated?"

"Ran would be more accurate. From what I heard, Washington foolishly threw himself into the fray above Kip's Bay but could not deter his troops, so intent were they on racing for the hills."

"Congratulations," she said, forcing a smile.

"I believe we had a wager." Grant sipped his wine and waited for her response. His upper lip sweat profusely. Was he nervous about courting me, Anne wondered.

"The rebellion is defeated then?" she asked.

"Not quite. General Howe did not press the attack."

"Again?"

Grant leaned in towards her as if they were co-conspirators. "You are quite forward, but, unfortunately, correct."

"If Washington lives to fight another day, then our wager is not yet resolved."

"No, I suppose you're right," he said, refilling his glass. "But we have yet to set the stakes."

"What have you in mind?" Anne placed her goblet down, better than spilling her wine when she heard Grant's terms.

"The winter calendar in New York will be full of festivities…" Grant paused, clearly choosing his next words with care. "…I desire your companionship."

"And if the rebels do put up a good fight?"

"I will stake your Father's business and declare him dressmaker and haberdasher to the nobility."

"Then we have a wager," Anne said, spitting into her palm and offering it to the General.

"I do admire your *pudeur*," he said, spitting as well. He clasped her hand, dwarfing it in his own.

"I apologize if I appear the coquette. That's not my intention." Although Grant's hand felt slippery as an eel, Anne did not release it. "One more condition," she said.

"Go on."

"If I win, you will step side and inform Major Whitcomb that he has your permission to court me."

"That is acceptable – as long as I too can add a condition."

Anne nodded. Fair is fair. And their hands were still locked.

"If you lose, you will provide your companionship in my bedchamber as well as in more public places." Grant laughed heartily as he broke free of her grip.

Color drained from Anne's cheeks. She might have just snatched defeat from the jaws of victory.

***

Monday dawned with the first crispness of autumn. Feeling fit at last, I bounded from my tent eager to return to Norwalk harbor. A squirrel darted from the bushes, looked my way, then took off down the road towards the waterfront. Perched in a walnut tree, an orange-breasted robin tweeted merrily away. Good omens, I thought.

For the first time since I left Coventry in January, I wore civilian clothes, my brown suit and a round-brimmed hat appropriate for a schoolmaster. My attire returned thoughts of my family on the farm, but the memories had flattened. Stephen rolled up my uniform and tucked it into his haversack, promising to wash it thoroughly for my return.

Although shrouded in fog, the silhouette of the *Schuyler*, a single-masted sloop, was clearly visible. Captain Charles Pond, a fellow Connecticut man and renown privateer, had reviewed my letter of marque from General Washington last night, agreeing to transport me across the Sound to Huntington and pick me up on the beach there next Monday morning. He and his crew were already on board when we arrived.

"Are you sure?" Stephen asked. "There's no shame in returning to the battlefield."

I glared in response, my thoughts already consumed by my chosen mission. I was a Ranger now, and proud of it. There would be no turning back.

"Your buckles?" Stephen pointed down at my shoes. "I have yet to encounter a schoolteacher who displays silver so ostentatiously."

"Ah, you're correct, friend. They do not comport with my calling." I knelt, removed the offending ornaments, and handed them over. "For your safekeeping."

"Godspeed," Stephen said, as he saluted. "I will be counting the hours until your safe return."

"Huzzah," I replied, clapping his shoulder, indulging in a long look at my boon companion. "A week's journey, that is all."

"Step lively, Hale," Captain Pond called. "The tide does not wait."

***

Forgetting all Puritan decorum, Anne splashed her spoon into her meat pie, splattering her frock with gravy at the rumble of the approaching coach on Monday afternoon. Her family was finally reunited! She swept Phineas, then Mother, into her arms before they even reached the front door. Her brother, just fifteen, was now as tall as she, and boasted a broader chest. As Anne feared, Mother had not fared well in Halifax, her complexion wrinkled as a prune, her weight light as a scarecrow.

Father, the last to step down, paid the coachman for the ride from the Staten Island ferry. Anne led the way inside, introducing George and Rose, requesting them to add places to the table. As the family settled, Father pulled Anne aside. "We'll talk about General Grant later," he said sternly.

"No need. We have reached an agreement. One that *you* will find most satisfactory, I believe," she replied, savoring the look of anticipation on Father's face. While she might have to suffer the General this winter, Father could not lose.

Ale, cider and conversation flowed freely around the table as the Wheatons shared stories. Caleb was missed, particularly by Phineas who expressed his own desire to enlist in the Queen's Rangers as soon as Major Rogers would take him. Anne could see that Father beamed at the prospect of his two sons serving the Crown, although his words echoed Mother in expressing consternation.

Sadly, she realized that her contribution had already faded from center stage. She was a woman, after all, expected now to marry, ideally a man of wealth and status, tend the home fires and produce heirs. No need to fret over military matters any longer.

After dinner, Father and Phineas went for a walk into the village, while Anne looked after Mother. "Where's Becky? Did she remain in Halifax?"

"A grizzly mauled poor Becky in April when she went to pick spring berries. The child never had a chance," Mother replied, shaking her head. "A most gruesome sight."

The "child" was older than me, Anne thought. "We should have freed her," she said quietly. "And paid her a decent wage to stay on."

"Why would we have done that?" Mother asked as she poked about the parlor. "And don't discuss the matter with Father. He was quite disappointed to lose his investment."

George came in, setting a low fire to take the chill from the room. Mother reclined on the settee, unfolding the quilt at its foot and wrapping it over her knees. Anne gasped as *Cato* fell to the floor.

Mother picked up the book, recognizing it immediately. "From Schoolmaster Hale?"

Anne nodded. "I couldn't part with it. The words are timeless. And books are so hard to come by."

"Balderdash. I am not too old to know that this drama is propaganda for the rebel cause."

"But…"

Mother cut her off. "You still carry a torch for the schoolmaster…even though he is a traitor to our King. And you were betrothed to another man. A nobleman at that."

"Your words are harsh."

"My heart has grown cold, my patience with this rebellion worn thin."

"It will be over soon - this rebellion," Anne said. "We have routed the Continental Army. Washington will shortly sue for peace."

"Not soon enough," Mother said, turning away, staring into the flames. "And then?"

"Then?"

"What will become of you? Father has told me you have rejected the overtures of General Grant. He is a bit old, but what other prospects do you have – a widow of modest means and a reputation as a tart."

"A tart?" The sobriquet, especially coming from Mother, buckled Anne's knees.

"Do you not think hints of your 'conjugation' with Mayor Matthews reached Halifax?" Mother furrowed her graying brows, as if puzzled, searching vainly for clues to her own maternal failings.

Anne never considered herself a loose woman, frisky perhaps, but not immoral; others, however, obviously held her in different regard. Damn them, she decided, thrusting her chest forward. "Do not believe all rumors, Mother."

"As you wish." Mother fiddled with the blanket on her lap.

"Father never mentioned such malicious gossip."

"He is too proud."

"And hopeful that my 'associations' will bring him good fortune."

"That too."

"I may have a new suitor: Major Richard Whitcomb – he served with Geoffrey in Scotland."

"Show me you have forgotten the schoolmaster." Mother handed the book to Anne. "Toss this rubbish in the flames."

Anne hesitated. *Cato* was much more than a token from her former schoolmaster. Its romantic notions of liberty, rebellion and sacrifice had comforted her on bleak nights in Boston and lonely days in the wilderness. Its verses provided hope for a better world. A clean slate for all men and women. Major Whitcomb...

The front door burst open; Father and Phineas bounded inside, laughing. Her younger brother humped over, exaggerating a grimace as he pantomimed dragging a heavy load. "Father told me how we made the rebel prisoners lug their cannons across the field," he said. "And aim them at their own forts."

But, did Father tell you about the mercenary Hessians slaughtering helpless men, Anne wondered. Or the profits he hopes to earn from prison ships anchored in the harbor?

"Anne, dear, I'm waiting," Mother said, pointing at the book still in Anne's hand.

Her fingers caressed the leather binding, worn soft by her fingers – and Nathan's. It was only a book, words she had already committed to memory. If the rebels could survive this summer, then she might find opportunity to further their cause.

Anne sailed the manuscript into the hearth, watching it sizzle. She silently recited Nathan's last words to her as the pages crumbled to ash - to happier climes and safer shores. Perhaps they would meet again.

***

Robert Rogers traipsed down the Flatbush Road on Monday evening, anxious to reach the Matthews' farmhouse before dark. The bulk of his command remained in the city, flushing out any remaining rebels, but he had moved out, along with a dozen of his men, when a messenger from Caleb arrived. Unfortunately, the damn boy could only provide secondhand details of Hale's travels. The captain, dressed as a schoolmaster, had slipped away, sailing from Norwalk harbor at dawn, destination unknown, but highly likely Long Island.

Rogers had too much at stake to leave spycatching to his young sergeant. Hale had to head this way; there was little information of value for him to glean out east. Rogers planned to lodge in Flatbush tonight, as he had several times in the past month, and then fan out with his men in the morning. He had included Obey, one of Caleb's recruits, in his dozen because he claimed knowledge of the back roads and Indian paths. Caleb would cross the Sound by whatever boat available and pick up the search from that end. Hale would be trapped between them.

Anne had set out a plentiful supper - meats, cheese, pudding and ale – and insisted that Rogers sleep in the keeping room, while his men camped outside. He had saved her life after all. When plates were cleared, Anne asked the valet to bring up an aged port from the cellar. Her father and strapping young brother, who looked like he would soon make a fine Ranger himself, joined them in the parlor, while her mother retired for the evening.

"What's the news from New York?" William Wheaton asked, pouring an ample dollop of the ruby treasure in all four glasses. "Is Washington's demise imminent?"

"Unavoidable, but not yet imminent, I'm afraid."

"Aren't Clinton's Regulars hot on the chase?" Wheaton asked.

"Most certainly. They forayed up to Harlem Heights yesterday, expecting an easy go of it, but the rebels put up quite the fight."

"Quite the fight?" Anne's face brightened at the news, most surprisingly Rogers thought, but she quickly rinsed her emotions.

"We lost almost a hundred men, another two hundred wounded, but the confrontation was even more dear for the rebels. Tom Knowlton, one of Washington's few experienced commanders, met his demise."

"How many rebels did we kill?" In his excitement, Phineas spilled his port all over his shirt, a waste of expensive liquor.

"Not quite as many," Rogers replied. "Washington's claiming victory. Rallying his troops. And the citizenry."

"And my son? May I inquire how Caleb is faring?" Wheaton's scowl reflected fatherly concern. Anne, however, appeared to have discovered the holy grail in her port glass, barely glancing up at the question.

"Caleb is a sound young man," Rogers replied, still studying Anne. She and her brother were close. Why were her ears not perked to the conversation? "He leads a mission for me in Connecticut right now, but should be crossing to Long Island in the morning."

"Connecticut?" Anne asked, emerging from her trance. "Caleb's wife resides in Greenwich."

"Wife?" Rogers asked angrily, the news taking him by surprise. Did the youth tarry for a conjugal visit? And let Hale escape?

"My brother's married?" Phineas corkscrewed his lips as if to spit out a vile tonic.

"His marriage was the price of our freedom," Anne said. "It is a long story best told another time."

"The woman's from a good Tory family, I understand," Wheaton added.

"I don't care if she's the King's daughter. We have a spy to catch," Rogers replied. *And my fortune may hinge on it.*

"A spy?" Phineas, at least, was all ears.

"Masquerading as a schoolmaster. With the powder scar of a soldier," Rogers said. "Shouldn't be too hard to find."

Anne stilled, her lips locked, fingers squeezing her glass till Rogers thought it might crack. He had spent his life leading men, reading their thoughts, assessing which path they might take in the heat of battle. Anne was as fearless as her brother, but more cunning. And she harbored a secret; he was sure of it. "The rebel's name is Hale. Captain Nathan Hale," he added, purposely feigning nonchalance.

He swore color drained from Anne's cheeks, but, before she could speak, Phineas shouted, "Hale was my schoolmaster in New London."

"The man was always spouting rebel dogma," Father said. "Good riddance to him."

"Schoolmaster Hale saved you from the mob, Father," Anne said, her tone as sharp as a cobbler's awl. "Or *you* might have swung from a tree limb."

"If *Captain* Hale is captured out of uniform behind our lines, he will hang, won't he?" Father asked, almost gleefully.

"Most certainly," Rogers said, standing.

"You are truly despicable, Father," Anne shouted as the dam guarding her emotions cracked, her secret now obvious. She stomped upstairs and slammed shut the door to her room.

"My apologies for upsetting your daughter," Rogers said to Wheaton. "Please excuse me. I must check on my men."

"It is I who should apologize. My daughter's emotions overwhelmed her good senses. As is wont to happen with women," Wheaton replied, handing him a fresh bottle of port. "Here, take this libation with you. To cheer your men."

Rogers walked out the front door, bottle in hand. While it was no crime to harbor feelings for a rebel, it might be treasonous to act on them. Would Anne defy her father, her brothers, and her King and try to warn Captain Hale?

He surveyed the farmhouse from the outside. Country homes often had hidey-holes and secret passages. The façade appeared straightforward, but the proportions appeared off in the rear. An unmarked bulge that he was certain was no chimney led from the attic to the scullery. He stepped inside the scullery, uncovering the hidden door and ladder in only a few seconds.

Anne Wheaton was a woman with balls, Princess had said. Rogers had risked his life to see her to safety, grown fond of her in a paternal way, but couldn't allow her to jeopardize his future. He replaced the camouflage around the secret door and went outside, finding an apple tree with a view of the scullery. He sat against the trunk, popped the cork from the port, and savored a long swig from the bottle. He'd sit here all night, if necessary.

***

Anne paced angrily in the cramped bedroom upstairs, regretting that she had turned over the master to her parents. Did she hate them? Tonight, perhaps, but she knew her anger would pass; however, she did accept that the fissures in their relationship were deepening, like ice-cracks on a frozen pond. At some point, the floes would separate and there would be no middle ground.

She listened as Father and Phineas clambered up the stairs. Doors shut, piss tinkled into chamber pots, beds creaked. After the house quieted, Anne lay down, still dressed, but could not sleep. She paced again, silently reciting *Cato* in a misguided effort to still her mind.

Nathaniel was out there, possibly close, stalked like a deer by the Rangers. Could she even find him, let alone save him?

Rogers had said that Nathan now masqueraded as a schoolteacher. As such, he would likely visit schools pretending to seek employment. There were only three, maybe four, schools of a reasonable size between Flatbush and Huntington. She could leave a message for him at each. The journey would take less than half a day on horseback, perhaps a full day on foot.

Fortunately, Anne had stored her writing implements in her room. She composed a two line story: his father was seriously ill, Nathan needed to return home at once. Signing as Marcia, Cato's daughter, she added the character's final prayer for her father: *let him but live, commit the rest to Heaven.* She copied the brief missive four times, tied each parchment with a red ribbon, and tucked them into her undergarments.

She also pinned a note to her parents' door, claiming that the Van Cliffs had relations in Oyster Bay that required a fitting for new clothes. She planned to return by suppertime.

The tall case clock tolled four times as Anne finished. She toed gingerly into the hall, minced towards the bookcase, and withdrew *The Iliad.* Why unlatch the secret passage? If she was truly traveling on farm matters, there was no need to slink down a ladder. She walked down the main staircase, listening for Rogers' snores from the keeping room, but heard only the scatter of a mouse. And the pounding of her heart.

A half-full glass of port remained on the parlor table. She slugged it in a single gulp, opened the front door and stepped into the pre-dawn darkness, the moon obscured by a bank of clouds. An owl hooted a long mournful tone. A goat bleated in reply. The stable was around back.

Anne tripped in the vegetable garden, sprawling into the turnip patch. She rose slowly to her knees, finding herself staring directly into the business end of Robert Rogers' pistol.

"And where are you off to at this wee hour, Miss Wheaton?" he asked, his words slightly off kilter. Spilled port blemished his fringed shirt, his pistol hand tremored.

Anne stood, equal in height to the Colonel. "No business of yours," she replied.

"Ah, but you are wrong. I am tasked with monitoring the countryside for subversive activities." Rogers' hand steadied, his tone hardened. "And General Howe has invested in me the authority to detain and interrogate anyone I deem suspicious."

"I'm off to Oyster Bay. To fit a gentleman and his wife for their holiday wardrobe."

"And the name of this gentleman?"

Anne bit her lip. "Nehemiah Longfellow," she said, slowly retrieving the name of Father's contact from deep in her memory, like a bucket from a well.

"I will send two of my men to accompany you then. For your safety, of course," Rogers said.

"There is no need. I can fend for myself, as you well know."

"There may be rebels on the road. They are dangerous sorts."

"Fine then. Can your men hold pins and needles while I take my measurements?"

"Miss Wheaton, do you take me for a durgen? You are about to embark on a foolhardy attempt to save your schoolmaster, Hale, from his appointment with the gallows."

"I resent that accusation."

"The ink smudge on your skirt is still wet. Whom have you been writing letters to this evening?"

Anne reflexively tucked her right hand into her pocket. Rogers' eyes gleamed hunter-sharp at her mistake.

"Can I search your person? Perhaps you have hidden correspondence in your buntlings?" He stepped closer, his breath reeking of alcohol.

"No, you certainly may not." Anne squirmed at her own stupidity: she could no more save Nathan than she could cure the pox.

"Then I suggest you return to your room. And perhaps we can forget this encounter ever happened. Or would you prefer to swing alongside your schoolmaster?"

Rogers had treated her most gently, waiting alone so there would be no other witnesses. She could not squander this generosity. "Thank you, sir," she said before turning back towards the house, careful not to trip again in the darkness.

"My debt to Princess is now paid in full," he called after her.

Anne took the stairs two at a time, stifling a scream of relief when she saw her note still pinned to her parents' door. She tore it down and retired to her room, offering a silent prayer for Nathan before drifting off to sleep.

***

A steady drizzle fell at dawn on Tuesday, pattering a mournful reveille on the window pane in my room at the Flying Cock in Huntington, a poor substitute for the bleat of a bugle and the rustle of men. I had lain awake most of the night, plotting and revising my itinerary for the week. As the dull light seeped through the shutters, I tossed off my night shirt and fumbled with my waistcoat, snagging a button, looking in vain for Asher to assist me.

I breakfasted alone at the far end of the common table in the Cock's public room, the buxom serving girl, Molly McDonald, bringing me porridge, boiled eggs, and a cup of tea, a beverage frowned upon in Continental Army camps. Three other travelers, none in uniform, dined as well, paying me no mind. I was unaccustomed to anonymity, restless in my silence.

When I stepped yesterday from the *Schuyler* onto the beach, I was nervous and clueless, half-expecting a drum and fife corps to greet me. I spent the day getting my bearings in town, making a few polite inquiries about the local schools, and testing my cover, which almost crumbled when I gasped at supper upon hearing that the Continental Army had been routed at Kip's Bay. Fortunately, my miscue went unnoticed amid the din in the tavern, which surprisingly appeared split between neutrals and royal supporters.

The war seemed more distant here, far from the burning issue it was in New England. While men had read the Declaration of Independence, the defeat of Washington and our army last month had doused any flame it might have sparked. Most expected the revolution to end before winter, and saw no reason to support a losing cause; it was bad for business and certainly not worth dying for. The words stung, but increased my resolve to prove them false. To that end, I edged closer to my fellow diners.

"I'm up to my snout in pork. I'll not buy any more," a prosperous merchant by the weave of his purple silk cravat announced, pounding his tankard on the table.

"What am I to do with my pigs then?" his companion, a homespun-attired farmer, asked, a pleading look souring his face.

"It's not my fault the redcoats have moved out. Marched off to New York City, I believe. Left only a token garrison here."

"I'll take a third off our usual price. My wife will toss me into the pigpen if I don't slaughter those animals."

"Half off."

"Done." The men shook hands on the deal and turned to peeling their eggs.

Molly appeared at my side with a fresh pot of tea, and a smile that hinted at possibilities beyond breakfast. "Schoolmaster Hale, will you be supping with us again tonight?"

I brushed off the tea, but returned the smile. "Yes, I believe I will," I replied, standing.

"Good luck in your inquiries today. St. Paul's School is just across the green, and the Three Sisters is a few miles up the Smithtown Road. John Warden is the director. A good man, he hoists a pint or two here on his travels."

"You're most helpful."

"Would you be in need of dinner? I can pack fresh bread and cheese for your journey."

"Thank you kindly. I will be in need of refreshment."

"I'll see that you're well-sated then." Molly appeared to give her hips an extra sashay as she returned to the kitchen. The flirtation, albeit brief, revived my spirits.

I hastened up to my room, tugged off my shoes, and removed the folded parchment containing my notes from yesterday. My Latin was a bit rusty, but passable. I dipped my quill and added a summary of the breakfast conversation I had just overheard. General Washington would want to learn of the concentration of British forces in New York, and the paucity of redcoats stationed here on the Island. I also added my thoughts on the "neutrals", whom I surmised were more likely "closet" rebels. They might provide clandestine support for our Cause and emerge into the sunlight should events swing our way on the battlefield.

The rain stopped by the time I finished writing, although the cloud cover didn't break. I nodded to Molly on the way out, as well as to her father, Tom, the Cock's proprietor.

St. Paul's was my first stop, the master, Reverend Tyndale, most welcoming, but far too garrulous. Two hours later, after grilling me on the works of Plato, Cicero, and Swift, he opined that no employment opportunity existed at present, but he would keep me in mind for the future. I tried to turn our closing conversation towards Payne's pamphlets and Hamilton's essays, but Tyndale would not take the bait.

Molly's dinner, packed neatly in a haversack, saved my life on the Smithtown Road. I stopped to eat on a bluff overlooking the Sound, gazing across the water at my beloved Connecticut. As I grappled with a jar of honey, an unexpected treat, two familiar faces walked towards me, pushing a cart flopping with freshly caught flounder. Flaming Tories from the Cardinal and Crow in Greenwich, they were, most fortunately, inebriated and not particularly interested in greeting a bystander. Regardless, I dropped my head, practically dipping my nose in Molly's honey pot, until they passed.

My visit to the Three Sisters' School proved well worth the walk. Determined to avoid another lengthy dialogue on the Greek classics, I shifted the discourse promptly to *Common Sense*, careful to disguise my true colors. Warden also feigned discretion, but could scarcely contain his enthusiasm for the Glorious Cause. After we sniffed each other out with a few more questions, like dogs in heat, I confirmed that we were of like mind. Warden promptly suggested a meeting with a gentleman from Setauket, a town further east, who might prove of assistance. We agreed to meet again on Saturday at the Flying Cock.

I arrived back at my lodgings just as the last pastels of daylight drained from the sky. After transcribing my notes and tucking them back into my shoe, feeling quite pleased with my day's work, I sauntered downstairs to supper. Molly set me a place in the corner, away from both the bar and her father, and brought a pitcher of ale.

"Your dinner was a godsend," I said before filling my tankard.

"Made the honey myself."

"I licked the pot clean." I struggled to fix my gaze on Molly's cherry lips, but my attention drifted south to savor the twin delights framed by her bodice.

She checked her father, occupied with two boisterous patrons. "There's plenty more where that came from."

Molly was true to her word. She slipped into my room after the Cock closed, wearing only a robe which crumpled to the floor in short order.

***

Rogers and his men bivouacked in the woods outside Oyster Bay on Tuesday night. He feared he had grown soft; the release of the Wheaton girl weighed heavily on his mind. He was certain she had written a warning to Hale, though he couldn't figure out how she had thought to deliver it.

Why had he not confiscated the incriminating documents? Anne would have been his pawn forever, a useful one at that since she appeared to be well-ensconced with the British high command. Alternatively, if Hale somehow slithered through his net, he would have at least had one traitor to turn in to General Howe. Now, all his eggs were in one basket. Hale.

A fast rider from Caleb's command arrived just as Rogers broke camp on Wednesday morning. The inexperienced sergeant had started his search far out in Oysterponds, too far out in Rogers' opinion, and worked his way west to Setauket before stopping for the night. Neither party had encountered Hale yet. He must be somewhere between them.

Rogers divvied up his men for the day's search. He would lead half along the North Shore, the route he expected Hale to take, while the other half would head south towards Hampstead. Obey, Caleb's recruit, would be his right hand. The Black had a sharp edge, a quality most desirable in a Ranger, as well as a local's knowledge of the ambages through the woods and marshes. Rogers knew he could ill afford any more sentimentality.

***

When I awoke at sunrise, Molly was gone, my fingertips musky-sweet with her scent. My jitters returned as I dressed but I calmed myself with the knowledge that I was one day closer to the end of my mission. However, I could not tarry here. I would need to follow the redcoats to New York if I hoped to provide General Washington any useful intelligence.

Last night's calisthenics stirred a powerful hunger in my belly. I was the first one down to breakfast, my full belongings in tow; Molly served me cold tea.

"I suppose you won't be supping with us tonight," she said, looking through me as if I was a window pane.

"No. My quest takes me…south to Hampstead," I said, careful to conceal my true destination.

"Got what you were looking for, did you?" she mumbled as her father approached, lingering closer than he had the day before.

I decided not to complain about the tea, gobbling down my meal. Needless to say, no offer of honey was forthcoming. I thought to tell Molly I planned to return on Saturday, but decided against it, saying only a brief farewell as I paid my reckoning and departed.

The morning was cloudless, though breezy, a harbinger of autumn. Horses, wagons and pushcarts, as well as a stream of pedestrians, bustled along the Shore Road, clogging the intersection at Horse Neck that led north to Queen's Village. I picked my way through the traffic and proceeded west, planning to reach Brooklyn before nightfall and either stay in a public house there or board a ferry across the river to New York.

"Hail, schoolmaster," a vaguely familiar voice startled me. The merchant with the purple cravat approached, likely returning from Oyster Bay, today sporting apricot neckwear.

"And to you, sir."

"Beware," he said, pulling me to the side of the road, "…there's Queen's Rangers ahead. Vile men, accosting proper Englishmen as if we were rabble."

"Most appreciated," I replied. "I will keep my guard."

"There's a cut through, just a ways on the left, marked with a cairn. It will help you shinny around them."

I found the short-cut without difficulty; the path, deserted, plunged down one grassy dune, up another, then descended again, safely out of sight of the main thoroughfare. Savoring the salty, sea air, I began to whistle a tune, *Yankee Doodle*, then quickly caught my error, changing to *The Captain's Tart*, a fond reminder of more carefree days.

In my reverie, I missed the footfalls of an advancing traveler, a squat Black, uniformed in a green jacket, bobbing through the thicket thirty yards downhill. It was Obey, Van Cliff's man, now wearing the colors of the Queen.

Obey looked up, recognized me, and reached for a pistol looped across his chest. Unarmed, as a schoolmaster would be, I tensed, hemmed in by hedges, my only option to launch my body at my enemy.

To my astonishment, Obey didn't draw his weapon. Rather, he pivoted, forged his way into the dense greenery, and busied his fingers with the fly on his breeches. With his broad back facing the trail, he appeared intent on relieving himself, not impeding my progress.

"Go on, Captain Hale," he said over his shoulder as he shook his pintle. "Do not traverse this way again. We are searching for a spy from Washington's army. Dressed as a schoolmaster."

Enough said. I broke into a trot, muttering a brief word of thanks as I passed.

"Our slate is wiped clean now, Captain," he called after me before proceeding in the other direction.

I didn't slow until I reached the outskirts of Oyster Bay. If the Queen's Rangers were here, then Caleb Wheaton was here as well, a confrontation I did not relish, especially on these terms. How did the British learn of my mission? Certainly not from Hempstead, Hull or Wright. Or Colonel Knowlton.

I mentally retraced my other contacts as I walked west. Were enemy spies imbedded in our Ranger camp or inside Mortier House? What about Lara the strumpet, Darby Appletree, Molly at the Flying Cock, Reverend Tyndale, John Warden? Any one of them might have surmised my true intentions and reported my presence.

It didn't matter, I realized. My cover was blown; and, I would have to pass through British lines in any direction I traveled. Since I had no safe houses to hide me, and I could not simply fly back to Harlem Heights like a bird, I might as well continue to gather intelligence and evaluate my options each day. But, no more visits to schoolhouses or dalliances with bar maids.

I reached Jamaica in late afternoon, supped there, and proceeded onward towards Brooklyn, traveling the very road the redcoats had trampled last month en route to the Guana Heights. No one appeared to be searching for a schoolmaster, or even looked too closely in my direction.

For an hour, I walked fifty yards behind a company of green-jacketed Hessians, belting out marching songs in their undecipherable tongue, before they turned off on a path that meandered into the brambles. A battalion of light infantry camped alongside the road in

Bedford. A battery of artillery, four and eight pounders, lined the shore near the ferry. I memorized locations, armaments, troop size, and regimental insignia to add to the journal secreted in my shoe.

A ferry to New York tethered idly at the landing, so I hopped aboard. The ferryman waited for three more passengers before pushing off. I kept my head down as he rowed across the East River, its waters still in the moonlight. I wondered where Asa, Captain Caulk and the *Laughing Lady* had sailed off to, but cut my reminiscences short.

We docked at Murray's Wharf in under an hour, just as the watchman lit the evening lanterns. Redcoats were thick along the quay that only weeks ago was home to the Continental Army. I found a ramshackle tippling house on a dead-end alleyway, updated my journal by candlelight in a nook in the public room, and shared a bed with a glazier from Gravesend who noted most proudly he was installing a picture window in General Howe's private yacht.

***

Rogers was apoplectic by the time he connected with Caleb in Huntington on Wednesday night. How had Hale slipped through their trap? The luscious hues of his dream plantation in Virginia were fast fading to ash. He ordered the Rangers, a score of men, to line up on the village green; the good citizens of the town scampered to the fringes at the sight of his motley crew, armed and menacing.

"You sniveling turds!" he bellowed, marching up the line and back again. "Did you bury your heads so far up your arses that you allowed a simple schoolmaster to stroll past you?"

"He never came our way, sir," Caleb answered. "I would have recognized him on sight."

"Well, he didn't come our way either. Perhaps he vanished like a pixie into the vapors?" Rogers did not lower the volume of his tone, or its venom. He made another inspection tour, looking each man in the eye, searching for a flinch or quiver, any tell of deceit. Nothing.

Obey anchored the end of the line, standing as ramrod straight as a dumpling of a man could, insouciantly so for a Black, Rogers thought. Needing to make an example of someone, he slammed his fist into Obey's gut, expecting to double him over, but the man weathered the blow with barely a shiver. "Where were you, boy? Caleb vouched you could fight like a caged grizzly."

"Fiercer than that, sir. But the schoolmaster did not cross my path."

Rogers read Obey's eyes, he was not lying. The colonel's fury ebbed, replaced by cold calculation. Perhaps Hale was here in Huntington - hiding, or ill, or burying his head beneath the skirts of some local tart.

"Wheaton, you accompany me," he said, pointing to the sign of the Flying Cock, a rooster soaring across a cerulean sky, fixed above its doorway. "The rest of you spread through town. Knock on every door. Poke in every barn and stable."

A comely wench, a pleasant distraction from the task at hand, greeted them at the Cock's door and led them to a table. Caleb stepped lively in her wake.

"Will you need a place to sleep this evening?" Molly asked.

"We're not here to sleep," Rogers replied. "We're here to find a rebel spy. Posing as a schoolmaster."

"Have you seen him?" Caleb asked.

"A rebel spy, you say?" Molly rolled her eyes.

"You wouldn't know it, of course," Caleb continued. "He has a most honest countenance, capable of charming even the most God-fearing woman."

"A powder scar on his cheek as well," Rogers added.

"I haven't seen such a nefarious person. But I'll be certain to look out for him," Molly replied, pivoting sharply towards the bar. "I'll fetch you a pitcher of our finest ale."

Caleb sat, appearing content to rest and ogle the wench, but Rogers remained standing. He surveyed the room, half-filled with peddlers and farmers. "We have work to do," he said, tugging his young sergeant to his feet. "Wander about. Engage in conversation. Turn up a lead."

After thirty minutes, the two Rangers returned to their table, no wiser for their efforts. The promised ale had not arrived, the voluptuous maid out of sight.

The publican, gray-haired but still boasting a full set of teeth, approached bearing a bottle of whiskey and two glasses. "Our finest scotch. At my expense," he said.

"To what do we owe this honor?" Rogers asked, filling his tumbler to the brim.

"You inquired about a schoolmaster. He lodged here the night before last. And the night before that. My daughter's memory was faulty. She's not been right since her mother passed last year."

"The schoolmaster might have bewitched her. As he did my sister," Caleb offered.

"Or perhaps he tickled her fancy," Rogers added. "Wouldn't want that rumor to circulate, would we?"

"No sir," McDonald replied, head down, apparently fixated on a roach wriggling across the floor.

"Did she happen to know where the schoolmaster was headed?" Rogers asked.

"He told her south, towards Hampstead."

Rogers sipped his whiskey, licked his lips, and smiled crookedly. "Your whiskey's quite fine, but your daughter's lying. There's little chance Hale would have gone south. No military value in that direction."

"That's what she said. I swear it."

"Well, you'd better jar her memory then." Rogers took a long swallow. "Or perhaps, you'd prefer me to do it."

"No need. I'll talk to Molly myself."

"While you're at it, ask her if Hale made any promise to return."

McDonald nodded and stepped away. Rogers refilled his glass, while Caleb nursed his liquor. The innkeeper returned shortly.

"Molly swears the spy said south. And the rake made no commitment to return," he said.

"That's all?" Rogers asked, imbibing again. "It appears your daughter was on quite familiar terms with the man."

"He visited St. Paul's school on Tuesday. And Three Sisters near Smithtown as well. John Warden, the proctor there, is not shy in his criticism of the Crown." McDonald spilled his words with increasing velocity.

"We'll pay both schools a visit tomorrow. Been quite some time since I've been in a classroom," Rogers chuckled.

"You'll be in need of supper and a bed then?" McDonald asked. Rogers answered with his most menacing glare. "On the house, of course," the innkeeper added.

Much to Caleb's obvious disappointment, Molly did not re-appear at supper. Or at breakfast on Thursday morning. Her father, however, handed them a basket of bread and cheese as they departed, as well as an offer to enjoy the hospitality of the Flying Cock again this evening.

Rogers sent Caleb and five men south, just in case Molly was telling the truth, while he marched with the remainder across the Huntington green to St. Paul's. Reverend Tyndale immediately confirmed his meeting with Hale, boasting that he had seen through his disguise and sent him on his way. The good reverend blanched, however, when Rogers inquired why he then had not reported Hale to the proper authorities. Rogers did not waste any more time on the old windbag, choosing to head east straightaway.

John Warden was teaching Latin to class of teenage boys when Rogers knocked on the schoolhouse door. "We need to talk about your interview with Nathaniel Hale," he demanded.

"The schoolmaster?" Warden asked.

"The captain in the Continental Army."

The principal's face soured, as if he was about to retch. "My class adjourns in two hours."

"Your class adjourns now." Rogers stepped into the room, lined with three neat rows of tables and benches. A British flag hung over the hearth. The boys swiveled to face him, mouths agape. "Out. All of you!" He pointed the way with his pistol. He didn't have to ask twice.

Rogers had Obey and two others join him in the now empty classroom, while the rest stood guard outside. "Sit down," he commanded Warden. "I want to hear all about your conversation with Hale. Don't skimp on the details."

"He only stayed an hour, maybe less."

"Go on."

"I sounded the man out on Socrates and mathematics, long division in particular, but he was lacking, so I sent him on his way."

"Hale was lacking? A Yale graduate?" Rogers sneered as he approached Warden, saw the man tremble, a trickle of sweat dripping into his eye.

"Yale? He did not mention…"

Rogers backhanded the schoolmaster across the face. "You're lying." He motioned to Obey. "Bind his hands and feet."

"What are you going to do to me?" Warden whimpered as Rogers' men carried out their orders, leaving him trussed like a hog. Obey held him upright.

Rogers knew from experience that the threat of torture often accomplished more than the act itself. Most men broke quickly; only a select few could withstand extended pain. Warden did not appear likely to fall into the latter camp. He withdrew his hunting knife from its scabbard and tapped it on the table. "We can start with your eyes? Two is a luxury, don't you think?"

"No!" Warden started to bawl.

"Well then, what more do you have to say?"

"We discussed *Common Sense*, Payne's pamphlet." Warden's breath was so ragged he could barely croak out the sentence.

Rogers nodded, allowing his silence to speak for itself. He rested his blade on Warden's cheek. The proctor shrunk away but Obey held him steady.

"Hale said he would be traveling west towards New York."

"As I expected," Rogers replied, keeping his blade in place. "Will Hale return here?"

Warden shook his head. Rogers slowly slit his cheek, drawing blood. "You're lying."

The blood, mingled with tears, trickled to Warden's lips, then down his jawline, but the proctor remained silent.

Rogers slit the other cheek. "Don't make me take your eye," he said.

"We arranged to meet on Saturday at noon. At the Flying Cock." Warden's head slumped.

Rogers motioned to Obey. The Black grabbed Warren's hair and yanked his head upright, holding it still. Rogers waved his blade back and forth in front of Warden's eyes. "Hale had better show up. For your sake."

***

Thursday dawned dry and hot, unseasonably so for late September. Thoughts of Molly, unsuitable for sharing, stirred me awake before the grim reality of my mission pushed them aside. I tucked my schoolmaster's jacket in my haversack, assuming instead the role of a prosperous Connecticut landowner, looking to establish contacts with New York's new masters.

The sun arched above the East River as I walked along the wharves towards the Battery. Stevedores, already shirtless and sweating, were unloading cattle and hogsheads from merchant vessels that must have lain at anchor in the Lower Bay waiting for the British occupation to begin. The pursuit of profit once again trumped the pursuit of liberty.

I made note of the merchantmen's names, as well as the particulars of the men-of-war that dotted the harbor, familiar hulks including the *Rose*, the *Phoenix*, the *Eagle* and the *Halifax*. A squadron of Regulars appeared to be constructing a new redoubt facing Governor's Island. The remainder of the shore defenses held no surprises, since my men had built many of them, although I swallowed hard seeing the ramparts manned by redcoats. The city streets bustled; nevertheless, I feared I would arouse suspicion if I tarried in any one spot too long.

By mid-day, I had wandered to the west side. Under the spire of Trinity Church, I purchased a pail of oysters, a workingman's meal, from a pushcart and dined standing among a handful of others.

"Hot, ain't it?" a red-haired carpenter, his apron flecked with sawdust, commented to no one in particular.

"Even hotter up on Harlem Heights," another aproned man replied. "I hear the rebels put up quite the fight. Sent the lobsterbacks scurrying for cover."

I wanted to shout a huzzah, but restrained my emotions, cracking open a shell and guzzling its slimy contents.

"Howe must be pissed as all hell," the red-head continued. "He's locked up New York tighter than a virgin's cunt."

"Sentries and roadblocks at every gate," his mate replied.

"How'd you get in?" the red-head stabbed his finger at me.

"By sail," I replied.

"Well done," the workingmen chorused.

I ordered an ale from the peddler, which he splashed into a battered leather cup which looked as if it had come over on the *Mayflower*. I pretended to admire the church as I sipped, hoping to engage in more conversation; however, a familiar figure, one I had hoped never to see again, slipped into the corner of my eye. Ian

Lawrie, the traitor, sauntered down Broadway, obviously inebriated, his arms linked to two harlots.

Pulling my tricorn down low over my forehead, I bustled across the boulevard. As Lawrie roared with laughter, the hairs on my neck bristled; but, fortuitously, he was enraptured of his companions, not me. I breathed easier as the threesome swung off for the Holy Ground.

Would Lawrie cross my path again? Or another man - or woman - who recognized me from my months camped in New York? I couldn't take the chance; I had to leave the city tonight. Returning to my crude lodging, I removed my shoe, transcribed my new notes, and drew a map highlighting the location of the new fortification.

As I stepped back into my shoe, I despaired at the absurdity of my spycraft. Did Washington not think British officers could read Latin? Would they not search my footwear if they suspected me of espionage? Yet, here I was – alone in enemy territory following instructions from my commander.

I must admit I was tempted to abort my mission and immediately rejoin the Rangers on Harlem Heights. To do so, I would have to negotiate the British pickets, who might be on the look-out for me; however, I knew the terrain well and could possibly slip around them. The prospect of stepping from the shadows, uniting with my friends and brothers, and again fighting like an honorable gentleman tipped the scale towards walking north. On the other hand, my scheduled meeting in Huntington on Saturday with John Warden and his "friend" from Setauket was a prodigious counterweight.

If I could lay the groundwork for a network of rebel supporters, our next agents might have a safe haven in enemy territory. Even more promising, I could establish a line of communication to Warden and other like-minded men already living in occupied territories; then General Washington would have a reliable and steady source of intelligence for the duration of the war. And our commander-in-chief would not have to ask another volunteer to serve undercover, a most disagreeable state that choked my windpipe with bile every waking minute.

I did not grapple long with my decision: the good of the Cause far outweighed my own safety. I had to return to Huntington even though Caleb Wheaton and the Queen's Rangers might be lying in wait. I packed my modest belongings, walked down to Murray's wharf and boarded the first ferry to Long Island.

***

Anne awoke each day with the dread she would learn that Nathaniel had been captured and executed. Thursday had been no different; she barely touched her breakfast porridge. She spent the morning in the yard, supervising the servants and slaves as they salted and barreled vegetables. After the mid-day meal, which she only nibbled, she toured the nearby woods with George to mark the trees that should be felled to stock the winter wood pile. While a drop in temperature would certainly be welcomed this afternoon, it would not be long before the cold brought privations to everyone on the farm.

Anne dismissed the help in late afternoon. As she splashed her face with a bucket of well water, she heard the unmistakable clop of an approaching horse. Her stomach clenched as she toweled off and walked around to the front of the house.

An elderly Black, impeccably attired in the Van Cliffs' green livery, braked his coach at the door. He stepped down, tipped his hat and handed her a sealed parchment. "I'm to await your response," he said, bowing deeply, his close-cropped hair streaked with silver.

Anne read quickly. It was an invitation to sup at the Van Cliffs this very evening, its urgency and mystery suggesting an ulterior purpose. Her neighbors were quite the intriguing couple – he a wealthy Dutchman and regular patron of the Holy Ground, and she an Asian. Anne wanted to accept immediately, but was hesitant to undertake any activity that might incite Colonel Rogers. He had treated her generously, far more so than her feeble attempt to warn Nathan had warranted. Would he consider a visit to the Van Cliffs a suspicious event? Hardly since they were staunch Tories. Would he even learn of it? Not likely either. She replaced her mob cap with a pink bonnet, informed Father of her destination, and climbed into the carriage.

The scene inside the Van Cliff manor confirmed Anne's intuition. The table was set just for three with everyday pewter, the shutters closed despite the heat. Peter paced back and forth in front of the hearth, which mercifully was not lit, while Elizabeth, wearing a high-necked day gown, carried a tray of meats and cheeses.

"Our apologies for such short notice, but we need your help," Peter said. "Our Sally is in grave danger."

Elizabeth nodded before hurrying out of the parlor.

"Go on," Anne said, now noticing the absence of the young kitchen maid.

"We have learned there is a bounty out on her head in Georgia colony." Peter pushed open a shutter with his one good hand and peered out. "Slavecatchers may turn up on our door any day now."

"So Obey informed you of the 'disposition' of the men from Virginia?"

"Yes. He said you were a true friend of the Cause."

"I am," Anne replied.

Elizabeth returned bearing a bottle of wine in each gloved hand. Peter took one of the bottles and filled three flagons. "Then will you help us spirit Sally to a safer place?"

"Will not the British garrison here in Flatbush protect Sally, as your property?" Anne asked.

"They may, or they may not," Peter replied. "General Grant has yet to declare, but I fear he is no friend of the Black."

"The general is not progressive in his thinking," Anne noted.

"Obey said you have contacts in Connecticut. The abolitionist movement has taken seed throughout New England, unlike here in New York."

"Yes, but I will need to secure the assistance of my brother, Caleb. It is his wife who resides in Connecticut."

"Obey has spoken highly of Caleb, but how will you reach him?" Peter asked, motioning for Anne to sit.

"He's campaigning here on Long Island. I expect he will turn up at the Matthews' shortly." Anne took her place at the table and sipped her claret.

"We may not have much time." Peter helped himself to a slice of beef.

"The farmhouse has a secret room. If you fear danger is imminent, bring Sally straightaway." The prospect of adventure spurred Anne's appetite. She ate heartily for the first time this week. As she stabbed the last morsel of cheese on her plate, she thought it time to ask the question lodged most deeply in her mind: "How did you two meet, and marry?"

The couple exchanged a glance, ripe with long-term companionship. Elizabeth cradled a fearsome dragon's head pipe, carved in intricate detail from meerschaum, a soft, white mineral found only on the Turkish coast. Anne recalled Father talk wistfully of the exotic meerschaum pipes with several patrons at Wheatons, but had never actually seen one before.

Peter spoke first. "I was a captain for the Dutch West India company and sailed to Africa several times in the triangle trade. Although I profited handsomely, I also saw the evils of slavery first hand and recognized how grievously I had sinned."

"And I was a slave…," Elizabeth said, speaking up for the first time. She tooted earnestly on her pipe, filling the room with a pleasant, floral aroma. It was unheard of for an Englishwoman to smoke but more common among the Dutch. "…snatched by pirates from my village on the China coast when I was twelve and brought to Africa. Peter bought me at auction in Whydah."

Elizabeth's voice sounded deeper than her slight frame suggested, more alto than soprano, Anne thought. Years of pipe-smoking must have taken their toll on her vocal chords.

"We are not married in the eyes of the church," Peter added quickly. "I pray that does not offend you."

"No offense taken," Anne said. "You're doing the Lord's work."

Riding home in the coach, Anne began to formulate a plan. Darcy might prove more helpful than Thankfull. Rogers had contacts as far north as Canada. While she could not save Nathan, she vowed to do her part to fight for freedom, one runaway slave at a time.

Smoke-smell drifted down the Flatbush Road. What was burning? Not the farmhouse, she saw as the coach approached. She asked the driver to take them up to the Heights. Flames danced from rooftops across the river, lighting the city skyline in a macabre glow. Had the rebels torched New York?

***

On Friday morning, I awoke to the sight of a smoldering city. From my window at the Cornell House just outside Brooklyn village, I saw charred mansions, tottering taverns and roofless tenements. Redcoats and citizens lined Broad Street, toting buckets of water up from the river. Two bodies swung from a tree on the bank, ropes tight upon their necks. Suspected arsonists, I thought, likely rebels acting on their own, since Washington had strongly vetoed the destruction of New York.

The Samaritan in me wanted to stay and fight the fire, but I had to begin my journey to Huntington. I decided to explore the southern shore of Long Island today and lodge in Hampstead tonight, avoiding the Shore Road and hopefully the Queen's Rangers, as well as the temptation of another liaison with Molly. I would head north to Huntington on Saturday morning for my noon rendezvous with John Warden. After our dinner, I planned to walk east, stopping overnight in Suffolk, and then loop to Oysterponds on Sunday to complete my mission. In seventy-two hours, I would be back on the beach in Huntington, awaiting the *Schuyler* and my sail to safety.

***

Rogers supped alone at a table in the back of the Flying Cock on Friday evening, content that his trap was set. The tavern was crowded, buzzing with cheerful, if not besotted, voices. Pipe smoke clouded the air. He surveyed the patrons, looking for any outward sign or sound of rebel sympathies, but saw none.

He suspected Hale would return tonight, rather than tomorrow, to see Molly if nothing else. Tom McDonald wanted to send his daughter abroad to relations in Jericho, but he had ordered her to stay. Nothing like a honey pot to attract - and distract - an adventurous young man.

Caleb had pleaded to be present at the capture, but Rogers couldn't risk Hale recognizing his former pupil, so he sent the sergeant, Obey and three others east on a phantom mission. The rest of his men were deployed along the roads from Oyster Bay and Hampstead. They were to dress as civilians, identify Hale, the tall schoolmaster with the powder scar on his cheek, and follow him. Unless he turned and ran, they were not to confront or detain him.

Rogers wanted the prize all to himself. He gnawed the meat off a chicken bone and sipped his ale, his eyes glazed with dreams of glory.

***

453

The southern coast of Long Island was desolate. All I saw were endless beaches, low-slung barrier islands, dunes as tall as barns, and the frothy waves of the Atlantic Ocean curling to shore. The sea breeze kept the temperature comfortable, enabling me to walk briskly with little fatigue. I encountered no military presence unless I included a solitary redcoat and his girl enjoying a picnic in the sand. The image sent my thoughts drifting to the women who had touched my life in the past year: Prudence's bright smile and tragic death, Anne's intellectual fierceness albeit misguided, Princess' exotic beauty and savagery, and finally Molly's pillowy bosom and lusty riposte.

I strolled into Hampstead shortly after mid-day, the fifteen-mile journey hardly wearing the tread in my leather soles. Stopping in a public house, one of only two customers early on this weekday afternoon, I refilled my canteen with ale and scarfed down a dinner of freshly baked bread and ham. Had I known the shore would be deserted all along? Had I welcomed a day free of stress after my close calls in New York? Feeling guilty, and perhaps anticipating a reunion with Molly – against my better judgment - I decided to press on to Huntington, another twenty miles, before dark.

Shadows lengthened as I peregrinated through Oyster Bay and turned right along the Shore Road towards my final destination. I sensed a presence over my shoulder, but dismissed it to fatigue. Or paranoia – the loneliness of my mission striking my resolve like axe blows on a tree trunk. Sooner or later the tree would have to fall.

The blue sign of the Flying Cock was a welcome sight, promising relief for my thirst, hunger, and weary feet. Huntington, at last, I thought, almost home. Captain Pond and the *Schuyler* were within reach.

Molly was tending to a table of powder-wigged merchants when I arrived. I waited at the door, somewhat nervous about her reaction after I had left without much explanation. On the other hand, I had rarely failed to woo the fairer sex with soft words and my winsome smile.

I nodded to Molly as she returned to the bar, a tray of empties in hand. Her first glance at me was encouraging, but she quickly swiped it clean. Her shoe must have caught an errant plank because she stumbled, her flagons crashing to the floor. I raced to help her retrieve them, bending low while other customers appeared to shrink away.

"We have no rooms here tonight. You should leave." Kneeling, she spoke in an urgent, hushed tone.

"No room here? Even for a lonely friend?"

"At once," she added as she stood.

"Schoolmaster Hale, how good of you to return to our humble establishment," Molly's father's voice boomed as he hastened to my side. He pushed his daughter towards the bar with one hand, and steered me from her with the other. "Right this way, sir."

I was quite surprised to be welcomed so heartily, and stalled to get my bearings. "But, Molly said…"

"Nonsense, our Royal Suite was just vacated. It is available for your respite." Tom McDonald pointed towards an empty table in the rear, positioning himself between me and the front door. "After you have dined, of course."

I would have had to force the publican aside to reject his generous offer. Before I even settled in my seat, he brought over a pitcher of ale and a board of cheese. Famished, I ate heartily. And drank with just as much gusto. Before I finished the cheese, McDonald arrived bearing a plate crammed with a shank of lamb, carrots and boiled potatoes, and a second pot of ale. My head down, buried in my supper, I barely heard the scrape of the chair next to me.

"Mind if I join you?" A gravelly voice, tinged with a northern New England accent, asked. A freshly shaven man, dressed in a black frock coat and tricorn, stood patiently waiting for my reply.

"Yes, of course, sit down, sir." I replied, almost embarrassed at the riches on my plate.

"Robert Jones," he said, extending his hand. "From New Hampshire originally."

"Nathaniel Hale," I replied. "A Connecticut man." Since Tories still regularly traveled from my home state to Long Island, I saw little harm in this revelation.

McDonald rushed over with a second platter of food and a bottle of whiskey, leading me to surmise that Mr. Jones was a regular patron. "I'm here to trade furs. You?" Jones asked.

I hesitated, my guard up at the question. "I'm a schoolmaster. In search of a new school."

Mr. Jones poured two tumblers of whiskey. "To new opportunities," he toasted.

I raised my glass to second his toast. The whiskey went down smoothly, clearly a beverage of the first rank. As we ate, Jones regaled me with tales of life in the wilderness, trapping beavers and evading Indians. I was enthralled, his stories sounded so like the ones I had read in my youth. I tossed down a second round of the fine scotch.

"God save the king!" "Hang the rebel traitors!" Rum-sodden cheers emanated from the front of the Cock.

Mr. Jones belched. "Tory bastards. Damn them all to hell," he swore just loud enough for me to hear. I was flabbergasted but held my own tongue in check.

McDonald cleared our plates himself, set a slice of apple pie before each of us, and poured us each a tumbler of ruby Madeira.

Jones appeared to wait for the innkeeper to step out of listening range. He looked circumspectly around the room; no one appeared to pay us any mind. "To Mr. Hancock and his Congress in Philadelphia," he offered in a hushed tone.

A fellow rebel, cloaked in disguise just like me. "To Congress and the Glorious Cause," I replied, sipping my Madeira.

"I suspected you were a friend all along," Mr. Jones said with a wink. "Are you truly a bum-brusher?"

"I was once, but not any longer. I'm here to gather intelligence for General Washington." I knew I shouldn't boast but couldn't help revealing myself to my new friend. As a trader who traveled frequently, he might prove an invaluable asset to our intelligence efforts.

"I knew it," Mr. Jones replied, pouring himself a second port.

I held up my hand to decline. "I've had enough for tonight. Perhaps we could meet again in the morning? To discuss future opportunities."

"Excellent idea. At seven promptly?"

"Seven it is." I stood, more wobbly than I expected, and made my way upstairs. The door to the Royal Suite was ajar. I stumbled inside, hoping to find Molly waiting. But I was alone.

***

Rogers waited until Hale's shoes vanished from sight before rising from his seat. The naive captain had proven easier to play than a penny whistle.

"Well done," he said to Tom McDonald, alone washing down the bar. "And keep your daughter under lock and key. Or you'll both face the wrath of the Crown."

"No worries, sir. I've shackled Molly to my bedpost."

His Rangers, several now wearing their green jackets, waited outside. He positioned them in a cordon around the tavern. Hale would not be leaving tonight, or receiving any visitors. His days as a free man were over.

***

I slept well, the best night's rest I had enjoyed on Long Island. The long walk, buttery liquor, and camaraderie of my new friend had obviously agreed with me. Nevertheless, the dread of discovery returned as soon as I rolled over, the risk of capture pressing like an anvil on my chest. My right index finger involuntarily rubbed the hairy mole of my neck, but I did not allow it to linger there.

Today was the day to consider success, not failure. If my meetings with Robert Jones and John Warden went well, I could set the foundation for an intelligence network that might be able to alter the tide of the war. And Warden had mentioned a man from Setauket; he might be the third wheel on our cart. Perhaps Jones also had like-minded friends who could aid the Cause.

I was the first to breakfast, sunlight streaming through the open door. Disappointingly, Molly was not in sight, although her father greeted me with a hearty welcome. He guided me to a table in the rear and placed a current broadsheet for my perusal. It had news of the British victory at Kip's Bay but little else of interest. I wondered about the fire that had raged in New York. McDonald brought a plate of eggs and a cup of tea.

The tall case clock chimed seven times. Robert Jones was running late. I finished my meal while I scanned the gazette again, searching for an advertisement for furs. Surely Jones would want to trumpet his wares, but I could find no such notice.

"Schoolmaster Hale," Jones' voice boomed. "A good morning to you."

"And to you sir," I replied, folding the newspaper.

To my surprise, Jones was accompanied by two men, younger and rough-looking. While they carried no pistols, I noticed a knife, a menacing hunter's weapon, in the belt of the shorter man. A tool of his trade, no doubt, but generally not displayed at breakfast in a respectable public house. McDonald approached empty-handed, as if he was unsure if the men were here to dine.

"What are you staring at, man?" Jones bellowed belligerently. "Why have you not brought our meal?"

"Yes, sir. Of course, sir," The innkeeper hurried away.

"My kinsman, Walter and Tremont, are interested in your story, Hale. Thought you wouldn't mind sharing it," Jones said.

"I'm a schoolmaster, university trained, in search of a school," I replied, feeling extremely uncomfortable at being thrust into the center of the ring so abruptly.

"School you say?" the short man laughed. "Haven't seen the inside of one of them since I was a tyke."

McDonald arrived with a heaping tray of breakfast. Jones' relations shoveled food into their mouths as if they hadn't eaten in a week, while Jones himself ate at a more refined pace. I was growing more uncomfortable by the second, but didn't want to offend Jones whom I still hoped would anchor my future intelligence efforts.

When his kinsman had devoured every last scrap, Jones turned to me. "Now, Hale, enough balderdash. What is the true nature of your business?"

"I'm a master of school." I mixed up the words in my agitation. Warning bells clanged loudly in my brain.

"Did you not tell me last night that you were here to gather intelligence for General Washington?" Jones pressed. "Was that a falsehood? A scoundrel's boast to lure me into a traitorous admission?"

"No. I mean yes. I mean no. I'm no scoundrel." I was riding a runaway filly and couldn't tug the reins with enough force to slow her down.

"Which is it, man?"

"I'm a simple schoolmaster, sir. That is all," I replied, tapping my right shoe on the floor to pace my breathing. My notes and maps were hidden in that shoe, I realized. Panic flooded my brain, but I fought it back down.

"I must have been mistaken last night. Too much whiskey perhaps," Jones said, standing, shaking his head. He motioned his kin to rise. "We should leave the schoolmaster to his breakfast."

Chairs scraped. Dogs barked in the yard. A goat bleated. I saw my dream of an intelligence coup fading to dust, men laughing at my inept recruiting efforts. "Wait. Please sit," I heard myself saying. "We have more to discuss."

"Seize him!" Jones pointed his spoon at my chest. "He's a traitor to the King!"

"What?" I stammered.

Jones' kinsmen lunged for my arms. I struggled but couldn't break free. The hunting knife tickled my throat. I went limp in my captors' grasp.

"I am Lieutenant Colonel Robert Rogers of the Queen's Rangers and you are under arrest for espionage."

I was speechless. Robert Rogers? The hero of the Seven Years' War? I had seen Rogers in camp outside Boston. The vibrant man accusing me looked nothing like that haggard old crone.

"Take him away, boys," Rogers said. His men lugged me out the front door. Molly peeked out of the back room, tears in her eyes.

A crowd now waited; a fisherman spit in my face; a washerwoman tossed a horse turd in my direction, but fortunately her aim was faulty.

Obey stood alongside several other Rangers who gaped at me as if I was a two-headed dwarf. The Black kept his proud gaze steady although I swore he blinked as I was dragged past. I had enough of my wits not to acknowledge him and add his death warrant to my own.

"I'm a schoolmaster," I shouted, deflecting attention. "This is all a misunderstanding."

"Captain Hale." Caleb Wheaton stepped from behind Obey, strutting towards me in his green jacket. "I do believe you are out of uniform."

***

Rogers led the procession down to the waterfront, commandeering the first vessel he saw in the name of the King. He would take Hale to New York by sail, much less chance of escape or rescue than an overland journey. Caleb, although he had disobeyed orders and returned too soon, would lead the guard detail; no man in his troop would watch the prisoner more closely.

Before Hale was tossed aboard, Rogers ordered him searched, confident he would find incriminating evidence. Hale was too young and green not to have made a mistake. And Washington had no spycraft in his arsenal, at least according to the British spies in the Continental Army camp.

Caleb shoved Hale roughly as he rifled his pockets. Rogers whacked his young sergeant on the side of the head with the flat of his palm. "That is not how you treat an officer," he shouted. "Captain Hale deserves respect. He serves his cause to the best of his ability."

Caleb pursed his lips, seething, but said nothing. His search turned up only a silver watch and a handful of coins.

"His shoes. Check inside his shoes," Rogers ordered as he stuffed the loot in his sack. Hale flinched.

Caleb steered the prisoner towards a flat rock and sat him down, pulling off first his left shoe, then his right. Two folded parchments fluttered to the ground.

"Ah, what do we have here?" Rogers could barely contain his satisfaction.

Caleb unraveled the first, and scanned it. "It's written in Latin. Not my strong suit, but I can see a list of several our regiments deployed on the Guana Heights." He picked up the second sheet. "And this one's a map. Pinpointing the location of our new battery inside New York." He handed both to Rogers, feigning solemnity.

Rogers was too pleased by the discovery to smack the insolent sergeant again. He could now deliver the prisoner and the evidence to General Howe tied neatly with a red ribbon. Hale's fate was sealed.

It was a half day's sail to New York, the swirling waters of Hell Gate at the head of the East River posing the only danger. Hale was subdued, his head only lifting when they passed a merchant brig, the Whitby, just converted into a floating prison, anchored in Wallabout Bay. Moans of the sick and wounded, pleas for help, and a ripe array of curses echoed from its hold. General Howe had acted smartly to position the vessel out of sight, sound and smell of the city.

Captain Hale was lucky, Rogers thought. His end would be quicker and more merciful than the protracted torture of his fellow rebels captured on Long Island.

Coming into view around a bend in the river, New York still smoked from the fire which had been extinguished less than twenty-four hours ago. Rogers ordered the crew to bypass the city proper and dock at the Beekman estate, Howe's country retreat and part-time headquarters, several miles north. The manor, located atop Mount Pleasant, was, until last month, the summer home of James Beekman, a rebel supporter and wealthy dry goods merchant.

They tied up next to the *Britannia* where a quartet of musicians unpacked their instruments on deck. As Rogers marched Hale, guarded by Caleb and three others, up the dock, they passed Betsey Loring, outfitted in a scarlet gown, leading three elegantly dressed women in the opposite direction.

The general was occupied when the Rangers and their prisoner arrived at the main house, a rather mundane Dutch-gabled cottage. They waited outside the rear stoop for almost an hour before being summoned. Four Regulars assumed Hale's escort, dismissing the Rangers.

Rogers followed them inside, awed by the elaborate furnishings, far more elegant than the exterior of the home would suggest. The procession stopped in the study, a mahogany paneled room with a view of the river outside its stained glass window. The fireplace was framed with Delph tiles depicting Biblical scenes. Howe sat behind a black-lacquered desk, writing furiously with a gold-plumed quill. Rogers forced his way forward.

"A rebel spy, Captain Nathaniel Hale, apprehended in Huntington this morning," he proudly announced.

"A most serious charge," Howe said, barely looking up. "What say you Hale? Do you deny the accusation?"

"I'm a schoolmaster, sir. I was in Huntington in search of a new position," Hale replied.

Rogers handed the general two parchments. "We found these in Hale's shoe."

Howe put aside his own papers and read Hale's notes. "It appears you were in New York on Thursday when several despicable rebels set fire to the city."

Hale seemed genuinely astonished. "I had no involvement whatsoever in that heinous act, if in fact it occurred as you claim," he declared.

"What was a supposed schoolteacher doing in the city then? Drawing maps of our defenses as well?" Howe laid the notes on his desk and stood, resting his elbow on a black marble mantel. "Do you take me for a fool?"

"No sir," Hale replied.

"Are you guilty of arson or espionage then?" Howe asked. "Your fate will be identical either way."

Hale breathed deeply and stood as erect as his bonds would allow. "Espionage, sir. I acted directly under the orders of my commander-in-chief, General George Washington."

"Well said, young man," Howe appeared to focus on Hale for this first time. "Under the rules of war, I pronounce a sentence of death by hanging to be carried out at dawn tomorrow."

Hale's shoulders sagged but he held his head high. "I respectfully request a firing squad. It is an end more fitting an officer and   gentleman."

"I'm sorry, Captain Hale, but the gallows is the only fitting end for a spy," Howe replied as the clock struck four. "I must be going," he said. "God be with you, Captain."

Rogers lingered as Hale was led away. "I deployed twenty of my men on Long Island for a week to snare Captain Hale," he said.

"Well done, Colonel," Howe said, striding purposely towards the door. Rogers followed.

"My expenses, sir, were quite high."

"Yes, submit a report to the exchequer and we will reimburse you in due time."

"I was hoping for an additional stipend…" Rogers voice trailed off as Howe kept walking. His request must have struck a nerve because Howe wheeled, his face flushed.

"Wars are expensive, man. And you expect an additional stipend? For doing your duty?

"Above and beyond my duty, I believe."

"Go and plunder Westchester, then. Make life miserable for any man there who supports the rebels." Howe clapped Rogers on the shoulder. "Now, I truly must depart. Mrs. Loring is waiting aboard the *Britannia*. A splendid evening for our first soiree of the season, don't you think?"

Where is my invitation, Rogers thought? Am I not a senior officer of the Crown? He palmed a white porcelain statuette of a dove, stashing it in his pocket as he followed Howe out into the foyer. Caleb waited in the garden.

***

I forced the wobble from my knees as a cordon of four Regulars marched me outside. Colonel Rogers and Caleb Wheaton stopped mid-conversation, according me the deference reserved for a dead man walking. They were the victors, for now at least, but, in perhaps the only vanity left to me, I refused to acknowledge them. I did reflect briefly on Anne. What fight would she fight? Despite her protestations of loyalty to the Crown, I had no doubt liberty was her passion.

We marched between ruler-straight rows of peach and apricot trees en route to the greenhouse, an octagonal structure with a glass dome, reminding me of a pagoda I had seen glazed on a Wedgewood plate displayed in the window of Mr. Beekman's finery shop in New York. While I knew the penalty for espionage was death, I did not actually comprehend that I could be executed until the general had announced my sentence. I gagged as the guards locked the door and assumed their positions outside.

Gathering my wits, I stalked about my prison, noting a knee-high shovel in one corner, an empty clay vessel large enough to hide a hound in another, and an empty piss-pot in a third. There was a chair and desk as well, but it was devoid of any quills, keys, knives or other instruments which might further my escape. A half-dozen lemon trees and assorted florals produced a quite pleasant aroma, certainly far better surroundings than a dank, dark dungeon. Unfortunately, I was not scheduled to reside here long.

As twilight settled, quite likely my final sunset, the greenhouse cooled down from the day's heat. An open window would have been helpful, but I understood that was not to be. Shortly thereafter, a sergeant entered bearing a tray with a bowl of stew, a spoon, and a solitary candle.

"May I request a bible and writing implements?" I asked.

"I will inquire of my superiors, Captain Hale," he replied before exiting.

Although I had little appetite, I sat down to my supper in the flickering candlelight. My death would not be on the battlefield but on the gallows, as foretold by the mole on my neck after all. I prayed my father and brothers would understand that I had served the Glorious Cause nobly, and would not be shamed by the nature of my demise.

A rustle outside, down by the river, startled me. Colonel Knowlton and the Rangers? Coming to my rescue? I bolted to the window but could see nothing outside the ring of lanterns surrounding the greenhouse. I would need a weapon. The shovel? Before I could find it, the door opened and the sergeant returned, emptyhanded.

"Do not get your hopes up Captain. It is only General Howe and his mistress returning from their evening festivities," he said. "They can be quite boisterous on occasion."

I struggled to keep my composure. "My writing implements?"

"Sorry, sir. The Provost Marshal denied your request."

"Not even a bible?"

The sergeant shook his head. "Cunningham's not a military man. He doesn't have much respect for rebels, even a captain such as yourself."

I wanted to be angry at Cunningham's insolence, but found I had little energy.

"I'll be back at sunrise, sir," the sergeant said as he left and bolted the door.

The moon, a crescent, was high in the sky, easily visible through the dome. I vowed to stay awake all night long. I paced for a good hour, maybe two, desperately trying to devise an escape plan, but I could not conceive one, short of throwing myself at my guards when they came for me at dawn. Then I would likely be beaten and shackled in irons, and still hung. An even more dishonorable death.

Sitting, I turned my mind to *Cato*. The Roman senator had chosen suicide rather than succumb to Caesar. I could also choose to die bravely, if not as stoically. I began to plan my final words on this earth, words that might bring comfort to my family and hope to my fellow rebels.

"What pity is it that we can die but once to serve our country!"

Cato's farewell infused me with purpose. I decided to revise it, however, since I did not seek anyone's pity. The British officers who would be present at my execution would surely recognize the reference and understand that I too was a gentleman who sacrificed his life in opposition to a tyrant. I prayed my final words would resonate loud and long enough to reach my father's ears. After rehearsing my parting soliloquy many times, recognizing that I would have to deliver it under extreme duress, I allowed myself to lie down and doze.

A knock on my door awoke me. The sun was already up. An officer, a fellow captain, entered my cell. I scrambled to my feet, brushing off my shirt and trousers. Had my execution been postponed?

"I understand Cunningham, Howe's devil-catcher, has treated you most uncivilly, Captain Hale," John Montresor said.

"I have been denied the most basic elements accorded a condemned man," I replied, harboring a breath of hope that Montresor brought news that my execution had been stayed.

"Cunningham appears delayed on other matters," he said. "I will provide to your spiritual needs in my quarters, provided you swear on your honor that you will attempt no escape."

"I swear it," I replied. My fate remained unchanged.

Since we were surrounded by guards, Montresor allowed me to walk with my hands unbound. He inquired as to my family and my education, noting the quality of my Latin. I took pride in his compliment albeit ruefully since my Latin had ultimately condemned me.

I gazed northward. We were close enough to the front lines that my rescue was not out of the question. Where was Stephen this morning? Little John? William Hull? My brothers? My sister Rose whose stitching I would wear to the gallows? General Washington? I served in my own way for them all, and prayed they would not forget me.

Montresor's lodging, a canvas marquee battered by years of service, overlooked the river. After setting up a chair and field desk in the sunshine, and laying out Bible, quill, ink and paper as well, he retired inside. My guards staked out a perimeter, but at sufficient distance to allow me some privacy.

I didn't want to write. I wanted to run, jump, wrestle, laugh, love, cry. But I forced my hand to set down my thoughts, first to Colonel Knowlton, informing him that I had completed my mission and urging him to carry on to victory, and then to my brother, Enoch.

I did not hear Captain Montresor approach. William Cunningham waited alongside my guards, chafing like a dog on a leash.

"It's time," Montresor said, reaching for my letters.

***

Rogers followed the execution procession down the winding road from the Beekman estate to the Artillery Park. Hale, his posture defiantly upright, was seated on a bed of hay in the rear of a farmer's cart, pulled at a walking pace by a coffee-colored draft horse, and surrounded by a squadron of redcoats. In London, he had seen such processions from the Tower to Tyburn, the streets lined with spectators out for an afternoon's entertainment, but the way today was largely empty. It was the Sabbath after all.

Rogers had sent the bulk of his regiment up to White Plains but had waited outside the greenhouse since dawn, along with Caleb Wheaton. When Hale was first led to Captain Montresor's tent they thought he might have received a last minute pardon, but William Cunningham's appearance assured him that Hale would shortly meet his Maker. The Devil-catcher was accompanied by a deputy, whom Caleb recognized as Sam Hale, Nathan's cousin.

Rogers sympathized for the condemned man, seeing two of his longstanding antagonists present at his demise. But, Hale, of course, did not have much time left for contemplation if, in fact, he "saw" anything at all at this point.

They reached the park in less than an hour. Cunningham pointed out a tree, an oak; one of the redcoats tossed a rope over a stout limb hovering fifteen feet or so off the ground and fixed a noose. An efficient hangman could snap his victim's neck at the first drop, while a bumbler could leave his victim sputtering and shitting for several minutes. Little wonder why Cunningham had moved the gruesome spectacle from the Beekman grounds; Howe would not have wanted his beloved mistress to watch.

Caleb followed the wagon as it approached the makeshift gallows. The boy's first execution, Rogers thought, a necessary passage in the life of a ranger.

"Don't get too close," he shouted.

Rogers himself lingered on the periphery, keeping one eye on the hills to the north, and one hand on his pistol. With Tom Knowlton dead and the Continentals trapped atop Harlem Heights, George Washington was likely plotting his own escape rather than the rescue of his spy, but Rogers had learned in the wilderness never to underestimate a cornered enemy.

He shuffled his feet impatiently, anxious to be off to Westchester. There was silver to be earned, and perhaps a haughty Virginian to be captured, he thought rather pleasantly.

When the wagon was in position, Hale's guards stood him up directly underneath the noose. Cunningham appeared anxious to proceed, there was no chaplain to administer a final absolution, but Sam Hale shouted to give his cousin a last word.

Captain Hale spoke, several men up front respectfully nodded, but Rogers could not hear the oration.

"Swing the rebel off," Cunningham commanded, likely before Hale had even finished. The executioner whipped the horse's flank; the beast bolted forward.

Rogers only watched the body dangle for a minute or so before signaling to Caleb. They walked together back towards the Beekman property.

"I want you to return to Flatbush and tell your sister Hale is dead," he said.

"It's time for her to move on," Caleb replied, already a wiser man.

***

A black crow lodged on the window sill adjacent to the Wheaton's pew at the meeting house, pecking on the frame for several seconds before soaring skyward. Although normally not superstitious, Anne had little doubt the bird was a harbinger of bad news. Minister Wyndham droned on for another two hours, well past mid-day, but she hardly heard a word. When at last his voice faltered, she was the first of her family to the door.

General Grant, who must have conveniently arrived late, was already outside. "Miss Wheaton," he said, gesturing they should talk privately. "About our wager..."

Between Nathan, Rogers and the Van Cliffs, she had not dwelled on her victory, but now she feared the general was going to welch on his payment. "Yes, sir. I understand the rebels put up quite the fight on Harlem Heights."

Grant shook his head, as if mourning the loss of a loved one. "That they did, most unfortunately."

"So I have won our wager."

"I propose we press the bet." The general rejoined the living, his expression exhibiting the eagerness of a traveling snake oil salesman. "We will squash Washington and his army before the year is out."

"I am not a gambling woman." Anne started to refuse, but paused. "However, I will consider your proposal once Wheaton's Emporium is firmly established in New York."

"You will?" Grant beamed. "Excellent, excellent. I will speak with your father immediately."

"Thank you, sir. Now, I must be going."

"You do not suffer again from a weak constitution?"

"No sir. I am quite well." Anne turned to leave.

"Miss Wheaton? Have you forgotten the second part of our wager?"

"Your courtship?"

"Would you still require me to retire from the field in favor of Major Whitcomb?" Grant asked.

"No." She held back a chuckle as the general floundered. The events of the past week, involving both Nathan and the Van Cliffs, had swayed her to realize that the value of Grant's patronage outweighed her romantic interest in the major, which had never reached a fever pitch anyway. "Not yet at least," she added.

"Then will you accompany me to General's Howe's October soiree? We missed the first one last night, I'm afraid."

"I would be honored. Now, please talk to Father and Mother. I do not want them to think I'm a brazen tart standing here flirting with you in view of our entire congregation."

"Of course." The general bowed his farewell.

Anne hastened up the Flatbush Road, a knot tightening in her stomach. Caleb waited on the front steps of the Matthews' manor.

"Let's walk, sister." He took her hand and led her around back towards the fields. She followed meekly, knowing full well the words she would hear.

"Captain Hale is dead," Caleb said. "He was executed this morning for espionage at the Artillery Park on Manhattan Island."

"How did he die?"

"Most bravely."

"No, brother. What was the manner of his death?"

"He was hung."

"A most ungentlemanly demise. Nathan deserved better."

"He was a spy, sister. He understood the rules of war."

"Nathan was an honorable man. A fervent believer in a just cause." Anne turned away, fighting back tears. "Was he allowed a last word?"

Caleb nodded. "I regret that I have but one life to lose for my country."

Anne smiled, recognizing the reference to *Cato*, feeling the touch of Nathan's hand reaching out to her from the grave. "That sounds like Nathaniel."

"I pray I am as resolute when my time comes," Caleb said. He handed her Nathan's watch. "You should see that this is returned to his family."

She nodded. Silver watches and gorgets. The earthly remains of the men she had loved and lost.

They walked to the end of the vegetable garden and back in silence. "I fear Hale's words will echo throughout the Continental Army," Caleb continued.

"They will resonate for generations, brother."

"If that is so, we will never squelch this rebellion."

"Once the candle of liberty is lit, it is impossible to extinguish."

"I fear we are on the wrong side of history then."

Caleb was no longer a hotheaded youth, as much now a man as Geoffrey - or Nathan. "There is a way to shift to the right side, brother," Anne said.

"I will never desert my King."

"Nor will I. But Sally, the Van Cliff's slave girl, may be in need of our help. Bounty hunters from Georgia search for her as we speak."

"Can we spirit her to safety?" Caleb asked.

"We can. And must."

"Then I will assist you in any way possible."

"Blood brothers forever." Anne linked her arm inside Caleb's elbow as they climbed the steps to the house.

"We have but one life to lose," he replied.

"No, brother," Anne said. "We have but one life to live."

EPILOGUE

"...Hale was, first of all, not a man who could easily avoid attention, being above average height and bearing facial scars acquired in a gunpowder explosion. And he was a particularly bad choice for this mission because his cousin, Samuel Hale, was a Tory, General [William] Howe's deputy commissary of prisoners, and at this very moment with Howe's forces. [Nathan] Hale was completely ignorant of the espionage tradecraft and ill-suited for the job of agent. The general reason for the failure of his mission is obvious—it was a thoroughly amateurish undertaking in a business that permits few mistakes. Furthermore, the young captain's superiors arranged no cover story to account for Hale's absence from the [Continental Army's] Rangers, most of whom already knew what Hale was to do in any case. The possibility that the British might have their own spy in the American camp seems not to have occurred to them. Hale was given no secret ink, no code or cypher, nor was he given any training..."

Maj. Gen. E.R. Thompson and Gen. Judicial Affairs O'Toole
Military Intelligence officers
Analysis of Hale's mission – 2002

For over two hundred years, the rumor circulated that Sam Hale was behind his cousin's capture; however this theory was finally discredited when the memoir of Consider Tiffany, a Connecticut merchant and Loyalist, surfaced in 2000. It corroborated two other diaries which mentioned that Robert Rogers had tracked, entrapped, and apprehended Nathan.

The British allowed Nathan Hale's body to swing for three days as a warning to the rebels. His carcass was stripped, spat upon, and pinned with crude cartoons. His final resting place remains unknown.

On the evening of Hale's hanging, Captain Montresor visited the Continental Army camp at Harlem Heights under a flag of truce. He met with General Putnam, General Reed, and Captain Hamilton. Montresor's primary aims were to discuss a prohibition on illegal weapons, sawed-off nails inserted in musket balls, as well as a prisoner exchange, likely involving Generals Stirling and Sullivan, but he also mentioned Hale's execution. William Hull accompanied Washington's return message to learn more details of his friend's death.

Enoch Hale grew worried about his brother by late September after he had received no letters for several weeks. He traveled to the Continental Army camps and heard whispers of Nathan's demise, but did not receive official confirmation until he met with Colonel Webb on October 26th. He searched for his brother's belongings but could not locate Asher Wright who was off at war. Nathan Hale's effects did not reach his family home in Coventry until June 4, 1777.

As a wily politician dealing with a restless Congress, George Washington did not publicly admit his mistakes either on the battlefield or behind it during the disastrous summer of 1776. He did, fortunately, learn from them. Washington kept the Continental Army on the move, primarily inland away from the reaches of the Royal Navy, until 1778 when the mighty French fleet first arrived. During this time, he orchestrated an outstanding intelligence network in and around New York, most notably the Culper ring, which served the patriot cause until the end of the war. It is not unreasonable to believe that Hale's mission laid the foundation for this network.

Ben Tallmadge became Washington's Director of Military Intelligence and was the chief architect and administrator of the Culper ring. He also fought in several actions, earning the rank of lieutenant colonel by war's end. Tallmadge went on to serve as postmaster of Litchfield, Connecticut and then as representative to Congress from 1801-1817.

William Hull fought bravely throughout the Revolution, gaining the rank of lieutenant colonel as well as the public recognition of General Washington and Congress. He served as governor of the Michigan territory from 1805-1812 and as a brigadier general in the War of 1812. On August 16, 1812, mistakenly believing he was far outnumbered, Hull surrendered Fort Duquesne to the British. In 1814, he was court-martialed, convicted, and sentenced to death. President James Madison pardoned him in recognition of his long service record. Hull published his memoirs in 1824 which succeeded in somewhat clearing his name before his death a year later.

Stephen Hempstead was captured by the British in 1777 and paraded naked in a horse-drawn cart. After his release, he returned to active duty and was wounded in 1781 defending New London from a raid led by the traitor Benedict Arnold. He moved out west to St. Louis after the war and lived to the ripe old age of seventy-seven.

Asher Wright lived even longer, dying in 1844 at the age of ninety. His memoirs, published in 1836, as well as those of Hempstead and Hull, are primary sources for details on the espionage mission of Nathan Hale.

Samuel Hale sailed to England in 1777, leaving behind his wife and son. There is no record that he reunited with his family or returned to America. He died in 1787.

Mayor David Matthews escaped from prison in Connecticut late in 1776 and reclaimed his post as Mayor of New York. He joined Provost Marshal William Cunningham in the starvation and plunder of rebel prisoners of war. After the war, he evacuated to Cape Breton Island in Nova Scotia and became active in its governance.

Shortly after Hale's execution, Robert Rogers and his Rangers were ambushed in Mamaroneck, New York. Rogers escaped but his reputation never recovered. He was relieved of his command the next spring, replaced by the legendary John Simcoe. Rogers returned briefly to England where he received a commission to raise another company of Rangers in Canada. During this effort, he was captured and jailed. Once again, he escaped, this time returning to England for good in 1783. He died there, a derelict, in 1795.

At arguably the most dire time in our nation's history, Captain Nathaniel Hale stepped forward when all others retreated. His valiant sacrifice became the first step along the Continental Army's road to victory. He is the state hero of Connecticut; his statue stands eternal vigilance on the campus of the Central Intelligence Agency in Langley, Virginia.

THE END

Maps

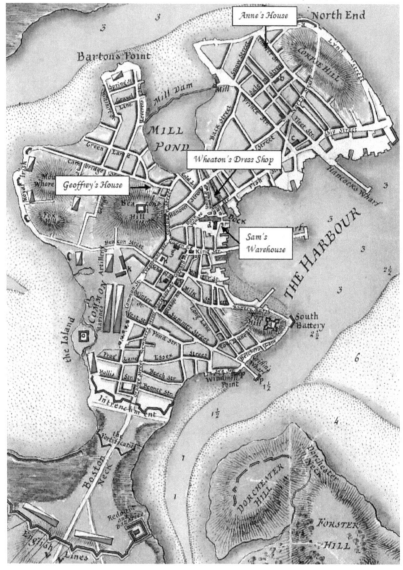

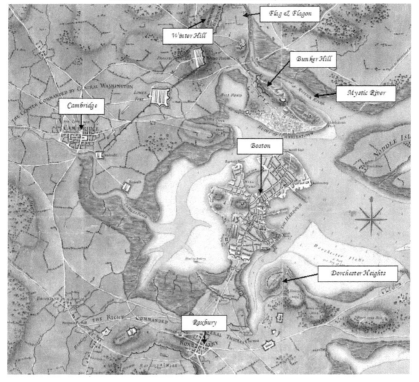

MAP OF THE TOWN OF BOSTON
AND SURROUNDING AREA, 1776

http://i.imgur.com/D6aw2Ji.jpg

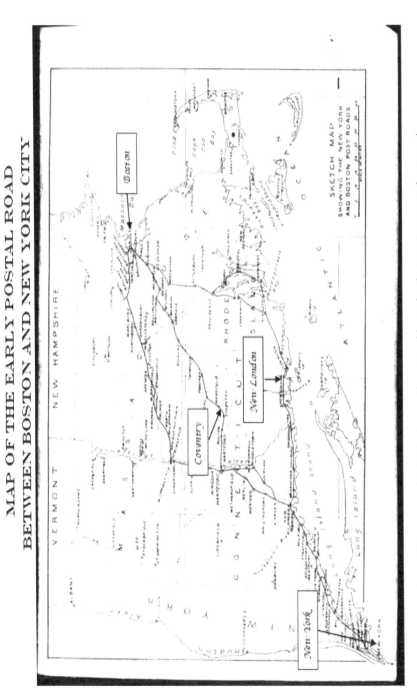

MAP OF THE EARLY POSTAL ROAD
BETWEEN BOSTON AND NEW YORK CITY

https://www.constitutionfacts.com/founders-library/early-american-postal-system/

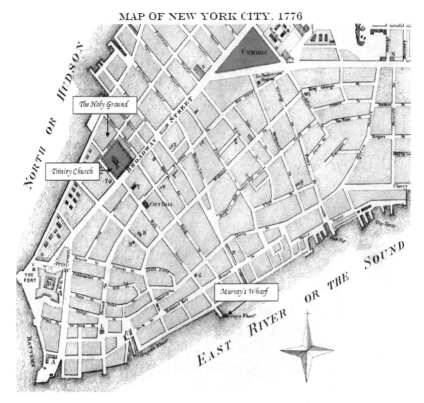

MAP OF NEW YORK CITY, 1776

MAP OF THE CITY OF NEW YORK AND ISLAND OF MANHATTAN, 1776

The King's Bridge

Greenwich Village

Bowery Lane

New York City

https://www.mapsland.com/maps/north-america/usa/new-york/large-detailed-old-map-of-new-york-city-and-of-manhattan-island-with-the-american-defences-in-1776.jpg

MAP OF WESTERN LONG ISLAND – AUGUST 1776

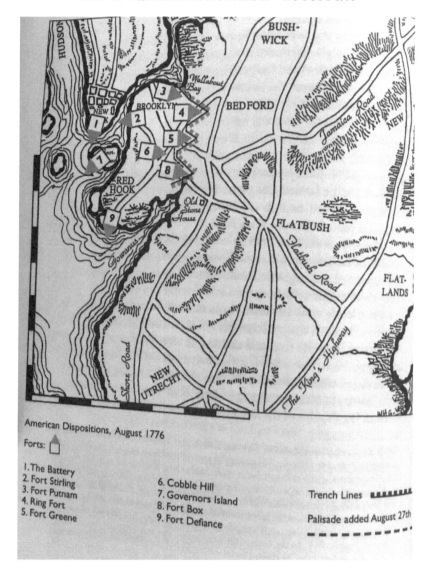

American Dispositions, August 1776

Forts:

1. The Battery
2. Fort Stirling
3. Fort Putnam
4. Ring Fort
5. Fort Greene
6. Cobble Hill
7. Governors Island
8. Fort Box
9. Fort Defiance

Trench Lines

Palisade added August 27th

MAP OF CENTRAL LONG ISLAND

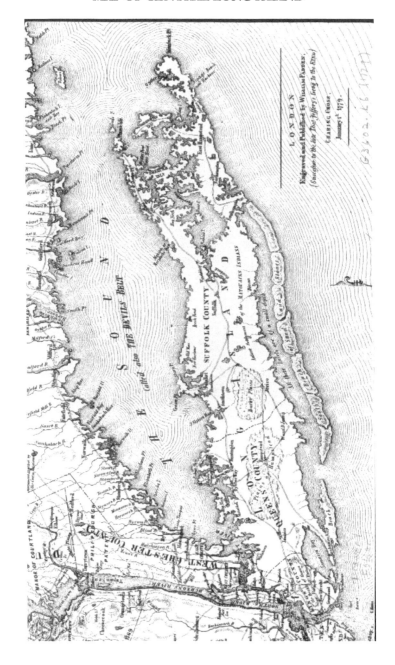

Alphabetical Listing of Significant Historical People

General William Alexander (Lord Stirling)
General Benedict Arnold
Private Tom Brown
General John Burgoyne
General Henry Clinton
William Cunningham
Benjamin Franklin
Margaret Gage
General Thomas Gage
General Horatio Gates
General James Grant
General Nathanael Greene
Enoch Hale
Captain Nathan Hale
Samuel Hale
General William Heath
Stephen Hempstead
Private Thomas Hickey
General William Howe
Captain William Hull
Sir William Johnson
Colonel Tom Knowlton
Colonel Henry Knox
General Charles Lee
Betsey Loring
Joshua Loring
Provost Marshal William Maroney
Mayor David Matthews
Salem Poor
General Israel Putnam
Colonel Robert Rogers
Peter Salem
General Joseph Spencer
General John Sullivan
Lieutenant Ben Tallmadge
Governor William Tryon
General George Washington
Colonel Charles Webb
Phyllis Wheatley
Reverend Eleazer Wheelock
Ebenezer Williams

Timeline of Key Historical Events

<u>1775</u>
April 19 - Battles of Lexington and Concord

May 25 - Generals Howe, Clinton and Burgoyne arrive in Boston

June 4 - Rogers sails from England

June 15 - Congress appoints George Washington commander-in-chief

June 17 - Battle of Bunker Hill (Breed's Hill)

July 1 - Hale accepts lieutenancy in Colonel Charles Webb's Connecticut regiment

July 2 - Washington arrives in Cambridge, MA

July 7 - Hale resigns from the Union School

Sept 1 - Hale promoted to captain

Sept ?? - Rogers lands in Maryland; walks to Philadelphia; Franklin signs his travel pass

Sept 11 - War council rejects Washington's plan to attack Boston

Sept 26 - Hale establishes camp on Winter Hill, MA

Oct 10 - Rogers in New York; Governor Tryon confirms his land grants

Oct 18 - War council rejects Washington's second plan to attack Boston; British Navy firebombs Falmouth, NH

Oct ?? - Hale wrestles with men, receives scolding from Webb

Nov ?? - Hale and Hull sign re-enlistment papers; Hale copies rules of officer conduct

Nov 13 - Rogers visits Reverend Wheelock in New Hampshire

Nov 29 - Captain Manley of the *Lee* captures the *Nancy* and her armaments

Dec 5 - Thirteen Continental Army officers petition to reward Salem Poor, a Black, for his service on Breed's Hill

Dec 10 - enlistments expire for Connecticut militia; many go home

Dec 11 - Martha Washington arrives in Cambridge

Dec 16 - Rogers meets with General Sullivan in Cambridge

Dec 25 - Washington calls for re-enlistments - will accept free Blacks

Dec 26 - Hale arrives home for the holidays

1776
Jan 10 - Thomas Paine publishes *Common Sense*

Jan 17 - Colonel Henry Knox arrives in Cambridge with cannons transported through the wilderness from Ft. Ticonderoga

Jan 30 - Hale arrives in Cambridge; camp moves from Winter Hill to Roxbury

Feb 16 - War council rejects Washington's third plan to attack Boston

Feb 17 - War council approves Washington's fourth plan: fortify Dorchester Heights and counter-attack Boston if Howe assaults the Heights

Mar 4 - Continental Army occupies and fortifies Dorchester Heights - takes all night

Mar 11 - Washington forms his Life Guard unit

Mar 17 - British evacuate Boston

Mar 18 - Hale leaves for New York

April 5 - Hale arrives in New York

April 13 - Washington arrives in New York City

May 31 - Hale leads raid on *Asia's* supply boat

June 27 - Rogers arrested in New Jersey; taken to Philadelphia

June 28 - Tom Hickey hung for treason

June 29 - British armada sighted; land troops on Staten Island

July 4 - Declaration of Independence signed in Philadelphia

July 9 - Washington reads the Declaration to the troops in New York
July 9 - Rogers escapes from prison in Philadelphia

July 12 - British warships bombard New York; Admiral Richard Howe arrives

Aug 6 - Rogers receives commission from General Howe to establish Queen's Rangers

Aug 20 - Hale is in Long Island (Brooklyn); writes last letter to Enoch

Aug 22 - British troops cross the Narrows to land at Gravesend Bay

Aug 27 - Battle of Long Island (Brooklyn)

Aug 29-30 - Washington engineers the evacuation of Long Island (Brooklyn)

Sept 1 - Washington commissions Colonel Tom Knowlton to form a Ranger unit

Sept ?? - Knowlton recruits Hale (and his brothers); Hale is ill but accepts

Sept 14 - Hale receives his order for transport to Long Island on any armed vessel

Sept 15 - Hale and Hempstead march up the coast to Norwalk, CT
Sept 15 - Battle of Kip's Bay; British take New York

Sept 16 - Hale arrives in Huntington, Long Island
Sept 16 - Battle of Harlem Heights

Sept 20-21 - Fire ravages New York

Sept 20 - Hale meets Rogers in tavern near Huntington

Sept 21 - Rogers arrests Hale at breakfast

Sept 21 - Hale faces General Howe at Beekman mansion

Sept 22 - Hale hung at the Artillery Park near Beekman mansion

Sept 22 - Captain Montresor meets with Putnam, Reed and Hamilton under a flag of truce

Bibliography

"5 Courtship Rituals from Colonial America." *Mental Floss*, 3 July 2013, mentalfloss.com/article/51525/5-courtship-rituals-colonial-america.

"6 Revolutionary Taverns." *New England Historical Society*, 12 June 2017, www.newenglandhistoricalsociety.com/6-revolutionary-taverns/.

"14th Continental Regiment." *Wikipedia*, Wikimedia Foundation, 17 Jan. 2019, en.wikipedia.org/wiki/14th_Continental_Regiment.

18th Century Songbook, www.americanrevolution.org/songs.php.

"19th Continental Regiment." *Wikipedia*, Wikimedia Foundation, 10 Oct. 2016, en.wikipedia.org/wiki/19th_Continental_Regiment.

"A Colonial Gentlemen's Clothing: A Glossary of Terms." *A Colonial Gentlemen's Clothing: A Glossary of Terms: The Colonial Williamsburg Official History & Citizenship Site*, www.history.org/history/clothing/men/mglossary.cfm#neck.

"A Colonial Lady's Clothing: A Glossary of Terms." *A Colonial Lady's Clothing: A Glossary of Terms: The Colonial Williamsburg Official History & Citizenship Site*, www.history.org/history/clothing/women/wglossary.cfm.

"A Football History: from Its Origin to Now." *Topend Sports, Science, Training and Nutrition*, www.topendsports.com/sport/soccer/history.htm.

A Short History of Boston's Beacon Hill, www.beacon-hill-boston.com/History. *A Short History of Boston's North End*, www.north-end-boston.com/History.

"A Tale of the Lost Beekman Mansion." *Untapped Cities*, 30 Dec. 2018, untappedcities.com/2012/04/18/a-tale-of-the-lost-beekman-mansion-2/.

Abass, D.K. and Rod Mather. "The History of the HMS Cerberus and HMS Lark." *NOAA Ocean Explorer Podcast RSS*, oceanexplorer.noaa.gov/explorations/08auvfest/background/history/history.html.
Abrams, Jeanne E. *Revolutionary Medicine: The Founding Fathers and Mothers in Sickness and in Health*. NYU Press, 2013.

Adams, Hannah. *A Summary History of New-England, from the First Settlement at Plymouth, to the Acceptance of the Federal Constitution: Comprehending a General Sketch of the American War.* University Microfilms Intl., 1978.

Addison, Joseph. *Cato.* Createspace, 2017.

"Anarchy in Action." *New England Town Meetings - Anarchy in Action,* anarchyinaction.org/index.php?title=New_England_town_meetings.

Anderson, Virginia DeJohn. *The Martyr and the Traitor: Nathan Hale, Moses Dunbar, and the American Revolution.* Oxford University Press, 2017.

Bakeless, John. *Turncoats, Traitors and Heroes.* Da Capo Press, 1998.

Bangs, Isaac and Edward Bangs. *Journal of Lieutenant Isaac Bangs.* New York Times, 1968.

Barnett, Rachael. "Food Preservation." *Role of Women in Colonial America,* roleofwomenincolonialtimes.weebly.com/food-preservation.html.

Battle of Bunker Hill: Composed by a British Officer, the Day after the Battle, June 17, 1775. Sold, Wholesale and Retail, by L. Deming, No. 62, Hanover Street, 2d Door from Friend Street, Boston, 1832.

Battlefield Signals, Jan. 2018, www.warnersregiment.org/Battlefield Signals.html.

"Bed Time, Eighteenth Century Style." *Bed Time, Eighteenth Century Style,* twonerdyhistorygirls.blogspot.com/2010/06/bed-time-eighteenth-century-style.html.

Bell, J.L. "The Myth of Provost William Cunningham." 10 Oct. 2007, boston1775.blogspot.com/2007/10/myth-of-provost-william-cunningham.html.

Berkin, Carol. *Revolutionary Mothers: Women in the Struggle for America's Independence.*

"Boston 1775." *Boston 1775,* boston1775.blogspot.com/.

"Boston National Historical Park (U.S. National Park Service)." *National Parks Service,* U.S. Department of the Interior, www.nps.gov/bost/index.htm.

Boyle, Beth Maxwell. *Early Lighting 6*,
www.ramshornstudio.com/early_lighting_6.htm.

Bradford, James C. *The American Revolution: a Visual History*. DK Publishing,
2016.

"Brandywine Battlefield Historic Site." *Ushistory.org*, Independence Hall
Association, www.ushistory.org/brandywine/special/art06.htm.

"British Red Ensign Flag." *Revolutionary War and Beyond*, www.revolutionary-
war-and-beyond.com/british-red-ensign-flag.html.

Brown, Richard H. and Paul E. Cohen. *Revolution: Mapping the Road to
American Independence 1755 to 1783*. W.W. Norton & Company, 2015.

Burns, Robert. *The Merry Muses of Caledonia*. 1911.

"Cato, a Tragedy." *Wikipedia*, Wikimedia Foundation, 22 May 2019,
en.wikipedia.org/wiki/Cato,_a_Tragedy.

Chernow, Ron. *Washington: A Life*. Penguin Books, 2010.

"Colonel Webb's Seventh Connecticut Regiment." CTSSAR,
www.connecticutsar.org/colonel-webbs-seventh-connecticut-regiment/.

"Colonial America: the Simple Life." *Colonial America: the Simple Life*,
colonial-american-life.blogspot.com/.
Colonies and the Mail, postalmuseum.si.edu/exhibits/current/binding-the-
nation/starting-the-system/colonies-and-the-mail.html.

Colonial Clothing - Revolution and the New Republic 1775-1800,
www.americanrevolution.org/clothing/colonial7.php.

Coming of the American Revolution, www.masshist.org/revolution/index.html.

"Common Sense Quotes by Thomas Paine." *Goodreads*, Goodreads,
www.goodreads.com/work/quotes/2548496-common-sense.

"Connecticut Line." *Wikipedia*, Wikimedia Foundation, 22 May 2019,
en.wikipedia.org/wiki/Connecticut_Line.

"Continental Army." *Wikipedia*, Wikimedia Foundation, 28 May 2019, en.wikipedia.org/wiki/Continental_Army.

Cooper, James F. *Tenacious of Their Liberties: the Congregationalists in Colonial Massachusetts*. Oxford University Press, 2002.

"Courtship and Marriage in the Eighteenth Century." *Courtship and Marriage in the Eighteenth Century : The Colonial Williamsburg Official History & Citizenship Site*, www.history.org/history/teaching/enewsletter/volume7/mar09/courtship.cfm.

Craft, Susan F. "Colonial Quills." *Colonial Quills*, 28 Jan. 2013, colonialquills.blogspot.com/search/label/colonial American slang.

Cross, John David. *The First Americans*. New Word City, 2016.

Crusader12. *Library Company of Philadelphia: New Yorker Ads*, librarycompany.org/treasures/ad19.htm.

Daigler, Kenneth A. *Spies, Patriots, and Traitors: American Intelligence in the Revolutionary War*. Georgetown University Press, 2014.

"Declaration of Independence: A Transcription." *National Archives and Records Administration*, National Archives and Records Administration, www.archives.gov/founding-docs/declaration-transcript.

Dine, Ranana. "Scarlet Letters: Getting the History of Abortion and Contraception Right." *Center for American Progress*, 8 Aug. 2013, www.americanprogress.org/issues/religion/news/2013/08/08/71893/scarlet-letters-getting-the-history-of-abortion-and-contraception-right/.
"Early American Coins." *Early American Coins - Littleton Coin Company*, www.littletoncoin.com/shop/Early-American-Coins.

"Early American Currency." *Wikipedia*, Wikimedia Foundation, 7 Apr. 2019, en.wikipedia.org/wiki/Early_American_currency.

Fife, Drum, and Bugle During the Revolutionary War, fifeanddrum.army.mil/kids_fife_drum.html.

"Flag Timeline." *Ushistory.org*, Independence Hall Association, www.ushistory.org/betsy/flagfact.html.

Fleishman, Cooper. "38 Slang Terms from Colonial Times That Need to Be Brought Back." *The Daily Dot*, The Daily Dot, 16 Apr. 2018, www.dailydot.com/unclick/18th-19th-century-vulgar-slang-terms/.

Fleming, Thomas. *How Good a General was George Washington? (The Thomas Fleming Library)*. New Word City, 2012.

Fleming, Thomas. *The Loyalists (The Thomas Fleming Library Book 1)*. New Word City, 2013.

"Flintlock." *Wikipedia*, Wikimedia Foundation, 13 May 2019, en.wikipedia.org/wiki/Flintlock.

"Founders Online: Home." *National Archives and Records Administration*, National Archives and Records Administration, founders.archives.gov/.

Franklin, Benjamin. *The Old Mistresses Apologue: Known as Advice to a Young Man on the Choice of a Mistress*. Janus Press, 1975.

Gallagher, John J. *Battle of Brooklyn*. Da Copa Press, 2009.

Genealogy Trails History Group. "Nathan Hale Biography." *Genealogy Trails History Group*, genealogytrails.com/conn/tolland/nathan_hale.html.

"General Charles Lee Leaves His Troops for Widow White's Tavern." *History.com*, A&E Television Networks, 13 Nov. 2009, www.history.com/this-day-in-history/general-charles-lee-leaves-his-troops-for-widow-whites-tavern.

"George Washington Digital Encyclopedia." *George Washington's Mount Vernon*, www.mountvernon.org/library/digitalhistory/digital-encyclopedia.

Getty, Katie Turner. "The Route Is by Way of Winnisimmet: Chelsea and the Refugees." *Journal of the American Revolution*, 30 Jan. 2018, allthingsliberty.com/2018/02/route-way-winnisimmet-chelsea-refugees/.

Giffin, Phillip R. "Samuel Blachley Webb: Wethersfield's Ablest Officer." *Journal of the American Revolution*, 19 Sept. 2016, allthingsliberty.com/2016/09/samuel-blachley-webb-1753-1807/.

Goodwin, Doris Kearns. *Leadership in Turbulent Times*. Simon & Schuster, 2018.

Grosvenor, Edwin S. *The Best of American Heritage: New York*. New World City, Inc. 2017.

Gunning, Sally Cabot. *The Widow's War: A Novel*. Harper Collins, 2009.

Hagist, Don N. *British Soldiers, American War: Voices of the American Revolution*. Westholme Publishing, 2012.

Hambucken, Denis and Bill Payson. Soldier of the 1775 American Revolution. The Countryman Press, 2011.

Hartgrove, W. B. "The Negro Soldier in the American Revolution." *The Journal of Negro History*, vol. 1, no. 2, 1916, pp. 110–131., doi:10.2307/3035634.

"Hints of Nathan Hale." *TURN to a Historian*, 3 Apr. 2014, spycurious.wordpress.com/2014/04/03/hints-of-nathan-hale/.

"History of American Women Blog." *Lucy Flucker Knox | History of American Women Blog*, web.archive.org/web/20110404015629/http://www.womenhistoryblog.com/2009/04/lucy-flucker-knox.html.

"History of Marshfield, Massachusetts." *Wikipedia*, Wikimedia Foundation, 28 May 2019, en.wikipedia.org/wiki/History_of_Marshfield,_Massachusetts.

Hochstetler, J. M. "Wedding in Colonial America." *Colonial Quills*, colonialquills.blogspot.com/2011/05/wedding-in-colonial-america.html.

Holliday, Carl. *Wit and Humor of Colonial Days: 1607-1800 (Classic Reprint)*. Forgotten Books, 2015.

Hutson, James. "Nathan Hale Revisited A Tory's Account of the Arrest of the First American Spy." *Nathan Hale Revisited (July/August 2003) - Library of Congress Information Bulletin*, www.loc.gov/loc/lcib/0307-8/hale.html.

"I've Been Scent from the Past: 17th and 18th Century Perfumes." *The Pragmatic Costumer*, 22 Dec. 2015, thepragmaticcostumer.wordpress.com/2013/07/02/ive-been-scent-from-the-past-17th-and-18th-century-perfumes/.

"International Swear Words to Love and Use: Colonial Style!" *By All Writes LLC*, 25 Nov. 2014, byallwrites.biz/2014/11/25/international-swear-words-to-love-and-use-colonial-style/.

"Johnson's Regiment of Militia." *Wikipedia*, Wikimedia Foundation, 2 Sept. 2016, en.wikipedia.org/wiki/Johnson's_Regiment_of_Militia.

Johnston, Henry P. *The Campaign of 1776 Around New York and Brooklyn (Illustrated Edition)*. Amazon Digital Services, 2013.

Johnston, Henry Phelps. *Nathan Hale, 1776; biography and memorials (1901)*. Amazon Digital Services, 2010.

Johnston, Henry Phelps. *The Record of Connecticut Men in the Military and Naval Service during the War of the Revolution, 1775-1783*. Reprinted for Clearfield Co. by Genealogical Pub. Co., 2003.

Jones, Paul Anthony. "30 Excellent Terms From a 17th Century Slang Dictionary." *Mental Floss*, 18 May 2017, mentalfloss.com/article/500833/30-excellent-terms-17th-century-slang-dictionary.

"Joshua Loring." *Wikipedia*, Wikimedia Foundation, 22 Apr. 2019, en.wikipedia.org/wiki/Joshua_Loring.

"Josiah Wedgwood." *Wikipedia*, Wikimedia Foundation, 2 May 2019, en.wikipedia.org/wiki/Josiah_Wedgwood.

Kalman, Bobbie. *Historic Communities: 18th Century Clothing*. Crabtree Publishing Company, 1993.

Kilmeade, Brian and Don Yaeger. *George Washington's Secret Six: The Spy Ring That Saved the American Revolution*. Sentinel, 2013.

Lancaster, Bruce and John Harold Plumb. *The American Revolution*. Houghton Mifflin, 2001.

"Learn." *African-Americans in the Continental Army and the State Militias During the American War of Independence | Museum of the American Revolution*, web.archive.org/web/20130203080341/http://www.americanrevolutionce nter.org/reflections/african-americans-continental-army-and-state-militias-during-american-war-independence.

Lee, Charles. *The Lee Papers*. New-York Historical Soc., 1873.

"List of Delegates to the Continental Congress." *Wikipedia*, Wikimedia Foundation, 12 May 2019, en.wikipedia.org/wiki/List_of_delegates_to_the_Continental_Congress#D elegates_who_attended.

Loeser Consulting. *Historical Flags of Our Ancestors - American Revolutionary War Flags*, www.loeser.us/flags/revolution.html.

Loyalist Institute: Queen's American Rangers, Cavalry Officers, www.royalprovincial.com/military/rhist/qar/qarcav1.htm.

"Loyalist Lucy Flucker Meets Patriot Henry Knox at a Boston Parade." *Women of Every Complexion and Complexity*, womenofeverycomplexionandcomplexity.weebly.com/loyalist-lucy-flucker-meets-patriot-henry-knox-at-a-boston-parade.html.

Martin, Joseph Plumb. *A Narrative of a Revolutionary Soldier*. SIgnet, 2010.

MayflowerHistory.com, mayflowerhistory.com/cross-section/.

McCullough, David. *1776*. Simon & Schuster, 2006.

Meltzer, Brad. *The First Conspiracy: The Secret Plot Against George Washington*. Macmillan, 2019.

Miller, Tom. "The Lost 1745 Kennedy House -- No 1 Broadway." *The Lost 1745 Kennedy House -- No 1 Broadway*, 1 Jan. 1970, daytoninmanhattan.blogspot.com/2012/07/lost-1745-kennedy-house-no-1-broadway.html.

Mohegan History, www.dickshovel.com/moh.html.

Moore, Frank. *Songs and Ballads of the American Revolution*. Hardpress Ltd, 2013.

Morgan, Edmund Sears. *The Genius of George Washington*. Norton, 1981.

Nash, Gary B. *The Unknown American Revolution: The Unruly Birth of Democracy and the Struggle to Create America*. Penguin Books, 2006.

"Nathan Hale Homestead Coventry Connecticut Landmarks." *Historic Site Downtown Connecticut Landmarks*, www.ctlandmarks.org/nathan-hale.

"Nathan Hale's Mission." *Central Intelligence Agency*, Central Intelligence Agency, 4 Aug. 2011, www.cia.gov/library/center-for-the-study-of-intelligence/kent-csi/vol17no4/html/v17i4a03p_0001.htm.

"Native American Indian Weapons." *Native American Weapons: Bows and Arrows, Spears, Tomahawks, War Clubs, and Other American Indian Weaponry*, www.native-languages.org/weapons.htm.
Nevins, Allen. *The Life of Robert Rogers*. Amazon Digital Services, 2016.

O'Donnell, Patrick K. *Washington's Immortals: The Untold Story of an Elite Regiment Who Changed the Course of the Revolution*. Atlantic Monthly Press, 2019.

Olasky, Marvin. "Did Colonial America Have Abortions? Yes, but ..." *WORLD*, world.wng.org/2015/01/did_colonial_america_have_abortions_yes_but.

"Online Library of Liberty." *The American Revolution and Constitution - Online Library of Liberty*, oll.libertyfund.org/groups/65.

O'Reilly, Bill and Martin Dugard. *Killing England: The Brutal Struggle for American Independence (Bill O'Reilly's Killing Series)*. Henry Holt and Co. 2017.

O'Reilly, Edward. "New York's Last Colonial Mayor." *New-York Historical Society*, 7 July 2015, blog.nyhistory.org/profligate-abandoned-and-dissipated-new-york-citys-last-colonial-mayor/.

"Orient, New York." *Wikipedia*, Wikimedia Foundation, 30 Nov. 2018, en.wikipedia.org/wiki/Orient,_New_York.

Pavao, Esther. "General Charles Lee." *The American Revolutionary War*, www.revolutionary-war.net/general-charles-lee.html.

Phelps, M. William. *Nathan Hale: The Life and Death of America's First Spy*. ForeEdge, 2015.

Philbrick, Nathaniel. *Bunker Hill*. Penguin Books, 2013.
Philbrick, Nathaniel. *In the Hurricane's Eye: The Genius of George Washington and the Victory at Yorktown*. Viking, 2018.

Philbrick, Nathaniel. *Mayflower: A Story of Courage, Community, and War.* Penguin Books, 2006.

"Phillis Wheatley." *Wikipedia*, Wikimedia Foundation, 27 Mar. 2019, en.wikipedia.org/wiki/Phillis_Wheatley.

"Pieces of Eight." *Pieces of Eight: The Colonial Williamsburg Official History & Citizenship Site*, www.history.org/history/teaching/enewsletter/volume3/march05/iotm.cfm.

"Pilgrims v. Puritans: Who Landed in Plymouth?" *The Historic Present*, 18 Oct. 2011, thehistoricpresent.com/2008/05/12/pilgrims-v-puritans-who-landed-in-plymouth/.

"Plan of the Rebels Works on Prospect-Hill. Plan of the Rebels Works on Winter-Hill." *The Library of Congress*, www.loc.gov/resource/g3764s.ar091700/.

"Porcelain." *Wikipedia*, Wikimedia Foundation, 29 May 2019, en.wikipedia.org/wiki/Porcelain.

Powell, William S. "A Connecticut Soldier Under Washington: Elisha Bostwicks Memoirs of the First Years of the Revolution." *The William and Mary Quarterly*, vol. 6, no. 1, 1949, p. 94., doi:10.2307/1921863.

Procknow, Gene. "Did Generals Mismanage the Battle of Brooklyn?" *Journal of the American Revolution*, 20 Apr. 2017, allthingsliberty.com/2017/04/generals-mismanage-battle-brooklyn/. Random House, 2007.

"Revolutionary Drummers." *Revolutionary Drummers : The Colonial Williamsburg Official History & Citizenship Site*, www.history.org/history/teaching/enewsletter/volume2/october03/drummers.cfm. *Revolutionary War - Sons of the American Revolution - Rufus Landon, Revolutionary War Drummer*, www.revolutionarywararchives.org/landon.html.

Richardson, Susan. Greenwich Before 2000. The Historical Society of the Town of Greenwich, Inc., 2000.

Roberts, Kenneth. *Rabble in Arms*. Down East Books, 2013.

Rogers, Robert. *A Concise Account of North America .: To Which Is Subjoined an Account of the Several Nations and Tribes of Indians Residing in Those Parts, Etc.* 1765.

Rogers, Robert. *Journals of Robert Rogers of the Rangers.* The Irregular Press, 2016.

Ross, John F. *War on the Run: The Epic Story of Robert Rogers and the Conquest of America's First Frontier.* Random House, 2009.

Rowland, Tim. *Strange and Obscure Stories of the Revolutionary War.* Skyhorse, 2015.

Schecter, Barnet. *The Battle for New York.* Penguin Books, 2002.

Schellhammer, Michael. "Nathan Hale: A Hero's Fiasco." *Journal of the American Revolution*, 28 Aug. 2016, allthingsliberty.com/2013/03/nathan-hale-heros-fiasco/.

Schenawolf, Harry. "American Revolutionary War Cockades in Washington's Army." *Revolutionary War Journal*, 30 Dec. 2017, www.revolutionarywarjournal.com/cockades/.

Schenawolf, Harry. "British Army Uniforms during the American Revolutionary War." *Revolutionary War Journal*, 30 Dec. 2017, www.revolutionarywarjournal.com/british-army-uniform/.

Schenawolf, Harry. "Holy Ground: New York City's Red Light District During the American Revolutionary War." *Revolutionary War Journal*, 30 Dec. 2017, www.revolutionarywarjournal.com/holy-ground/.

Schenawolf, Harry. "Music in Colonial & Revolutionary America." *Revolutionary War Journal*, 29 Dec. 2017, www.revolutionarywarjournal.com/music-in-colonial-america/.

Scott, Ian Hugh. "The Largest Ice Free Harbor in the World." https://ezinearticles.com/?The-Largest-Ice-Free-Harbour-in-the-World&id=3073033. "Search Results from George Washington Papers." *The Library of Congress*, www.loc.gov/collections/george-washington-papers.

Second Continental Light Dragoons, www.dragoons.info/our_past/.

Seymour, George. *Documentary Life of Nathan Hale*. Kessinger Publishing, 2006.

Shaara, Jeff. *Rise to Rebellion: A Novel of the American Revolution (The American Revolutionary War Book 1)*. Balantine Books, 2011.

"Siege of Boston." *Wikipedia*, Wikimedia Foundation, 3 May 2019, en.wikipedia.org/wiki/Siege_of_Boston.

"Sixth-Rate." *Wikipedia*, Wikimedia Foundation, 22 May 2019, en.wikipedia.org/wiki/Sixth-rate.

Shepherd, Joshua. "Revolutionary War Olympics: The Games Our Founders Played." *Journal of the American Revolution*, 28 Aug. 2016, allthingsliberty.com/2016/08/revolutionary-war-olympics-games-founders-played/.

Smith, David. *Whispers Across the Atlantick*. Osprey Publishing, 2017.

Smock, Geoff. "From Wannabe Redcoat to Rebel: George Washington's Journey to Revolution." *Journal of the American Revolution*, 7 Oct. 2017, allthingsliberty.com/2017/10/wannabe-redcoat-rebel-george-washingtons-journey-revolution/.

Soldier - Chapter Five, www.americanrevolution.org/soldier/soldier5.php.

"Spices in the 18th Century English Kitchen." *Savoring the Past*, 15 Nov. 2012, savoringthepast.net/2012/11/15/spices-in-the-18th-century-english-kitchen/.

Spuffard, Francis. *Golden Hill: A Novel of Old New York*. Scribner, 2017.

Stark, Caleb and John Stark. *Memoir and Official Correspondence of Gen. John Stark, with Notices of Several Other Officers of the Revolution. Also, a Biography of Capt. P. Stevens, and of Col. R. Rogers, with an Account of His Services in America during the "Seven Years War."*. 1860.

Stephenson, Michael. *Patriot Battles: How the Revolutionary War was Fought*. Harper Collins, 2009.

Stokesbury, James L. *A Short History of the American Revolution*. Harper Collins, 2008.

Surgery - Amputation, www.americanrevolution.org/surgery/surgery37.php.

Tallmadge, Benjamin. *Memoir of Col. Benjamin Tallmadge.* Amazon Digital Services, 2015.

"Tattooed War Clubs of the Iroquois | | Lars Krutak." *Lars Krutak | Tattoo Anthropologist*, 10 Feb. 2018, www.larskrutak.com/tattooed-war-clubs-of-the-iroquois/.

Taylor, Dale. *The Writer's Guide to Everyday Life in Colonial America.* Writer's Digest Books, 1997.

The Associated Press. "Nathan Hale Blundered Into a Trap, Papers Show." *The New York Times*, The New York Times, 21 Sept. 2003, www.nytimes.com/2003/09/21/us/nathan-hale-blundered-into-a-trap-papers-show.html.

"The Capture of Charles Lee." *TURN to a Historian*, 15 May 2014, spycurious.wordpress.com/2014/05/15/the-capture-of-charles-lee/.

"The Early American Postal System." *Constitution Facts - Official U.S. Constitution Website*, www.constitutionfacts.com/founders-library/early-american-postal-system/.

The Famous Webbs, webb.skinnerwebb.com/gpage3.html.

The Journals of Each Provincial Congress of Massachusetts in 1774 and 1775: and of the Committee of Safety: with an Appendix, Containing the Proceedings of the County Conventions-Narratives of the Events of the Nineteenth of April, 1775-Papers Relating to Ticonderoga and Crown Point, and Other Documents, Illustrative of the Early History of the American Revolution. Dutton and Wentworth, Printers to the State, 1979.

The Mariners' Museum: Birth of the U.S. Navy, www.marinersmuseum.org/sites/micro/usnavy/03/03b.htm.

The Old Stone House in Brooklyn, theoldstonehouse.org/.

The Revolution's Black Soldiers, www.americanrevolution.org/blk.php.

"Theater in the United States." *Wikipedia*, Wikimedia Foundation, 6 Apr. 2019, en.wikipedia.org/wiki/Theater_in_the_United_States.

"Thomas Paine: Common Sense." *Ushistory.org*, Independence Hall Association, www.ushistory.org/paine/commonsense/sense2.htm.

"Tinderboxes in the Home." *Tinderboxes, Flint and Steel, Tinder, Striking Light and Fire at Home*, www.oldandinteresting.com/tinderbox.aspx.

"To Bathe or Not to Bathe." *To Bathe or Not to Bathe : The Colonial Williamsburg Official History & Citizenship Site*, www.history.org/foundation/journal/Autumn00/bathe.cfm.

Tooley, Lynn. "Colonel Charles Webb's Regimant, 1776 - 19th Continental." *Colonel Charles Webb's Regimant, 1776 - 19th Continental | Connecticut In The Revolution | American Wars*, www.americanwars.org/ct-american-revolution/colonel-charles-webb-regiment-1776.htm.

Tucker, Phillip Thomas. *How the Irish Won the American Revolution: A New Look at the Forgotten Heroes of America's War of Independence*. Skyhorse, 2015.

Ulrich, Laurel Thatcher. *A Midwife's Tale: The Life of Martha Ballard, Based on Her Diary, 1785-1812*. Vintage 2010.

United States Postal Service. *Colonial Times*, about.usps.com/publications/pub100/pub100_002.htm.
Washington, George. *George Washington's Rules of Civility and Decent Behavior*. Rowman and Littlefield Publishers, Inc., 2013.

"Weaving, Spinning, and Dyeing." *Weaving, Spinning, and Dyeing: The Colonial Williamsburg Official History & Citizenship Site*, www.history.org/foundation/journal/winter07/weaving.cfm.

Wheatley, Phillis. *Poems on Various Subjects, Religious and Moral*. London: A. Bell, 1773; Bartleby.com, 2010.

"William Cunningham, The Provost Marshal." *Access Genealogy*, 16 July 2011, www.accessgencalogy.com/america/william-cunningham-the-provost-marshal.htm.

Winslow, Erving. "A Loyalist in the Siege of Boston." *The New England Historical and Genealogical Register. Notes and Queries*, LVI, 1902.

"Witches and Witchcraft The First Person Executed in the Colonies." *Witches and Witchcraft - CT Judicial Branch Law Library Services*, www.jud.ct.gov/lawlib/history/witches.htm.

Yurtoğlu, Nadir. "Sandwiched Between Omens of Discord and Rum, the Infamous Mrs. Loring Announces Marriage Vows." *History Studies International Journal of History*, vol. 10, no. 7, 2018.

Zellers-Frederick, Andrew A. "Struggle for a Lighthouse: The Raids to Destroy the Boston Light." *Journal of the American Revolution*, 1 July 2018, allthingsliberty.com/2018/07/struggle-for-a-lighthouse-the-raids-to-destroy-the-boston-light/.

Zerbey, Nancy. "New England Architecture: Guide to House Styles in New England." *New England Today*, 29 Mar 2019.

Contemporary Thrillers by Scott M. Smith
(Published on Amazon under the name SM Smith)

The Fourth Amendment

Darkness is Coming

ABOUT THE AUTHOR

Scott M. Smith

After a thirty year career on Wall Street, Scott retired in 2014 to pursue a lifelong passion to write. His cybersecurity novel, *Darkness is Coming*, won Distinguished Favorite in the Thriller category in the NYC Big Book Award competition. In 2017, he began researching the life and times of Nathan Hale, the official hero of his adopted home state of Connecticut. The effort resulted in *The Spy and the Seamstress,* as well as several in-depth articles published in the prestigious *Journal of the American Revolution.* Two of Scott's articles were selected for inclusion in the *Journal's* annual compendium of its best writings. Connect with Scott at www.scottmsmithbooks.com.

Made in United States
Troutdale, OR
09/20/2023

13064788R00286